HIGH
RISK

Also by Simona Ahrnstedt

All In

Falling

Published by Kensington Publishing Corporation

HIGH
RISK

SIMONA AHRNSTEDT

KENSINGTON BOOKS
www.kensingtonbooks.com

KENSINGTON BOOKS are published by

Kensington Publishing Corp.
119 West 40th Street
New York, NY 10018

Copyright © 2016 by Simona Ahrnstedt
First published by Bokförlaget Forum, Sweden
Published by arrangement with Nordin Agency AB, Sweden

All Kensington titles, imprints, and distributed lines are available at special quantity discounts for bulk purchases for sales promotion, premiums, fundraising, educational, or institutional use.

Special book excerpts or customized printings can also be created to fit specific needs. For details, write or phone the office of the Kensington Sales Manager: Kensington Publishing Corp., 119 West 40th Street, New York, NY 10018. Attn. Sales Department. Phone: 1-800-221-2647.

Kensington and the K logo Reg. U.S. Pat. & TM Off.

eISBN-13: 978-1-4967-0624-9
eISBN-10: 1-4967-0624-2
First Kensington Electronic Edition: April 2018

ISBN-13: 978-1-4967-0623-2
ISBN-10: 1-4967-0623-4
First Kensington Trade Paperback Printing: April 2018

10 9 8 7 6 5 4 3 2 1

Printed in the United States of America

Prologue

There was so much to be afraid of in this house. At least if you were a child. The strange food. The angry voices. Never knowing what would happen, when she would be given a beating.

But the basement was still worse.

It was cold and smelled awful.

She shrank back against the wall with her forehead on her knees, felt abandonment like a lump in her stomach. Like a wound in her heart. It hurt to be alone, detested. She was used to it by now, but it had never been this bad before.

It was dark, too. And she was hungry.

She sniffed into her knees. Felt so afraid, no matter how brave she tried to be.

She wouldn't cry.

No matter what they did to her, she wouldn't cry.

Chapter 1

Ambra Vinter looked down at her notebook. Ideas for articles, the phone number of someone she'd interviewed, and a reminder to herself that she needed coffee. The last part was underlined twice. She didn't demand all that many things in life, but drinking coffee in the morning was one of them.

"Ambra, are you listening?"

I was trying not to.

But since the voice belonged to her immediate superior at *Aftonbladet,* news editor Grace Bekele, Ambra replied with as much diplomacy as she could. "It would be great if you could send someone else. I was on a job in Varberg last week. And I just got back from the fire in Akalla."

Ambra attempted a pleading look. There had to be some other reporter Grace could send on this particular lousy job. A young, hungry journalist who wasn't yet as cynical as she was, someone who would appreciate being able to leave their desk.

"Except I want you to go." Grace made a sweeping gesture with her slender hand, and her long, pointed nails glittered. She looked like a supermodel, but it was for her dynamic leadership that she was renowned. And Ambra knew that Grace would win this battle, just as she always did.

"Where was it again?" Ambra asked. Her clothes smelled of smoke. She never got used to how quickly a fire could spread. Three minutes and there were flames everywhere. No fatalities, which was a bad angle, but good all the same. Families should never die in fires three days before Christmas.

"Norrland, like I said."

"Norrland's huge. Could you be more specific?" Ambra had good reason not to want to go north, lousy job or not.

"Norrbotten then. I have the place here somewhere."

Ambra waited while Grace riffled through the papers on her over-loaded desk. They were at the Breaking News desk, the very heart of the machine that was the *Aftonbladet* newsroom. It was two in the afternoon, and it was pitch black outside. Freezing rain and sudden gusts of wind battered the windows. The weather report was head-ing up the home page, of course. Unusually good or unusually bad, the weather was always on the main page online, because it was something that always sold. It was the day's most-read article, with almost one thousand clicks a minute.

Ambra leafed forward to an empty page in her notebook and said, as obligingly as she could, "What exactly do you want me to do in Norrbotten?"

Grace picked up a few stacks of paper and almost managed to knock over a mug of stale coffee. No one had their own desk, not even the editors. Grace was one of four news editors who manned the desk, round the clock, every day of the year. The other editors, everything from Sports, Entertainment, and Crime to Foreign Affairs, Investigative, and Culture, were spread around the room like satel-lites orbiting a never-sleeping hub.

"The note was just here. I want to say it was Kalix," said Grace.

Always something to be grateful for. She obediently wrote down *Kalix* in her notebook.

"You'll be interviewing Elsa, ninety-two. Call up and arrange a meeting. I should have her number, too. It came in through the tip service. I had a feeling it could be something."

"Great," Ambra said, managing not to pull a face. The tip service was *Aftonbladet*'s digital space for ordinary people to submit news tips and earn 1,000 kronor if it paid off. In 99.99 percent of cases, it didn't, but Ambra wrote down *Elsa* anyway and then rubbed her forehead.

"Elsa's a person, at least?" she asked.

The question wasn't irrelevant. Once, she was sent out to inter-view a certain Sixten Berg, twenty. Sixten turned out to be a white-crested cockatoo who could sing and dance along to "Hooked on a

Feeling." The interview became an amusing paragraph with a funny video clip online. Not quite what Ambra dreamed of during her journalism training.

Grace pulled out a neon yellow Post-it note. "Here. Elsa Svensson, born 1923. She had an affair with one of our prime ministers and evidently gave birth to his secret love child."

That made Ambra look up. "Recently?" she asked skeptically.

Grace raised an elegant eyebrow. "The woman's ninety-two, so no, not in this century. But she's never talked to the press before and she seems to be a real Norrbotten original. Could be a good story. Long, interesting life story, exotic place, you know? And it's perfect for Christmas. People love that kind of thing."

"Mmm," Ambra replied without any enthusiasm. "Which prime minister?"

"One of the dead ones. You'll have to double-check."

"Didn't they all have a load of illegitimate children?" Ambra really didn't want to do this. Give her double homicides and traffic accidents any day.

"Come on, Ambra. This one is practically made for you—it's what you're good at. Guaranteed to bring in a load of clicks, and I'm under orders to do more of this kind of thing; it sells like mad. Plus, the woman specifically asked for you."

"Of course," said Ambra. It happened sometimes. The readers wanted to meet a specific reporter.

She glanced over toward the window again. An electric Advent chandelier flickered irregularly at her. The entire media world rested on numbers of clicks, because that meant advertising revenue. And there was no ignoring the fact that, in practice, she was probably only one reshuffle away from losing her job. Her career had been on what could only be described as a downward curve for the past few years. If she didn't play ball, she would end up on night shift. Taking the night shift was a one-way street; those who went down it never came back. They lived like nocturnal pale creatures, translated pointless articles from English, and died a spiritual death. She gave up.

"Photographer?" she asked.

Grace nodded. "Local freelancer. You can contact him once you're there."

"Okay." Ambra got up. There was no point going home now. She would grab a coffee; buy an ice-cold sandwich from the staff room vending machine; call Elsa, ninety-two; and stay at the office to do some research. Hurrah.

"And you'll send me the info you have?" she asked.

"I want a first piece as soon as you can. If it's really good, maybe we can run a couple. Norrland Christmas, reindeer, cozy snow feeling, stuff like that."

Ambra rocked on her heels.

"Was there something else?" Grace asked.

Ambra paused.

"I know it's short notice and a long way to go, but you should be able to get home before Christmas." Grace's tone was stressed but friendly, and Ambra knew her boss meant well, but it wasn't exactly her holiday plans that were the problem. Ambra had exactly one relative— her foster sister, Jill—and she and Jill hadn't celebrated Christmas together for the past few years.

It wasn't that it was beneath Ambra to talk to the ex-lover of a dead celebrity either. A journalist was never meant to be forced into a humiliating piece (a rule *no one* cared about), but Ambra had worked on Entertainment and done far worse things. No, this was about the fact that she had serious issues with going north.

"I'll figure it out," she said with a repressed sigh. Her private life was no one else's business.

"I know you will." Grace's eyes were steady on her from across the desk.

At thirty, Grace was just two years older than Ambra. She was already an experienced news editor with one of the toughest papers in the division. And as though her relative youth and gender weren't enough of a handicap, Grace was also black. Born in Ethiopia, she'd moved to Sweden as a child and was some kind of academic genius. Grace Bekele was legendary in the media world, and when she looked at Ambra like that, Ambra was prepared to walk over burning coals. Or go to Kalix.

"Thanks."

"And listen, I know you want that job with the Investigative desk. I didn't forget. I'll put in a good word for you with Dan Persson, if I get the chance."

Ambra didn't know what to say; gratitude was such a difficult feeling. But that was her dream. Working for *Aftonbladet*'s Investigative desk, hunting down scoops and writing longer articles. Rumor had it there would soon be a vacant position there. They rarely came up, meaning there would be a lot of competition. Most likely all of her colleagues and competitors. But if she didn't make a mess of things in the next few weeks, then maybe she stood a chance. Providing she managed not to offend the editor-in-chief too much. Maybe it was just as well she went away for a while, now that she thought about it.

"Thanks. I'll leave tomorrow." Her mind was already thinking through the various possible angles as she automatically checked off what she would pack and which equipment she would need.

"Hold on," said Grace. She held up another Post-it note, an orange one this time, shaped like an arrow. "Found it. I was wrong. It's not Kalix after all. Sorry."

So long as it's not Kiruna, Ambra had time to think before Grace said, "The woman lives in Kiruna. I always mix up those two. Anyway, it's pretty much the same thing."

She uttered the words with the nonchalance of someone who thought that Stockholm was as far north as civilization stretched. The vast expanse of Norrland was a blank sheet even for well-educated city dwellers. But Ambra knew better. After all, there were varying degrees to every hell.

Kiruna. *Of course* it was Kiruna.

She snatched the note from Grace's hand and left the desk.

Why did it have to be Kiruna, of all places? A town she never wanted to visit again. A place where she had shivered, cried, and hated more than anywhere else in the universe.

Ambra passed the Web-TV studio and the Crime desk; she walked by Investigative and glanced longingly into their office, one of the few departments allowed to work with the door closed. She grabbed a mug of coffee and her laptop, managed to avoid her nemesis, Oliver Holm, and slumped onto a free couch. She started up her laptop and logged in. The mail program opened. Twenty e-mails in ten minutes. Nineteen of the messages were hate mail on an article she'd written about sexual harassment at a gym, published the day before. She scrolled through them and knew that she should forward the worst to the security department, but she didn't have the energy. She had been working for too long now to care about anonymous misogyny. Tomorrow, she would write about illegitimate children in Kiruna instead.

She dialed Elsa Svensson's number and sighed impatiently while she waited for an answer. She assumed it would be a while before she made it back to her apartment, her TV, and her couch.

Chapter 2

Tom Lexington threw a log onto the open fire. Although the house was well insulated, the fire provided some welcome extra warmth. Outside, it was four below zero, and the snow was coming down heavily. He would have to dig himself out if he wanted to leave the house.

Tom stared at the fire. When he focused on the flames and the crackling of the wood, he felt almost normal. He reached for another log. As he threw it onto the fire, he heard the quiet hum of his cell phone on the coffee table. He got up to see who it was. *Lodestar Security Group, switchboard.* Work.

He scratched his stubbled chin, knew he should answer—it could be important—but he didn't have the energy today. Instead, he shuffled into the kitchen and then couldn't remember why he'd gone in there. He paused, staring out the window at the snow and the trees. Waiting for the weather report on the radio. Suddenly, a loud, popping sound came from the speakers. A jingle for the next program, which was about hunting. Tom's hands started to shake. Then his thighs. His field of vision shrank, and he struggled to breathe. It happened quickly, less than a second between hearing the noise and feeling as if he was about to collapse.

He groped for the countertop to prop himself up. His heart was pounding as though he were in combat. Suddenly, he was no longer in the house. No longer in the woods outside of Kiruna, in a winter landscape of freezing temperatures and snow. He was in the desert. In the heat. In the hellhole where they'd interrogated and tortured him. His blood was rushing through his veins so fiercely that it was as if the ground was trembling beneath him. Memories flashed before his eyes like a film. He forced himself to breathe in through his nose and out through his mouth. But it didn't help. He was *there*.

He braced himself and then brought his hand down on the counter with all his might. The pain shot up his arm and into his body, and it did actually help. It hurt like hell, but the pain cut through his panic attack, and he was back in the room again.

Tom took a deep, shaking breath. The flashback had lasted only a few seconds, but he was soaked through with sweat. His legs were unsteady as he took the few steps to the pantry and grabbed a bottle of whisky. He didn't think about how many empty bottles were already beneath the sink, just poured the whisky down his throat and then turned on the faucet. Kiruna was north of the Arctic Circle and the water in the pipes was ice-cold, but he drank it greedily. As he put down his glass, he heard his cell phone again. He went into the living room and picked up the phone from the coffee table.

Mattias Ceder, he read on the screen. Again. Mattias had been calling him all fall. Tom hadn't answered once. He rejected the call and took the phone with him into the kitchen, where he poured another whisky. Two seconds later, it started to ring again. He peered down. Mattias Ceder, of course. The man always was a stubborn bastard. At one point in time, Mattias and Tom were best friends, brothers-in-arms. Back then, they would have given their lives for each other without a moment's hesitation. But that was a long time ago. Plenty had changed since then. Tom studied the phone until it fell silent. It beeped to signal a message: *Could you answer the damn phone sometime?*

He took a big gulp, poured more whisky, swirled the glass.

It was years since he'd last talked to Mattias. When they were young men, they could talk about everything, but that was before Mattias betrayed him.

Tom looked down into the sink. It was full of mugs, plates, and cutlery that he hadn't had the energy to load into the dishwasher. The woman who cleaned would be here tomorrow, so he let it be, well aware that he never used to be the kind of man who let other people clear up his mess.

He grabbed the glass, the bottle, and the cell phone and went back into the living room. It wasn't the first time he had struggled with PTSD—he'd been a soldier in one way or another ever since he was eighteen. He had been in combat, seen his comrades die, been injured. That kind of thing left its mark, and he'd suffered from both anxiety and flashbacks before, after particularly difficult experiences. But nothing like this. These memories appeared as though from nowhere. An unexpected sound, light, or smell, practically anything could set them off, and then suddenly it was as though he were *there,* back in captivity. The whole thing was entirely out of his hands. If things were different, maybe he could have talked to Mattias about it. Mattias was a soldier, too, had been in tight situations, knew how it could be. The type of thing civilians would never understand.

Tom emptied his glass. His head was spinning slightly. He grabbed his phone and wrote to Mattias: *Go to hell.*

It felt good to send that, actually. He stared at the screen to see whether he would get an answer, but nothing came. If Mattias called again, he *might* answer, he decided. He was drunk now, could feel it, knew that his judgment was clouded, that he shouldn't call anyone, not while he was crashing like this. But he dialed the number anyway. Not Mattias. Someone else. He tumbled onto the sofa and listened to the ring.

"Hello?" Ellinor answered.

"Hi, it's me," he slurred.

"Tom." She sounded sad as she said his name.

"I just wanted to hear your voice," he said, attempting to speak as normally as he could.

"You need to stop this. You're just torturing yourself. You shouldn't be calling me."

"I know." He should take a shower. Shave, pull himself together. Not keep calling his ex, week in, week out. "But I miss you," he said.

"I need to hang up." Tom heard a faint sound in the background.

"Is *he* there?"

"Bye, Tom. Take care." Ellinor hung up.

Tom stared straight ahead. Calling Ellinor was a mistake, he had known that in advance. But how was he meant to go on without her? He really didn't know. All his years of military training had been about just that. Being able to force yourself to do the impossible.

Forcing your body to continue, even when it wanted to give up, even when things seemed hopeless and despite devastating losses. It was about not thinking of anything but the task at hand.

He lay down with his head on the armrest and stared up at the ceiling, felt memories of his captivity begin to wash over him again. While he was being held prisoner, his thoughts of Ellinor kept him going. Memories of her smile, the longing to be with her again.

Calling her was idiotic. He was drunk and not thinking straight. But coming up here was still the right thing to do. Kiruna was where Ellinor was, and he wanted to be close to her. He would do anything to win her back. Anything.

Chapter 3

It really was freezing in Kiruna, Ambra thought as she moved, shivering, between the airplane and the terminal building. The wind tore at her jacket, and she half ran behind her fellow passengers. They had passed the Arctic Circle long before they landed, and up here in the north of the country, the sun had set on December 10 and wasn't expected to rise above the horizon again until January. Right now, in the middle of the day, the light seemed more like dusk, but in just a few hours' time, it would be completely dark.

She had only hand luggage with her, and so she hurried through the arrivals hall, toward the exit and the bus. The feeling of unease grew with each step. The snow was piled up in yard-high banks, the ground covered, too, and she slipped in her too-thin boots. A pack of eager huskies howled behind a steel mesh fence. Still shivering, she climbed on board, bought a ticket to Kiruna, and sat down by a window. Snow, snow, snow. The unease was practically physical now. The bus started up.

She was ten when she'd arrived in Kiruna for the first time. It was just a few days before Christmas then, too, which might be why everything felt especially tough now. A stressed social worker with pale, curly hair and darting eyes had spoken to her, explained that Ambra couldn't stay with the family she was currently living with. She remembered how she'd clutched her teddy in her arms. She knew she was too old for a soft toy, but he had been her only security.

"What's your teddy called?" the social welfare secretary asked, with that artificial tone adults always used.

"Just Teddy," Ambra whispered.

"You and Teddy are going to live with another family now. You'll have to ride the bus yourself, but you're so big now, Ambra, it'll be just fine. It'll be an adventure," she said with false cheer.

Ambra boarded that bus with her teddy and a small box containing her mother's and father's possessions.

"Someone coming to meet you?" the bus driver had asked. Ambra nodded, didn't dare say that she didn't know.

The bus driver was kind, offered her strong, minty throat tablets and talked to her all the way there. But once they arrived, her worries grew. It was the first time she had ever seen so much snow. She was wearing all the warm clothes she had, but she was still freezing. She kept close to the bus driver as he helped the other passengers lift their bags from the luggage compartment. What if no one came to meet her? What would she do then?

"Are you the foster kid?" she heard a cold voice say behind her.

Even before she turned around, she knew it wouldn't be good.

"Were you getting off here?"

Ambra jumped and returned to the present.

The bus driver was giving her an encouraging look in the rearview mirror. They were at her stop.

Ambra got up, grabbed her bag, and hurried off the bus. She trudged forward and managed to make it to her hotel, the Scandic Ferrum, without falling flat on her face. As she entered the warmth of the lobby, she stamped the snow from her feet and was greeted by a young receptionist. She checked in and headed up to her room on the second floor. It was icy cold inside, and she pulled a fleece sweater from her bag, placed her laptop beneath one arm, and went back down to reception.

"It's really cold in my room," she said.

"We've been having trouble with the heating," the receptionist explained. "We're working to fix it, but I'm afraid I don't have any other rooms available."

Ambra decided to work in the hotel restaurant. She sat down at one of the tables with her computer in front of her. The place was full of lunch guests—completely normal people, she assumed, but they still gave her the creeps. Her eyes scanned the room over and over again, and she kept checking the entrance, afraid that someone from her past might appear, however unlikely that was.

Their names were Esaias and Rakel Sventin, the people who became her new foster parents. Esaias was tall and strict, Rakel pale and silent with her hair in a thick plait down her back. They had five sons, four older boys from Esaias's first marriage, and one between them, a year older than Ambra. Esaias ruled the family with an iron fist.

"Sit back there," he said to her when he eventually picked her up from the bus. He pointed to an old car, and Ambra climbed in. She didn't have any choice. Esaias Sventin reached for her, pulled Teddy from her arms, threw him into a trash can, and then closed the car door.

Someone dropped a tray, and Ambra was dragged back to the lunch restaurant. She glanced around, her heart pounding, and she shuddered when a tall, thin man came into the restaurant. A wave of repulsion, almost fear, washed over her before she realized that, of course, it wasn't Esaias, just someone who looked vaguely similar to him. But her body remembered.

She sipped her coffee and placed a hand on her cell phone. *I'm a grown adult,* she repeated to herself. It was her constant mantra. Every second, defenseless children were suffering all over the world. Far too many of them lived a life much worse than what she herself had had to endure. If only she could leave Kiruna, she would feel peaceful and happy.

Her cell phone screen flashed. News was arriving all day. She skimmed through the latest, shared a link on Twitter, uploaded a photo to Instagram. She was a modern-day reporter, the kind they always talked about at editorial meetings and reshuffles, the kind who should be "out among the readers." Many of her coworkers grumbled, some thought themselves too good to be writing on social media, but it actually suited her perfectly, and her online platform was probably one of the main reasons she still had her job. So she made an effort to be noticed digitally.

"You wouldn't be Ambra Vinter?"

She looked up at the man standing by her table. Young, slim, and *very* handsome. Thick winter coat and heavy boots. A huge Nikon camera on a wide strap over one shoulder. A bag of lenses on the other.

"You're the freelancer," she said.

"Tareq Tahir," he confirmed. They shook hands, and he sat down opposite her. Ambra studied him furtively as he put his camera on the table. Tareq had to be twenty, maybe twenty-one. Plenty of photographers were young; the best always got into the field early. He had thick eyelashes, dark brown eyes. A manly, sexy mouth. Sensitive, strong fingers that fiddled with his camera.

Tareq flashed a white smile at the waitress, who hurried over to their table to ask if he wanted anything. Ambra had been forced to go up to the counter to order her lunch, coffee, and refill. Not one waitress was interested in coming over to serve her. But then again, she didn't look like she was in a boy band either.

"So, how's it going?" Tareq asked once the waitress dashed away. "Have you got hold of her?"

Ambra worriedly shook her head. She had a problem. She'd spoken to Elsa Svensson the day before. The ninety-two-year-old had an unexpectedly clear and lively voice, and she seemed more than happy to talk, said she was looking forward to their meeting. But as Ambra was boarding the airplane, she'd received a message saying that Elsa wanted to push back their meeting.

"I tried calling her several times, but she didn't answer."

"What do you want to do?" Tareq asked.

Ambra knew Elsa's address and had considered just heading over there, but that kind of thing could lead to a recoil effect. People were tricky like that. Not everyone appreciated journalists turning up at their house and asking to come in. Strictly speaking, she didn't even know if Elsa was home. The old lady might have packed up and left Kiruna. It happened. People who promised to talk often changed their minds at the last minute. They had every right to, but that didn't stop it from being annoying as hell.

"Do you know her?" she asked.

Tareq gave her an amused look. "You mean everyone knows everyone in Kiruna? It's not actually that small."

That wasn't what she meant; it was just a desperate question, a way of trying to solve the problem of their missing interview subject.

She knew exactly what Kiruna was like. Of course not everyone knew everyone. In fact, the inhabitants were fairly good at letting everyone go about their business undisturbed. A foster child could, for example, come to school with bruises, untreated ear infections, and fractured bones without anyone seeming to notice. She was being unfair, of course. Kiruna wasn't the only place like that. It was that way almost everywhere, because they lived in a crappy world.

Ambra scratched her hairline. The hat she was wearing was itchy, but it was so damn cold that she kept it on.

"Are you from here?" she asked Tareq, though she suspected she knew the answer; he had virtually no dialect.

"Nope, born and raised in Stockholm. I moved up with my mom after high school. She met a guy from Kiruna and fell in love with both him and the area. I'm just visiting her. I'll be back in Stockholm after New Year's. I'm starting a photography course."

"But you already work for *Aftonbladet?*"

"I got lucky and found a load of freelance work."

She interpreted that as meaning Tareq was pretty damn good. Judging by his appearance, he had roots somewhere in the Middle East. Iraq, she would guess. If his parents were immigrants, then he probably hadn't had anyone to give him a leg up in the business, which meant that getting photography work for a major national paper must have been a near-impossible task. But he'd managed it.

"You did a few jobs for Entertainment, right?" she asked, remembering what Grace had said. "How did you like it there?" she asked as neutrally as she could. In her opinion, Entertainment was a damn sewer. They reported on society events, news at the edge of journalism. They couldn't ask critical questions and were treated badly by everyone—the celebrities, their own bosses. It was awful. Unless you enjoyed chasing reality TV stars and monitoring Instagram accounts.

Tareq's fingers stroked the smooth lines of his camera. Short, clean nails; dark strands of hair; masculine hands. And then that gentle, polite voice. He was incredibly nice. And attractive.

"You were there too?" he asked.

"Yeah," she replied without elaborating. It had been her worst year as a reporter. All she could hope was that she would never have to lie in a bush waiting for some unfaithful celebrity to leave their lover's apartment again.

"So bad." He laughed with an empathetic look in his warm eyes. "I thought it was fine. But maybe not what I want to do for the long run," he added.

Handsome, nice, *and* diplomatic. Tareq would go far. Ambra felt a sudden, inappropriate urge to pull off her hat and plump up her hair.

The waitress came back with Tareq's order. He clutched the condensation-covered glass of orange soda.

"Fanta is my vice," he said, smiling at the waitress who looked as though she wanted to start a family with him.

After the waitress reluctantly left them, Ambra glanced down at her cell for roughly the tenth time. She was itching with restlessness. To put it bluntly, she was costing the paper money up here if she didn't produce anything. She was already trying to come up with alternative pieces in her head. Something about snow, maybe? Or the plans to move the entire town away from the mine shaft?

Tareq gulped down his soda and pushed the glass away. He got up and grabbed his camera and lens bag. "I just wanted to come in and say hi. Is it okay if I go out awhile? I have some things I can be doing while we wait. Just let me know as soon as you hear anything."

Ambra nodded, watched him leave with long, quick steps, and then allowed her gaze to sweep across the restaurant. The Scandic Ferrum was in the middle of town, and it seemed to function as some kind of gathering point. Businessmen and women shivering in thin jackets at one table. Mothers in practical winter clothing, feeding their babies purées and fruit at another. A group of firefighters over by the counter.

She studied them for a while before she checked her phone. Sent the latest message to Grace and waited impatiently to see whether a bubble containing three dots might appear, an indication that a reply was on the way. She wanted to know what she should do if Elsa Svensson didn't turn up.

Nothing.

She opened Instagram instead, wondered whether she should call Jill, but then her cell phone flashed and vibrated in her hand. Grace had finally replied: *Heard any more?*

Ambra replied with quick, practiced movements: *Nope. Should I wait?*

She almost hoped that Grace would tell her to go home. But no: *Yeah, wait. Did Tareq turn up?*

Yup.

Grace ended with: *Keep me updated.*

Ambra put down her phone. She drummed her fingers on the

table in frustration. She'd drunk far too much coffee and was feeling shaky and slightly ill. She glanced up at the counter again. The firefighters were gone. A solitary man was left, buying a coffee. He was wearing a thick, unbuttoned winter coat, a plaid shirt, and a T-shirt beneath it.

While Ambra thought about what to do next, she studied the man. There was something about him she couldn't quite put her finger on. He was silent, standing tall like a mountain. Broad shoulders. Long-haired and bearded, too. He looked like a tough guy, a real Norrland cliché; all that was missing was the snowmobile and the gun. Ambra turned away. She'd always had trouble with the beefed-up, macho type.

The man came toward her table with a mug of coffee, and she cast another quick glance at him. *FBI,* it said on the T-shirt beneath his shirt. She squinted at the text beneath it. *Female Body Inspector.* Jesus, that was tasteless. She pulled a disgusted face and couldn't stop herself from muttering, "Nice shirt," just as he walked by.

"What?" The man stopped. His voice was dull and hoarse, and he looked at Ambra as if she had just appeared from thin air, as if he was so deep in thought that he hadn't even realized he was around other people.

She could make out zero sense of humor in what had to be the darkest eyes she had ever seen. Every warning bell she had was ringing.

"Did you say something?" he asked, and his eyes narrowed on her. They were bloodshot, and his beard looked unkempt. Then there was the chauvinist slogan. It was a joke, she knew that, but she had written so many articles about trafficking, child prostitution, and honor killings. About young women treated as objects, or worse. About perfectly ordinary men who murdered their girlfriends or wives in a jealous rage, simply because they thought they owned them and their bodies. His T-shirt was disgusting, even if it was meant to be humorous.

She knew she should apologize, stay quiet, ignore him. "You're not funny, if that's what you thought," she said instead.

The man froze, and she tensed. *Just take it easy, Ambra. He looks dangerous.* The man continued to stare at her, as if he didn't understand what she meant. A shiver passed through her. It looked like he was about to say something, but then he shook his head and moved on.

Ambra slumped back in her chair. The blood started running through her veins again. She didn't dare turn around and look for him. There was something in his eyes, something in the way he held himself that told her he wasn't someone she should provoke. The hairs on the back of her neck were on end, and she assumed he was sitting somewhere behind her. Christ, she hated this town.

Chapter 4

Tom glanced over to the woman who'd just snapped at him. He'd been so lost in thought that he hadn't heard what she said, just noticed she was angry. From where he was now sitting, he could study her from behind, and with his back to the wall he had the best possible view of the restaurant. His eyes quickly swept the room before he looked at the woman again. All he could see, beneath the layers of clothing, the scarf, and hat, were a few dark curls. He'd automatically noticed her pale skin when she snapped at him, her dark brows and almost glowing green eyes.

She wasn't from Kiruna, that much was clear from both her clothing and her attitude. And from something more difficult to define, in the way she held herself and the way she moved. Kiruna natives were rarely in a hurry, and they moved at a different tempo, never with that intense efficiency. She was a big-city girl, he was almost sure of that. Typing away on her computer, constantly checking her phone. Every now and then, she would scan the room and take a quick sip of her coffee. Everything she did was quick, as though she were surrounded by some kind of high-voltage energy.

Tom took a drink. They had good coffee here at the hotel, and he liked how big the restaurant was. Ever since his time as a prisoner, he struggled with feeling confined. The hotel was one of the central meeting places in Kiruna. A lunch and coffee spot during the day, a bar at night; sooner or later, the majority of Kiruna residents came here.

He scanned the room again. It was automatic, taking in his surroundings. Making a note of who was waiting for someone, who might represent a threat. He did it without thinking. Read faces to see whether they meant anyone harm, checked hands for weapons. Men and women alike.

The restaurant was pretty busy, just two days before Christmas. On weekdays the hotel held conferences, but now the guests were mostly tourists and vacationers. Kiruna was a popular destination. People went dogsledding, tried to hunt down the Northern Lights, went skiing. Or else they took a night trip on snowmobiles, across the frozen Torne River, stopping for coffee by a roaring fire. The huge car manufacturers sent people north to test-drive their new models in wintry conditions, and many car ads had been filmed in and around Kiruna. And then there was Esrange, the rocket range and research center, not far away. Scientists, both Swedish and international, were drawn to it. But the dark-haired woman with the intense eyes was neither a test driver nor a space scientist; Tom was sure of that.

He found his gaze being constantly drawn to her, and he didn't know why. She was so hostile and thorny that somehow her presence forced its way through the haze he was stuck in, and now he couldn't ignore her. Judging from her back, she was currently hammering away at the keyboard. Did that mean she was a writer? No, they weren't usually so ill-disposed. The few writers Tom knew were pretty quiet; they spent most of their time daydreaming. There was no real reason for him to care. It was just that he couldn't work out why she was so angry. Her fury seemed to be aimed at him in particular. Like he had done something, personally, to her. But he had a good eye for faces, and he was sure they had never met before.

He saw her check her phone again, and then it struck him: She was a journalist. Not a local reporter, but from one of the big-city papers. It all fit. But why was she here? What could be so important that a reporter from the capital—he was almost certain she was from Stockholm—would travel all the way up here a few days before Christmas?

Maybe she had relatives in Kiruna and was just getting some work done between family gatherings? Stockholm journalists often had roots in smaller towns or villages, Tom knew. He'd met so many journalists over the years. Educated and instructed them in safety. Flash points and the edges of war zones were always crawling with reporters, crazy thrill seekers. He'd argued with many of them, because journalists argued constantly. Been annoyed at them and their meddlesome belief that they were the only ones *really* standing up for democracy. Been interviewed and misquoted. Seen them leave people high and dry in pursuit of high reader numbers. Twist the facts and start crusades. No, he didn't like journalists.

Tom looked down at the table. He could still feel the aftereffects of that morning's panic attack. This was one of his bad days. It was incredible that it could vary like that, completely without logic. He never knew when the panic would well up, when a sound might make him overreact. The firecrackers the kids were running around with didn't make it any better. It was still a week until New Year's, and firecrackers were forbidden, but they were still going off everywhere.

A few days earlier he had found himself jumping into a snowdrift, entirely involuntarily, when one went off behind him. His heart was racing, he had tunnel vision, and it was only when he came to his senses that he realized he had thrown himself onto a child, as though to protect it with his body, and that the child was now beneath him, its hysterical mother to one side, pounding him on the back. The kid howled, the mother shouted, and Tom mumbled an apology and hurried away.

The journalist got up. She was talking on her cell phone and took a moment to stretch, to roll her neck and shoulders. She pulled a face, as though the movement was painful. She had long legs, but otherwise none of her body was visible beneath all her layers. Not that he was checking her out. It was just something he noticed. While she talked, her eyes were constantly on her computer, like a hawk.

And then everything changed.

Tom forgot the journalist and everything else.

Because *she* came into the restaurant, and he almost stopped breathing.

Ellinor.

Jesus, it was really her.

Did he come here to the hotel because, sooner or later, everyone came here, and he knew maybe Ellinor would too? Honestly, he didn't even know anymore. His brain wasn't working like normal. Sometimes, he wondered whether he was going crazy. But he was in Kiruna because of Ellinor, hoping that despite everything she still needed him, that she missed him the way he missed her.

He followed her movements at the counter. She was blond and straight-backed. Healthy and happy, a sporty woman who loved skiing and swimming, who loved children and animals—the entire world, apparently, other than him, Tom Lexington.

She placed her order and then glanced around the room. Her eyes scanned over the guests.

Tom was perfectly still.

And then she spotted him.

She froze midmovement. Tom simply stared. Ellinor stared back. All other sounds disappeared. It was as if a corridor formed between them. Tom held his breath, didn't dare move. *Please, don't go* was all he could think.

He had made so many mistakes where Ellinor was concerned.

If she stays, I'll take it as a sign. Please, don't go.

Give me one more chance.

She paused.

He continued to hold his breath as the memories washed over him.

He'd first met Ellinor Bergman in Kiruna when he was twenty-one. Ellinor was eighteen, with soft blond hair and a mouth that was almost always smiling. They met in a bar. She was at a table with a couple of friends, and he was at another with his.

"Do you live here?" he asked when they bumped into one another by the bar.

"Yeah. You?"

"I'm studying to become an officer. I'm here on an exercise with my old battalion."

"Ranger?" She smiled.

Tom nodded. Might have expected her to seem impressed. Most girls were when you told them you were a ranger and an officer.

"My dad's in the military," she explained.

"What do you do?"

"I'm in school. Today's my eighteenth birthday. We're out celebrating."

"So maybe I can buy you a birthday drink?" Tom said, feeling incredibly worldly.

She let him.

They talked all evening. Ellinor got both drunk and flirtatious, and Tom tried to keep up, though he had never been the flirting type.

They didn't sleep together that evening. He knew right away that Ellinor was more than just a quick lay, and so he wanted things to move slowly. Plus, she still lived at home. He chased her over the weeks that followed. Took her to the movies and to dinner. It didn't take long before he was in love. And it wasn't surprising at all: Ellinor was easy to spend time with. Happy and positive, easygoing and bright natured. A kind, uncomplicated girl. And pretty, too.

They had sex for the first time at her house one evening, when her parents were away. He wasn't a virgin, and nor was she. It was good, and he knew she was The One. Nothing felt complicated with Ellinor. When he had to study, she found things to do on her own. She had plenty of friends, had lots of activities, and was full of energy. His studies and his education sent him across the country, but he would travel back to Kiruna to be with her as often as he could.

"I don't want to live in Kiruna forever," Ellinor said when she graduated high school.

He kissed the tip of her nose. "So where do you want to live?"

"In Stockholm. With you."

And so when Tom graduated, they moved to Stockholm together. They bought a flat and felt like adults. Ellinor went to college and worked extra from time to time. Tom worked a lot. Weeks could pass and they would barely see each other.

They had their downs, of course, but what couple doesn't? Once they had been together four years, they bought engagement rings.

"It feels so right, Tom," she said as he pushed the ring onto her finger. For him, it was a sign that they would be together forever.

Life went on. Ellinor got a job as a teacher at an inner-city school, took different courses and enrolled in further education, changed jobs. Tom worked hard. The years passed, and though he spent a lot of time abroad on secret operations, they were like any other big-city couple. Or so he thought.

Until one June day earlier that year when Ellinor was standing with her head against the door frame into the kitchen, which they had just renovated. She looked at him and sighed. "Tom, we need to talk."

At first, he barely noticed her strange tone; his thoughts were elsewhere. He looked up from his paper and asked, "Can we do it later? Work's been pretty intense."

She crossed her arms.

"Work's always intense. I want to talk. Now." It seemed as if she was psyching herself up, and he sensed catastrophe. "I slept with someone else."

The shock felt like a physical blow. "Who?" he asked as he fought back the feeling of unreality.

"It doesn't matter."

"It matters a lot to me. Is it serious?"

"That I slept with someone else? Yeah, it's pretty serious."

And then she started to cry. Tom felt remarkably shut off. Work really was incredibly intense at that moment. His company, Lodestar Security Group, was expanding at record speed. They specialized in complicated transactions, and one of their clients in Baghdad had just lost staff in a suicide attack. "I don't know what to say," he said impotently.

"You aren't angry? Don't you feel anything? Nothing?"

"I love you, Ellinor. What more can I say?"

She shook her head. "So don't say anything. It was never your strong point. I want to leave you, Tom. This isn't working anymore."

"What isn't working? Tell me. Please. I'll do anything."

"But it doesn't matter now."

He couldn't understand how it had happened. It really did come out of the blue for him. At that point, his strongest feeling was still one of unreality. "I know I've been working a lot."

"It's not just that. I've made up my mind."

"Please, Ellinor. You can wait, can't you? We can talk?"

"I don't know if there's any point."

His cell phone started to ring. It was from Iraq. "I need to take this," he said automatically.

She gave him a look but said nothing, just let him go.

He worked like a machine for two days straight. Ellinor sent him a message to say she was going to her parents' house to think. Ellinor's parents liked him, he liked them, and Tom thought it was a good idea; maybe they could talk to her. But it was actually the last time he and Ellinor spoke in months. Would he have acted differently if he had known what would happen?

The very next day, Tom got a call from a friend that led to his going to Chad, which led to an armed operation, a helicopter crash in the desert, and being taken prisoner. Back home, everyone thought he was dead. The trip, which should have taken only a few days, which should have been a diversion from the crisis Ellinor and he were going through, changed everything. It was four months before he finally returned to Sweden, in October. By then, Ellinor had already rented out their apartment, moved back to Kiruna, and moved on.

What a fucking expression.

Moved on.

They hadn't seen one another since that day in June, he realized, as they continued to stare at each other across the hotel restaurant.

He'd called her the minute he was free and back home in Sweden. She was glad he was alive. But he hadn't wanted her to visit him in the hospital, and then she hadn't come down to Stockholm at all, said it would be better if they didn't see each other.

But now Ellinor took her tea from the counter and started to slowly, almost hesitantly, walk toward him. Tom barely dared breathe. He searched her face for a sign of . . . anything. She looked like she always did. It had to mean something that she was here, that she was on her way over to his table, that they were finally going to *see* each other.

If Ellinor would just give him one more chance, he would fix everything he had destroyed, become the man she wanted, the man she deserved. Seeing her again . . . He almost held his breath.

She reached his table, cocked her head, studied his chest, and said, "That shirt, Tom. I would never have thought that of you." She raised an eyebrow, and at first he had no idea what she was talking about. Then he connected the dots and looked down. Apparently he was wearing a plaid shirt, though he had no memory of having put it on. And beneath that, a black T-shirt that he'd pulled on without giving it a second thought. Upside down, he read the white text on what he had assumed was one of his usual black T-shirts. *FBI,* it said in huge letters. *Female Body Inspector* beneath it.

Ahh. That explained a lot. Both Ellinor's amazed look and the prickly journalist's response. He quickly glanced over to her table, but she seemed to be absorbed by her laptop.

"It's not mine," he explained, though they shouldn't be talking about T-shirts. "The woman who cleans and does the washing for me has a son. It must be his. I guess she washed our things together."

Ellinor studied him.

"You look tired," she eventually said. She was still on her feet. He wished she would sit down, drink her tea opposite him like she used to, say she had changed her mind, that she hadn't moved on at all.

But she remained standing, continued to inspect him. "And you've lost weight," she added.

Tom ran a hand over his forehead. "I'm okay," he lied.

"You're drinking too much."

He gave her a bewildered look. How could she know that?

She smiled again, that soft smile which Tom had practically etched into the inside of his skull when his jailers did unbearable things to him. "Can't keep anything a secret around here," she said with an apologetic shrug. "One of the girls who works at the liquor store is in my book group. You've met her. She said you came in and bought a load of liquor, repeatedly. You never had a problem with alcohol before."

"No," he agreed. But that was, of course, before those months in which he had been abused on a daily basis by men who hated him and everything he stood for. Back home, he had been given scripts for all kinds of pills, but that was where he drew the line, the psycho-pharmaceuticals. He self-medicated with alcohol instead. Very smart.

"You have to stop calling me," she said quietly.

It was so embarrassing, that he had been reduced to someone who called his ex when he was drunk. But that was also the problem. He didn't see her as his ex.

"What do you see in him?" The words came from nowhere, and he regretted them immediately.

Her shoulders slumped. "Tom . . ."

"Sorry. Can you sit down for a while?"

She glanced around, then slinked into one of the chairs and put her cup down on the table.

"I'm so sorry, I know it's my fault you feel this way."

"It's not your fault." *Or not just yours anyway.*

"You know what I mean." She blew on her tea.

"You ended things before I left. You couldn't have known what would happen."

"I thought you were dead. That's what they told us."

"So you moved back up here?"

"Yeah."

"How long had you been seeing him, before you told me?" *Days? Weeks? Months?* He had no idea. Did he even want to know? She'd ended things, he'd left, and while he languished in Chad, she'd built a new life for herself.

Ellinor's fingers moved along the edge of the cup. "What does it matter?"

"It doesn't, I guess."

"I'm sorry. The last thing I wanted was to hurt you. And it was awful to think you'd died. Especially after . . ." She trailed off and stared down at her tea.

"After you broke my heart?" Tom attempted to sound lighthearted but suspected he failed miserably.

Ellinor looked pained. "Sorry," she said. "That was never my intention. But things were bad between us for so long. You have to agree about that."

Tom didn't agree at all. To him, everything had been fine, and the fact that she was unhappy had come like a lightning bolt from the heavens. "Are you really happy with him?" It felt completely impossible. How could she be happy with someone *else?*

"Yes, I am. I'm happy. With Nilas."

Nilas. What kind of name was that?"

"You really don't look so great. Shouldn't you talk to someone?"

"I have. A psychologist."

Her face lit up. "That's great. That's good to hear."

He pulled a face. He didn't like psychologists.

The breakdown had happened on one of his first days back at work. He'd been taken straight to the hospital on his return to Sweden; he was undernourished and infected. The day after he left the hospital, he went into the office. All he wanted was to work. It was raining, and the leaves were yellow. The first two days were fine. But on the third day, he was in a meeting. A Swedish businessman had been kidnapped in Pakistan. They were discussing whether to take on the task of trying to rescue him. It was nothing unusual. That type of request was very common, and it was one of their fields of expertise. They were talking about weapons and various strategies when he suddenly felt ill. At first, he thought it was a stomach bug, that he must have eaten something bad. But then his body started to shake.

He had never experienced anything like it.

At the same time, he also started sweating, and he thought that it would be too damn ironic if he died of a heart attack right then, after everything he had survived.

"Tom?" one of his colleagues asked worriedly.

The question sounded as if it were reaching him through water.

Afterward, he could remember only fragments of loud voices, phone calls, and a trip to the hospital in an ambulance. An overworked ER doctor ran an EKG, took tests, and listened to his chest.

"It's a panic attack, nothing to worry about," the doctor announced, and then hurried away, probably to see someone who was actually sick.

Since Lodestar had incredibly expensive private health insurance, the head of HR insisted that Tom talk to a psychologist as a follow-up.

"Acute stress disorder, panic attacks, and probably undiagnosed PTSD," the psychologist said, studying him over her steel-rimmed glasses.

"Not so bad," he said with an artificial laugh.

"I'd say it's fairly serious."

"But it'll pass?"

The psychologist studied him awhile. "That depends."

"On what?"

"On you." Typical psychologist.

"So what should I do?"

She wrote something in her notepad. "What do you want?" she asked. It was as though she *couldn't* give advice.

"I want to be cured. I thought that was obvious."

"Of course. But what do you plan to do once you feel better? What do you *want?*"

And Tom sat there in that expensive psychologist's clinic, thinking that all he wanted was to have Ellinor back.

The very next week, he decided to take a time-out from work, from Stockholm, from everything, and left for Kiruna. But Ellinor was stubborn. She didn't want to see him, didn't see any point in it. Though now she was here. That had to be a sign.

"I miss you," he said now.

Ellinor stirred her tea more quickly. "Tom . . ." She looked away, bit her lip.

"Can't you give me another chance?" he asked. If he could just get Ellinor back, everything would be fine. He was sure of it.

"I have to go now." She got up, clutched her purse. He looked at her fingers. She wasn't wearing her ring. Of course. Her eyes followed his gaze. "When they told us you were dead, I had to go through your things. Our things. I sent your ring to your mom. It was awful for her, thinking you'd died. Do you want my ring back, by the way? You paid for it."

"No, it's yours," he managed.

She seemed to hesitate, as though she didn't know how to say good-bye. *Don't go,* he wanted to say. Stay. Don't leave me.

"Take care, Tom," she said.

He watched her leave, stayed at his table, drained of all the energy he thought he had managed to scrape together.

What was he going to do?

He glanced over to the table where the prickly journalist was sitting, but she must have left while he talked to Ellinor. Her computer was gone. The only sign of her was a white cup with a faint lipstick mark.

Chapter 5

Ambra stamped her feet against the cold and peered in through a store window while she thought. Should she call Grace to say that this job was going down the drain? Grace probably had at least ten other reporters out in the field right now. Hundreds of national and international news reports to read and prioritize, hour in and hour out. One lone reporter, way north of the Arctic Circle, who couldn't get hold of a low-priority interview subject was hardly very important.

She wanted to get back to Stockholm and the office. Wanted to be where the action was, loved the pulse and the energy of the newsroom and hated this dump of a town. Imagine if something huge happened right now, and she missed it because she was here?

There was a time, just a few years ago, when she got to report on important things, to write articles that made a difference. That was before they got the new editor-in-chief. After that, everything went downhill. She and Dan Persson didn't click at all. Just thinking about it made her stomach ache. She wanted nothing other than to work for *Aftonbladet,* it was that simple. She knew a lot of people thought she was confident, but she really wasn't. She didn't want to lose her job. Couldn't. Because if she couldn't be a reporter, she genuinely didn't know what she would do.

She started to walk as she blew hot air between her palms and her gloves, trying to warm up her hands. She passed a tourist shop. The place was crowded with people, offering snowmobile rides, trips to see the Northern Lights, dogsledding, and ice fishing. She stopped. The window was full of Sami Christmas decorations, souvenirs, and fluffy hats. Packages wrapped in red ribbon gave the place a cozy holiday feeling. Her eyes fell on a pair of earmuffs. They were the world's lamest accessory, but when she was a kid she had wanted a pair so much she practically hadn't been able to think of anything else. Not that she ever got any. She hadn't gotten any Christmas presents at all.

She turned away. She'd promised herself not to care about the approaching holiday—it was just a few days she needed to get through—but she could feel her mood worsening the closer the damned day came. A young girl was coming toward her with a man, presumably the girl's father. They were chatting, the man holding the girl's hand tight, listening, nodding, stroking her hair. Ambra swallowed, looked away.

As she quickly crossed the road, her cell phone rang.

Praise God and Hallelujah, finally! She quickly accepted the call as she plugged in her headset. She pushed the headphones into her ears.

"Hello, this is Elsa," she heard on the other end of the line.

"Hi! How are you?"

"Good, thanks." And then it sounded as though Elsa giggled.

Ambra glanced at her watch. It was only five o'clock. "I'm so glad you called. Could I come over? Now? Or tomorrow?"

"No, no, not tonight, I'm expecting company. And tomorrow is Christmas Eve day."

"I can do tomorrow," Ambra said quickly, hoping Elsa wasn't going away or hosting thirty-six relatives at home. People rarely had time to meet on Christmas Eve, the biggest holiday in Sweden. "Is that okay for you?"

"Absolutely."

"Could we come over to your place? It'll be me and a photographer."

Silence.

"Elsa?"

Elsa giggled again, and Ambra could have sworn she sounded drunk. "Sorry. That's fine, dear."

"So tomorrow morning at ten?"

Elsa said they were welcome, and Ambra hung up, hugely skeptical about the entire piece. She pulled out one earbud and continued to stamp life into her feet. Her cell phone rang again. Shit, had she changed her mind? But this time, it wasn't Elsa.

It was Jill.

"Are you at work?" Jill asked the moment Ambra answered.

"Nah, in Kiruna." Ambra caught sight of her reflection in yet another store window, phone in hand, headphone in ear. Sometimes, it felt like all she did was talk on the phone. "You?" Jill was an artist, and she spent more time on the road than she did at home.

"I'm so tired, I can hardly remember what the town's called. What're you doing there? I thought you hated Kiruna."

Ambra saw her reflection smirk. "I hate most things."

"True. Me too. Everything fine with you? Sure you don't want a Christmas gift?"

"Completely sure," Ambra replied firmly.

Jill earned roughly the same in one week as Ambra earned in a year, so things quickly got strange when it came to giving gifts. Having one of Sweden's most successful singers as a foster sister wasn't always easy.

"I'm due onstage soon," said Jill. "And I've been invited to dinner with some county governor afterward, so I just wanted to call and say hi before. I'd prefer to skip the dinner. It'll be all canapés and champagne and five courses and a load of boring people."

"Sounds better than my evening."

"Nah, it gets boring in the end too. Well, I need to go warm up my voice. Don't work your ass off. Kisses."

That was something new Jill had started doing. Ambra remembered seeing it on Instagram too. *Kisses*. She hated it. Jill moved in a bizarre world of artists with strange rules of interaction that Ambra had never understood.

"Bye," she said, ending the call.

She looked up at the sky. That was something she remembered from her childhood. How bright the stars were up here. Did astronomers ever get into conflicts like she did at the newspaper? Arguments about being the boss's favorite, competition for interesting jobs, e-mails from anonymous haters. Of course they did. The entire academic world was like a soap opera. Early in her career, she wrote a report on professors who took bribes to raise their students' grades at a particular Swedish college. Her first death threat arrived after that article. She still had it, in a frame, on her desk. Macabre, maybe. Though not as macabre as threatening a young, female journalist with anal rape. There hadn't been any mention of that in the job description. Being called whore, slut, and traitor on a daily basis.

Ambra decided to keep walking. Yes, she was freezing her ass off, but she needed to clear her mind. The snow crunched beneath her feet as she crossed the road. The air was so cold that it glittered in the glow of the street lamps. The scent of ginger cookies and mulled wine hung over the streets. That familiar fragrance of companionship. *But it'll be over soon, and then it's an entire year until next Christmas.*

She was still trying to pep herself up when the façade of the hotel appeared. She hurried toward it. A man came out of the entrance and headed straight toward her along the sidewalk. Wasn't it the same man, the one from the restaurant earlier? The one with the sexist T-shirt? He seemed to be deep in thought. Ambra was on the verge of stepping into the road, but then she decided to stubbornly continue on the sidewalk. The man was getting closer. Would he move to one side? Nothing suggested that. Maybe it was stupid of her, but Ambra kept walking straight ahead, on a collision course, her pulse rapidly picking up. He still hadn't seen her. Was she invisible, or what? The man's head was bare, and he wasn't wearing gloves or a scarf. His chunky boots crunched in the snow. She had time to see that he was wearing pants with pockets on the sides. Maybe he was some kind of construction worker?

And then they crashed into each other.

Not hard, he looked up and swerved at the last moment, but since Ambra refused to move a millimeter, their upper arms and shoulders collided with a faint rustling sound. She shuddered a little, almost imagined feeling his warmth through the layers of coats separating them. She saw the surprise in his eyes, then recognition, and then he was gone. It sounded like he mumbled something, maybe a "sorry," but by then she had already picked up the pace and was almost at the hotel. She hurried in through the entrance without turning around.

What a weird guy.

And what a crappy day this had been.

Chapter 6

Jilliana Lopez stretched across the hotel bed in her suite. She was still wearing her stage clothes—a tight sequin dress, shiny pantyhose, and super-tight spandex underwear—but she had pulled off her red booties and was wiggling her toes. Her dress glittered at the slightest movement. Today's show ended with "Ave Maria," her showpiece, and she'd been given a standing ovation by the hundred or so Christmas guests. A good show, all in all. And now she was full of the special feeling she always had after a performance. Exhausted and worked up at the same time. Full of impressions but devoid of feelings. She was also a tiny, tiny bit hoarse. She would have to be careful with her voice—she was fully booked for the next two years.

She raised her legs into the air and studied them. The boots were pretty, but they were tight and her toes ached. *Everything* ached.

"When am I next free?" she asked her assistant, Ludvig, who was darting around the hotel suite with silent, effective movements. Jill squinted at him. Without lenses, she was practically blind, but even when she was wearing them, her vision wasn't great. She squinted even more. Ludvig was sweet. "How old are you, exactly?" she added. He looked terrifyingly young.

"Nineteen." He pushed a strand of blond hair behind his ear, but it fell forward again immediately. He had done the exact same thing at least ten times in the last minute.

Ludvig was her first male assistant. The record label had sent him, and it had gone surprisingly well. Nineteen. Technically, he was legal. He pushed his hair behind his ear again. Young men were usually very energetic. "And I guess you want to be an artist?" she said, giving up the thought of seducing him before she even finished the question. She didn't sleep with people who worked for her. Things got too messy. *Been there, done that.*

"I'm in a band," Ludvig said, picking up the red booties and putting them in the closet. He didn't elaborate, and Jill didn't ask. Wannabe artists were thirteen a dozen. It was awful, really, the music world. New, hungry youngsters were constantly snapping at your heels. And the others, those who were more or less successful already, were just waiting for a chance to drive a knife into your back. Though you would still exchange hugs on the red carpet. She groaned. The spandex was like a straitjacket. She raised one hand in the air. Ambra sounded low when they'd spoken on the phone, she thought absentmindedly as she studied her long red gel nails. Red wasn't really her shade, despite her dramatic Latin coloring. There was something in the gaudy Christmas red that made her own skin tone look almost vulgar. Pornographic. Ugh, she *hated* it. She would take off the nails as soon as the Christmas shows were done.

"You asked when you were free," Ludvig interjected, interrupting her thoughts. Jill liked that, the way he kept on top of things. It was an unusual quality, especially in a young man.

"You have two shows on Christmas Eve," he continued. "But then you have a few days off before the New Year's shows start. The first is in Örebro city. The Swedish National Public TV, SVT, is coming to film. Skansen, the Sconce, on New Year's Eve. And then the televised *Melodifestivalen,* the Melody Festival, starts."

Crap, that damn circus. Can I really manage another year?

"I haven't decided what to do about that," Jill said, still thinking. Why was Ambra down? Was it because it was Christmas, or was it something else? You never knew with Ambra, and they weren't great at confiding in each other. Neither of them liked this time of year. They just handled it differently. Jill made sure she was fully booked with shows and concerts. She had done so ever since her breakthrough on Swedish *Idol*. As long as she was booked up, laughed a lot, and kept moving forward, she had no time to be sad. But Ambra had a tendency to wallow a little.

Jill looked at Ludvig, who was now shaking a feather boa as he hummed a Christmas tune. Jesus, it suddenly struck her. If he was nineteen now, he must've been about seven when she'd had her breakthrough. How could twelve years have passed already? Where had the time gone? Ludvig placed a huge bouquet of roses into a vase.

"I don't understand why people always give me flowers," said Jill. She was never in the same place for longer than a day, sometimes even less than that. Did people think she took them with her? "They should give me money instead."

Once, in an interview, Jill had mentioned that she loved yellow roses—the kind of nonsense statement she sometimes made because of a sponsor, because it felt right in the moment, she couldn't remember. But now she was constantly being given yellow roses. She hated them.

"I think they're pretty," said Ludvig.

"Upload them to Insta, and you can have them. Or give them to someone in the hotel, I don't care."

She would rest for another five minutes, and then she would get up and change. But Jesus, she was exhausted. Was it normal to be so tired? Was she getting old? She closed her eyes to fight the panic. But she had been doing the same Christmas show since October, working her way northwards from Ystad, Malmö, and Helsingborg in the south, and now she was finishing things off in the north of the country. No surprise she was tired. She *wasn't* old.

She rolled over onto her stomach, pressed her chin to her chest, and stretched her neck. Her hairline itched. There was so much spray, foam, and glitter in her hair that it felt like plastic beneath her fingers.

She reached for her cell phone, posed for a selfie, and uploaded it to Instagram. She handled most of that stuff herself. She had a good sense of what her followers liked and started to write in English long before her label even entertained the thought. The minute she switched to a more internationally accessible language, her account exploded, and she now had close to two million followers. That wasn't much in a global context, but the number was growing all the time.

"I need a hit in English," she philosophized as the likes started to pour in. And she should upload a moving image, she thought. The fans always went crazy for video clips.

Most of her fans were sweet, but it never took long for the first haters to appear. She didn't want to read what they wrote, but she also couldn't stop herself.

Your lips are ugly.
Looks like you've put on weight.
Jesus Christ, you're ugly.

She held up the phone to Ludvig.

"Sometimes I wonder what's wrong with people."

"You know most of them love you," he said.

She kept scrolling; it was like an addiction. "It never feels like that's enough," she said. Some of the haters were names she recognized from years back. She wondered what was going on behind their evil comments. Most online trolls had male aliases, but that didn't necessarily mean a thing. Private accounts, of course. She blocked the worst of them, but new ones were constantly appearing. In just a few minutes, she had several hundred likes. The majority were sweet, but a feeling of unease lingered over her, like dirt that won't scrub off. She only had herself to blame for reading them, she knew that, but still.

"Sometimes I think about just quitting social media," she said, half joking and half serious. She needed to focus on writing new material, not allow anonymous bullies to make her feel bad. It took up so much energy.

"Don't let the haters win. You know you have loads of fans who worship you."

Or at least the person they think I am, Jill thought cynically.

For the most part, she was satisfied with her life. Maybe not happy, exactly, but only idiots were happy. She was in the position she had been fighting for all these years. She knew the price of fame was loneliness and, from time to time, hate, and she was generally prepared to pay that price. But sometimes a melancholy she really couldn't understand came over her. She had everything. Who was she to feel sad? She turned off the screen and put down her cell phone. The best way to handle the problem was always to ignore it.

"Will you upload something else to Insta for me? From the show?" she asked Ludvig.

"Of course. You want to approve it first?"

She shook her head.

"Which shoes were you thinking for dinner?" Ludvig held up a pair of Manolo Blahniks.

Jill hesitated. They were nice, but her feet were so sore. And her stage clothes were so tight it felt as if they were about to burst. She would probably have to take it easy with what she ate for a while. Her metabolism wasn't exactly getting better with age. All she wanted was to stay in her room, drink hot chocolate, and eat cheese sandwiches. God, she would kill for that. When did she last eat cheese? Cream? Chocolate? She ate nothing, worked out constantly, and she still weighed more today than she had at the same point last year. They'd had to let out her dress a half centimeter. Ugh. Was she getting old *and* fat? No one would love her if she was fat. They would tear her to shreds.

"I'll wear those," she said with a firm nod toward the Manolo Blahnik shoes. "And the pink Diane von Furstenberg dress." If she kept on all the tight underwear, it would work. And that was just what she needed to get herself into a good mood again.

Feeling shit hot. Flirting. Mingling.

She would eat two tiny bites of every course, max. She would just push the rest of the food around the plate and talk about how good it was, about how full she already felt. That classic strategy. Small bites and no dessert. She would treat herself to a glass of wine too. A large one, white, because that contained fewer calories. She could say she didn't like red. Good plan.

She could already feel her energy returning. Nothing got better by lying in a hotel suite, feeling sorry for yourself. You had to choose happiness, live in the now . . . she tried to remember other mantras. Love herself? Aim for the stars?

She got up from the bed, went over to the dressing table, and picked up a brush. "How far are we from Kiruna, do you know?" She began to brush the spray from her hair. She was useless at geography. And all other subjects. She had failed almost everything at school and hadn't even bothered applying to senior high school. Singing was all she could do.

"A few hours by car, I guess," Ludvig replied.

Should she make a stop in Kiruna? Say hello to her foster sister?

Jill turned around and waited while Ludvig unzipped her sequined dress.

She would dress up, in high heels and lipstick, and she would deliver. Because if there was one thing Jill Lopez could do, it was deliver. After that, she could think about Ambra.

"Write on Insta that I'm allergic to roses now. Especially yellow ones."

Chapter 7

As Tom walked to his car, his thoughts were on the angry woman he'd just run into. Again.

For the second time, he'd been so lost in thought that he didn't see her coming. Not before they almost collided on the sidewalk. He bumped against her upper arm and then caught a glimpse of a knotted brow and a stubborn mouth. She seemed angry, and he wondered whether rage was her default setting. When he turned around, she was already on her way inside, which meant she was probably staying at the hotel.

There was something about her that he couldn't quite put his finger on, as though he could hear her through the bubble he was trapped inside. But he couldn't understand why. She was overwrought and hot-tempered, clearly easily provoked; unless it was just him, in particular, she had a problem with. But there was something else, something that almost wouldn't let go. He had never met her before, he was sure of that. Recognizing a face in a millisecond could be the difference between life and death in his line of work. Of course, most things were the difference between life and death in his line of work, but though they had never met, there was something vaguely familiar about her. It bothered him that he couldn't work out what.

He quickly stepped to one side for an old lady who was approaching on a kicksled, then turned off onto the next street where his car was parked. He'd stayed in the restaurant for a long time, leafing through the newspaper without being able to read, staring out the window, and hadn't realized how much time had passed. That wasn't like him. He was usually hyperaware of time. He really wasn't himself at the moment. But seeing Ellinor today, it felt like . . . Tom couldn't describe it, even to himself.

Putting complicated feelings into words wasn't something he'd ever been good at; he'd always been more of a practical problem solver. Give him a machine gun to assemble or a building to storm— those were challenges he could manage without any problem. But this whole thing with Ellinor . . . He genuinely didn't know how to move forward now, could no longer think logically. He'd been reduced to panic attacks that he never knew when to expect.

That scared him.

He had been in a bad way before, of course. No one who'd spent the last twenty years doing the things he had could survive without a few internal scars. But it had never been so bad that a few drunken evenings with his colleagues couldn't fix it. European debriefing, they called it. You went out, talked to people with similar experiences, drank copious amounts of beer, and everything felt better.

But not this time; things actually felt worse now than when he first got home. At first he'd felt hope, but all these weeks in Kiruna had brought him precisely nowhere.

He was used to being competent, to making things happen; he could do things few other people on earth could manage. And yet he couldn't win Ellinor back.

Tom glanced around, temporarily disoriented, then spotted his car and unlocked it. Out of sheer habit he had disconnected the internal lights so that they wouldn't come on and make him a sitting target in the dark. It was over the top, but these precautions were practically in his blood.

He climbed inside and placed his hands on the icy wheel. The paralyzing fear that he wouldn't actually be able to fix this, that for the first time in his adult life he was faced with a problem that he wouldn't be able to solve through stubbornness, cunning, or even pure force, threatened to overwhelm him. His arms felt weak. His legs feeble. He could taste blood in his mouth. Where was that from? Or was it in his mind?

Back in Chad, he occasionally lost his grip on reality. They'd treated him so badly. Threatened him with execution, told him he was going to die, placed automatic weapons against his chest, his forehead. Forced him to his knees. There was no preparing for how that felt, the way you eventually almost hoped for death. Though you also wanted to live at any price. He'd shared some of this with the psychologist. Only a fraction of it, of course, but still more than he had told anyone else in a very long time. How his captors enjoyed his helplessness, how they hit, kicked, and interrogated him for hours on end. How the lack of control over his own body felt. How he worried about everyone back home. The psychologist listened intently, with a calm gaze, but he still hadn't been able to share more than the most superficial parts. His habit of hunkering down and keeping quiet was too deeply ingrained. He didn't know whether it was the psychologist or himself that he was trying to protect by not going into the details of what they'd done to him. Because that was what he did, he protected people by keeping it all to himself. Ellinor never asked, and he never told her. Was that wrong? He had always thought of himself as strong. Not invincible, of course, but almost. Was it everything he had kept to himself that was now on the verge of destroying him?

Tom's chest suddenly felt so heavy that he had to rest his head against the wheel. He breathed in the leather smell of the new car and tried to calm himself down, but it didn't work. His mind was spinning, and he lost control of the deep, stabilizing breaths he had been trying to take. His breathing grew quicker and quicker, until it felt like he wasn't getting any air. His body tensed, and then his heart began to race, faster and faster, like it wanted to break free of his body.

Not now, he thought in desperation. Not again. It was as if the car seat started to vibrate beneath him, and those vibrations spread upward through his body.

He tried to remember what the psychologist had taught him. She had gone through what happened to the body during a panic attack, and it hadn't been completely useless. He tried to concentrate.

"It's anxiety, Tom. It's awful. But no one goes crazy from anxiety. Nor do they die, it just feels that way. Try to cope, one second at a time."

Tom tried.

He really tried. The sweat was pouring down his skin. His hands gripped the wheel, his tunnel vision worsened. This was one of the worst panic attacks in a long time. This was a seven on a scale of one to ten, he thought dimly, as organ after organ—lungs, heart, blood, and muscles—were struck by anxiety. Maybe an eight after all.

"Zero is no anxiety, and ten is unbearable. The majority of us can cope with a two without any trouble," the psychologist said.

Tom started to lose control of his thought process. His entire system was battling the instinct to fight or take flight. His shoulders were tense, his body shaking. A nine now. He couldn't see properly, gripped the wheel so tightly that his knuckles turned white. Was he about to die? It felt that way.

"It's a normal biological reaction, it's just that it happens in unexpected situations, that's what's so terrifying about it. You need to train your body not to react to it. It's good if you keep moving. That helps to break down some of the chemicals your body produces."

I should move, he thought faintly. His body was full to bursting with the adrenaline and noradrenaline pumping through his veins. But he didn't have the energy to get up. All he could do was sit in the icy car and try to make it through. One second at a time. During his training, he pushed himself way beyond the limits of what most people could handle. Every course he took aimed to break down soldiers through extreme physical and psychological pressure. Not allowing them to sleep, forcing them to dive in forty-four-degree water. Elite soldiers broke down and cried. They were taunted, degraded, mocked. Day in and day out. And he'd survived it all. But these attacks broke him in a completely different way. His muscles felt exhausted. His strength vanished and was replaced by a bitter feeling of defeat.

At last, the panic started to ebb away.

His vision returned.

The prickling sensation disappeared. He could move his fingers and almost breathe normally. A seven. Then a six.

Thank God.

A five.

A few more breaths, then I start the car.

Definitely better now. He could relax his shoulders. See properly.

He started the engine, glanced in the rearview mirror. Indicated left before he pulled out, though the street was deserted, and soon left Kiruna behind him.

The thermometer showed seven below zero, and the temperature continued to sink as he drove out into the forest. Rationally, he knew the anxiety would always pass sooner or later, but during every attack there was an underlying fear that this time might be different. That he would go crazy.

When he got home, he parked in the garage and did his usual lap of the yard, checking the locks and windows on the various buildings before he slumped onto the couch, completely exhausted.

He didn't have the energy to light a fire. His stomach growled. Panic attacks used up a huge amount of energy, he had learned. He had gone into Kiruna to buy groceries but then had completely forgotten to do so.

From the couch, he peered out through the panoramic windows. They were huge, impractical windows to have up here, considering the winters were so cold. But this was an expensive house, built by a billionaire with delusions of grandeur, and the views out onto the forest and snow-covered expanses were magnificent, both day and night. The moon was bright, and he thought he could see a hare in its winter coat before he tipped his head back and closed his gritty eyes.

Working in special forces had taught him to never give up. He had worked in some of the worst parts of the world, led secret operations in Somalia, been a bodyguard in Iraq, and driven convoys through Afghanistan. He had lived through situations that felt helpless and still managed to turn them around, time and time again. And not once had he ever considered giving up. Always thought of himself as too stubborn, too experienced, too *stupid* to give up. He had seen colleagues crash and burn over the years, but never expected it of himself. Had never actually thought he had any limits, always assumed he was the one who could handle and cope with the most.

But here he was. Looking out at snow that glistened in a thousand shades of white, silver, and blue beneath the light of the stars, thinking that it might have been better for everyone if he'd died back in Africa.

Chapter 8

You never knew what an interview would be like, Ambra thought as she sat opposite Elsa Svensson with a crocheted cushion behind her back. Elsa had unruly white hair and dark brown eyes. She looked like a kind fairy godmother. But you *never* knew beforehand. Sweet old ladies could be psychopathic killers. It didn't happen often. But it did happen.

Once, Ambra interviewed a middle-aged woman who collected egg cups. In her soft, gentle voice, she explained that she had gotten fed up with her constantly unfaithful husband. She tied him up on a kitchen chair; tortured him using an iron, a screwdriver, and boiling water; and eventually strangled him using a washing line. Afterward she stuffed his body into the freezer in the garage.

So. You never knew what would happen.

Ambra doodled in her notepad and waited while Tareq took pictures of an obediently posing Elsa.

Tareq studied the photos on his camera and then nodded to let Ambra know he was happy.

"I've gotta go," he said apologetically.

As Tareq said his good-byes, Elsa grabbed a turquoise shawl from the couch and pulled it over her shoulders. "I'll make some coffee," she said, heading off into the kitchen. Ambra waited in the living room. In all likelihood, her trip up here would be pointless. That was the most common outcome, that the tips they followed up on didn't lead anywhere. Elsa didn't seem to have dementia, and maybe Grace was right, there could be a story here, but it still felt like a long shot. She looked around the room. Elsa's apartment really didn't seem particularly special. Crocheted table cloths and yellowed pine furniture, like every other pensioner's home Ambra had ever visited. Pink hyacinths in matching copper pots. Neat pelmets and a cozy feeling.

Elsa was born in 1923. What had a woman from that generation seen and experienced? War, peace, the struggle for women's rights, and everything in between. And on top of that, an illegitimate child with a prime minister known for having affairs. What would that be for the paper? A quarter page?

Ambra glanced out of the window. Elsa's apartment was high up; the sun was beneath the horizon, but she could still make out the mountains in the distance. There was smoke rising from the mine, the trucks carrying the ore moving in a steady stream. She remembered that mine. It was like an ancient beast out there. They'd visited it once, while she was at school. Going beneath ground was horrible, and her classmates had laughed at her and . . . As though from nowhere, the memories washed over Ambra.

Life in Kiruna was so unlike anything she had experienced before. She was used to moving schools and classes, used to departures, new people, and foster families. But it was so cold. And so dark. They spoke so differently, and none of her classmates had been interested in a withdrawn Stockholm kid who lived with the strictly religious Sventin family.

"Why do you talk so weird?"

"Don't you have any parents? Didn't they want you?"

She'd kept to herself during recess, heard her classmates whispering, wanted to get away. And then she got sick. Really sick.

"You're going to school," Esaias Sventin had said as Ambra sat at the breakfast table and tried to swallow the lumpy oatmeal. That was all they ever served. Apparently jelly was a sin. Like so much else at the Sventins'.

"My ear hurts so much," she'd said. She didn't really want to stay home—she hated the cold wooden house—but she felt so ill. And her ear was pounding and aching.

"Which?" he'd asked bluntly.

She'd pointed to the right one. Her nose had been running for days, and she was shivering. She just wanted to get back into bed. Listlessly, she stirred her porridge, and was completely unprepared for the blow. It struck her right above her tender ear, and she'd screamed at the explosion of pain. The others sat in silence. Rakel looked down at the table. Their sons glanced at once another.

"Stop your complaining, child," Esaias had said, and that was that.

Ambra fainted at school that morning, collapsed and woke to find the other children standing around her and staring. The school nurse was kind and smelled nice, and Ambra had wanted to stay with her forever.

"You have an ear infection. You need to see a doctor," the nurse said. She called the Sventins. No one had time to pick her up, of course.

"Can you manage to walk?" the nurse had asked with a worried look.

Ambra nodded, ashamed that no one cared about her. She made her way home on shaking legs. She told the Sventins what the nurse had said, but the family believed in beatings and prayers.

They did *not* believe in doctors, hospitals, or antibiotics.

"This is God's way of showing that you aren't pure, that the devil lives inside you. You must pray to be healthy," Esaias warned.

God clearly had other plans, because Ambra only got worse and worse. One day, her eardrum burst. Puss started oozing out.

"Maybe we should take her to the hospital," Rakel had said hesitantly.

"It's in God's hands," Esaias said, and with that the discussion was over.

Ambra survived, but even today her hearing was worse in her right ear.

And now she was back in Kiruna. God clearly had a sense of humor, at least.

"Have you tried coffee cheese before?" Elsa asked when she returned with a tray and started setting out napkins and cups. She opened a round foil package. Ambra doubted that many Stockholmers knew what coffee cheese was, but she did.

"Yes. I like it a lot. I'd love a piece."

"Is everything all right?" Elsa studied her closely.

"Yeah."

Elsa placed a flat, white piece of coffee cheese on a napkin. People sometimes added small chunks of it to their coffee, hence the name, but Elsa added a lick of cloudberry jelly and handed the napkin to Ambra. The cheese was delicious, firm and squeaky against her teeth. The cold cloudberries were sweetly sour.

"Is it okay if I start?" Ambra put down her spoon.

Elsa nodded.

"I wonder if you could start from the beginning. Maybe tell me about how you met the prime minister? Is it correct that you had a child with him?"

Elsa took her coffee the Norrland way, drinking it from the saucer with a lump of sugar between her teeth. She put the saucer back on the table. "How much of what we talk about will end up in the paper?"

Ah. The inevitable question. "That really depends, if I'm completely honest. Ultimately, my editor will be the one to decide. If you could start from the beginning . . . ?"

"I understand. Yes, we met up here—he came to Kiruna to take a course."

Ambra made notes while Elsa talked. The story wasn't enough— she recognized that immediately. An old prime minister that half of their readers would never have even heard of. An illegitimate child, born in undramatic circumstances, who went on to live a perfectly ordinary life.

"What does your son do today?"

"He's a social worker."

Just two or three years earlier, it probably would have been enough for an article in the paper, but that was no longer the case. People demanded more sensational content now. Ambra scratched her forehead. Would it even be enough for a short paragraph?

"Could you tell me any more about the prime minister?" She didn't want to let Grace down. Maybe she could find a personal angle, something no one else knew. But the man was known for his affairs, and several lovers and illegitimate children had emerged over the years.

"He was like most other men. It didn't last too long. I wanted to keep the child, and that's what happened."

Ambra decided to wrap things up. It could be something brief on a slow news day, and Tareq had managed to take a few good pictures.

Definitely not worth the journey up here. Oh well, these things happened, and she had at least eaten a little coffee cheese. She glanced at the ornate grandfather clock behind Elsa. Could she make an earlier flight? Not that she had anything to rush back for. The Christmas break stretched out in front of her, three empty, work-free days.

"Why did you decide to talk about this now?" she asked absentmindedly.

"I've been asked to give an interview before. It happens on a regular basis. A neighbor calls a paper and wants to sell the story. I always said no in the past, didn't think it had anything to do with anyone else."

She was right there. "But you said yes this time. Why?" Ambra asked.

Elsa studied her for a long moment. "Because of you," she eventually said.

"Me?"

"When they said they were calling from *Aftonbladet,* I said yes. On condition that you did the interview."

There it was. She'd thought Grace was exaggerating.

"Well, thank you for your confidence," she said politely.

"We've met before, you and I," said Elsa.

Ambra shook her head apologetically. She had no memory of that, but then again she had also met a great many people. "Where?"

"Here in Kiruna. I was here while you lived with the Sventins. I know how bad things were for you with them."

The hairs on Ambra's arms stood on end. She didn't know what to say, but she thought this was one of the worst aspects of faring badly as a child. Realizing that people had known what was going on but no one had come to her rescue. . . . Some wounds took longer to heal than others.

Elsa's face crumpled. "We tried to help you. But Esaias had a strong influence over the people in charge. I wrote letters. I called. But I couldn't do it. I'm so sorry."

"It was a long time ago," Ambra said, still shaken. Growing up as she had, always wondering why adults broke their promises, never took her side, never believed her. It was no coincidence she was now a reporter who fought for those without a voice. It was more than a job. It was a calling.

"I always wondered what happened to you. Then one day I saw your name in *Aftonbladet*. I've followed your career ever since, and I wanted so much to meet you, but I do understand if you think I'm crazy."

Ambra leaned back in her chair, trying to process the information.

"Sorry if I gave you a shock. I'll make some more coffee, give you a chance to gather your thoughts a little."

When Elsa went out into the kitchen, Ambra got up. What a turn of events. She didn't know how to react to this. She went over to the bookshelf and studied the spines. Something Elsa had said was bothering her, something she needed to follow up on before she left. There was a stack of what looked like photo albums on a sideboard, and Ambra got the same feeling again. There was something Elsa had said that she ought to be asking about.

Elsa returned with the coffee. She put the tray down on the table.

"I thought of something," Ambra said, suddenly remembering.

"Yes?"

"You said the prime minister was here on a course, that you met there. What was the course?"

Elsa's fingers moved across the photo albums. They looked old, big and with intricate gold detailing.

"A lot of people came up here," she said slowly. "Mostly foreigners, actually. For a while, we were completely overbooked."

"You ran the course the prime minister came up here to take?"

"I ran the first one myself. Then my wife and I did it together."

It took a second or two before Ambra managed to process her words.

"You were married to a woman?" There was no mention of that anywhere.

Elsa's fingers moved across the photo album again, this time with a melancholy expression on her face. "We were registered partners; we couldn't get married before 2009. Even then, the priest tried to stop us. There are strong conservative forces up here. We had to go to another church. But yes, we were married. Ingrid died last summer."

"I'm sorry."

"Thank you. It's fine now. She was older than I, and we had many wonderful years together. She wouldn't have wanted me to be sad. I scattered her ashes in the square here one night." Elsa giggled, and Ambra could suddenly imagine her as a young woman with light hair and a mischievous glimmer in her eye. "I'd rather you didn't write about this, if you don't mind."

Ambra nodded. She absentmindedly took a few sips of the coffee Elsa had poured. "I promise," she said, wondering whether she should start getting ready to leave. She liked Elsa. It felt good to know that someone had cared, even if it hadn't made any difference.

"What was the course?" she reminded her. Maybe the prime minister had been interested in reindeer herding and signed up for a course on the history of reindeer keeping. Or maybe he liked carving things from birch bark? On top of creating children out of wedlock, that was. She checked that her computer was properly packed away.

"This was the sixties. It was a little more common back then," said Elsa.

The zipper on her bag stuck, and Ambra replied without looking up: "What was more common?"

"Sexual experimentation."

Ambra stopped pulling at her bag. She must have misheard. "The course can't have been about *sex?*"

Elsa cocked her head. "Yes, I suppose so. Different types of relationships, a focus on closeness. People came here and lived out the ideas we taught."

"Now it sounds like you ran some kind of sex camp. Are you telling me the prime minister came up here for something like that?"

Elsa waved her hand impatiently, as though Ambra had misunderstood the entire thing. "Not just him. We had lots of participants. We were very famous, in our own discreet way, if I may say so. Let me show you. Could you pass me that?" She pointed to the photo album on top of the pile.

Ambra handed it to her while her brain tried to process this new information. Sex camps? In Kiruna?

"I promised Ingrid I wouldn't talk about it, not before she was dead. She was much more private than me. And I wasn't planning to say anything at all. But it's completely different now that it's you. Ingrid wouldn't have had anything against it. We really were so worried about you."

Elsa sat down on the couch and opened the album on her knee. Ambra sat down next to her. She could see pictures and clippings between the rustling sheets of tissue paper. Elsa stroked the pages with one hand. "In our courses, I must say that Ingrid was very free. I loved that about her. We both took part. The sixties, you know," she said, as though that explained everything.

Ambra leaned forward and studied the images. "But that's . . . ?" she said, amazed.

Elsa smiled and nodded. She turned the page.

"And that's . . . her. Is it really? And him?" Ambra studied the pictures of world-famous faces. The majority were black-and-white photographs: square, old-fashioned images. A young Elsa appeared in several of them. In a light fur hat and elegant skiwear.

"No one has seen these pictures in a long time. The course belonged to our past. I suppose we became more prudish with the years."

Ambra's fingers brushed against the edge of one photograph. "They came here?" These were some of the world's most famous people from the late fifties and early sixties. Presidents. Artists. Movie stars.

"Oh yes," Elsa said, pointing to an American president, well known for his film star looks. An iconic blond actress was by his side. "These two were here several times."

"At sex camps?" Could it be true? Ambra studied the pictures carefully. She was skeptical by nature, but they looked genuine. She recognized a number of the landmarks from the area.

"Why has no one ever written about this?"

"We were very discreet. And up here, people don't gossip. Many people earned a lot of money from this type of visitor."

It wasn't completely unthinkable. Ingrid Bergman had been hidden away by her home village when she returned to Sweden. The care shown to Prince Daniel Westling and the Crown Princess in his hometown was legendary, and there hadn't been a single leak to the press.

"Plus, back then, there was no Internet or anything," Elsa said.

Ambra hesitated. There was a story here, that much was clear. But it would also mean more time in Kiruna, and she wanted to get away. She could just pretend the interview had come to nothing and head home. No one would be any the wiser.

But this was *too* good. It ticked all of the boxes. Unusual sex, secret networks, and genuine celebrities—check, check, and check. Her brain was already thinking of headlines and introductions. Pictures and angles.

"Elsa, is it okay if I call my boss and tell her about this?"

"I don't know."

"It doesn't bind you to anything, but I'd like to know more."

"Yes, I suppose so." Elsa nodded hesitantly, but that was all the encouragement Ambra needed.

"Could I go into the kitchen to make the call?"

"You do that. I'll dust the other albums down a little. We kept going right into the seventies—there are more pictures if you'd like to see them."

Ambra pulled out her cell phone and dialed Grace's number as she left the room. She waited impatiently. The minute Grace answered, she said, "You know Elsa in Kiruna?"

"What? Ah, yes," Grace replied vaguely. Ambra could tell that her mind was on a thousand other things.

"It's nothing like what we were expecting. You need to hear this." She quickly recapped. "It's like Norrland porn on Ecstasy," she finished up.

"Pictures? Do you have pictures?" Ambra smiled at the excitement in her boss's voice; she knew Grace would like this.

"Loads."

"We need exclusivity, make sure of that. Buy them. Has she talked to anyone else? Local paper?"

"No one."

"You need to make sure it stays that way. Talk to her. Damn, it's Christmas Eve tomorrow. Can she meet you? Do you need to get home?"

"I'll talk to her. I'll stay as long as I can."

"What's the angle?" Grace asked.

"*Aftonbladet* exclusive—Kiruna's secret sex nest."

Grace was silent for a moment. "Or: The pictures reveal—secret orgies. Try to convince her. And we need video. Can you film? Tareq should have a video camera. Otherwise we'll send one up."

There was silence at both ends of the line.

"Good work," Grace then said, and Ambra could hear she was pleased. She wished making Grace happy didn't mean quite so much to her. She ended the call, sent a quick message to Tareq, and then went back in to Elsa.

Chapter 9

Tom put his second beer down on the counter. The hotel bar at
the Scandic Ferrum was practically deserted, which wasn't strange.
It was Christmas Eve after all, it was snowing heavily, and all normal
people were at home with their families, eating Christmas dinners, exchanging gifts. He'd thought this was just what he needed. Getting
out and grabbing a beer in a bar, as though it was any old day. Since
the majority of his adult Christmases had been spent working, he
wasn't expecting to have any strong feelings about it. Just like any
other night. But now he wondered if there was any more pathetic
feeling than sitting alone at the bar in a nearly empty hotel at three in
the afternoon on Christmas Eve.

The bartender gave him a questioning glance every now and then,
but otherwise stared expressionlessly at the TV in one corner.

Tom's eyes swept across the room and the tables. The wallpaper
featured a pattern of different forest animals, there were stuffed
ptarmigans in a line by the bar, and chandeliers made from reindeer
horns hung above the tables.

And then there was her. She was still sitting there. That woman.
Endlessly tapping away at her computer. She occasionally glanced
down at her notes on a pad next to it. She had a cup of coffee that
the bartender had refilled a few times.

Tom sipped his beer. After a while, he allowed his gaze to wander
back to her. She seemed lost in her work, and so he studied her a little longer. Her scarf was wrapped around her neck, her hat pulled
down over her hair, and she was wearing a knitted sweater. She

scratched her forehead every now and then, shifted in her seat, wrinkled her nose. Her entire being was intense. Quick movements and a constantly changing expression. Occasionally, she mumbled something and shook her head, as though she was part of some heated dialogue even though she was alone at the table. Then she would throw herself at the keyboard again. It was forty-five minutes since he'd first started watching her, and she hadn't looked up once.

"Did she eat already?" Tom asked the bartender.

"What?"

Tom nodded toward the woman. "When did she last eat?"

"No idea," the bartender replied, and turned away.

At four-thirty the woman stopped writing and started fiddling with her phone instead. Tom ordered another beer, deliberated with himself.

"How's it going?" he eventually called out.

The woman looked up at him and then peered around the room in surprise, as though she had only just realized where she was. "Are you talking to me?" she asked.

"You and I are the only ones here. You working?"

She glanced at her computer and then at him. "Why do you want to know?"

Good question. Tom raised his glass to her. "Merry Christmas."

She grabbed her coffee cup, raised it halfway, and in an ironic tone said, "Merry Christmas." She put the cup down without drinking and gave him an apologetic look. "Out of coffee," she explained.

Tom opened his mouth, but trying to talk across such a distance felt stupid. He got up from the bar and walked over to her. She followed his movements with narrowed eyes. Pulled at the sleeve of her sweater and bit her lip, guardedly rather than invitingly.

"Am I bothering you?" Tom asked with a gesture to the computer and everything else she had spread out around her.

She shrugged.

He chose to ignore her ambivalence. "Are you a journalist?"

"Yep."

"What are you writing?"

"I'm filing an article about the sexist T-shirts worn by the men of Kiruna," she replied without blinking.

Aha. He smirked at her. "In three parts?"

"At least." But she seemed to relax a little. The tension of her mouth relaxed, and her shoulders seemed to sink.

"I know why you reacted like that. But that T-shirt . . . it wasn't mine," he said.

She looked up at him skeptically. "It wasn't mine in the *I didn't have sex with that woman* kind of way?"

"It wasn't mine in the *It belonged to someone else and is now in the trash* kind of way," he said firmly. When he'd seen what was written on it, he'd thought it awful himself. He raised a hand as though swearing an oath. "One hundred percent true. You staying at the hotel?"

"Yeah, I'm staying here," she said, and stretched. Tom's eyes briefly focused on her breasts beneath her fluffy sweater.

"First time in Kiruna?" he asked.

A brief silence before she replied, "No. Are you staying here too? At the hotel, I mean."

"No. I'm just waiting for Christmas Eve to end. Only a few more hours."

She nodded and stretched her neck.

"Stiff?"

"Very. I lost track of time. Jesus, I've been sitting here so long. But it's submitted now."

They looked at one another. He could have gone back to the bar. They didn't know each other, and he wasn't sure they would even get on. But it felt good to talk to someone.

"I asked the kitchen to make me a little food," he said as the silence started to grow awkward. "You want some? They had a Christmas food platter."

She leaned back in her chair, raised an eyebrow, and gave him a questioning look. She had pretty eyes—gently tilted, very serious, and piercing, as though she knew about most things in this world. They were green and made her look like an alley cat. "You thought we could sit together?" she asked, as though he was suggesting a foreign custom and she just wanted to check she had understood him. But then she gestured to the chair opposite. "Sure. I'm Ambra."

"Tom," he said, sitting down. "So, how's it going? With your T-shirt report."

She had closed the lid of her laptop when he sat down. A woman used to being cautious with information.

"Really well," she replied as the bartender appeared with a sigh.

"I'll have what he's having, Christmas food and a beer," Ambra said, and she took off her hat. She ran her fingers through her hair. Glossy, dark brown curls. As she plumped it up, he could smell shampoo or some kind of spray. It smelled good.

"Where do you work? For a paper? Or are you freelance?"

She studied him for a long moment, as though weighing whether she dare tell him.

"*Aftonbladet*," she eventually replied.

"Last name's Vinter, right?" He remembered reading something by her; he was almost sure he had heard the name before.

"Yeah." She sounded much more prickly now, more like the arrogant big-city girl he'd assumed she was. "What about you? You have a last name?"

"Lexington," he replied as the bartender appeared and started to place napkins and cutlery on the table. "So you're here over Christmas?" he continued.

"Could say that. And you, do you live here?"

"For the moment."

The bartender returned with the food. Two generous plates of herring, potato, gravlax, smoked salmon, crisp flatbread, and butter.

"You want schnapps, too?" the bartender asked with, if possible, even less enthusiasm than before. Tom gave Ambra a questioning look.

"A small one?" she said, hungrily studying the food. "I want to celebrate being done. Let's have both beer and schnapps."

Tom nodded. It was definitely that kind of night.

Each was handed a frosty glass of liquor, pale yellow Norrland aquavit. Ambra sipped her shot, cautiously to begin with, and then she resolutely downed the entire glass. Tom did the same, and then ordered two more.

It was that kind of night.

They started on their food. Ambra must have been starving, because she wolfed down everything that appeared at their table. It was only after her third aquavit, the cold cuts, a hefty portion of Jansson's temptation—the traditional salty, creamy Swedish casserole dish made of potatoes, cream, onions, pickled sprats, and bread crumbs—and another beer that she put down her cutlery and groaned gently. She took a paper-thin slice of the smoked reindeer that had appeared on the third plate. Her cheeks were slightly flushed, and when she unwrapped her scarf, he automatically looked up at her. Her breasts were small, but Tom liked them in all shapes and sizes—he was pragmatic like that. Plus, hers looked good beneath her knitted sweater. He had already decided that.

"So why were you working on Christmas Eve?" he asked, tearing his eyes from her body. He wasn't really the type to stare. Ambra sipped her liquor and put down the glass. The bartender had eventually just left the bottle on the table, and Tom continued to refill both their glasses. Ambra's index finger moved around the edge of her glass, and he followed the movement. She had nice fingers. Nice breasts, nice eyes. He was definitely getting drunk.

"I was finishing up an interview," she replied.

"On Christmas Eve?" It was a sacred holiday for Swedes. People worked only if they really had to.

She gave an apologetic shrug. "I'm bad at taking time off."

"Workaholic?" he asked.

She raised an eyebrow, and seemed to be thinking about his question.

"No, I just don't have a life or any interests," she replied, and then she giggled. It seemed he wasn't the only one who was drunk. When she wasn't prickly and defensive, she was actually pretty cute.

"No family?" he asked. She didn't wear a ring, but that didn't necessarily mean anything. They'd made small talk while they ate. A little about the weather (cold), the hotel (drafty, according to her; standard for Kiruna, according to him), and the food (both were more than happy). But she hadn't mentioned anything personal. Though nor had he. Tom was, by nature, paranoid. Operatives were forced to choose between two extremes, he thought as he studied her over his glass: being paranoid or being dead. He lost his train of thought.

"I have a sister, but she's traveling right now and we never celebrate Christmas together anyway. What about you? Why are you here all on your own?" She reached for a ginger cookie, added a slice of blue cheese, and pushed the whole thing into her mouth.

"I haven't celebrated Christmas with my family since I was a teen," he said, swirling his schnapps glass. He should have called his mom, he realized now. And his sisters. His thoughts returned to Ellinor. Right now, she was probably sparkling alongside Nilas, unwrapping gifts or gazing into an open fire.

She finished chewing and reached for more. "Do they live here?"

"My family? No."

"What about a girlfriend?"

Tom paused, but then he shook his head. "You?"

"Nope, I'm single too."

The air grew charged. She twisted a lock of hair between her fingers. Tom had always liked women's hands. Hers were small and delicate, and he found himself fantasizing about what she could do with them.

"But are you from here? You don't have an accent," she asked, and he tried to pull himself together.

"Not at all. But I did do my military service here, about a hundred years ago now. Ranger battalion."

"Ranger?" Tom saw her glance at his arms, and it was a real struggle not to flex his biceps. He wasn't as bulky as he'd once been, but he was still in good physical shape, and she didn't seem to have anything against it. He looked into her green eyes. She wasn't just cute, she was *really* cute, he decided.

"When?" she asked, blinking slowly. Her eyelashes cast long shadows over her cheeks.

"Ninety-seven to ninety-eight. I was up here a few times after that. I got into the Officers' Program with the Military Academy, and then I did exercises up here."

"Officer, huh? So, Tom Lexington, are you still in the army?" Her voice was low, suggestive.

"Nope," he said.

"What do you do, then?" she asked. Her catlike eyes studied him, her lips wet from the beer she had just drunk.

Tom thought about his lonely evenings, his panic attacks, and bleak prospects for the future. This was the down side to getting involved with people, the reason he had avoided everyone since coming up here. The reason people like him preferred to spend time with those similar to them. How much should he tell her? The woman was a reporter with one of Scandinavia's biggest papers, after all. But it was a long time since he'd last worked on anything top secret, and what he was, what he had done, that was no secret at all.

Or: not everything anyway.

"I'm between jobs right now," he replied vaguely, and held up the schnapps bottle in question. It was almost empty. Ambra held out her glass. Tom split the last of it between them.

"How do you like your job? Is it fun?"

She leaned back and studied him, as though she knew exactly what he was doing—diversion. She sipped the last of her schnapps, and he suddenly realized what he had recognized in her, the thing that had been niggling at the back of his mind. She wasn't just some ordinary middle-class girl. Not at all. He had seen people like this before. He just hadn't made the connection. But he could see it now. He'd met plenty of street kids—in Asia, the Middle East, most recently in Chad. These were children who didn't trust anyone, who were used to fighting for survival every waking second, both mentally and physically. Always reading their environment. And Ambra's eyes had the exact same look as those kids' usually did.

"Working for *Aftonbladet* is just the best." She sounded sincere.

"Why?"

"Nothing beats being present while history's being written. Finding the perfect mix of news and entertainment. I've never wanted to do anything else, not work for TV or for a weekly magazine."

"Nothing?"

"Nope."

Tom couldn't help but smile at how passionate she sounded. He recognized the feeling. It was something he usually felt himself when he was out on an operation.

He was drunk. His emotions nicely blunted, without the slightest anxiety. It was like they were cut off from the rest of the world. The snow was falling outside and Ellinor was celebrating Christmas with Nilas somewhere, but he cared less than he had in a long time. If he focused on Ambra and avoided thinking about anything else, life was almost bearable. The alcohol helped, of course. His eyes moved over her again. That helped too. Looking at her.

Her eyes told him that she saw the way he was staring at her breasts. He didn't remember what they were talking about.

Her cell phone rang.

"I need to take this, excuse me. It's my boss."

Tom glanced at his watch. It was eight o'clock. On Christmas Eve.

"You stay here. I'll go," he said. He got up and went to the restroom. When he came back, Ambra was finished with her call, and she was swigging her beer straight from the bottle. She looked like a world-class reporter, with her jerky movements and alert posture, as though she might leap from her seat at any minute, wave her press pass in the air, and start to push corrupt politicians and stubborn holders of power up against the wall.

"What did your boss want?" he asked.

"She just wanted to check something. And see how things were."

"So how are things?"

She took another swig. "I hate Christmas," she said quietly.

He knew that much already. "What has Christmas ever done to you?"

"It's not Christmas specifically. I hate anything to do with family holidays. Christmas, long weekends, Easter."

A frown appeared as she talked. Tom leaned forward to better hear what she was saying, and he saw that she had long, thick eyelashes and a pretty mouth. It looked kissable. Even when she spat out her questions or statements, her mouth looked soft. He already knew he was drunk; the table was covered with bottles, and he heard himself slur the odd word. But he wasn't falling down drunk, just comfortably full and nicely woozy. Life didn't actually suck right now.

"I never met anyone who hates holidays before," he said, but he recognized himself in her words. He, too, liked working more than time off.

"My entire existence and identity are linked to my job." She raised the bottle to her mouth, and he studied her lips as they wrapped around the neck. "I told you I didn't have a life," she reminded him, wiping her mouth with the back of her hand.

"Other than a sister?"

"She's my foster sister. We met when we were teens. What about you? Why are you alone on Christmas Eve?"

He shrugged. "It just turned out that way. You know."

Ambra nodded slowly at Tom's words. She knew exactly how it could be. She stole glances at him through her lashes. Tom Lexington. She certainly wasn't expecting this of her Christmas Eve, to be sitting here with a man, almost flirting. No, they were definitely flirting. She was often on the road with her job, and yes, she had ended up with locals before, both at bars and occasionally (twice) in bed. It was fun to have company sometimes, but she wasn't the kind of social person who gained energy from everyone she met. Plus, she was relatively uninterested in one-night stands (not for moral reasons, but they were just so *boring*) and had resigned herself to spending Christmas with nothing but her beloved computer for company.

Yet here she was.

With Tom Lexington, a former Kiruna ranger who clearly had no one to spend Christmas with either.

He didn't look too bad. If you liked the big, serious, beer-drinking, macho type. Black eyes. Black hair and beard. Black clothes, black, black, black. He was mysterious, but that didn't matter; it was refreshing that he talked so little about himself. He drank a lot, considerably more than she, and she had drunk far too much. He also seemed pretty low. Yes, their time together was unexpectedly fun, but she hadn't heard him laugh even once. At most, his lips would curl occasionally, which was probably meant to be a smile. Though maybe it was just Christmas that was getting him down. God knows she understood if that was the case.

He wasn't exactly handsome, but he was sexy in a tough-guy kind of way. She didn't usually fall for the strong, silent type, but she *was* attracted to him. Though that could just be the beer and the schnapps talking. And the fact there was no one else around. But still. There was something rugged, lumberjack-esque about him.

"What are you thinking about?" he asked.

"Woman starts talking to a stranger. You'll never guess what happens next."

His eyes shone. She could easily see herself rolling about with Tom in her bed one floor up, imagine those hands undressing her, being pushed down by him, kissing and making love, discovering whether he was a clumsy or a firm lover. With that huge body and those hard eyes, he would have been terrifying if he hadn't been so unboorish.

He was definitely checking her out, even if he thought he was being discreet about it. It happened so rarely that she didn't mind. And he was doing it nicely, stealing a glance and then quickly focusing on her face again, nodding at what she said, asking follow-up questions. She felt his eyes on every single part of her body, felt them in places she would like his fingers to be, his mouth. Yes. They were the only ones there. He seemed to have the basics of social competence, and she really was drunk. Plus, she had been writing an article about sex orgies for hours.

"Ambra. That's an unusual name," he said, and his dark eyes panned down over her sweater for a nanosecond or two. She felt butterflies in her stomach.

"I think it's Italian. My mom chose it. It's from a painting, I think."

"Is she dead? Your mom?"

Ambra nodded. She didn't want to talk about it, not now. She couldn't remember any Christmases with her mom and dad, but every now and then she felt a faint sensation that might have had to do with them. A scent, a feeling of joy and security.

Tom swirled his glass. The lighting in the restaurant was low, and Ambra hadn't seen the bartender in a while. Maybe he had gotten bored of them and gone home, they had been in the restaurant for so long. There was a candle burning on the table, and the flame flickered in Tom's eyes. When she'd seen him for the first time, he scared her. She had an easily aroused, deep-seated fear of aggressive men, but he was so calm, seemed so stable, that her fear quickly subsided.

She often met military men through her work, and many of them liked to talk about how mentally stable they were, only to prove themselves to be surprisingly high maintenance. But Tom seemed genuinely level-headed.

"What's the best thing about your job?" he asked quietly.

"Being in the newsroom." She loved being a reporter, writing, interviewing people, but nothing beat the feeling of walking into the office. The people were a little smarter, a little funnier there; it was one of the best places on earth. "I think it's the feeling that anything's possible. That anything could happen. That today could be the day we make history. It's hard to explain."

"What about the worst?"

"Not everyone likes you. I don't have anything against constructive criticism, but let's say I get my fair share of hate and online trolls. Some of them can be really serious."

"How?"

"I don't want to quote them, but it's definitely a case of men who hate provocative women in the public eye."

"Sounds awful."

"Yeah. And it would be good if I didn't argue with my boss so often. I seem to rub our latest editor-in-chief the wrong way. I can be a little . . ."

"Angry? Judgmental?" he suggested. But he smiled.

She laughed. "Difficult, I was going to say. I should be better at keeping quiet sometimes." She shouldn't have told Dan Persson that the paper had taken a step back when it came to feminism, for example. Or argued against *all* of his suggestions.

"But then you wouldn't be so good a journalist. What's it like being out in the field? Like you are now."

"It depends. But I heard an incredible story yesterday. About a secret sex camp up here. Can you imagine?"

He smirked. "Not really. Is that what you were writing about before?"

"Yeah, it'll be in the paper tomorrow morning. The first part anyway. The rest will depend on how well the next interview goes." Elsa had gotten tired, and they had decided to meet a second time. "Secret sex means lots of readers."

"Sounds . . . quite tabloid."

"I guess so."

The bartender unexpectedly returned. He cleared their table, the empty bottles and stacked plates, and replaced the candle that had burned down. "We're closing soon," he said sullenly. "You want anything else?"

"Coffee?" Tom asked.

"Nah, I think I actually want to keep drinking. Like you said. It'll be good once today is over."

They sat in silence.

The bartender brought two beers to their table and then disappeared.

"I like talking to people too," Ambra continued. "Understanding what makes them tick. Maybe that's my strongest driving force. Curiosity. Or justice. Not letting people get away with bad things. Ah, I don't know." She put her hand on the table. Tom looked down at it and put his a short distance away.

The air thickened. Did he notice it too? She was aware of everything about him. His hand, he had such big hands. His presence. His serious eyes.

"It's past midnight—officially Christmas Day," she said slowly, moving her hand closer to his, feeling the warmth of his skin over the short distance between their hands.

"Yeah."

She pulled at the label on her beer, no longer thirsty. "Should we get the check?" she asked quietly.

He nodded. He paid the entire thing, despite Ambra's protests. "Not up for discussion," he said bluntly, and she gave in.

"Did you drive here?" she asked once the bartender cleared their table.

"Yeah."

"You aren't planning on driving home? Since you've been drinking?"

"No," he said, looking her in the eyes.

Silence. They would never see each other again. The air was so charged, the sparks were practically flying between them. They had established that they were lonely, both of them. It was as though it had already been decided. She swallowed. Wanted him.

*   *   *

Inside Tom, a small voice whispered that he should be heading home. Now. That he definitely shouldn't be sitting here, exchanging meaningful looks with Ambra.

But he'd also drunk copious amounts of alcohol, so he couldn't drive.

Plus it was freezing cold and it was snowing.

It was also Christmas. There would be almost no taxis in Kiruna at this time of day, and definitely none that would drive him out into the woods.

And so on, to infinity. The reasons for staying at the hotel seemed endless.

She was lonely.

He was lonely.

There was something between them, definitely.

Tom hesitated. Had he known all along that this was how it would end up? He honestly had no idea. Somewhere, deep down, he suspected he would have come to different conclusions if he was sober. But the chemistry was there. They'd flirted like hell. And the fact was, it was a long time since he'd last had sex. Maybe it was just what he needed.

Ambra got up from the table. She teetered slightly, and that decided things.

"I'll walk you to your room," he said, putting a hand beneath her arm.

"Okay," she said.

Though she was no longer unsteady, he didn't let go of her. Something happened inside him the moment his hand wrapped around her arm. A buzzing in his body, an inhalation that stopped in his chest and then . . . Desire. It was desire he was feeling.

They remained like that, her fragrant hair against his cheek. At the very back of his mind, he heard a voice: *This is an incredibly bad idea*. But he ignored it. Ambra looked up at him. Her long eyelashes trembled. His thumb moved against her sweater, imagining the skin beneath it. She was warm under his hand, and an image flashed before his eyes, the two of them wrapped around one another in a cool, wide hotel bed. Her with so much passionate energy and such

long legs. And him . . . A moment of forgetfulness and human contact, wasn't that just what he needed?

"Come on, I'll walk with you," he said, and his voice sounded
hoarse. He would follow her up. And then he would see.

Yeah, right.

They made it to the elevator. The lobby was deserted. Outside the
spinning glass doors, the snow was pouring down.

It took a while for the elevator to arrive. Without really thinking,
Tom raised a hand and trapped one of her bouncing curls between
his fingers.

"I . . ." he began, but then he trailed off.

His hand moved in beneath her silky hair. She looked at him without blinking, and he saw her chest rising beneath her sweater. His
hand cupped the back of her neck and he slowly pulled her toward
him. She followed the movement, raised her face toward his. He
bent down gently, lowered his face, and then his lips grazed hers. She
made a slight sound beneath his mouth, and her hand moved onto
his upper arm, caressing it lightly. She closed her eyes, and he did the
same. It was a simple kiss, no tongues, very little body contact, just lips
meeting, hands and fingers moving on top of skin and clothes and
hair. But it was a kiss that promised more, and Tom groaned quietly.

The elevator pinged. Christ, they were still in the lobby. He opened
his eyes. She did too. They smiled at one another, slightly embarrassed. Her cheeks were flushed, her eyes bright. The elevator doors
opened. He really shouldn't . . . But he followed her in. They each
stood against one wall, said nothing during the short ride. When they
reached her floor, Ambra moved ahead of him. Her hips swayed gently. The lighting was low, and the hotel was silent around them, as if
they were the only people inside, in Kiruna, in the entire world.

"This is me," she said, stopping in front of a door. She fumbled
slightly with the key card before she managed to push it into the
reader, and then she turned to look at him. She had the palest skin
he had ever seen, as if she never spent any time in the sun, as if she
lived at night and consisted mostly of snow and stardust and everything else that was white. When he looked closer, he saw that she
had a small dot to one side of her mouth, a black beauty spot.

He kissed her again. Pushed her backward, against the door,
heard her pant, and then their tongues met and it coursed through

him like a bolt. It was a long, long time since he last kissed anyone but Ellinor, and Ambra felt shockingly different. Shockingly good. He kissed her almost aggressively, desperately. Pushed her harder against the door, let his tongue explore her mouth, heard her pant. She raised a hand to his chest, pulled back slightly, her hair messy, her lips swollen from his kisses.

"Wait," she said breathlessly. "Shouldn't we go in?" She studied him questioningly, and it was as though that broke the spell. Like waking from a pleasant but unrealistic dream. He didn't want this, did he? *Couldn't* do this. He was in Kiruna for something completely different, couldn't jeopardize that with a woman he didn't even know.

"Tom?" she said when he didn't reply.

He took a step back. Her hand fell to her side.

"It's best if I go," he said.

"What?" She looked at him with her big, questioning eyes. There was an invitation in that look, as clear as if she had uttered the words. *Stay here with me.*

And why not?

Ambra Vinter was a grown woman, alone in an unfamiliar town. He was single, free, or at least uncomfortably lonely.

There was no good reason to say the words Tom heard himself utter: "I shouldn't have come up here."

Ambra blinked. The glimmer in her eyes was gone.

"I'm sorry," he said, and he was. Sorry and probably crazy. It wasn't as though Ellinor would appreciate his abstaining from sex for her sake. It wasn't as though his plan to win her back was even working; if anything it was the opposite.

"Why? There's nothing to be sorry for," Ambra said. Her tone was almost breezy, but Tom sensed he had hurt her. He wanted to explain that he hadn't been with a woman for so long, he didn't trust himself, that she seemed so lonely and that he was even more so and that it just felt wrong, even while it also felt frighteningly right. But what he said was: "Will you be okay?"

She looked at him. "Will *I* be okay? Yeah. Don't worry."

"Ambra, I . . ."

"Good night, Tom."

She quickly turned around, pressed the door handle, tore the key card from the reader, slipped inside the room, and hastily closed the door behind her.

Tom remained outside, irresolute. He listened, but he couldn't hear anything.

Great job, Tom, really smooth. He raised his hand to knock, but then thought better of it. He looked at his watch. One o'clock in the morning. He headed downstairs to find someone who could give him a room for the night.

Chapter 10

Ambra held her breath and waited until she heard Tom's footsteps disappear on the other side of the door.

Then she closed her eyes, put her forehead against the wall, and moaned as quietly as she could.

That had to qualify as the ultimate humiliation. She was literally the only woman as far as the eye could see. In a town where there was a real shortage of women. With a completely single guy. Inviting him back to her room, and being open about it.

And then being turned down.

Ambra opened her eyes, staggered into her room, and clumsily started to undress. Her head was spinning; she wasn't used to drinking so much. She managed to unbutton her jeans, but then her fingers stopped cooperating. She pulled off her sweater instead, and collapsed onto the bed. She almost wished she was more drunk. There was no chance she would have forgotten this by tomorrow. Maybe even ever. She groaned miserably. Why did he say no? She'd never had her sister's confidence, or looks for that matter. She really wasn't an expert when it came to men. She was far from a bombshell, she was well aware of that. But those few times she did *put herself out there,* she had never been turned down in such a humiliating way.

She wished she could tell herself that she didn't know what had gotten into her. But she had flirted, entirely deliberately, with the strong-but-silent Tom. Somewhere in the middle of their spontaneous Christmas meal, the mood between them had changed and she'd started to see him less as a buff, macho guy and more as a potential bedmate. She tried to kick off her shoes as she lay across the wide bed. The thing was, she'd assumed Tom was on the same wave-length. The thought hadn't even struck her at first. But then she saw the way he was looking at her. And she started paying more and more attention to the way he listened to what she said, filled her glass, and so many other small things that she'd interpreted as inter-est. Not interest-interest. But attraction, a flirt, a one-time thing. Two lonely souls in a bar in Kiruna. She'd thought that the tension was there. And he seemed slightly vulnerable. That had an effect on her, sent her mind down risky paths. She'd checked his hand. No ring. No indentation from a ring. She rubbed her face. Didn't he say he was single? No? Plus, they kissed.

Jesus Christ, they *kissed*. And what a kiss it was. It made her entire body warm, hot. God, it was sexy. But then he dumped her. This was verging on unbearable.

She managed to kick off one of her shoes, but she didn't have the energy for the other. She just lay where she was with her pants un-buttoned and one shoe on her foot. Tom wasn't handsome like a model, not in any sense. Big and angular, with too-long hair, some-where between unshaven and grizzly. He was far from the ideal man in her world. Nothing like the type she usually fell for. Intellectual, know-it-all men who spouted empty phrases the minute things got complicated. So it wasn't automatically a bad thing that Tom was differ-ent. But Tom definitely *wasn't* the type of man who usually fell for her.

So no wonder he'd turned her down.

She felt so humiliated she didn't know what to do. If she were to write a list of her most embarrassing experiences as an adult, this would definitely be up there. And, of course, she couldn't just drop all thoughts of what had happened. No, that would be far too healthy. Instead, she started to go through the things she had said.

It was like a table tennis match between them. He batted back any questions he was asked. Tom Lexington clearly didn't like to talk about himself, and he managed to make her say considerably more than she usually did. But it wasn't so much what she'd said (however much she wished she had kept quiet about always being alone at Christmas; God, that sounded pathetic) that was the problem, more what she'd *done*.

Ambra groaned again. There was no end to how embarrassed she felt. She had bitten her lip and played with her hair and carried on.

Laid her hand next to his. Made out with him, invited him in. And then he said no.

She covered her eyes with her hand and moaned.

This kind of thing happened. All the time. Men had no obligation to perform just because a woman fluttered her eyelashes. They really didn't.

But still. Jesus Christ.

If it was possible, she now hated Kiruna even more.

She lay with her arm over her face for a while. But her head was spinning, so she opened her eyes and stared up at the ceiling instead. There was a crack running from one corner to another. Always cracks in hotel ceilings.

She glanced at her watch. It was late, she should get some sleep. But instead she dwelled on how stupid she felt. And then, exhausted from working hard and drinking too much, she fell asleep on top of the covers, still wearing her jeans and one shoe. Her last thought was that, despite everything that had happened, that was still far from being the worst Christmas Eve she had ever experienced.

Chapter 11

Mattias Ceder leaned against the door frame and studied the sight of the newly woken Tom Lexington. The sheets were crumpled and twisted, as though Tom had been tossing and turning in his sleep.

Mattias was in the doorway of the hotel room for almost an entire minute before Tom even started to stir. That was worrying. The Tom he knew would have leaped out of bed before an intruder even managed to turn the door handle.

"I was just wondering when you'd wake up," he said loudly.

Tom sat up. "What the hell are you doing here?" His eyes were bloodshot, his voice rough and grumpy. He seemed disoriented.

Mattias wasn't the least bit surprised. Tom had sounded drunk on the phone early this morning. He stepped into the room and pulled the door closed behind him. "You called and asked me to come, so here I am."

Tom looked at him with suspicion. "I did? When?"

Mattias glanced at his watch. It was nine-thirty in the morning. "You called me at two. You were blind drunk and said you needed to talk to me. That you were in the Scandic Ferrum and that I should come here."

"You're lying."

"Nope," Mattias said. He genuinely wasn't lying this time. But it wasn't surprising that Tom didn't remember their call. He'd been barely coherent, hyperventilating and slurring. Raving about soft lips. Talking about anxiety attacks and awful mistakes he had made. The

truth was, the call terrified Mattias. He had known Tom a long time—
the two men had experienced both war and loss together—and Tom
had *never* sounded like that before.

"How the hell did you get in?"

Mattias held up the key card he'd grabbed from a cleaning cart.
He could probably have asked the hotel to let him in, but where was
the fun in that?

Tom snorted and rubbed his eyes. "I can't believe I called you of
all people."

"But you did, so I came."

Maybe it was a temporary confusion that made Tom call. Maybe it
was a subconscious cry for help. Mattias didn't care which. He was
here now, and he wanted to strike while the iron was hot.

Tom grabbed a T-shirt and started to pull it on. His arm got
caught, and he swore and started over. "Did you come from Stockholm?"

"Karlsborg. By plane."

Tom gave him a skeptical look. It was in Karlsborg, that small town
on the western shore of Lake Vättern, that they'd met for the first
time. The two men worked and studied there for a few years, and
both knew there weren't any regular flights from the town. But Mattias had got lucky, and sometimes that was all you needed. That, and
the right contacts, of course. He'd been celebrating Christmas in
Karlsborg, at a dinner with friends and coworkers, and when Tom's
call came in he was still awake, reading in one of the guest rooms. A
few phone calls later, he was sitting inside a roaring Hercules war-
plane heading north. A group of special forces guys had given him a
ride and dropped him off just over an hour ago, before they flew on
to some secret location. He took a cab to the hotel.

"Get dressed, then we can talk," he said.

"I am," Tom hissed.

Mattias studied Tom, who had managed to pull on the T-shirt and
was now struggling with his pants. He and Tom were officers, elite
soldiers, and certain habits ran deep. It made no difference how you
woke a former special forces officer, no difference how tired or hungover he was. Two seconds later, he would be getting dressed, ready
to go out into battle. But Tom really did look awful. Worn and di-

sheveled. His huge body was covered in scars and marks from badly healed wounds, and even Mattias, who was used to violence and its effects, felt uncomfortable at the thought of what Tom must have been subjected to if it left behind those marks.

Tom ran his hand through his unruly hair and buttoned his pants, which hung too loosely from his hips. Though the physical changes were evident in Tom, that wasn't the main difference. It was something else. In the past, everyone knew that you could give Tom Lexington a seemingly impossible task, drop him behind enemy lines, and trust that he would do what was necessary. He was the one everyone turned to once all other options were exhausted, once the situation seemed hopeless. Even when he and Mattias were out on duty, sometimes for days on end under the most awful conditions, Tom never looked this haggard. Today he looked as if he had one foot in the kingdom of the dead and was no longer sure where he belonged, among the living or those who had given up. His hair was long and dull; he was grizzled and had dark shadows on his face. But it wasn't even that. Mattias was used to seeing Tom dirty, grizzled, and long-haired—certain tasks demanded it. It was his eyes. There was something missing from them. For the first time, Mattias was forced to admit that maybe it was true after all, that the rumors he had refused to believe were right: Tom Lexington was a broken man.

"I need coffee," Tom croaked as he pulled on his socks and boots.

Mattias took a step into the room. No point speculating. He couldn't see a bag, no overnight things. So, Tom wasn't living here permanently. It bothered him that he didn't know where Tom had been living these past few months. He didn't like not knowing things. Not for the first time since last night, his thoughts turned to the unthinkable. Had Tom checked into the hotel because he planned on doing something stupid? Men with Tom's background, with his experience . . . Regardless of what people thought, the most common cause of death for soldiers like Tom wasn't enemy violence. It was suicide. That had been in the back of his mind the entire time, of course, and that was why he had hurried up here. One of the reasons anyway.

"Why don't you answer your phone? I've been calling you all fall," he said.

"I was busy," Tom replied as he bent down to tie his boots.

Mattias crossed his arms. "Really? With what?"

Tom gave him a dark look. "I don't need to explain myself to you, let's get that damn clear."

"I know, it was just a question."

Yet another furious look. "This really isn't a good day for me."

Mattias thought to himself that it was probably a while since *any* day was good for Tom. The man's ability to bear what, in reality, was unbearable was definitely greater than most people's. Back in Karlsborg, he was like a machine: stable, effective, and unbreakable. But everyone had a breaking point. Everyone.

"Can we talk downstairs? They're still serving breakfast in the dining room. Maybe we could sit there?"

But Tom shook his head. "I don't want to go down there. I did something stupid. . . . I met . . ." He trailed off and grimaced. "I just want to leave."

"Back to your place?" Mattias asked accommodatingly. "You do have a place up here, right? Or are you living in the car?"

"I have a house. We can go there. But just so you shut up. Give me two minutes." Tom grabbed his wallet and keys, shoved them into his pocket, and headed into the bathroom.

"Though *I'm* taking the car keys and *I'm* driving," Mattias shouted after him. The room reeked of alcohol. Tom would be in no fit state to drive for hours.

Tom seemed to hesitate. But he had called Mattias because he needed help; that had to mean there was a straw to clutch. And right now, Mattias was just glad for the smallest of things. "It's icy as hell, you're hungover, and you don't want to mow anyone down. I'm driving, okay?" he said persuasively. Kindness was often the best way to manipulate people. Not least when they were in crisis. And Tom was always reasonable.

Tom muttered some curse words but fished the keys from his pocket. He threw them at Mattias, who caught them without looking.

"Show-off," Tom snarled as he vanished into the bathroom.

Ten minutes later, they were on the road out of Kiruna.

Mattias stood by Tom's kitchen window and studied the forest and the snow-covered landscape while Tom made coffee.

"I forgot how cold it is up here," Mattias said, his eyes following a roe deer as it vanished between the tree trunks. The silence in the forest practically hummed with cold. Snow wasn't his favorite of the elements. Tom, on the other hand, began his military career up here, with the mythical ranger battalion, and had always liked snow. Mattias was at the Armed Forces Interpreter Academy in Uppsala—itself just as mythical—during the same period. They had always complemented one another.

"I can't believe it's nearly ten years since we started at Karlsborg," Mattias continued while Tom doggedly rattled the cups. "Time goes fast," he added.

Tom raised an eyebrow at the platitude.

Mattias and Tom had joined the special forces in Karlsborg during the same year, and both had completed their training, which lasted just over twelve months. The same couldn't be said of everyone. The eliminations both before and during training were brutal. Some of the recruits couldn't handle the constant physical and psychological pressure, others were terrible at keeping secrets, and some just weren't smart enough. Sometimes, up to ninety percent of a year's intake might be weeded out.

Without a word, Tom handed him a cup of coffee, brewed in an advanced-looking machine—thankfully. Mattias had never understood the Norrland preference for boiled course-ground coffee. He took the cup. Tom served it black, without asking. He probably remembered that was how Mattias liked it. Tom's memory was both an asset and a curse. Mattias sipped with satisfaction.

Tom was standing with his hip against the kitchen island, drinking from his cup with his eyes fixed somewhere in the air.

Mattias wondered how to approach his second task. All fall he had been trying to make contact with Tom. This was his opening, but he would need to tread carefully.

"You have a good team at Lodestar," he began, feeling his way forward.

Tom didn't say anything, just gave Mattias a look that said he knew exactly what he was doing. Working him. Well, it made no difference.

"None of them would tell me where you were." Tom's team was

loyal to their boss. They hadn't given anything away, hadn't shared any information at all. But Tom always did have the ability to make people give their all. The best leaders were like that—they forged strong bonds. There were many bad private security firms in the field. And a handful of good ones. Tom's Lodestar was one of the very good ones. If you hired them, you got world-class experts.

Silence again. But Mattias was counting on that. Everything would have been much easier if he hadn't betrayed Tom in the past, of course. What a damn mess that had been.

Tom gave ten years of his life to the Armed Forces and to his country. First military service and officer training, then just over two years in the special forces before he quit when Mattias turned against him. After that, Tom turned to the private security sector. He started off working for a foreign company, risked his life in countries like Iraq, Syria, and Liberia. Then he returned to Sweden. Demand for men (and women, for that matter; there weren't many of them, but they did exist) with Tom's training, competence, and experience was enormous, so Mattias assumed Tom had been able to pick and choose. He eventually joined the small Lodestar Security Group. The press release said that he joined as managing director, but what that title meant in practice was something Mattias could only speculate. Under Tom's leadership, Lodestar established itself as the market leader in just a few short years. In international circles, the Scandinavian security company was relatively small, but when Mattias asked around, it had a good reputation. Now, its leader had emigrated to Kiruna. Why? Tom was still young; he would soon turn thirty-seven and should still be at the top of his game. He shouldn't look like a wreck and be living in the woods.

"No one at work knows I'm here," Tom said, breaking the long silence. "I have some things I need to work out on my own."

What kind of things? Mattias thought, but he knew better than to ask.

"People have been wondering," he said instead.

"People?"

Mattias put down his cup and made a vague gesture with one hand. Everyone was wondering, of course. But above all, he was curious. Because all this, it was so unlike Tom. Running away. Taking off without telling his colleagues where he was going. Abandoning his friends.

"What are you doing up here?" As far as Mattias knew, there was no longer anything linking Tom to the area. And he knew most things about Tom Lexington.

Father dead. Mother and three sisters with families spread around the Stockholm area. A job that paid handsomely. A big, newly bought apartment in the city. A materially rich life. Yes, he'd been taken prisoner earlier that year, but he'd survived, he'd been treated. He was an old elite soldier with a tough shell and a thick skin. It shouldn't have broken him. Right?

Tom shook his head dismissively, sipped his coffee, and slipped back into silence.

"Are you here on a job?" Mattias continued. Interrogations often went this way. Asking questions over and over again, innocent questions, the same questions to different people, piecing together tiny fragments of information. There was nothing up here for a man who was an expert in the things Tom was an expert in. Unless the Russians were getting ready to invade. But Mattias would have heard about that.

"Does it look like I'm working?" Tom asked drily.

No, he looked like a bum, Mattias thought. The silence spread through the room once again.

Mattias waited. There wasn't a sound from outside, no cars, no planes, nothing.

He patiently continued to wait. Tom always was a stubborn bastard. Yes, what he'd done to Tom was lousy. And maybe—*maybe*—he would have acted differently today, but still . . .

"It's been years now. When are you planning to forgive me?"

"Forgiveness is a bullshit concept. As though we can forgive."

"Maybe not. But I'm sorry, and I'm asking for your forgiveness. Again."

"Fuck off."

Mattias sighed. "You're too damn stubborn. Always have been."

Tom snorted.

Mattias wondered whether he should provoke Tom into a fight.

Would it help to clear the air, using their fists? But they were too old for that kind of childish solution, and Tom, even in his weakened state, would probably knock the shit out of him.

"Come on. What're you doing in Kiruna? Why are you doing this whole hermit thing?"

Tom scratched his neck. Put the cup into the sink. Sat down in a chair.

Mattias sat down opposite him.

"Ellinor lives here," Tom eventually said.

Aha. A piece of the puzzle. Ellinor Bergman.

In a line of work where broken relationships were the rule, Tom Lexington and Ellinor Bergman had been the exception. The couple everyone expected to last forever. Which just showed that you never knew. Mattias studied Tom's tormented face. Something still didn't add up. Tom and Ellinor had broken up in the spring. They weren't registered at the same address anymore. How did she fit into this?

"Are you together again?" he asked in an attempt to solve the puzzle.

"No."

"But she's here too?"

"Yeah, in Kiruna."

"I don't understand."

Ellinor did some kind of feminine job, he seemed to remember. Something caring and gentle, a nurse or in a kindergarten. No, something else.

"She lives here now. Works at the school," said Tom.

That was it. Teacher.

"With her new man."

The penny dropped. Ellinor had moved on. And Tom . . . had not.

Mattias leaned back in his chair, swung one foot across his knee. "So, you're here to . . . ?"

Tom stared into the distance. Mattias studied him, the dark circles beneath his eyes, the hunted look on his face.

"I need to have a talk with Ellinor," Tom eventually said. "She can't be serious about all this. I just need to sit down and *talk* with her."

Christ. Mattias tried to hide his shock. This was bad.

"You don't understand. I can fix this."

He never would have expected this from Tom. It explained the state he was in. Captivity, torture, and a relationship going down the drain on the top of that. "Was that why you were at the hotel? Is Ellinor staying there?"

"No. I was there to drink my way through Christmas. I met a journalist, a woman. We drank together, and I was completely gone. We . . . I made a fool of myself, I guess." He rubbed his eyes. "Why did you come here, Mattias? Really?"

The moment of truth.

"This has to stay between us. I've been asked by the chief to start a counterterror group. Our job's to map and analyze different threats to the country. It's going to be a priority team within the Forces, and I'm building the group myself. It's going to be small, a specialist group with key competencies in different areas. I've started interviewing already. Not just inside the military, also cryptographers, academics, hackers."

"The chief made the right decision, then. Sounds like the perfect job for a master spy," Tom said drily.

Mattias gave him a steady look. "I want you."

"You can't be serious."

"Why not?" Tom's analytical abilities and field experience were unsurpassed. He would be an incredible addition. Mattias had wanted Tom on the team ever since he got the go-ahead. He'd come up to Kiruna because Tom wasn't doing well. But it would be misconduct if he didn't try to recruit someone with Tom's competence, especially now when he had such a golden opportunity. "Whether we like it or not, there's a war being waged against Sweden, an advanced information war. You could think about it, at least?"

Tom crossed his arms dismissively. "I have other things to deal with."

Mattias studied his nails. "And how's that going for you?" he asked quietly.

Tom said nothing. His stomach growled.

Mattias glanced at his watch. Almost lunch. He hadn't eaten since he'd left Karlsborg. "Are you hungry?" he asked.

Tom shrugged, but his stomach rumbled again. "There are cans. You can cook."

Mattias decided to settle for the moment. The first rule when trying to win people over was to identify their needs and satisfy them. Tom always was grumpy when he hadn't eaten.

"I'll whip up something."

Tom listened to Mattias banging around in his kitchen. He leaned against the backrest and closed his eyes. Mattias was too damn annoying. But he *was* hungry, and Mattias had always been good with pots and pans. Maybe he could wait until after they ate to throw him out. One bonus of being angry with Mattias was that he hadn't given any more thought to his embarrassing faux pas with Ambra Vinter. He raised his hands to his face. Jesus, what a mess.

It wasn't long before the smell of food started to drift from the kitchen, and he realized he was starving.

"Pasta with mushrooms, cheese, and freeze-dried cream." There was a long pause. "I think anyway. The contents of some of these cans are pretty similar. You've heard of fresh food, right?"

But the smell coming from the kitchen wasn't half bad, and when Mattias served up the meal, Tom ate greedily. Afterward Mattias loaded the dishwasher while Tom brewed more coffee, an entire pot this time. They sat down at the table, talked about cars for a while, then the weather, not quite relaxed but at least not as tense as before.

"Is this your place?" Mattias asked as he poured another cup of coffee.

"No," Tom replied, but he didn't elaborate. It was none of Mattias's business. The previous year, Tom was involved in an operation to rescue a kidnapped nineteen-year-old before he was to be executed by Islamists in Somalia. The young man was the only son of a Norwegian oil millionaire, and the luxurious house in Kiruna belonged to the grateful father. Tom was allowed to borrow it whenever he wanted. Mattias asked a few general, everyday questions about the place. Tom replied that there was a garage, several bedrooms, and a billiards room.

"And a sauna," he added. Mattias was a Swedish citizen, but his mother's family came from the Åland Islands, and Ålanders had a passionate relationship with saunas. Mattias said something about there being a lot of yard to tend, and then Tom mentioned that there was a brand-new snowblower in the garage. Uncomplicated, manly subjects. Mattias always was good at that. Making small talk about nothing, asking questions, making people feel comfortable. The problem was that you never knew if it was all just a game. He was a master manipulator. Officially, Mattias was a researcher at the Swedish Defence University, but Tom had always suspected that was a cover—which had now been confirmed. Mattias was far too smart not to have been recruited by MUST, the military intelligence agency. He was a born spy. He spoke fluent Russian, French, Arabic, and Farsi, and he was easily the best interrogator Tom had ever met. He was diplomatic, well educated, and always so damn easy to talk to.

He was the most slippery, deceitful person Tom knew.

All operatives within the special forces were given code names before they met their coursemates. It meant they could work and fight together for years without ever knowing one another's real names. One man was given the name Mast because he was tall. Others had neutral code names like Olsson. There were five Olssons in Tom's training course. A kid from Mora was called The Doctor because he was a devil at sewing up wounds. Tom became Grizzly on account of his dark hair and bearlike size. Mattias Ceder was The Fox. Not because he was especially foxlike, but because he was so damned cunning. The Fox knew how to get into anyone's psyche without using violence or torture, just using conversation.

"Everyone wants to talk, everyone has a need to be listened to," Mattias used to say. Maybe not the most dramatic approach, but it was effective. His calm, stubborn questions gave the kind of results torture never could. "Hitting someone isn't effective, because eventually they'll talk just to avoid more pain. Using logic is more subtly undermining," he'd said, getting secrets out of everyone.

Tom stretched out his legs. He could handle ten foxes if he had to. He would listen awhile longer, as polite thanks for the food. But if

Mattias talked too much, he would throw him out. The Fox could talk to the snowdrifts while he slowly froze to death.

Tom sipped his coffee.

Yes, he could definitely feel a real sense of satisfaction at the thought of throwing Mattias Ceder out into the woods if he said anything too annoying. He placed his hand on the table and gave Ceder a cold look. He would call it Plan B.

Chapter 12

Ambra screwed up her eyes, didn't want to open them. If she lay perfectly still, maybe she could go back to sleep.

She *shouldn't* feel sorry for herself, she thought. Making a fool of herself really wasn't the end of the world. Far worse things happened. *Think of all the people with cancer. Or people fleeing war. Those who can't escape the bombs or famine.*

She started to sweat. Swallowed and swallowed until she couldn't hold back any longer, rushed into the bathroom, and just managed to fling open the lid before she threw up, hunched over the toilet.

Afterward she sank to the cold stone floor.

Even if there really, *really* were much worse things to care about, anxiety washed over her. Ugh, she didn't want to be herself right now.

She rubbed her forehead, sniffed, and slowly got up. Everything went dark, and she had to grab the sink to stay upright. She waited it out and then drank water straight from the faucet. She avoided looking at her reflection as she hurried back to the bed.

She would visit Elsa again that afternoon. She hoped she would feel better by then. Jesus, she couldn't remember when she was last so hungover she couldn't work. Never, in all likelihood.

Ambra pulled the covers over her head and tried to think of more things that were worse than being turned down by a man outside your hotel room at Christmas, but she couldn't. The kiss. Oh, God, *that kiss.* Tom knew how to kiss, which just made everything worse. She groaned beneath the covers. In a few days' time, she would probably have forgotten the whole thing, but right now she wished—intensely, in fact—that she could turn back the clock and start over. She would spend Christmas Eve alone, in her room, and never start up a conversation with Tom Lexington at the bar. Never feel attraction or desire, never imagine she could see the same thing in his eyes.

She threw back the covers. She needed fresh air. And some pain-killers. She knew, deep down, that what had happened wouldn't make the slightest difference in the long run. She would probably never see Tom again. He wasn't important. And, at some point in the future, she would probably meet a man who didn't find her so repulsive that he said no when she came on to him, pressed herself against him. Intellectually, she *knew* all this, but sadly her intellect wasn't exactly in control right now; regret and shame had free reign. She rubbed her eyes. Yesterday's mascara crumbled beneath her fingers, and she had slept in the same clothes she had been wearing all day. So, the plan was to take a shower, find some painkillers, drink a gallon of coffee, and then prepare for her interview. And, very important: forget everything to do with Tom Lexington.

Her cell phone was almost dead, so she staggered to her feet again; found the charging cable; checked Twitter, Instagram, Facebook, and her e-mail; concluded that World War III hadn't broken out while she slept; and lay down on the bed as another wave of nausea washed over her. She would go straight from the interview to the airport and head home. God, she couldn't wait to leave Kiruna and get back to Stockholm. She had managed to find a seat on one of the overbooked planes, and she made a promise to herself, there and then, that she would never come back here. They would have to fire her. Her job meant everything to her, and she was willing to step up and do most of what they asked, but there was a limit to how low she could sink, and as far as she was concerned, she had reached that level yesterday.

She feebly waited for the next wave of nausea. The minute it passed, she dragged herself into the shower, rinsed off the makeup and dirt, and washed her hair. She felt slightly better after she found some clean clothes, and when she made it down to breakfast without bumping into Tom (the horror!), she decided she might survive the day after all. She would do the interview with Elsa and then leave this godforsaken town.

With a mug of steaming coffee beside her, she opened her laptop.

It took a while to get started, but she managed to come up with a few more interview questions and skim through her notes. After a second cup of coffee and a sandwich, she felt marginally recovered. As the breakfast buffet was cleared away, her anxiety abated, and she started feeling like a person again.

Yes, her job was her very best friend.

At ten-thirty Ambra took two more painkillers, hoped her stomach and liver would cope, packed her toiletries and the last of her clothes, checked that she hadn't forgotten anything, then zipped up her bag. She was meeting Elsa at three, and her flight home was at eight. Since she had a little time to kill, she decided to take a walk to help with her hangover. The last thing she did was to pull on her hat, scarf, and gloves; zip up her coat; check out; and leave the hotel through the revolving doors.

It was Christmas Day, and the snow-covered streets were completely deserted. Every store she passed was closed; not even the hot dog kiosk down by the bus station was open. She slipped on the snow. A lone kicksled sped past, and she saw someone walking a dog, but otherwise the town was empty. Christmas Day in Sweden was the dullest day of the year. Yet her headache started to disappear, and the cold air felt invigorating. She struggled up a hill, looked in through a store window, shivered a little. It would be good to get home this evening.

But she needed to see Elsa before that. She hoped the old lady would be in a talkative mood and that it would lead to a great article. She promised herself to make the story about the sex camps as dignified as she could.

She turned onto yet another deserted street and passed Elsa's pink building, but it was far too early to knock, and so she continued her walk.

With its eighteen thousand inhabitants, Kiruna was a small town, and she had already been up and down most of its streets. She cut across a parking lot, making her way away from the town center. She was starting to feel warmer now.

Suddenly, she caught sight of the big, red church up on the hill. It was one of the town's main landmarks, but she had been avoiding it. Did she dare go up there? The outside of the church was illuminated, and there were lots of people heading up the slope. Ambra hesitated, but then she slowly followed the stream of people. She stopped at a notice board for upcoming events. A Finnish preacher would be appearing, a midnight mass would take place, a . . . Suddenly, a movement, a feeling, or maybe it was a sound, caught her attention. She slowly turned her head. The hair on her arms stood on end, and her mouth went dry. She barely dared look, afraid to be recognized. Was she mistaken?

But no, she wasn't, not this time. There he was. In the flesh. It wasn't a figment of her imagination, it was the real Esaias Sventin. She felt dizzy, as though she'd stood up too quickly. He passed so close to her that she could almost make out his nauseating scent, but he didn't notice her. It was him, though. And close behind him was Rakel Sventin, his wife, with her plait and headscarf and everything.

Her skin prickled. It was them. So, the church still made its premises available to them. The Laestadian sect. The madmen. It was a scandal. They shouldn't be allowed to set foot within the Swedish church, much less to preach there.

Ambra was about to turn around, wanting nothing more to do with them, wanting only to run, when she noticed something she hadn't seen at first, due to the number of people. Esaias and Rakel weren't alone. There were two children between them. She watched them go. Who were they? Grandchildren? They couldn't be foster children, could they? Somehow she'd always assumed that they'd never taken in any more foster children after her. It was always so obvious that they hated her. And they were too old now, weren't they? Hesitantly, she followed them. She still had almost an hour before her meeting with Elsa.

There was no music coming from the church, but that didn't surprise her. Music was a sin. She stood there. Watched the Sventins enter the church, the two children between them. They seemed to be girls. Maybe around ten years old.

Ambra herself was ten when Esaias and Rakel took her to church for the first time. It was her first real church service. At most, she had been to a handful of school events in modern churches, full of pale wood, vases of summer flowers, and songs by Astrid Lindgren on the piano. Always alone, of course. At all the end-of-school events, Lucia processions, and parents' meetings. This church was red on the out-side but dark and black on the inside. Low, mumbling voices rose to-ward the ceiling. Old people sitting on the pews, black Bibles in their hands. Only the men spoke in Laestadian churches, only the men preached. And once the preacher had been talking for what felt like an eternity, Ambra squirmed on the hard bench. Her feet didn't reach the ground, and the backs of her thighs hurt.

"Sit still," Esaias whispered threateningly.

She sat as still as she could. But she had pins and needles in her legs. And the people were so strange. When she glanced to one side, the woman next to her was crying silently.

The preacher's words were strange too. Strumpets. Temptations. Demons. Sinners. A man in the front row suddenly got to his feet, and words that sounded like they belonged to another planet began pouring from his mouth. Ambra stared. More people started crying. They hadn't eaten before they came, and she was so hungry. She squirmed.

"Sit still!"

She really did try. But one leg had gone to sleep, and it hurt. She tried to raise her leg.

Esaias grabbed her arm so hard that she gasped. He placed one of his big hands over her mouth to silence her. It stank.

"It's the devil in you. Sit still, I said," and he grabbed her cheek in-stead, pinched so hard that her eyes grew dark. The tears started to flow, but Ambra didn't dare move an inch. She endured the pain, sat completely still until Esaias let go of her.

When the service finally ended and they went home, the others sat down at the table.

"You can watch. You'll get your punishment after dinner."

She stood there and watched them eat, waiting for her punish-ment. Foster parents had hit her before. One foster mom pulled her hair, another pinched her. She was often pushed around by older children, relatives, or others who simply allowed themselves to take their anger out on someone who couldn't defend herself. But Esaias hit her. Beat her with a cane on her back and behind.

He would breathe heavily afterward, as though it was hard work hitting a child only a fifth of his size. "Go to bed," he commanded.

But her bed was wet. Someone had poured water into it. She didn't dare say anything, just climbed in. She had been hit before, heard evil things, but she had never been punished in this calculating, systematic way. And that evening was only the beginning.

Ambra watched the church doors close behind the couple and the girls, and she stopped below the steps, uncertain what she should do, overwhelmed by the sight of them, almost panic-stricken. What was awaiting those two children inside?

"Is everything okay?" she heard a kind voice ask. She turned and saw a woman around her age, with long blond hair under a hat with light fur covering her ears. White overalls, white fur boots. She looked like a winter angel.

"Yes, thanks," Ambra replied hesitantly.

The woman smiled. "You groaned," she said as an explanation, and a white ball of a dog suddenly appeared next to them. The woman was holding the leash in her hand, Ambra saw now. And she seemed completely normal. Not like one of the Laestadian madmen but like a normal Kiruna resident with a soft, Norrland dialect and the healthy appearance of someone who spends a lot of time outdoors and knows how to dress for the weather.

Ambra nodded firmly. "I'm fine. Just a little hungover," she added, pulling a face.

The woman laughed. "You're not from around here, are you? Can hear it when you talk."

"I'm a journalist. I'm here on a job."

"Are you the one talking with Elsa? My mom heard it from one of her friends. Nice to meet you."

"I'm actually going to see her now."

"Let me know if you need help with anything up here," the woman said cheerily. She took off one glove and held out her hand. "My name's Ellinor Bergman."

"Come in, dear," Elsa said when Ambra knocked on her door at three on the dot. They went into the living room again. Ambra sat down in the same chair and breathed out, still jumpy at having seen the Sventins.

"How are you?" Elsa asked with a concerned look.

Ambra shrugged noncommittally. "Did you think about what we discussed?"

"There's a lot to consider," Elsa said. "I've lived here my entire life, I was twenty-one when the second world war ended. I'd long been thinking about creating a retreat up here, long before anyone even knew what a retreat was. It was a huge success even during its first year. The prime minister came to the very first one, in 1958."

"Did you fall in love?" Ambra asked. This really was an entire lifetime ago.

Elsa shook her head. "Not in love, exactly. At least I didn't. But he was charming, and one thing led to another, as they say. I got pregnant. I wasn't very young, particularly not by those days' standards, and I so dearly wanted to keep the child. By then, Ingrid was already in my life. We were terribly in love. All that love when I was approaching forty."

"Were you ever interested in women before?"

"No. I knew that lesbians existed, of course, but I never thought along those lines. Meeting Ingrid was like a miracle. And in many ways, Olof became *our* child, mine and Ingrid's. He grew up without a father, but he was surrounded by warmth and love all the same. Times were so different then, it's almost impossible to imagine today. More judgmental, but also simpler, freer."

"Sounds almost idyllic."

"It was a blessing to be able to experience it. I'm so grateful. Ingrid always dreamed of being an artist, and with me she was able to do that. We could afford to live how we wanted to. For a while, everyone came here. Not just film stars and celebrities, but many others seeking sanctuary. Rumor spread that this was somewhere they could be in peace, be themselves. Homosexuals. People with questions about their gender identity, their sexuality. Gradually, we moved over to mindfulness and art courses, less sex." Elsa clutched the cross she wore around her neck before she continued. "Ingrid's family were Laestadians, just like the family you lived with. It was difficult for her, because when she chose me she was completely driven out, as though she had stopped existing. If we were out walking and saw her family, they pretended not to see her. It was terrible. We had to fight for our love on all fronts."

"But Elsa, that's why you should talk," said Ambra. She was moved by the story and knew that both Grace and their readers would love it. "Your story is so much about our equal worth as humans, about love, and tolerance."

"And celebrities." Elsa smiled.

"That too. And I'm not going to lie, celebrities sell papers, and I definitely want to write about your camp, your retreats, and what you did there, but I want to write about the rest of it too. It's a beautiful story. Unique and universal at the same time. We need this."

Elsa seemed hesitant. "I don't know . . ."

"What do you think Ingrid would have wanted?" Ambra asked.

"She was very private, but she was also brave in many ways. You remind me of her, actually." Elsa smiled, and Ambra knew she had managed to convince Elsa. A surge of triumph rushed through her.

The doorbell rang. "That's probably Tareq," Ambra said. "I'll get it."

"My mind is made up," Elsa called after her. "You're right. I'll do it. For Ingrid's sake."

"The thing about tantric sex, it's hugely overrated, if you ask me," Elsa said as she slurped her coffee through a sugar lump. "It was really just something fun we tried one year. But most people found it boring, so we moved on."

Ambra smiled. Elsa was fantastic. Once she'd made up her mind, she really was telling them *everything*.

"What did you do instead?" she asked.

"Some of the women who came here had never had an orgasm, so we ran an orgasm school. This was before YouTube—there are videos online now, of course."

"Of course," Ambra mumbled. She glanced at Tareq, who was filming behind her. He nodded calmly; he was catching it all. To be on the safe side, Ambra was also recording Elsa on her phone. She already had several great quotes.

"Just between us, there was quite a lot of smoking, too, but only marijuana. A little grass, that was all, never hurt anyone."

Ambra said nothing, just glanced at Tareq from one side again. They would probably have to cut out some of the weed-smoking parts, but otherwise it was perfect.

"Elsa, this is going to be great," Tareq eventually said. "Ambra, you happy?"

Ambra nodded, and Tareq started to pack up his equipment while Elsa went out into the kitchen. Tareq was sweet, Ambra absent-mindedly thought as she watched his long, deft fingers on the equipment. Handsome and young, wiry and strong, like many of the best photographers were. They were strong from hauling their equipment around all the time. And he was kind. She should have flirted with him instead.

He looked up and smiled. "Hey, a few of us are going out tonight. Come along if you want," he said, getting up and swinging his bag onto his shoulder.

"That would have been great," she said honestly. "But I'm flying back tonight."

"Okay. I'll be in touch once I check the film. But this is going to be great. Good work."

"Nice boy," Elsa said once Tareq left.

Ambra closed her notepad. She had enough now. Grace would be happy. "How does it feel?"

"It was good to have you here. Partly because of the interview, but also to meet you. Are you sure you're all right? If you don't mind my asking."

So, Elsa had noticed she wasn't herself. Ambra smiled reassuringly. "Yeah. I'll send your quotations so you can check them over," was all she said.

"That's fine, dear." Elsa looked as if she wanted to say more, but she held back.

Well. The interview was over. Grace wanted the story to run over two days. The first article tomorrow, December 26, and the second the day after. Tareq would work on the raw footage, and an editor would polish it up and upload it to the website. Elsa offered the black-and-white photos for no cost, but Ambra insisted on paying her 10,000 kronor. Grace would probably kill her if she found out, but it was still cheap, and it wasn't like the paper didn't have the money.

Everything was done, and she would probably never see Elsa again. That was the strange thing about this job. You met people, listened to their stories, grew close to them, felt moved, and then parted ways for good. Plus, with Elsa, there had been another dimension to it.

She paused. She wasn't originally planning to share any personal information with Elsa. But this whole trip was so strange. Elsa's revelations. Tom Lexington. The Sventins. "I saw them," she said tentatively.

Elsa clasped her hands in front of her stomach. "Where?" she asked. It felt good, that she understood.

"Outside the church."

"Ah, of course." Elsa leaned forward and took Ambra's hand in hers. It was warm and smooth, like heated tissue paper. "You're very pale. Was it difficult?"

"I saw him and Rakel. It was awful. But the worst thing was that they had two children with them. Do you know if they have grandkids?"

"It's not impossible. They had a lot of children, if they're still in the community . . ."

"Sect. It's a sect."

Elsa nodded. "If their sons are still in the sect, they must be grown men, married, probably with children of their own. That's what they do, they marry one another and have lots of children."

"Yeah, I guess so."

"How did it feel to see them?"

"He was so old. Her too."

"They ruined so much."

"Yes." Ambra sighed.

"Would you like something to eat?"

"I have to go." It was almost six, and she didn't want to miss the plane.

"If you want to talk, I'll be here the rest of Christmas. Maybe you could come for lunch tomorrow?"

Ambra really wished she could say yes. "I'm sorry, I'm flying home today."

"Another time then," Elsa said warmly.

"Yeah," Ambra replied, though she knew the likelihood was virtually nonexistent.

*   *   *

After saying good-bye to Elsa, Ambra took a cab to the airport. The snow was coming down heavily again, and she clutched the seat the whole way there. By the time she arrived, it was practically a full-blown storm. She paid for the cab with her private Visa card—she didn't have the energy to worry about receipts and expenses—and opened the door. The departures hall was full of people, and she knew even before she checked the screens that something wasn't right. The loudspeaker system was booming, people were talking hysterically, exhausted children were crying. She pushed her way over to a screen. The flight to Stockholm was cancelled because of a technical fault.

"All planes to Stockholm are fully booked over the next few days," said the harried woman behind the check-in counter.

"So how am I meant to get home?"

"We have one seat left, via Oslo."

"I'll take it," Ambra said. She had to get away. Behind her, she heard someone burst into tears. She turned around. A heavily pregnant woman carrying a small child in her arms was crying dejectedly.

"Did you want that seat?" Ambra asked after a short, selfish pause.

The woman blew her nose and nodded.

"Take it," Ambra said with a sigh.

"Thank you."

After an hour, she had no choice but to accept it: She was stuck in Kiruna. She ended up on a standby list, hailed a cab, and went back to the hotel. She sent Jill a message, looking for sympathy, and received a sad emoji in reply.

"Do you still have my room?" she asked, and the hotel checked her in. She slumped onto the bed and sent a message to Grace saying she didn't know when she would be able to leave Kiruna. It was Christmas, and the flights were booked to bursting.

OK, keep me updated.

Her fingers drummed her cell phone. What should she do now? Stuck in a town she hated.

Should she get in touch with Elsa and see whether the invitation to lunch was still open? Ten minutes later, she had been invited over the next day. That was something.

Ambra lay back down on the bed. Now that she was here, should she do a little digging into the Sventins? She would have to think about it, she decided, studying the room service menu. She put it down. Grabbed her phone and scrolled through her contacts until she found Tareq's number. She hesitated for a moment, but why not?

Can I still hang out with you tonight?

His reply came quickly. *Yeah! Cool! We'll be at the Royal from nine on.*

Ambra opened her computer and got an hour's work done. Then she applied a little lip gloss, ran her fingers through her curls and spritzed them lightly. She gave herself a stern look in the mirror. She wouldn't let Kiruna break her. She refused to feel anxious because of this town. She would take control of her feelings and she would have fun.

"You hear that?" she said to her reflection. "We're going to have fun."

She left her room at nine, went down to reception, and asked for directions to the Royal.

Chapter 13

Tom checked out the noisy club and decided that there was probably nowhere he wanted to be less. Someone was singing karaoke on a small stage by one wall. Disco balls turned on the ceiling; their blinking lights bothered him and he looked away. The walls were covered in reindeer antlers, animal skins, and Sami art. The bar had a special on drinks containing vodka, cloudberry, and lingonberry. He used to come here when he was young, but the place had completely changed since.

"Looks different from how it used to," he said, watching two flannel-shirt-clad, intertwined men.

"It's Christmas, there's not much choice," Mattias replied, nodding to the bartender and gesturing that they wanted two beers.

Tom watched two young men kiss at the bar. Mattias handed him a beer, and they sat down at a table. They had been talking about fishing, old acquaintances—*not* about work—back home, and somehow Tom had let Mattias talk him into getting out, around other people, for a while. Mattias had that ability. To be convincing.

"The Christmas Day Gay Bar is meant to be the best place to hang out in the whole of Norrbotten. I read that somewhere," said Mattias.

"If you say so," Tom replied. He didn't actually care what type of place it was. It was the noise levels and the flashing lights he was struggling with. Ten minutes and then he would leave, he decided, glancing at his watch as someone started trashing a new song over on the stage. The singers finished up and were rewarded with clapping and cheers.

"You could try looking a little less . . . I don't know, mercenary-ish," said Mattias.

"What are you talking about?"

Mattias shoveled a handful of nuts into his mouth. "Try to look like other people do, Tom. You're scaring the locals."

"You can always go back to Stockholm if it doesn't suit you."

"Yeah, so you said. Twenty times."

"I . . ." Tom began, annoyed, but he trailed off.

Both he and Mattias were sitting with their backs to the wall. It was an old habit. That way you were guaranteed a good view of everyone else and you couldn't be attacked from behind. It meant Tom could see right across the club, and his eyes spotted a familiar face. It was dark, but he recognized her immediately.

Ambra Vinter.

She was at a table with a group of young men. They were drinking, downing beers, and she laughed and flicked her hair every now and then.

Shit.

"Someone you know?" Mattias asked, looking over to the table at the same moment Ambra caught sight of Tom across the crowded room. She froze midlaugh, then sat completely still with her hand wrapped around her beer. The flashing lights danced over her face. For a moment Tom thought she would ignore him completely, but then she gave him a quick, cool nod and turned her attention back to her friends. Her dark hair bobbed whenever she and the others laughed.

"Who's that?" Mattias asked.

Tom paused. "A reporter I bumped into."

A curious glimmer appeared in Mattias's eyes. "At the hotel? She's not the one you made a fool of yourself with?"

This was the irritating thing about Mattias. He didn't miss a thing. So damn annoying. Tom shrugged. Mattias's eyes lingered on Ambra. She had turned so that Tom could see her in profile. She was pretty like that, from the side; she had a straight nose and soft cheeks. She looked angry. Angry and dismissive.

"Come on, let's go over and say hi," said Mattias.

Don't think so. But Mattias was already on his feet, making his way over to her. Tom glared after him, but it seemed even more idiotic—if that was possible—to stay at the table by himself, so he reluctantly got up and followed.

Mattias said something, and everyone at the table, Ambra and the four younger men, turned to look at Tom as he arrived.

"This is Tom," said Mattias. "This is Tareq." He continued the introductions, saying the names of the others, though Tom immediately forgot them. They were young, handsome, and happy, and they made him feel old and cynical. By their age he had long been a hardened soldier.

"And you know Ambra, of course. Sit." Mattias himself was already sitting. He gestured to the only free seat, next to Ambra, a narrow space on the end of a pine bench.

"Hi," Tom said stiffly.

Ambra gave him an almost imperceptible nod in reply and then looked away. She shifted as far as she could along the bench and seemed about as comfortable with the situation as he was.

The four young men, however, greeted them enthusiastically. Their table was covered in beers and glasses and snacks, and it wouldn't have been much of a stretch to guess that they were drunk.

"Sit," Mattias repeated. Tom did as he was told and perched on the end of the bench, next to Ambra. She moved farther away, but no matter what he did he couldn't avoid a certain level of physical contact. He tried his best to find a position that didn't involve squashing her or falling off the bench. He pulled at the neck of his shirt.

"Tom said you're a journalist, Ambra. You from up here?" Mattias asked.

Ambra pushed back her dark curls, though they immediately fell loose again, and Tom caught the scent of something through the beer haze. A flower, perhaps. Or maybe a fruit. Something feminine, in any case. He remembered smelling the same thing when they kissed.

"I'm from Stockholm, just here on a job. Or was. My plane was canceled, so I'm stuck here for at least one more night. You? Do you live in Kiruna?"

Mattias swigged his beer. He seemed completely at ease. "I'm just visiting."

"So what do you do?" Ambra asked after a moment's silence. Tom tried to move his leg, but doing so just made her tense further.

Mattias flashed her an open smile, as though he didn't have a secret in the world. "Me? Nothing special. A little consultation work. Information."

A typical standard response for someone who worked in secrets. Vague answers about something so uninteresting it never led to follow-up questions.

"In which area?" Ambra asked. Tom looked down at his beer, and he was close to smiling. Maybe she was just being polite. Maybe she had caught a hint of something. It served Mattias right. Let him sweat a little.

"Boring bureaucracy for the most part," Mattias replied with a nonchalant shrug.

"Mmm-hmm." Ambra sounded skeptical. When she lifted her glass, their thighs touched. She had nice thighs, soft and warm.

Mattias held up his empty glass. "I'm going to the bar," he said, and he squeezed out and walked away. The table was less cramped now, and Ambra quickly moved along the bench. Tom listened to the others' conversation. After a while, Tareq got up and disappeared. Ambra's fingers drummed the table in time with the music. She still hadn't said a word to Tom. One of the other young men got up and left with another guy. Someone started to sing another terrible karaoke version of a famous song. The noise levels rose, if that was possible. Suddenly Tom and Ambra were alone at the table. She sipped her beer, put down the glass with a gentle thud, and glanced around with a dogged expression on her face.

"Didn't mean to chase everyone away," Tom said, but his joke fell flat.

A tense silence without any eye contact.

"Sorry about your flight," he said after what felt like a never-ending moment.

"Thanks," she said.

More tense silence.

"About yesterday," he started, tense and uneasy.

Ambra made a pained sound. "Please. We really don't have to talk about it. Can't we just pretend nothing happened?"

"Sure," he replied, half relieved and half . . . something else. Their kiss had been fantastic, after all. Hot. Sexy.

They sat in silence again.

Mattias seemed to have vanished. There was no sign of the others either. All Tom wanted was to go home. Back to the silence and the solitude.

The increasingly loud environment, the noisy people, the temperature, which seemed to have increased by several degrees . . . He started to sweat. Shit, not now. Flickers appeared at the edge of his field of vision. All of a sudden it was as if someone had cranked up the heat and taped shut all of the windows. His internal systems were screaming for him to get up, run from the threat, the anxiety, himself. He clutched his beer glass, stared at the table, tried to breathe calmly. How much time had passed? How strong was it? A five, surely no more? Six? Breathe, Tom. *Shit, shit, shit.*

"Hey, are you okay?" Her light touch on his arm almost made him leap up. Ambra's face looked concerned, her tone much softer than before. But he couldn't get his breathing under control. He couldn't sit here and have an attack. He wiped his forehead with the back of his hand, tried to force his shoulders to relax. Couldn't speak, not right now. This was the worst part of it, the total lack of control.

Ambra handed him a bottle of mineral water.

"Here, drink," she said.

He did, and breathed out deeply. Drank again. The flickering faded a little. Definitely a five now. Maybe even a four? He wiped his forehead again. Breathed, jaggedly and heavily.

"What happened?" she asked after a while. He could feel her trying to meet his eye, but he avoided it. Needed to stabilize first. He breathed in again. Calmly, nicely. Relax the legs. Don't squeeze the glass until it breaks.

"Tom?"

"Nothing. I'm all right now." Definitely better. He could even talk.

Ambra's voice did actually help. It was calming and helped him to focus on something other than his runaway body. He tried to move his fingers, his toes, to force the blood out into them rather than pooling in the bigger muscle groups. A weak four now. The instinct to fight or flee retreated, and he could start to think again. He searched for something to say, something unconnected to what he'd just experienced. It was so damn embarrassing. "Did you see Elsa again?" he asked.

"Yeah. But are you really okay? You look terrible."

He made a dismissive gesture with his hand. "I'm fine." He forced himself to look at her, to meet her gaze. Those green cat eyes were studying him worriedly. He breathed in through his nose, out through his mouth, and tried to focus on her eyes.

"Tom . . ."

He shook his head. "Tell me about Elsa," he said. He rubbed the back of his neck; it was drenched in sweat, and he drank more water.

"I liked her a lot, actually." Ambra smiled tentatively. Her eyes still looked worried, but he could feel that his pulse was definitely slowing. He clutched the bottle of water, focused on Ambra's voice, on her eyes, on her throat above the neck of her sweater. She seemed to like those knitted sweaters—this one was dark blue—and they were sexy. Soft and feminine. A nice contrast to her prickly antipathy toward him. His eyes lingered on the curve of her breasts. That helped too.

"I don't know any old people, isn't that weird?" she continued.

Tom's eyes quickly moved back to her face. The tightness around his chest had loosened. He was drenched in sweat and thirsty, too, but his body was no longer out of control. "You don't? No old relatives?" he asked.

"Not one. My grandparents are all dead, and their parents too."

"No others?"

"Nope, I don't have a single relative."

The words came out so easily, as though it was just an unusual detail she was revealing, a slightly amusing anecdote. But the only people Tom knew without any relatives were the survivors of war.

"Parents?"

"Dead. Dad died of heart problems when I was four, and my mom died later that year, just before I turned five."

The same neutral tone of voice. As though she was telling someone else's story.

"So where did you grow up?" he asked. There had to have been someone. Didn't she mention a sibling?

"Social services took care of me. I was a foster kid."

Her fingers played with the label on the glass bottle. She had slender fingers. Short nails painted a dark, glossy color he found vaguely erotic. He remembered the way those fingers had clutched his upper arms the night before, how her entire body pressed against his. She didn't say any more, avoided his eye.

They had clearly returned to the tension of earlier. He knew he should make his excuses and leave. This was too much. The atmosphere. The attack. But she looked so small. Like she really was as alone as she'd just said. He glanced around the room and then back at her. She was pulling at the sleeves of her sweater, and he wanted to say something that would make her relax, smile. An image of their kiss in the hotel corridor came back to him, an intense memory of her lips against his, the quiet sounds she made.

"Last night . . ." he started, but he was interrupted by Tareq returning to the table. Ambra's face lit up in relief. Tom studied the considerably younger and more handsome man with a frown. A thought struck him. Was something going on between the two of them?

"Everything good? You gonna be okay?" Tareq asked without sitting down. He was rocking on his heels.

"What do you mean?" Ambra asked suspiciously, her face turned to him. She patted the empty seat next to her. "I'm here with you—are you going to sit?"

Tareq shook his head and gave her an apologetic look. "I just wanted to come see if you were good. I met someone." He gestured over to the bar.

Ambra crossed her arms. "Are you kidding me? You're leaving again?"

"Not leaving. Just sitting over there." Tareq flashed his blinding smile. "Plus, you have Tom."

"Yeah, you have me," Tom murmured.

Ambra ignored him. "So you're dumping me?" she asked Tareq.

He held up his arms in appeal. "There's dumping and dumping. Please?"

Ambra snorted.

"He's a firefighter *and* he plays ice hockey," Tareq continued.

Tom didn't say a word, but he followed their exchange with interest.

"I'll snitch to Grace," Ambra sulked, but he could hear she had given up. "Tell her you're unreliable. You'll be covering C-list celebrities' weddings once I'm done with you. Fine, fine, go."

Tareq smiled, thanked her, and disappeared back toward the bar.

Tom couldn't help it. He was happy that Tareq turned out to be gay. Ambra watched him push his way over to a big blond man by the bar.

She leaned back and put one arm on the armrest. "This visit to Norrland is going to go down in history as the trip when every man I met dumped me," she said.

Tom was close to smiling. "What a negative attitude. The night is young. I'm sure you'll find someone, if that's what you want." They both looked out at the sea of laughing, dancing men. Ambra raised a long, dark eyebrow.

"Well, maybe not *here*," Tom agreed.

She pushed a strand of hair from her face. Dark hair, pale skin. She was an attractive woman. Right then, he couldn't believe he had said no to her. If only the circumstances were different . . . There was just something about her.

"It's been a strange trip," Ambra said drily.

Ambra looked over to the bar. It was crowded with men and the odd woman. Tom followed her gaze, and while his head was turned, she took the chance to sneak a look at his body. It was so long since she'd last had sex, and even though the man was a damn idiot, there was something about him she found undeniably attractive. He was wearing a black T-shirt—without any slogans this time—and he had enormous biceps. She wasn't the only one stealing glances at him. Lots of the other people were too.

She hadn't been given a single one.

Like she said, this trip was far from an ego boost. But still, it was good that Tom had turned up like this. After her initial shock, she'd played it cool and eventually managed to salvage some of her battered pride. She glanced at him again. It was pure reflex. Such a shame it hadn't gone anywhere with them. All her girly parts were drawn to him.

"Did you say something?" Tom turned around and was now looking at her attentively. She could have sworn something happened between them, and she found herself lost in his serious eyes. But she had already gone through this once.

She shook her head. "Nope. Nothing."

Silence.

And a little more silence. Ambra scratched her ear. Crossed her legs. Glanced around the room. If she hadn't given up her seat on the plane, she would be home by now.

"How's it going over here?" Mattias was back.

Tom shrugged.

It was all very well to be primitively attractive, a strong, silent type, but Tom really wasn't very talkative. She still didn't fully understand what he was doing in Kiruna. She looked at Mattias Ceder again. His entire being oozed secrecy. And then it all fell into place.

"You two are in the military, right?" she said, feeling pretty pleased with herself.

Tom didn't say a word.

Ambra waited. Leaned back, crossed her legs. And yes, she was aware that Tom kept stealing the occasional glance. Good for her, but bad for him. He should've taken his chance when he had it.

"I maintain that I'm a technical advisor," Mattias eventually said.

"You said consultant before."

"Then that's what I'll maintain," Mattias replied without blinking.

Ambra thought for a moment. "And if I ask off the record?"

"Off the record, I'm still a consultant," Mattias replied with a smile.

She bit her nail, thought deeply. Curiosity was difficult. The reporter in her wanted to run off and Google them immediately. She had already looked up Tom, of course, but there was nothing about Tom Lexington online. That was highly unusual. He didn't have Facebook, wasn't on LinkedIn, and while people sometimes avoided social media, there was *nothing* about him anywhere. Not a single paragraph, not a line, nothing, nichts, nada. That in itself was suspicious. She would put money on Mattias being just as invisible.

She turned to Tom. "What have you been doing since you finished whatever it was you did in the military?"

"Captain." He looked away.

Ambra scratched her neck. List of things that were easier than getting any answers out of Tom Lexington: Turning things to gold. Waking the dead. Wringing water from a stone.

"The ex-military types I've met are those pumped-up, macho guys who stand on the sidelines, screaming things at people in security courses," she thought aloud. She wasn't fond of men like that.

Mattias grinned. "Tom works on courses like that."

Ah, information. Tom probably knew plenty of survival-related things that he could teach others. Though it would be good if he was doing a little better himself. She thought back to the panic attack she'd witnessed earlier. Intuition told her it wasn't his first. Or his last. There was something that didn't add up here, but she couldn't quite put her finger on it. "Do you run those courses up here?" she asked, searching for a way in.

Tom shook his head again.

"He's here because of a woman," Mattias said with a wry smile.

Ambra's fingers stopped drumming. *What?*

"What the hell, Mattias," Tom snapped.

"I just thought we should lay our cards on the table. I didn't know it was a secret."

"It's not exactly common knowledge. There was no reason to tell her."

Funnily enough, Ambra thought the exact opposite. Actually, it was highly relevant information. "As I recall, you said you were single," she pointed out in a tone she thought was the perfect balance between cool and mildly interested. Everything made a whole lot more sense now. Another woman. Of course.

"It's complicated," was all he said.

Yeah, well when were things *not* complicated?

"Does she live here?" *And where is she now? Why didn't you cele-brate Christmas together? Why did you flirt with me? Kiss me?*

"Technically, it's over between us. But even if it's over, it's . . ."

Ambra held up a hand. "Complicated. I get it. It's okay." And it was okay, in its own depressing way. At the very least Tom hadn't dumped her because she was the least attractive woman in town; it was because he was in love with someone else. That was probably as it should be, and as soon as she recovered from the news that he was taken, then . . . But he *had* said he was single. Or had she just imagined that?

She tried to remember; she really was drunk last night. This was a lot to process. He had a girl. Or, sort of. He was a former soldier. But he still hadn't said what he really did. The reporter in her told her there was a story here, somewhere.

Right?

Maybe Tom and Mattias really were boring consultants or advisors who ran mind-numbing courses and did such uninteresting work that a trip to a gay bar in Kiruna was the most exciting thing they had done in years. Maybe they were here to test out a secret new model car. That would've been newsworthy, at least. Grace would have wanted her to explore it anyway. But honestly, she would rather lie naked on a bed of nails than write a story like that. New cars, was there anything more boring? If there was, it would be karaoke.

Someone was back behind the microphone again, and she could hear the sound of yet another disco tune. Ambra spotted Tareq, that traitor, enjoying it from right up by the stage. Despite everything, it had been a good night. Christmas would soon be over. She was comfortably tipsy—not like yesterday, just nicely relaxed after a few beers. And she had ended things with Tom on a better note. It was good. A calm, relatively uneventful evening in Kiruna. It could have been much worse.

And then Ambra felt it.

It started as a low murmur over by the entrance. People elbowing one another in the sides. Whispering, turned heads, wide eyes. The noise rose, and the buzzing spread through the room. Conversations were interrupted and then started again. The excitement grew, became impossible to avoid. It could be anything.

But somehow Ambra knew exactly what was happening. She had experienced it before, and knew there were few people in the world who could have this impact on a room. She happened to know one of them very well.

She was sure of it before she even turned around.

Jill had arrived in Kiruna.

Chapter 14

Jill Lopez stepped into the lively club, then came to a halt in the middle of the floor. Though she was wearing her contact lenses, she still couldn't see all that well, and so she stood there, taking in the room and the atmosphere, trying to orient herself without squinting.

The room was mostly full of men, almost exclusively men, actually. Rustic décor—everything seemed to be made from pine and reindeer skin—but she was met by a special kind of energy. It took a while before she realized what it was. A gay bar. Perfect. She'd decided to come here on a whim and had already forgotten what the place was called. Ludvig had organized everything, and she'd begun regretting it when she was only halfway there, wondering what she was doing, but now she was here.

She slowly made her way forward through the whispering, photo-taking crowd. Plenty of celebrities complained about all the cell phone cameras, as though their star status was somehow disconnected from the public, but not Jill.

The first six years of her life had been devoid of any love. Then she was adopted by a childless Swedish couple. That was the short, PG version in any case. The one without the violence, terrible conditions, and a life journey that might have ended in drugs and death. Instead, she discovered music, and that was the story the papers told, focusing on her natural talent and success. Jill loved her fans and the devotion they gave her. She posed for selfie after selfie, working her way through the sea of people. Ambra was here, thank

God, sitting at a pine table with a huge man dressed entirely in black. Jill sensed rather than saw them.

She signed a few autographs, glanced over to the table, and gave Ambra an apologetic smile. Almost there. The black-clad man said something to someone next to Ambra, and Jill spotted another man. He was big, too, but not quite so broad-shouldered. More wiry, with brown hair, a serious face, and knife-sharp eyes that looked her up and down. She noticed a quick flash of recognition and then nothing. That was actually quite unusual, and she felt an unexpected wave of irritation. Surely he had more to offer than that?

She posed for a few more selfies, blew a kiss, and then made it over to the table.

"Hello," Ambra said, not getting up. They never hugged, and part of Jill was grateful for that; she hated the forced hugs and kisses on the cheek she was always being subjected to. Ambra never was the hugging type anyway. Though maybe it was because both of them had been too fucked up by their childhoods to act like normal people.

"Hi," Jill said, and she studied the two men. They were straight; she could see that immediately. She gave Ambra a speaking look.

"Tom, Mattias, this is my sister," Ambra said obediently. "Jill," she added, as though they didn't already recognize her. Jill couldn't remember the last time she met anyone who didn't know who she was. Barely a week passed when she wasn't in a paper. She was the face of a global beauty brand, and she was often on TV.

"Hi," the man with the dark eyes said. Tom.

"Hey," said the other. Mattias.

"What're you doing here?" Ambra asked.

It was a good question. "I was in the neighborhood . . . ?"

Ambra shook her head. "Last time we spoke, you were almost 200 miles away."

It was a pure impulse, from start to finish. But it was also a long time since they'd last seen each other, and she was so tired of Ludvig and hotel rooms.

"We left after your message, checked in, and I asked for you at reception. I ditched my assistant at the hotel and came here."

"You're insane. Why didn't you call first?"

Jill shrugged, didn't want to admit that she hadn't said anything because she was afraid of a no. Better to travel up unannounced than to be turned down over the phone.

"I always wanted to see . . ." She trailed off, couldn't quite remember where she was. She glanced at the two men again. No glittering eyes, no flirty laughs, nothing that even remotely suggested they saw her as a woman, as a sex object, or the celebrity she was. What a strange pair. But that was Ambra. She hung out with weird people. Maybe it was a bad idea to turn up unannounced after all. Ambra always did hate surprises. But Jill was restless, it was a few days until her next show, and she'd never had much control over her impulses.

"How do you know one another?" she asked. She couldn't work out the strange trio in front of her.

"We don't know one another," Ambra said as Tom replied, "Ambra and I celebrated Christmas together."

"Celebrated Christmas together?" Jill asked, intrigued. Ambra never celebrated Christmas. That was something they had common, their hatred of the holidays. Ambra because she dreamed of impossible things, and Jill because she just hated everything that didn't revolve around her.

"We ate and we drank, that's all." But Ambra looked embarrassed, and Tom squirmed in his seat. Did she dare hope her sister had gotten laid? Probably not. Ambra was useless when it came to men.

"And you?" Jill said, turning to Mattias. "How do you fit into this triangle?"

"I got here this morning, so I don't really fit in at all." His voice sounded educated: He spoke clearly and with some kind of upper-class accent. He sounded smart. She didn't like smart men. Ambra called it her education complex; Jill called it self-preservation. Another man came over, but unlike all of the others at the table, he was grinning.

"This is Tareq, my freelance photographer." Ambra introduced him. Tareq was young, dark-haired, and looked like a model.

"Jill Lopez. I'm a huge fan," he said, his voice full of reverence.

"Glad to hear it, Tareq," said Jill. Finally. Someone acting normally.

"Like Ambra said, I'm a photographer. Would it be okay if I took a few pictures?"

"Tareq, she's not here on business," Ambra said warningly.

"I'm sure I can handle a few photos," Jill said. She got to her feet, smoothed out her dress, and posed. Several of the other patrons took the chance to snap a few photos. From the corner of her eye, she saw Ambra, Tom, and Mattias watching the spectacle.

Jill sat down, and Tareq snapped a few more pictures before he put down his camera. "My God, I had no idea you were friends. I follow you on Instagram."

"We're sisters," said Jill.

Tareq gave Ambra an accusing look. "You never said you were related to an icon."

"Mmm, I wonder why," Ambra replied drily.

"We don't talk about it much," said Jill.

The truth was, they never talked about the other publicly. They never commented on each other's posts on social media. Jill never discussed her background in interviews, and Ambra never said anything about anything, so the fact they were foster sisters wasn't common knowledge.

"What are you doing up here?" Jill asked. Had they already talked about that? Ah, she couldn't remember. She stretched out her legs and studied them while Ambra talked. When she looked up, she realized Mattias was staring.

"Are you listening?" Ambra asked, and Jill nodded, though she had only been half paying attention while Ambra talked about some old lady she'd interviewed. Of all the things Ambra thought important, it was her job as a brow-beaten, underpaid journalist that Jill understood the least. There was always some poor soul Ambra wanted to write about, someone who needed saving or rehabilitating. She didn't get it.

Loud music started to rise above the murmur, and Jill smiled. It was one of her songs. A five-year-old disco tune still played so often that she would probably be able to live off the royalties from it alone. It was one of three or four songs she always had to sing at shows or fans would be disappointed. She waved a thanks to the barman, and he turned up the volume. She laughed, and he blew her kisses with both hands.

"Please, Jill, could you get up onstage and sing?" A beefy blond guy who couldn't have been much older than twenty had come over to their table. Several others joined him, forming a choir of pleading. She felt the weariness in her body, really just wanted to sit down. But she flashed them a glittering smile. "One song," she said, getting to her feet. People applauded. She quickly bent down to Ambra. "Where are we?"

"Kiruna," Ambra mimed, and rolled her eyes.

Jill stepped up onto the small stage and looked out at the room. The faces toward the back were hopelessly blurred. Silence spread throughout the club.

"Hi, Kiruna," she said, and the applauding and whistles went on until she gestured for them to stop.

She hadn't warmed up her voice, and she had no idea which song they were planning. Cell phone cameras were held in the air. She shook her hair behind her back, grabbed the microphone with both hands, closed her eyes, and waited for the music to start.

Mattias Ceder couldn't take his eyes off Jill Lopez. There was some kind of light source behind her, and at certain moments it looked as if she were surrounded by a halo. Her dark hair fell over her shoulders in waves, and her long, ring-covered fingers were wrapped around the microphone. When she closed her eyes to hold a note, the hair on his arms stood on end.

Christ Almighty.

He knew who she was, of course; *everyone* who didn't live under a rock or in a cave knew who Jill Lopez was.

But he liked opera and classical music. Literature and theatre. Things that spoke to his intellect and made him into a better person. It was all about having good taste and an understanding of culture. Everything about Jill Lopez verged on the vulgar, too sexy, too intense.

But this was the first time Mattias had ever heard her sing live.

That *voice*. It was much darker than he expected. Deep and sensual. She filled every trite line about love and passion with meaning, made it resonate within him, as though he was the man who had left her, the man who made her search for love, the man she longed for. It was the pop equivalent of being mowed down by a steamroller. Not one note of it was false, not one feeling seemed fake.

Once she was finished, Mattias didn't even think to applaud. He was completely overwhelmed.

"Your sister can really sing," he heard Tom say to Ambra in what had to be the understatement of the century.

Up onstage, Jill shook her hair again. She smiled and started singing along with the notes of a ballad. A song about a love that overcame both time and space. Mattias knew it was trash, low-brow culture, but listening to her was like being hauled through an emotional mangle.

After yet another song, an uptempo tune that caused the energy in the room to simmer over, followed by a fierce round of applause, she came back over to them, beads of sweat on her chest and a swing in her step. She slumped down onto the bench beside him, and he caught a warm and fruity scent that reminded him of sun-kissed beaches, exotic spices. Mattias racked his brain for something suitably polite, distant, and socially acceptable to say.

"Do you write your songs yourself?" he eventually asked. That would have to do.

Jill pushed her hair from her face. Her skin was damp, and thick, dark wisps stuck to her décolletage.

Mattias forced himself to look her in the eye.

"I write everything myself. The lyrics and the music."

"So you studied music in college?"

Jill laughed. "I can't even read the music. I'm completely self-taught."

"You were fantastic," he said honestly.

"Thanks. Could you pass me some water?"

She crossed her legs, and he followed the movement with his eyes. They were probably the most gorgeous legs he had ever seen. He poured her some water. She reached out and brushed against his hand, which was still holding the glass.

Mattias pulled back—not quickly, as though he had felt something, but slowly, casually. He watched as she scrawled her autograph onto a napkin for a fan.

"How long have you . . ." he began, but it was impossible to have a conversation with her. They were constantly being interrupted. She agreed to a couple of selfies, but then it was clear that she was getting tired. Mattias glanced at his watch—it was past midnight.

"I need to go back to the hotel to sleep," Ambra said, yawning behind her hand. "You going to stay and keep turning heads, or have you had enough attention for one evening?" she continued with a glance at her sister. It was hard to imagine two more different women.

"You can never have enough attention," Jill replied, but she seemed relieved. "I'll go with you. So we have time to talk. I leave early tomorrow."

The women got up. Mattias and Tom did the same.

Tom turned to Ambra. "Night," he said in his usual, brusque way. Ambra shoved her hands into her back pockets and nodded in reply. Jill shook Tom's hand.

"Nice to meet you," she said, and then she held out a hand to Mattias. He shook it. Her hand was a little sweaty but surprisingly strong. She left behind the scent of perfume. He was close to raising his hand to his nose to smell it. But Tom would have broken down in mocking laughter, and Mattias was glad he managed to stop himself in time.

"What's going on between you and Ambra?" he asked once they sat down again.

"Nothing."

Lies. There was something between them. He'd just spent practically the whole evening stealing glances at her. "But you like her?"

"I don't think anything of her. She's a journalist. I don't like journalists."

"No," Mattias agreed. Journalists could be difficult for men like them. "The sister was damn hot," he said.

"Guess so."

The noise level rose, someone started to sing a hard rock version of an ABBA song, and people were starting to undress over by the stage.

"Enough socializing for me," Tom said, getting to his feet. "You can drive."

Mattias, who had barely drunk one beer, drove them back to Tom's place.

"I can check in to a hotel," he halfheartedly offered. He was exhausted, had been on the go for almost forty-eight hours. He was also unexpectedly unsure of where he stood with Tom. He'd come to manipulate Tom, but it had also done him good to see him again, to talk almost like before.

Tom shrugged. "You can stay, it's a big house. But you'll have to take care of yourself."

Mattias made up a bed using sheets from the closet in the guest bedroom. He undressed, folded his clothes, and placed everything in a neat pile.

Tom disappeared to another part of the house after doing a quick sweep of the grounds. Mattias lay down. What a day. Seeing Tom. The club. Jill Lopez.

He fought it for a minute or two before giving in. His hands moved beneath the covers. With a feeling of guilt, he recalled her almond-shaped eyes, luscious golden skin, ample curves. He jacked off, silently and efficiently, as though he were twenty again, back in the barracks.

If no one knows it happened, it's almost like it never did, he thought. But it still felt embarrassing.

Chapter 15

Tom woke the next morning, December 26, with his heart pounding in his chest. He opened his eyes and gasped for air as if he had just broken the surface after a long dive. Two seconds passed, and then he remembered where he was, remembered that he was no longer in captivity. Kiruna. House. Safety.

Jesus Christ.

He'd dreamed that they were hitting him. Over and over, abuse that lasted for hours. They had varied the method of torture from time to time. Even with blindfolded eyes, you learned to tell the difference between what they were using. Power cables. Canes. Fists.

On shaking legs, he went out to the kitchen in an attempt to stave off the panic attack that was trying to break free. It wasn't the first time that an incredibly realistic nightmare had set off an attack. He filled a glass with water, put it down on the countertop, and tried to take calm and steady breaths. Alcohol, which had dampened his anxiety so well last night, was essentially a poison that made the body launch an offensive in an attempt to stop it. As long as he was drunk, he could suppress the anxiety. But once the alcohol started to leave his body, each of his systems was ready and primed, meaning that the anxiety grew worse than before. It was a vicious, never-ending cycle. But he didn't have the energy to worry about that right now. Instead, he stared out at the trees and the snow while he focused on his breathing. His alcohol consumption would have to be shelved away as just one more thing to feel guilty about, along with all the others.

Outside the kitchen window, the snow glittered in the light of the full moon and he focused on the white landscape while waiting for his body to calm down. For a brief second, he considered a quick pick-me-up. The bottle of whisky was in the cupboard, and it would feel so good to lose himself in it. But it would also be the final proof that he had passed the limits of normal behavior. He drank a glass of water instead.

The anxiety wouldn't subside. Images from his dream flashed through his mind. Automatic weapons pressed against his forehead. Kicks to his belly, boots to his head. Cigarettes being stubbed out on his flesh.

He rubbed his eyes, needed to try to think about something else. He'd been on the verge of a significant attack in the bar last night, he remembered. Talking with Ambra had helped. For the most part, it was hard work to have other people there when he felt so vulnerable, but there was something so damn calming about those green eyes, as though nothing shocked or scared her, as though she were a soldier who had been to war. Which was a ridiculous thought. Ambra Vinter was small and slim, about as far from a soldier as you could get. She'd looked pretty yesterday, albeit in her usual prickly way. She was like a porcupine, just cuter. He smiled at that. Thinking about Ambra helped. And now he remembered something she'd said. She was stuck in Kiruna, didn't she say that? Something about a cancelled plane. What was she doing today—working? He refilled his glass, drank slowly, felt his body calm down. If the circumstances were different, he might have invited her for a coffee or a walk, he thought. Strange. It was so long since he'd thought about any woman other than Ellinor. But Ambra was fun to talk to, and she was sharp.

He put down his glass. He hadn't read a tabloid paper in so long, but he suddenly had the urge to read something she had written. So, after a quick shower, he went to his closet, dug out the laptop that had been lying there these past few weeks, sat down at the kitchen table with a cup of coffee, opened his web browser, and surfed to aftonbladet.se. He typed Ambra's name into the search bar and hit Enter. The articles lined up, stretching back in time. He started from the beginning, preferring to be methodical.

Tom had written many reports of his own over the years, and he'd completed the officer program, but he had never considered himself a particularly good writer. Ambra, on the other hand, she was incredibly good.

The first of her articles was from a few years earlier. Back then, she worked primarily on the entertainment pages. Kept an eye on celebrities, wrote about society weddings and who was in a relationship with whom. He leaned back in his chair, struggled slightly to see her in the role of gossip columnist. Then there was a year of articles on different types of crime. Murders, assaults, disputes. Depressing reading about society's worst side.

He studied her byline picture from back then. Crossed arms and a serious face. In the years that followed, she had done a little of everything. Short articles about both domestic and foreign news. The occasional longer piece. Then her name began to appear beneath short, nondescript paragraphs about a wide variety of subjects. He got the feeling that something must have happened. A personal crisis, maybe? Hadn't she mentioned something about not getting on with her boss? In her latest byline picture, she seemed even more serious, almost angry. Her dark hair was pulled back, there was practically no sign of her unruly curls. He studied the image for some time. Aside from the angry expression, she didn't look much like herself. It wasn't surprising he hadn't recognized her. She was much prettier in reality. His eyes lingered on her face, and he remembered the way she looked last night, how he kissed her the night before. Their kiss was fantastic. The kind of kiss you remembered for years to come.

Her latest article was the piece on Elsa Svensson and the sex camps, published that morning. It was long, personal, funny, and written in a tone he recognized. He could hear Ambra's voice behind the words. He realized he was on the verge of a smile. It was okay that they'd ended up in the bar yesterday, he and Mattias. Because seeing Ambra had been fun.

He shut the lid of his laptop and looked at the clock. Almost ten. Mattias was still sleeping.

What the hell was he going to do about Mattias? It felt strange having him there. Strange and worryingly familiar. You developed a very particular type of relationship in the special forces, one unlike anything else. He and Mattias had been so cold that they'd shivered together, lain down in mud and lost the feeling in their feet while they watched their targets. Swum until they literally sobbed with exhaustion. Lost friends and saved each other's lives. Under those circumstances, you grew close in a way an outsider would struggle to understand.

Which meant that the betrayal, when it eventually came, was so much worse.

They were deployed to Afghanistan in 2008. Both were fully trained, working as secret operatives. They would be there for six weeks, which was too damn short. It would be impossible to get anything done. But that kind of thing wasn't up to them—they just went wherever they were told.

They stayed in a camp with regular Swedish forces, an Afghan force, and a handful of Americans. The mood in the camp was low when they arrived. There had been plenty of losses but very few successes.

"A Taliban leader is planning a suicide attack," the commanding officer informed them during their briefing that evening.

Tom and Mattias exchanged a look. They would be leaving immediately. Precisely how they wanted it.

"We're going to attack this building, to the right of the mosque."

They followed the group tasked with localizing and neutralizing the Taliban leader that night. They left in two helicopters, armed to the teeth, hanging from the sides. It was a complete cliché, but it was also pretty cool, sweeping across the town like that. Tom studied the map he kept in his chest pocket one last time. Frowned.

"There are two mosques," he said to Mattias. Their intel only mentioned one.

"Is it the right building?" he asked the commanding officer.

"We're here," someone suddenly said, and he never got an answer to his question. He shelved his anxiety. You couldn't start causing trouble during an ongoing mission.

They jumped from the helicopter, ran over to the house. On the agreed-upon signal, Tom kicked in the door.

The assault force was made up of Tom, Mattias, and six other soldiers. There were guards outside and in the trees, and they had snipers positioned in strategic locations around the building.

Tom had worked with many different nationalities and knew there were good guys and jerks in every group. The testosterone-fueled American he was paired up with that night, a man whose entire vocabulary seemed to consist of "fuck" and "asshole," shouldn't have been there.

"You two. Right." The commanding officer gestured with quick hand movements.

"Fuck," the American said, making a point to spit on the ground.

Tom shook his head. He didn't know this guy. It was like working with a live grenade. They went in. Heard a low mumbling over the radio, but nothing more. Everything they saw suggested it was an ordinary house they were storming. But Tom had a bad feeling about it and was just waiting for the mission to be aborted and for them to be ordered back to base.

Suddenly, a small figure peeled away from a mattress on the floor. Tom saw the thin body through his night vision goggles. The whole mission felt wrong. *It's just a kid, this is an ordinary house, we're in the wrong place,* he had time to think before the American opened fire next to him, suddenly and without warning. Each of the soldiers was armed with automatic weapons. On default mode, those guns spat out six hundred bullets a minute, ten a second.

The tiny body shuddered and was torn to pieces before Tom's shocked eyes.

He threw himself forward, shouting: "Stop, for fuck's sake. Stop, it's just a kid. Stop."

"All clear," Tom heard over the radio. It was the wrong house, he was completely sure of it. He looked down at what was once a living child. All that was left was blood and scraps of flesh.

"Withdraw," the commanding officer ordered, and they left the building.

When the helicopter landed back at base, Tom was so angry he could barely talk. He tore off his helmet, threw it to the ground along with his gun, and screamed at the American: "You bastard, he was just a kid!"

The American spat on the ground. "Fucking whatever. One less terrorist-to-be."

It was as though a black veil was drawn over Tom's eyes. He

launched himself at the American and managed to land one good right hook before the two men fell down the slope. They rolled around in the dust, hitting and kicking without any finesse, until they were finally pulled apart. Tom was blind with rage. Mattias hauled him back to their barracks.

"He shot a kid. He's a psychopath."

Mattias nodded and shoved him onto his bunk. "It was the wrong house. A fucking fiasco."

"It's wrong. Completely wrong."

"I know. But you need to calm down."

The very next day, the Taliban managed to detonate a suicide bomb at a local market. Forty people died, the majority of them women, children, and the elderly.

"If we attacked the right house, we could've stopped this," Tom said bitterly to the Swedish operation commander, a lieutenant colonel he respected.

"It was dark. We get bad intel sometimes. This is what happens. Let it go, Tom, for everyone's sake," the lieutenant colonel told him.

He was right, of course. Inaccurate information was far from unusual. But Tom couldn't drop what had happened. There was a difference between bad intel and dead children. He was a soldier, and there were certain rules you followed as a soldier, because otherwise you were no better than the Taliban, the jihadis, or any of the other terrorists they were fighting.

There was right and there was wrong. That was what he believed and, ultimately, defended. Democracy. Freedom. What was right.

Tom wrote a report about what happened. He sent it from Afghanistan, got back to work, and made sure to stay as far away from the American as he could.

When Tom returned to Sweden, he asked for a meeting with the head of the army. His request was granted.

"They asked me to call in a witness," he said to Mattias. "Would you come?"

"Tom, are you really doing this?" Mattias asked. He sounded concerned.

"I have to. Would you come?"

"I'll come." Mattias avoided his eye.

Tom and Mattias attended the meeting at HQ along with five lawyers from the Armed Forces, plus two men in anonymous suits who didn't introduce themselves and whom Tom suspected belonged to the intelligence service. There were also two witnesses from camp and a large number of high-ranking military men, their chests covered in medals. The commander in chief sat silently and severely behind his oversized desk. Tom wasn't offered a seat. It was a clear demonstration of power.

But Mattias was by his side. Tom was sure his friend, his brother-in-arms, his comrade, would back him up.

After Tom gave his brief, concise report, Mattias got up. He was calm, seemed focused, as he always did.

And then he drove the knife into Tom's back.

"Captain Lexington wasn't himself even before we left for Afghanistan. He overreacted then, and he's overreacting now. He hasn't been himself for a while."

Tom thought he must have misheard.

"We can't rule out that the perpetrator was armed," Mattias continued.

An icy chill spread through Tom. "The perpetrator? There was no fucking perpetrator, it was an unarmed child."

"It was dark, it was chaotic. We can't rule out that he posed a threat."

Mattias met Tom's eye, and Tom couldn't see a thing in his gaze. It was completely neutral. Not that he knew how a person was meant to look when they betrayed their best friend. Mattias lied, and Tom's military career was over. He couldn't stay. He had given them ten years of his life, believed in their ideals and spirit. But now it was over.

Tom quit the very next day. Left the Armed Forces, never to return.

That was eight years ago.

And now Mattias was here, in Kiruna, pretending to be his friend in an attempt to bring him back into the Forces.

But Tom was done with that; he knew it with certainty. Until yesterday, he thought he was done with Mattias Ceder, too. Now, he wasn't sure. Part of him wanted to throw the traitor out, tell him to go to hell. But another part remembered their friendship.

* * *

"I'm going to buy groceries," Tom said when Mattias got up just after ten. He skidded up onto the main road and then stepped on the gas until the snow swirled around him. The temperature gauge in the car showed seventeen degrees. For Kiruna, that was practically spring.

After he made it to the grocery store, he bought bread, cheese, and orange juice, and then his eyes scanned the shelves of paperbacks. It was a long time since he last read a book.

While he was working abroad, he devoured plenty of books: fiction, nonfiction, and biographies, most things in fact. Reading was a great way to wind down. When you were in a tight situation, the adrenaline would rush through your veins in a way you couldn't imagine. He had been shot at by everything from terrorists to ordinary criminals, hunted by pirates, preyed upon by carjackers, and he'd fought the Taliban. In situations like that, you needed to be able to function without thinking. Otherwise, you would die—that was the evolution of the battlefield. It was afterward that you felt the reaction, and it could be powerful. Those who didn't manage to wind down never lasted very long. Tom saw plenty of men go crazy after a battle because they never came down from their adrenaline high. Some soldiers and operatives used sex to relax, others worked out, many drank. But Tom liked to read.

In school, reading was always torture. He didn't know why, but everything to do with letters was a nightmare for him. Being forced to read aloud in front of the class, hearing the laughter when he struggled, practicing and practicing and still not keeping up. He felt stupid, and it wasn't until he began his training to become an officer that things got better. He wanted to graduate so badly, he forced himself to study constantly and one day the letters just started to play ball. It was like his brain managed to forge a new circuit, and everything finally fell into place. Shit if he knew what happened.

He chose two paperbacks from the bestseller list, paid, and packed up his things. Just as he left the shop, he heard a skidding sound, someone shouting, and then he was knocked to the floor by an enormous creature that appeared from nowhere.

It was a dog—a huge, shaggy, gray thing—that collided with him. Its withers came up to somewhere on Tom's thigh. The dog was dragging a leash behind it, and without even thinking, Tom put his foot on the handle just as the dog got ready to run off. It stopped with a jerk, and Tom bent down and quickly grabbed the leash. The dog pulled at it angrily, its ears flat and teeth bared. Tom hesitated. He'd seen far too many people attacked by angry packs of dogs to dismiss the danger. But there were a few kids outside the shop, and so he kept hold of the leash, at arm's length now, wondering what the hell to do next.

What kind of idiot kept a dog like this in town? He studied the trembling, bristling monster. It looked more wild than tame. Who even owned a beast like this?

"Oh, God, thanks," he heard, and a breathless Ellinor came running toward him.

She was the last person he was expecting to see.

"This is your dog?" he asked incredulously.

"She got loose. She's not used to me," Ellinor panted. The animal followed her with its eyes, laid its ears flat against its head, and stared. Not that Tom could read a dog's body language, but it felt like it was trembling when it pressed itself against his legs. It wasn't angry, it was scared.

"What's it scared of?" he asked.

Ellinor took off one of her gloves and wiped her forehead. She puffed a little. "Something startled her. I wasn't ready, and she pulled free. She's ridiculously strong. Strictly speaking, she's Nilas's responsibility."

Nilas. The veterinarian. The man Ellinor had inexplicably decided to leave him for. The irresponsible idiot who clearly owned an unpredictable dog and had no problem leaving Ellinor to run around after it.

Tom stood still, with the leash in his hand and Ellinor's eyes on his.

"There you are. I was getting worried!"

Ellinor turned around.

Nilas.

Tom couldn't even think that awful name without pulling a face.

Ellinor waved. "Don't worry, she's here."

Nilas came to a stop. He took off one glove and held out a hand. "You must be Tom," he said.

"Must I?" Tom replied, not reciprocating the handshake.

Ellinor's eyes narrowed, but Nilas just smiled. "Good of you to grab Freja. I'd best take her. She's friendly, but dogs can sometimes bite when they're scared. Come, Freja."

Nilas reached for the leash. Freja growled faintly, low in her throat, and Tom studied Nilas with a mean smile. "Funny, she doesn't seem all that happy to see you. Maybe you're not so good with animals after all."

"We think she was mistreated by her last owner," Ellinor explained. "Nilas has been taking care of her because she was in such bad shape." She raised her chin and said: "Nilas is fantastic with animals."

"Freja," Nilas said, patting his thigh encouragingly.

But Freja continued to tremble against Tom's leg, and he was already regretting getting involved. He was completely uninterested in the crazy animal. Irritated, he held out the leash; he just wanted the whole thing to be over and done with. But Nilas didn't take it. Instead, he studied Tom as though he'd just had an idea. Since one of Nilas's last ideas was to sleep with Tom's fiancée while Tom himself was in living hell, he was sure he wouldn't much like this new one.

"I am actually looking for someone who can keep Freja for a while. We already have two dogs, and they're so lively they stress her out. She needs peace and quiet."

Tom said nothing. It wasn't his problem.

Ellinor placed a hand on Nilas's coat sleeve. "Tom doesn't like animals," she said. It wasn't true; he had no feelings either way. Ellinor, on the other hand, loved all animals.

By now, Freja was no longer trembling against his leg. Instead, she started to scratch herself behind her ear, a huge paw clawing at her thick gray coat with frantic energy. Tom studied her. "What is she, anyway? Devil dog?"

Nilas put on his glove and stood up straight. "She's probably a mix. Mostly Irish wolfhound. They end up huge. She's still a puppy."

"A puppy?" The dog had to weigh at least sixty-five pounds. How much bigger could she get? Freja gave a quick bark and then crashed down across one of Tom's feet. She lay down right on top of it, crossed her front legs, and lowered her head.

All three of them looked down at her. She didn't seem to have any intention of moving. Tom tried to move his foot. She whined.

"Worst-case scenario, we'll have to put her down," said Nilas.

Ellinor raised a hand to her mouth and turned pale. Tom gave Nilas a suspicious look—he wouldn't put emotional manipulation past him. Freja, still lying on his foot, had now started licking something on the ground, but other than that she looked pretty healthy.

"Tom, you can't let her be put down," Ellinor said. Somehow he was now the villain in this whole tale. He should have just let the dog run off.

Tom glanced around, as though he was attempting to find someone who could confirm the bizarreness of the situation he found himself in. A woman with her head bowed and a bouquet beneath her arm was just coming out of the grocery store. He recognized her, he realized, because it was Ambra Vinter. She seemed to be trying to sneak past without being seen.

"Hi," he shouted loudly.

She stopped, looked up, met his eye, and hesitated, as though she really just wanted to hurry on.

"Oh, hi!" Ellinor said cheerily. Ambra looked as if she had given up all hope of passing by without being noticed. She nodded to Tom and then turned to Ellinor.

"Good to see you again," said Ellinor.

"Hi, Ellinor," Ambra said. She greeted Nilas and glanced guardedly at Tom.

"Hi," he said again. Had she really been planning on sneaking past? Ambra shoved her hands into her coat pockets.

Ellinor looked back and forth between them. "You two know one another?" she asked.

"Yeah," Tom said with a nod, at the exact moment Ambra shook her head and said, "No."

Ellinor cocked her head. Freja scratched herself again, her entire enormous body shaking.

"We bumped into each other the other day," Ambra said vaguely. It was clear the entire situation bothered her.

"Ambra is working up here," Tom said, though no one asked.

"I know." Ellinor nodded, placing a hand on Ambra's arm. "She's here to interview Elsa Svensson."

Ambra gestured to the bunch of flowers beneath her arm. "I'm actually on my way over there now. She lives around the corner. I didn't realize you two knew one another. You wouldn't be . . . ?" She paused, embarrassed.

"Tom's ex," Ellinor filled in with a kind smile.

"Thought so."

The silence spread. Nilas hadn't said a word since he'd greeted Ambra. He just studied them, glancing at Freja every now and then. He stood there looking reliable, in a Norrland kind of way. It felt strange that Ellinor was with Nilas now. It felt wrong. Like a misunderstanding that Tom could fix if only he could sit down, draw up a plan, form a strategy. If he could just *do* something.

Tom looked at the dog, which was sitting on his foot. Ambra scratched her nose and pushed her hair from her face. Ellinor, on the other hand, glanced between Ambra and Tom, a slight frown on her otherwise smooth brow, as though she was trying to work out if there was anything to read between the lines.

"I'm going to be late," Ambra said suddenly, not to anyone in particular. She gave Nilas a quick nod; gave Ellinor a quick, slightly awkward hug; and then glanced at Tom. It was impossible to tell what she was thinking.

"Ambra . . ." he started, at the exact same moment that she said the world's shortest "Bye" and hurried away. Leaving him, Ellinor, Nilas, and the dog to their fate. He didn't blame her.

"Sweet girl," said Ellinor.

Sweet? That wasn't quite the word he would use to describe Ambra. Ellinor watched her until she turned the corner. "Is something going on between you? Or am I just imagining things?"

Was there something between them? He remembered the noises Ambra made when he pushed her up against the hotel door.

"No," he replied firmly, and then a slobbering noise by his feet caught his attention. Freja had started chewing his shoelace. Drool was running down his boot. *What the hell*.

"She likes you," said Nilas.

"I doubt that," Tom said, with a glance in the direction Ambra had gone.

"I mean the dog likes you," said Nilas. "I'm not so sure about the girl. But the dog, she likes you."

Tom yanked his boot from beneath the dog. It was covered in slobber. Freja shook herself. Tom held out the leash to Nilas. He'd had enough of this circus.

Chapter 16

"We can surely have a little sherry before lunch," Elsa said, opening a kitchen cupboard and taking out two small glasses and a bottle. She poured the liquor and handed Ambra a glass. Ambra wasn't certain she had ever tried the stuff before, but she sipped it politely. If she'd had a grandmother of her own, she would have wanted to drink sherry with her. Elsa studied Ambra. "How are you?"

The meeting outside the grocery store had had a stronger effect on Ambra than she expected. But she didn't want to burden Elsa with that. "I'm fine. Thanks for inviting me over."

"I hope everything resolves itself with the flights. I'm sure there'll be a spare seat soon. And your article was so lovely. You're very talented."

"You think so? Thanks." She was happy with the first, introductory piece. The actual interview would be published tomorrow.

"Are you hungry? Sit, and I'll serve up. I made moose steak. Real food. Do you like that?"

"Sounds delicious." The smell of the food was comforting. Meat, sauce, and potatoes. Proper Swedish food. She traced the squares on the tablecloth with her finger.

"Are you sure everything is good? Did something happen? Is it the Sventins, did something else happen there?"

Ambra shook her head. "It's just this whole Kiruna trip," she said, not quite honestly, because her thoughts were mainly on that strange scene with Tom outside the grocery store.

She gently pulled at the tablecloth. Tom was in love with Ellinor, she was sure of that. And it wasn't surprising. The woman was super gorgeous; she was blond, seemed nice and sweet and soft-edged. All in all the perfect woman. It was depressing.

Elsa brought out a jug of lingonberry juice.

"Sometimes I don't understand myself. Or other people," Ambra thought aloud.

"Are you thinking of anything in particular?" Elsa asked as she placed a pot holder on the table, followed by a pot. She sat down opposite Ambra and held out the dish of potatoes. Ambra helped herself, allowed Elsa to serve her thin slices of meat.

"Relationships, I guess. I don't get why they're so hard. For me, at least." She heaped lingonberries, sauce, and pickles onto her plate, Elsa said bon appétit and they started to eat.

"It's delicious," Ambra said between bites. It was so rare for her to eat home-cooked food. She just wanted to stay in Elsa's cozy kitchen, eating homemade dinner, listening to the radio, and feeling normal for a while.

"They're hard for everyone. Some people never learn to master them. Relationships, that is," Elsa said.

Like me, Ambra thought. That was how it felt. As if she hadn't learned all of the rules for navigating people without making a fool of herself. Without being abandoned. A small, illogical part of her often wondered whether there was something inside her, some quality that meant she genuinely wasn't worthy of love. The grown-up, rational part of her knew it was nothing to do with her. It wasn't her fault her parents had died, that she was passed around in an imperfect system of foster homes. But it made no difference what her brain told her. She still had a nagging suspicion that, at some fundamental level, there was something lacking with her. That everyone she met would notice it sooner or later. That no man would ever look at her the way Tom looked at Ellinor.

"Maybe I'm a lesbian and don't even realize it," she said.

Elsa took another potato and laughed. "I doubt that, even if it is a lifestyle I'd recommend."

"I'll remember that."

"Why was it that you ended up with the Sventins?"

"My mom died and there was no one else, so social services placed me there."

"That's terrible."

"Yeah." Ambra didn't remember any details from her early childhood, before everything changed. Sometimes she wasn't even sure she knew the things she knew. Maybe those scents and odd, vague memories she thought she could remember were all just made up. A broad, smiling mouth and sad eyes. And, even earlier: two people who laughed a lot and who represented safety.

"Mom died of a brain hemorrhage. It was Christmas. They didn't find me until a few days later." Ambra was in bed next to her when the police broke down the door. She didn't remember any of this, but she had once read her file. "I guess that's when I started hating Christmas."

The girl was found in bed next to the deceased mother, dehydrated and exhausted.

Social services took care of her after that. For a while, a very distant relative took her in. She shared a room with two siblings and could vaguely remember colorful walls and sliced bread for breakfast, but they didn't want to keep her. *The family feels the child is too much trouble,* she later read in her file. Apparently a five-year-old orphan could be so difficult that you got rid of her. There wasn't anyone else after that, and so she ended up in her first foster home. Somewhere around the tenth, she finally lost count.

Elsa lifted her sherry glass and studied her for a long while. "But something else is bothering you today, isn't it?"

Ambra nodded. Elsa was perceptive. Or maybe she was just easy to read. "I met a man up here."

"I see."

"He's not for me, it's not that." She heard herself stumble over her words. She paused, took a breath, and continued, more slowly this time: "Anyway. I liked him and thought the feeling was mutual. But I misjudged the whole thing. It turned out he wasn't at all interested." She sounded quite indifferent, she thought. Like a grown woman telling a funny anecdote, not a foster kid with a gaping hole of abandonment in her soul.

"That's always difficult. Feeling rejected."

"Yeah."

They sat in comfortable silence. It felt good to have her feelings confirmed.

"Men fall for a certain kind of woman, I think," Ambra continued. Elsa was almost one hundred. She had to know things.

But Elsa slowly shook her head. "Men aren't a uniform species. They fall for different types, just like we do."

Her words sounded smart, in and of themselves, but they didn't match up to Ambra's experience. "What do *you* think men want, then? Really?"

Elsa gave her a slight smile. "I lived most of my life with a woman, so I may not be an expert on the subject. But I don't think you can generalize like that. Men are different. Just like women."

That was what everyone said, but it didn't make *sense*.

"Go on," Elsa said, putting down her cutlery.

"So, this is what I think," Ambra began. "We're always told to be ourselves. But what if you're just not all that nice a person? Being yourself isn't so smart then. My theory is that lots of women have realized this and are playing a role instead. Depicting an uncomplicated version of themselves. They're happy, kind, accommodating. And they aren't lying, exactly, but they're also not being themselves. They show off girlish qualities, renounce themselves, and it works. It's like someone gave them a manual." Ambra fell silent. She had never seen any manual herself.

"And you feel you've been duped?" asked Elsa.

"When you grow up without any role models, without any kind of thought-out parenting, you end up with knowledge gaps." There was so much she'd had to work out on her own. How to insert a tampon. How to buy bus tickets. How to hide your money so that no one from your foster family could steal it. How to plan your homework, be a friend, behave when you were in love. How to try not to cry when the entire class laughed at the fact you spoke weirdly. How to be aware of dangers and protect yourself.

"I read advice columns in newspapers and a load of relationship books, then I tried to act following the advice they gave."

"Sounds like you really made an effort."

Ambra smiled. "I guess you could say that. But I really wasn't a success."

Though she still wasn't sure if it was just her sources that were wrong or whether she really did have some kind of social defect. Jill was also abandoned as a child, but she knew what to do. Everywhere

Ambra turned, there were people who knew the social codes and how to use them. Who taught them that? Or was it an innate skill? Ambra was good at her job, at least the parts of it that had nothing to do with office politics. She could get people to talk in interviews; maybe she radiated something that made people take the risk of confiding in her. It was everything *outside* of work that she found so damned hard. Bosses. Men. Friends. Tom. She constantly felt as if she was doing things wrong. "I often feel like a UFO," she summed up.

"You should be yourself. There are plenty of crazy men out there, so there must also be plenty of crazy women for them," Elsa said.

Ambra smiled. "That doesn't sound much like solidarity."

"You shouldn't feel solidarity with someone just because they're the same gender. And stupidity has nothing to do with gender, it's everywhere."

"So why do you think some women find it so easy to meet some-one?" she asked, which was what she *really* wanted to know, after all.

"I think, honestly, that a lot of them simply settle." Elsa got up and fetched the bottle of sherry.

"I guess so," said Ambra. She turned down more sherry but said yes to coffee.

They cleared the table and washed up together and then took their coffees out into the living room. Ambra sat down on the couch, Elsa on the rocking chair, slurping her coffee. Ambra smiled at the sound, found it soothing.

Elsa put down the saucer. "I want you to know that I think you're an exceptionally good person. Your parents would be so proud of you," she said.

And just like that, Ambra felt a lump in her throat. The thought that her mother and father would actually be proud of her wasn't something she had ever realized before.

"Tell me about them."

"My mom loved everything Italian. She studied art history and worked in a little gallery before I was born. She's the one who wanted to name me Ambra, after a painting she saw in Rome. Dad was a watchmaker." That was what she remembered, in any case.

"They sound like good people."

"Yeah, they were. Normal." Ambra often thought of them that way. As normal people.

"Life isn't fair," said Elsa.

Ambra thought of all the people she had met over the years. The widows of murdered men. Parents whose children had died. Victims of accidents. Refugees. "A lot of people have it much, much worse," she said. She knew with all of her heart that that was true. On the whole, she had *nothing* to complain about, not really.

"Your parents died. That's the worst thing that can happen to a child. Even if other people do experience terrible things."

Ambra shook her head, knew she was lucky compared to many others.

"Ambra—that was the medieval word for amber. Did you know that amber also comes in different colors, not just gold? Blue is the most rare. And then there's green." Elsa leaned toward her, studied her closely, and then smiled. "Like your eyes. You have unusual eyes. Ingrid would have loved to paint them. She gave me a figurine made from green amber once. It should be over there somewhere." She pointed to a book case, and Ambra got up.

In front of the books, there were a number of different ornaments and keepsakes. Small boxes, picture frames, tiny figurines. A vase of dried flowers. Stones, miniatures made from reindeer horn. She loved looking at things like that.

Everything she'd inherited from her parents' home had gone missing; she didn't know how, but a little disappeared with every move until finally there was just one box left. A small box of things. A few photos. A worn Winnie the Pooh. A couple of paperbacks with her mom's name on the inside cover. Dad's antique watchmaking tools; a set of tiny screwdrivers in a case. Her parents' wedding bands and a charm bracelet that her dad gave to her mom when Ambra was born. Ambra had loved that bracelet.

The box disappeared after Kiruna. Esaias Sventin swore she took it with her when she ran off, but she hadn't. And now it was gone. Her entire past had been taken away from her. She often looked in antique stores, surfed auction sites looking for anything that reminded her of the few things she remembered of her parents. A pattern on some porcelain woke vague memories. A vase that resembled a feeling she had.

"Is this the one?" she asked, holding up a green frog. Immediately, a memory washed over her, one she had long since forgotten. *Mom's little frog*. She stroked the little green creature. Mom had called her *frog* because she was never still, she was always hopping around. The memory floated by, shapeless and fleeting, like always. But she was almost certain it had happened.

Elsa held out her hand and took the figurine. "Yes, that's the one. Ingrid bought it on a trip to Kenya."

"It's beautiful," Ambra said. Her throat felt tight, and her eyes stung a little. She sat down on the couch and pulled up her knees.

"I've decided to stay in Kiruna a few more days."

"Is it because of the man you mentioned?"

"What? No, not at all." She felt herself blush, but this wasn't about Tom. "I want to get in touch with the case worker who was responsible for me when I was here." She wanted to find out whether the Sventins still fostered children. Imagine if those two girls were foster kids and were forced to endure the same kind of things she had. It was unbearable even to imagine.

"What are you hoping to find?"

"Don't know." It was Christmas, so maybe she wouldn't find a thing. But she never planned to come back up here again, so if she was going to do anything, it had to be now.

"Let me know if I can help."

"Thanks."

They drank their coffee and the conversation moved on. After an hour or so of chatting, Elsa seemed tired. It was time to leave.

"Thanks for having me over," Ambra said after she carried the cups into the kitchen and washed them up.

"Wait a second." Elsa disappeared. Ambra heard a faint rustling, and then Elsa returned with a small parcel wrapped up in thin tissue paper. "I want you to take this. Open it."

Ambra unwrapped the paper. It was the little green frog. She gave Elsa an uncertain look.

"But . . ."

"No, I want you to have it. It's a gift from me and Ingrid."

Ambra stroked the little green figurine. The color was so intense it was almost glowing. "Thank you," she said quietly. She folded the paper back over the frog and gave Elsa a warm hug.

"Let's stay in touch," Elsa said.

Ambra nodded.

When she came out onto the street, it was almost four in the afternoon. She looked up at the sky. It was perfectly clear but dark. She zipped up her jacket and wondered whether she should check to see if the movie theater was open or whether she should just go back to the hotel, sit down at her computer, and get a little work done.

"Hi there," a shadow said, emerging from the darkness.

She jumped. *What the hell*. Tom Lexington. "You scared me," she said accusingly.

"I didn't mean to," he said.

"Why are you sneaking around, scaring people?"

Tom gave Ambra an apologetic shrug. It really wasn't his intention to startle her. He had spotted her coming out of the doorway and made himself seen.

"Sorry. But I'm not sneaking around. I'm walking the dog." He pointed to Freja as she sniffed about in the snow. They had been out for hours, ever since he'd left Ellinor and Nilas, walking around the whole of Kiruna, but Freja still didn't seem the least bit tired. "She wanted to come this way. Maybe she has a boyfriend around here somewhere?"

"Probably. Men always cause trouble for us women."

In Tom's opinion, it was at least as often the other way, but what did he know? If the past few days had taught him anything, it was that he was useless with women. Aside from the dog kind, perhaps.

Ambra studied the shaggy animal. "I didn't realize it was yours."

"She isn't. Her name's Freja."

They both looked down at the colossus, which was now digging for something in the snow. "I think she might have a screw loose," he added.

Ambra smirked, and a warm sensation spread through his chest. He liked it when she smiled.

"Have you been outside since we met earlier?"

He nodded. It felt good to have cleared his thoughts. Good to avoid Mattias, to get a little exercise.

"Listen, I wanted to apologize for the way I acted outside the store. It was a weird situation for me. Ellinor's my girl. My ex, I mean."

"Yeah, she said."

"And Nilas is her new . . . uh . . . guy."

Ambra kicked the snow gently with one foot. "Strange situation," she said neutrally.

"Freja is his dog."

She looked up at that. Raised one of those long eyebrows slightly. They were like jet black slashes on her pale face. "And you're taking care of her?"

"Only temporarily." He would take Freja back that evening. Or maybe tomorrow. She wasn't any trouble, not really, and one night here or there didn't make much difference.

"I'm sorry too. For everything."

But Tom shook his head. Ambra hardly had anything to apologize for. "How was Elsa's?" he asked.

"Good. Nice. She's interesting."

"Are you going back to the hotel?" he asked. "Or are you headed home today?"

"I'll be here another day or two."

"We can walk you to the hotel, if that's all right? The dog still needs to walk off a little energy. I don't know where she gets it from."

Ambra nodded and Tom whistled to Freja, who came running.

Ambra laughed as they started walking. "She listens to you."

"Yeah, it's like I'm some damn dog whisperer. Hey, I read your articles."

"You did? Which?"

"All of them, I think. Don't sound so surprised. I do actually know how to read. They were interesting. You're a good writer."

She gave him a skeptical look.

"That was meant as a compliment," he said.

"Hmm."

"What?"

"Nothing. I was just a little taken aback."

They walked in silence again. Ambra seemed lost in thought, and Tom kept his eyes on Freja, who seemed thrilled at their extended walk. Every now and then she looked back at him, as though to make sure he was still there. She was a strange dog. Or maybe all dogs were like her.

"It's so incredibly clear up here," Ambra said after a while. She was looking up to the sky, where the stars were shining brightly. Their walk ended much too quickly; they were already at the hotel. She stopped by the entrance and shivered. "And so cold."

Without thinking, Tom reached out to brush away a couple of snowflakes that had landed on her. And suddenly, from nowhere, the idea that he should pull Ambra close, sweep her into his arms and warm her shivering body, kiss that soft mouth, explore it a little more thoroughly, came to him.

"You aren't wearing enough," he satisfied himself by saying.

"I know. It's a pure protest. I refuse to adapt to Kiruna."

"Why?"

"I hate Kiruna."

"You'll freeze to death," he pointed out, but he couldn't stop himself from smiling. It felt like typical Ambra to defy the weather gods and an entire city.

"I think I already have, actually."

"Why do you hate Kiruna so much?" he asked.

"I lived here when I was a kid. It wasn't a good time."

"No?" He grazed her shoulder, brushed away some snow, and then pulled back his hand.

"No. Elsa mentioned the Northern Lights would be visible tonight," she said.

He wondered what could have happened while she lived here, what could be so bad that she changed the subject like that, but instead he looked up toward the clear sky. "Probably. You like them?"

"No idea. I've never seen them."

"But you lived here." How was it possible that she had never seen the lights?

"I must've missed them. Or repressed it."

"But you've been on a snowmobile before?"

"Nope, never done that either."

"Then of course you don't like Kiruna. You missed all the fun parts."

"Which are?"

"Looking at the Northern Lights. Riding snowmobiles."

She smiled, waved away a snowflake that had floated down onto her forehead.

"It's fun," he said, and an idea suddenly came to him. "Are you working tonight?"

"I think so. Why?"

"We could ride snowmobiles and watch the Northern Lights. I know a good place."

"In the middle of the night?" Her tone was deeply skeptical.

"That is when the lights are visible," he pointed out. "I can pick you up here at eight."

She seemed to hesitate, followed Freja with her eyes and bit her lip. "Are you sure?" she eventually asked.

Warmth spread through his chest again. "I'll drop Freja off at home and then pick you up. It'll be fun, you'll see."

"And cold."

"That too." He was so close to bending down to kiss her on the nose, but he managed to stop himself in time. He had already crossed some kind of boundary with his impulsive idea. He raised a hand and patted her arm instead, as though she were one of his men.

"Dress warm."

Chapter 17

"What are you going to wear?" Jill asked over the phone. She had left the hotel and Kiruna early that morning, before breakfast, constantly on the go.

Ambra looked down at herself. She had borrowed a pair of ski pants, a long-sleeved T-shirt, and some thick socks from reception. "Everything I have, I think. It's not exactly the kind of date where you dress up." She thought for a moment. "It's probably not even a date."

"Maybe just as well. Remind me to take you shopping for some cute clothes sometime. Do you even own anything other than knitted sweaters and jeans?"

"Of course I do," Ambra lied. Going shopping with her sister was probably at the top of her list of Humiliating Things I'd Rather Not Do Ever. She clamped her cell phone against her shoulder with her ear, pulled on a hat, and quickly glanced in the mirror. She was barely visible beneath all the layers, and she was already sweating. She hesitated, but her vanity won out and she applied a little lip gloss.

"Is his friend going with you?" Jill asked breezily.

Ambra paused. "Who? Mattias? I don't think so." *I hope not.* "Why are you wondering that?"

"A girl can wonder."

Was Jill interested in Mattias? Or did she just want to worm her way into Ambra's life? Jill had a tendency to do that; she would sweep in, take over Ambra's friends, outshine her, and blind everyone with her fame and her striking beauty.

"No, it's just the two of us," she said firmly.

"Just say if you want any tips on how to act. I'm not saying you're the biggest nerd when it comes to men, but honestly, Ambra, you have plenty to work on."

Just what she wanted to hear after all of her doubts. "Thanks a bunch for the pep talk." She thought for a moment, eventually worked up the courage, and asked. She hoped Jill wouldn't be too harsh. "What is it I need to work on, exactly?"

"Oh, you know. Pull in your thorns. Don't start talking about the patriarchy or politics before you've even said hello."

"I don't do that."

"And it doesn't hurt to smile from time to time, that's all I'll say."

Ambra stared into the mirror, annoyed that she had gotten herself into this discussion. "You should see me now. I'm smiling like crazy."

Jill laughed. "So, when was the last time you slept with someone?"

"That really doesn't feel like something I want to talk to you about."

"Do you at least have any hot underwear?"

"I'm wearing around eight thousand layers of clothing. No one's getting anywhere near my underwear today."

It was one thing for *her* to have dirty fantasies about Tom, but they were just that: fantasies. Jill's life played out in a different dimension. She probably couldn't even imagine what it must be like to be an ordinary mortal woman whom men weren't constantly falling in love with.

"So long as you aren't wearing those granny panties." Jill sighed.

"But they're so comfortable," Ambra protested guiltily. Granny panties were a woman's best friend—that was her private opinion on the subject. Plus, nothing was going to *happen* tonight.

"Oh, God. Sometime, I should . . ." Jill began, and Ambra groaned loudly, convinced she couldn't cope with any more criticism veiled as concern.

"Bye, Jill, I've gotta go," she said quickly. She hung up just as her sister said what sounded like "I'm sure there's a cute bra in AA at one of those special stores in the Old Town."

When Ambra got down to the lobby, Tom was already waiting for her. He was wearing a thick winter coat that looked as if it was designed for a month-long polar expedition, covered in zippers and pockets. With it, he had on salopettes and chunky boots, and there was something so damn appealing about him, standing there in the lobby. He was like a tank or a fortification. Someone you could take shelter behind. He looked her up and down.

"You need proper clothes. It's already close to zero out there, and it's only going to get colder."

"This is everything I have," she said, feeling the thorns Jill mentioned shoot out.

"We'll figure something out," he said smoothly.

They walked outside, and he nodded toward a huge black Volvo. She climbed into the passenger seat.

"Where are we going?" she asked. No one knew where she was headed. Her cell phone was in her pocket, but the battery always ran out at record speed up here in the cold. Plus, the coverage was far from perfect. Even if Tom seemed safe and she was attracted to him, she didn't know the man. Her instincts were usually good—they'd saved her on a number of occasions—but they didn't seem to work properly around him. They were constantly pulling her in different directions. Sometimes she wanted to make out with him, and at other times she was almost afraid. And now they were in a car on the way to . . .

"Where are we going?" she repeated.

"My house," he replied. The snow swirled outside the car, whipped up into a smoke all around them.

"Why?" she asked sharply.

"To find you some warmer clothes and pick up a snowmobile. You're not allowed to drive them in town, so we need to go to my house. I have spare clothing, too." His voice was calm and warm and she relaxed a little, forced herself to trust him. They turned off and headed straight into the forest. Her anxiety returned. "Where are we now?"

"I live out in the woods, is that okay?"

She paused, but then nodded.

They drove in silence, deeper and deeper into the forest, until eventually he pulled up outside a low, dark house.

"Is Mattias here?" she asked.

"He's probably working. He promised to watch Freja. Do you want to go in and say hi?"

She shook her head. He turned on the light in what looked like a huge barn. Benches down one wall, hooks holding thick outer clothing, cupboards. A neat line of boots, all different colors and sizes. It looked completely normal.

Tom pointed to a pair of pale gray overalls. "It gets really cold when you're out, so I grabbed these. I hope they fit. There are thick gloves and proper boots," he continued. She nodded, a little overwhelmed by the amount of clothing she was expected to wear.

"And here's a balaclava. You can wear that under your helmet, instead of a hat." He held out a soft white hood.

"It'll protect your cheeks and chin. What kind of socks are you wearing? If they're cotton, you need to switch to wool. Cotton is the worst thing to have next to your skin. Here." He handed her an unopened pack of soft, thick socks, and she wondered whether he had bought them for her sake. Though maybe he had a whole box of women's socks somewhere.

"I'm going to die of heatstroke," she protested, but she did as he said and obediently pulled on the wool socks and the overalls, then shoved her feet into the enormous boots. Tom seemed to know what he was talking about, and she had no desire to freeze to death.

"You'll thank me later," he said, handing her the balaclava. She pulled it on and tucked in her hair. He held out a helmet and, with a look of concentration on his face, helped her to adjust and fasten it.

She held her breath. Being helped with the equipment like that was an intimate feeling. He was so close to her, his fingers so warm on her skin. She fluttered her eyelashes and felt herself blush.

"Ready?" he asked.

She nodded, and they moved into the garage. Two huge black snowmobiles glittered at them.

"You can sit behind me," he said, starting to move one of them outside.

"I wouldn't mind having my own," Ambra protested, and she pointed to the other machine.

"They're easy to ride. It's basically just a case of starting the engine and steering. But it's dark out, and the terrain's unfamiliar. That can be dangerous, and your safety is my responsibility. I'll drive."

She climbed onto the snowmobile behind him and tried to pretend that it didn't feel at all strange to press her thighs against his legs and wrap her arms around his waist.

Tom started the engine with a few twists of the wrist, turned around, and said, "You need to hold on tight." She slid a little closer, felt her breasts being squashed beneath all of the layers. Tom shook his head, reached back and wrapped an arm around her, and pulled until Ambra was clinging to his back like a bandage.

"Uff," she said.

"Okay, let's go," he said, increasing the gas. They started off so fast that Ambra almost flew backward. She locked her arms around Tom's waist in a death grip.

He swung out into the forest, and she squeezed her legs around him as they turned. The trees rushed by, the snow whirled, and Tom sped up again; it was as though they were floating, just gliding over the surface of the snow, and she felt excitement bubble up in her chest. She *loved* it.

The cold almost knocked the breath out of her, and she felt grateful for all of the layers. Wilderness surrounded them, tall pines, untouched snow, and above them a sky that stretched out to eternity. The stars shone in the cloudless sky, and she felt the urge to reach up and grab them, they felt so close. It was like being in a magical land.

They drove through the forest. Occasionally, the track turned— sometimes it was just a long, straight stretch and Tom sped up. At one point, they sped across a flat plain.

"Is this a meadow?" she shouted in his ear.

"It's a lake," he shouted back, speeding up so that they flew across the frozen, snow-covered water. After they had been driving for a while, Tom slowed down and they came to a stop.

"Try to get your circulation going," he said, starting to take the bags from the snowmobile.

While Ambra rotated her arms, bent her knees, and jogged on the spot, Tom set up some kind of wind shield using poles and tent material. He dug a snowbank and placed furs on the ground, then, to Ambra's intense fascination, he lit a fire, right on the snow. He built a pile of thick pine branches and sticks, then lit it. "I came up here earlier to prepare," he explained as he fed the fire, first with a handful of birch bark that he took from a bag, then smaller sticks, and last with logs that he fetched from beneath a dense pine. "So long as you've got wood, you'll be fine."

They sat down on the furs, side by side, with the snowbank behind their backs and the crackling fire in front of them. Tom dug out a thermos, unscrewed the lid, and handed her a cup of steaming coffee.

"It's like being out with a scout," she said as Tom sipped his coffee.

He smiled. "A kind of scout, maybe. But making fire, I could do that in my sleep. Are you cold?"

Ambra thought about it. It *was* cold, her cheeks and the tip of her nose were icy, but otherwise she was unexpectedly warm.

"Do you do this kind of thing often?" she asked.

"Depends what you mean. I'm used to being outside, but just sitting down to look at the sky without waiting to attack or be attacked, that doesn't happen so often. Sadly."

"Do you still do that kind of thing?" she asked carefully.

Tom was silent for so long that she was sure he wouldn't answer. "I don't usually talk about it," he said gruffly. "If I do, can you promise it'll stay between us?"

It was a question she had been asked so many times before. She was a veritable vault of secrets by this point, her own and others. "I promise," she replied. She meant it. So long as Tom didn't confess to a murder, she would stay quiet.

"I was an operative in the special forces," he said.

She had figured out that much already, that he wasn't just an ordinary ranger. He was some kind of specially trained elite soldier.

"Before. Though not now, so it's not confidential anymore."

"So what do you do now, if it's okay that I ask?"

This time, Tom stayed silent for so long that she didn't think he would answer.

"I work for a company called Lodestar. I'm the CEO and something called Operations Director," he eventually said.

Lodestar sounded vaguely familiar. "Private security, right?"

"Yeah, partly in Sweden, for bigger companies and the occasional individual. But mostly abroad. In high-risk countries."

She quickly racked her brain for everything she knew about private security; it was about playing bodyguard and chauffeur in dangerous conflict zones, navigating foreign cultures and war-torn countries. Risking your life. It wasn't a job for amateurs.

"Thanks for your confidence," she said, catching his eye. He looked at her for a long while without saying anything, and she wondered what he was thinking. Why did he invite her out here? She saw his eyes glisten, and he gestured up toward the sky. "It's coming now," he said, and Ambra followed his line of sight. They had an uninterrupted view from where they were sitting, with their backs to the woods, kilometer after kilometer of snow-covered landscape in front of them, and a clear night sky above.

The Northern Lights started to dance across the heavens. Strands of color, mostly greens and yellows, and the occasional pink or purple glow. Slow at times, and then at high speed. Rising green waves, turquoise columns of light.

"Wow," she whispered, wide-eyed. Explosions, swirls and spirals, red, green, yellow, every color; it was like watching the very birth of the universe. As though the Norse gods were crossing the sky. Or as if she were on another planet.

"Let me know if you're cold. I don't want Sweden's best reporter to freeze while she's my responsibility," he said after a while.

She smirked at the overdone compliment. "I'm not your responsibility," she said, but she wished it didn't feel quite so good to know he cared. There was something protective about him that she was unused to. She would never forget this, she thought as she looked back up at the sky.

Tom forced himself to stop staring at Ambra. He watched the celestial performance instead. If he spent too long looking at Ambra, he might start to think about kissing her. He snuck a glance at her out of the corner of his eye and saw her sitting with her head bent back, following the Northern Lights with wide eyes. His eyes lingered on her mouth, remembered how it felt beneath his. She shivered.

"Come on," he said firmly, getting up and holding out his hand. "We need to get our circulation going a little."

While Ambra circled her arms and stretched her back, Tom fetched a small spade. He quickly dug a square hole and packed down the snow to form a neck support at one end.

"What are you doing?" she asked as she did some kind of squat. She was starting to sound out of breath.

"That's enough," he said. "Breathe through your nose. The air's cold."

He had packed for all eventualities, and he now placed two insulated mats in the bottom of the hole. "Lie down," he said.

She looked suspiciously, first at the little camp he had built and then at him. Always that cautiousness.

"It'll be warm," he explained. "And it means we don't have to crane our necks the whole time."

She sat down. Tom sat next to her and then draped a huge animal skin over the two of them. They lay back against the neck support. Ambra was completely still. It *was* an odd situation, but their combined body warmth and the insulated mats should keep them warm for hours. He had slept outside when it was forty below zero before. With the right equipment, it was perfectly fine. He had lain like this countless times before, shouldn't be affected by the physical closeness. But it was different with Ambra. Her body brushed against his, and he was ultra aware that she was there. He took off a glove and searched for his pocket with one hand.

She tensed. "What're you doing?"

He pulled out a bar of chocolate in reply. Not a tough, nutrient-filled bar, but real milk chocolate with chopped nuts and raisins. Ambra's eyes glittered. He handed it to her, and she broke off a big chunk and handed it back to him. They lay there like that, eating chocolate and watching the Northern Lights, warm beneath their layers of furs, clothes, and insulated materials.

Ambra was much more relaxing to spend time with than he had thought. She hadn't criticized his background, hadn't asked whether he had killed people, whether he was a mercenary, nothing like that.

"How long does it last? And is there any more chocolate?" she asked.

He handed her the rest of the bar. "Another hour at least. Do you want to head back?"

"No. Who knows if I'll ever see them again."

He glanced at her and then back up at the sky.

They lay next to one another in silence, and his mind emptied; he just admired the sky, breathed. When he next glanced over at her, she was asleep. He shifted a little and told himself that it was just because he was stiff and needed to change position, but he put an arm behind her.

Her eyelids fluttered. "Sorry, I didn't mean to fall asleep. I'm awake now," she mumbled.

"We can go if you like," he said.

She shifted gently and then became motionless again.

"Ambra?" No reply. She had dozed off again. Tom followed the stars' movements across the sky, comfortably at peace with his surroundings. Ambra wasn't moving an inch; she was sound asleep. But she looked peaceful, and it was warm in their little nest, so he let her be. The temperature continued to drop; the snow crackled in the chill. A branch, weighed down with snow, broke with a dry snap. He could hear the quiet rustling of an animal somewhere, maybe a fox. Tom didn't think they needed to worry about predators, and so he just lay there, remarkably comfortable to have a dozing Ambra by his side.

The Northern Lights slowly died out, the occasional green band crossed the sky and then disappeared, leaving behind only sky and stars, the moon and the endless snow-covered landscape. Ambra stirred.

"How long did I sleep?" she asked, her voice drowsy.

"Awhile."

She turned to him. Sleep had made her face relax. Her prickliness was gone. She was just a soft woman with warm eyes. The hat she had pulled on when she took off her helmet was no longer straight. She had her scarf wrapped around her, and in the moonlight her skin seemed almost silver. Tom studied her pretty features, those dark eyebrows, that straight nose, her broad mouth. She looked up at him and Tom lowered his face toward hers, toward lips that had been tempting him. She raised her head to meet his lips, looked at him with wide-open eyes. He almost brushed against her mouth. Their breath had already met—he could smell her, wanted to kiss her more than anything else—when a loud sound made her tense and open her eyes. An owl hooting. It sounded close. Tom paused, and Ambra blinked.

"What was that?" she asked.

"Great gray owl, probably. There are a load of birds of prey up here."

He pulled away, told himself he was relieved that they'd been interrupted before he did anything hasty. Why was he so drawn to her? And why did he invite her out here? During all the years he and Ellinor were together, they had never taken a nighttime trip to watch the Northern Lights. This was something he had done with Ambra only.

Tom got up and moved over to the fire. He squatted down, deep in thought, and scooped snow onto it until it was completely extinguished. The night closed in around them. He stayed where he was, his mind empty.

"Tom?" Her voice sounded so small. "Where are you? It got really dark."

"I'm here," he said. He moved back over to her and held out a hand.

She took it, clung to him.

"Let's go home," he said.

"Yeah, I'm pretty done with nature now," she said. Neither of them mentioned their almost-kiss.

When Ambra climbed onto the snowmobile behind him, he didn't need to tell her. She pressed herself against his back, wrapped her arms around his waist. He started the engine, and the noise roared up in the silence. He twisted the handle and they sped off over the snow once more.

Chapter 18

She would have to decide what she was going to do today. Ambra peered at the things she had spread across her hotel bed. The notepad full of thoughts and angles, her computer, cell phone, and a map of Kiruna and its surroundings that she got from reception.

Stay here and investigate her former foster family or head home and go on as normal, that was the question.

The list of things *in favor* of investigating:

She was already in Kiruna, so she might as well make the most of the opportunity.

It would be a way of getting "closure" (ugh, she hated that word).

There might be a story in it (maybe).

And what if more kids were being subjected to the same things she had. What if. That last point was circled over and over again. It would be almost unbearable if that was the case.

She got up from the bed and hunted for her skin lotion. Jill was always being given things for free, and she would send Ambra a bag of them every now and then. This particular cream contained cloud-berries, apparently, which was very fitting, considering where she was. She rubbed it into her skin and kept thinking.

The list against investigating Esaias and Rakel Sventin:

Most things.

She got up and stared out of the hotel window. She had looked up the Sventins' address. They still lived in the same old house. *What should I do?*

Deep down, she already knew the answer.

Her driving force was to defend those who lacked a voice, to write about appalling conditions, to gain redress, and to fight for democracy. To reveal faults.

The whole thing would have been considerably easier if it wasn't the Sunday right after Christmas. She still called social services, a helpline.

"My name is Ambra Vinter. I'd like to talk to whoever is responsible for foster home placements in Kiruna," she said calmly. She was in her professional role. Over the years, she must have talked to several hundred bureaucrats and public officials, maybe even several thousand.

"Anne-Charlotte Jansson takes care of that. But she's on vacation until after New Year's," the voice on the end of the line informed her.

"Is there anyone else?" Ambra asked impatiently.

"I'm sorry, everyone is on vacation. If it's an emergency, you should call 112."

She left a message for Anne-Charlotte Jansson to call her back, adding that it was urgent, and then Ambra went down to eat breakfast with her laptop beneath her arm. Since neither the Internet nor the heating worked especially well in her room, she stayed in the dining hall with her nose buried in her laptop.

She went to aftonbladet.se and caught up with her colleagues' latest work. Walls were being built in Europe, and interest rates would either be raised or lowered. After that, she surfed around a little, read everything she could about the foster home system, about children who had suffered, about laws and regulations. At noon, she got up, her body ridiculously stiff.

As soon as Tom had dropped her off at the hotel, she'd fallen asleep instantly in her bed. She probably wasn't used to so much fresh air. Now, many hours later, indoors among the lunch guests and the murmur of conversations, it felt surreal that they had lain beneath the animal furs together. It had been amazing. The snowmobile ride, the star-filled sky, the Northern Lights. The almost-kiss . . . Christ, she was turned on when that happened. She wished she could send him a text to thank him for the trip, but she didn't have his number. And, of course, there were no hits when you Googled him.

She sat back down at her computer and explored the Lodestar Security Group home page. It was a nice-looking site. Somber colors and people in suits sitting in some kind of office environment. Keywords like *security, global, professionalism*. It was completely impersonal, as though they had bought generic photographs directly from a photo bank. No staff members were mentioned by name. No contact address, just a switchboard number. But she could read between the lines.

This company provided tailor-made private security in a number of the world's most unstable countries. She knew that Tom was a former elite soldier, and she assumed that the majority of Lodestar's employees had a similar background.

Aftonbladet had recently hired an award-winning security policy journalist. He probably knew plenty about this type of business. Should she give him a call and do a little digging? She wrote herself a reminder and continued to scan the site. She could call the Lodestar switchboard and ask whether they could pass on a message to Tom. But something made her hold back.

As she sat there, surfing the elegant, impersonal website, it was as though she finally realized what type of man Tom really was. It scared her a little. He wasn't a dry, suit-wearing boss or an eloquent media type. Violence and brutality were his everyday. No, she probably didn't dare get in touch after all. Besides, if he wanted her to contact him, he surely would've given her his number. Or gotten in touch himself. She was, like any normal person, perfectly visible online. She was also woman enough to think that he would call if he cared. He was about to kiss her again last night, wasn't he? Right? Yeah, he was, so she couldn't be so terrible with men after all. Tom liked her.

Ambra got up from the table again, packed away her laptop, and paced restlessly into the lobby. As she stood there, studying a cabinet of Sami handicrafts, her cell phone rang. It was Grace.

"I thought you were taking some time off," Ambra said.

"A few of the news editors are sick, so I'm helping out." Ambra was well aware that Grace was as much of a work addict as she was, that she didn't have anything against doing an extra shift. It was a dangerous approach, of course. And like everything dangerous, it was irresistible for story-seeking journalists.

"I just wanted to check that everything was okay," Grace continued. "You did a great job on that piece with the old woman. I've heard compliments from a number of sources."

Ambra looked down at her feet. She wasn't comfortable taking praise. "Thanks," she said.

"Did you make it back from Kiruna like you planned? Wasn't there some kind of issue with the plane?"

"I'm actually still here. There's something I want to check out."

"But will you make it home by tomorrow? You're working then, right?"

Shit, she hadn't thought about that. "Grace, I worked extra. I came up here over Christmas. I assumed I could take a few days off."

"Didn't you just hear me say we're short of people? I need you in the office."

"But I'm onto something up here. I want to write about foster home placements and kids who end up suffering."

Grace usually liked softer stories. The male news editors always wanted people to write about corrupt German car manufacturers, Russian presidents, and the North Korean nuclear threat—the harder, the better—but Grace consistently fought for stories about the most vulnerable in society.

But now she groaned. "That kind of thing's always a mess. One person's word against another's. And all the authorities are bound by confidentiality. No, forget it," she said.

"I contacted social services. The story could be linked to a religious sect." There was always room for sects in the news world.

"Do you have a contact? Really? Someone who'll speak out?" Grace sounded skeptical. Ambra heard a clatter in the background.

"Not yet, but I . . ."

"What the hell, Ambra. You know better than that. This'll never work. I can't have you up there writing that kind of crap story."

"We're talking about *children* here," Ambra said, angrily starting to pace around the lobby.

She heard Grace cover the mouthpiece and shout at someone before she came back on the line. "Lots of kids have a crap time. I want you to come home now. There's plenty for you to write about here."

"I want to do something important."

"Don't be so damn difficult. I'm expecting you to be in the office in line with your usual hours. You won't get any special treatment from me, if that's what you were thinking. You want to write about kids having a tough time, Stockholm is full of them. Go down to the emergency services center and listen to all that shit. We have five domestic disturbances involving mothers who were beaten to a pulp by their husbands while the kids watched. Children who've been thrown out, barefoot, in the snow. So unless you have someone from social services in Kiruna willing to put their name and title to a statement about placing kids with satanists, you can damn well fly back down here and come to the office." Toward the end, Grace was practically screaming.

Ambra kept quiet. Her jaw was clenched. "I'll head home then," she said sullenly.

"You do that." Grace hung up.

Annoyed at Grace, Ambra went back to her room, pulled on her coat, and left the hotel. She was still free right now; she could do what she liked. She walked to the bus station and found she was in luck, she didn't have to wait. She climbed onboard and sat down at the very front. She looked out of the window. Snow and more snow. How could there be so much of it?

The closer she was to her destination, the more she recognized. Plenty had changed over the years, but so much was still the same, and memories of the house and the street names washed over her, made her sit stiffly in her seat. She hadn't expected to react so strongly. When the bus pulled up and she stepped outside, unease washed over her. She slowly walked the short distance from the bus stop to the house where she'd lived during her foster time in Kiruna.

She'd lived with the Sventin family for just over a year. She arrived at Christmas, and her period had started that spring. There was so much that she had repressed, but she remembered how painful it was, how little comfort she was given, and how Esaias became obsessed by the fact she was changing. Eventually, his talk about the devil and the demons she carried inside her became unbearable. She ran away, back to Stockholm, and lived on the streets with lonely refugees and other runaways before social services found her and placed her in another home. It was a sheer miracle that she made it through that time unscathed.

And now she was back. She'd come out here on a whim, hadn't really thought it through, and wasn't prepared for the emotions that were now welling up inside her. She slowly approached the red wooden house with her heart pounding in her chest. They still had the same mailbox—funny how the memory could wake so many feelings—an ordinary black mailbox made of steel. There was no smoke rising from the chimney. The house seemed empty; it was pitch black inside and no one had cleared the snow on the walkway. Damn it, this was badly planned on her part. She wondered whether she should peer in through the windows, but she couldn't bring herself to get that close.

She felt physically sick. Her stomach ached. Her body remembered that time better than she did. She was so damn scared when her first period arrived, because she didn't understand what was happening to her. The cramps hurt so much, and the feeling when it ran out of her, as though she was peeing herself, and then when she saw it was blood. She was terrified, afraid she was dying. She didn't dare say anything and bled onto handkerchiefs and bedclothes and her underwear. Rakel was furious about the mess she made. And then Esaias grabbed her by the neck and dunked her into a tub of cold water. She didn't remember what happened next; her head was empty.

No, she couldn't stay here any longer.

She hurried back to the bus stop, waited an eternity for a bus, and was practically frozen solid by the time she made it back to the hotel. Her room was chilly when she stepped inside. She took off her gloves and felt the radiator, which was ice cold, but she didn't have the energy to call down to reception and complain. Instead, she lay down on the bed still wearing her hat and scarf.

She listlessly bit one of her nails. Took out her cell phone and called Jill, but only got her voice mail. She realized she should do something sensible, but instead she ended up surfing Instagram. Jill had uploaded pictures from some party yesterday.

Ambra put down her phone. All the happiness she'd felt on the snowmobile trip was completely gone. Tom hadn't been in touch, the Sventins were on her mind, and Grace was angry. It was hard not to feel like a failure. And to add insult to injury, her immediate future involved enduring a night in a cold hotel room, then somehow trying to get home from Kiruna even though all of the planes were full.

* * *

"So you watched the Northern Lights, you said. Nothing else?" Mattias wiped the countertop, hung up the dishcloth, and gave Tom a skeptical look.

"Nope, nothing else," Tom replied. He took a bottle of mineral water from the refrigerator and reached for a glass. Paused when he remembered how close he had been to kissing Ambra again, how her mouth almost tempted him. But nothing happened. So, no, nothing else. Not exactly.

Mattias leaned back against the counter and crossed his arms. "Is her sister still in town?" he asked neutrally.

"Why?"

"No reason. Just making conversation. How're you feeling today?"

"Stop asking how I feel all the time."

Tom turned away from Mattias's piercing gaze and looked out the window. He was aware of it himself—his mood was at rock bottom again. He couldn't shake it off today, the anxiety just beneath his skin. It was so damn annoying. He was used to always being in control, of himself, his body, his feelings. If he at least knew why.

He'd been in a great mood yesterday, out in the forest with Ambra, but he woke with a headache and palpitations, and since then things had gone downhill. He hated that his moods were so illogical, that he swung from one extreme to another without knowing why. Mattias had offered to take Freja out both that morning and at lunch, but it almost felt worse that Mattias felt obliged to help out.

As though she could sense he was thinking about her, Freja came over to him. She wagged her tail and he petted her.

"Is it okay if I get the sauna up and running tonight?" Mattias asked as he watched the dog.

"Do whatever the hell you want," Tom replied. He hadn't used the sauna once, didn't even know if it worked.

"Or I could check into a hotel," Mattias said. It wasn't the first time he had offered.

"When does your plane leave?"

"I managed to talk my way into a standby seat tomorrow. If you need some time alone, I can go into town."

"Lay off," said Tom. The idea felt ridiculous. The house was several hundred square meters.

"How are you doing, really?" Mattias asked.

"I need to go out," he snapped. If Mattias asked once more, he would explode.

"Take the dog with you," Mattias shouted after him.

Freja was beside Tom, in the passenger seat. She was looking out the window with interest, but she would turn to look at Tom every now and then, as though to make sure she wasn't doing anything wrong.

It was time to give her back to Nilas. He was hardly in any shape to take care of a dog.

He turned off onto Ellinor's street. Slowed down, tried to see whether anyone was home. His cell phone was back on the counter in the house. There was a light on in Ellinor's kitchen. He kept the engine running. Freja studied him tensely. He reached out to her, let her sniff at his hand, and then he petted her gently behind one ear. Her fur was coarse, and she trembled beneath his hand.

"You can't stay with me," he said.

She looked up at him with her big, pleading eyes.

"Ah, what the hell," he muttered, driving away. He glanced at Freja. "Tomorrow," he said to her, noticing that she was paying attention to him. "Don't start getting any ideas. I'm giving you back tomorrow."

What difference would one more day make? It wasn't like anyone had been in touch asking about her.

"Come on, we'll go into town instead." Freja gave a short bark and he stepped on the gas, leaving Ellinor's house behind him.

There were plenty of dogs in Kiruna—hunting dogs, sleigh dogs—and he managed to find a huge pet store, where he bought a sack of dry food; two big bowls; a collar; and a new, sturdier leash. Freja allowed him to clip the collar around her neck, and then she obediently waited for him to attach the new leash. He let her nose around, followed her wherever she went, and suddenly they were outside the Scandic Ferrum, Ambra's hotel. He slowed down, wondering whether she was still there or whether she had managed to find a seat on a plane.

"Come on, let's go in," he said to Freja, and he managed to squeeze them both in through the revolving glass doors.

"Is Ambra Vinter still here?" he asked at reception.

"She is. Would you like me to call up to her room?" the reception-ist asked with a watchful eye on Freja's impressive size.

"Hello?" He heard Ambra's voice on the line. Guarded, brief.

"Hi there. This is Tom," he said. "Lexington."

"Ah. Hi. Why are you calling me on this phone?"

"Because I'm at your hotel. In the lobby. Want to come down?"

She appeared almost immediately, her hands in her back pockets, the same sauntering walk, her thick scarf wrapped around her neck several times.

"Hi," he said. He realized his mood was already better. She had such a strange effect on him, and it took a while before he managed to identify the feeling. Happiness. He felt happy whenever he saw her.

She pushed her hair from her forehead, stuck out her chin. Her lips were pink and glossy. "Hi. Thanks for last night. I wanted to send you a message to say thanks, but I don't have your number."

The idea of exchanging numbers had never crossed his mind. This thing between them, it couldn't go on. Could it? Though why not? They had a good time together, so why deny himself that?

Ambra reached out toward Freja. The dog sniffed cautiously.

"Did you manage to get any more sleep this morning?" Tom asked. She looked pale, with dark circles beneath her eyes, and a sudden wave of protectiveness welled up inside him. There was something so fragile about her, something brittle.

"Yeah, thanks. But I'm absolutely freezing. My room's so cold, and it's freezing down here too." She wrapped her arms around herself.

"Is everything all right, Ambra?" he asked, studying her more closely. She seemed down, not just cold and tired.

"It's been a weird day. . . . It doesn't matter. I'm glad you stopped by. It felt strange not to be able to get in touch."

"Yeah," he agreed. But the lobby really was drafty; the minute the doors opened, a cold wind came blowing in. Ambra pulled her sleeves down over her hands, rubbed her knuckles together. Her frozen appearance gave him an idea.

"The house where I'm staying has a sauna," he said. "We're going to get it going tonight."

She gave him a pair of raised eyebrows in reply. He liked that ges-ture, he realized. Arrogant, questioning, expectant.

"Mattias is an Ålander," he explained. "They are islanders and have an unhealthy relationship with saunas. It's like a religion to them."

"Yeah, so I've heard. I interviewed a fisherman from Åland once. Sea, fishing lines, and his sauna—that was all he was interested in."

"Want to stop by? Warm up a little?"

"You're kidding, right?"

"Nah, it's actually pretty nice. Have you done it before? Been to a sauna?"

Ambra shook her head.

"Not that, either?" There was so much Tom couldn't understand about her. She was experienced, had seen things the majority of people never would, but there were also a number of everyday things that she hadn't done during her time in Kiruna, like ride a snowmobile or watch the Northern Lights. In fact, she'd told him practically nothing about her time up here.

"You have to come. It's nothing weird, really, more like a hobby or a sport."

"Aside from the fact you're naked?" she drily pointed out.

"We have towels. Bring your sister if you want."

Her eyes narrowed. "Is this just a way of getting to Jill?"

"No," he said, surprised. "Why would I want that?" He thought for a moment. "Though now you mention it, Mattias would probably be happy if she came along."

"I see."

She looked anything but positive.

He wasn't really the type to insist, but it suddenly felt like a great idea to invite her over. Mentioning her famous sister was mostly a way of making her feel more comfortable with the whole idea.

"Come on," he said convincingly. "I can't believe you've never tried it. And you'll warm up in the sauna, really warm up, I can promise you that."

"And everyone will be wearing a towel?"

"Definitely. We have some huge towels we can wrap ourselves in."

"And there won't be any rolling about in the snow? Or whipping one another with birch branches?" Her cheeks blushed slightly.

"I promise, on my honor, not to whip you with a birch branch or anything else," he said solemnly.

The thought of seeing her again that evening, talking with her, hanging out with her, listening to her and bickering with her, was surprisingly pleasing. He would bring in the wood, light a fire, put on some music. They . . .

"No, Tom, I can't." Ambra interrupted his thoughts with an apologetic smile. "Sorry, I can't. And Jill's not here anymore."

Okay. He looked at Freja, who was whimpering on the floor. He was disappointed, he suddenly realized, and had been hoping she would say yes.

"Thanks for stopping by anyway, and thanks for the invite," Ambra said.

He was about to say that they could do it another day, but they would probably never see each other again.

Freja was still whimpering. "I guess I need to take her outside," he said, though he had absolutely no desire to leave just yet. It felt so strange that this might be the last time they ever spoke.

"Okay." She looked at the dog and then up at him. Long, dark eyelashes, and those slanting eyes of hers. She raised her palm to him in some kind of good-bye.

At the very last minute, Tom remembered. He found a pencil stub and the receipt from the pet store, scrawled down his number, and handed it to her.

She took it. Looked at him. He stepped toward her and gave her a quick hug. She tensed in his arms, but then she wrapped hers around him. For a second, she hugged him back, awkwardly.

"Call me if you change your mind," he said quietly.

She nodded. He turned around and urged on Freja, who was eagerly pulling toward the exit. When he turned back, Ambra was already gone.

Ambra hit her head against the elevator wall. Why did she say no? With a sigh, she opened the door to her room. She should have said yes to the sauna. Her cell phone started to buzz.

"You called?" she heard Jill chirp on the other end.

"Gaaaah."

"What's up?"

"I'm an idiot."

"Oooh, wait a second, let me stop the music and you can fill me in. Ludvig! Turn off the music. Right. Go."

"There's nothing to tell. I'm just such a loser."

"Before I get excited, it's not work, is it? Please tell me it's a man."

"Tom Lexington stopped by."

"And?"

"Nothing. That's all."

Silence.

"Jill?"

"Ambra, my dear, dear sister. You *have to* get yourself a life. Twelve-year-olds have more exciting love lives than you."

"I don't know what's going on between us. He's nice, we have fun together. But he has an ex he isn't over yet." *And he has really hard eyes and sometimes has panic attacks he doesn't want anyone to know about.*

Jill made a disapproving sound. "Another woman? Don't sleep with him. End it, immediately. You don't need that kind of crap."

"I can't end it, because there's nothing going on. But he is nice. And he asked me out, which no one else has in a long time, okay?"

Jill sighed deeply. "So damn tragic."

"Yeah, I know. How's Örebro? I saw on your Insta you went to some party," she said, changing the subject. Jill's glamorous existence was about the closest she would ever get to a life.

"Ludvig! Where are we?"

She heard some murmuring.

"We're back in Norrland," Jill chirped. "I was invited to a party at the Icehotel, so we came back up. We rented a huge car."

That was Jill in a nutshell. Wild, impulsive, restless. "How was the Icehotel?"

"Cold. Lots of vodka. A really cute reindeer herder."

Something suddenly clicked inside Ambra. "Hey, isn't the Icehotel in Jukkasjärvi? Are you still there? That's only like half an hour away from here."

"I guess so. Where are you again?"

Ambra clutched her cell phone tight and managed not to groan. "Jill. Stop messing around. Listen to me now. I want you to come over here, to Kiruna."

"When?"

"Now."

"Why?"

"We're going to go to a sauna."

"Ha ha, so funny."

"I'm serious. You're going to come over and give me moral support."

Deep, deep sigh.

"Mattias will be there," she tempted her.

I think. I hope. Maybe. Or would she rather go to the sauna alone with Tom? Those arms, those shoulders. In a sauna. Covered in sweat.

"Which Mattias?" Jill asked.

Ambra felt like slamming the phone against the table. She hated it when Jill was obstinate like this. "You *know* who I mean. We talked about him yesterday. I saw the way you were looking at him when you were here. If you come over here now, I swear I'll owe you a favor."

Long, calculated silence. Oh, she would pay for this. Ambra knew it in every inch of her being.

"I'll come. On condition that I can take you shopping in Stockholm. Women's clothes, including underwear and shoes, and probably also accessories. Anything knitted, denim, or cotton is forbidden."

"Fine, fine. But you have to be nice when you get here, not some fucking pop diva."

"Let's not ask for the impossible. Ludvig! We're going out in the car. Kisses, Ambra."

"I hate it when you say that," Ambra shouted back. But Jill had already hung up. Ambra pulled the scrap of paper with Tom's number from her pocket. Ha! She was going to take a sauna with Tom Lexington.

Chapter 19

Jill leaned between the front seats and stared out through the windshield. "According to the GPS, you should turn off here," she said to Ludvig, pointing to the right, out into the forest.

Ludvig didn't reply. He hadn't said a word the entire drive. His body language made it perfectly clear what he thought about her forcing him to drive them there. Jill, on the other hand, couldn't care less; he worked for her.

"You sure he's all right?" Ambra whispered.

Jill fixed her hair and leaned back. "He's pissed. He wanted to stay in Jukkasjärvi and drink blue cocktails out of ice glasses."

"Are you going to bring him into the sauna?" asked Ambra.

"Nah, he can drive around or something, pick us up later. Will we get any food?" Jill was starving, wasn't sure she could hold back today, even if she would be around others. God, she felt like letting loose. Not just uploading pictures of food and desserts she then didn't eat, but actually *eating*.

"He said there would be dinner when I called," Ambra replied.

"Do you think he's a good cook? He looks more like the type who'd club a moose to death and then eat it raw in his cave."

"He's fully civilized. I'm sure we'll get good food." Ambra sounded touchy. Was she nervous?

The GPS said something, and Jill shouted: "Ludvig! Turn here!"

"I knoooow."

Jill stared out through the window. The branches of the enormous trees were bowing under the weight of all the snow. "So much forest. And snow. Hope we're not going for a walk."

Ambra looked at her. "But you're dressed so practically."

"At least I don't look like a Christian social worker," Jill replied.

As ever, Ambra was wearing pants and a sweater. They weren't exactly ugly, but nor were they cute or flattering. Jill shoved her hand beneath her clothes and straightened her bra. Jesus, everything felt tight. Today's outfit was a little on the impractical side—she agreed with Ambra about that—but this wasn't her usual gang, and she felt a sudden pang of uncertainty. She usually hung out with people who admired her, who wanted something from her. People she didn't feel inferior to.

She remembered Mattias Ceder perfectly well. Remembered how smart he sounded. Mattias looked like the kind of person to take 40,000 credits worth of classes in college, while she barely made it through high school and hadn't opened a book since. Singing was all she was good at, and usually that was more than enough, but whenever she was among educated people, she felt stupid. Then there was the intense, silent Tom. She didn't understand him at all, and actually found him pretty scary. No, she needed these clothes tonight. She might not be smart or have a good education or an important job, but she was hot.

She was here for Ambra, she reminded herself. Ambra liked Tom, and Jill couldn't remember when something like that last happened.

Mattias lifted the big, shiny char onto the chopping board and started to fillet the fish. He enjoyed cleaning fish, preparing it.

"Did you catch that yourself?" Tom asked. There were plenty of options for ice fishing around them, but Mattias shook his head. He hadn't been fishing in a long time. "But I bought it from one of those vans selling fish, so it's from the area." He expertly cut out the fillets and placed them on the chopping board. After that, he quickly removed the bones, fins, and fat. "Could you drain the potatoes?" he asked, nodding toward the stove.

Tom took the pot and drained the water from the almond potatoes. Mattias took out shallots, wine, and cream and made a quick sauce; he chopped some dill and folded in a couple of egg yolks, seasoned with mustard. He had managed to get hold of good-quality ingredients, and he enjoyed cooking, but he was starting to feel like it would soon be time for him to leave Kiruna. He'd been planning to leave that evening, but that was before he heard Jill Lopez would be coming. One more day, he decided. Her sex appeal was probably overexaggerated in his mind. Just as well he got it out of his system now, so he could stop with the sexual fantasies every night.

Tom closed the refrigerator door, opened a beer, and handed it to him. Mattias drank straight from the bottle and studied Tom, who was staring into thin air with a frown. Mattias put down the beer and transferred the fish to the oven.

"So I guess you like her? The journalist?" Mattias asked.

Tom shrugged. "She's okay."

Tom had a bottle of champagne in the refrigerator and he also smelled good, so Ambra was probably more than that.

"They're here," Tom said. Mattias hadn't heard a sound, but Tom always did have unnaturally acute hearing. A moment later, Freja started to bark. Mattias looked at the dog.

"The pooch, what's the deal with her? Are you going to give her back?"

"Yeah."

Mattias now heard the car pull up outside. Freja growled deeply and followed them to the front door.

Tom opened it, and the snow swirled inside. Ambra Vinter was on the porch, stamping her feet, wrapped up in a scarf and hat.

Jill Lopez was behind her.

With all of her sex appeal.

Jesus Christ, the woman looked like she could melt the North Pole.

"Hi," Tom said.

"Welcome," Mattias said. "Come in."

Ambra floated inside in a cloud of snowflakes and subzero air, and then Jill swept by, wearing sky-high heels, a pale brown coat, jingling jewelry, and glossy lips. She looked fantastic. Vulgar, curvy, hair-raisingly hot.

After the two women took off their coats, unwound their scarves, pulled off their hats, and checked themselves in the mirror (Jill, not Ambra), they waited with Tom in the living room while Mattias fetched the champagne. Jill took the glass he handed her, her long fingers stroking the crystal. Ambra nodded in thanks.

Tom raised his glass. "Welcome," he said.

The two women sipped their champagne—a really good bottle, Mattias thought approvingly, if expensive and flashy, but definitely nothing to be ashamed of. He liked his wine the way he liked his women: sophisticated, elegant, tasteful. He studied Jill. Who wore patent leather heels in weather like this? She was wearing a figure-fitting dress made of what Mattias was sure was expensive cashmere. It clung to her curves like a second skin and was belted tightly at the waist. Her jingling earrings grazed her neck, and a huge necklace drew his eyes down to her exceptional décolletage. Ambra glanced guardedly around the room while Jill stood in the center, her back straight and her jaw confident.

"This house isn't half bad," she said. "When Ambra told me we were going to a cottage in the forest, I thought it would be a hovel."

"Cottage?" Tom said with a questioning look at Ambra.

She pulled an apologetic face. "I only saw the barn," she said.

"Hmm," he said, running his hand over his bearded chin. "Want to see the rest of it?"

The women nodded.

"While you show them around, I'll finish the food," Mattias said. His eyes happened to land on Jill again. It was hard not to, there was so much of her. Curves, high heels, body-skimming clothes. Jill flashed a slow smile.

"What?" he asked.

Her eyes darted across the apron he had forgotten to take off before they arrived. "Nothing. You are cute as a housewife," she said, turning around.

Ambra stared out of the window in the living room. The house, which Tom was apparently borrowing from an acquaintance, was built on a slope, and this side looked out onto forest and an open expanse of meadow. During the day, the views out of the enormous windows must be incredible. The entire house was oversized somehow, masculine. The ceiling height had to be approaching seven meters in the living room, and it was full of huge couches, thick reindeer skins, and an enormous open hearth where a fire was crackling away. Beams on the ceiling, and then those huge windows.

Tom appeared next to her. He smelled great. Freshly showered. He was wearing a black sweater again. No slogan, plain black, and tight across his chest and arms. If he was anyone else, she would have assumed he was showing off his muscles, but he seemed to completely lack that kind of vanity. Aside from the fact that he smelled so good. She sniffed gently.

"I'm glad you changed your mind and decided to come," he said quietly. He didn't smile, but his eyes were warm.

"I'm a little nervous about the sauna part," she admitted, sipping her champagne.

"We'll take care of you, I promise." His voice was comforting, and she knew that if there was one thing she could rely on, it was Tom's ability to take care of a person. "Are you hungry? Mattias has made enough food for an entire company."

She swirled her glass a little. "How big is a company, exactly? I've always wondered."

"Smaller than a brigade and bigger than a platoon." His dark eyes glittered, and she felt herself being drawn to him. He was a mystery, this man. What did it mean that he'd invited her over? What did he want from her? Did he want *anything?*

"And yes, I'm hungry," she said. The smells coming from the kitchen were fantastic, and the champagne had already gone to her head.

They sat down at the table in the living room, with the snow outside and a crackling fire not far away. Candles lit and lights dimmed. She cast a glance at Jill. Even she was impressed, Ambra could see it. Good. You never knew with Jill. She could be a real pain if something didn't live up to her expectations.

Ambra was next to Tom, with Jill and Mattias opposite. As Mattias served the food, Tom poured white wine into huge glasses.

They toasted. Ambra and Tom looked at one another, and it felt utterly surreal that they were sitting there, in the middle of the woods, at what most resembled a couples' dinner party. Ambra tried to remember whether she had ever been to one. The closest she could remember was a piece she wrote about a dinner party that ended in murder in Örebro. She sipped her wine, decided not to mention it. She met Jill's amused eye over the table and prayed silently that her sister would behave.

"What's on your schedule going forward, Jill?" Mattias asked.

"I have a show in Stockholm on New Year's Eve, and then it's spring, new shows and a tour."

"Are you going to be on the Melody Festival this year?" Ambra asked as she poured more sauce and helped herself to salad. It was a huge televised musical competition. First in Sweden, dragging on for weeks on TV, then a big finale in one of the European capitals, complete with scandals, drama, and maximum publicity. Jill had competed on the glittering TV show once, came in second, and had a smash hit with her entry.

But Jill shook her head. "I don't know, I need to make up my mind pretty soon." She ate a forkful of fish, potato, and sauce. "I do need a new hit—it's been a while. But I'm a bad loser. I can't handle faking happiness for someone else," she added.

Mattias laughed gently. Jill smiled and ate another forkful.

"You're very different, for sisters," Mattias said, studying Ambra and then turning back to Jill. He was right, they couldn't be more different.

"I'm youngest," Jill said.

"One whole year younger," Ambra said drily. ·

"We don't have any biological connection, and we're not really even proper foster sisters," she continued, using air quotes as she said the last part. "But we've stuck together since our teens."

Tom didn't say much, but he listened intently, topped up their wine, and nodded every now and then. There wasn't a centimeter of Ambra that wasn't aware of his presence.

"Go on," said Mattias. He had an incredible ability to make people want to talk. Calm, attentive.

"I ended up in the foster system when I was young," Ambra began. "By the time I was fourteen, I'd been with so many families I lost count. I'd run away a number of times, and social services didn't know what to do with me. I'd given up on everything." She nodded to Jill, who continued their story.

"And I was adopted from Colombia," she said. "I was in an orphanage there for the first few years of my life, but then I was adopted by a crazy Swede and her equally crazy husband. One day, I decided I'd had enough and ran."

Jill was good at that, lightening her hellish childhood with a cou-

ple of amusing sentences. In truth, she had been dumped on a rubbish heap in Bogota, found, and then left again on the steps of an orphanage run by nuns. Jill never spoke about it, but Ambra assumed
things hadn't been easy in the orphanage. She'd read enough horror
stories about what went on in similar institutions. After that, Jill
ended up with the mentally ill, alcoholic Swedish lady and her awful
husband. Jill's childhood had been a living illustration of *out of the
frying pan, into the fire*.

"We met by chance one summer," Ambra said.

"How?" Mattias asked. He seemed so warm and empathetic. Someone you wanted to trust with all of your secrets.

Ambra glanced at Tom. He was studying her intently. He was on
her side, she realized. He would never let anyone hurt her. Wherever
had that exaggerated thought come from?

"I'd run away from my adoptive family," said Jill. "I refused to live
with them anymore. Not that they wanted me, either. I think they
hated me." Jill once told Ambra that her adoptive mother said they
were planning to adopt a different, younger child but that they had
been talked into taking Jill. "I've regretted it every day since," her
adoptive mother had added. Toward the end, they'd forced Jill to live
in the garage and threatened to send her back to Colombia.

"I was placed on a farm in the countryside," Jill continued. "With a
woman who kept horses and took in difficult girls."

"Did you stay there?"

"Yeah, until I turned eighteen. But by then I'd already started
touring. It did me good to live in the countryside. It was really calm
out there."

"Until I turned up," Ambra interjected.

"Yeah, and then all hell broke loose," Jill agreed with a laugh.

Ambra was fourteen. She had long since left the Sventins. The
new foster family she was living with hadn't wanted to take her on vacation with them. They weren't allowed to do that. Foster kids were
entitled to the same standard of living as all other family members.
Or that's what it said on paper, anyway, though Ambra had been
through almost everything by that point, and nothing surprised her.
So the family left, and she was sent to a farm in the countryside by
her stressed social worker. They were always stressed. Always running off to something more urgent.

"Doesn't sound like you found each other right away," said Mattias. He refilled their glasses.

"Not exactly." Ambra smiled. Jill was a full-fledged bitch even as a thirteen-year-old, and Ambra hadn't trusted a single soul by that point.

"It was hate at first sight," said Jill.

Ambra nodded. "We fought like animals." It was no exaggeration; they'd clashed almost every day in the beginning. Ambra was convinced she was going to be sent away. But the woman who ran the farm—Renée—stuck it out. She managed to give Jill the attention she needed and she also gained Ambra's trust. The years they spent on the farm were an oasis for both of them. A turning point.

"What happened?" Mattias asked.

"Since we didn't manage to kill each other, we became friends instead. Gradually," said Jill. It was a difficult process, but one day, when Ambra was being picked on in school, Jill beat up the bully, and their relationship changed. Or maybe they just matured.

"Jill started singing and I started studying," Ambra added. She was tired of teachers who shook their heads, principals who pursed their lips, and she had been torn between dropping out of school or really knuckling down. Even today, she was deeply grateful to her teenage self, who had possessed enough brain cells to make the right decision.

"I had my breakthrough on Swedish *Idol* when I was sixteen, and that changed everything," Jill said.

"Sounds like it was good for you?" said Mattias.

She nodded. "Singing probably saved my life. And Renée meant so much to us. She encouraged our friendship and sisterhood. Since neither of us have any biological siblings, we decided to be one another's sister. It's been that way ever since. And no matter which way you look at it, it's the longest relationship either of us has ever had."

"What happened to Renée?" Tom asked quietly.

"She died," was all Jill said. She looked away.

Renée's death was a damn tragedy. The one good thing about it was that, by that point, both girls were older than eighteen. No more foster homes. Jill went off on tour and Ambra decided to study journalism.

"She had cancer," said Ambra. Shitty illness.

Jill held out her glass. "No more about that," she said encouragingly. Ambra nodded. It was far too nice an evening to be delving into gloomy thoughts. But she did miss Renée. Often.

"More wine?" Tom asked.

She nodded. His arm grazed against hers when he picked up the bottle.

"Sorry," he mumbled.

"Don't worry," she mumbled back, wanted to touch his arm, run her fingers over those strands of hair, smell him a little more. Freja came over and positioned herself between them. Ambra gently stroked her rough coat. Freja laid her head on Tom's leg for a moment and then she turned to Ambra, sniffed, and did a loop of the table.

Jill studied the dog, though she didn't say anything.

"Ambra, how's your work going up here? Are you doing any more interviews?" Mattias gave her a warm smile.

"Not right now. There's one thing I'm looking into," she said. She didn't elaborate. Spying on her old foster parents seemed too disturbed.

"Do you like your job?" he asked.

"A lot."

"Ambra's passionate about saving the world," said Jill.

She didn't say it in a mean way. And she wasn't completely wrong. Ambra put down her cutlery and breathed out.

"Full?" Tom asked.

"That was incredibly good," she said, noticing that even Jill had cleaned her plate.

"Have you ever been to the Icehotel?" Tom asked her as Jill explained that she had just come from there.

"No."

"It's actually pretty cool," said Jill. "You should go over there, Ambra. Now I'm stuffed. What do you say, time to get undressed?" She gave Mattias a flirty look.

He nodded, though his expression didn't change. "We can have dessert later. The sauna's warm. Tom, if you show them where to get changed, I'll clear the table."

Ambra and Jill followed Tom downstairs.

"You can use this as a changing room," Tom said as he turned on the light.

The women looked at each other. The house didn't just have a sauna in the basement, as Ambra had assumed; the entire lower level was made for relaxing. One wall consisted of individual shower booths, and against the other there were armchairs, small tables, and wicker baskets. Tom moved around the room, lighting the candles. The mosaic tiles glittered in varying shades of copper.

"You're both so quiet," Tom said as he opened a cupboard and took out some towels.

"I don't know why, but I assumed it would be some kind of bachelor's sauna, full of cans of beer and other unhygienic things," Ambra said. Jill nodded in agreement.

Tom smirked. "Nah, we got rid of all the unhygienic stuff before you got here. The left-hand shower can be for the ladies."

Ambra took the pile of towels he held out to her. They smelled freshly laundered, and they were almost laughably soft amid all the grand manliness of the house.

After she and Jill closed the door to their changing room, she heard Mattias arrive. Soon after, they heard the mumbling of the men's voices from the other room.

"What do you think?" Ambra whispered as she took off and folded her jeans.

Jill raised a perfectly penciled eyebrow and gave her a long look. "That you should invest in a wax, maybe?"

Jill herself was wearing a G-string and a lacy bra from some ridiculously expensive brand, and it was clear she was waxed clean. She was so beautiful it was painful, Ambra thought, withstanding the impulse to look down at her own utterly ordinary body. Jill was naturally olive colored, as if she had a constant tan. She was much curvier than a model, but she was perfectly proportioned, as though she had already been Photoshopped. Yes, Jill had a personal trainer and was constantly on a diet, but it was completely insane that a person could look like that. And wearing a G-string and delicate lace—things very few women could get away with. Ambra took off her cotton panties, soft and comfortable, but hardly sexy. She didn't have much of a bust, and her bra had seen better days. But still . . .

"I'm glad you came with me," she said honestly. Jill was her family, and it didn't matter that she was *too* hot.

"Of course you are. They seem nice enough, they seem like

straight-up guys, but you did the right thing not coming alone. I have pepper spray in my purse."

Ambra was fairly sure that neither Tom nor Mattias was a man who could be stopped with a little pepper spray. "Are you interested in Mattias?" she asked, still whispering.

Jill shook her head. "He's far too decent. And a little snobby, with his wines and all the books he's read, don't you think?"

Ambra thought Mattias was sociable and polite, and he had mentioned *one* book he liked, in passing, while they were discussing literature. But Jill always did have a complex when it came to her education, and she usually preferred men who were a little more . . . one-dimensional. Plus, she could see Jill was lying. She liked him, all right.

"What about Tom?" Ambra asked as nonchalantly as she could.

"He's super cheery, isn't he? You two are a good match." Jill stepped out of her G-string and unclasped her bra. Ambra handed her one of the towels. Jill wrapped it around herself and managed to look like an ultraglamorous film star, even in pale gray terry. "He was checking you out," she said.

"What?" Ambra didn't like how eager her voice sounded. She needed to control herself better. But she had noticed it too.

"You said he has another girl?"

"An ex. Ah, I don't know." Ambra wrapped a second towel around herself and almost drowned in all the soft material. She wiggled her toes on the heated floor. "But you're the one who said he was looking at me. I have no idea what he thinks of me."

"Men. They're either boring as hell or completely incomprehensible," Jill said. She opened the door to a toilet, sat down, and started to pee, completely unembarrassed.

"You could close the door," Ambra pointed out.

"I don't like closed doors. Listen to me now. You're a hundred times better than I'll ever be. Loyal and super smart. You're one of the people they'll want to keep around if the world's about to end and they need to choose the thousand smartest people. You're one of the best, Ambra. And any man who can't see that really doesn't deserve you."

Ambra stared at her, astonished. "Thanks," she managed to say.

Jill wiped herself, flushed, and quickly washed her hands. "Just be careful. Those tortured, silent types, I don't get what it is about them that some women find so attractive. You don't think you can fix him, do you? That never works out, I swear."

"Thanks for all the advice I didn't ask for. But don't you think the relationship between them is weird?"

There was something going on between Tom and Mattias, she just couldn't quite put her finger on it. Something bubbling beneath the surface.

"No idea. But you know I don't really care about other people's problems. Come on, let's go get a look at some male bodies."

They quickly showered. Ambra wrapped the towel around herself again and crossed her arms to guarantee it wouldn't fall down when she stepped out of the shower.

The men came out at the same time, and it wasn't the most re-laxed situation she had ever experienced. Four people who barely knew one another, wearing only towels. She tried not to stare at Tom, who had a towel wrapped around his waist and nothing else. She looked at him, counted to one, two, looked away for a while, and then peered at him again. She had met enough military, ex-military, and wannabe-military types to be able to separate the wheat from the chaff. Tom and Mattias were the real deal. Tom was a fighter, a man who was used to—possibly even comfortable with—deathly vio-lence. The result was roughly 50 percent troubling and 50 percent sexy. It was strange. She had met men like him before, at least in terms of appearance, without feeling the slightest attraction. In fact, the opposite was true. The safety courses the paper sent her on were always led by men like Tom Lexington. Big, tough men who were more than happy to fix their eyes on you and roar: I'VE BEEN DOING THIS FOR TWENTY YEARS. YOU DO THAT IN REAL LIFE, YOU'RE DEAD. HEAR THAT? YOU'RE DEEEEEAADDD.

Except Tom never roared, tensed his muscles, or showed off. He was more like an experienced predator. Silent and observant. And, like she said, sexy.

She gave herself two more seconds, and her eyes darted across his naked torso. Je–sus. Christ. Muscles everywhere. A little black hair. Dark nipples. Rock-hard abs. Lots of scars.

She didn't dare look at Jill, convinced that her sister would know exactly what she was thinking and blurt out something that would make her way more embarrassed than she already was. Ambra had done far more unusual things than this: traveled with shit-hot men without any makeup, gotten changed in front of men, a load of things that she didn't care about. She wasn't the least bit self-conscious in front of Mattias, for example, even though he, too, was wearing nothing but a towel. But Tom . . . he affected her, made her feel conscious of her own body and what it might get up to.

Mattias held open the door, and Ambra stepped into the sauna. The heat hit her like a wall. The wood crackled, and Mattias picked up a copper bucket and poured water onto the heater, causing clouds of steam to rise. There were huge windows out onto the woods and the darkness, and it was so hot that she started sweating immediately. She studied the sauna as Jill puffed and panted and commented on the heat from behind her.

Three benches, two half-naked men, an unpredictable foster sister, and her.

There was no telling how this would end.

Chapter 20

Tom was last into the sauna. It felt strange to be doing this, taking a sauna with Ambra. The whole house was suddenly so full of life. Mattias, a dog, two women. A *couples' dinner,* for God's sake. And the very obvious fact that Ambra was nearly naked. She was usually wearing so many layers when they met, but suddenly all he could see was bare, glistening skin wherever he looked. Maybe it was his generally weakened state that made him react so strongly to her nudity? He hadn't been himself for so long now, maybe there was some kind of chemical imbalance in his system, one that made him unable to tear his eyes away from her. It was damned obvious, in any case.

Jill sat down on the lowest bench. Ambra paused, but then she took a step up and sat down on the middle one. She sat with her back completely straight, pressed her knees together, and held on to her towel with both hands. Like a prim and proper schoolteacher.

"You good there? Don't want to sit up here?" Mattias asked. He was making his way to the top bench.

Ambra shook her head. Small droplets of sweat were already glistening on her skin. "It'll be too hot for me."

"Are you just going to stand there?" Mattias asked, giving Tom a telling look. *Stop staring.*

Tom tore his eyes from Ambra and climbed up to the top bench. The sauna was a generous size, and during the day the view from the windows was incredible. Right now, all they could see was the snow, stars, and darkness outside.

Jill straightened the towel over her generous bust; lay down; stretched out her long, golden legs; and gave a contented sigh. A typical sauna sound. Ambra wiped her forehead and checked her towel again, pulled it down over her thighs.

It was far too hot to talk, and silence descended over them. Ambra massaged her shoulder with one hand. She was glistening with sweat now. Strong, slender fingers continued to knead her shoulder and neck. Bare arms, sweaty hair, pale skin. It was arousing, Tom thought, drowsy with the heat. This was his first ever sauna with women; he hadn't realized how different it could be, how sensual a woman's skin could look when it slowly started to glow in the heat, to glisten with sweat.

He shifted in his seat, would rather not get an erection. He closed his eyes and leaned back against the burning hot wall, heard the noise of the women breathing in and out; he could make out Ambra if he really focused—her breathing was quicker than Jill's. Mattias made barely a sound. He was trained to be silent, just like Tom. The sound of the crackling heater was relaxing, the hiss when a drop of water turned to steam hypnotizing. He was aware of a number of scents, too—the steam, the wooden benches heating up and giving off a smell of resin. And then Ambra. Every time she moved, he caught the gentle fragrance of her skin.

Tom's muscles started to relax, and with that relaxation his stress and constant alertness dimmed slightly. It felt restful. For months, he had forced himself not to feel a thing, had turned off his body to enable himself to cope. But now he felt more full of life than he had in a long time. He'd barely thought of sex once since his period in captivity, and hardly since he'd returned home either. But now . . . With his head against the wall, he allowed himself to sink into his fantasies.

It was like a slow-motion film playing behind his eyelids, small scenes appearing to him. In his mind, he leaned forward until the scent of Ambra surrounded him, until he was so close that he could stick out his tongue. Carefully, he licked her warm skin, tasted the salt of her sweat, maybe even the soap from the shower, a residue of her perfume.

He opened his eyes, rubbed his chin. Shit, he was starting to get turned on by his fantasies.

Ambra's chest rose and fell; a bead of sweat formed on her temple, ran down her jaw and over her breastbone, disappearing into the tempting cleft above the top of her towel. She made the same movement again, massaged a tendon or muscle. Tom moved down onto her bench. She jumped, and he moved away from her, sitting with his back against the wall. She did the same, moved over to the opposite wall so that they were sitting opposite one another. She re-arranged her towel, but he managed to catch a glimpse of a thigh, a hint of a dark shadow.

"Warm?" he asked, trying to make himself as harmless as possible. They were trained in that kind of thing in the special forces. In how to vanish into the background, to avoid drawing attention, how not to provoke.

"Yeah, but it's nice." Her eyes moved over his body, swift but defi-nitely noticeable. Tom knew what she could see. The scars.

"Sorry," she said, looking away.

"Don't worry. Ask if you like."

"Are you sure?"

"It's totally fine," he said. Mattias glanced at him, but he kept quiet. "It's fine," Tom repeated, with emphasis this time.

She nodded to his shoulder, and Tom's fingers moved to the scar.

"That's one of the least heroic ones. We were out marching, run-ning, with our weapons drawn. I tripped and managed to shoot my-self."

He was nineteen when it happened, hadn't know anything about anything. Everything was simpler back then, even if it had hurt like hell. His pride had also taken a thorough beating.

"This one's from a wild dog," he said, turning his calf to show her two long, pale scars. "Machete. Knife. Stiletto," he continued, point-ing to wound after wound. "I don't even remember what this one was," he said, showing her a scar on the back of one hand.

"Looks like an axe," Mattias said.

"Right, exactly, an axe." Tom nodded.

He wiped his forehead. He'd barely drunk any wine, stuck to water at dinner, but he felt sick, almost dizzy. Could this talk of his old wounds really be the cause?

He'd realized Ambra was curious and hadn't realized it could be tough for him. But talking about his scars, memories of how he had been shot, stabbed, year after year, memories that never used to bother him in the past, made his pulse pick up. He tried to breathe calmly, couldn't embarrass himself by having an attack now.

"Jesus, what exactly do you do?" Jill asked. She was propped up on her elbows, staring at him with wide eyes. He'd forgotten about her while he was talking. But now his heart was beating so hard that he couldn't hear properly; blood was coursing toward his primed muscles. The sauna suddenly felt much, much warmer, almost unbearably so. As though through a tunnel, Tom looked down at his legs. One of them had started to shake against the bench. Shit, not now. Jill said something else, but Tom didn't hear her. He got up from the bench in a quick, jerky movement.

Mattias looked at him, concerned. "Tom . . ."

"I need to cool off," he said, hating the way Mattias kept an eye on him like that, hating that he wasn't himself.

"Me too, I'm way too sticky," said Ambra.

She got up, and he forced himself to stand still and hold the door for her, but then he hurried into one of the showers, closed the screen, leaned forward, and breathed deeply.

He felt better already. The heat in the sauna must have made things worse. He turned on the shower and raised his face to the cooling water. This was even better. The shaking was gone, his heart was calmer.

He could hear Ambra splashing around, and that too had a soothing effect. The cool tiles beneath his feet, the gentle jets of water, the sound of another person. He let out a deep sigh. God, that was good; it was over.

"Tom?" Her voice sounded worried on the other side of the wall.

How much of the attack had she noticed?

"Yeah?" he replied

Silence.

She was in there, naked, he suddenly realized. On the other side of the wall. The water he could hear over there, it was hitting her body, sloshing down her shoulders, arms, stomach, thighs.

"Is everything okay?" she asked.

He grabbed the shower gel and worked it into a lather. So, she had noticed something. Of course. She was observant. "Don't worry," he replied, making his voice steady and loud to calm her down and to be heard over the water. He waited to see whether she would say anything else. While he waited, he had no problem imagining her in his mind. It helped to think about her. He lathered himself quickly and roughly, felt his body return to some kind of normal state. He'd made it.

"I'm fine," he said, rinsing himself off. Hopefully that was it for this time.

Ambra listened to Tom on the other side of the thin wall. He was still in the shower. He'd had another of those attacks. Mattias had seen it, too, but Jill hadn't noticed a thing.

She shouldn't have brought up his scars. There had to be a whole load of trauma there; she'd seen red circles that looked like scars from cigarette burns, for example, but she hadn't been thinking. He was like a map of battles fought and attacks survived. And torture.

She listened to the noise of his shower and felt herself perking up under the cool jets of water. She pumped soap from a luxurious-looking bottle and started to lather herself up. The soap was creamy and the foam thick, and she ran her hands across her body. It felt good. With her eyes closed, she gave herself over to the feeling of the jets of water and the fragrant soap. She slowly massaged the lather beneath her arms, took her time washing her stomach, thighs, thought about Tom.

She smiled at the sensual feeling, left one hand to linger between her legs. It was so long since she last felt anyone else's hands on her body, and so she allowed herself to stand there like that, lazily moving her fingers and bringing up an image of Tom, his glistening muscles as he sat there on the bench in the sauna. Broad shoulders and black strands of hair on his chest, a narrow trail that disappeared beneath his towel. To pull down that towel, follow the dark trail with her fingers . . . God, she was actually quite turned on now. She brought one hand to her breast, lathered it up, touched herself gently. Tom had been checking her out in the sauna, she was sure of it. For a moment, she could have sworn it was hunger she saw in his eyes. Jesus, it was so erotic, feeling as if someone was hungering for you. In her mind, she allowed Tom to stare at her while she slowly let the towel drop to the floor, saw him admire her body, desire it. And then he came toward her as she slowly lay down on the bench. His big, warm body came down on top of hers, covered her, weighed her down as his knees parted hers.

"Ambra?"

She almost jumped. He sounded so near. When she turned off the jets of water, the room was silent. He must be done already. How much time had passed exactly? Did he hear anything? Would she have to stay in the cubicle forever now?

"Everything okay in there?"

"Yup, all fine," she squeaked, one hand still between her legs. She looked down, saw the foam and water disappearing down the drain. She should probably get herself a real life soon. "I'm good," she said in a more steady voice.

"Want to go back into the sauna? Or do you want a robe?"

"A robe, please."

"I'll leave one for you out here."

When he told her she could come out a moment later, Ambra padded out of the shower. There was no sign of Tom, so she quickly pulled on the robe and tied the belt tightly around her waist. She stretched her neck again. Her hotel bed was so incredibly uncomfortable, and she had been hunched over her computer far too much since she arrived. She was ridiculously stiff. Did that mean she would have to take up yoga and Pilates and all that crap? *Maybe I should start jogging,* she thought without enthusiasm. Shame you couldn't get into shape by working. She would be incredibly fit if that were the case.

She rubbed her neck, tried to stretch it.

"Stiff?"

She jumped. "I don't understand how you can be so quiet."

"Sorry. Old habit. Life and death, you know." He was wearing a T-shirt and pants. He handed her a glass of mineral water. "Your neck?"

"I guess I'm not made for sitting hunched over my computer all day."

He smiled. "The youth of today." He sipped from his own glass and gave her a dark look over the top of it. "Want a massage?"

"Are you kidding?" Ambra managed to keep her tone light, uncertain whether he was joking, but her shameless body was dancing with expectation, shouting: DO I WANT YOUR HUGE HANDS ALL OVER MY BODY? YESSS!

Tom shrugged, as though it made no difference to him, and Ambra realized she would probably regret it for the rest of her life if she didn't take him up on his offer.

"But you should know that I'm pretty great at it," he said nonchalantly.

"Maybe a little, then," she said, hoping she sounded cool enough, as though this was an everyday occurrence for her—accepting impulsive offers of physical contact. But, seriously, aside from sex and world peace, was there anything better than a massage?

"Sit down," he said, nodding to one of the chairs. She did as he said and leaned back, suddenly nervous, against the backrest. Tom moved behind her without a sound. It really was crazy how quiet he could be. Maybe this was a terrible idea. And maybe—probably—her judgment had been clouded by the heat, what she had been up to in the shower, and because it was *Tom*. But she really did like massages; she spent all the health and wellness money she got from the paper on appointments with people who would knead and pull at her misused muscles. Though this was almost *too* intimate, she thought. Tom wasn't an anonymous, certified spa masseur being paid to fake that they liked what they were doing. Tom was someone she reacted to physically. A man who . . .

She almost scooted out of her seat when she felt his hands on her shoulders through her robe.

"Do you want me to pull it down?" she asked, her voice hoarse. She cleared her throat. *All righty then, time to get yourself together.*

"No, it's fine," he mumbled, and his fingers moved in beneath the soft terry fabric at the collar. God, it felt incredible. Strong fingers, warm palms, a little roughness from his calluses.

"Though you should probably breathe," he said quietly as his fingers sought out yet another tender, overworked muscle group, moved across it, searched, stroked, pressed.

"That feels so good," she mumbled.

"Breathe," he repeated, and she obeyed.

He found yet another tender spot, and applied pressure with his determined fingers. He had big hands, and when his fingers found her neck muscles, Ambra heard herself groan. She couldn't stay quiet. Tom didn't say a word, just continued the massage. Other than her occasional stifled groans, the room was silent.

He worked his way down her neck, on to her shoulders, and it felt as if she were floating away. If she pretended he was a stranger, she found it much easier to relax. Soon enough, she wasn't thinking at all, just feeling. Her muscles softened until they were like butter. She had gone to heaven, she thought through the haze. His movements slowed down, a palm stroked her shoulder, and through her relaxed fog she noticed a change. A hand moved into her hair. Deft fingers worked their way through her curls, massaged her scalp. It was still a massage, but there was something different about it. A finger ran along her collarbone. She saw her breastbone rise beneath her robe, more quickly than before. He must have seen it too. A rough finger grazed her neck, stroking just beneath her ear, more a caress than anything else. All she could hear was the roar in her own ears, the sound of her blood surging and her heart fluttering against her ribs.

Tom's hand paused, a couple of warm fingers on her neck, one on her collarbone. Her mouth was dry, as though she'd forgotten to swallow for a long time; in fact, it was only a few seconds since he'd started touching her like this. She shifted gently in the chair, turned her head, felt her hair brush against his palm, saw his hand on her shoulder. Short, neat nails, dark strands of hair on the back of his hand, yet another of his countless scars.

She could barely breathe; everything was happening in slow motion as she turned her head and saw Tom's face over her shoulder.

"Nice?" he mumbled. Their eyes met, her with her robe now a little pulled down over her shoulders, him with his hand on her body.

"Very." She saw the bulge in his pants. Every time she breathed in, she saw his hand follow the movement. Every part of her was aware that Tom really did have his fingers on her bare skin; that she was completely naked beneath her robe; that his eyes, dark as the night, weren't leaving hers for a second; that he wasn't blinking; and that she didn't know what was going on. His fingers caressed her neck. She looked up at him again. She moved her shoulders slightly, and her robe slipped farther down her arms. She was breathing heavily, her eyes fixed on his.

"I shouldn't," he mumbled as his mouth approached hers, and

Ambra thought: Yes, you really should. And then his lips met hers, barely touched them, but it still sent a shockwave through her body and into every erogenous zone she had. She panted beneath his mouth. It moved across hers, she parted her lips, and he made a low sound. She twisted in her chair and placed a hand on his shoulder. She pulled him toward her without breaking the kiss, felt his hand move down, across her chest. Ambra stretched with all of her being, her entire body yearning toward that hand, and then, *of course,* the door to the sauna opened with a thud and Jill came out.

Tom pulled away and backed up.

Ambra was perfectly still.

"What's going on here?" Jill asked. "What did I miss?"

Ambra looked up at Tom. He turned away and opened a cupboard. Ambra pulled the robe up over her shoulders and got to her feet. "Nothing's going on," she said.

"I'm going to take a shower," said Jill. She studied them both. She always did have an uncanny ability to sense tension in the air. Foster kid damage. "What were you up to?"

"Nothing," Ambra repeated.

"Nothing," Tom said, closing the cupboard with a bang.

Jill raised an eyebrow but didn't say anything else, just stepped into the shower cubicle and pulled the door closed behind her.

Ambra looked over to Tom again, caught his eye in the mirrored door. There was a pained look on his face, as though he'd done something he really regretted. It was hard not to be annoyed at the man. Hadn't she already moved on from the whole Tom Lexington thing before he appeared out of nowhere wanting to see her? Yes, she had. She wasn't the one to suggest the sauna, the time together, the massage. It was him, him, him.

"I'll go up and make coffee," he said, quickly crossing the floor. He didn't look at her before he disappeared upstairs.

"So, what happened?" Jill asked when she came out of the shower. She untangled her hair with her fingers.

"Nothing, really. But I wish it had," Ambra added. "Even if it would've just been a one-time thing for him."

Jill gave her a pitying look. "No, you don't. You're terrible at meaningless sex. You have to be more like me, more hardened, to be able to handle relationships without any feelings getting in the way. And you have far too many feelings for that. It's tragic."

"Guess so," Ambra said gloomily. She didn't want feelings. She wanted to be cool and carefree. And she wanted to make out with Tom. "But you said I should have sex," she pointed out.

"Everyone should. But not with him."

She hated that Jill was probably right.

The door to the sauna swung open again.

Ambra and Jill looked at each other. They had completely forgotten Mattias. He scratched his chest and peered around. "Is everyone done with the sauna? Where's Tom?"

Jill, who took the opportunity to sit in one of the deep cane chairs, stretched out her legs and waved a hand in the air. "He went upstairs. He's a real social genius, your friend."

Mattias's eyes lingered on her legs. "Not everyone can be as smooth as me."

"You think? How smooth are you, exactly? If you don't mind me asking." Jill's eyes glittered dangerously.

Ambra sighed. She was virtually invisible when these two got going. She started to search for her clothes. Next time someone asked her to a sauna, she would say no thanks and lock herself in her room with a kilo of candy. She grabbed the last of her things, went into one of the toilets, and got dressed.

"I'm going up," she said when she came out, but she may as well have been talking to herself. Jill and Mattias were deep in some intense conversation, and neither of them heard her.

Well, she'd get her dessert in any case.

Chapter 21

The rest of the evening wasn't as tense as Tom feared.
It was way worse.

While Mattias served dessert and Tom made coffee, Ambra didn't say much. She helped to put the cups onto a tray, and when she went to fetch the milk, she paused by the refrigerator door. Tom realized she was looking at the picture of him and Ellinor, a photograph from their ten-year anniversary at Ellinor's parents' house. It was an old picture. He happened to bring it up to Kiruna with him, and he'd hung it on the refrigerator door without really giving it a second thought. He wished she hadn't seen it.

Ambra opened the refrigerator, took out the carton of milk, and kicked the door shut again. "Nice picture of you," she said breezily.

Did she mean it? Her tone was curt.

"What are you two whispering about?" Jill shouted from the table. Ambra carried the tray over. "Lay off," she replied to her sister, and then disappeared from the room.

Tom watched her leave. He hadn't handled any of this very well.

Tom added another log to the fire before he went back to the couch and sat down. If it wasn't for Jill and Mattias talking and laughing nonstop, the rest of the evening would have been deadly quiet.

". . . then he snorted cocaine all morning and was on the verge of missing the live broadcast. But all the old ladies like him, so now he's the main presenter on Channel One." Jill had her head cocked, and as far as Tom could tell, Mattias was genuinely interested in her crazy, tall tales about the Swedish celebrity elite. Maybe it really was fascinating to listen to gossip direct from such an informed source. But Tom couldn't concentrate. He glanced at Ambra, who was curled up at one end of the couch, listening with an absent expression on her face. She had probably heard all of Jill's stories before. She would nod politely at something Mattias said every now and then, but it was clear she had withdrawn into her own world.

Jill said something Tom couldn't hear, and Mattias laughed loudly.

"Want more coffee?" Tom asked, holding up the pot to Ambra.

"No, thanks, I'm fine," she said, her voice exaggeratedly polite. She smiled stiffly, and Tom couldn't think of anything else to ask her. Mattias was laughing loudly at something Jill said, and Ambra looked as if she wished she were a thousand miles away. Tom could hardly blame her. He'd acted like an idiot. It was as though he had suffered a temporary meltdown. A chemical reaction he couldn't contain. But Ambra's warm, fragrant skin beneath his fingers, those small, stifled sounds of enjoyment she made, they all made him want to kiss her. And then his body just took on a mind of its own and started thinking ahead, about considerably more than a kiss. About how it would feel to pick Ambra up from the wicker chair, for example, to feel her arms around his neck, her legs around his waist; slowly parting her robe and moving inside, skin against skin, making love to her against a wall, a table.

It was somewhere around then he should have stopped massaging her, of course. Instead, he bent down toward her inviting mouth without thinking of the consequences. Tom, who never did anything without a Plan B, C, or D, had leaned down to kiss Ambra Vinter without anything resembling a backup plan for everything that could go wrong. He really couldn't understand it. He'd never believed you could have feelings for two women at the same time, that it was just bullshit made up by men who wanted an excuse to cheat. He loved Ellinor, and winning her back was the only reason he was up here.

Ambra was attractive, there was no doubt about that, but he'd met attractive women before. Normally he didn't have trouble keeping his short-term attraction and long-term goals separate. He'd never cheated on Ellinor, never even came close. And that was the rub, at least for him. He had never deceived his woman. They did once have a long break, many years earlier, during which he had a couple of short relationships, just as he assumed Ellinor had. He wasn't a virgin when they first met, either. There were a number of sexual experiences from his youth that he definitely didn't want to have gone without. But ever since the worst of his teenage hormones died down, he had never allowed his dick decide what to do. As an operative, he was flexible, that was the very basis of being an elite soldier— adaptability and flexibility—but he didn't act on sudden impulses. Shit, he didn't even *have* sudden impulses. Or not before he met Ambra Vinter anyway.

"Ambra, you have some of those, too, don't you?" he heard Jill say.

"Sorry, I didn't catch that. What are you talking about?"

"Online haters," said Jill.

"Jill was talking about how much crap she gets on Instagram," Mattias added.

Ambra nodded. "Everyone does, journalists and artists, but women suffer more. And if you're young, it can be really terrible."

"What's done about it?" Mattias asked with a frown.

"Threats and hate toward women aren't exactly priorities," Jill said. "I have one troll who regularly threatens to cut off my breasts and rape me. With a hammer and a broken bottle, most recently. The police have dropped the case every single time, so now I don't even bother reporting it."

"Is it the same for you, Ambra?" Mattias asked.

"Yeah. Some of them are really violent. Several appear again and again."

"But what do your bosses say?" Tom asked. He was leaning forward with his forearms on his thighs, studying her seriously.

She shrugged, a gesture that could have meant absolutely anything. Did she get threats? He would love to have a word with her haters, if that was the case. Ideally with the assistance of a baseball bat.

She was curled up even smaller in the corner of the sofa, with her feet tucked up beneath her and her hands pulled inside her sleeves.

Tom got up, grabbed a blanket, and handed it to her.

"Thanks," she said, draping it over her legs. Her hair was dry now, and curlier than ever. Sitting like that, she looked ridiculously young, more like a teenager than a journalist with one of the country's biggest papers. Her entire being was a study in contrasts. On one hand, a cynical reporter who covered gang murders, natural disasters, and abuse. On the other, a young woman who had never been to a sauna or seen the Northern Lights. He put down his cup and wished he could think of something to say.

Ambra reached across the coffee table and grabbed her cell phone, just to avoid Tom's gaze for a while. Jill was laughing again, and Mattias was grinning. The evening really was becoming unbearable. She was trying her best, but her mood had plummeted rapidly. She tried to catch Jill's eye to signal that she wanted to leave, but her sister was far too busy flirting with Mattias. Jesus, they were going for it. Her phone buzzed, and she read the newsflash.

"Did something happen?" Tom asked, and she wished she didn't feel a thrill every time she heard his low voice say something.

She nodded and put down her cell phone. "Serious car crash in Skåne."

"They've been having really bad weather down there."

"Yeah."

"Though it's been pretty bad up here, too."

"Yeah."

It was an idiotic conversation, as if they were two strangers in an elevator or something. She thought about the picture on the refrigerator. Tom looked away, and she curled up beneath the blanket, wishing she'd have the guts to bring up what had happened. What was the etiquette after you just happened to kiss someone anyway? And what was Tom Lexington up to? Was he a player after all? He seemed so straight-up, but then he went and kissed her like that, and he kept pictures of Ellinor in his kitchen, and Ambra didn't understand a thing. Was there something between them or not? Didn't he realize the mixed signals he was giving her? And what about her— how could she even get herself into this bizarre situation? She glared at Jill, who was in the process of uploading her hundredth Instagram picture, this time of Mattias's lingonberry cheesecake.

Freja, who'd been dozing by the fire up to that point, lifted her head, got up, sniffed Jill, and then moved on to Mattias, who was busy brushing something from Jill's shoulder. She reached Ambra, sniffed the rug, and then padded away and expectantly sat down by Tom's feet.

"I'll take the dog out," he said. He seemed grateful to get away.

* * *

Once he left, Ambra moved around the living room as Jill talked about a British talk show she had been on. Ambra had just taken a paperback down from a shelf and started to read the back cover when she heard Tom stamping his feet in the hallway, and Freja came charging back into the room. She ran over to Ambra. Her fur was cold. "Good to get out?" she asked, scratching the dog behind the ear. Freja closed her eyes and seemed to be enjoying it, so she petted her a little more. When she eventually looked up, she realized Tom was watching her.

"It's getting late," she said.

He didn't reply.

"Jill, do you think we could call Ludvig? Ask him to come get us?"

"Already?" Jill seemed surprised.

"I have to get up early," she said. Somehow, she had managed to book a seat back to Stockholm, and right now she wanted to leave this part of the world more than ever.

"When does your plane leave?"

"After lunch, but I need to work first," she lied.

Jill pulled a face.

Ambra wearily shook her head. "Can we just go?"

Jill made the call, and after a seemingly endless fifteen minutes, she said: "He's here now."

Thank God.

They said their good-byes in the hallway. Mattias helped Jill with her coat; Tom held out Ambra's jacket and helped her pull it on. She hurried to push her arms into the sleeves and to move away. They exchanged a few quick hugs and then they were finally outside.

Ambra slumped into the backseat. She rested her head against the window. She was completely exhausted.

"Why were you so weird?" Jill asked while she pointed out directions to Ludvig.

"I'm tired," Ambra replied dismissively. She *was* tired, tired of this whole Kiruna adventure. She wanted to get home, back to normal life, to the office. Once she was home, she would try dating again, she promised herself. Normal, uncomplicated, available men.

"I had a great time anyway. Those two are really fun, or Mattias was. You were so cold to Tom, though. What happened between you?"

Ambra gave her a cold look. "I'm surprised you even noticed. You spent the whole night flirting with Mattias. I thought you said you didn't have anything in common."

"We don't. It was a bit of harmless flirting. Why are you so blue? What were you expecting?"

"I don't know."

"You said it yourself, he has a girl."

"An ex," she pointed out. "Who has a boyfriend."

"Yeah, yeah, I still think you should be happy to get rid of him. Try to think of it like that."

She hated it when Jill did this, argued against her feelings. "Could you let me be sad for a while before you start all the positive pep talks?"

"But no man is worth feeling sad over." Jill sounded as if she genuinely didn't understand. She hit the back of the driver's seat with one hand. "Ludvig! You need to turn off soon!"

"I know. I still have a GPS," Ludvig replied grumpily.

"Turn off here," Jill said, waving her hand.

"I *knoooow*."

Ambra tried to ignore their constant bickering by looking out the window, staring at snow-covered pines as they rushed by.

She would definitely let it go. Really soon. Nothing had even happened, she told herself as they left kilometer after kilometer of forest behind them. Everything was normal. There was no reason to feel like a failure. No reason to be disappointed. Maybe she just misunderstood everything and Tom and Mattias were discussing how awkward she was at that very moment. She just needed to get back on her feet. Back in the saddle.

It was a horrible expression. One that foster parent after foster parent had used whenever she fell, whenever she hurt herself, whenever someone pushed her, whenever she was sad. "Back in the saddle, Ambra. Dry those tears, Ambra. Pay no attention to her, she'll stop soon enough."

Jill was right, she just needed to let it go.

She would do it, she really would. She just needed to work out how first. How to ignore her reactions, her feelings. How to ignore the fact that it genuinely *hurt*.

Back in the saddle, Ambra.

She leaned her forehead against the window and watched the forest rush past, silent, dark, and threatening.

Chapter 22

Ambra stowed her computer into her bag. She quickly double-checked the cupboards, the bathroom, and beneath the bed to make sure she hadn't forgotten anything, but everything was packed away. *It will be good to go home,* she thought as she pulled on her jacket, to leave Kiruna and all its failures and memories behind her. She had managed to talk her way into a late checkout and decided on another quick trip that morning to the house where the Sventins lived, again on a whim. The place still looked completely abandoned, and she wasn't even sure what she was hoping to achieve by going back. She had left another message with the social worker and then returned to the hotel to pack up the last of her things.

She would make it in to the office that afternoon and had promised to submit an article later that day, so Grace was no longer pissed. The taxi she ordered wouldn't be coming for a while, and so she lay down on her bed with her cell phone, scrolling through her news feeds. The world seemed to be in one piece. Unless you lived in Syria, that was. She absentmindedly opened up Jill's Instagram feed. Her sister had uploaded pictures of yesterday evening. Champagne glasses, an open fire, but also a picture where Tom was visible in the background. He probably wouldn't appreciate that, she thought with a smirk. When she read through the comments, she saw how hate filled they were. Jill hadn't been exaggerating, some of them really were hair-raising. Ambra reported the worst of the comments and put down her phone. She realized that the trip to Kiruna had been good in one sense: For the first time in a long while, she felt like she wanted to meet someone. A man, that is.

An acquaintance from another paper had been in touch over Twitter recently, asking if she wanted to go out. Should she say yes and arrange to go for a coffee with him once she was back in Stockholm? It would do her good to get out more. Stand up to her fears, do something other than work.

It was also good to have met Elsa. Ambra had taught the older woman how to send text messages and take pictures with her cell phone, and after a few minor autocorrect errors, they now sent short messages to one another. Elsa seemed especially fond of the emoji function, and her latest message to Ambra was full of flowers, planes, and waving hands.

The small frog from Elsa was wrapped up in a pair of socks in her purse. She would put it on her bedside table, alongside the only photograph she had of her parents and an insanely expensive and impractical candlestick from the super exclusive Swedish store Svenskt Tenn that Jill once gave her.

She would just have to focus on the positives of coming up here and try to repress the rest. In a few days' time, she wouldn't care anymore. And by this time next year, it would be nothing but another bizarre memory among all the others she'd collected over the years. One of many in the memory bank. Do you remember when you did a live TV report with your sweater inside out, ha ha? Or when you had to step in to do an interview with a furious politician and she tore strips off of you? Ha ha. Or, funniest of all, when you thought that ex-soldier in Kiruna liked you? Ha ha haaaa.

She heard a knock at the door. Ambra assumed it must be the cleaning staff wanting to come in, because she had waited until the last minute to leave her room.

"Come in," she said, propping herself up on her elbows. When no one answered, she got up and went over to the door.

Tom Lexington.

You have got to be kidding me.

"Hi there," he said, filling the entire door frame with his size and presence.

Ambra lowered her hand to the handle and squeezed the metal tight. This was where she was meant to come up with something witty to say. Or slam the door.

"Hi," was all she managed.

He peered over her shoulder, into the room where her luggage was packed and ready.

"Are you leaving?"

"My cab will be here soon."

He pushed his hands into his pockets and leaned against the door frame.

"I wanted to stop by before you left," he said.

She dragged the tip of her shoe against the floor. "You could've called. Or sent a message."

"Guess so," he said.

She was silent. Dragged her foot again, debated for a moment, and then resigned herself to it. She may as well come out and say it. She braced herself. "Sorry I was in such a bad mood yesterday."

He shook his head. "It was my fault. You don't have anything to apologize for. I don't know what happened. I shouldn't have, you know . . ."

"It doesn't matter," she said.

"You're cool, that's what I mean. It's been fun, spending time together these past few days. And it did me good, to get out, to talk with you. It really meant a lot to me. I'm grateful for it. But I told you about my situation."

Jesus, she wasn't sure how much more of this apology she could handle. "You don't need to explain," she said, but he continued anyway.

"I don't know what happened. I lay awake all night thinking about it. I don't want you to think I had any ulterior motive. I haven't really been myself lately, you know, and the sauna was hot, and maybe it was the wine . . ."

"It's okay, Tom," she said, resting her cheek against the open door. She wasn't pissed, she wasn't angry. It *was* okay. Jill was right, this whole being someone's comfort lay thing wasn't really for her. She'd been attracted to Tom and then read her own feelings into the situation. Yes, she felt embarrassed, stupid. But they were *her* feelings, not his. No big deal. She would go home and sleep with the Twitter journalist instead, she decided.

"Thanks for coming by," she said.

"It didn't feel right to part on bad terms."

"Yeah," she agreed.

"Maybe we can be friends?"

"Sure. Friends, sure." She groaned inside.

He seemed relieved. "I can carry those down for you," he said, pointing to her bags.

After a short pause, she said yes; she didn't want to seem ungrateful now that they were apparently going to be *friends*. They took the elevator down to the lobby, where she quickly checked out, and then they found themselves standing outside the hotel.

"You don't need to wait with me," she eventually said, hoping he would get the message.

He brushed some snow from his face. A number of flakes had settled in his black hair, small white stars in the darkness.

"That's what friends do, isn't it? Wait with one another."

"Suppose so."

They waited.

And waited.

"It's cold," she said, huddling up inside her jacket. She was about to freeze to death. "Maybe we should wait inside?"

"There's no cab coming," he said firmly.

"It's coming," she said.

"Nope." He picked up her bag and started to make his way toward the parking lot.

"What are you doing?" she shouted, jogging after him. "The cab will be here any minute."

"It's not coming." He threw her bag into what she recognized as his car.

"Am I being kidnapped?" she asked, irritated.

He closed the trunk lid, opened the passenger side door and held it open for her. "Jump in, I'll give you a ride."

"But the cab . . ."

"Get in."

Tom pulled up outside the Kiruna airport fifteen minutes later. He parked by the terminal building, climbed out of the car, and lifted Ambra's bag from the trunk.

"I can take it," she said, holding out a hand.

"I'll carry it in for you," he said decidedly, ignoring the obstinate look in her eye. The bag was heavy, and he still felt guilty; he needed to do something for her.

She walked ahead of him, and Tom followed her jerky movements with his eyes. It was good they had straightened things out, that they could part as friends.

Tom waited as she went to pick up her boarding pass. She was taking her bag as hand luggage, and he knew she had her beloved computer inside. Strange how quickly you could get to know a person.

She turned around.

"So," she said.

So.

New Year's Eve was approaching, and the airport was busy. All around them, people were checking in bags, skis, and strollers. "Thanks for the ride," Ambra said as Tom held out his hand to her. She had pulled off her hat when they went inside, and her hair was a wild mass around her face.

He told himself he was just going to straighten one particularly unruly lock, but somehow his hand wasn't satisfied with that. After he straightened that one curl and saw it bounce back, his hand continued the movement. Suddenly, he found himself stroking her cheek in a tender, lingering gesture. She froze and stared at him. His fingertips were coarse, so he kept his touch gentle, just wanting to see whether she was as soft as he remembered.

She was.

He let his fingers rest against her silken skin.

Standing in the middle of Kiruna's little airport, stroking Ambra's cheek, should have felt like a mistake, but it didn't. It felt like the smartest thing Tom had done in a long time.

"What are you doing?" she mumbled, her brow furrowed. Tom's entire palm was on her cheek now, however that had happened. Ambra blinked slowly, but otherwise she held his gaze. She didn't seem to be a particularly vain woman, and he assumed that those long black lashes of hers were real.

"Thanks for the past few days," he said quietly.

She inhaled, as though she had forgotten to breathe and was now compensating for it with one long, deep breath.

"Tom?" she said.

"Yeah?"

He should stop touching her. But Ambra looked up at him, her eyes like mountain lakes and birch glades in spring. And then it felt as if she was moving her cheek against his palm, only a slight movement but enough encouragement for Tom's fingers to slide back toward the nape of her neck, in beneath her curly hair. It was like touching a cat or mink fur, she was so incredibly smooth, and he heard someone breathe out and knew that the sigh had come from him.

Point of no return.

Every operation Tom had ever been on had one, a point of no return, and he was close.

Then, once Ambra was on her plane to Stockholm and disappeared from his life, possibly for good, her scent would linger on his fingers as a reminder, he thought. He passed the point where he might have been able to turn back, took one last step and held on to her, not hard but determinedly, lowered his mouth to hers, and then, finally, finally, he kissed her. Finally got to continue what he'd started yesterday, dreamed of last night. His mouth moved against hers. Their lips met, tentatively. He angled his head, gently brushed his tongue against her lower lip, and she allowed him in, parted her lips, invited him to taste her, to feel her welcoming warmth.

Tom pulled her closer, so firmly that he heard her pant; pressed her to him, felt her mold to his shape, felt a leg slip between his thighs. His hands moved in, beneath her coat, around her back, down past her waist, and onto her hips. He grabbed her ass and pulled her even closer, kissed her properly now. She was still just a stranger to him, but his hands and body were fast learners, enjoying the fact that she had a soft, round ass beneath her jeans, passionate arms exploring his body, and an eager mouth. She clung to him as though they were in the middle of a natural disaster and he was her only hope of survival. Tom moved one hand between their bodies and raised it to her breast, cupped the soft weight of it. She groaned faintly against his mouth, made that feminine movement of pressing her breast against his hand, and then he groaned, too, ran his thumb over her nipple, which he felt harden through her layers of clothing.

They kissed like that, passionately and erotically, until he sensed a change in her. She stopped moving in his arms, gently pulled away, placed one hand on his chest, and pushed him back. She didn't say anything, just breathed heavily, and studied him as though she was trying to understand what had just happened.

"What happened to being friends?" she said with a wry smile.

Good question.

"I have no idea," he said, pushing one of those incessant locks of hair from her face. His finger followed her temple, her cheek, and then wandered down towards her collarbone. She gave off such a strong, energetic impression that he didn't always notice how young she looked. Every time she took a breath, her collarbone rose and fell beneath his hand. He could sense all her vulnerable points, her pulse, her throat, her veins.

"This was a bad idea," she said, though she didn't sound too convinced.

"Yeah," he replied, taking her face in his hands and kissing her again—hard, eager, with an open mouth and tongue. Her palms flew up to his chest, onto his arms, and then around his neck, where they nestled into his hair. Tom groaned as Ambra pushed her body against his again. He hadn't realized quite how starved he was when it came to physical contact. He pressed his mouth against hers, used his tongue, kissed her recklessly, uncontrollably, heard her whimper.

And then someone swerved to avoid something in the crowded departures hall; maybe it was a baggage cart, maybe someone stumbled and bumped into Ambra. Tom's arms wrapped around her protectively.

"Sorry," said the woman who had bumped into her.

"No worries," Ambra mumbled.

The woman moved on, and Ambra laid her cheek against his chest. Tom's hands were clasped behind her back, his chin in her hair, and he breathed in the scent of her. She shifted gently but stayed in his embrace, now with her nose against his breastbone. How long had they been making out like teenagers? A minute? Five? Even longer? He had no idea. It was as if everything his brain usually kept track of—his surroundings, the way people were moving, how much time had passed—ceased to exist. He let go of her, took a step back, and rubbed his face. A loudspeaker barked that the flight to Stockholm was now boarding.

She straightened her clothes. "That's me," she said.

"Yeah."

Her face was flushed, her mouth looked like it had just been kissed, and he felt a jolt in his heart. They would probably never see each other again. "Hope you have a good flight home," he mumbled.

She smiled, turned, and walked away toward security.

Tom waited, confident she would turn around. But she didn't, and then she was gone.

Gone.

Chapter 23

After Ambra's plane landed, she took the Arlanda Express train into Stockholm. Now that she was on her way to the office, Grace was calming down. Ambra had spent the whole journey from Kiruna working. She replied to e-mails, wrote a few short pieces she sent as soon as she had Wi-Fi, and even started sketching out two more articles that Grace wanted her to turn in after lunch.

She barely thought about the kiss in the airport.

Aside from the fact she thought about it nonstop.

She stepped from the train and headed toward the *Aftonbladet* building.

It had obviously been a farewell kiss, and she didn't expect anything more; no follow-up calls or continuation of any kind. It was perfectly clear that Tom wasn't serious about her. But still. What a fairy-tale kiss. And what an inexplicable man Tom Lexington was. She knew she should be annoyed that he couldn't decide whether they should be friends or make out. But it was hard to be angry at someone who had just given you the best kiss of your life. Because while Tom Lexington might be incomprehensible, damaged, and in love with the sprightly, blond Ellinor, the man knew how to kiss. What they'd shared in the airport in Kiruna easily came first, second, and third on Ambra's list of Best Kisses of My Life.

She swiped her pass to get into the building, took the elevator to the seventh floor, said hi to the others on the Breaking News desk, and then slumped into her seat, switched on all of her screens, and logged in.

"Welcome back," Grace said, using her hand to cover the microphone on her headset.

Ambra said hi, then went to get a cup of coffee, grabbed the last banana from the bowl and a few leftover dark chocolate pralines from a box (did anyone like dark chocolate, really?), and returned to her desk.

Back in her seat, she quickly checked her Twitter feed. The journalist from *Dagens Nyheter,* Henrik Stål, hadn't replied to her message about going for a coffee. She really wasn't having much luck lately.

Last time she had sex was also with another journalist. They dated all summer. Dinners, long conversations about Important Things, and then sex, always at her place. He talked trash about his ex-wife every time, and then he'd gone back to her, just in time for fall. According to his most recent Facebook update, they were in love, had never been happier, and were going to renew their wedding vows in Dubai.

How nice for them.

At the Christmas party before last, Ambra had flirted intensely with one of the IT guys. He was engaged now. To a twenty-year-old trainee from the Viral desk. Ambra wouldn't go so far as to say it was a pattern, that the men she was more or less interested in ended up dumping her, moving on, and meeting the love of their life; that would be too depressing. But what was it people always said? The lowest common denominator in all your failed relationships is you.

The question was whether there were more men like Tom. Like him, only, well—*available*. Did they exist?

Grace finally hung up. "What's going on?" she asked with her eyes on her own monitor. That was how things were. All conversations were subordinate to the news feed.

"We've got a traffic accident at the top of the Södertälje Bridge. And then new pictures of Princess Estelle in the lineup. Do you have a couple of minutes?"

Grace glanced around. "Couch?"

They sat down on the couch, both their cell phones facing up, ready to act if anything happened.

"Okay, this thing about the foster family," Ambra began.

Grace nodded and started to peel an orange. The scent of citrus spread through the air. "I thought about what you said, I promise. But listen, that kind of social services thing—you know how it can bounce back. It sounds like the kind of story that might blow up in our faces. The more you dig into it, the more they close ranks, and then you'll find yourself being reported by everyone." Grace put a slice of the orange into her mouth. "Is there any particular reason why you're so into this story?"

No one at the paper knew about her background. In fact, she rarely talked about her childhood at all. It was odd how much she'd blabbed in Kiruna. But something had happened up there. Not just with Tom, but with her. The memories came flooding back. It was Esaias Sventin's fault that her hearing was bad, that she didn't own anything belonging to her parents, that she didn't trust people. She was a grown woman now, and she could live with that. But the idea that he and Rakel might be fostering other children . . . that they were allowed to go on . . .

"I think it could be a good piece, I just need a little time," she replied neutrally.

Grace chewed and then swallowed. "Have you been thinking about the position with Investigative?"

Ambra nodded.

"I think you'd fit in well there, even though I don't want to lose you from Breaking News. But you need to come up with something better than this story about social services. You know how many people want that job."

Oh, Ambra knew. They both looked over to Oliver Holm on the Society desk. The editor-in-chief, Dan Persson, was standing beside him. The young guys of the office were gathered around him, laughing and slapping each other on the shoulders.

"Did you have anything else?" Grace asked.

Ambra shook her head. She couldn't help but think of Tom Lexington and his mysterious background. What had he been through? And: was there a story there? A story good enough for an Investigative piece? She wanted to ask Grace. Grace was phenomenal at finding angles and judging how newsworthy a story was, but Tom had told her those things in confidence. Ambra reluctantly held back. Oliver laughed again.

"You did a good job with the old lady," Grace said, gathering up the orange peel.

"Elsa Svensson."

"Right. Make sure you catch up your hours today."

"Grace, there's one more thing. Do you know anything about elite Swedish soldiers?"

"Why?"

"I met a guy who works in private security. You know, kidnapping courses, bodyguards, that kind of thing."

"That whole area's a jungle, it's completely unregulated. I know the UN keeps an eye on some of them. That there have been attacks abroad. That there's been talk of international legislation."

Ambra was impressed. That was Grace to a tee. A cornucopia of general knowledge.

Grace's phone started to flash on the table. "Karsten Lundqvist's our expert in that kind of thing. He wrote about it last year, I think. Talk to him," Grace said as she picked up her phone. Ambra's started to buzz at the same moment.

Huge fire in asylum centre, Central News Agency reports.

"We'll run it as a flash," Grace said, getting to her feet.

Ambra was already moving.

"Do we have any pictures? Video?" Grace shouted, receiving a thumbs-up in reply. Ambra got down to work.

When Ambra arrived home much too late two days later, the day before New Year's Eve, both her refrigerator and freezer were empty. She had been working virtually nonstop, and she was exhausted. She listlessly stared at the empty shelves in the refrigerator. Oh, and it was her birthday, too.

She always steeled herself for the day in advance. Told herself it would be okay. That it was just like any other day. All that was true.

But the fact still remained.

Today was her birthday, and she felt like the loneliest person on earth.

Eventually, she managed to find some crisp bread and a jar of mackerel in tomato sauce. She put the open sandwiches onto a plate and sat down on the couch.

Jill had forgotten, of course. As usual. It was stupid to feel so low, really. She didn't have any expectations; no one even knew what day it was. Her birthday wasn't something that had ever been celebrated. Constant upheavals and different family situations weren't exactly conducive to cozy parties or birthday dinners. She knew of people who had big family celebrations, and she'd seen them in movies and on social media, studied the way people interacted, talked, laughed, passed plates to one another. Sunday dinners. Family gatherings. Inside jokes and homemade desserts.

But none of that was for her.

She *knew* that.

She took out her computer, thinking she should have just stayed at work. An e-mail pinged into her in-box. She clicked to open it.

Congratulations Ambra Vinter, the subject line read.

She opened the e-mail.

> Hi Ambra,
> Happy birthday. We wanted to celebrate by offer-
> ing you a 10% discount on anything in our shop.
> Best, Anton at Sexoteket AB.

She studied the accompanying pictures. Dildos in a range of "girly" colors. Underwear that tasted like chocolate. Something she couldn't make out at first but then realized were "authentic feeling" fake breasts.

And here she was, thinking no one cared. Sexoteket clearly did. She had bought something from the online sex shop once, a long time ago. It wasn't even anything interesting, just a book she needed for an article that she couldn't find anywhere else. But now they sent her an e-mail every year. She thought about replying to Anton and asking him to remove her from their mailing list, but instead she closed the lid of her computer, nibbled at her crisp bread, and scrolled through Instagram. People were out for dinner with their partners, showing off their cute kids, away on weekend trips. A famous author was out at a restaurant with her girl gang. An artist, who according to Jill self-medicated with psychopharmaceuticals and kept her weight down using cocaine, had uploaded some pictures of raw food.

Ambra brushed the crumbs from her chest. She should at least have bought wine. She shuffled out to her tiny kitchen. She'd been given a bottle of liqueur at some point, hadn't she? Jill gave it to her, though she didn't know why. There it was, neon and unopened. Should she? Ambra found a clean egg cup and took it and the bottle back to the couch. She turned on the TV and started one of her favorite episodes of *Lyxfällan,* a Swedish reality TV show about people in dire financial straits who were helped back on track by two angry coaches. A young man cried when he was forced to sell his video games.

She poured the liqueur into the egg cup, toasted herself, and then drank it in one go. Refilled it and discovered that if she held her breath while she drank, she practically couldn't taste it.

After the third shot, she went back to the kitchen and fetched a bigger glass. You could say what you liked about liqueur, but the more of it you drank, the better it tasted.

Chapter 24

Tom placed the last of his groceries into the bag. Swedish flatbread, dog food, fruit. The store was almost empty; everyone was probably at home making dinner, watching TV, hanging out with their friends, or whatever else normal people without posttraumatic stress disorder did in the days between Christmas and New Year.

"Hey," he heard behind him.

He turned toward the familiar voice. "Hi, Ellinor," he said, pausing with his bag in his hand. Ellinor was carrying a bag from the Swedish liquor store, Systembolaget, and he could make out a bottle of champagne. Right, it was New Year's Eve tomorrow. "You on the way out too?" she asked. Tom nodded, and they left the store together.

"Hi, Freja." She laughed when the dog, which had been waiting outside, started wagging her tail. Somehow he still had Freja. He wasn't sure how it had happened, but he'd put off calling Ellinor and Nilas. By now, he looked forward to the regular walks and the exercise he got from having the dog.

"How are you two doing? She looks much happier."

"We're fine," he replied as he untied the dog. Ellinor followed him to his car. If she asked to take Freja back, then of course he would hand her over without hesitation. But it made no difference to him if he kept her awhile. He opened the trunk and put the bags inside. Freja was already waiting by the passenger side door.

"Anyway, I just wanted to say hi," said Ellinor. "You seem happier too." She laid a gentle hand on his arm and smiled at him. "Happy New Year, Tom." And then she left.

He sat down in the car and started the engine, but something resembling hope suddenly filled his body. Freja, who loved sitting up front next to him, barked. He reached out and petted her head. "Did you hear that? Ellinor said I looked happier." It was a minor victory. He would improve upon it. No more drinking from now on.

"Come on," he said when they pulled up at the house. Freja jumped from the car and started sniffing around in the snow. Tom carried the groceries inside and unpacked the fruit, vegetables, and juice. He was eating better now, he realized. It wasn't a conscious decision; it had just happened. He was getting more exercise, too, thanks to Freja.

He moved around the house, tidying up a little, and glanced at the corner of the couch where Ambra had sat. Their kiss was nice, the one at the airport; a fucking fantastic kiss, actually.

He continued toward the sauna, made sure everything was locked up. He spotted something white in one of the booths. When he lifted the delicate object down from the hook, he realized it was a white camisole. He caught a whiff of perfume and immediately recognized the scent. Ambra. It was hers. She had gotten dressed quickly after the massage. She must have forgotten it. He stood still for a moment, the soft white top in his hand, and then he climbed the stairs, deep in thought.

He poured a glass of juice and looked out the kitchen window. It felt good to have the house to himself. Mattias had left for Stockholm the day after the sauna, and he didn't miss him. But he could see Ambra before him, the way she stood here, in his kitchen, sipping champagne with a glimmer in her eye. He draped the camisole over the back of a chair and went to find his cell phone. He quickly wrote: *Hey. How are you? Tom.*

He hit SEND. Paused with the phone in his hand. Should he have written anything else? Would she reply?

His phone made a faint buzzing sound. He took the juice and his cell phone into the living room, wanting to sit down on the couch and read the message in peace and quiet. He peered at the display expectantly.

I'm fine, thanks. You?

He quickly replied: *Good, thanks.*

He hit SEND again, but suddenly worried he'd been too short. He should have said something else. He wrote: *What're you up to?*

Was she in Stockholm now? He wondered where in the capital she lived. A small apartment in the center of town? A new condo in one of the suburbs? Or did she live with someone? Another message beeped. He had turned up the volume so he didn't miss anything. She replied: *Nothing.*

He sat like that, with the phone in his hand, thinking. She wasn't very talkative. Was she busy? Pissed? Should he have gotten in touch sooner? Why was he doing it now? He scratched his forehead. He wasn't used to trying to work out the meaning behind a single word. But if she didn't want him to keep messaging her, she would let him know, wouldn't she? Yes, he decided, and so he wrote: *Nothing?*

It took her a while to reply, and Tom got up from the couch. He stacked wood in the fireplace, lit it, waited impatiently, finally heard her reply arrive. The message was longer this time: *I'm watching a TV show. People who've completely ruined their finances get help from two angry men who make them feel guilty. It's awful really, but it's my vice. One of them anyway.*

He wasn't sure whether she was joking, so he asked: *They show that kind of thing on TV?*

He sat with the phone in his hand, waiting. Another message arrived: *You've never seen Lyxfällan?*

He typed a quick reply: *I don't watch TV much.*

Her reply came immediately: *Snob.*

Tom laughed. Freja raised her head and gave him a confused look. His phone beeped again: *I'm drinking liqueur. I never drink.*

He could almost hear her voice when he read those words. He smiled and typed: *You did at Christmas. You were drunk.*

Long pause. Maybe it was a bad idea to bring up that evening? But he liked the memory. Ambra was cute when she was drunk. She looked relaxed and happy. Like she did after the sauna. And after the kiss. She replied: *Yeah, true. I drank a whole lot up there. Weird Kiruna.*

Hmm. What should he say now? He wasn't so used to this. Making small talk. And through a phone. Should he bring up the kiss? Though maybe she'd forgotten it. Another message arrived. This time, it read: *Today's my birthday.*

Tom read her words several times. Was she out celebrating? Or did she have people over for a birthday dinner? But she'd mentioned TV, so something told him she was alone. He took a chance and wrote: *Can I call you?*

He sat there with the phone in his hand, waiting. She didn't reply.

Ambra looked down at the phone in her hand. Read the latest message from Tom over and over again. *Can I call you?* She wasn't expecting that. But then she wasn't planning to tell him it was her birthday, either. She glanced at the bottle of liqueur. The level of liquid was now considerably lower, which probably meant that technically she was drunk again and incapable of good judgment. Did she want to talk to Tom? She thought for a while before she wrote: *Yeah.*

Of course she wanted to talk to him. Their text conversation was the best thing to happen to her all day.

Her phone immediately started ringing.

"Happy birthday," he said when she answered. "Am I interrupting anything?"

He had a good phone voice. Calm and deep.

"Thanks. And no. I'm just chillin' at home."

"Can I ask how old you are?"

"Twenty-nine. One more year to thirty."

"Practically a baby."

"How old are you?" she asked.

"I'll be thirty-seven next birthday. Do you hate birthdays too?"

"Not quite that bad. What are you up to?"

"I'm at home. Sitting on the couch."

If she closed her eyes, she could just see Tom in front of her. Long legs outstretched, probably wearing black. She thought she could hear crackling. Did he have a fire going? Was there any more cozy sound than crackling, breaking wood in an open fire?

"The Northern Lights are visible again tonight. Do you have snow in Stockholm?" he asked.

"A little. Not like in Kiruna." And in that instant, Ambra experienced something she would have never expected: a longing for Kiruna.

"Do you have any plans for this evening?" he asked.

Ambra glanced at her watch. It was eight. She was planning to go to bed at nine so that this lousy day could come to an end. "Not really."

"What have you been doing since you got back from Kiruna?"

She put down the liqueur and lay back on the couch, curled up with the phone and Tom's voice. "Working, mostly. Is Mattias still there?"

"No, he left the same day as you. I haven't spoken to him since."

The kiss at the airport hung between them. He hadn't mentioned it. Should she? Was it better to pretend nothing had happened or to nonchalantly say, thanks for the kiss by the way, I've been thinking about it pretty much nonstop these past few days. She eventually settled for, "Is Mattias your best friend?"

"No. Maybe in the past, but our relationship is a little more complicated than that."

Ambra thought that Tom seemed to have a lot of complicated relationships, but who was she to judge. Her own relationships weren't exactly light and breezy. "So who is your best friend, then?"

If he said Ellinor, she would hang up, she decided. But he was silent up there in Kiruna.

"Oddly enough, it's probably my friend David. We've known one another a long time. He was a huge support when I got back to Sweden. He's the kind of friend who's there for you, one hundred percent. But we're not in touch right now. Not after Chad."

It took Ambra a moment to process what Tom had just said. The journalist in her reared her head through the haze of alcohol. She sat up on the couch, felt the goose bumps on her arms. "Chad? What were you doing there?"

Long silence.

"You don't have to tell me—forget I even asked," she eventually said; she both did and didn't want to pump him for information.

She heard him take a deep breath. "I was there on a job last summer. I was taken prisoner."

That wasn't quite what she was expecting. "Who by?"

Long silence. "Local thugs."

"Shit."

"Yeah."

"For how long?"

"A long time. Listen, I probably shouldn't be talking about this."

"It's okay," she said. "I've drunk so much liqueur that I'll probably forget everything we talk about by tomorrow."

He made a low noise. If she didn't know better, she would have thought he was laughing.

"What do you like about David?" she asked as she tried to find a notepad and a pen. She wondered what was required of a man to be Tom Lexington's best friend.

"We've known each other a long time. He's reliable, loyal. A real friend."

"But you lost contact?"

"It's complicated."

Of course.

"So who's *your* best friend?" he asked.

"Jill, I guess. Though it's complicated for me too. Jill travels a lot."

"And you're pretty different too?"

Aha, so he had noticed. "Yeah, we're pretty different. I like a lot of people at work, but I don't spend much time with colleagues." *I should get better at it,* she thought. What was she afraid of?

"No one else?"

"Nope. I moved around a bunch during my childhood, different foster homes all the time, so I never really managed to make friends before it was time to leave. Plus, I was ridiculously shy." She lay down with the armrest beneath her neck. "Being a grown-up is easier. Do you still have Freja?"

"She's here. I should probably take her out now."

"Thanks for calling to say happy birthday," she said.

"It was good to talk to you. Hope the rest of your birthday is good."

"You too." She pulled a face. "I mean, I hope you have a good evening."

After they hung up, Ambra lay on her side on the couch. She pushed a pillow beneath her cheek and reached for the remote to turn up the volume on the TV again. She glanced at her notebook on the coffee table. She had completely forgotten about it. She picked it up. *Chad,* she read, followed by two exclamation marks. The whole thing was underlined with a thick line. Beneath that, she had sloppily written, *Is he a bad guy??*

She poured a little more liqueur and sipped it as yet another episode of *Lyxfällan* came on. But her thoughts were elsewhere. Why the hell was Tom in Chad?

Chapter 25

"What do we have on the fire in Kista?" Grace asked the next morning.

Always these fires.

"I talked to the police. They suspect arson," Ambra replied.

"Perfect. Could you write something on it?"

"Already am."

Ambra quickly finished the piece and sent it to the online editor, who published it on the website. *Aftonbladet* had long since moved almost completely online. They still ran a paper edition, but the focus was on the Internet. That was where they were visible, and everyone fought to be featured at the top of "page one." Grace was the bottle-neck through which all news passed.

Ambra started on her next piece, a train crash in Hallsberg. It was nine o'clock, and the live feed from their web TV had just started. She kept one eye on that as news from the BBC, CNN, and the rest of the world rolled in on the monitors around them.

Whenever she had a spare minute, she dealt with her e-mails, but her in-box was constantly filling up. A piece she'd written on inequality between the sexes had been published yesterday. It was short, based on a dry scientific report, maybe 200 characters at most, but it contained a great quote from a well-known female scientist. That piece had ended up in some hidden corner of the website, but it made no difference how short it was or how low down it was posted: the hate mail had been pouring in since yesterday. She scanned through the messages and wondered how Åke, Göran, and whatever else they were called managed to get so agitated. While she did so, she dialed the number for social services in Kiruna. She read a message from Hotmail user Lord_Brutal900 as she listened to the dial tone:

I'll shove a chainsaw up your disgusting feminist cunt.

He was one of her regular haters, and that message was relatively tame compared to what he usually wrote. She deleted it and wondered who he was. A middle-aged businessman who hated feminists? An acne-ridden teenager who didn't know any better? A woman? No, female hate was different. The paper's policy was that you should report anything out of the ordinary. But she didn't want to seem weak, so she just deleted them. Once, on Twitter, she had—in the heat of the moment—outed a particularly crazy idiot who sent her disgusting messages from the e-mail address connected to his job with a medical research company. Dan Persson wasn't amused, and she was given a reprimand. She deleted a few more messages and then heard a voice on the end of the line.

"I'm looking for Anne-Charlotte?" Ambra said.

"Sorry, she's on vacation."

Jesus, people took long vacations. Ambra left another message for the social services worker, rolled her stiff neck, and got up from the chair to stretch.

Why had Tom called yesterday?

Not that she wasn't happy about it—she was—but she couldn't make sense of their relationship. In movies and in books, everyone was always so good at reading other people's motives. They could always see or sense what the other person was thinking, feeling. And maybe some people really could do that, but honestly she sucked at it. What she interpreted as attraction might be nothing but a way to pass the time on Tom's part.

She grabbed her notebook. At least she understood her work.

So. What was Tom Lexington doing in Chad? She searched the Internet. Tom's company, Lodestar, was active both in Sweden and abroad, according to their home page, but she couldn't find anything about Chad specifically. The site was full of generic phrases about global this and international that, but it didn't mention any specific countries. She thought for a moment and then typed in "Tom Lexington + David," but she didn't expect to find anything. She had already established that Tom was invisible online. She clicked around at random, read aimlessly, scrolled through picture after picture, and then, suddenly, a picture of Tom appeared. She studied it more closely, unsure whether she was just imagining it. There was no mention of his name anywhere: The picture was from a shareholders' meeting the previous year. She stared at the picture. Yep, it was definitely Tom.

Security was high when Hammar Capital called an extraordinary general meeting, she read beneath the picture. The article, which was eighteen months old, was about how Hammar Capital, a Swedish venture capitalist firm, had hijacked the huge Investum company. Ambra had zero interest in the world of finance, but the saga had dominated the headlines and front pages for a couple of days as it all played out, so much so that even she remembered it. Clearly Tom himself had provided them with security back then. She would never have thought that a man with his expertise would work on something like that; it seemed more like glorified guard duty. She read on. Hammar Capital was owned by David Hammar. She knew that much. The bad boy of the finance world. The stone-cold venture capitalist. Who then married the daughter of the owner of Investum. Natalia. Who, in turn, was the sister of the jet-setting Alexander De la Grip. Ambra brought up a few pictures of Alexander De la Grip and studied them. Jesus, he was insanely good looking.

So, Tom's best friend, David, could be David Hammar, right? They looked roughly the same age. When she Googled David Hammar, she saw that he was born in the same year as Tom, though that didn't necessarily mean a thing. She sat there with the picture of Tom on her screen. He had a beard there, too, but it was shorter, neater. Wearing a dark suit and a discreet earpiece. Well built. That had to be an advantage in certain contexts; people respected you. But it must also be difficult to blend in, she guessed. She started to close the tabs and images open on her screen, and was just about to close the entire browser when her eyes fell on the pictures of Alexander again. In one of them, he was standing next to a red-haired woman. They were posing on a red carpet, at the premiere of what looked like a kids film. Isobel Sørensen, she read beneath the image. She was incredibly beautiful, too. Two tall, beautiful, glamorous humans, they looked as if they were from another planet. But what caught Ambra's attention was the child they had with them. A serious boy, standing between them, with Alexander's hand on one shoulder. Marius, she read. He looked about seven or eight. She read the text, and the hairs on the back of her arms started to stand on end, a clear signal that she was onto something. *The couple married last fall. They have also begun proceedings to adopt Marius, originally from Chad.*

There it was.

The connection.

Chad.

Ambra quickly glanced up from her computer and then delved back into the depths of Google. Could it be a coincidence? She read about the red-haired woman. Isobel Sørensen, now De la Grip, was a doctor. She specialized in general medicine and was a researcher at the Karolinska Institute. Before Isobel began her research post, she worked for Doctors Without Borders and the nonprofit Medpax organization (Ambra couldn't stop herself from rolling her eyes here; Isobel sounded like some kind of superwoman), which ran a pediatric hospital in Chad.

Aha. Chad again.

She leaned back in her chair and stared into space. Suppose Tom's best friend really was David Hammar. David had a brother-in-law, Alexander, who was married to a woman who had not only worked in Chad but was also in the process of adopting a child from there, and all around the same time that Tom was apparently being held prisoner. Was there a story here? Or was she letting her imagination run away with her? Why would a former elite soldier from Sweden travel to Chad? What exactly was he doing there? And why was he taken prisoner? How did he get free? The more she thought about it, the more the questions stacked up. What was the story here, and where could she find more information? Imagine if there was a scoop here, a real revelation?

She read through her notes again. The natural thing would have been to ask Tom, of course. But what if he wasn't being quite so straight with her after all? It was clear the man had plenty of secrets, and there was an occasional hardness in his eyes that sent chills through her. Plus, she was sure he wouldn't appreciate her snooping around, so she would need a good explanation. She decided to wait before she talked to him, but something was still bugging her. She was genuinely curious, and there were huge gaps here, gaps she would love to fill in. After a moment's deliberation, she sent an e-mail to the paper's security expert, Karsten. No harm in that. She would talk to him first, then . . .

"Ambra." She heard Grace's voice from her desk.

Ambra tore herself from her thoughts. "Yeah?"

"Ten-year-old hurt by New Year's fireworks. Could you call up and get confirmation?"

Ambra nodded. Two minutes later, she was completely consumed by her work again.

Late that evening, Ambra wandered home. She had done an hour's overtime, always found it difficult to tear herself away from the action. She lived on Västerlånggatan in the Old Town, the medieval heart of Stockholm, and she loved to walk, people watch, and window-shop. When she looked up, she saw rockets and fireworks lighting up the dark sky. They spread their white, yellow, and blue light for a moment and then disappeared. Jill was doing a show at Skansen tonight, in the open-air museum's huge, live-streamed New Year's celebrations. Ambra knew she could go over there if she wanted to. But Jill would be preoccupied, and Ambra had no desire to freeze by standing outside until twelve. She sent her sister a message, wished her a happy new year and good luck, and decided not to say anything about her forgotten birthday. Jill was who she was.

A few of her colleagues from the office were going out, and one of the girls had invited her along, but she didn't know them well and said no, which might have been stupid. Next year, she would be better at saying yes. Their main TV anchor, Parvin, a woman Ambra respected immensely, was throwing a dinner party. But everyone would be in pairs, sophisticated people, and Ambra knew she would feel just as lost there, and so she had mumbled something about how she would love to next year and said no. She regretted that slightly now. There had been some talk of meeting up with a girl from Crime, but then she went and got herself a boyfriend and gradually disappeared into thin air. The curse of a single life: being dumped the moment a potential partner came along.

She heard the sound of a text from her pocket and fished out her phone. It was from Elsa. Decorated with fireworks and champagne emojis: *Happy New Year, my dear.*

She sent a reply, shoved her phone back into her pocket, and felt a warm sensation in her chest. She liked Elsa. It would be fine. This was just one day like any other.

Chapter 26

The loud crack of the gunshot sent Tom's body from 1 to 100 in a fraction of a second. Pulse, heart, lungs; all were working to full capacity. Another shot. Adrenaline coursed through his veins. *Where's it coming from? Can I see the shooter? Where can I take cover?* And then another shot. He tried to orient himself, but he couldn't see a thing.

Need to breathe, need to stabilize myself, need to take cover.

His head was pounding, and he was having trouble controlling his breathing. The surplus of oxygen made him dizzy. He forced himself to hold his breath, breathe out, wait. His heart was racing. He always tried to keep his heart rate in check during battle, to control his breathing and calm his nerves, but this time he didn't quite manage.

Take it easy. Focus. Locate the enemy.

He blinked rapidly. He couldn't see, and for a moment his sense of panic increased, but then he realized it was only sweat clouding his vision. He wiped his forehead with the back of his hand. He didn't hear any more shots. His back was against something. A wall? Different noises now. What were they? Barking. A dog barking. Freja. He could see the dog now. She was jumping up and down in front of him. Her barking reached him as though through a tunnel. He got up, into a sitting position, hadn't even realized he was lying down, that it was the ground he'd felt against his shoulders and back. He leaned against the wall and glanced around. He was inside the storeroom, but he had no memory of how he got there. He'd been going to fetch something and heard the shots.

No, not shots, he realized now that his body was calmer. They were fireworks. He breathed out, felt his pulse slow further. Jesus Christ. It was *fireworks* he was hearing.

He had been on the way out, someone set off some firecrackers or rockets in the forest, the noise echoed between the trees, and his body had immediately switched to autopilot and reacted as though it was under attack. He wiped his forehead, got up on shaking legs. Freja wagged her tail.

"Were you scared?" he asked. "I was scared as hell." His heart was beating at something like one hundred beats a minute now. He brushed snow from his pants, happy no one had witnessed what had just happened. So damn embarrassing.

He was used to shots being fired, had spent years of his life on shooting ranges, in drills, and in war zones. There were many nights where he had slept through the sound of guns being fired without a problem. You just got used to it. There was no way he should react to the sound of fireworks like that. Those bangs weren't even all that similar to the short, dry sound of real shots. But something had gone wrong and it seemed like a memory, a flashback—he was suddenly *there* again, in the heat, in hell.

He shook his legs, rolled his shoulders and neck. Looked out at the treetops. When the next round of bangs started, he was better prepared, but he still felt his body tense. Another crack and his heart started to pound. Damn it, on an intellectual level he knew the situation wasn't dangerous. Yet more noise, this time a series of sharp bangs that thundered above the trees.

Freja barked agitatedly.

He returned to the house and took a firm grip of the snow shovel. "Come on," he grimly said to the dog. "Let's try this whole exercise thing."

He started to shovel snow with powerful movements. Freja leaped around him, ran off and returned, dug like crazy in the snow, and barked encouragingly at his shoveling. After twenty minutes of determined work, Tom was drenched in sweat and his chest was heaving. But he no longer felt afraid; he was no longer anxious. When he heard the next bang, he barely reacted.

He drove the spade into a snowdrift, leaned against it with one arm, and glanced around.

I'll be damned. It actually worked.

By the time he'd cleared the entire yard and went back inside, his body was exhausted but calm, and after he took a shower he felt almost normal again.

He poured a glass of water, stood with one hip against the counter, and gazed out the kitchen window. His cell phone was on the worktop. David Hammar had called while he was out, then sent a message, a New Year's greeting and a few words about how Tom was welcome to come over, at as short notice as he liked. He really did need to get in touch with David. The two men went way back. Lodestar was responsible for Hammar Capital's security, and he and David used to go out and drink beer together. After Chad, David had been a rock. They were friends, but Tom knew that over the years he had distanced himself from David. His line of work made it easy to separate yourself from those you cared about. But David was a good man, a real friend. He really should call back.

He stood there with the phone in one hand, a glass of water in the other, hesitating. Eventually, he put down the glass and dialed the number before he had time to change his mind. Not David's number, not yet. But still, one step in the right direction.

"Hey, Johanna, this is Tom Lexington," he said when the receptionist answered.

"Tom," she said. She sounded astounded, almost reverential.

Johanna was a former special forces officer whom he'd recruited a few years earlier. She had been out in the field on a number of operations, but she was currently pregnant with her first child and was manning reception. Tom would never send a pregnant operative out on a dangerous mission. It was that simple.

"Hi. How are things?"

"Good, boss," she said, and her surprise was replaced by friendly efficiency. Johanna was one of the best operatives Tom had ever worked with—quick-thinking, invisible when she needed to be, reliable.

"How's everything at the office?" he asked. It was New Year's Eve, but Lodestar was always open, always working.

Over the past few weeks, just the thought of work had made him anxious. He was incredibly ashamed of that fact, but it wasn't something he could control. He still felt a sense of unease now, but it was good to hear Johanna's voice, to hear that everything seemed fine. He had abandoned his men, but they were coping, and that was reassuring. They were a good group.

"It's really quiet here today," she replied.

"I wanted to ask someone to forward my mail. I'm in Kiruna right now. I'll send the address."

"I'll do that right away. Do you need anything else?"

"Sorry I haven't been in touch before now."

Johanna was silent for a moment, as though she didn't know how to reply. "We were a little worried," she eventually said.

It was never his intention to worry people. It was just that he felt like an enormous burden on the entire company. People outside of the field always thought that dying was an operative's worst fear, but what they really feared most was letting down their colleagues and others, doing a bad job, putting others in danger. Embarrassing themselves by not doing what they were meant to. It was that feeling that had eventually overwhelmed him last fall, that he was a burden on his team.

"I'm sorry about that, Johanna," he said truthfully. He had allowed himself to deteriorate, both physically and mentally. Those men in Chad hadn't just taken control of him while he was there. They'd stolen part of his life back home, too. But he would try to change that now. He would regain control of himself. "I'll send instructions," he said.

"I'll organize everything ASAP, boss. Just send me the address."

After he ended the call, Tom went out into the study. He paused in the doorway. Before he'd left Stockholm, he'd quickly filled a box with things. It contained the picture of Ellinor—the one on the refrigerator—plus a few reference books; a well-thumbed copy of *The Art of War,* which Mattias had once given him; and a load of papers, above all documents and pictures from the Chad operation. So far, he hadn't been able to bring himself to look at them, but it was finally time.

Slowly, and with a growing sense of unease, he started to go through the various folders, reading and sorting them into piles. He knew better than anyone that he had done things he should pay for. He had killed people. During operations and in battle. But those he killed were participants in a war, and in war both sides always suffered losses. That said, the world of private security was full of gray zones and deviants. Psychopaths and sadists often sought out jobs that would give them the ability to murder, abuse, and rape. He knew plenty of terrifying instances when private security forces had murdered and tortured innocent people. Tom never tolerated that kind of thing, of course; as far as he knew, he never hired those kinds of men. Inflicting violence was never really the primary task in his role; it was more a tool to be able to carry out his work. The aim was always to cause as little damage as possible.

The raid on the tiny desert village in Chad last summer had turned into a real battle. It was wildly chaotic. They'd attacked in the dead of night, aiming to rescue Isobel Sørensen, a field doctor whom they had managed to localize to the village through their surveillance. Tom flew in with the helicopter from one side while the men on the ground advanced using night vision goggles. Conflict at night, in a built-up area, was the most difficult type of battle. Bad vision and split-second decisions could easily result in bloodbaths and civilian losses.

He didn't *think* any innocents were killed, but it was hard to know for certain. The minute he was back on his feet once he returned to Sweden, he contacted all of the men involved in the operation, gathered all of the material and pictures they had. Everyone he spoke to said that the rescue of the doctor had taken place without civilian losses. But you never knew. One stray bullet could have killed a villager—worst-case scenario a woman or a child—and that thought was hard to live with.

The whole rescue had been an illegal operation, carried out on foreign territory, and not sanctioned by any authorities. Yes, they'd rescued a civilian doctor from the hands of bandits, but still. Guilt and doubt gnawed away at him. He took out the photographs and studied them closely. They had been thorough with their documentation, before, during, and after. They'd carried out surveillance to establish who was in the area. During the attack, the soldiers wore cameras that sent images to a computer, and then one of the men documented the aftermath of the attack. Destroyed houses and other objects, dead and injured people. The whole thing looked professional, no civilian casualties. But had he made any mistakes? Had he given the wrong orders at any point?

When Freja came in and looked up at him with pleading eyes, he realized he had been sitting with the documents for several hours. They went out into the kitchen together. He fed her, made a sandwich for himself, and then glanced around the room as Freja emptied her bowl in less than thirty seconds.

"You want to go out?" he asked, swallowing the last of his sandwich. Freja gave a quick bark, and he pulled on his coat again. The odd firework lit up the sky, but the noise no longer bothered him. As he trudged through the snow, keeping one eye on the dog, he thought back to when he and Ambra rode the snowmobile. He'd forgotten to mention the top when they'd spoken yesterday. Their conversation was so good that he'd completely forgotten why he'd called her in the first place.

He glanced at Freja. "What do you think? Should we go back in and give her a call?" Freja barked loudly, and they returned to the house.

"Ambra Vinter," she answered on the second ring. She had a trustworthy voice. Calmer and softer on the phone than in real life.

"Hey, it's Tom."

"Yeah, I saw that." Her end of the line went quiet, and he suddenly felt stupid; was he bothering her in the middle of some festive New Year's meal? He glanced at his watch, hadn't realized it was so late.

"Are you out?" he asked.

She laughed quietly, and the sound sent a slight jolt through him. He went to the couch, lay down, and closed his eyes; he could just see her in front of him, those deep dimples, those guarded eyes, and that soft mouth curling into a smile at one side. The kisses. He remembered them, every single one. The unexpected, drunken kiss on Christmas Eve. The warm sauna kiss here in the house. And then the super-erotic kiss at the airport. He had cupped her breast then, could still remember its soft, warm weight in his palm, held on to it as a fantastic private memory.

"Just between us, I'm at home," she replied. "Alone. With my computer and the TV. What about you? No parties in Kiruna?"

Tom almost laughed. "Not exactly. I shoveled the whole driveway and went out with Freja. Doesn't get any more exciting than that."

They fell silent. He raised one leg, brushed some dust from his pants, felt like a teenager who had called up the cutest girl in class and now needed to think of something to say. "I just felt like calling you," he said.

"How are you?" she asked. Her voice was easygoing, but he knew what she meant.

He thought back to his anxiety attack that morning. "It was tough before, but it's okay now," he said, wondering whether he would have been this honest with anyone else. But Ambra was great in that sense. She was direct, didn't tiptoe around. Ellinor did. He didn't like that, he realized, though he'd never thought about it before. The tiptoeing around difficult subjects, the avoidance.

"Have you talked to anyone about it?" she asked.

"I talk to you," he said.

"You do?"

"I've told you more than most others," he said. It was true. Other than a handful of colleagues, David, and the men who were with him in Chad, no one knew what had happened down there.

There was a long silence on her end. He waited, comfortable just to listen to her soft breathing. "You never actually told me what happened, what you went through."

"It's a long story. Maybe some other time."

"Okeydokey."

He heard her breathing again, and could almost smell the scent of her, her warmth and softness. "Listen, Tom Lexington. Now that we're on the phone, making small talk, you think we should talk about that kiss . . . ?"

She trailed off.

He brushed some more dust from his leg.

"The one at the airport, I mean," she added. "Or in the sauna."

"I remember," he said. As though he could have forgotten any of those kisses. "I don't really know what happened," he said honestly. Now, looking back, with twelve hundred kilometers between them, he couldn't explain it, the explosive attraction he suddenly felt.

"They were pretty good kisses," she said. Still in the same easygoing tone.

"Agreed. Though you know my situation. With Ellinor, I mean."

"Yeah, I do. I just wanted to bring it up so we, well, you know. So we can stop thinking about it. Put it behind us."

"Sure," he agreed.

Long silence. Tom clutched his phone. Did she want to hang up now? Did he? Definitely not. He wanted to hear her low voice in his ear, to see her in his mind. She made him feel calm. And turned on. And happy.

"Can I ask you something?" she said.

Her voice sounded thoughtful, and he wasn't quite sure he wanted to hear the question, but he said: "Sure."

"If Ellinor turned around and said she wanted you back, would you want that?"

"Yes," he replied. Because it was true.

Wasn't it?

"Okay," she said. "Thanks for being honest."

"I'm sorry I . . . That I gave you mixed signals."

"Yeah. Though nothing serious really happened. You haven't been doing too well, right?"

"No, but that's no excuse. I think things are looking up. And if Ellinor and I are going to have a chance in the future, I don't want to mess that up by . . ." Tom trailed off. He could hear her gentle breathing on the other end of the line, way down south in Stockholm.

"Don't worry, Tom. It was a nice kiss, but it's like you said, it doesn't mean anything in the long run."

Had he really said that? That it was meaningless? It sounded like she was fumbling with something. "What are you doing?" he asked as he heard fireworks over the line. He glanced at his watch. It wasn't long until midnight.

"I was looking for the remote. Jill's doing a show on TV, and I promised to watch. But it hasn't started yet."

"Just say if you want to hang up."

"I'm happy to talk."

"Did you always want to be a journalist?" he asked, pulling himself together a little. He looked over at Freja, but she was sleeping by the fire.

"Feels like it."

"Why?"

"It was Renée's idea. She said it was a way of fighting for the weak, being their voice in society, and I guess it is in a way."

"So you fight for the weak?"

"I try. I mean, I work for a tabloid, but that's essentially my driving motivation. It's a tough world, but it's the only one I want to be in, because if you want people to read what you write, *Aftonbladet* is where you should be. It's the same if you're passionate about providing the public with correct information, so they can make informed decisions. There are so many shitty sites out there; someone needs to fight that battle, be objective. Or does that sound arrogant?"

"No, it's obvious from your writing that you care."

"I'm not all that proud of everything I've done."

"No?"

She sighed. "There are things I've written that affected people badly, speculative things. You can't always choose the angle or the headlines that'll be used."

Tom knew what she meant. He had witnessed people being hung out to dry, people who deserved better than running the gauntlet in the media.

"What about you? Have you always wanted to be—whatever you are?"

"Not to begin with. But it suits me."

"Yeah, I can imagine. Hey. When we spoke last, you said you were in Chad when you were captured?"

Tom looked up at the ceiling. Of course she couldn't let it go. The word *Chad* had just slipped out. He didn't normally have any problem keeping quiet about sensitive things like that. Though he also didn't talk to other people all that often. It was easier that way. Avoiding civilians. But talking to Ambra really was easy, which also meant it was easy to slip up.

"Is it because I'm a journalist that you don't want to say anything?" she asked when he didn't reply.

It was still true that he didn't have a particularly high opinion of journalists. Most of them were thirsty for something sensational. They were usually interested only in things that went wrong, and since so much of the information around his job was classified, they never had access to the bigger picture. Those fragments of information they did occasionally manage to bring together in a scandal often meant something completely different to those who knew the whole story. But that wasn't something intelligence officers or operatives could share. It was secret, and so they had to hold their tongues, accept whatever was written or said about them. And yet he found himself trusting Ambra more and more. "What do you want to know?" he asked.

"What were you doing in Chad?"

It wouldn't be the end of the world if she knew. As long as she didn't write about it. As long as she didn't know everything.

"Off the record?" he asked.

"Of course."

He weighed his words before he replied. "It was a private rescue operation. A job I took on for a private individual."

"A Swede?"

"Yes."

He could practically hear her thoughts now. It was something he liked about her, really, her determination. In many ways, he was the same. Stubborn. Goal-oriented. Focused on the solution.

"I can't say much more about it," he warned.

"Just one more thing, and you don't have to reply if you don't want to. Was the operation a success? You were taken prisoner, I know that much. But what about the person you were meant to rescue?"

"She's fine."

"A woman?"

He sighed. "No more, Ambra."

"Sorry, I got a little eager. I didn't mean to pry. Thanks for telling me. There are so many fireworks here."

"I can't really hear you," he said, could barely make himself heard over the fireworks. He glanced at his watch. Five to twelve.

"I'm going to watch TV now. I'm glad you called. That we could talk."

"Me too. Happy New Year, Ambra."

"Happy New Year, Tom."

Chapter 27

"So what would be a scoop then?" Ambra asked the next morning.

Aftonbladet's security expert, Karsten Lundqvist, blinked at her in pain. His plaid shirt was crumpled, his hair a mess, and he smelled as if he hadn't showered. "Could you speak more quietly? My brain hurts."

"Good night?"

Karsten closed his eyes. "Come, I need coffee." He got up and Ambra followed him into the kitchen. There was a faint scent of liquor and mints hanging over the entire newsroom, and most people looked pale and hungover—aside from a few of the most self-righteous parents of small children.

"I'm never drinking again," Karsten said as he opened and closed cabinet doors. The shelves were all empty, so he grabbed a mug from the overflowing dishwasher and rinsed it sloppily. "You want any?" he asked, holding up a jug of dark, muddy-looking coffee.

Ambra shook her head. "Scoop," she reminded him, leaning back against the worktop. Karsten looked awful; the country wouldn't be getting any deep analysis from him today. But she wanted to try to talk to him all the same, while everything in the office was still quiet.

"Could you start over from the beginning? More slowly this time," he said, taking a sip of coffee.

"What mandate does the Swedish military have when they're abroad?"

"The Swedish military is only allowed to assist, and to defend itself. Nothing offensive. They're very firm on that. Unlike the Americans and the Brits, for example, who just shoot at whatever they want."

"Does that also apply to the special forces? That they're only allowed to defend themselves?"

"Yup. So, in answer to your question, if, for example, a Swedish soldier shot an unarmed civilian abroad, that would be a scoop. If you could prove it, that is. And that's the near-impossible part. They keep the lid on that kind of thing."

"What about the private sector?" Ambra asked.

Karsten scratched his bristles. "If we're going to keep talking about this, let's go back to my desk," he said. "I'm going to die unless I sit down."

Ambra followed him back through the office. He slumped down into his swivel chair. Ambra pulled another chair over to his desk, placed it back to front, and sat down with her chin on the backrest.

"Those private security types are anything from chauffeurs and bodyguards to soldiers with access to military equipment, helicopters, the whole arsenal. Internationally, in particular, it's about offering private war services to whoever can afford them."

"Private war? That sounds crazy."

"It can be. Madmen and sadists are all drawn to that kind of violent work. Not all the companies manage to weed them out."

"Jesus."

"Plenty of abuse occurs. It's no secret."

"And they don't get punished? I mean, murder and torture are still illegal."

"Rarely. The whole thing isn't made any easier by the fact that they operate in countries where there isn't a functioning government or police force. The number of unrecorded cases is huge. You've heard of Blackwater, right? What they did in Iraq was horrific."

Ambra nodded. She had read about the infamous security firm that ran riot in Iraq, killing civilians during the war. Abuse, torture, executions, and all paid for by the American state.

"What about Swedish private security firms?" she asked, feeling slightly nauseated. Was this the kind of thing Tom did? He was just a completely ordinary man, right? Wasn't he? Suddenly, she wasn't sure. Was he capable of the kind of thing Karsten was talking about? He was a former elite soldier, ran Lodestar, so the answer to that question was probably in some part yes. She shuddered.

Karsten took off his glasses, tore off a piece of tape, wrapped it around one arm, and then pushed them back onto his nose. "I think I sat on them yesterday," he said with a sigh. "A hell of a night, yeah. You need to know anything else? Before I expire from my hangover."

"Are they good? The Swedes. Compared to international companies, I mean."

"Ah yeah. The Swedes are generally appreciated abroad. There are a few companies here with a good reputation, even globally. They're run by former elite soldiers, people with tactical know-how who've been in tight situations. They have firsthand knowledge of trouble hot spots, dangerous countries like Iraq, Afghanistan, the Congo. You know."

She nodded. "So what do they do there? In those countries?"

"They provide security, to Swedish companies, ambassadors. Security analysis, surveillance, knowledge. If a Swedish company wants to establish itself in a war-torn or unstable country, let's say Libya or South Sudan, they bring those security experts with them, people who can take responsibility for keeping their staff safe, who know the country."

Ambra thought for a moment. "Sounds much more civilized than murdering civilians and waging private wars," she said. It sounded more normal.

"Though the Swedes do end up in more offensive situations, too. There are rumors of all kinds of things."

"Like what?"

"Different operations. I think the Swedes have been involved in rescue operations, for example. There are a couple of unconfirmed cases I've always wondered about."

"Like what?"

"A Swedish engineer went missing in Pakistan, for example. Everyone assumed he was being held prisoner—we even wrote about it, his family was distraught. But suddenly he reappeared in Sweden, and there was a lid on the whole thing. Someone brought him home."

"Who?"

"If you have the money, you can buy that kind of expertise."

"People who'd travel to Pakistan just to rescue someone?" she asked skeptically.

"People who will go absolutely anywhere and rescue absolutely anyone."

It sounded like an action film. "What would that cost?"

"Rescuing someone who's been kidnapped? Hard to say. Depends on a lot of different things. The country, the kind of equipment you'd need. If you have to hire extra men, maybe even mercenaries."

"An educated guess?" she begged.

Karsten shrugged. "Assuming everyone involved wants somewhere in the region of two thousand dollars per day, plus all the bribes, vehicles, and weapons. One, maybe two million dollars?"

"And people actually do this?"

"The most common thing is to pay the ransom. Plenty of international companies have insurance for that kind of thing."

"So how much does that cost?"

"The ransom? Maybe ten million? The downside, other than the huge amount of money, is that it takes a long time. People can end up being held for years."

"So it's quicker to attempt a rescue?"

"Yeah. But it also has its downsides."

"Like what?"

"That it doesn't usually work," Karsten replied drily.

After her conversation with Karsten, Ambra went back to her desk deep in thought. The office was still quiet, so she could allow her mind to wander while she kept an eye on the news feed. She opened the Lodestar Security home page and clicked through the anonymous pictures. What exactly did this streamlined company get up to? And Tom—who and what was he, under the surface?

She leaned back in her seat. Tom radiated calm and steadfastness, but there was also a hint of something that for want of a better word she would call danger. Had she completely misjudged him? Missed something during the time they'd spent together? What happened in Chad last summer? All she knew was what he told her. That he rescued a Swedish woman. That he was captured and held prisoner. She assumed he wasn't lying, but really she had no idea. Something told her he was good at lying. She so wanted to put her questions to him directly, but if he discovered she was snooping about in his past, he would clam up immediately. She was sure of it. Because that's what she was doing, wasn't it? Snooping?

She got up and stretched her back.

Maybe she should drop the whole thing. Was it even interesting to anyone but her? It was hard to be objective, to work out whether it was the journalist in her who had caught wind of a story, or whether it was nothing but curiosity about a man she was attracted to. She sat down again and leafed through her notes. She had tried to create some kind of time line for Tom Lexington, filled it with what she knew about him. Which wasn't much.

Military service in Kiruna from 1997 to 1998; he was a Norrland Ranger. When she Googled what that involved, it seemed to be mostly about surviving under extreme conditions. After that, the Military Academy combined with exercises for a few years. He became a captain, if she remembered correctly. And then he trained to become a special forces operative in Karlsborg. That lasted roughly one year. The whole thing was incredibly secretive, but she had put together everything she could find and guessed that Tom must have finished his training to become an elite soldier roughly ten years ago. By then, he was an expert in most things: parachuting, diving, explosives, and gathering intelligence.

But what happened next? How long did he stay in the special forces, for example, after he took his exams? Surely a few years, at the very least. At some point, Tom Lexington left the military and moved over to the private sector. Why? Was it for the money? She read in an online forum that a man with his experience and competence could earn up to 200,000 kronor a month in the most dangerous countries. But something was bugging her here. Tom said that joining the military felt as if he had found his place in the world. She could see it in his eyes, hear it in his voice when he said it had been more than a job, more like a calling. So what made him leave? She wished she knew *when* he'd left the military, because right now that was one huge hole in his time line, until he turned up as a partner in Lodestar Security Group. She had managed to find a press statement about that. His name wasn't given, only his title. She glanced at his time line again. To be honest, it was mostly gaps and question marks.

And the biggest question mark of all: What exactly happened in Chad last summer?

Ambra continued to twist and turn the facts. Tom had organized the rescue of a Swedish woman. In all likelihood, an armed rescue. Could it be the field doctor she'd read about? Isobel De la Grip, the superwoman. She was a Swedish citizen, she had been in Chad, and she had a connection to Tom—through her brother-in-law, David Hammar. Was that logical or was it nothing but a long shot?

Ambra Googled Isobel De la Grip and managed to find a cell phone number for her. She sat there with the number on the screen. She was about to cross the line. If she called Isobel and Tom found out . . . That would be the end of the phone calls and the flirting. But she was a journalist in heart and soul—she couldn't *not* do it. She dialed the number.

"Hello, this is Isobel."

"Hi, my name is Ambra Vinter, I'm a reporter at *Aftonbladet*. I'd like to ask you a few questions, if that's okay?"

"Of course."

"It's about your work in Chad."

"Yes?"

"Could you confirm that there was an incident there last summer?"

Long pause.

"I thought you wanted to talk about my work as a doctor. I'm not interested in talking about all that."

"All that? What happened? Were you held prisoner in Chad?"

"I'm sorry, but I can't have this conversation. Bye."

And with that, the line went dead.

Ambra sighed. Yup, that was a success.

She ate lunch alone, eavesdropping on stories about people's New Year's Eves. Afterward she loaded her plate into the dishwasher, poured herself a coffee, and headed back to her desk. She really should be working, but she couldn't quite drop the whole Tom story. She would have to straighten things out. She opened the image of him she had saved, the one of him providing security for that board meeting. She couldn't deny that he turned her on. But her job was to influence politicians and opinion, to work against the antidemocratic forces in society. It was a role she took seriously. If Tom was responsible for killing civilians in some kind of illegal operation, she couldn't be his friend. She was sure of that. They would end up on different sides.

These increasingly serious thoughts were interrupted by her phone ringing. It was an unlisted number. She didn't like to answer anonymous calls. Nine times out of ten they were made by crazy people. After a moment's hesitation she rejected it. She didn't have the energy to hear any rambling or conspiracy theories right now.

At around three, she went back to Karsten. This time he was slumped forward over his desk with his head in his arms, and there were open packs of painkillers and Resorb on his desk. He had a glass of water, a soluble tablet fizzing away in it.

"Feels so reassuring to know that you're responsible for reporting on the security of the nation on a day like this," Ambra greeted him.

Karsten looked up at her and grimaced. His face was gray. "By all means, sit down," he muttered. He forced himself into an upright position, grabbed a pen, and used it to stir his glass. He sipped the liquid and wiped his mouth with the back of his hand. "Ugh, this stuff's disgusting."

"I was completely sober yesterday," Ambra said helpfully.

Karsten grabbed his forehead and swallowed a few times. "Don't you have anything to do over on Breaking News?"

"Nah, it's quiet. People are pissed—there's basically no exciting angle on the fact that New Year's Eve was unusually quiet."

"So what do you want now?"

"Have you heard about anything that happened in Chad? Anything that could be linked to Swedes?"

"Like what?"

She deliberated with herself. "A kidnapping. A rescue mission. Conflict."

"When?"

"This summer."

"I can check, but it might take a while. I have a friend with the Ministry for Foreign Affairs. There are a few other channels I can check, too. But first I need to use the bathroom," he said, abruptly getting to his feet and disappearing.

Deep in thought, Ambra returned to her own desk. Her cell phone was ringing, a private number again. After a moment's hesitation, she answered: "Ambra, *Aftonbladet*."

"Hi, this is Lotta, you were trying to get hold of me?"

"I was?" The name Lotta didn't ring a bell.

"I work for social services in Kiruna. I had several messages from an Ambra Vinter. Is that you?"

Ambra stopped mid-movement. "Lotta? As in Anne-Charlotte Jansson?"

"Yes. I'm actually still on vacation right now, but it sounded urgent."

Ambra rushed to start making notes. "Thanks so much for calling back. I'm a reporter with *Aftonbladet*, and I wanted to ask you about some foster home placements your department has arranged, with one family in particular."

"I can't give out that kind of information just like that."

No, she knew that, but she tried anyway. "The Sventin family. Do you know of them?"

"As I said, technically I'm still on vacation. I just wanted to get back to you." Her voice sounded much cooler now. Or was Ambra imagining it?

"I'm grateful you called," Ambra said, trying to sound as trustworthy as she could.

"We never talk about cases over the phone. Or by e-mail."

Ambra noted that she had left an opening. This Lotta might be willing to talk face-to-face. "I understand. When are you back to work?"

"Tomorrow. I'll be in my office."

Ambra thanked her again and they said good-bye.

She glanced at her watch. In a few hours' time, her working day would be over. Once today's shift finished, she had five days' vacation. She twisted and turned the options, but she had already made up her mind.

She was going back to Kiruna.

Chapter 28

Mattias Ceder had been working hard all week, ever since he got home from Kiruna, and the long hours were starting to take their toll. Today was Saturday, supposedly his day off, but it made no difference what day it was, the nation was always under attack. And as a result, Mattias was always working. Despite that, the weekend pace at HQ on Lidingövägen was slower than during the week. The majority of the military leadership worked normal office hours, and everyone there today was like him: workaholics and/or trying to keep up with the never-ending external threats to the country. Terrorists, aggressive nations, and hackers paid no attention to Swedish laws about forty-hour weeks and overtime.

So far, Mattias had managed to write an analysis of the terror threat linked to a state visit, a report on a suspected foreign spy, and an A4 sheet on modern interrogation techniques that would be sent to the Ministry for Foreign Affairs later that week. It was time for the first of the day's two interviews. Recruitment often took place on the weekend, and it suited him perfectly.

He got up and went to greet the woman waiting outside his room.

"Filippa," she introduced herself with a firm, dry handshake. She was thin and pale, completely unremarkable, with light brown hair, pale eyes, a knitted sweater, jeans, and a battered old purse.

"Thanks for coming in on a Saturday," he said, showing her into the room.

Filippa was a hacker Mattias had heard of through his contacts at the Royal Institute of Technology. It was Sweden's elite education center, and a hotbed for computer geniuses. As well as a breeding ground for possible intelligence agents. She sat down opposite him. With her cautious body language and soft voice, she gave the impression of being young and insecure, but Mattias knew better. Fillipa *was* young, just twenty-two, but she already had a degree in computer science and, according to Mattias's source, there wasn't a computer system in the world that the young hacker couldn't get into. All he needed to do was recruit her before someone else did.

"Okay to start?"

Filippa nodded, and Mattias began the interview with the usual, general questions, to sound her out a little. Shyness didn't necessarily have to be a problem, but nor could it be paralyzing. In his new super team, every member would need to be able to hold their own among other experts. They talked about moral judgments, and Mattias skirted around the subject, asked questions in different ways, wanted to get a sense of what she really thought about right and wrong, life and death, war and peace. Political orientation wasn't so important—Mattias was a firm believer in mixed groups—but those with prejudices were always impossible to work with. They couldn't take in the facts but just viewed everything through their black-and-white filters. Dangerous people.

"Why do you want to work for us?" he asked.

She flashed him a quick smile. "I like hacking," she said.

"Why?"

"It's an intellectual challenge. And I'd be able to do it legally here."

The interview lasted forty-five minutes, mostly a chance for him to gain a first impression. But Mattias had a good feeling about her.

"We'll be in touch about a second interview," he said as they parted.

He went down to the cafeteria and bought a salad, which he ate back up in his office. He worked another hour and then welcomed the day's second prospect: a retired cryptologist. At sixty-seven, the man was on the verge of being too old, but Mattias wanted a mixed team. It was true that young people had an intellectual flexibility that older people often lacked. Plus, the young had an innate understanding of how social media worked, which was invaluable in this day and age, when so many threats were made using the Internet and terrorists kept in touch via Facebook groups. But a mixed-age group also resulted in unexpected viewpoints, and a good cryptologist often took many years to form.

After the interview, Mattias decided to put the sixty-seven-year-old on his maybe list. It would have been great to discuss the two interviews with Tom, he thought, not for the first time that week. Tom was an incredible sounding board. He saw beyond the obvious; he was calm and methodical and could make creative associations and analyses like no one else.

Mattias moved over to his tiny window. This was his official office. In his other room, the unofficial one, there was no window at all.

It was dark out, but the courtyard was lit by spotlights. There were a number of discreet guards stationed out there. He still didn't know what to do about Tom. The trip to Kiruna had always been a long shot, but it did feel like a victory that they'd talked about what happened. The fact was that Tom still hadn't forgiven him, much less started to trust him. And he was damaged, both physically and mentally, that was also obvious. They hadn't spoken since he'd left Kiruna. Mattias scratched the bridge of his nose. Maybe he should give up? There were other people he could try. But no one like Tom Lexington. Tom was the best, and Mattias wanted the best. He stared out at the snowy courtyard.

It was here, at HQ, that he'd betrayed Tom all those years ago. Even today, he could remember the expression on Tom's face, dreamed about it sometimes, how he had frozen when the extent of his betrayal sank in. Mattias had been so nervous that day that he could barely talk when he got up and uttered the words that protected the unit but ruined his friendship with Tom. In an abrupt voice, he said the words he had been practicing all night:

"Captain Lexington wasn't himself even before we left for Afghanistan. He overreacted then, and he's overreacting now. He hasn't been himself for a while. We can't rule out that the perpetrator was armed," he said.

Tom stared at him furiously after he spoke. It wasn't often that Tom got angry, but when he did it was a terrible sight. Like the devil himself had his eyes trained on you. "The perpetrator?" he barked, his voice echoing across the room and the medal-clad men. "There was no fucking perpetrator, it was an unarmed child."

Mattias cleared the expression from his face. If Tom would just calm down, maybe he could save them both. "It was dark, it was chaotic. We can't rule out that he posed a threat," he said in a convincing tone, trying to make Tom realize that saving the unit was their first priority. What had happened was unfortunate, but there was no point dragging it out. For everyone's sake.

But Tom just stared at him, and then he turned to the medal-wearing men who would decide his fate. "We killed a defenseless child. I don't give a shit about this fucking demonstration of power. What we did was wrong, and you're so afraid for your own asses that you should be ashamed." The thing was, he was right. But it made no difference. After that meeting, Tom's career in the military was over.

What he had done was necessary, Mattias thought, following a lone conscript with his eyes. But if he was faced with the same dilemma again today, he didn't know whether he would make the same decision. What he did know was that the nation needed Tom. Somehow, he had to get him onboard.

Mattias read through a few more applications and put those he wanted to interview into a separate pile. He would call them personally on Monday. He opened Twitter, scrolled through his feed, and immediately noticed a troll attack, a fake article by someone paid to spread disinformation by a foreign power. It was well written, seemed perfectly genuine at first glance, and it was spreading fast—even disseminated by so-called Swedish patriots. He scrolled through the discussion and wrote down a few points, made a note of several names he wanted to look into more closely. The sooner the new group came into being, the better. He moved on to Facebook, checked a few of the accounts he had on his radar. So many of the threats to their open society and democracy were made on social media these days. People actively spreading lies and misinformation with the aim of causing damage, stirring up hate and worry. An increasingly large part of his job was devoted to keeping an eye on them, these people who deliberately and systematically undermined the country. This information war went on twenty-four hours a day. The enemy mapped people out, spread articles that caused divisions, played people against one another. It was a classic divide-and-rule strategy, and it worked depressingly well.

He left the tabs open and paused for a moment with his fingers poised above the keyboard. Eventually, he typed in the address of Jill's Instagram page. Strictly speaking, there was very little information war going on there, but he couldn't help it. There was just something about Jill Lopez that fascinated him. She was the polar opposite of the women he usually dated in every respect. Jill was extravagant, almost vulgar at times, uneducated, and extremely visible on social media, about as far from the discreet academics he was most comfortable with as you could get. And yet he couldn't stop himself from going back to her Instagram page time and time again. Every day, in fact, since he got home from Kiruna.

He studied her latest posts. She'd performed at Skansen on New Year's Eve, and now she was in Copenhagen. She really did seem to be constantly on the move. Judging by her pictures, she had performed for the Danish Crown Prince Couple yesterday and been on a shopping trip in the capital today. Most of the images were of her, in different poses and locations, and if it hadn't been for the amusing, slightly sarcastic captions, he would have found the whole thing incredibly self-obsessed. But during their dinner in Kiruna, she'd explained that it was a way of building her brand, constantly uploading pictures of herself, that it was what her fans and record label demanded.

Other than the fact that Jill was incredibly attractive, he couldn't decide what it was he found so fascinating about her. He'd never been particularly interested in beautiful, attention-seeking divas. And that was probably the answer to his question. Because Jill was more than that. She had a kind, self-deprecating side. It was partly visible in her own comments beneath the images, but he'd noticed it back in Kiruna, too. And she had a vulnerability that showed itself from time to time. She wasn't just some spoiled, glamorous star. She talked easily about the orphanage in Colombia where she spent the first few years of her life, but afterward she had looked away. While they drank expensive champagne, she returned to the unhappy adoption as an amusing anecdote, but then he had seen the looks she exchanged with Ambra, seen the pain the two women shared and probably avoided talking about, even with one another. And on the couch, in front of the roaring fire, she had talked about the online hate she experienced, giving the impression that she took it all in her stride, but no one could be completely unaffected by what she went through.

Mattias scanned through the comments on her latest uploads. Below some images, there were nearly a thousand. On the most recent selfie from Copenhagen, she had 112 comments and three thousand likes. Most of them were kind, full of hearts and various emojis, but some were also incredibly hostile.

Your tits are starting to sag.
You really think you're something, don't you, bitch?
Everyone can tell exactly what she wants.

He assumed Jill's team reported the worst of them, but new comments were constantly appearing, so she had no real way of protecting herself. He clicked on one of the worst users, but it was a private account. Of course. Bullies and trolls were cowards, always hiding behind anonymity.

He frowned. Thought for a moment and then dialed Filippa's number, told himself it was a good chance to test her abilities on a real-life situation.

"Could you get into a private Instagram account? A locked one?"

"Send it over and I'll do it," she said.

Mattias opened three of the worst and sent the links to her. He went to fetch a coffee and an apple, talked to a plainclothes colleague, and by the time he got back Filippa had sent him all the information. Fantastic, he would make sure he looked into it further.

He closed the lid of his computer. It would be a terrible idea to call Jill, of course. They had nothing in common, and she was a walking security risk. But she had also been on his mind all week, and one phone call surely wasn't the end of the world. He debated with himself for half a minute or so, until his common sense lost out and he dialed her number, the private one.

"Hello?"

He heard her deep, husky voice after the very first ring. Somehow, he hadn't expected her to answer, even though he was calling her cell phone. It was Saturday night. Shouldn't someone like Jill be out at a gala, on a red carpet somewhere?

"This is Mattias Ceder," he said.

Long pause. "Who?" she asked.

A smile tugged at his lips. He'd been able to see straight though people ever since he enrolled at the Interpreter Academy; he was one of the military's best interview leaders, and he knew a lie when he heard one.

"We met in Kiruna, at Tom Lexington's place," he said politely.

"Aha. The consultant. How are you?"

"Good, good. How are you?"

"Fine. I'm in Copenhagen. Nice city. If you like Danes."

He laughed. It sounded as if she'd had enough of them. "I bought your CDs."

"CDs, how very twentieth century. Which, if you don't mind me asking?"

"All of them."

He heard her deep laugh again.

"So have you listened to them?" she asked.

He had spent every night listening to the CDs, allowing her pure voice to fill his apartment. "Yep. And I wanted to take you out to dinner to talk about them. When are you next in Stockholm?"

"What makes you think I want to see you again?" Her tone was light and flirty.

He could play games, if that was what Jill Lopez needed. Some might even say it was what he did best. Playing the game. "Do you?" he asked.

"Maybe. I'm back in Stockholm on January sixth."

That was four days' time. "I'll book a table for the seventh."

"I do need to eat."

"Yeah, you do. I'll make a reservation and see you then, Jill Lopez."

She hung up without another word. Mattias shook his head, equally happy and concerned that he had called.

Chapter 29

"Hi, Tom, it's Isobel. I hope you're well. Listen, could you give me a call back? I know I've left a bunch of messages, and I don't want to hound you, but there's something I need to talk to you about. Just give me a call, whenever you can. Take care."

The message from Isobel De la Grip was the last one left on Tom's voice mail. He put down his phone. For so many weeks, he hadn't been able to bring himself to do it, but now he'd listened to every last message. It took a while. A few times, when he'd gotten David's concerned voice or his mom's anxious questions in his ear, he'd felt the panic rising, but he needed to take back control of his life. He couldn't go on like this, and so he forced himself to keep listening. He would call Isobel later.

He looked down at the floor in the study where he had all of the documents from Chad spread out. More had arrived with the mail Johanna had forwarded on to him, and Tom had spent the past few days carefully going through everything, arranging papers, reports, and images across the floor, sorting them into piles, reading and thinking.

He now had a good overview of what had happened in the village after his crash. He turned up the volume on the radio and sat down at the table. When the weather report came on, he turned up the volume further. It was as he'd thought. A snowstorm was expected over the next few days.

"What do you say? Should we go into town and stock up a little?" he said to Freja, who sat up and scratched herself with her back leg in reply.

*   *   *

After buying batteries, an extra flashlight, candles, and matches, Tom walked over to the grocery store with Freja. He left her outside while he went in to buy fresh produce. He picked up a few bags of dog food, paid, and went back out to collect Freja, who was waiting impatiently. He gave her a treat before he untied the leash. She wolfed it down without either breathing or chewing. He petted her and she closed her eyes, pressed herself against his leg.

"Hi there," he heard. He looked up. It was Ellinor. Her cheeks were flushed from the cold, and the weak sun made her pale hair glow. She had a small white dog with her. It seemed they were constantly destined to meet like this.

"Hi, Freja. You and Tom seem to have found one another." Ellinor bent down and stroked the dog, which gave her a dismissive wag of the tail and then started sniffing the fluffy little dog.

"She gets me out. It feels good," he said, realizing he felt better today. More exercise, better food, and less alcohol all meant he was sleeping better. He still woke from nightmares drenched in sweat, but he could at least fall asleep again now.

"Where's Nilas?" he asked.

"He's on call in Kalix. A horse." She smiled again, and things almost felt like before, relaxed and normal. As though they were making small talk about what to have for dinner or to buy her sister for her birthday.

Ellinor looked at him, and something passed between them. It almost seemed as if she wanted to give him a hug, but then she just said good-bye, waved, and left, quickly, through the snow.

Tom headed back to his car. It had started to snow, and Freja was bounding around trying to catch the flakes on her tongue, barking at the piles of snow. Tom was in a good mood, too, he realized as he watched her. Maybe things really were about to turn around. He loaded the groceries into the trunk and closed the top. He was standing with one foot on Freja's leash when she suddenly barked and ran off.

"Freja!" he shouted. She was harmless, but she was also big, and he didn't want anyone to be afraid. He watched her go and saw her jump up at someone.

"Freja!" he repeated, starting to run toward the dog and the person she had attacked.

"Don't worry," he heard. It was Ambra. He slowed down, surprised, and saw Freja jumping up and down in front of her. Ambra was laughing at the excited assault and bent down to grab the leash.

"You should take better care of your dog," she said as he reached her.

Tom took the leash and gave the dog a stern look. Freja didn't seem to feel the least bit guilty. She was trembling with excitement at having found Ambra for him. "Okay, okay, good girl," he muttered before he took a closer look at Ambra. Same coat as before, same huge scarf and hat pulled down over her forehead. A red nose and those brilliant green eyes were practically all he could see. But it was her.

"Aren't you in Stockholm?" he asked.

Ambra shrugged, and he wanted to smile at the familiar gesture. "I'm just here to check out a few things," she replied vaguely. "It's cold," she added. Their breath was like clouds, and the wind bit their cheeks.

"It's going to get worse. You really should invest in a warmer coat."

"I know. My protest against Kiruna isn't so functional, sadly." She pulled her scarf even tighter.

"When did you get here?" he asked, trying to make the dog calm down. She was still completely beside herself.

Ambra patted Freja on the head. She was wearing thick gloves, but Freja still seemed pleased. "Yesterday."

He noted that Ambra had been in town twenty-four hours without letting him know. She wasn't obliged to tell him anything, but he still felt a little surprised. "Same hotel?" he asked.

"Yup, though this time the heating in my room works, which is a huge improvement."

"Where are you headed? Do you have time for a coffee?"

"I'm going to see Elsa."

Tom wanted to spend time with her now that she was here, felt a sudden and inexplicable desire to be sociable. That was all it was, he told himself. Spending time with another person today, talking with them.

"If you're here tonight, maybe I could take the fourth estate to dinner?" he said.

She looked hesitant. "I don't know," she said.

"What if I tempt you with the Icehotel?"

"Isn't that miles away?"

"Nah, not by car. They have a great restaurant, Lappland's best chefs. You can't keep coming all the way to Kiruna without seeing the Icehotel."

"And here I was planning to eat takeout in my room," she said, but he could hear that she was warming to the idea. Maybe she was just as desperate for company as he was.

"I have it on good authority that there's no takeout food left."

Her eyes glittered. "Oh really? In the whole of Kiruna."

"Large areas of Norrbotten, actually. People are having to see one another and eat in restaurants if they don't want to starve."

"Is that right?"

"I saw it in the newspaper, so it must be true," he said.

"The great takeout famine?"

"Exactly, so you read about it too?"

She laughed, and he realized that he really did want to take Ambra Vinter out to dinner, flirt a little. Jesus, he didn't even know if he could flirt. "Come on," he said persuasively. And he wasn't the persuasive type.

She shook her head, as though against her better judgment, and he dealt the final blow. "It's on me. Not just the food, secrets too."

Her green eyes shone as he knew they would. The woman was too curious for her own good, and he was exploiting it shamelessly.

"Secrets? Truly? How could I say no to an offer like that?"

And he smiled, an inexperienced smile, aimed at her; he felt happiness warm his chest. "No, I know, it's irresistible. I'll pick you up at the hotel."

Chapter 30

Ambra couldn't get over the fact that Tom Lexington was actually *flirting* with her. That smile . . . It was so rare, the effect was even more powerful. When Tom smiled, she just wanted to snuggle into his arms and rub herself all over him. It was rather undignified, that he had that effect on her. She should have known they would bump into each other; Kiruna wasn't all that big. She had even thought about getting in touch. But so much about Tom was complicated, and she already had enough drama in her life. But then Freja spotted her, and now Tom was here, being handsome and overwhelming, wanting to eat dinner with her. She didn't have anything planned for that evening, or any other evening in Kiruna for that matter. Going to dinner with Tom sounded like a great idea.

Though it might also sound like the dumbest thing she could do.

God, she shouldn't trick herself into thinking they could just be friends, that she could handle this. But, of course, she found herself nodding yes.

"Six o'clock, outside the hotel," she said.

"Great. See you then. Try not to freeze to death before that. Freja, come!" His voice was commanding and his movements firm. His entire being seemed bigger and more powerful than last time, and the breath caught in her chest. This was so gloriously dangerous. She forced herself to look relaxed and waved to him and Freja, ridiculously happy that they would be meeting again that evening.

She kept walking, to Café Safari, the small, yellow wooden building where she was meeting Elsa. As soon as she stepped inside, joining the throngs of tourists, Elsa appeared and gave her a long, warm hug. They made small talk in the line and then each ordered a slice of smörgåstårta—Swedish sandwich cake, layers of white bread, mayonnaise, shrimps, salmon, and veggies—and coffee.

"You can't get smörgåstårta in coffee shops anywhere in Stockholm," Ambra said happily. She loved the savory delicacy.

"Can you manage something sweet too?" Elsa asked.

"Always," Ambra replied, choosing a chubby piece of princess cake. Elsa picked a chocolate cake and placed it on the tray. They sat down upstairs, by one of the windows looking out onto the mountains and a last hint of the pinkish sun.

"When does your train leave?" Ambra asked, delving into the layers of prawns, mayonnaise, and sliced cucumber.

"Not until two-thirty." Elsa was going to visit a friend. Ambra suspected this friend was a new love, because Elsa looked incredibly chic with her colorful scarf and newly set hair. She brought a big piece of smörgåstårta to her mouth. It was both gratifying and a little depressing that a ninety-two-year-old woman seemed to have more momentum in her love life than she did.

As they ate, they talked about Elsa's son, the number of tourists, and the snow festival at the end of January. Ambra went to fetch more coffee.

"Thank you, dear," Elsa said.

"People should eat cake more often," Ambra said as she cut into the green marzipan and whipped cream with her spoon.

"Yes. Cakes and chocolate. Ingrid always said chocolate was proof of God's existence."

"Are you a believer?"

"Sometimes. Maybe." Elsa stirred her coffee, seemed to be thinking about something. "I asked around a little, about the Sventins. Those girls you saw—they aren't their grandkids."

"So they're foster kids?" Ambra had been hoping to hear the opposite. She put down her spoon.

"Yes."

"Jesus. I thought, hoped, that they were too old. This is a scandal."

"Yes." Elsa gave Ambra a concerned look. "I don't know whether I should tell you this . . . But Esaias Sventin is giving a sermon today. At the church."

"He is? Kiruna Church?" So he had become a Laestadian preacher. That didn't surprise her; he was strict and unforgiving—it suited him perfectly.

Elsa nodded. "I don't know how they can allow it, how that sect can be allowed to use Swedish Church property, I mean, but he is." She looked down at her little wristwatch. "In thirty minutes. Do you want to go?"

Did she? Listening to his hateful voice. She had no choice, not really. She nodded.

"I'll come with you," said Elsa.

Ambra was tense with nerves as she and Elsa approached the red church a short while later. She held open the door for Elsa, and they sat down at the very back. The dark, uncomfortable pews filled up with people. Women in long skirts and kerchiefs, their hair tied up. Men in simple, austere clothing. Pale children. Ambra's palms were sweating, her shoulders tense.

There were no lights on in the church, and the visitors sat on the benches in silence, their heads bowed, as though waiting for damnation. She studied their tense faces and was struck by the sense that they were all insane. Some argued that Laestadianism was a beautiful Christian community, that it was about a wholesome, simple life and love. But to her it was nothing but the evil and madness that, as a child, she had only barely survived.

And then he came in.

Esaias Sventin.

Just thinking his name made her retch.

She watched him as he passed. He looked older. When she'd lived with him, he was in his thirties, just a few years older than she was today. The Laestadians married young. Some daughters were betrothed when they were just nine. Esaias now had streaks of gray in his short hair. He wore black trousers and a black jacket, a white shirt without a tie. Wearing a tie was a sign of male vanity. He looked out at the congregation. Would he notice her? Could he feel she was here?

"Want to leave?" Elsa whispered beside her. Ambra heard her as though through a fog. She was having trouble breathing, clutching her gloves tight in one hand. She shook her head. Esaias opened his mouth, and his voice—which had also aged—echoed across the church hall.

"Laughter is the instrument of the devil," he began. She recognized those words, had heard them over and over again.

"Temptation is everywhere. The devil and his demons are everywhere. Sin is everywhere," he continued.

This constant obsession with driving out the devil, sins that had to be atoned for. He used to force her to eat. Rakel served huge portions, and when Ambra couldn't manage everything, he would force her to eat and eat until she threw up. "Those are the devil's demons coming out of her," he would say.

There were variations on how the demons and sins were meant to leave her body. "Wash away the sin," he might say as he dragged her over to the sink, filled it with ice-cold water, and pushed her into it until she thought she was about to die. Living in that house was like walking on eggshells, always being afraid, never knowing when they would crack. "Burn out the devil with pain," he would say as he struck her with a belt. If she closed her eyes, she could still remember the terror and the shame.

She sat perfectly still on the bench, didn't want to relive those memories, didn't want to be here anymore. Esaias's voice roared in her ears. As an adult, she could see he was crazy, but she was still shaken by the memories that came flooding back to her.

"Ambra?" Elsa's voice was trying to reach her, but Ambra could barely hear, the roar in her ears was so loud.

"Come on. Let's go, this was a mistake," Elsa said encouragingly.

Ambra nodded and gathered her things. They got up. Ambra made the mistake of looking over at Esaias one last time. The movement must have caught his attention. He always did have eyes like a hawk, reacting to the smallest of movements. He caught sight of her, straight across the church hall. His lips moved, but she couldn't hear what he was saying.

He stared at her.

Flickers started to appear at the edge of her field of vision, the air left the room, her throat tightened.

"Come on, Ambra," she heard Elsa say. She felt the old lady's hand clasp hers and pull her away from the row of pews.

"Sinners and whores! They are everywhere!" Esaias's words roared after her as she fled.

When Ambra reached the steps, she paused for a moment to catch her breath.

"I shouldn't have suggested it," Elsa said with remorse.

"It's not your fault. It's his," she said doggedly. He was crazy. And two children were now experiencing the same hell she had once been subjected to.

They walked slowly toward the train station in silence.

Ambra waved good-bye to Elsa, waited until she saw the train leave, and then allowed herself to react. She was shaking like a leaf. Jesus, what a day. And she still had her meeting with social services to go. She definitely deserved to be taken to dinner after this.

"Hi, I'm Lotta," said a woman wearing a silver cross around her neck when Ambra registered at reception a while later.

"Ambra Vinter. Thanks for agreeing to meet with me."

Lotta wore the same tense expression that Ambra had seen on countless social workers. A woman Ambra once interviewed, an experienced manager in one of the country's most socially challenging areas, called the process that most social workers went through "vision meets reality." They were constantly experiencing burnout, or worse: becoming cynical, hardened, or indifferent. Many took sick leave or resigned, which only led to an even greater burden on those left behind, who were given more and more cases with increasingly limited resources. It was a depressing, endless downward spiral.

They sat down in Lotta's room, which was full of journals, files, and stacks of paper. Documents about suffering, children needing help, and families. Ambra said no to coffee. The dark atmosphere of the room was already affecting her. Lotta placed one palm on a stack of documents, as though to reassure herself that they were still there. Or maybe to prevent Ambra from launching herself at them and starting to snoop. There was a withered hyacinth on the window ledge, competing for room with yet more papers. Ambra wondered whether Lotta met the children she worked with in this room, or whether they went somewhere more welcoming.

"You asked about the Sventin family. I can't discuss individual cases, but what I can say is that to date we haven't received any complaints." Lotta pursed her lips.

Her words almost sounded rehearsed. But social services and the press often found themselves on a collision course. It didn't necessarily mean she had anything to hide.

Ambra tried to look as reflective and understanding as she could. "I understand, you're bound by confidentiality. But they do still have foster children? That can't be confidential."

"I can't comment on that."

"But is it correct that they have two girls right now? Who aren't their biological children?" she persisted.

Lotta opened her mouth, but before she had time to speak, the door opened. A nearly bald man appeared in the doorway. He had a few wisps of white hair combed across his scalp, and his face was flushed. He gave Ambra a stern look. Out of the corner of her eye, she saw Lotta virtually shrink back behind the table.

Not a good sign.

"What's she doing here?" he asked.

Ambra got up and held out her hand. "My name is Ambra Vinter. I'm a reporter with *Aftonbladet*. Are you in charge here?"

He didn't offer his hand, of course. "I'm Ingemar Borg, and I'm the manager here. Why are you here? You have no right to be here."

"I'm just asking routine questions. I'm not looking to harass anyone," she continued as calmly as she could.

"You're the one asking questions about the Sventin family, aren't you? You should know that they meet all the criteria for a family home. They're experienced and have made a real contribution for over twenty years now. They're specialists in children no one else wants."

Well, he had no concerns about confidentiality, at least. "You make them sound like saints." Ambra had trouble keeping the acid tone from her voice.

The man took a step toward her. "I recognize you."

"I work for *Aftonbladet*, as I said. Maybe you saw my byline?"

"No. I *know* you. What was your name? Ambra. You lived with them, didn't you? I remember all our kids. You were one of them. Lied and ran away. What are you up to? Are you even here for the paper?" He took another step toward her.

She didn't remember him at all. But she was a child back then, and the majority of adults were just anonymous, uncaring strangers.

"Make sure she leaves," he said to Lotta, whom Ambra saw nod out of the corner of her eye. He turned on his heel and left, the door still wide open.

Lotta swallowed and swallowed. She clutched the little silver cross around her neck. "I'm new here," she said in a stifled voice. "I should never have agreed to this meeting. He's right, we never had any formal complaints."

"But?"

Lotta gave her a pleading look. "I can't risk my job. I need to ask you to leave. I'm completely snowed under with work. This was a mistake."

"I'm leaving. Thanks anyway."

"Is it true, what he said? You lived with them?"

Ambra gathered her things and pulled at her scarf. "You have my number. Call whenever you like. If you want to talk."

"But what do you want from us?"

Ambra looked at the terrified social worker in the crowded, depressing room. "For no one else to go through what I did," she said, and left the room.

Ambra walked back to the hotel. It was dark, and the air was so cold that it stung her nose whenever she breathed in. Shivering, she hurried to her room and took a long, hot shower.

She applied some lipstick and filled in her eyebrows; she was fond of her bold brows. And her dimples. She put on a little eyeshadow and hoped the haunted expression she saw on her face would disappear during the course of the evening.

Just before six, she went down to the lobby. At one minute to the hour, she saw Tom's huge black car pull up outside the hotel. She liked that he was on time.

He leaned over and opened the passenger side door from the inside. Ambra jumped in and sank into the luxurious leather seats. She turned her head and looked into his dark, dark eyes. Today had been a strange day, and her defenses were down. Who was Tom Lexington, really? A nice, normal guy she was attracted to? A crazy ex-soldier? Could a person be both? She was well aware that the dumbest thing she could do would be to cross some kind of professional line with him—which, technically speaking, she already had. Every instinct she had was screaming at her. This was a potentially dangerous man with far too many secrets.

But she didn't have the energy to be sensible. Not today. She had survived Esaias Sventin. She could probably survive one dinner with Tom.

"Hey."

"Yeah?"

"I'm looking forward to tonight," she said honestly.

"Me too." He tore off, and the snow sparkled in the winter darkness as they drove towards Jukkasjärvi.

Chapter 31

It took thirty minutes to drive from Kiruna to Jukkasjärvi. Tom was focused on the road ahead. The visibility wasn't great and Ambra was deep in thought, so they didn't say much. He kept to the speed limit but still had to slam on the brakes when three startled deer ran out on the road, right in front of their headlights. The deer quickly disappeared into the forest on the other side.

"Christ, they came out of nowhere," Ambra said, her voice shaken.

"I saw them," he said reassuringly.

He parked outside the Icehotel and noticed that she was shivering.

"It's the river, it lowers the air temperature," he said as they walked toward the hotel, surrounded by tourists in overalls and guides in ponchos made from reindeer skin. There were fires burning in huge iron barrels, the low hum of snowmobiles.

"It's so blue," she said in amazement. The ice really did shimmer in tones of the sky and the sea.

"The ice from the river is that color," a guide said helpfully.

"It looks like something from space," she said, and Tom agreed. They entered the hotel and walked around with groups of Japanese tourists; Swedish couples; and hordes of Germans, Americans, and Danes admiring the rooms. Each was unique; some were just small boxes, but others were entire suites, with spectacular decoration. And everything was cut and sculpted from snow and ice.

"They build a new one every year," Tom read from the brochure. "The sculptors come from all over the world. They create a room each, with different themes."

They were standing in a room containing a huge peacock made

from snow and ice. The icy patterns on its tail feathers glittered blue. Even the bed in the middle of the room was made from ice, covered in reindeer skins. The floor was snow. "Could you imagine spending the night here?" he asked, though he suspected he knew the answer.

"No. It's beautiful, but too claustrophobic. You?"

"Maybe. Want to see the church?"

They stepped inside. Their breath was a cloud around them, but the temperature was a balmy twenty-three degrees, not nearly as bad as the fierce cold outside. "Absolutely everything is ice," she said, glancing around. The benches, the pulpit, everything glistened so cold and white.

"Let's go see the ice bar," he suggested. She looked a little pale, but she nodded and they walked over. A glittering ice staircase awaited them, booths made of ice, with reindeer skin-covered benches to sit on. The place was almost full, the music loud and the noise level high.

"It's like being inside a frozen soap bubble."

Tom ordered a drink for each of them, small cocktails in square ice glasses. They were almost impossible to drink from.

"It's frozen solid." She laughed as she tried to loosen her glass from the ice table.

After they finished their frosty drinks, they walked over to the restaurant.

"It looks like Narnia," she said as they passed illuminated ice sculptures between ancient, snow-covered pines.

The restaurant was warm and welcoming, and they sat down by the window table Tom had booked.

"I didn't think it was possible to get a table here. Isn't this place super popular?" she asked, studying the menu the waiter handed to her.

Tom simply hummed. He'd had to call a certain Norwegian billionaire to get the best table, but he didn't plan on telling her that.

"Have you been here before?" she asked.

"No." It was strange. They had lived in Kiruna for so many years but never eaten here. Ellinor always said it was too touristy.

"You don't think it's too touristy?" he asked.

She smiled, and her dimples appeared. "I am a tourist, so it's a good fit. But I'm so hungry I'm shaking. Can we order appetizers?"

Tom tore his eyes from her tempting dimples and ordered Kalix caviar for both of them. The orange delicacy arrived on top of a huge block of ice, with diced onion, sour cream, and small buckwheat waffles.

"It's a work of art," Ambra breathed.

"It's the local caviar, and the very best quality. The people of Norrbotten keep this to themselves."

"This might be the best thing I've ever eaten." Ambra sighed, sipping the champagne he had encouraged her to order. The color was back in her cheeks. Earlier, in the car, she'd seemed so tense he had seriously considered calling the whole thing off. He sipped his low-alcohol beer. She looked happy. Something, he realized, she rarely did. Usually, Ambra Vinter looked as if she were carrying the weight of democracy and the world on her shoulders. He liked her like this, giggly and bright eyed from expensive champagne, her dark locks reflecting the candles on the table. He caught her eye. Ambra twisted a lock around her finger and stuck out the tip of her tongue to catch a stray roe that had caught at the edge of her mouth. She picked up her glass and smiled at him over the rim. Champagne suited her. "How's Freja?" she asked.

"I gave her a new chew toy before I left, so I hope she isn't attacking my shoes or the furniture while I'm gone." She laughed.

They talked about everyday things while that special energy they had started to buzz between them. He asked about an article he had read. They talked about skiing (she had never been), about whether she should have wine or beer with the main course, and about gossip in the Swedish media—columnists who could barely write, editorial writers with megalomania, which attention-hungry celebrities would do almost anything just to appear in the paper. "There's one actor who always talks about how much he hates the tabloids in interviews and who calls us roughly every six months to ask why we haven't written about him in so long."

"Weird. So, what did you do today?" he asked as a waiter brought new cutlery and glasses for the main course.

"Saw Elsa, ate with her." She pulled gently on her ear, seemed to hesitate. "After that, I did an interview with a social worker."

"Was that why you came to Kiruna?"

"Yeah."

"Is it a secret interview?"

She played with her knife, ran her index finger over the table-cloth. "Not secret, exactly, but it's not really official either. Just something I'm looking into."

"Did it go well?"

She shook her head. "No." She looked down at the table with a frown. Her long lashes cast shadows over her cheeks. "It went badly."

"Want to talk about it?" he asked quietly.

He waited as she was served the red wine she'd ordered. Tom continued to drink his beer. Once the waiter disappeared, she said, "I have to say, these trips to Kiruna, they're definitely eventful. I met someone . . ." She fell silent. Her tense expression was back. Tom waited. She started over.

"I went to church today."

"In Kiruna?"

"Yeah. The father of the foster family I lived with was there."

"You were a foster kid up here?" He didn't remember whether they had talked about this before. But that would, of course, explain why she used to live here. He hadn't thought of that.

She nodded, twisted her glass. The red wine swirled inside the bowl. "Yeah. When I was ten. One of many foster families. One of the worst, actually."

"How many were you with?"

"Not sure. More than ten, in any case. I didn't stay with some of them very long. If they don't think you fit in, you move on."

"And if you don't like them?" he asked, feeling the anger bubble inside him.

She gave him a sarcastic look. "No one listens to the child. It makes no difference how it's supposed to be—that's the way it is. I don't actually remember how many families got sick of me. But that man. I ran away from him when I was eleven. It felt surreal to see him again. And the way I reacted was crazy."

"How?" he asked. He felt the hairs on his arms stand on end. What had the man done to her?

"It was like my body reacted automatically. I was thrown back to that time, felt all those old feelings. It was horrible." She took a deep gulp of her wine and looked up at him.

He definitely recognized that. But his flashbacks were from things he had experienced as a grown man, things he was trained to endure, things he had, in a sense, chosen to expose himself to. She was just a child. A small, orphaned girl.

"What happened when you lived with them?" he asked. Did they hit her? Other kinds of abuse? His grip tightened on the glass.

She had put her glass down and was sitting with her hands wrapped around her upper arms, as if she was freezing, though the room was warm. "All kinds of physical abuse. Punishments. Slaps. Psychological things too. Things I only really realized were completely sick once I was an adult. Nothing sexual," she added. As though that made it any better.

"Jesus," he said with emphasis.

"Yeah. And I know there are kids living with him and his wife now." Her voice broke slightly. She cleared her throat, tensed her jaw. "Anyway, I saw him in church today. It was tough."

She grabbed her glass and took a couple of sips. Her hand trembled, and Tom had to hold back from getting up, going over to her chair, pulling her into his arms, and saying that next time someone wanted to hurt her, she should come to him. Next time, they would have to go through him.

Ambra twisted her glass again. "When you see him—shit, I can't even say his name—objectively, you would never suspect a thing. It's a really strange feeling. That we can't tell what people are really like just by looking at them. Even today, that's one of the things I find most difficult. He's so decent on the surface. Calm and polite. Respected in the community. Everyone listens when he preaches. But he would change when he was at home. It was terrifying. The monster waiting inside," she said, taking a deep breath.

Tom nodded. He'd met plenty of monsters in his time, knew exactly what they could be like. Evil wasn't visible on the surface.

"In the end, you start to doubt your own experience," she said thoughtfully. "You think that you're overreacting, that you deserved a beating. That you're spoiled. Ungrateful. Even today I have trouble processing certain things I experience. It's hard to explain."

She gave him a lopsided smile. "I feel like I'm ruining the mood a little."

He wanted to place his hand on hers, tell her he liked their conversations, regardless of whether they were easygoing or serious.

Ambra was unlike Ellinor in so many ways. Ellinor didn't like difficult things, and he had automatically protected her from all the negative aspects of his work. She was a fundamentally happy and positive person, and she came from a stable, secure family. Ellinor looked to the future, and she had a phenomenal ability to shake off anything bad or unhappy. Tom always liked that about her, the fact she didn't get bogged down by things. But now he wondered whether that had actually helped drive them apart, the fact they never talked about the difficult things. Was that why he was attracted to Ambra? Because she was so different, new, and fascinating?

Though that wasn't the whole story, he knew. He liked Ambra because she was who she was. And because she was pretty, of course. There was no point denying that. Not strikingly beautiful like Ellinor. Ambra was like a complicated, well-crafted mechanism that you had to get near to appreciate.

"What?" she asked with a smile over the edge of her glass.

He was saved from answering by their food arriving. She had chosen the reindeer with juniper and lingonberry; he opted for the elk fillet with rösti and blueberry jelly. He was happy to have something else to focus on for a while. He needed to process his thoughts a little. It was desire he felt for Ambra—there was no point denying that. He'd been living like a dead man for so long, and now he was starting to feel alive. With life, sure as fate, came desire. It wasn't so strange. He was a man. She was a woman.

"My God, it's so good," she moaned, and he nodded.

They ate in comfortable silence. Ambra sipped her red wine and seemed to relax again. She was wearing a thin top the same color as the blocks of ice, and she had small, glittering stones in her ears. A memory of her long leg between his thighs fluttered through his mind. The way she looked when she closed her eyes and groaned into his mouth. What would she look like when she came?

"How are you doing?" she asked. "How are the panic attacks? Still as bad?"

It felt good that she asked straight out. It did him good, as though some of the shame lifted.

"It's okay," he replied honestly, spearing a piece of meat. "Better." She put her cutlery to one side and gave him an encouraging look. "I promised you secrets, I know. Ask away."

"How did they capture you?"

"I was in Chad, like I said. A rescue operation for a Swedish citizen."

"A woman," she pointed out.

"Yeah, a Swedish woman. My helicopter crashed; it was a ball of fire. My men assumed I was dead and left me behind."

"I didn't read about it anywhere."

There were Westerners in captivity all over the world, Swedes among them. The media knew about most, though they didn't tend to write about them out of consideration for their safety. But no one had ever found out he was being held in Chad.

"How long did they keep you prisoner?" she asked when he didn't say anything.

"A few months."

"Is that why you've been feeling like you have?"

"Yeah, I get flashbacks from things that happened."

She studied him with a steady gaze. "Sounds really damn tough. I've seen how powerful the attacks are. What a story. It's incredible."

"You can't write about it," he warned her.

"No, of course not." She glanced furtively at him. "Unless I can convince you? I really need a good scoop right now."

Her words were jokey, but Tom heard only the journalist in her. He shook his head.

"Definitely not. What I told you was in confidence. It can't end up in any newspaper."

"Got it," she said, holding up her hands.

"Want dessert as compensation?" he asked.

Her face lit up. "Definitely. The more the better. Dessert's almost better than a scoop."

Tom waved for the waiter to bring the dessert menu, then watched in amusement as she deliberated between arctic bramble panna cotta and seaberry mousse.

"You order one and I'll order the other. We can share," he offered.

After the desserts arrived, she asked, "Have you ever tried arctic bramble?"

"I didn't even know such a thing existed," he replied honestly.

"It's one of the best berries," she said, picking up a ruby-red berry from her panna cotta and holding it up to him. "They ripen under the midnight sun."

"Is that true?" he asked skeptically, digging his spoon into the mousse.

"No idea," she replied with a grin.

He laughed, and since she had already wolfed down most of her dessert, he pushed his over to her. "Here, take mine too. Have both."

She pulled it closer. "Thanks. Dessert overload. Just what I need after a day like today. Do you want to try the panna cotta?"

He shook his head, liked to watch her stuff herself full of sweet things. "How long are you staying this time?" he asked.

"I don't know. It depends."

Her words hung in the air between them. She scraped the bowl clean and licked her lips.

"How long can Freja cope without you?" she asked.

"I need to go home soon," he said. He had never realized how much responsibility it was to have a dog.

It was snowing gently when they went outside, huge flakes that caught in Ambra's hair and eyelashes. He didn't want to drive her back to the hotel just yet. It was so cold that the snow crunched as they walked over to the car. From time to time, their arms bumped and she didn't pull away. He wanted to put an arm around her, but instead he walked around the car and opened the door for her.

"Thanks," she said.

He grabbed the scraper and cleared the ice that had formed on the windshield. Afterward, he climbed inside and started the engine, but he didn't pull away. He debated with himself.

"It's not so late," he said.

"It's early," she agreed. Her voice was neutral.

"I'd like to stay out, but I need to get back to the dog."

"I understand," she said, looking at him.

"Want to come?" he asked.

She blinked.

"I can give you a ride back later," he added. *Unless you want to stay, of course.* He wanted to see her in his house again, curled up on the couch. He wanted to be with her.

Ambra looked at him for a moment. "Sometimes, Tom Lexington, I don't understand you at all. What happened to just being friends?"

"We *are* friends," he said.

"Maybe. But that's not all. Admit it."

"I like you."

"I like you too. And I'd like to go to your place. Even if you are the most difficult man in the universe."

"I'm not that bad," he said, putting the stick into gear and stepping on the gas. But maybe Ambra was right, he thought. He didn't know what he wanted anymore.

Chapter 32

So, she was back at Tom's place again. Ambra shook her head. He came out into the living room with Freja's leash in his hand.

"I'll get a fire going when I'm back, but I need to take her out first," he apologized. Freja barked and wagged her tail. Her huge body was trembling with joy.

"I'll manage," Ambra said, glad she wasn't expected to follow them outside. It was snowing more heavily now, and even the short distance from the car to the house had been enough to make her shiver.

"Make yourself at home. I need to take her for a good walk or she'll tear the place to shreds, but we'll be back soon." He gestured to the dog with his head. "Come on, you beast." Freja barked and almost knocked over a table on her way out.

Ambra waited until she heard the door close before she peered around the room. She moved over to the bookcase and aimlessly scanned the shelves. There was a small pile of Swedish paperbacks, but most of the books were in Norwegian or English. She absent-mindedly flicked through a book on the Northern Lights.

She strained to see whether she could hear them coming back, but when she didn't hear either Tom or Freja, she moved on, out of the living room.

What exactly did "make yourself at home" mean?

The house had a lot of doors. She would like to take a look inside a few of them, she thought, moving through the house.

Hmm, that looked like a gun cupboard. Made from thick metal.

Secured with what seemed like some kind of advanced combination lock. Ambra had no connection to weapons herself, but everyone up here probably had guns. Or was that just prejudice? She *hoped* the cupboard was full of hunting rifles and nothing else. Otherwise that was illegal, wasn't it? Even if you were ex-military? All she knew about Swedish gun laws was that most things were illegal, aside from weapons for hunting if you'd taken a course and had a license.

She studied a closed door. Damn, she was curious. Was Tom hiding something, or did he just not like open doors?

"Hello, we're back!" she heard from the hallway.

She hurried back into the living room. Freja came running in and shook herself, sending snow flying across the room. She ran over to Ambra and started sniffing her leg. Ambra scratched the dog behind the ear as she listened to Tom making noise in the kitchen. When he came in, he held out a bottle of beer.

"We didn't really do what we had planned, so I'll probably have to take her out again in a while. Just say if she gets too irritating," he added with a nod toward the dog.

"It's fine. She seems to like me." She noticed he was still drinking low-alcohol beer, so clearly he was serious about his offer to give her a ride back later. He smiled, and his eyes were warm.

Ambra swigged her beer and glanced at him. She had never really bought into the idea that you could be physically attracted to someone without any kind of intellectual connection. But she still wasn't sure about Tom and who he really was. And yet, she really wanted to have sex with him.

Tom was crouched down in front of the fireplace. He methodically cleared away the ash, added new wood, and built up a small pyramid of logs. The stack didn't take long to start crackling. The flames rose upward. Ambra sat on the couch and put down her beer. She didn't feel like drinking any more.

"That has to be the best sound," she said.

He mumbled a reply. The fire smelled great too. And was so warm. She sighed gently with contentment.

Tom came back and sat down on the other end of the long couch. Ambra pulled her cell phone from her bag. It was almost dead, the battery on red. "I didn't bring my charging cable," she said.

"It's the cold."

"Yeah, do you have one for this?" She held up her phone.

He shook his head. "Only an older one. Do you even have any coverage?"

Ambra studied the bars on her dying phone. "Barely," she admitted.

"It's difficult to get Wi-Fi out here in the forest because we're so isolated. I'm on a different provider, but it doesn't always work."

She put down her phone, didn't like how dependent on it she felt. She curled her legs beneath her.

"Are you cold?" he asked, immediately getting up and fetching a blanket for her. She draped it over her legs and studied him thoughtfully. The atmosphere had changed. It was one thing to spend time together in a busy restaurant, but now she was alone here, and they didn't know one another. Not really. Though maybe she was just paranoid. Trust wasn't exactly one of her greatest strengths.

"Are your parents still alive?" she asked. He was so solitary, like one of those enormous boulders dragged into the middle of nowhere by a glacier. But he had to have come from somewhere.

"My dad died a long time ago. Mom is still alive. And I have three sisters, though we don't talk much."

Ambra twisted the fringe on the blanket and wondered how that felt, to have blood ties with someone and then decide to have nothing to do with them. She understood it could happen, of course. You couldn't choose your family. But still. Having a living mother, several siblings, people you looked like, relatives.

"Why don't you talk to them?"

"It's my fault. I couldn't do it, not while I was feeling so bad."

"Aren't they worried?"

"*Everyone* is worried. That's the problem."

"What was it like before you left? Were you close?"

"It's complicated," he said with a deep sigh and a furrowed brow. Tom and his complicated relationships.

"My mom cried when I joined the special forces. I guess she knew what it involved. You have to live a parallel life. She felt like she lost me."

"Did you enjoy it there?" she asked, though she suspected she knew the answer. A certain look appeared on his face whenever he talked about the special forces.

"Yeah, I did."

She didn't ask any more. No one said as little as special forces men. Not even their press spokesman talked to the press. Part of her assumed that they loved the secrecy of it.

Tom got up from the couch and stoked the fire, added more wood. "Would you prefer coffee?" he asked over his shoulder.

She smiled at the way he didn't miss a thing. "Maybe a little tea?" she said.

He went out to the kitchen, and when he came back she took the steaming mug he handed her. He was drinking coffee. It smelled good, strong. She strolled over to his bookcase, sipped the tea, and allowed her eyes to wander; she loved gathering information that way.

"When was this taken?" she asked when she spotted an old photo. It was of Tom and three other young men, all in green army clothing. Their faces were painted, and they seemed to be in a plane.

"It's old," he said. "We were just about to jump, somewhere above Lake Vättern. An ordinary day, an ordinary exercise."

"You look so happy," she said, studying the picture more closely. She had never seen him like that: grinning, carefree. Not weighed down.

"Yeah."

"Was it during your training?" she asked.

He seemed to hesitate, but then he quickly nodded.

"Was that where you met Mattias?"

"Yeah, we met in Karlsborg. Probably the best time of my life."

She knew a little about the training they underwent there so she said, skeptically, "But you basically get tortured there?"

He shrugged. "It's not for everyone. I can't explain it. They test you in difficult situations until they know what you can do, know that you'll perform when it counts most. Every man wonders whether he could handle it. Those of us who went through the training, we know we can. It's some lame manly thing, I guess."

She put the picture back on the shelf. "I know it's not the same thing as training to be in the special forces, but I've done a few safety courses. They send us on them all the time."

"People handle that type of pressure differently," Tom said.

"Yeah, I know. I've seen tough CEOs break down, hardened war reporters act completely irrationally when they're put under pressure."

"And you?" He was looking at her with interest.

She flashed him a blinding smile. "I loved it."

Tom smiled. "Have you ever needed to use any of what you learned?"

"Only mentally. I've never been in a really tight spot."

"That's the most important part, the mental toughness."

Ambra gave him a skeptical look. "Really?"

"Yeah. Survival is about knowing which risks are worth taking, and that's something you can learn."

"How?"

"Simple things really. Pausing. Accepting the new conditions. Exploring what options you have."

"And then what? Scream for all you're worth?" She smiled, and her eyes got caught in his. She turned away and moved on to the next object she found. It was hard to think rationally when he was looking at her so hungrily. "What's this?" she asked, and she realized that she sounded slightly breathless. It was a small plastic toy, and it seemed completely out of place in its masculine surroundings. "A bear?"

When he took it out of her hand, his fingers brushed hers, and she felt a tingling rush. "I got it as a gift when I left my unit. It ended up here with a lot of other things from my office. It's a grizzly bear." He was silent, twisting and turning the little toy before he said, "That was my codename in the special forces. Grizzly. No one outside of Karlsborg knows that."

"No one?" she asked, thinking of Ellinor.

But he shook his head. "No one but you."

She studied him for a long moment. "Grizzly suits you," she eventually said. He put the bear back onto the shelf. "Maybe I should go home," she said reluctantly. It was snowing more heavily now, and it was getting late.

"Do you want to?" he asked quietly.

She slowly shook her head.

"I like talking with you," he said, and his eyes moved across her face, lingered on her mouth. He smelled faintly of coffee and mint, and she loved that he had clearly brushed his teeth when he went out with Freja, that he smelled so good. All she wanted was for Tom to kiss her.

Their dinner, the entire evening, had been leading up to this moment. He ran a finger down her temple and then stopped and looked at her. She leaned forward and he kissed her. Ambra closed her eyes. Let all the other senses take over, noticed his smell, his taste, his roughness. She loved his mouth, his lips. His tongue, oh yes, definitely his tongue. Tom kissed powerfully. Not gently, not awkwardly, there was no question there, just a kiss that took control. He raised a hand to the back of her neck and pulled her toward him. She did the same, her other hand on his bicep, and trembled slightly when she felt his muscular arm. There was something so primitive about these kisses, and it was divine. He shook his head.

"Damn, I don't know what to say," he said. His dark eyes were impossible to read.

Nothing, she thought spontaneously. Don't say anything, keep going. She was completely overwhelmed by the attraction she felt. And he felt it, too, that much was clear.

"Ambra," he said. It sounded so sexy, her name in his mouth, though they should be kissing more and talking less. She looked at him and tried to show all those feelings in her eyes. *Kiss me.*

His rib cage, rising beneath his tight shirt, his pecs, his biceps—all his damn muscles. And then he kissed her again and Ambra clung onto him and let herself be swept along.

She placed her hand on Tom's chest, and he groaned into her mouth as she pressed herself against him, pressed her entire body against his hard arousal, urging, encouraging, and *finally,* his enormous palm moved to her breast and the effect was almost electric. Ambra felt his hand through the thin material, heard his breathing in her ear, took in the scent of him, the smell of fire and wood, coffee and winter. He brought her cheek to his warm skin. He was breathing more heavily now, his thumb moving deliberately over her nipple. His hand snaked in beneath her shirt, over her bra and then under that too. Ambra couldn't hold back a pant. He cupped her breast, bit her ear gently, and mumbled something she couldn't hear. She pressed herself against him, dragged her nails down his chest, over his T-shirt. Tom wrapped an arm around her waist, pulled her tight, panted . . .

And then they were interrupted by a bottomless howl. It was Freja, who had positioned herself by their feet and started to wail. A deafening sound that made it very difficult to kiss.

"Quiet, Freja," Tom said, though he laughed as he said it. "I'm sorry. I forgot she needed to go out again. It's usually pretty urgent when she sounds like that. Might as well get it over and done with."

"Sure," Ambra said, and Tom pulled her into his arms and kissed her until she whimpered against his mouth, until her hands were on his upper arms, moving across his back, up to his neck. Jesus, this was madness. All she wanted was to get under his shirt, to feel him, but Freja was still howling and Ambra pulled herself free and started to laugh.

"You'd better go out. That way we won't have any accidents."

Chapter 33

Tom pulled on his coat, gloves, and scarf. When he opened the door, the snow swirled inside. The temperature had dropped dramatically. Freja barked angrily at the weather.

"Out with you," he told her.

The dog threw herself outside. He followed her, hunched over against the snow, trudging through the drifts. The question was whether he would even be able to make it back to Kiruna tonight. Though maybe he wouldn't need to. Quickly and willingly, he got lost in thoughts of Ambra.

Sexy, hot thoughts of smooth limbs and quick hands. Soft lips and a fragrant, welcoming body waiting for him.

He felt like a normal man around her, not a weakened freak or a violence machine, just a person. He wanted to discover and explore every inch of her. See which other arousing sounds he could coax out of her. Wanted to take off one piece of clothing after another, peel them away and unwrap her like a gift. Explore and caress. Kiss her until her lips were swollen and her cheeks flushed.

His cell phone started to ring, and he hurried to pull it from his pocket; maybe Ambra was worried. But it wasn't Ambra. It was Isobel De la Grip. He peered after Freja indecisively. But she had found an interesting snowdrift and was ignoring him completely. His phone continued to ring. He didn't want to talk to Isobel. He wanted to hurry back to Ambra. But this wasn't the first time Isobel had called him lately, so maybe it was just as well he got it over and done with.

"Hello, this is Tom Lexington," he answered.

"Tom! I'd almost given up. I'm so glad you answered, and sorry for calling so late. How are you?"

Tom liked the redheaded doctor. He also admired her work in the field—she had gone through things most people couldn't even imagine. When she asked how he was, he knew it was out of genuine concern.

"Sorry I didn't answer. I've had a lot on my mind."

"I understand, please don't feel bad. I didn't mean to chase you. I just wanted to ask you something. Do you know a journalist named Ambra Vinter?"

Tom stopped dead. That was probably the last thing he was expecting. "Why?" he replied guardedly.

"She's a reporter from *Aftonbladet*. She called me. Wanted to ask questions about the rescue mission in Chad. She asked all kinds of things. I know you haven't said anything, but there aren't many of us who know what happened."

"This is the first I'm hearing about it," Tom said.

He gripped the phone in his hand, felt a weight building on his chest, could barely believe what he was hearing. "When did she call you?"

"A few days ago. I'm so worried. I don't want to be a burden on you. I know you've had more than enough to deal with. But we agreed not to say anything. We've run into problems with the adoption."

"I thought it was all done."

"So did we. But it's some bureaucratic crap, and I'm terrified the authorities will say no if they find out how Marius got here, if they find out what happened down there. I just wanted to check whether you knew anything. Has she been in contact with you? Alexander and David haven't heard from her." Isobel, who was one of the most composed people he knew, sounded worried, almost on the verge of breaking down. And it was all Ambra's fault.

"I'll look into it, Isobel. Thanks for calling. And don't worry, I'm sure it's nothing." He kept his tone brief and calm, but inside he felt ice cold. What the hell was going on? What was he missing?

"I don't know what I'll do if we lose Marius."

"I know. I'll take care of it."

She was silent. "Thanks, Tom," she eventually said.

"No problem," he replied, but the guilt weighed him down. He was the one who had talked. Ambra's information had come from him. It was the oldest trick in the book. A pair of pretty eyes, a little attention and some kisses, and that was all it took for him to spill secret after secret. He'd even *offered* to tell her more if she went to dinner. How stupid could a man be?

He shouted for Freja and trudged back toward the house. He would have to accept that he'd been tricked, that Ambra had betrayed him.

He silently opened the door. Listened but couldn't hear any sounds. What was she doing, taking the chance to snoop around while he was out? How much had she already seen? The paranoia was taking hold of him.

He moved inside without a sound, but there was no sign of her. He silently took off his coat and dropped it to the floor, allowed his instincts to take over. Gestured for Freja to lie down. He gently opened the door. Ambra wasn't in the living room. Not in the kitchen either. He moved toward the hallway and the doors there. One of them was slightly more ajar than he'd left it. He'd trusted her. He still hoped he was wrong, that Isobel was mistaken. He pushed the door to his study. It swung open without a sound. Ambra was in the middle of the room, looking at the documents spread out on the floor.

"What are you doing?" he asked, and she jumped.

She turned around, and did at least have the decency to look guilty. "I didn't hear you coming."

"What are you doing in here?"

"I was going to the bathroom and the door was open." She moved her arm in a sweeping gesture over the documents. Reports from Chad. Pictures. "What is all this?" she asked.

"I can't see how that is any of your business." He tried to assess the situation objectively. Twisted and turned everything she had asked him since they'd met, skillful questions.

He could barely believe it, but Ambra had pumped him for information. It was painfully obvious now. She was a journalist with a tabloid. She made her living uncovering things. And then she'd stumbled over this. No, not stumbled, he had given her a possible scoop. Exposed Isobel. Other sensitive information. If Ambra had had time to read any of the documents, she would know that people had died because of him.

Everything he'd said to her was in confidence. It was a long time since he'd last felt so deceived, so betrayed, a long time since he last *was* so badly betrayed. He'd even told her his fucking code name. Not that it was confidential anymore, but even so.

He took a step toward her.

"I was looking for the bathroom," she repeated, her voice strained, "and I know I shouldn't have come in here. I'm sorry. I told you I'm curious, and then I saw it was about Chad, and I shouldn't . . . I can see you're really mad. Sorry. I'm sorry, I didn't mean . . ." She wrung her hands looking distraught.

He couldn't tell if she was acting. The attraction he felt for her knocked out all of his usual instincts.

"Why did you call Isobel De la Grip?" he asked.

Ambra swallowed again. He could see her slim throat working. Didn't she realize how exposed she was out here, all alone with him? How easily he would have been able to hurt her if he was that type of man? Her lack of caution made him even angrier.

"What do you mean?" she asked. Her voice trembled toward the end of the sentence, giving her away.

"You know what I mean," he exploded. "Are you spying on me?" He could hear how furious he sounded. He *was* furious, not the least at himself, that he had let himself be so affected by her that it clouded his judgment. That he never suspected she might have an ulterior motive. That he'd allowed himself to be deceived.

Suddenly, the light on the ceiling flickered. The room went dark for a moment before it came back on. The storm was affecting the power. Ambra's face was tense.

"I think it's best if I go back to the hotel," she said, and her chest heaved beneath her thin blouse.

"Not quite yet. We need to talk a little, you and I. But first: Get out of here!" He moved to one side, saw her hesitate.

He waited. The light went out again, came back on. The power seemed close to cutting out.

"Go," he said.

She left the room without looking at him. Her scent lingered in his nostrils, and he had to force himself to focus on reality, not the fantasy he had tricked himself into believing. "You can't write about Chad—you know that, right?" he said.

She didn't reply.

"Ambra . . ." He laid a hand on her shoulder. She jerked away as if he had hit her.

"Actually, I don't think you can tell me what I can or can't write. There were documents in that room talking about firefights and dead villagers. Who killed them?"

He crossed his arms. The light in the hallway flickered, and he thought he could hear the storm coming. "It's more complicated than that."

"Everything's so fucking complicated with you." She trudged back to the living room, and he followed her. Freja was waiting for them, looked up anxiously, as though she could tell something was happening.

"You need to realize that this is serious. What I told you, it was in confidence."

"So you aren't denying you killed people in Chad?"

"I can't talk about that. How much have you told your bosses? Who else have you mentioned this to?"

"Come on."

"Seriously, you have to back off."

"I don't have to do anything. It feels like we're done here. I want to go back now."

He was so angry with her. And with himself. How could he have let himself be duped this way? It was embarrassing. "The roads are almost snowed closed. You should've thought of that before you started playing master spy," he snapped.

"No. I want to leave. Now. If you aren't going to give me a ride, then I'll have to . . ."

She really didn't get it. He grabbed her hand hard, pulled her down the hallway, and tore open the door. Wind and snow swirled inside. The storm had really arrived. Going out would be suicide.

"Be my guest," he said sarcastically.

She stared at the storm. The snow was pouring down.

Tom dropped her hand and gave her a furious look. "Whether you like it or not, sweetheart, you're stuck here with me."

Chapter 34

Ambra was trying not to show how scared she was. But Tom frightened her. What she'd done was wrong, she knew that. You didn't snoop around the way she had. But she'd peered in through the crack in the door and seen the documents spread out; then somehow she found herself taking a step into the room and saw the pictures. They were images of war and devastation. She saw what looked like dead people, mutilated bodies, saw reports about firefights and losses.

This was serious, she thought as her heart pounded and Tom stared at her with ice-cold eyes. The images could be proof of something really terrible. She was afraid now. Tom was suddenly a different person. A stranger who terrified her. The light on the ceiling flickered again. Jesus, she really hoped it was only a temporary power issue. Tom stepped toward her, and she flinched instinctively. He frowned. She was breathing heavily. Her very first foster home. There was a man. He was the first one to hit her. He used to scare her and then hit her. She still had trouble dealing with sudden movements. She had taught herself not to be afraid, but now she was so terrified she wasn't quite in control.

The lamp flickered one last time, she saw Tom's face, and then they were plunged into darkness.

"What's going on?" she asked, aware of how scared she sounded.

"The power's out," was all he said. She could only just make him out, a compact darkness amid all the other darkness. She blinked, couldn't see anything. Her cell phone was out of power. No one knew she was here. She'd been so stupid, so careless. The darkness was penetrating, and she was finding it difficult to breathe.

"Ambra? What are you doing?"

She tried to think clearly and logically. Tried to stop breathing so damn hard. She could feel the cold sweat beneath her arms.

"Ambra?"

"What?" she said, her voice small.

She heard him move. She hadn't moved an inch. Part of her knew she might be overreacting, but she couldn't think straight.

"I need to see if I can get the power back on," he said curtly. The grown-up part of her knew his hand wasn't raised to hit her; he was just grabbing the door. But she didn't really know him at all. He was twice her size, strong as a bear. And he had pictures of dead people in his office. Panic threatened to take over. As he moved out into the dark hallway, she heard his footsteps, but otherwise he was silent.

"What are you doing?" he asked.

"Nothing." *I don't want to be here. I'm so scared I can't think.*

"I need to find a flashlight that works. There are candles in the kitchen. And the fire is still going."

He disappeared again. She was at a crossroads. Should she go back to the living room, deeper into the house? Or should she stay in the hallway, where she was closer to an exit?

She had to pull herself together. Act. She was capable, not helpless. *Think, Ambra.* She couldn't stay here, which meant she had to get away. That was her only option. But how? If Tom wouldn't give her a ride, she would have to come up with something herself. But even if she made it to the car, it wouldn't be able to handle the storm. It would get stuck in the snow straight away.

The snowmobile!

Keys, she had seen keys somewhere. She closed her eyes and racked her memory. The kitchen. She'd seen keys on a hook in the kitchen. It said *snowmobile* above the hook. She could hear him rummaging around in the house. Her heart was pounding.

"Ambra?" he shouted again.

She couldn't tell whether he sounded angry, irritated, or something else.

"What?"

"I'm downstairs, trying to get the backup generator going."

Perfect. She hurried to the kitchen as fast as she could. He had lit a gas lamp in there. She found the hook and the key for one of the snowmobiles. The clinking sound made her hold her breath, but he was still making a noise downstairs and didn't seem to notice anything.

She paused. What was she doing? It was cold and snowy outside. But she hated the fact he was refusing to give her a ride, that he scared her. To hell with him. She sneaked back out into the hallway. She fumbled along one wall and found what she was looking for—overalls. She pulled them on. Managed to find her scarf, hat, and gloves. Drenched in sweat, she pulled on shoes. Paused again. Was this really a good idea? But she'd had enough. He had shown her how to start it, said it was easy. He would just have to come into town to pick up the snowmobile tomorrow; she was only borrowing it. It wasn't far into town. How hard could it be? And she had warm clothes; she would make it. He wouldn't decide whether she stayed or left. It was her choice. He could go to hell.

Ambra left the house and closed the door quietly behind her, gasped for breath in the wind, pulled her hat down onto her head, did up the zipper as far as she could, and then hurried toward the garage through the heavy snow and whipping winds.

She made it without any trouble. It wasn't locked, and she opened the door with a pant, propped it open. The air was calm inside. The shiny black car glittered threateningly at her, but there, there were the two snowmobiles. Still no sign of Tom. She took down a helmet from the wall. For a moment, she thought about going back to the house, but she sat down on one of the snowmobiles and studied the controls, tried to remember what he'd done, what he'd said.

She pulled on the helmet over her hat, fastened it, put the key into the ignition, and started the engine. She gripped the handles, took a deep breath, bit her lip, and accelerated. The snowmobile took off so quickly that she almost lost control when it flew out of the garage. But she clung onto the handles, turned gently, and then she was really speeding ahead.

Tom was right, it was super easy to drive. She'd done it! The snow whirled around her and she hunched down behind the handle bars.

The thing was insanely fast. She steered it away from the house, and the snowmobile sped across the ground. When she turned around, she saw the house disappear from view, and then the forest enveloped her. She was on her way. At this rate, she would be back in Kiruna in no time. If the police stopped her, she would ask for a ride, but in this weather they would surely let her drive in town, even if it wasn't allowed? She would soon be back in her room, in her bed, and once she managed to charge her cell phone, she would send Tom a message to pick up the snowmobile.

After a while, her initial excitement started to fade. It was much colder and darker than she had expected. Didn't everyone say that the snow made the night brighter? But it was terribly dark, despite the snowmobile's powerful headlights. And despite her layers, she had started to shiver. She was almost there, it couldn't be far now. As long as she stuck to the road, it would all be fine.

She squinted, had trouble seeing through all the snow. Was she still on the road? It was hard to tell; it felt as if the trees were closing in around her. Shouldn't there have been a road sign or something by now?

She slowed down, glanced around, continued, but a few minutes later she was forced to admit it. She had no idea where she was. She was lost, like an idiot.

There was nothing but forest and snow and darkness all around her. The wind whipped at her face, and she was now so cold that her teeth were chattering. She sped up again, but the sinking feeling inside her grew.

She had overreacted, been a typical, naive city girl about the weather, and she'd let her fear take over. In doing so, she had gotten herself into something that might be a much, much bigger threat than Tom Lexington ever could be.

Chapter 35

Tom heard a noise upstairs. It sounded like the front door closing. Hadn't he closed it properly earlier? He wiped his hands on a rag and wondered what Ambra was doing up there; he hadn't heard from her in a while. It felt good to get away from her for a few minutes. He'd been so angry before, but now he felt calmer, realized he might have overreacted. He still felt betrayed, but he was also partly to blame for that.

With a sigh, he gave up on the backup generator. He couldn't get it going. It was sloppy of him not to check it earlier. He cocked his head and listened. The house was completely silent. Freja whimpered anxiously.

"Don't worry," he hushed her as he heard a low humming noise outside. At first, he didn't know what it could be. It sounded like a snowmobile, but it couldn't be. Could the storm sound like that?

He put his tools back into the box and headed toward the stairs.

"Ambra?" he shouted.

No reply. Freja sniffed the air. Something wasn't right. The atmosphere in the house felt different; he couldn't explain it any better than that. He quickly climbed the stairs, searched using his powerful flashlight. The house was silent and seemed empty. Ambra wasn't on the couch or by the fire. She wasn't by the gas lamp in the kitchen, either.

The sound of the engine was louder now. It was outside, definitely one of the snowmobiles. It tore off. Tom went over to the front door, which blew shut at that exact moment. He turned the handle. What the hell was she doing? The sound of the snowmobile vanished.

When he opened the door, the wind swirled inside. He couldn't see a thing. Ambra and the snowmobile were already gone. But he didn't understand. Ambra had to realize it was crazy to drive off like that. He hurried into the kitchen. Sure enough, the keys were gone.

Confusion and irritation were slowly replaced by unease. He'd been angry before, he knew that, but was it enough to drive her to this? It was hard to believe. She didn't think he would hurt her, did she? No, he couldn't believe that. He'd been so hurt, felt so stupid, but that was all. What should he do now? Would she manage to find the main road? Would she try to make it to the hotel? The snow was still coming down heavily, and the temperature was dropping steadily. If she didn't make it, she could be in serious trouble.

He looked down at Freja. "What do we do now?" The dog whimpered in reply.

With growing unease, he went back into the kitchen, took down the keys for the other snowmobile, continued into the living room, and blew out all the candles. The fire was still burning, and he put up a fire shield in front of it. He pulled on his boots, took out a rucksack, and packed a foil blanket, a bottle of water, a knife, a fire striker, and a flashlight. He added a rope, too. Should he stay in the house and wait? But what if something happened to her? If she drove off the road, crashed?

He quickly pulled on a snowsuit and gloves. "Stay," he said to Freja.

As he walked over to the garage, it felt as if he was about to be blown over. With a deepening sense of panic, he started the second snowmobile and set off. He had a really bad feeling now. Ambra was a city girl, probably didn't realize how quickly a person could get hypothermia, how dangerous it was. How quickly you lost your judgment in the cold. He knew how to track and he knew the terrain, but if she had gone off-road it would probably be impossible to find her. He drove off, tried to stick to a slow-enough speed to track her but quick enough not to lose precious time.

After an hour or so of searching, he was starting to get seriously worried. Did he dare hope she'd made it all the way to Kiruna? He wished he could call the hotel to ask if she was there, but he had no coverage at all out here in the forest.

The question was whether he should go back to the house and try to call from there, or whether he should keep looking. But if he made it back, managed to get through to the hotel and Ambra *wasn't* there, that would be crucial time he had wasted. Because there was no doubt: It could be a matter of life and death now.

He drove in wide circles. An hour and twenty minutes had passed. It had to be at least twenty below zero, but the wind chill made it feel even worse. His eyes scanned the snow.

And then he saw it.

The snowmobile. It was on its side, looked like it had crashed into a tree.

He sped up, drove over, and jumped off. Ambra was lying beside the snowmobile, curled up on her side in the fetal position.

He got onto his knees beside her. It seemed like a gentle fall. Her helmet had protected her, and she wasn't lying in a strange position, but you never knew.

"Ambra!" he shouted over the wind. She didn't respond.

How badly hurt was she? He lowered his cheek to her mouth to check if she was breathing. He felt a faint breath and almost shouted with relief. He took off his gloves and wrapped his hand around her wrist, but he couldn't feel a pulse. When a person's blood pressure fell, that was where it vanished first. Instead, he managed to bring a finger to her neck. He felt a pulse, weak but regular.

"Ambra? Can you hear me?" No reply. He unzipped her jacket and managed to get through all of her layers, placing his knuckles against her breastbone. He hated the idea of hurting her, but if she didn't wake up she would need to go to the hospital. She didn't seem to have hurt her neck. The ground beneath her was soft and she looked okay, but he wasn't sure. He pressed his knuckles against her breastbone and saw her face twist into a grimace. "Ow."

"Ambra," he said, relieved beyond all words. If she was breathing and had a pulse, he wouldn't need to give her CPR, which would have been a nightmare in these conditions.

"Do you know who I am?"

"Tom," she said. Then she fell silent. The question now was whether to take her to the hospital or back to the house. The journey to the hospital would be long and dangerous; she was talking normally and her pupils reacted to light when he shone the flashlight in her eyes.

"Ambra," he said as he started to wrap the foil blanket around her.

He left her helmet as it was. "Do you know where you are, what happened?"

"Stop asking stupid questions," she muttered, and he smiled despite the terrible situation. She sounded like herself, and that was all he wanted to hear.

"I'm taking you back now," he said.

When he picked her up, she seemed lifeless again. He climbed onto the snowmobile with her in his arms and started the engine. He drove off as quickly as he dared.

The minutes back to the house felt like hours. Ambra didn't stir once in his arms, but he focused on the ground ahead of them, on what he would do when he made it back, how he would do it.

He drove up to the door, quickly carried her inside, and laid her down in front of the open fire, still wrapped in the foil blanket.

The house was cold and dark, but he had to get the snowmobile back into the garage—it was the only means of transport he had if the storm continued, cutting them off from the outside world. And it was also better to warm her up slowly. Her heart might stop otherwise.

Tom parked the snowmobile in the garage and ran back to the house as quickly as he could. Ambra was where he had left her, with Freja by her side.

He pulled off her gloves, sat down, and managed to take her helmet off.

"Are you awake?" he asked. When she didn't reply, he pinched her cheek gently.

"Stop it," she mumbled. He stroked her forehead, carefully checking for bumps or cuts. Nothing. Her chest was moving slowly, and the sense of relief made his heart ache.

But she was far from being in the clear yet. The house had no power, no warm water. The risk of a collapse was huge if she didn't get the right care; Tom knew that, he had covered this kind of thing countless times in his training. Get the body temperature up, slowly and steadily. He grabbed his Swiss army knife and started to cut off her clothing, first her overalls, then her jeans, from her ankles up to her waist, careful that he didn't nick her skin. She would probably be furious that he had ruined her clothes, he thought as he took off the belt, without damaging it. In fact, he almost hoped she would be. Because an angry Ambra meant a living Ambra. And there was no other way of getting soaked jeans off.

He couldn't get her shoes off, and so he had to cut those off, too, after which he pulled off her socks. Next, he cut her shirt open. She was wearing a camisole beneath it, and that went the same way. He didn't even think. He just pulled off her panties and bra, looked away, covered her with a blanket, and then started to search for frostbite on her hands and feet. It was hard to say, but she didn't seem to have any serious damage. She had a few marks that would turn into deep bruises, but she didn't seem to have broken anything, and her chest was still rising and falling.

After he went to fetch another blanket, he spent more time looking for wounds, swellings, anything that might suggest internal injuries. She *seemed* fine, but he didn't dare say that for certain.

Once she was dry and properly bundled, he started to work on building up the fire. As it burned, he went to get pillows, which he placed beneath her head. Her face was no longer quite so gray, and Tom finally felt confident enough to go take his own outer clothing off. He pulled on a dry T-shirt and pants.

She still hadn't moved, but she was a much better color now, and her chest was moving regularly. When he took her pulse, it already felt much stronger. He quickly went to grab a flashlight and a thermometer. He boiled some water and filled a cup, added spoonful after spoonful of sugar. Back in the living room, he checked her pulse again, and noticed she had more color in her face.

"Ambra, open your eyes," he said. Her eyelashes fluttered, and her pupils contracted when he shone the light into them. "How are you feeling?"

"I'm freezing. I hate freezing."

"I need to take your temperature," he said, sticking the thermometer into her ear. He heard a beep and looked down: ninety-three degrees.

"Do you know where you are?" he asked.

"Think so," she mumbled. She sounded like she had just woken up, slightly confused, but not like she was hallucinating.

He quickly lit all the candles he could find and placed them around the room. He would let her stay here, where it was warm, he decided. He carried two thick mattresses down from upstairs and laid them next to one another. He made up a bed by the fire.

"I'm going to pick you up now," he said.

"Yeah, yeah," she muttered. He lifted her onto one of the mattresses. She looked so small, weighed almost nothing in his arms.

Still shaken, he looked down at the woman who could easily have died out there in the forest. Was there someone he should call? What would he say? That he had terrified Ambra so much she'd risked her own life to escape him? He checked his cell phone. There was no service in the storm, so that decided that.

He touched her skin; she was still cold, and he took her temperature again. It was rising. He sat down next to her. She needed to drink some liquid.

"Ambra, you need to wake up."

"Why?" Her voice was drowsy and slightly irritated.

He lifted her head and placed another cushion beneath it. "Open your mouth," he ordered, and when she eventually did as he asked, he gave her half a teaspoon. "Three of these, then you can sleep, okay?"

She sighed deeply but opened her mouth and allowed him to feed her. "Now I need to rest," she mumbled, and then she was gone again.

Tom watched Freja, who was wagging her tail miserably. He carefully lay down next to Ambra. She didn't react. He felt her forehead and her hands. She was slightly less chilly. He pulled gently at the covers he had placed on top of her. She was so still. He glanced at Freja, who gave him a wretched look and laid her head on her front paws. "It'll be fine, girl," he promised. The best source of heat was actually skin-to-skin contact, but he made do with creeping in beneath the covers so that there was a sheet between them. She felt warmer. He shifted closer.

"I'm so scared," she suddenly mumbled. Her voice sounded small, and since her eyes were still closed he doubted she knew where she was or what she was saying. She frowned and then sobbed, a silent, tortured sob. "Don't say a word, please."

"Ambra, you don't need to worry," he said, struck by the fear in her voice. Was that his doing?

She shook her head but didn't say any more. After a moment's hesitation, he took her hand and held it, listened to her breathing. It wasn't quite steady, but he thought she was sleeping, not unconscious. She was so small beside him, giving off practically no warmth at all.

"Sorry," she said after a moment. Her voice sounded tortured. "I was stupid, I know, sorry. Please."

"It's fine, Ambra," he said, stroking her hand.

A concerned look had appeared on her face again. "Just don't tell Tom, I was so scared of him."

"You don't need to worry," he whispered, over and over again.

All his life, he had tried to help people. And as a soldier, he had always seen it as his duty to protect women and children in particular. What he'd subjected Ambra to . . . He felt ruined. Wretched. She was under his roof and she had fled. Out of fear of him. Because he scared her. He had betrayed everything he believed in, all of his ideals.

After a while, she started to stir, and she turned with a groan, her back to him. Tom waited, a breath in his throat, but it seemed she was still asleep. He didn't want to leave her, and it seemed as if his closeness helped to calm her, so he lay down on the mattress beside hers. His hand lingered on her slender shoulder. She was breathing calmly now, no nightmares, no anxiety. But he really didn't want to leave her, wanted to keep an eye on her, and so he pulled a blanket over himself and lay there next to her. If anything happened, if she felt afraid or in pain, he would notice immediately. The fire crackled. Freja moved over to his feet, and they lay there like that, all three of them, until eventually he fell asleep.

Chapter 36

Ambra woke slowly with a terrible feeling inside her. Something was wrong, she knew it before she was even awake, long before she opened her eyes. All she wanted was to stay asleep, didn't want to face whatever had scared her.

Was she a grown woman, or was she a child?

It was one of her recurring nightmares, that she was still a foster child at the mercy of someone else. But no, she didn't live with the Sventins anymore, nor anyone else for that matter. She was a grown woman; she'd had her own home and a real job for years.

So why was she so scared? Was it a nightmare, or had something actually happened? Was she sick?

Something had happened, she could feel it, something she didn't want to think about. She was so cold last night, must have forgotten to close the window. And she almost felt as if she had been drugged. Was she hungover?

Reluctantly, she opened her eyes. She would never be able to get back to sleep now anyway.

She wasn't home; she saw that immediately. The room was dark, but she wasn't home. Where was she? She was genuinely disoriented. How could she not know where she was?

She tried to blink the sleep and the grit from her eyes, but it was too exhausting. And she couldn't get her brain to work. She gave up, closed her eyes, felt herself float away. So good.

"Ambra? How are you?"

Someone was touching her forehead, forcing her to come back. A low, worried voice. "You slept for twenty hours. Are you awake? You need to drink a little more."

All she wanted was to sleep; she was completely exhausted.

"Ambra?" Someone was shaking her now, not hard but firmly. "You *need* some liquid."

"I'm so tired," she whispered. It sounded more like a croak.

"I'll help you sit up."

"Tom?" she asked, confused. What was Tom doing here? Wasn't he in Kiruna? Wait. She was in Kiruna. Or was that just a dream?

"Don't go back to sleep. Come on, I'll help you." He pulled her arm and helped her to sit up against the pillows. She was so drained that she slumped backward. But then she realized she really was thirsty. Her mouth was so dry she could barely swallow.

"Drink this. Slowly," he said, handing her a cup of tea. She pulled a face when she tasted it. It was far too sweet.

"Drink."

She drank half of it before he took the cup away from her. "You can have some more in a minute," he said.

She licked her lips. They were dry. "What happened?"

"Do you know where you are?" His eyes were serious.

Ambra looked around. "Your house," she said. But she still didn't understand. What was she doing in his living room? On the floor? Had she fainted? She couldn't remember a thing.

"You took one of the snowmobiles and drove off. I found you in the forest just in time. You'd crashed, and you were lying in the snow, freezing cold and unconscious."

His words were difficult to decipher. It was hard to see the logic in them. Ambra reached for the cup, and he handed it to her.

"You can have some soup later," he said as she drank more of the tea. He spoke slowly, but Ambra still couldn't quite keep up. Jesus, she had such a headache. It was like an iron band around her head. And her body hurt so much.

She moved and realized she was naked. Did they have sex? She really couldn't remember, she thought with panic. But she could remember that she'd been afraid, terrified. She pulled the blanket around her. "Why aren't I wearing any clothes? What happened? Did we . . . do something?"

Tom shook his head. "Nothing happened—you have my word—nothing like that. We fought, I got mad. Then you drove off on the snowmobile. You don't remember?"

She racked her memory. Snowmobile. Snow. It did sound vaguely familiar. She looked over to the window. Snowstorm. She remembered.

"You just disappeared," Tom continued. "I drove around looking for you. When I found you, you'd crashed into a tree. I brought you back here. Your clothes were soaked through, so I had to take everything off. I swear nothing else happened," he repeated.

She believed him. She twisted a little, felt the sheet against her ass and her breasts; as far as she could tell, she wasn't wearing a stitch. Maybe she should focus on something else, but had Tom undressed her? Everything? She cleared her throat. "I'm still thirsty," she said.

He nodded and went out to the kitchen. While he rattled around in there, she shuffled into a sitting position and pulled the covers up over her shoulders. Freja was lying with her head on her paws, watching her. "Hi there," Ambra said, and the dog got up and came over to her, letting Ambra scratch her under her chin.

By the time Tom returned, Ambra's brain was starting to work again.

"Rehydration," he said, and she took the glass. She sipped the liquid and studied him over the edge of the glass.

"You scared me," she said, suddenly remembering the way he'd changed.

He sighed deeply. "And *you* almost scared me to death. When I found you out there . . ."

"I was scared," she explained.

He seemed genuinely confused. "Why?"

"You were so angry."

"Yeah, I was angry. But you didn't think I would . . . that I'd **hurt** you?"

She sighed. "It's something I struggle with. It's ingrained in me, I know that. But I was so scared, and I don't know . . . I didn't think. I just wanted to get away." They were old feelings, and from a logical point of view they didn't make much sense. She just couldn't handle feeling powerless. But logic didn't always help—she had been terrified and panicked.

"You were spying on me. You called Isobel. I have a right to be angry."

"Yes."

He seemed serious, determined, and, yes, still a little scary, but he had risked his own life to save her, and she wasn't afraid anymore. "My clothes, where are they?"

He gave her an apologetic look. "They didn't make it."

"Not even my underwear?"

He shook his head. "Sorry."

Ambra looked away. She couldn't stop herself from blushing. So this man had undressed her, down to her bare skin, while she was unconscious. That would take a while to process.

"The power's still not back on. I heated water on a gas stove. There are gas lamps in the bathroom. You can wash yourself, if you want. I put out a toothbrush. And you can have these." He held out some thermal long johns, a fleece sweater, and a pair of socks—his own, of course. No male underwear, at least, she thought. She probably wouldn't survive that embarrassment. She took the things from him.

"How did you get my clothes off?" she asked.

"They were soaked through and you were freezing cold. I was in a hurry, so I had to cut them."

Of course. She got to her feet, wobbled. Tom shot up like a rocket and put an arm around her waist. "I'll carry you," he said as Ambra clutched the clothes and the blanket so that it wouldn't fall off her.

"Please, I want to do it myself. I need to pee and to be alone. I don't *need* to be carried."

Tom looked like he wanted to protest.

She took another step. Her head was spinning. But she could do it. She took another step. And another. She would make it.

"I understand if you want to close the door, but don't lock it," he commanded from behind her.

"Sir, yes sir," she muttered. But she really was dizzy and incredibly weak, so she decided Tom probably had a point. She would hurry to get dressed, she doggedly decided. If she collapsed in the bathroom and had to be rescued again, she at least wanted to be dressed.

She quickly washed, dressed, and brushed her teeth. The sweater and long johns were soft and far too big. She had to roll back the sleeves several times, and the trousers dragged on the floor no matter what she did, but they were cozy and she felt much better now she was dressed. Her belt had survived, and when she tightened it around her waist the long johns stayed up. She pulled on the thick socks and the fleece, which practically reached her knees. She felt a little more like a person again.

"There's no power, we have no service, and there's still a storm outside, at least one more night," Tom told her when she came out. "But we've got enough wood and food to last a few weeks, so we'll be fine. Plus I have one of the snowmobiles."

At that point, Ambra pulled an apologetic face, but Tom waved it away.

"No criticism, I'm just thinking aloud. The way it's snowing, we'll have to dig ourselves out. You'll have to stay here tonight."

She nodded. Her stomach rumbled.

"I made a little food. I only have one camping stove. Swedish flatbread sandwiches and soup, is that all right?" he asked.

She was starving, so after she wolfed down the food, he made coffee and handed her biscuits with cheese and butter.

"Mmm," she said.

"How do you feel?"

"Much better." She was still exhausted, but considering she'd almost died in a snowstorm, she was surprisingly well.

"You don't have any frostbite. But you still might get a fever."

"Yes, doctor."

He didn't smile. "If you go sit down out there, I'll come. We need to talk."

Tom poured more coffee. Ambra curled up on the couch and tried not to think about the way they'd sat there making small talk . . . what was it, less than twenty-four hours earlier?

"Why are you so interested in what happened in Chad?" he began, getting straight to the point.

She didn't have a good answer to his question. Other than the fact that she had a tendency to be suspicious of people, and that her suspicions were often justified. "I think I was born curious," she eventually said.

He put down his cup. "I'll show you," he said. He got up and walked away, returning a moment later with a stack of photos, which he put down on the coffee table.

"This is what you saw. I'll tell you about it, and I'll answer your questions, but you have to swear that this stays between us."

Ambra's hands clasped her coffee and she nodded seriously. "I swear."

Tom started to lay out the pictures on the table. Photos from the desert, some dark, others blurred. Sand, smoke, weapons. She studied them while he began to talk.

"After I left the military . . ."

"When?" she interrupted him.

He shook his head. "Years ago. I moved over to the private sector, got a job with a British security firm. I worked abroad for a few years."

"Where?"

He paused.

"Come on, Tom."

She could see he was fighting with himself, but eventually he gave in and she felt a slight thrill of triumph. "Iraq. Afghanistan. Countries like that. Different places in Africa. But after a few years, I decided I was done with war. The jobs paid really well, but it was tough going and I wanted to come home."

To Ellinor, she filled in silently for herself.

"I started working in Sweden," he continued.

"Lodestar?"

"Yes."

"Did you do things that were illegal?" The question was verging on rude, but she had asked it now.

He looked down at his hands. Ambra waited. "Right and wrong don't always exist in these countries," he said slowly. "Not in the kind of work I do. I have a moral code of my own that I try to follow."

"Really?" Ambra couldn't help but sound skeptical. In her experience personal moral codes didn't mean much.

"I know how it sounds, but it's a way for me to stand up for what I did. I did a lot of routine work and administration these past few years, not so much active duty. But then that woman got captured in Chad."

"Isobel De la Grip?"

"Yes. She's an experienced field doctor. She was on her way to a pediatric hospital when she was captured by local thugs. Her boyfriend, or husband now, Alexander De la Grip, he got in touch with David Hammar. David called me for advice. No one knew what had happened to Isobel; we didn't even know if she was alive. It ended with us going to Chad to search for her."

"Sounds like a bad action movie."

"A lot of things in that line of work do. But we managed to find out where she was being held. It was a village, in the desert." He pointed to one of the pictures, which showed a village from a distance. She studied it and the other images. There was a grainy picture of Alexander De la Grip, several of various men bent over maps, all armed and dressed in fatigues. Merciless men. There was one of Tom, too. He was wearing sunglasses, his beard was short, his face dusty, and he looked serious. The picture was blurred, but it was Tom. She touched it.

"I recruited some freelance soldiers, and we planned an attack and rescued her," he said. "And then my helicopter crashed."

"But it was a village of civilians you attacked?"

"That was where they were keeping her. We didn't know if they were torturing her."

"Did any civilians die?"

"I've gone through all the information from the operation, read the reports from everyone who was involved. As far as I can tell, no civilians were killed. It was dark and there was a lot of fighting, but I work with professionals, not psychopaths. The whole thing was over in a couple minutes."

"But people died?"

"Not people. Soldiers. There's a difference. According to the reports, my men killed two, maybe three of the kidnappers. Maybe they injured people who died later—we'll never know. Those were the documents you saw. So if you ask me whether I ever killed anyone . . . yes. But not in Chad."

Ambra nodded. She didn't want to hear any more.

He sat back on the couch and studied her. "Now I want to ask you a couple of questions."

"Okay," she said, and she tried not to squirm under his piercing gaze.

"Was this why you came back to Kiruna?" he asked, watching her closely. She wasn't the only one with trust issues, she realized. She had hurt him, this unshakable man.

"To find out more about me? About this?" He gestured to the images on the coffee table.

"I came to look into my former foster family, to try to talk to a social worker. Whom I probably caused real problems for."

He looked as if he didn't entirely believe her.

"I wasn't even sure we would meet up here, as you might remember," she reminded him gently.

"Why did you call Isobel? Why didn't you ask me?"

"I didn't know how you would react. You might have gotten mad. If you can imagine such a thing."

"Yeah, I'm sorry about that."

"And I'm sorry I snooped, that I overreacted. Sorry. But I came here to look into *my* background, not yours. I swear."

"What the hell were you thinking when you took off like that? In the cold? You could've died."

"But you saved me," she said, trying to stifle a yawn. She was so tired. "I think I need to rest again." She was suddenly completely exhausted.

"You look drained," he said. "If you get ready, I'll make up the bed."

"Upstairs?"

"No, it's freezing up there. You'll have to sleep down here." He took their cups and went out to the kitchen. Ambra studied the pictures on the coffee table. She quickly took out her phone, which, by some miracle, still had four percent of battery left. She took a photo of the image of Tom. Some of the other pictures were visible in the background, but this was for her own use. She just wanted a picture of him. Afterward she trudged to the bathroom, brushed her teeth, and used the toilet. When she came back out, he had folded back the covers for her and was sitting by the fire, with his back to her. She pulled off her long johns, the fleece, and the socks, and she kept on only the long thermal sweater, which would have to act as nightgown. She lay down and pulled the blanket up to her chin.

The last thing she heard was "sleep well," and then she went out like a light.

When Ambra woke next time, she felt much more alert. The fire had died down, with just a single log alight in the open hearth. The room was dark, and it felt like the middle of the night. She heard a quiet snoring, and when she turned around she was surprised to see Tom asleep on the mattress next to her. She turned onto her side, her head resting on one palm, and studied his face. He was sleeping in his T-shirt, with a blanket over him. She reached out and stroked his forehead, the way he had hers. He made another sound, but he didn't wake. The blanket wasn't covering him completely, and she gently brushed her fingers over his chest. Her hand came to rest on his rib cage, which rose calmly beneath her palm. The man had saved her life, carried her in his arms, taken care of her. How hot was that? His skin was warm, but the house was cold; the tip of her nose was like ice, and she scooted toward him. For an elite soldier, Tom slept surprisingly deeply. She moved even closer and made an interesting discovery.

Tom had a hard-on. She could see it through the blanket. And then she felt his hand on her hip.

"What are you doing?" he asked huskily, turning his face toward her.

"You're awake?" she mumbled. She felt her blood start to pump more quickly, rushing to those parts of her body linked to sex. Her entire being was reaching out toward him and his presence.

"I think so. How are you? What are you doing?" His words were rambling.

He had turned onto his side, facing her, and their bodies brushed up against one another. Every time she took a breath, her chest touched his. Her nipples hardened. She slowly licked her lips, her eyes focused on him the entire time. Tom gave her an uncertain look. She didn't remember having seen him look that way before. She laid a hand on his hip, moved closer to him. He swallowed, his big throat working, and then he came to meet her, slowly until their lips were almost grazing each other's. Ambra gently swept her mouth over his. He lay perfectly still, and she almost didn't continue, but then she raised her hand to his cheek and parted her lips, and he did the same. As her tongue entered his mouth, his came to meet it. His hand moved up the back of her neck, and when he kissed her it was hard and eager, not the least bit hesitant or uncertain; it was more a frustrated explosion, and Ambra whimpered. His tongue swept into her mouth, demanding and powerful. Kiss after kiss, as though all of the feelings that had been bubbling between them were finally unleashed. She pulled at his shirt, wanted to feel more of his glorious skin. His hand was on the curve of her back, pressing her firmly toward him. He pulled at her top, murmuring something about her wearing too much, and then his hands finally found their way beneath it. Ambra leaned against his neck and panted into him when his palm moved over her breast; he kept it there, warm and rough.

"I want to look at you," he said huskily.

Ambra swallowed. But she withstood the impulse to pull down her top and helped him to take it off instead. She raised her arms, and he lifted it over her head, threw it to one side, and devoured her with his eyes. She shivered. His hand moved back to her breast. His eyes were jet black in the faint light of the low fire. Her small breasts had always made her feel unfeminine, but Tom's wild hands, hungry kisses, and very hard evidence of appreciation made her feel attractive and sexy. She shuddered.

"Are you cold?" he asked.

She nodded, though her shiver was mostly due to everything going on between them. He grabbed a fur and placed it over her. "Better?" She nodded again. His body enveloped hers, his knees found their way in between her legs.

"You take off your top too," she said, her gaze not leaving him for a moment.

He obeyed. Her eyes hungrily moved across his chest. She had seen it before, in the sauna, but right now, in the glow of the dying fire, so close up, he was almost too much. Muscular, a small patch of black hair on his chest, and a thin line down his stomach, scarred from battle. She would give anything to see him without a beard. But looking the way he did right now, there was a brutal sensuality to him, more wild than tame, and when his index finger traced an invisible line from her collarbone down to her breast, circling her taught nipple, she closed her eyes and gave herself over to the sensation of being desired. He bent down and took her other nipple in his mouth, and God it felt good. His hand stroked her stomach, her hips, her thighs. Ambra impatiently moved toward his big, slow hand, wanted it . . . ah, *there*.

He cupped her sex with his hand, looked her straight in the eye as he slowly explored her most intimate area. She didn't wax, had barely shaved in an eternity—it was like 1981 down there—but it didn't matter; she thought Tom was a man who didn't much care about that kind of thing. He caressed her, kissed her until she pantingly plastered herself against his hand, his mouth, his tongue.

"Ambra," he mumbled into her mouth. Over and over again. She pulled at his pants, wanted this so damn much. He let go of her, pulled back, left her.

God, what was he doing? Ambra gave him a warning look. *Don't even think about stopping*.

Tom laughed, though it wasn't a happy laugh, more a frustrated one.

"Are you on birth control?" he asked.

She shook her head. It was so long since she'd last had an active sex life. But he must have . . . ?

"I don't have any protection here," he said, sounding stifled.

Ambra propped herself up on her elbows. "Nothing?" she asked, unable to tell whether he was messing with her. "You have everything in this place. We could practically survive the apocalypse here."

He nodded. "Definitely. But there are no condoms. Sadly."

She slumped back down on the mattress. So. She couldn't take the risk. She never wanted to get pregnant by mistake. The world didn't need any more unwanted children with fucked-up parents.

Tom leaned over her. "But I can keep doing this," he said, stroking her stomach, cupping her again, moving his fingers in circles, deliberate, determined. No fumbling here, no more uncertainty, just a man who knew how to please a woman. Ambra parted her legs, raised them slightly.

"You're so damn hot," he murmured. It was as if he could read her reactions, interpret every noise she made. Those hands and fingers, those words; they were like magic. His lips on her mouth, his kisses, caresses. His fingers, gently inside her, and then a little less gently, a rhythm that suited her better than any rhythm ever had.

"Tom," she panted, and he kept going, kept going. Christ, he knew what he was doing. She could feel it building inside her. She threw herself forward and back, pictured him penetrating her, pressing himself into her, making love to her, and then it came. The release. It just came and came. It was literally the best orgasm of her life, coming in long waves, making her lose herself, her entire body tense, pressing herself into him.

"Jesus," was all she could say as his palm came to a rest on her, his wrist pressing down, gently, as she landed. She couldn't think. All she could do was breathe.

He leaned forward, kissed her tenderly, lay down on his back, and pulled her close. She lay heavily on his warm, bare chest, closed her eyes with her cheek above his heart, rested, let the last embers of her orgasm die out. She sighed.

"Good?" he asked quietly.

She nodded against his chest, couldn't talk, could barely think. God, what an experience. She raised one hand and stroked him languidly. His chest was covered with short, dark hairs. She grazed one of his nipples and heard a stifled groan. Mmm, right. He hadn't been satisfied yet. She liked him when he was like this, charged, on edge. She herself was completely boneless. She playfully spread her fingers across his skin, brushed his stomach. He started to breathe a little heavier beneath her cheek. Ambra propped herself up on one elbow and allowed her hand to move down, over his pants. He stopped breathing.

"You're so hard," she whispered, stroking the material.

"You don't have to," he managed to say.

But Ambra wanted to.

"Take off your pants," she whispered, and he did as she said. Pulled off his pants, underwear, and socks in one lightning-fast movement. He was big and hard. Nice looking, too. A thin line of dark hair, a little more by the base. His cock trembled as she looked down at it, and she wanted to reach out and touch its smooth warmth, gently cup her hands around his balls. Not all men were good looking like that, but Tom was a fine specimen, and he was sexy as hell. "Show me how you like it," she said.

He hesitated.

"Show me," she repeated, grabbing his hand and moving it downward, encouraging him to take hold of himself. She placed her own hand on top of his and followed his movements.

"Ambra," he managed to pant.

"Keep going," she said, moving her leg on top of his, feeling his coarse hair against her calf, pressing her thigh into him. He groaned, but he did as she said and continued to move his hand up and down. And then Ambra took over. He was warm, almost burning, smooth in his hardness, and her hand slid up and down as confidently as his had. Tom closed his eyes, wrapped one arm around her in an iron grip, clutched the sheets with his other fist. Pressed up against him, Ambra continued her caress. She liked it, and there was a kind of primitive sexual satisfaction in making this big, capable man dependent on her, even if it was just for a while.

"Oh God," he moaned, but she continued, felt him tense, grow bigger and harder, and then he came, into her hand, onto his own stomach, in hot, pulsing spurts.

"Oh God," he repeated, his voice shaking. He was holding her so tight that she could barely breathe.

"Tom, you're crushing me," she breathed, and his arm loosened immediately.

"Sorry. Jesus. Wait, I can't . . ." He panted, his chest heaving, and he brought one arm to his eyes. When Ambra laid her head back on his chest again, his heart was pounding against her cheek. She smiled at the sound. Tom's hand moved up, over her ass, her back, to the nape of her neck, and he angled her face toward his and kissed her deeply. She smiled into his mouth, then into his skin.

"Careful, you'll get sticky," he said. "Wait here."

He pulled away from her arms and disappeared. She heard the sound of water, comforting sounds, and then felt him slip back into bed beside her. She slid closer. He smelled like soap and toothpaste and was slightly damp, as if he had dried himself too quickly.

"You're cold," she said, and then they kissed again; they didn't say anything else.

Maybe they didn't have any words left, maybe they weren't needed right now. She curled up in his arms and they lay there like that, silent and thoughtful as the fire died out.

Chapter 37

When Tom woke, the sun was on his face. The whole living room was bathed in pale Norrland sunlight. The storm had finally passed. He propped himself up on his elbows. Ambra was lying next to him, her dark hair spread out on the pillow. She was sleeping deeply. Even in her sleep, there was something hot-headed about her, but she no longer looked anywhere near as exhausted, and she'd seemed completely recovered last night. . . .

He studied her beautiful profile. What had happened between them was incredible. *She* was incredible. Bold, wild, sexy. He was turned on at just the thought of what they'd done, what she'd done, the way her hands had caressed him until he came in a powerful orgasm. He leaned forward and kissed her shoulder, breathed in the scent of her.

He carefully crawled out from beneath the covers. Ambra was still sleeping, but Freja's tail was wagging expectantly, and he went out into the kitchen and filled her food bowl. This thing between Ambra and him, what was it, exactly? Aside from the fact it was incredibly arousing, like a sexual fantasy come true.

He'd woken that morning with a good feeling in his body, but the more alert he became, the more complicated the whole thing felt.

It was one of the most powerful sexual experiences he'd ever had, but what did it *mean?* Sex complicated things, that was a given. Messed up his head, too. Not to mention the fact that many things felt different during daylight than they did at night. It had been so dark, with the power still out, and they had been so close to one another, cut off from the world. That was how it felt. As if what he and

Ambra had done last night had nothing to do with any other time. He'd just saved her life, after all.

He ran a hand through his hair and stared out the window. Last night, it felt like a good idea to throw himself at Ambra; actually, like the best idea he'd had in a long time. But now he wasn't sure what to think about his own behavior.

He turned on the faucet and filled the kettle. The power was back on, and he prepared the coffee machine. The snow was up to the window ledge. He would have to go out and do some clearing if they were going to get anywhere. He considered ignoring the snow, ignoring everything going on outside, just staying inside with the woman with magic hands. But that was hardly a long-term solution, and besides, a little manual labor would do him good.

He went out into the hallway. Freja rushed after him and jumped up and down with excitement as he pulled on his coat. It took a good deal of force to open the front door and then to clear a path over to the garage. Freja barked like crazy at the snow everywhere, leaped into piles of it and then rushed back to the house as soon as Tom was done.

He turned on the coffee machine and listened to it bubble, poured two mugs, and went back into the living room, where Ambra had started to stir. She had pulled on the fleece top, but her legs were bare as she stood by the window looking out. She turned around when he came in.

"Good morning," he said, handing her a cup of steaming coffee.

"I see the power's back," she said, bending down over the mug and breathing in the steam with a smile. She was so beautiful like this, her hair a mess, relaxed, bare legged. He felt a pang in his chest.

"I have service, if you need to make any calls," he said.

She smiled, pushed her hair back behind her ears, and he followed the familiar gesture with his eyes. He took a step toward her, wanted . . . but at that moment, his cell phone started to ring on the coffee table. They both automatically looked over to it. *Ellinor,* he read on the screen; there was a picture of Ellinor laughing.

Damn. Tom glanced at Ambra, suddenly feeling uneasy. She just smiled and looked away, buried her nose in the coffee cup.

"Sorry," he said.

"No worries, answer it," she said in a neutral voice.

Tom went into the kitchen. "Hello?"

"Hey, it's me."

He had always liked that greeting of hers, the way she assumed he would know who it was. But now it suddenly bothered him a little. "Hi, Ellinor."

"I just wanted to check that you were okay. What with the storm and everything."

It was unexpected. That she was calling. That she cared. "We're fine. We had no power, but we made it," he replied.

"We?"

He paused. "Freja and I."

She laughed. "What are you doing?"

"Drinking coffee."

Freja barked, and he took that as an excuse to end the call. "I need to go, but thanks for calling."

"Good to hear your voice, Tom."

He hung up and headed back to the living room, deep in thought. Why was Ellinor calling him suddenly?

"Is everything good with Ellinor?" Ambra asked. She avoided looking at him.

"Sorry about that," he said.

Ambra shrugged. "It makes no difference to me."

Did Ambra expect them to talk about what had happened last night? Or should he act normal?

What even *was* normal once you'd suddenly noticed how pink and soft her mouth was, how beautiful the curve between her ear and her neck? How were you meant to act if you were constantly reminded of how her breast felt in your hand, how her small nipples had tickled your skin; if you then remembered exactly how she sounded when she came in an explosive orgasm against your hand? How did you just act "normal" then?

"How are you feeling?" he eventually asked, once the silence between them seemed almost endless. He had no idea what he should say.

"I'm good. I feel almost back to myself. Thanks again." She bent down over her coffee and took a small sip.

"When does your plane leave?" he asked.

"This afternoon. I need to get back to the hotel."

"I can give you a ride whenever you like," he offered. Should he say anything else? That the experience had been incredible for him? That even if she'd done it out of gratitude, it was more than he'd expected? That he would never forget it.

"Thanks. What should I do in terms of clothes?" She pulled at the long sweater. He would probably never be able to look at it again without having erotic associations, but he understood the problem.

Relieved, he put the coffee cup on the table. A practical problem to solve, that was just what he needed.

"Do you have more clothes and shoes at the hotel? I'll look for some boots and drive you over. We can probably take the car."

When Tom drove Ambra into Kiruna a while later, the bigger roads were already clear. The way they dealt with snow up here was like a military maneuver. The sun had already set, but the sky was still clear with some kind of half-light.

"Thanks for the ride," she said when they made it to the hotel. She tried to push back the sleeves of her jacket. They were constantly slipping down over her hands. "And thanks for everything. Everything you did."

"No problem," he said, though he wanted to say more. Something about how he needed to think. That he had never questioned his love for Ellinor before, that his whole head felt such a mess. But all he said was: "I'm glad it all worked out."

"It'll be good to charge my cell phone," she said, stamping her feet on the snow. "I'll leave your clothes with reception when I go," she added. Tom glanced at the jacket she had borrowed, the enormous boots she was practically drowning in.

"Sorry I had to cut up your clothes. I'll replace them, of course," he said.

"Actually, I think the etiquette when someone has just saved your life is not to take that person's money. It was just a pair of jeans and an old shirt. Tom, I'm really grateful—you know that, right?" She sounded serious.

"Yeah," he said. "I'm happy to give you a ride to the airport."

"Thanks, but not this time. I'll take a cab."

"Sure?"

He could see she had made up her mind, and maybe it was just as well.

Ambra nodded. She held out her arms to him and they hugged. He held her tight, breathed in the scent of her.

She took a step back. Smiled. "Don't worry. You don't need to feel pressured. I understand. We don't need to make this into anything more than it is."

He didn't know what to say.

"If you're ever in Stockholm, let me know," she continued, with that new, slightly cheerful voice he wasn't sure he liked. "If you want to, that is. No pressure. But if you want to."

He nodded. "Bye."

"Bye, Tom."

Tom stopped off at the gas station and bought paraffin, a generator, and some milk before he headed back to the house, deep in thought. Maybe it was just as well. They were too different, he and Ambra. And she seemed relieved to be leaving, hadn't seemed particularly concerned about whether they would see each other again. That was fine by him, he told himself, ignoring the fact it was a depressing thought.

While he parked the car in the garage and then let Freja out, he considered what they had talked about.

Had he said too much about Chad and his background? He'd trusted her more than he'd ever considered trusting anyone else.

When he carried the generator inside and started to tinker with it, his thoughts turned to what they'd done last night, and he found himself smiling. The way her body reacted to him was so damn delicious, the combination of passion and tenderness. The way his body responded to hers.

Later, he went out on the snowmobile, drove into the forest, and found the one she'd crashed. He trailed it back behind him. The whole way, his thoughts were elsewhere: on Mattias's offer of the job in Stockholm.

Tom hadn't been home to Stockholm for a long time. But he felt better now, and he had things he needed to sort out. He'd come up here for Ellinor's sake, but what difference did it make if he went down to Stockholm for a week or so? Maybe he needed a change of scenery. Plus, Ambra had said he could get in touch if he was ever in town. Maybe he would do just that.

That evening, he called Mattias.

"Tom, how are you?" Mattias sounded happy, if not enthusiastic.

"Am I interrupting?" Tom asked.

"Not at all, you can always call me."

Smooth as ever, but wasn't his tone a little curt? Calling Mattias had been an impulse. Tom scratched his neck, looked at Freja.

"Tom?"

"Yeah?" He heard low sounds in the background and glanced at his watch. It was seven. Was Mattias in a restaurant? Sounded that way. Low music, jingling.

"Are you still there?" Mattias asked.

"I'm here. But it wasn't anything particular."

"You sure? What happened?"

"Nothing happened," Tom said.

"Talk to me." It sounded like Mattias had covered his phone for a moment, but then he said, "I have time."

"I saw Ambra."

Mattias was quiet for a long moment. Tom could practically hear the cogs turning in his head. "So you're in Stockholm?" he eventually asked.

"No."

"She came back to Kiruna?"

"Yeah."

"To see you?" Mattias sounded concerned.

"No."

"But you met?"

Tom stared straight ahead. Yeah, you could call it that. They met, they kissed, they satisfied one another.

"Tom?"

"Yeah?"

A deep sigh from Mattias. "Why did you call, exactly?"

"To talk."

"But you aren't *saying* anything."

"I'm thinking about coming to Stockholm."

"Do it. Listen, I'm in the middle of something, but come down. I'll buy you lunch and we can talk more."

Tom ended the call with Mattias. He glanced at Freja. "What do you think I should do?"

But it was a rhetorical question. He had already made up his mind. He was going to Stockholm.

Chapter 38

Jill studied Mattias as he ended the call with an apologetic look. He looked handsome today: dark suit, no tie, pale blue shirt, clean-shaven, a glittering signet ring with some kind of military thing on it.

"Sorry. That was Tom," Mattias said, turning over his cell phone. He hadn't switched it to silent, but he wasn't playing with it the whole time either. There was nothing she found more off-putting than a man who couldn't put down his phone, so that was a bonus point for him there.

"What did he want?" She stretched out one leg. She was wearing knee-length suede boots today, and Mattias seemed to enjoy her legs in them. Judging by the way his attention kept catching on them any-way. Jill smiled and raised her glass of champagne, the bubbles rush-ing toward the surface. Mattias had ordered for the two of them, and he was something of a wine snob. Not that he was stuck-up in his snobbery—plus you would have to be crazy not to like Pommery. She took a big sip, loved the wooziness it gave her. Woozy and happy, was there anything better? It was as if all her concerns had disappeared.

"I have no idea what he wanted, actually. But I think he's having an affair with your sister."

That made Jill pause with her glass in the air. "He said that?"

"Not exactly. But I'm wondering. Have you heard anything about it?"

"I haven't talked to her in a few days. But Ambra can take care of herself. Though I think she could find someone better than him."

"Tom's a good man."

"If you say so." Should she be worried about Ambra? She wouldn't begrudge her a little sex, on the contrary, but with *Tom?* "Your friend, isn't he in love with some other woman?" she continued, studying Mattias through her lashes.

"Actually, I don't know. I thought so, but you saw the way he looked at her?"

Jill nodded. She had. She played with her glass. They were at the very back of the posh Cadier bar, waiting for their table in the dining room.

"What made you call me?" she asked. Men were always calling her up and asking her out. But those were men who, in various ways, were trying to use her. Mattias didn't seem to have any ulterior motive. Though men were very rarely surprising. They wanted to impress, boast, and fuck, but it was rarely more than that.

"I called you because I wanted to see you," he said calmly.

"We . . ." she began, but she was interrupted by a man forcing his way in between them. Jill had chosen a seat that would make her as invisible as possible, but it was hard to go out in Stockholm without being recognized. She sighed.

"Aren't you . . . ?" the man said with a grin, pointing rudely at her. Jill nodded, hoped he would go away. "My pals didn't think I would have the nerve to come over, but I recognized you." His eyes moved down over her chest before he turned toward a group of men who were waving and shouting at him. Damn it, he was going to cause a scene; she could feel it. She tried to catch the eye of a staff member, someone who could help her.

"You said hi. Now could you please leave?" Mattias said, though he didn't get up. Jill gave him a warning shake of the head. The last thing she needed was for Mattias to try to play the hero. She couldn't handle any more drama.

"This your old man or what?" the drunk man asked with a huge roar of laughter.

Mattias got up from his bar stool. He was shorter than the drunk man, lighter, and at least ten years older. "She doesn't want to talk to you. So either you leave on your own, or I'll help you out."

Jill put a hand on Mattias's arm. She wasn't exactly worried, but she knew this kind of situation could escalate quickly.

But then Mattias did something, Jill didn't see what, and suddenly the drunk man was on his knees in front of them. His face was twisted in pain and his breathing was strained. She stared.

"You took a fall," Mattias said with a cool voice. "I think you should go back to your friends now, and then I think you should leave." Mattias looked at his watch. "I'll give you two minutes." He moved, and the man gasped in pain.

"You're crazy," he panted.

Mattias bent down and said something into the man's ear. The man blinked firmly before he nodded.

"What are you doing?" Jill hissed.

Mattias sat back down on his stool, seeming completely unfazed. The other man got up from the floor, hesitated for a moment, and then stumbled off back to his pals. He said a few words and then they all got up and left the bar. Jill had never seen anything like it.

"What did you do to him? Was that some kind of judo move?"

"Yeah, kinda," Mattias said. He raised his glass and took a few sips. Jill studied him critically.

"I hate violence, just so you know." She was serious; she'd had enough violence in her life. More than enough.

"Same here," he replied.

"Your table is ready," a waiter came over to tell them.

Now there were members of staff around.

Mattias got up again and held out a hand in front of him. He walked behind her as she followed the waiter to the table.

Mattias was much bossier than she expected. He seemed so polished and sophisticated; she hadn't expected him to be so dominating. She didn't like men who tried to take charge of her, was used to being the one in control, and preferred it that way. But being out with a man who could make irritating idiots shut up wasn't all bad.

"Here you go." He pulled out a chair for her.

The restaurant offered international fine dining, and Jill could see Russian oligarchs, a foreign royal, a few Swedish financiers, and then completely ordinary people celebrating weddings or the like. She scanned the menu. It was expensive, even for Stockholm, and she wondered for a moment whether Mattias expected her to pay.

Nothing would surprise her. She had been on far too many dates that ended with her paying the tab. She could afford it, so she didn't care. She'd supported herself since she was sixteen, had always been the one to give to others, dated men she gave money, never the other way around. It gave her a feeling of control, of being the one

with the economic power. She didn't want to depend on anyone—
she and Ambra were alike in that sense. Aside from the fact that
Ambra earned a mediocre amount at *Aftonbladet,* whereas Jill was
economically independent several times over.

They each ordered steak. Mattias politely asked whether he could
choose the wine, and Jill nodded. She was an uncomplicated soul in
that respect; so long as she got drunk and avoided a headache, she
was happy.

"Was it true you bought my CDs?" she asked.

He looked up from the wine list. "Yup. And I listened to them.
Your voice is fantastic."

She froze a little. Roughly half the men she'd ever met said she
must have rhythm in her blood, considering where she was from.
She hated it. But Mattias didn't say anything of the sort; he just
seemed genuinely impressed.

"But it's not your type of music?" she asked.

He ordered a French wine before he replied. "I wouldn't have
thought so. But I like your music, a lot. I'm grateful I can widen my
horizons. What kind of thing do you listen to?"

Suddenly she couldn't tell whether Mattias was messing with her.
Had she ever been on a date where anyone asked what kind of music
she liked? It was actually quite strange that no one had asked. "I like
most things," she replied guardedly. "Jazz, pop, country."

"Metal? Classical?" he asked with a smile.

"I don't really think you can generalize. I like some songs, don't
like others. It's all part of my job to listen, so I guess I'm really an om-
nivore." She was so interested by their conversation that she forgot
to flirt. It really was relaxing, and she wondered whether it was all a
strategy on his part. Not that he needed any kind of strategy. Unless
he messed up somehow, she was fairly convinced she was going to
sleep with him.

They continued to make small talk about music, travel, and different wines as their food arrived. They ate their steaks; the wine he ordered was like poetry in her mouth, and for the first time Jill
understood the point of pairing the wine with the food. She reached
for her bag, her hand on her cell phone. She knew she should be taking pictures of the food, uploading them to Instagram. She paused.

Took it out. "Can I take a picture?" she asked, and, for the first time in a very long time, felt embarrassed.

His fingers drummed the table and he shook his head. "I'm sorry, Jill, but I can't be in any pictures."

She took a quick picture of her plate, wrote something meaningless, and uploaded the image, then grabbed her wineglass and took a deep sip.

"I have a job where I can't be visible in that kind of way."

"Yeah, I gathered as much."

"You're mad with me," he said.

"No," she lied, couldn't understand why she was reacting like a child. But he had every advantage. He knew about wine, he could handle pushy men, he had an *important* job. And he didn't seem at all charmed by her. They'd flirted in Kiruna, and he'd called her, but now she felt so unsure of him, unsure of whether she could really handle him.

"Jill?" he said.

"Tell me what you've been doing since I last saw you," she said, flashing him a quick smile. She would force herself to be happy. She smiled again, could already feel it working, away with all the negative thoughts, away, away.

"Working," he said, studying her closely.

She smiled again, felt like normal. "Not the whole time, surely?"

"Yeah, actually. And then I've been thinking about you a lot."

She laughed. She couldn't figure him out at all. There must be something about her he liked. "Thinking what?"

"How fun it was in Kiruna."

"Aside from the fact that Tom and Ambra sulked so much."

He waved his hand as though they were irrelevant. They were, after all. "The way you sang in that bar. If you knew how often I thought about that night." There was a glimmer in his eye, something primitive, and Jill felt a thrill rush through her. He was sexy in his controlled, restrained way. Especially when his eyes glimmered like that, like a wolf that had caught the scent of something. Yes, she would definitely let him have sex with her tonight.

The waiter came back to their table, asked whether they wanted dessert. Jill deliberated with herself. And then she heard him order chocolates, which were probably her favorite thing of all. If she was being honest, she probably even preferred chocolate to sex.

"How did you know?" she asked.

"I saw it on your Instagram."

"Half of that's lies."

"Yeah, but I took a chance on your love of chocolate being real." She chose a milk chocolate praline from the plate that arrived and nibbled at it appreciatively.

"I saw the kind of comments you get too," he said with a frown.

She pouted slightly, didn't have the energy to talk about her idiotic haters. She rested her chin in her hand, didn't care that she had her elbows on the table. She was tipsy and full-to-bursting. "They're idiots," she said dismissively.

"They're awful."

"Yeah, that too. But you can't let them see that you care, or it'll just get worse." She had learned that over the years. The haters were like hyenas, just waiting for a bared throat or the slightest sign of weakness. She saw Mattias's jaw twitch. Was he angry? "But they're not your problem. Or were you planning to fight them back too?"

"Maybe," he replied.

She took another chocolate, didn't want to think about those crazy people. "Where do you live?" she asked instead.

"In town."

She rolled her eyes. "Where in town? Is it a secret? Are you even allowed to go on dates?"

"Why wouldn't I be?"

"Because you're some kind of secret spy."

He shook his head. "I can go on dates." He slipped back into silence, seemed to be thinking.

"Mattias?"

"Yeah?"

"You need to forget those trolls. It'll drive you crazy otherwise, and then they've won. Okay?"

He nodded. Took a chocolate but didn't eat it, seemed to be thinking again.

She wondered what he was like in bed. Considerate? Firm, or maybe eager to please?

When she glanced at the time, she realized it was almost midnight. She didn't know where the time had gone.

Mattias waved the waiter over and took the check. He didn't even glance at her, just paid. When they got up from the table, she snuck a glance at the tip he had left. He was generous. Or was it just to impress her?

As they left the restaurant, she leaned in to him slightly, was looking forward to kissing him. He went to collect her jacket from the coatroom in the hotel lobby, helped her into it, and she leaned in to him again. He would take the chance right now, wouldn't he? But he didn't. She turned around, slowly. Looked at him, ran her fingers down her coat, stopping just above one breast.

He looked at her for a long moment, pulled on his leather gloves, and buttoned up his coat. "I got a call," he said, and his voice sounded apologetic.

"When?"

"Just now. In the coatroom." He placed a hand at the base of her spine and guided her gently toward the revolving doors. The air outside was cool and fresh. "I have to go back to work," he said as a huge black car rolled up toward them.

"In the middle of the night?"

He waved to one of the cabs waiting outside the hotel and held the door open for her.

"This wasn't how I was hoping the evening would end," she complained as she sat down in the backseat.

Mattias bent down, studied her, and then kissed her on the cheek—a long, lingering kiss.

"I'm sorry," he said. "Here." He handed her a bag with the Grand Hôtel's logo on it, and then closed the door. He waved one last time before he jumped into the huge black car that had pulled up behind the cab. The moment he closed the door, it drove off.

Jill told the cab driver her address and then opened the bag. Mattias had given her a box of chocolates. She opened it, took one out, and chewed thoughtfully as Stockholm passed by outside. Well, after tonight, it was fairly safe to say that Mattias wasn't a consultant after all.

Chapter 39

"Let's do the morning meeting now," Grace said, looking out across the office. She grabbed her cell phone and her headset and started making her way to the conference room.

Ambra followed her, finishing off the article she was working on at the laptop as she tried to avoid walking into anything. She hit one last key and sent off the piece, and then sat down. Representatives from the various desks came into the room and spread out around the table, and Grace wrote up the discussion points on the white board.

Oliver Holm was among the last to enter the room. Ambra groaned internally. She didn't realize he was even working today.

Oliver glanced around, flexed his muscles, and nodded. "Hey, man," he said to one of the men from the Foreign desk, thumping him hard on the back. They shared some private joke and laughed a private laugh, as though to show what cool players they were.

Ambra exchanged an eye rolling glance with the reporter from Entertainment.

"Okay, let's begin," Grace said with the marker pen in her right hand. "Cissi, what do you have on Crime today?"

Cissi, the crime reporter who'd found herself a boyfriend and abruptly stopped asking Ambra to hang out, replied, "Expecting a ruling on the park bench murder. We should have a flash for that."

Grace nodded and wrote it up on the board. "We'll help you with that. Society?"

"We're watching the parliament debate today. We'll be sending live."

"Web TV?" Grace asked, glancing over to Parvin, the paper's best-known TV anchor. It was Parvin who'd thrown the New Year's party Ambra had turned down. Ambra liked her.

"We're live at ten. We'll talk about the gang rape on a Finland ferry last night, the train disruption expected if a strike goes ahead. Someone also found a boa constrictor in a crate of bananas," she finished with a pained look on her face.

"That's good, no?" Grace asked.

Parvin shuddered. "Maybe if you don't hate snakes."

People laughed. Ambra glanced over to Oliver, who was looking at his computer with a smile on his face.

Oliver Holm was Ambra's age, but he had been with *Aftonbladet* for exactly one year longer. Oliver's grandfather was the news editor at the paper back in "the good old days"—in other words when the reporters were all tough, whisky-drinking men and the women were their secretaries. These days, the men at *Aftonbladet* were all feminists, officially at least. They wouldn't survive otherwise. But Ambra suspected that Oliver preferred the way things were before.

Oliver was one of the popular up-and-coming talents. He had experience in Washington, had been on long trips for work, had written about gang killings, liked tough jobs, went to the gym, hung out with the elite. He was a good writer, and if he wasn't such an ass, then maybe she would've been able to cope with his mixed talents. Oliver was a father, too; had custody of his two-year-old son every other week and was popular with the opposite sex. Maybe he treated other women better than he treated her.

"Oliver, do you have anything on that truck crash?" Grace asked.

"I got hold of the head of the rescue team. I'll give him a call soon."

"Great."

Oliver Holm would hardly be happy being an ordinary reporter, Ambra thought when she saw his satisfied face. Oliver wanted to move on to one of the bigger desks: Foreign, Politics, or of course Investigative. The desks where you could really shine, work on things that won major awards, where you got sent on prestigious jobs and invited to annual dinners with the bosses, if you really did well. She didn't blame him; she wanted the same things. Possibly minus the dinners.

"What do you have on Plus?" Grace asked. *Aftonbladet Plus* was their special feature segment: interviews and longer articles that cost extra to read.

The head of the Plus desk looked tired, unshaven, and gray-faced.

"Half my team's sick, but we have Oliver doing a series on murders of women out jogging. The unprovoked woman killer."

"What does that mean? That some killings of women are provoked?" Ambra couldn't stop herself from asking. "And why say woman killer? You would never say man killer."

Oliver groaned. "It's a good headline. Don't start with that crap again."

"We'll take another look at the headline," Grace said firmly.

"Of course," Oliver said smoothly, but he exchanged a sardonic glance with his direct manager.

Ambra remembered the first time she went out on a job with Oliver Holm. It was back in the very beginning.

She was new at *Aftonbladet,* but she had been doing some work for a small local paper ever since she was sixteen, and she considered herself experienced. After she finished her studies, she applied for various jobs and was accepted as one of the year's summer temps with *Aftonbladet*. They were fiercely contested positions, but she had good grades and all her experience with the local paper on her side.

When regular reporters went on vacation, the inexperienced summer temps got the chance to work on all kinds of things. Ambra had already covered a gang murder, traffic accidents, and press conferences. The temp who shone had the chance of being given a job once the summer was over. Ambra had made up her mind to be that reporter, to work harder than all the others. She was home alone in Stockholm that summer; Jill had started touring seriously, and Ambra could give the job her all.

After she had been there a month, she was given the task of going to report on a riot in the projects in Akalla.

"Take Oliver Holm with you," the temporary news editor said. Ambra went to introduce herself to Oliver.

"Want me to drive?" he asked politely, and Ambra nodded obligingly.

"Have you been working here long?" she said, trying to make conversation.

"Just a stand-in, one month. You?"

"Same here," she replied, nodding when their exit appeared. They were probably competitors, she realized. But he seemed nice and she wasn't worried, knew her performance was way above average.

As they parked the car, they saw columns of smoke rising into the air. There were a number of riot vans, and the police were setting up barricades. "Be careful," Oliver said gravely, and she thought his concern was kind of sweet. "Wait here and I'll go check where we're allowed to go," he said, disappearing. Ambra waited ten minutes. When he returned, all he said was, "We can leave. There's nothing to write about."

It was only once they were in the car heading back that she realized she should have protested, but she kept quiet. When they reached the office, Oliver went to speak to the news editor, and an hour or so later his piece was published: an article on the riot, full of action-packed eyewitness reporting. Her name didn't appear anywhere.

"What the hell is this?" she asked.

"What do you mean?"

"We went out there together, but you did the whole thing yourself."

"I preferred to do it alone. You didn't even dare go over. I was more hands-on."

"Are you joking?"

He gave her a questioning look. She didn't say a word. But it cost her the job that year. Oliver got the post. She applied for a new temp position the following year and eventually got herself a permanent job. And she had learned an important lesson along the way: Never trust anyone.

"And on Breaking News, Ambra is chasing people about the factory fire. How's that going?" Grace asked, bringing Ambra back to the present.

"I need to talk to the commander. A witness got in touch. She was about to be locked in."

"Perfect."

"Good to have some sob stories, too, to lighten the mood," Oliver said with a laugh.

It was his laugh that was hardest to defend yourself against. You were supposed to tolerate it, to show a sense of humor.

"Yeah, well I'll try to stick to your high level, Oliver," she said drily.

He crossed his pumped-up arms in front of him. "You can't take a joke, or what?"

For a second, her mood turned. "The problem is that your jokes are just so fucking boring."

The room was dead silent, and everyone was staring. Not at her or at Oliver, but at the door, which had opened without Ambra noticing. Standing in the doorway was *Aftonbladet*'s editor-in-chief, Dan Persson. And judging by the way he was looking at her, he had heard her every word.

She felt herself go red, probably until she was glowing like a stop sign. The room was still silent, as if she had farted loudly and no one knew how to react. How could she have such bad luck? The editor-in-chief never moved among the mere mortal reporters; he was rarely even in the office. What was he doing here?

"Lively atmosphere in here, I see. Grace, could I have a quick word?" he said.

Grace nodded. "We were done anyway," she said, disappearing from the room.

The meeting came to an end. Ambra grabbed her computer and walked back to her desk with heavy steps.

She buried herself in work until lunch, tried not to think about how she had embarrassed herself. People said stupid things all the time. Though not in front of his highness, the editor-in-chief. For a moment or two, she thought about asking Parvin whether she wanted to grab lunch, but her bravery deserted her. She walked down to the water's edge instead, along Norr Mälarstrand, letting the wind clear her mind. She allowed her thoughts to drift to something entirely different.

Tom.

Those kisses. The sex. *The feelings*.

Jesus, all these feelings she was developing for Tom. How did she even go about starting to sort them out? He had literally saved her life. How was she meant to react to something like that? And to everything else that had happened between them?

She looked out at the water, the lone gulls. What did she want from life, exactly? She wanted to write about important things and make a difference, of course. But what else? Did she want kids, for example? A family of her own? Did she even have what it took to be someone's life partner, someone's mother? Other people seemed so convinced that they were good enough for everything, but she constantly doubted herself. It wasn't exactly rocket science to realize it was linked to her childhood, but sadly it didn't help to know that people who were constantly abandoned developed this feeling of being different from everyone else; that insight didn't help at all. All the same, she couldn't quite shake it off. The one thing that never let her down was her work. Her job was her security, and over the years Ambra had thought that was enough. The men she met hadn't exactly been strong arguments in favor of anything else.

But now . . .

If anyone was to come up to her and say, Ambra, you can have Tom Lexington, how would she feel then? If Tom was available, not just physically but also emotionally, would she want him? Would she *dare* want a man like him? Because Tom was a real man. Not a man-child who was afraid to commit to anything, not an anxious intellectual with an easily bruised ego; he was the real deal. Not that it made any difference right now. She had given him an out when they'd parted in Kiruna. Typical her. Told him not to worry, played it so nonchalantly, all so she wouldn't get hurt later. Why did she say that? That it was okay. It didn't feel even slightly okay, and she didn't have an ounce of interest in trying to understand why he wanted stupid Ellinor rather than her.

She paused, turned around, bought a boring and expensive sandwich from 7-Eleven, and walked back toward the building with her head bowed. It was only when she was a few meters away that she noticed the small group smoking by the doorway. Typical. More humiliation, precisely what she needed.

She approached and tried to seem as indifferent and cool as she could. But it was difficult when she saw Dan Persson surrounded by a group of men. The Cool Dudes. The Guys. Dan Persson smoked, that was common knowledge, and more than one reporter had started hanging around outside, chatting; competing to see who could offer the boss a cig. The head of Investigative was there, too. He laughed at something Oliver said, and maybe she was imagining it, but it felt like they were laughing at her.

Ambra gave them a quick nod as she passed, and then she was finally inside. She had always suspected that Oliver added fuel to Dan's dislike of her whenever he got the chance.

She sat down at her desk. The smell of cigarette smoke lingered in her hair. She quickly checked the news sites, opened her e-mails, and read the latest from Lord_Brutal900 as she took a bite of her sandwich.

> You traitorous bitch. You think you're
> something. Why don't you just give up and throw
> yourself under a train?

She paused before she deleted it, then washed down her sandwich with coffee and scanned through the rest of her messages.

For the rest of the day, she barely looked up from her screen. It was only at seven that she finally switched everything off. By then, the last of the night shift had arrived. The people who never got to go out, who never met anyone, and who wrote articles that were the journalistic equivalent of empty calories and trans fats. She gave them a brief nod. They were pale, looked tired and disillusioned. Like they knew they were at the end of the line.

She caught sight of herself in the elevator on the way down, saw her bleak expression and realized she herself was probably a step closer to becoming one of those pale, ignored night reporters. She did up the zipper on her coat and stepped out of the elevator. No matter which way you looked at it, her career wasn't going in the right direction.

Chapter 40

Tom parked his Volvo on the street outside his apartment in Stockholm. It wasn't like him to be so impulsive, but once he'd made up his mind after the call with Mattias, he'd acted quickly. He'd packed that night and left Kiruna long before dawn the very next morning. He drove all day, saw the sun rise from the road, took short breaks along the coast, saw dusk transformed into darkness, and finally arrived in Stockholm, and Kungsholmen, late that night. It was a long journey, but he was used to challenging himself and had endured far worse in the past.

He entered his building and took the elevator to the top floor, unlocked the door, stepped inside, and put his bags down on the floor in the hallway. The apartment looked the same as it had when he'd left it just over two months earlier, bare and impersonal. There was a pile of mail, mostly flyers, on the doormat.

In the kitchen the refrigerator was echoingly empty, the majority of cupboards barely used. He put down the pile of mail, turned on the faucet, and took a jar of Nescafé from an otherwise-empty cupboard.

It felt strange to be back there, in a home that was his and his alone. By the time Ellinor had found out that he had "died" in Chad, she had already moved on and was in Kiruna with Nilas. While he was being held prisoner, she'd leased their apartment. As luck would have it, she put most of his personal things into storage, probably hadn't known what to do with them and hadn't wanted to burden his mother and sisters, who were grieving for him.

Tom filled the brand-new kettle and waited for it to boil. The past fall had been strange, to put it mildly, for everyone involved.

When he'd returned to Sweden from Chad, he'd spent a few days in the hospital. They ran tests, treated infections, gave him a drip with nutritional fluids. David Hammar came to visit him there, and when Tom asked, David recommended a realtor he knew.

The realtor came to the hospital, showed him pictures of three apartments, and Tom had chosen this one without even going to view it. He needed somewhere to live, and this place was closest to the office.

He took his coffee and moved over to the window. He could see water from every window in the apartment. The rooms were arranged in a line along the Karlsberg Canal, and after three months' imprisonment in the desert, he felt a sea view would be the best rehabilitation. So he bought it and moved in. The apartment was in great shape, recently renovated in shades of white and gray, but he had owned it for less than three weeks when he broke down at work and left for Kiruna, so it was still anonymous and virtually unfurnished. He'd bought a bed, a couch, and a dining table as soon as he was back on his feet, chose them solely based on whether they were available for immediate delivery. There were boxes of his things from storage stacked against the walls, but he hadn't unpacked even a fraction of them yet, had just taken out some clothes and tracked down the necessities. But despite the impersonal feeling and the stacks of boxes, it still felt good to be back, he realized.

With the coffee in his hand, he quickly toured the rooms before he returned to the kitchen. He spread out the mail on his kitchen table. The majority were ads, but he found a letter from his mother between a cheerful coupon offer and a Christmas catalogue from NK. She must have sent it just before the forwarding to Kiruna kicked in.

When Tom opened the envelope, he saw a Christmas card inside, full of his mother's neat writing. She was a teacher, taught Swedish to high school students, and was one of the few people who still wrote letters by hand. It had been tough when he had reading and writing problems at school, to have a mom who was a teacher. It should have made things easier, but he felt only shame, and her well-meaning attempts to help him mostly ended in arguments and harsh words from his side. Yes, he was only a child back then, but he still felt guilty about how he'd acted during those years.

> *Dear Tom,*
> *I think of you every day, and hope you are doing well.*
> *I hope you'll celebrate Christmas with us. You're more*
> *than welcome, and we're all longing to see you. Or if*
> *you want to come by between then and New Year, per-*
> *haps? We'll adapt to whatever you want, and I*
> *understand if you prefer to take it easy, I just want you*
> *to know that we're thinking of you and love you very*
> *much. I'm sending you a few pictures of the girls and all*
> *the grandkids.*
> *Big hugs, Mom*

She had enclosed a group picture of his siblings' children in Santa hats. Except for one of them who was wearing what looked like a Batman mask. He laughed. He had four young nieces. They had grown since he'd last seen them. He studied the photo and got that familiar feeling of guilt in his chest. He wasn't much of an uncle, or a brother. Or a son, for that matter.

Each of them had sent a message wishing him a happy new year. They loved and cared about him—he knew that—they were a loving, talkative, laughter-filled group, but he hadn't spoken to any of them all fall. Hadn't replied to their messages, hadn't stopped by, hadn't been in touch at either Christmas or New Year.

He was ashamed.

His youngest sister, the little one, was expecting her first child in the spring, but he hadn't even spoken to her. He looked down at the Christmas card, at the heart his mother had drawn beneath "Mom" and his feelings of guilt became almost unbearable.

His sweet mom.

The shock when she'd found out that her only son was "dead" last fall had hit her hard.

Tom grabbed his bags, carried them into the bedroom, and then called her. He couldn't even remember when they'd last spoken. He was in such bad shape when he got home, had so much to deal with, he'd avoided her.

Yes, he was a bad son.

"Hey, Mom," he said when he heard her familiar voice on the line. He could just see her. She still lived in the house where he and his sisters grew up, with her new husband. Though new . . . Mom and Charles had been married a long time now. She was probably still on Christmas vacation, though she was likely working anyway. Sitting with essays and exams, correcting, making comments. She was a popular teacher. He heard a quick intake of breath and then:

"Tom! I'm so happy. How are you?"

"I'm fine, Mom. Thanks for the Christmas greetings. And all the other cards."

"Are you sure you're okay?"

"Yes." He could hear the worry in her voice. She normally managed to hide it better, but things must have been tough for her lately. "I'm good, Mom. I went north for a while."

"But are you in Stockholm now? How long are you staying?"

"I don't know, awhile," he replied evasively. This was the problem. If he gave them a little, they immediately wanted more. Suddenly, he could see the house in Kiruna, the forest and the empty expanses in front of him, could practically smell the clean air, see the stars. He could just get in the car and drive back up there, ignore everything else, push back all the obligations and duties and expectations to another day.

"The girls are coming for dinner tomorrow. Would you like to join us?"

"Maybe another time." He couldn't deal with seeing them all at once.

"I can ask Charles not to be here if you'd prefer," she said silently.

Tom paused, shocked. She had never done that before, asked her husband to leave the house for his sake.

"No, no, there's no need for that. I just wanted to say hello, but I have to go now, Mom," he said. He couldn't handle more talking, suddenly felt emotionally drained.

They said good-bye, but the phone rang again the minute he hung up.

David Hammar, he read on the display. A friend he had also brushed off and ignored all fall, a friend who never let him down. Tom accepted the call, walked over to the window, and looked out. The sky was dark, no stars. The water was dark, too. He wondered whether the canal was already frozen over.

"Hey, David," he said quietly.

"It's damn good to hear your voice," David said. "How are things?"

"They're okay," he said, blocking out the anxiety that was lying in wait.

Tom especially hated showing any weakness around David. Not that he liked showing weakness to anyone, but David Hammar was so damn competent and larger than life.

"Where are you?" David asked, and Tom heard the sound of a child in the background. His daughter, Tom assumed, experiencing a moment of panic before he remembered that David and Natalia's daughter was called Molly. He had missed her christening, though he could no longer remember why. Probably a work trip he could have just as easily sent someone else on.

Tom hadn't been a good friend these past few years, had prioritized all the wrong things. "I'm home. In Stockholm. I was in Kiruna."

"So you're going back to work?"

"Not yet. I have a lunch planned, but otherwise I don't know."

David was silent for a moment. The child's babbling had also gone quiet. "Alexander and Isobel got married last fall," he said. "It was a quick civil ceremony, so they've decided to throw a party now."

"Yeah, they invited me," Tom said. He hadn't yet sent his RSVP, had totally forgotten about it.

"Are you going to come?" David asked, an insistent note in his voice.

Tom really didn't like the idea of going to a party, but now he felt almost as if he had no choice.

"I'll think about it," he said with a sigh.

"Yes, do. But come. And bring someone if you want."

After their call, Tom washed his cup, threw the ads and flyers into the recycling bin, wrote a shopping list, and turned on the broadband. He unpacked his bags, and just as he hung up the last sweater in the wardrobe, he received a message. It was from Ellinor. She was looking after Freja now, and stupidly enough he missed the dog already.

Ellinor had sent him a picture of Freja lying on a rug, chewing a bone. He called her. Looked out at the water again, toward the white walls of Karlberg Castle on the other shore. He and Ellinor had been to officers' balls in that castle. He used to study in its library, loved the military history of the place.

"How's Freja?" he asked.

"She's fine. How was the drive?"

"I just spoke to David."

"Wow, it's a long time since I've seen him. How is he? He has a kid now, right?"

"Yeah, a daughter. Molly."

Neither spoke, a tense silence. Would things have been different if he and Ellinor had a child? Maybe. But neither of them had wanted one. Right? Suddenly, Tom wasn't sure. Did they ever talk about it, or had he just taken for granted that their thoughts were the same? That they should wait.

"That's great," said Ellinor.

"He invited me to a party. A wedding party for Alexander and Isobel."

"Sounds fun. When is it?"

"A week this Friday. At the Gardens of Rosendal."

"Sounds perfect. Are you going to go?"

"Maybe, yeah, probably," he surprised himself by replying. And without thinking, he suddenly asked: "Want to come with me?"

"It would be great to see them all again," she said with a slight longing in her voice. Ellinor always did love a grand occasion; she was a social marvel. "But I can't. It wouldn't be a good idea, for many reasons."

"I understand." He did. And the strange thing was that Ellinor's name hadn't even been the one to first pop up when David suggested bringing someone, it was Ambra's. Asking Ellinor was nothing but a reflex. "Keep sending me pictures of Freja," he said.

"She's fine. Take care."

At ten-thirty the next morning, Tom left his apartment and walked the six or so kilometers to the Armed Forces headquarters on Lidingövägen. It was freezing cold, and there was snow on the ground, but a faint sun was illuminating the sky, and it felt good to get some exercise after spending the whole of the previous day in the car.

After a careful inspection of his ID card and being checked off an approved visitors list, Tom was allowed through the gates by a guard, then waited for Mattias in the entrance lobby. It was lunchtime, and there were people everywhere. Service men and women in blueish-gray uniforms, young soldiers in camouflage, intelligence staff in suits. There were considerably more women now than just ten years ago, a sign that even the military adapted to reality and admitted people based on competence rather than sex. Tom leaned back and allowed himself to blend into the background, made himself gray and ordinary, entertained himself by studying the people passing by. There were quite a few people in civvies, teachers, researchers, students, and then the odd man or woman who was meant to look like a civilian but whom Tom had no trouble recognizing as part of the intelligence service.

Mattias came down a staircase and walked straight toward Tom with his hand outstretched. "Sorry you had to wait. Are you in a hurry?"

"Not really."

"I'd like you to meet someone before we go get lunch."

Tom followed Mattias past another security check and into his office. A young woman turned around in the visitor's seat and studied them with a steady gaze.

"Tom, this is Filippa." Tom shook her hand. She was young, under twenty-five, with an ordinary, almost anonymous appearance.

"Filippa's a computer expert," Mattias explained once they sat down. "And a hacker. She can hack any laptop, iPad, or phone." Mattias seemed pleased. Filippa looked like a teenager, not some kind of superstar, but Mattias was good at recruiting people.

"Have you changed your mind?" Mattias asked once they said good-bye to Filippa and sat down at a table in a restaurant.

"I said yes to lunch, but otherwise nothing has changed," Tom said. He spoke firmly, but the strange thing was that he was no longer so sure. It had been a long time since he'd last set foot inside the Armed Forces building. He hadn't expected it to feel so much . . . like home. But feeling at home wasn't the same as wanting to come back.

"It was worth a try. What do you think of Filippa?"

"Is she as good as you say?"

"Better. She started out as an amateur hacker, but now she has a degree in computer science. Everyone's been trying to get her. But I got lucky. Turns out she's a patriot. What do you think?"

"She seems good, gives off a good impression. I think you should offer her the position, if you're asking for my advice."

"Tom, I could really use you here. We'll be doing some very important work, and you would be able to do what you do best."

"Kill people?"

Mattias scoffed. "Assess threats, analyze, lead people. You're starting to get too old for killing people."

"I have a few years left, surely."

"I wish I could make you change your mind. Is it because of me?"

"The fact you betrayed me in front of all my bosses? Yeah, I guess I'm a little petty about that kind of thing."

"I did it for our sake. For the special forces."

"I think you did it for yourself, for the sake of your career."

"Maybe. But no matter what motivated me, this is about you. Can you get over your grudge and be professional for the sake of your country?"

"I already have a job," Tom pointed out.

"I won't stop bringing this up."

Tom sighed. Mattias was stubborn. He had betrayed his best friend. He was difficult. He kept repeating all this to himself. But somehow he couldn't manage to work up his usual anger.

On the way home, Tom passed the *Aftonbladet* offices. He slowed down outside the enormous building, watched people coming and going, checked out the guards in reception. Their security was a joke. Newspaper offices were a strategic terror target, but he would probably be able to take the building with just a handful of men in less than fifteen minutes.

While he stood there staring at the building, Ambra suddenly appeared in the doorway. She caught sight of him and paused.

"Hi," he said with a grin. It felt too damn good to see her again.

She pulled on her gloves and shook her head. "The strange thing isn't even that you're here. It's that I'm not surprised. You have a tendency to just turn up."

"I'm in Stockholm," he stated the obvious.

"I can see that. But what are you doing here? Are you meeting someone from the paper?"

"Nah, I was just passing by," he lied easily. In truth, he had headed straight for the place. "I just wanted to check everything was okay."

"I'm on the way out," she said.

"A job?"

She nodded. "But why . . ."

She was interrupted by a man with a huge camera hanging over his shoulder. "Ambra, we need to go!"

"That's my photographer," she explained, hanging her press ID around her neck.

"Take care," he said.

She raised one of those black eyebrows of hers. Against her pale skin, they looked like dark brushstrokes. "I usually do."

Yes, he was convinced of that. He took a step toward her. "When do you get off?"

"No idea. It depends." The photographer made an urgent sound. "Sorry, I need to run."

"Can we meet again? Do you want to?"

"Do you?" Her green eyes studied him, unblinking.

"Yes," he said. If he took a deep breath, he could make out her scent.

The photographer waited, stamping his feet. Tom ignored him. "Where are you going?" he asked.

She straightened her hat. "Suspected suicide in Djursholm. I really need to go." She pursed her lips and then said, "Five. I finish at five, latest five-thirty."

"Fine, so should we meet then? Eat together?"

"Yeah. Should I make a reservation?"

He might be rusty, but things weren't so bad that he couldn't manage to organize a date. "Nope, I'll arrange everything," he said. And he leaned in and gave her a spontaneous kiss on the cheek. He just couldn't let her leave without touching her first. "See you at five-thirty," he murmured into her ear.

Chapter 41

Ambra watched the ambulance drive away from Djursholm, the most fashionable Swedish suburb; its lights weren't flashing. The police were still interviewing the neighbors. She had a few good quotes, and the photographer had photos from virtually every angle. They were done here, she decided.

This was a routine job that they never would have been sent to cover if it hadn't happened in an upper-class suburb and if the deceased hadn't been an important business leader. They were more newsworthy than ordinary people. The police officer she spoke to, a woman who had a good relationship with Ambra, told her it was probably just a perfectly ordinary heart attack.

She traipsed back to the car, allowing the photographer to drive, then stared out the window as they left Djursholm and pulled onto the E18 highway. She scrolled through the pictures she'd taken with her phone, listened to the photographer talk to the pictures editor. They passed Haga Norra. The Crown Princess lived in the castle there with her young family, in the middle of the huge, well-protected park, close to the waters of Brunnsviken. Djursholm, which they'd just left behind, was full of enormous villas and palace-like houses; it was home to Sweden's richest people. Jill included. But about twelve miles to the west, there were huge tower blocks where social problems and an appalling lack of services were the depressing order of the day.

She stared out toward the buildings. How different people's lots in life could be, and it was all so random. They turned off toward the city. They would soon be back in the office, and then she wouldn't have time to think about Tom, so she gave herself a few minutes here in the car, in between jobs. It was crazy that he'd just turned up like that. She grinned the rest of the way to the office.

She managed to finish all of her tasks, articles, and introductions by the end of the workday. No excessively dramatic events happened in Stockholm or anywhere else that day, so she said a few quick words to the nightshift and made it down to the exit by five-thirty. Tom was waiting outside as promised. No messages saying he would be late. No cancellations or last-minute changes of plan. If Tom said he would turn up, he did. He was wearing one of those super-advanced but understated ski jackets, a sober gray scarf, leather gloves, and sturdy boots. No hat covering his black hair, but he was holding a mysterious black bag in one hand.

He greeted her with a wide smile, and it was as though that smile of his had a direct connection to her erogenous zones. Her entire body trembled, and she hid the embarrassing fact that she was blushing by fiddling with her scarf and gloves.

"Can you handle a walk down to Kungsträdgården?" he asked, but then he glanced at her thin boots and shook his head. "We'll take a cab." He waved one over, opened the door, and slipped in after her. Ambra sank contentedly into the backseat. She wasn't used to being fussed over like this.

"How are you? No problems after you got so cold in Kiruna?"

"Nope, nothing. Where are we going?"

"You'll see."

"Macho," she mumbled, but it was a halfhearted protest.

The car was comfortable, Tom smelled great, and she would get to do something other than watch TV and eat leftovers after work. Plus, she would be doing it with one of the most attractive men she'd ever met. Somehow, Tom seemed a little more handsome every time she saw him. She glanced down toward the seat, where their legs were almost touching.

"How was work?" he asked.

"Pretty quiet, actually. It's unusual. But that can change in an instant. What did you do today? Are you working again?"

"I had lunch with Mattias, sorted out some paperwork, and then invited a beautiful woman out on a date."

It was on the cheesier side, so she rolled her eyes and tried not to let his response affect her. Jesus, he was practically irresistible when he was like this.

The cab dropped them off on Hamngatan. It was snowing, huge soft flakes swirling down, and the whole scene was ridiculously romantic. The store windows were slowly starting to fill up with spring collections, but there were still Christmas lights in the trees and on the buildings, twinkling away in the frostbitten night. There was a scent of mulled wine and roasted almonds in the air, and she could hear music from somewhere.

They walked toward Kungsträdgården, passing small stalls selling knickknacks and souvenirs alongside the empty fountain. There was another stall selling Norrland specialties, and Ambra paused. She looked around and sniffed the air. "Where is that smell coming from?"

Tom pointed toward a food truck. "You like waffles?"

"Are you kidding me? I love waffles," she said honestly, her mouth watering. The smell was incredible. "You want some? Or do you want to eat real food?" he asked.

"Waffles," she replied firmly. He ordered for both of them.

"Which jelly?" he asked as the waffle iron hissed and steamed as the batter cooked.

Ambra read the menu: raspberry, blackberry, strawberry. "All of them. And cream. And sugar." She smiled happily at him.

Tom pulled out a sheepskin fur from his bag, spread it out onto a rickety park bench, and went to fetch their paper plates. They sat there, beneath the glittering strings of lights, eating steaming-hot waffles with extra everything. Tom bought two more and wolfed down whatever she couldn't manage.

After they finished, Tom got up and threw away the napkins and plates. Ambra rubbed her hands together. It was cold, but she didn't want their date to be over yet. Maybe they could grab a coffee or a drink somewhere? Not that she knew anywhere nearby. She glanced around, but all she could see were the stalls and the tourists. She shouldn't have suggested waffles. She was stuffed already.

"Come on, frozen lady, you're shivering," he said. Ambra was hunched down in her scarf. They passed a stall selling purses, key rings, and accessories. Tom paused. "Choose one," he said, pointing to the hats.

"I don't need one, I'm fine," she protested.

"You're freezing."

Ambra was about to refuse, because there were limits to how fun it was to be bossed about, even if Tom was right and she was freezing. But right then, she caught sight of a pair of white, fluffy, sheepskin earmuffs. Just like the pair she'd seen in Kiruna. She pointed. "I want those. But I'll buy them myself." She reached for her wallet.

"Put that away," Tom said. He grabbed the earmuffs, paid, and placed them on her head.

They were wonderfully warm, and when his gloved hand grazed her cheek, she smiled at the considerate gesture.

"Come on. I thought we could go for a skate." He nodded to the artificial ice rink in the middle of the park. That was where the music was coming from.

"Ha ha," she laughed, assuming he was joking. But Tom held up his bag and opened it. Beneath the sheepskin, she spotted a pair of hockey skates.

Ambra shook her head, suddenly serious. This wasn't fun at all. "I don't want to," she said.

"But it's so much fun."

"I can't. I've never done it."

"Never?"

On every school trip, she would have to sit to one side because she didn't have any skates. No one had ever thought it was worth the effort to teach her, to treat her to even a secondhand pair of skates, and so she never learned. Now it was too late. "I can't," she repeated, giving him an angry look. This wasn't funny anymore. She *hated* being made aware of things she couldn't do.

"Ambra. I can teach you."

"No."

He looked frustrated. "But why?"

"I'll fall, cut myself to pieces." *And everyone will laugh*.

"What if I promise that you won't fall?"

She just wanted him to stop talking about it.

"I'm steady as a rock. I won't let you fall even once. Give it ten minutes, and if you still hate it, then of course we can stop, but I suggested it because I thought you'd like it."

"If I knock myself out, you won't think it's so fun," she said.

"You won't," he said confidently.

"That's ridiculous, you can't promise that."

"True. But I can promise I'll do everything in my power to keep you safe. I'm very good at that kind of thing."

She really didn't want to, but eventually she chose a pair of rental skates in the right size. They were pretty nice, she had to admit. All white with a thin fur edge at the top. She sat down on a bench, took off her own shoes, laced up the skates, and then tried to get up. She immediately wobbled, her arms spinning, her heart in her throat. But Tom, who was ready way before her, was there.

"Wobble as much as you like, I've got you," he said calmly.

She hated ice skating more than anything else on earth, she decided. And Tom was in second place.

"Try it. Wobble, hold on to me."

She clung to him as tightly as she could, just waiting for them to go crashing down. She was so angry she had tears in her eyes. But Tom wasn't lying. No matter how much she teetered or slipped, he never lost his balance, never lost hold of her. And he didn't laugh. That was the most important thing. He didn't laugh at her.

"It's so hard," she muttered, her heart beating wildly, trying to make her way across the slippery ice. The skates slipped from beneath her, but he held on. Maybe she wouldn't fall flat after all. She managed to coordinate her feet and skate forward thirty centimeters. She puffed out and relaxed slightly.

"It's a good idea to breathe," he said.

She didn't reply. But the worst of her fears started to abate, and every time she managed to glide forward, her self-confidence grew slightly. She relaxed a little more. Suddenly, she could hear the music again. Before, she was so afraid that all she could hear was the rushing in her ears, but now she could hear it. And she saw the twinkling lights hanging all around them. If she ignored the fact that she was probably the worst skater on the entire rink, then it wasn't a completely awful experience. And it did actually give her the opportunity to more or less plaster herself to Tom and his magnificent body, which, she had to confess, wasn't the worst thing in the world. Tom moved confidently over the ice, as if he were born on skates. When she managed to glance around without falling flat or waving her arms as if she was doing jumping jacks, she realized that although there

were plenty of good skaters—including a crowd of children all skating at least a hundred times better than she was—actually no one
was staring at her or laughing.

"Better?" Tom asked.

"A little," she reluctantly admitted.

"It's been ten minutes. Want to stop?"

But she no longer wanted to. She continued to cling to him, and
they skated in circles at a leisurely pace. She would probably never
be an ice-skating queen, but it felt good to do something she had always considered impossible.

"I'm ice-skating," she said with a laugh, both her hands clutching
his arm. She managed a few more minimal strides forward, and that
counted as skating in her world.

Somewhere after their third loop of the little rink, Tom took off
his gloves and shoved them into one pocket. He pulled off one of
hers and took her hand in his. "I need to keep you warm," he mumbled. They kept going like that, her hand in his, and after a moment
he turned around without letting go of her for a single second.

"What are you doing?" she squeaked. He was skating backward,
and took both of her hands in his.

"Bend your knees a little," he encouraged her.

Ambra did as she was told and concentrated on not falling. She
teetered, and panic coursed through her, but he stepped forward
and took her in his arms again, as steady as a rock.

"I've got you," he mumbled.

She clung to him. "Don't let me go," she said.

"I promise."

She would be aching all over tomorrow, but it was worth it. Music
and the scent of mulled wine, people skating, laughing, and smiling.
This was the kind of thing people fantasized about their life containing, but it rarely did. They slowly floated across the ice, being over-
taken by practically everyone else, but Ambra loved every second of
it. She was steadier on her feet now. It was all about the right combination of balance and fearlessness, she realized, even if she still clung
to Tom, leaned her head on his shoulder, reveling in the feeling of
being safe and taken care of.

She looked up at him as he looked down. His eyes glittered in the
colorful lights surrounding the rink, and he was so close that she

could make out every eyelash, every individual eyebrow hair, and he lowered his mouth to hers and kissed her, brushed his lips to hers gently, just a light kiss with his mouth closed and his lips soft, all while continuing to hold her steady. She probably wouldn't have been able to fall even if she tried to. She closed her eyes and allowed herself to sink into his kiss. His arms tightened around her, and they skated slowly around the rink until the music fell silent. She smiled at him, dazed.

"How are your feet?" he asked quietly.

"A little sore," she admitted, though that was an understatement. They had gone numb a long time ago.

"I'm impressed you managed so long," he said, steering her slowly toward the bench where they'd changed their shoes earlier.

"Sit down," he said before he bent on one knee in front of her. His breath was like a cloud around him, and Ambra studied the back of his neck as he grabbed hold of one of her skates. He untied the laces and slowly pulled the boot from her foot. She breathed out. Ouch, it really did hurt. He took her foot in his hand and massaged it gently.

"You'll feel it tomorrow," he said. She sat there on the bench letting him take care of her. Neither of them said anything more. She reached out and stroked his hair. It was smooth and cold, and she allowed her fingers to glide through it. He slowly pulled off the other boot.

"Tom," she said, and he took her hand and kissed her palm. It was such a tender gesture, his mouth against her skin, his bristly stubble, warm lips. She bent down and moved her forehead toward his, closed her eyes, and breathed him in, breathed in the moment. Jesus, she wanted him so hard, wanted him to want her. She couldn't quite get her head around it, the fact he was so attractive to her. It wasn't just that he was handsome and exciting and clearly knew how to do everything, including teaching her to skate. It was his entire being. The way he smelled. His body. His *everything*. This never normally happened to her, definitely hadn't happened with any other man. She could barely think. Wasn't he in love with another woman? He had been just one week ago, and Tom didn't seem like the kind of man who changed his mind so quickly. This could, in other words, be a highway to heartache. No good could come out of this. *But he bought me earmuffs.*

"I'll be right back," he said, getting up to return the skates. She got to her feet, and when he came back, he put an arm around her and pulled her close, as though it was the most natural thing to do.

If they'd had protection in Kiruna, they would have slept together in the house; she was certain of that. If she took what she could, now that Tom was in Stockholm, could it really be so dangerous? If she knew there was a time limit on whatever they had, she would be able to protect herself from getting hurt. Right? She pressed herself into him. Worst case, she would suffer a little heartache. People did actually survive that kind of thing. What was she meant to do now? Should she just ask? Imagine if he said no, if she'd misunderstood everything again? Though he had kissed her. That had to mean something?

"Ambra? Is everything okay? You're really quiet."

Say it now.

Want to go back to my place? Want to sleep with me? No strings, just your huge body against mine. But she was in too much of a cold sweat, disproportionately terrified. She couldn't bring herself to say the words, she just couldn't.

"I'm just a little tired," she said instead, almost pulling a face at herself. Was there any more idiotic phrase to say at that moment? He was the world's biggest gentleman; he would probably just say good night.

"You've had a long day," he said, as though to order. "Should we see about getting you home?"

Yeahyeahyeah, may as well. The evening had been almost too perfect. It couldn't go on like that, not in real life. She would go home and date the couch instead.

Chapter 42

Tom didn't want the evening to end yet. It was that simple. But Ambra was pale and silent next to him. She had probably been working hard these past few days, and now he had forced her onto the ice rink until she could barely stand up. Not so smart, now that he thought about it. He'd worn her out, and now he couldn't assume they would spend the whole evening together just because he wanted to.

"I live in the Old Town," she said. "It's almost easiest to walk from here." She straightened her earmuffs. She looked incredibly sweet in them.

"I'll walk with you, if that's okay," he said.

"If you like." Her tone was neutral, not exactly inviting, but he wanted to, and so he decided to interpret it as an encouragement. He wanted a lot of things, actually.

She had pulled away after their kiss. Or rather, it wasn't even a kiss, more an erotically charged touch, but Tom's entire body had stood at attention, been drawn to her, wanted to lay claim to her.

She was so pretty, with her obstinate eyes and intrepid courage. He could see how scared she was when he'd suggested ice-skating. It was heartbreaking when she admitted she didn't know how, and he might have bossed her about a little. He would have understood completely if she wanted to run a mile, but she swallowed her fear and refused to give in. It was admirable. And, unexpectedly enough, sexy as hell. Then he had kissed her, and he couldn't bring himself to say good-bye yet.

They passed the red walls of Saint James's Church and then the

Opera House, where guests in evening dress were smoking and laughing on the steps.

"Do you like the opera?" he asked.

"Not really. I saw *Madame Butterfly* once and cried the whole way home. She was forced to give up her child," she added when she saw his surprised expression.

"Not for you, in other words?"

"Lots of the so-called classics have a warped view of women, don't you think?"

"Definitely," he said, convinced she had a better idea of that kind of thing than he did.

They cut across King Gustav Adolf's Square and crossed Norrbro bridge. The parliament building was dark. The royal palace was covered in a dusting of snow, and as they made it into the narrow streets of the Old Town, the snow started coming down more heavily. The buildings glittered in their Christmas lights; there were fire barrels burning outside of restaurants. If they hadn't eaten waffles earlier, he would have suggested they get dinner, which was what he had initially planned. Maybe he could take her for a drink. While Tom debated with himself, Ambra came to a stop.

"This is me," she said.

Tom looked up at the peach-colored facade. It was an old building. The windows got smaller the higher up they were, and the whole building seemed almost lopsided.

"It was built in the sixteen hundreds," she explained. "I think they called it picturesque in the real estate brochures. My apartment is at the very top. No elevator, just a set of incredibly uneven stairs." She seemed to hesitate. "Want to come up?" she eventually asked.

Her tone sounded slightly reluctant.

"I'd love to see your place," he said as nonchalantly as he could. She quickly entered the door code and opened the heavy door. As she climbed the wide staircase ahead of him, he saw that the steps were worn and smooth and definitely looked like they could be four hundred years old. They climbed higher and higher. Eventually, she stopped in front of a door that looked like it belonged to a different era; it was dark and heavy. *Vinter,* he read on the mailbox. She unlocked it and showed him in.

"It's not so big," she said apologetically, hanging her coat on a bright red hook.

It really was small. A tiny hallway; a kitchen that only just had room for a table, three chairs, and a stool; and a small living room with a purple couch, a huge flat-screen TV, and some bookshelves on one wall.

"The floors slope so much that if I dropped a marble at one end it would roll to the other. But they're original, and there's something special about several-hundred-year-old boards."

"I guess so," said Tom, though he had never given much thought to antique floors before. The two windows in the living room were different sizes, and the ledges had to be close to fifty centimeters deep. The apartment was cozy: not tasteful, not modern, just cozy. Colorful and snug, and not quite what he had expected.

Ambra pulled at her sleeve as she often did. Was she nervous? Or just tired?

"Want something to drink?" she asked, heading to the kitchen. He followed her. The room was as colorful as the hallway and living room. A rounded, cream-colored refrigerator, shelves of mugs in different colors, mismatched bowls, and a bright yellow toaster. An elegant chandelier in all the colors of the rainbow.

"Your place is great," he said as Ambra opened the refrigerator.

"Thanks," she said, but then she frowned. "I've actually only got water to offer you," she added apologetically.

"Water is fine."

She took down two pale blue glasses from the shelves, mumbled an apology when she bumped into him. The kitchen was tiny, and he was in the way no matter where he stood.

"Do you like living here?"

She tested the water with one finger. "I moved around so much when I was a kid," she said, filling the glasses. "I rarely had my own room, never stayed anywhere particularly long, never felt at home. So when I got my first permanent position, I took out a huge bank loan and bought this place. Most of my salary still goes on the payments, but it was a good investment. It's gone up in value and it's my security, my base."

"Like a symbol of your independence."

"Exactly." When she handed him the glass, their eyes met.

He took a sip and put down the glass just as she made an unexpected movement. The room was so small that they inevitably came into contact. His extended arm brushed against her body, and the hairs on his arms stood on end. The air between them vanished. She was perfectly still.

"Tom," she whispered, looking up at him. Huge eyes. Vulnerable expression.

He took hold of her and pulled her close. She was still looking at him, intently, and then he lowered his mouth to hers and kissed her the way he had been wanting to for the past few hours, days. A real kiss.

Ah, but she tasted fantastic when her lips opened for him. Her tongue met his, eager and bold. Her hands moved up his chest, continued around the back of his neck, and she greedily returned his kiss. Tom's body responded, becoming hard, hot, and primitive. He pulled her to him until they almost fell back against the wall. Pots and other kitchen items rattled, but he just wrapped his arms tighter around her, couldn't let go, didn't care about anything else but the woman in his arms. Ambra tugged impatiently at his sweater, and then her hands were beneath it, on his skin. He felt fingers and nails, and it was like his brain short-circuited. He grabbed her thick sweater, tore it off, and threw it to the floor. She was wearing another one beneath it, so he impatiently pulled that off too. Yet another, thinner, beneath it. And another.

"How many tops are you wearing, exactly?"

"This is the last one," she said with a laugh, peeling off her camisole and then standing in front of him in a simple black bra and jeans.

"You're so beautiful," he rumbled, drinking her in. She rolled her eyes so he cradled her face. It felt important that Ambra knew he meant what he said, that his words weren't just empty compliments, that he wasn't the kind of man to say things he didn't mean. "Yes, you are," he said, his lips brushing against her chin.

She trembled, and he kissed her neck, too, lingering there feeling her panting and the pulse beneath her warm skin. He kissed her collarbone, nibbled at her silky skin wherever he could, heard her pant again. His mouth moved across her bra, and he heard her mumble something like *Oh God* as his cheek rubbed against it. He felt her nipple harden, felt a reciprocal wave of desire in his own body. This thing between them, it was an erotic madness; he felt almost wild with want. All he could think about was satisfying her. It was like a task he had been given, an operation. Ambra's fingers snaked around his neck again. He loved it when she did that, clung to him, laid claim to him. He wrapped an arm around her waist and pulled her tightly toward him, toward his throbbing cock. She whimpered as he fumbled with the buttons on her jeans, pushed a hand inside, and cupped her through her panties.

"Oh, Tom," she gasped.

He kept his hand there, between her smooth thighs, against her soft warmth and inviting wetness. She pushed herself against him, and he cast an eye at the table. It was small, but it looked sturdy; it would do. He lifted her up onto it. Her eyes glittered. Without a word, he started to pull off her jeans. She helped by placing her hands on his shoulders, wiggling backward. Then he managed to peel them off.

Jesus, she was hot. That black underwear against her pale skin, those fine features, long lines. She looked like a cross between a glittering fairy and a cocky superhero. He put a hand on her shoulder, pulled at her bra strap, wanted to see her naked. Now.

"Tom, wait," she said, placing a hand on his chest. He wiped his forehead. Her chest was rising and falling, and she studied him intensely. "Take off your sweater," she finally ordered after he had started to think she wasn't going to say anything more. He raised his arms and pulled it off, then stood bare-chested in front of her. He could feel his own heart thudding inside his rib cage, felt his muscles flex. She didn't seem to have anything against what she saw, because she smiled.

"Take it off," he said, nodding to her bra. She moved her hands behind her back and unclasped it. She had the most perfect breasts. He raised his hand to one of them, kissed her hard, pushed her back until she was lying with her elbows on the table. Moving in between her legs, he kissed her throat, her breasts, her stomach, breathed in the scent of her until he was dizzy with lust. He pulled at her panties, upward, so they strained against her slit. She moaned, so he bent down, kissed her through the moist fabric, used his teeth to nibble, tugged her panties until they slid into her slit, increased the pressure against her sex by pulling them upward.

"God, that feels good," she mumbled.

Watching her, he pulled the panties off, let them glide over her skin, down her legs, over her feet, before he threw them to one side. Her legs dangled over the edge of the table. He parted them with his hands, touched her gently, placed a hand on her stomach, stroked her almost glowing skin. Christ, she was beautiful. Naked. Parted. His.

"You don't have to," she protested faintly.

But Tom hadn't needed to do anything so much in a very long time. He bent down and licked her sensitive, trembling body. She panted, and he took his time, using his index finger to explore her, trying to find out what she liked, listening to her sounds, working his way forward, getting used to her taste, her smell.

"Don't you want to go into the bedroom?" she whimpered from the other end of the table, her voice lacking all conviction. No, he wanted to do nothing other than what he was doing right then. He spread his palm over her soft stomach and pushed her against the table, parted her legs, and began to lick her. She stopped moving, exhaled, deeply. He played with one finger, dragged it carefully along her beautiful opening, his tongue following closely, pressing himself against her. He felt her start to tremble, and smiled at the confirmation her body was giving him. He took his time nibbling the inside of her thigh. Her skin was as smooth as fresh snow, and he was rewarded with a gorgeous shiver.

"More?" he mumbled, parting her again and running the tip of his tongue over her most sensitive areas; tasting her, testing to see what made her shudder, made her pulse beat harder, his too.

"Yes, oh yes."

His finger moved downward, from one sensitive spot to another. Hidden, secret, exquisite spots. He loved to see her pleasure. Using his hands, he pushed her thighs even farther apart, took in her pink wetness, her damp, dark curls. She was a study in contrasts: soft and tough, light and dark, brave and afraid. He liked seeing her like this, exposed and vulnerable to him. Laid out like a feast. He bent forward again and licked her, methodically, pressed with two fingers, drew circles, used all his skill and intuition, as well as the raw desire that had built up in him, practically boiling in his veins, felt her swell, become hotter and tighter when he carefully moved his index finger inside her, felt all those amazing muscles contract around his finger, her thighs tense. It was intoxicating, watching this gracious, curvy, strong woman come apart beneath his tongue, his fingers, his movements. He closed his eyes, his senses heightened, kept up with her speed, pressed and licked and felt her drawing closer, felt her nails dig into his hair, one foot bracing itself against the tabletop. He grabbed her ass with one hand, used the other to caress her skin, to move over her, and then he felt it, the orgasm spreading out beneath his tongue and fingers like an underground explosion. It made her jerk and shake, and he continued until it ebbed away. He took in her scent and taste in his nose, his mouth, wanted to keep it, be intoxicated by it for as long as he could.

She lay on the table with her arms at her sides, her head slightly tilted, one leg pulled up. He kissed her stomach and she shuddered.

"Wait a moment," she whispered, her voice husky. There were goose bumps covering her pale skin.

"Are you chilly?" he mumbled, following the tiny bumps with the very tip of his index finger, watching the thrill shoot through her.

"A little," she replied, which he took as an excuse to take her in his arms, hug her entire body to his bare skin. A desire to protect, and something else he couldn't identify rushed through him. He nuzzled against her neck, held her even tighter, and then, just because he could, he stood up with her in his arms. He was strong, and embarrassingly happy to be able to demonstrate that to her. He hadn't even known he was the type, didn't usually show off in front of women.

"I should be protesting this," she said, but instead she wrapped her arms around his neck and breathed into his chest.

"Why?" he murmured into her hair.

"Because it's such a cliché. Plus, it's only about forty centimeters to the couch."

"You want to go there? To the couch?"

"Mmm."

Tom took the few steps into the living room and then sat down on the couch, with Ambra still in his arms. She was so soft he could barely think. He pressed her ass against his arousal, moved, groaned.

"Are you grinding against me?" she asked with a laugh.

"Yeah," he admitted.

She moved in his arms, and he gasped for air. "You don't want to have sex instead?" she asked.

"I'd love to," he said with emphasis. He paused a little, didn't want her to think he'd planned this, but . . . "I bought protection," he said.

She laughed against his skin. "Me too. Just in case."

She licked his neck, bit his earlobe. Tom couldn't remember when he'd last wanted anything as much as he wanted to have sex with Ambra Vinter in her tiny, colorful apartment. He would have given her the moon if she'd asked him to.

Her bedroom was as small and colorful as the rest of the apartment, her green wrought iron bed just wide enough for the two of them. He joined her beneath the covers, which she held up for him. The bed shook considerably and creaked loudly every time he moved, but it seemed to be holding up.

"It's an antique," she explained.

He nodded, his focus on something entirely different. He discreetly rolled on a condom, turned onto his side so they were face-to-face, breast to breast, nose to nose. He kissed her eagerly, pulled her leg over his thigh, parted her, caressed her smooth skin, adjusted his position, and finally entered her. It was better than he could have ever imagined. He groaned as her warmth enveloped him, lay completely still, just allowed himself to feel her, to hold her in his arms, to be inside her, to be so near.

"Tom," she breathed, clinging to him, pulling him tight, wrapping her legs around him. He slowly pulled out and then pushed inside her again, and again, made love to her, as slowly as he could, as intimately as he could, until his wildness took over. He was too starved to draw it out, the feelings too raw, too intense, so he placed a hand behind her neck and the other on her ass, pulled her tight against him until he was panting against her skin. It was verging on unbearably good, and he came, hard and shaking, deep inside her. Lost himself and disappeared.

"Tom?" He felt a soft hand on his cheek a moment later.

He blinked, still completely overwhelmed. "Sorry. Am I heavy?"

He shifted away, but Ambra followed him, wrapped herself around him. He kissed her smooth shoulder, heard the bed creak. Ambra laid her cheek on his chest, draped her entire body over his, and the most intense feeling of presence came over Tom. Here, in this tiny apartment full of tassels and small lamps and cheerful colors, he felt more at home than he had anywhere else. He stroked her fragrant hair. Played with a bouncy curl. She kissed his chest, ran an index finger through his hair. "Want to eat? I'm hungry again."

"Sure. Do you have anything here?"

"Nothing."

"What do you want?"

"Candy."

He kissed her on the nose and pulled himself free. "Then I'll buy candy. And I want to watch that program you were talking about."

Tom got dressed and went down to the store on the corner. He bought candy, freshly baked cinnamon buns, chocolate, and ice cream. When he came back, Ambra had lit candles and moved the duvet and cushions from the bed into the living room. They curled up on the tiny couch. She switched on *Lyxfällan*.

"You like this?" Tom asked after watching, astounded, for a while. He didn't understand a thing.

She shoved candy hearts and chocolates into her mouth. "A lot."

"Why?"

"There's nothing you just like?" she asked, reaching for more candy. Tom followed her movement. *You. I like you.*

"I don't watch a lot of TV," he said.

"Because of all your secret missions and rescue operations?"

"Exactly." He continued to watch the strange program, kissing her skin every now and then.

"Do you always have a beard?" she asked with a mouth full of candy.

"I wasn't born with one," he said.

"It tickles."

He brushed his chin against her face, and she gasped. "Stop, I'm so ticklish."

He playfully gripped her wrists. "You don't like my beard?" he asked, bending down farther.

"You wouldn't dare," she said, so of course he dragged his beard across her entire body until she was shaking with laughter beneath him. Eventually, she twisted and squirmed so much that they both fell from the cramped couch onto the floor. He landed with a thud and pulled her on top of him. She straddled him, and he lay there perfectly happy to find himself in a position between her thighs, with her breasts right above him. She turned off the TV, placed a hand on his chest, touched the scars on his body, bent down, and kissed them. His hands were on her ass, and when she leaned down towards him he grabbed her waist and flipped her onto her back, ready to conquer, besiege, capture.

"Caveman," she said, but her eyes were glistening, and he took a light grip on her wrists, pulled her hands above her head, and started to methodically explore her body with his lips and mouth. She giggled when he kissed beneath her ear, squirmed when he blew on her neck, but started breathing harder the longer he continued. He carefully brought his hungry lips to her hard nipple, moving them forward and back, and then did the same with the other. Ambra moved her hips.

"Tom," she pleaded.

"Shh," he mumbled into her skin. "I need to concentrate. Lie still."

He reached a small scar and moved his lips over it as softly as he could. Was this just an innocent, forgotten injury? Or had someone hurt her on purpose? Her life had been far too hard. If anyone ever laid a finger on her, he would track that person down and tear them to pieces, bit by bit, with great enjoyment.

When he let go of her hands, she turned onto her stomach. He studied her, placed his palm on her soft behind, stroked forward and back.

"I like your ass," he said.

"Good to hear," she said, giving him an inviting smile over her shoulder. Incredibly, he was hard again, so he didn't take long to accept her invitation. He grabbed a new condom, pushed her legs apart, steadied himself on his elbows, and entered her from behind. He made love to her again, against the uneven floor.

"Keep going," she mumbled, pressing herself back against him.

He hadn't thought he would be able to come again, but in this position he could get deeper inside her. He thrust into her, gently to begin with. But she groaned, and mumbled, "God, that feels so good," and he lost control slightly, thrust even harder, got lost in her tight warmth, allowed his hands to follow her spine, to move downward, and when she raised her ass toward him, pressed herself backward, he continued to pound away at her, harder now, against the floor. She panted and shifted beneath him, and he came again.

He heard a roar echo through the apartment, maybe it was his. He pulled out, kissed her between the shoulder blades. She was soaked with sweat beneath him, and his heart was pounding away against her back.

He lay down next to her, breathed out and studied her. "You didn't come," he said.

"I did before."

"But not now?"

She shook her head.

"Why not?"

"I don't come from just . . ." She bit her lip.

"From just?"

"I have to use my hands."

He turned onto his side, interested in what she'd said. He had always assumed that women mostly came from the act itself. Right? He wasn't sure.

"It was still good, though."

"But don't you want to come?" He had to say he wouldn't want to have sex without an orgasm. And he had come twice now.

"It's fine," she said. "It was great before. When you . . ." She trailed off, looked embarrassed. But Tom wouldn't drop the subject. He wanted to know what Ambra liked. And then he wanted to give it to her. To see her come again.

"When I licked you?" he asked, taking hold of her nipple and pulling at it.

She panted and nodded. "And the other thing."

"Can't you show me what you like?" he said.

She seemed unsure, so he leaned forward over her, kissed her swollen lips, caressed her shoulder, and moved down toward her hips, in between her thighs, pushed them apart. He lowered his mouth.

"No," she mumbled. "Use your fingers first."

"Show me," he commanded.

She lay perfectly still. Then she moved her hands. Parted and caressed herself, in much wider circles than he expected, gently used her nails, rose up on her ass. He parted her until she was exposed and touched her tenderly.

"Harder," she said. "And don't forget the area around it."

He smiled, liked it when she was bossy, demanding pleasure. And so he touched her the way she showed him, followed her instructions, heard her pants.

"Tom, I'm coming," she groaned, and he pushed one, then two fingers inside her, all while continuing to caress her with his other hand. She came against his hand, contracted and jerked until she brought her knees together. "Jesus," was all she said. He laid a hand on her hip, disproportionately pleased with himself. He liked giving her orgasms. He wondered how many more he would get to give her. Could women come multiple times, or was that just a myth? He would try to find out.

She shuddered again, beneath his hand. Maybe they should go to bed, or at least up onto the couch, but he couldn't move. He was going to be thirty-seven, after all, not a teenager anymore. Instead, he pulled the rest of the bedding onto the floor.

She leaned against his chest. Lay there while her breathing calmed. She played with his nipple. "Where's Freja while you're down here?" she asked breathlessly.

"With Ellinor," he replied without thinking. He regretted it the minute the words left his mouth. He felt her tense slightly.

"Okay," she said.

Shit, shit, shit. "Ambra, I . . ."

"No, no, don't worry."

"Sorry, that was insensitive of me."

"Really, don't worry."

He stroked her, traced the inside of her lower arm with his finger, wishing deeply he hadn't said anything. He had never thought it was possible to have feelings for two women at once. But what he felt for Ambra wasn't just desire, it was something more. He stroked her arm.

"Do you want to go to a party with me?" he asked quietly.

"A party?" she said against his chest, as though the word were alien to her.

He caught her hand and turned it over, kissed her wrist. "I would like it if you came," he mumbled into her warm skin. "My friend I told you about, David Hammar, he was pressuring me to go. And he told me to bring someone. Want to come?"

She sat up and studied him. "You want to take me to a party? With your friends?"

"Was it wrong of me to ask?"

She frowned. "It's just so unexpected."

"It's an ordinary party, nothing special. I understand if you don't want to," he said.

But she nodded. "Yeah, I do. Thanks."

Tom felt unexpectedly exhilarated. Suddenly, he had nothing at all against going to a party.

"Turn on your program again," he said with a wide smile, a smile linked to Ambra and orgasms and hopes for the future. He got comfortable beneath the covers and cushions and pulled her in close.

"Sure?"

"Definitely."

She turned on the TV and curled up next to him. He moved the bowl of candy in front of her, put his chin on her head, one leg over hers, embracing her. Sleepily he was drawn back into the bizarre program. With increasingly heavy eyelids, he listened to Ambra's catty comments and enjoyment of the candy. Somewhere between budget charts, crying, debt-ridden contestants, and the rustling of candy wrappers, Tom realized he was more content than he had been in a long time. Maybe ever.

Chapter 43

Ambra looked at the rows of clothes with indifference. The light in the store was giving her a headache. Or maybe it was the heavy perfume in the air. Or the fact she had just left work and was completely exhausted. After a shift, she usually felt more dead than alive, even without the added burden of shopping. She wished she'd had the nerve to cancel this date with Jill, but she hadn't.

So, here she was.

"But what does he mean? What do you think it *means?*" she asked Jill.

This was what she hated. Not understanding what things really meant. Having to interpret what was hiding behind words, acts, and gestures.

She liked Tom, and the sex was incredible. But sex was just sex. It was far too easy to read your own feelings and hopes into a smile, a hot kiss, a passionate weekend. Because the weekend they'd spent together *was* passionate. They'd made love and made love, and now she was full of feelings. But what did Tom feel? What would happen now? And what did it *mean* that he'd asked her to that party?

"I think it means he wants you to go to a party with him," Jill replied drily. She pulled out a dress, the fifth or sixth, or maybe tenth, Ambra couldn't bring herself to care. She wanted to think about Tom and sex.

"What about this one?" Jill asked.

Ambra looked down at the dress. Lace, with an open back. She pulled a face. "I hate lace."

"Maybe something more demure then."

The air was stale, and there were far too many people inside the store, whatever it was called. No matter where she turned, she saw upper-class girls with the same hairstyle, clothes, and body language.

She didn't want this, could feel it in every untreated pore and unwaxed body part.

She glanced longingly toward the entrance, but Jill shook her head in warning. "Don't even think about running off."

"Then can we hurry up a little?"

Even in ordinary situations, Ambra wasn't particularly keen on shopping for clothes, especially not in *boutiques*. But going shopping with Jill was even worse. A bit like going out with your own personal heckler.

"We could if you would actually *choose* something." Jill held up a glittery dress consisting of string and sequins. Ambra studied it suspiciously.

"Are those feathers?" She shook her head. No feathers.

With a look of exaggerated torment, Jill hung the creation back on the rack. "Should we do this another day, Miss Journalist?"

She was going to a party with Tom (God, she felt a thrill just thinking his name), so she had to find something to wear. Plus she had promised Jill a shopping trip, so she might as well kill two birds with one stone.

"No, I'll do better," Ambra said, trying to look energetic while a large part of her wanted nothing but to jump through the window.

How could people enjoy this? Everyone in the store looked like they had just stepped out of a fashion spread. Even if Jill was the biggest celebrity in the room, Ambra saw several others. The reporter in her would have much rather been interviewing people and ferreting out secrets than trying on clothes that would just make her look like she was playing dress up.

Jill ignored the stolen glances she was being given and held up two new dresses. One red and one yellow. Ambra shook her head.

"You're hopeless," Jill said. She was starting to look irritated.

"I'm tired," Ambra protested.

She had barely slept the past few days, just had incredible sex with Tom and worked like a madwoman. She got up early when she worked, and he had gotten up with her. Bought breakfast while she showered, made her sandwiches and coffee. Kissed her, walked her to work. Smelled so insanely good when they said good-bye. Acted irresistible.

"The sex was amazing," she said as Jill continued to search among the hangers. She pulled things out, studied them, hung them up again. Over and over.

Ambra traipsed after her. She needed to talk to someone about this. She lowered her voice. "It was so damn hot. I've never come so many times, and the orgasms . . . Unlike anything I ever experienced." She followed Jill. "Have you ever had an orgasm like that? One that feels like the best thing you've ever experienced, like you didn't think existed?"

"Mostly on my own," Jill said absentmindedly, taking out a dress with a delicate pattern and frills at the bottom and studying it critically.

"I came several times," Ambra said. She was usually just happy if it happened once. Half, even.

"Ugh, I don't want to know," Jill said, holding up the dress to Ambra.

"But you talk about that kind of thing constantly. You don't have any boundaries."

"When it's about me, yes. Keep your multiple orgasms to yourself."

Ambra glanced around to check no one was eavesdropping. "Do you come from the sex itself?"

"You mean the old in and out? Nah."

"Is that normal? To come without any hands, I mean?"

"Why are we talking about this?"

"Because I had to show him. He seemed to think that's how it is."

"His last girl probably made him think that. Some do. Ruin things for everyone else."

"You mean she faked it?" She had to say that the thought of Ellinor faking an orgasm perked her up enormously.

"I've done it so many times. Gets them to stop fumbling. But he's still with her, right? Ambra, you can't be hoping this is going to turn into anything if he is."

"But he seems interested. And I'm not hoping anything," she lied.

Jill seemed skeptical, but she changed the subject. "What about this? It would be better if you had breasts, but it should work." Jill waved the dress encouragingly.

Ambra automatically started to shake her head at the slinky blue dress—it looked expensive and a little slutty, not her style at all—when Jill said, in a low voice, "And before you say no, if you don't try this one, I'll film you, upload it to my Insta, say you're my sister, and tag every-one at *Aftonbladet*."

Ambra snatched the dress from her.

"Then we'll buy some shoes."

Ambra groaned.

Jill followed her toward the changing room. "And jewelry. And a coat. I saw one from Dior that would suit you. If you don't eat for a few days."

"I'm not buying a coat. And I refuse to starve myself. Coats should be roomy."

"Refuse all you like. But you can't wear a leather jacket or that ugly winter coat on top of an evening dress. Even poor people don't want that kind of thing. We're buying you a coat." Jill cocked her head, the way she always did when she wanted to manipulate someone and get her own way. "Let me do this for you. I forgot your birthday and I'm ashamed of that, so let me overcompensate."

"I'd prefer you be ashamed," Ambra said, still annoyed about her birthday. But she knew the discussion was over. She didn't have the energy to argue with Jill, not when her sister was in this kind of mood. Plus, her head was full of Tom Lexington.

Tom, Tom, Tom.

It was official, she'd fallen for him, she thought as she went into the changing room, undressed, and carefully pulled on the blue dress.

"And underwear. We need underwear. Are you still in there?" she heard Jill shout from the other side of the door.

"I'm here," Ambra said. The room was big and luxurious, with a little couch, several hooks, and gentle lighting. She could stay here. Rest.

Jill banged on the door. "Ambra?"

"Yeah yeah yeah." She struggled with the shoulder straps, adjusted the neckline. Jill was probably right, she would need different under-wear with this.

She turned around in front of the mirror and studied herself from various angles. She didn't actually *hate* this dress.

"Try these shoes." Jill opened the door, studied her, and then held out a pair of shoes. Slim, high heels, pointed toes.

"I won't be able to walk in those," Ambra said, but she took them anyway. They were the right size and were neither old-fashioned nor stupidly young. They were elegant, modern, and edgy.

It sounded as if they were whispering: *wear us, wear us*. Jesus, they were incredible. If she practiced every day and spent most of the party standing still, maybe it could work?

"Which hairdresser do you go to?" Jill had opened the door and stuck her head around the edge.

"Why?" Ambra looked in the mirror. She was pale and had dark circles beneath her eyes, but her hair looked normal. There was nothing wrong with her hair.

"So I know who to avoid. Doesn't matter. Ludvig can book you in with mine."

Ambra opened her mouth to protest, but she closed it again when she saw the mood Jill was in. Instead, she ran her hand over the shimmering blue fabric. She didn't dare look at the price tag. Would Tom like her in this? Would his eyes glitter dangerously when he saw her in the underwear Jill had handed into the changing room as a suggestion? Ambra took the bra and panties and studied them. Pale gray silk. A little lace. Tom was surely a man who liked lace.

She hung them up and stepped out of the changing room, still wearing the dress.

"Admit it, you think this is fun," Jill said.

"Though it feels wasted on me."

Jill held up two necklaces and squinted between them. "What do you mean?"

Ambra nodded toward her reflection. "As you're always pointing out, I'm not exactly a model," she said; all she could see was her lack of breasts and her soft stomach muscles.

"You're shit hot," Jill said, sounding unfocused. She put down the necklaces and picked up a pair of glittering earrings instead. They looked like snowflakes.

Ambra rolled her eyes. "Yeah, right."

Jill looked at her in amazement. "Are you serious now? You really think you're ugly? I thought we were just joking."

Ambra shrugged. She knew she shouldn't let Jill's comments bother her, regardless of whether they were serious or not. But Jill had been incredibly gorgeous since she was just fourteen. Hanging out with her, becoming invisible whenever Jill turned up, that kind of thing left its mark. It wasn't something she usually thought about, wasn't something she was proud of.

"Do you know how often I get negative comments about my appearance?" Jill asked.

Ambra gave her perfect sister a skeptical look. "Weren't you voted Sweden's sexiest woman a few years ago?"

"You've read what they write on my Insta? I'm too fat, too dark, too fake, too made up. And that's with me blocking the worst of them, the people who think I should kill myself for being too fat and too ugly."

"Ugh, I know, it's awful." It was so depressing. As though Jill had to be put in her place just because she was a woman and dared to be seen. "But do you let it affect you? Really, I mean?" she asked. Jill often boasted that things like that just bounced off her.

"Sometimes."

"I know it's hard work," she said, thinking that Jill didn't really understand what it was like for mere mortals. Plus, Jill never really took a position on anything, never had important opinions on anything. Everything was superficial.

"Ambra, you're so beautiful. Why can't you see that? Why can't you see what I see? A beautiful woman with perfect skin, great hair, fantastic eyes, and a completely normal woman's body."

Ambra squirmed uncomfortably. "Jill, you always get attention when we're out, but I'm invisible. You can't compare us. There are so many times we've been out and people have come up to you, said you're beautiful, given you compliments."

"People check you out too. Men."

Jill was about to put down the snowflake earrings, but Ambra grabbed them. They reminded her of Kiruna, of Tom, of the snowmobiles. "No, they don't," she replied.

Jill nodded firmly. "Yeah. They look, you just don't see them. You're so busy being prickly, angry, pretending you don't care about anything."

"That's ridiculous."

"Either way, you're really cute, and we're finally getting somewhere here. You taking those earrings? Good, then we just need to choose a bag to match. Something glittery."

When Ambra got home, she unpacked the various bags and boxes. Jill had paid the astronomical sum without even blinking, with a flashy credit card Ambra had only ever seen pictures of before. It was difficult, but Ambra decided to let herself be treated for once in her life, without immediately offering something in return.

Once was nothing.

She looked down at her treasures. Expensive costume jewelry in flat boxes, an evening bag; a glittery, unbelievably expensive clutch, still in its luxurious canvas pouch. The pale evening coat from Dior, which she would probably never wear again; the silk underwear, the dress and shoes.

Embarrassingly enough, she felt a lump in her throat. She had never received so many presents before, and she was clearly more superficial than she thought. What she felt for these things was pure love.

It could be fun to dress up after all. She ran her fingers over the thin, rustling tissue paper sticking up from an extravagant, glossy bag bearing the Prada logo.

Maybe even a lot of fun.

Chapter 44

Tom grabbed the car keys, locked his apartment, and went down to the front door. His car was parked on the street, and he had to scrape the ice and snow from the windows before he could leave. Aside from the fact that he missed his walks with Freja, it really did feel good to be home, he reflected as he climbed into the car. Ellinor sent him messages every day, both pictures and status updates. Today's message had already arrived, but just before he started the car he received another: *Are you going to the party on Friday, by the way?*

He replied: *Yeah.*

That's great!

It did feel good. Tom started the engine and drove away. The fact was, he was looking forward to the party. To seeing David Hammar. Saying hi to Alexander and Isobel De la Grip, congratulating them properly, partly on their marriage, partly on adopting Marius.

Tom suffered a bad conscience there. One of the recurring nightmares he tried to repress. Those dark eyes that had looked at him so trustingly.

He'd first met Marius in Chad last summer. A street kid who approached him, wanted to give him information, information that represented a breakthrough in their search for Isobel.

And then Tom treated him badly in return. Broke his trust by kidnapping him, a child. They had taken Marius into the desert and then locked him up in the Jeep so that he couldn't squeal to anyone. If Isobel hadn't brought the boy home with her once she was freed,

Marius might have died on the streets in Chad. And that would have been a child's life on Tom's conscience.

The anxiety tore at his chest, but he cast off those thoughts. He was getting better at fending off the attacks. Things had worked out in the end, he reminded himself. Isobel and Alexander loved Marius as if he were their own child, gave him all the security and care he had lacked before.

Tom turned on the windshield wipers against the snow, changed gears, and switched on the radio to distract himself. He heard the music, vaguely recognized the song being played. It was Jill Lopez, wasn't it? He relaxed, hummed along.

Yesterday was the first time he had been to the gym in a long while, and it felt good to work out in some other way than chopping wood or shoveling snow, to feel a little more civilized.

He hadn't seen Ambra since they'd parted ways outside her office the day before last, but she had been in his thoughts almost nonstop. He'd had to stop himself from sending her a message every five minutes. They'd made love practically all night, but she started work stupidly early in the morning and had barely gotten any sleep, so he was worried he had exhausted her. Or rather, that they'd exhausted one another. She had plans with her sister yesterday evening, but she was free today, and he had been hoping to see her. But then she agreed to work an extra shift. The woman worked far too much. She must be completely drained.

So what did he do now?

Should he suggest something? If so, what? He didn't want to seem pushy.

When his cell phone rang, he answered via Bluetooth as he pulled out onto the highway.

"Mattias here, how're things?"

"Good," was all he said. He couldn't quite work out where they stood with each other.

"I wanted to check whether you'd changed your mind, whether you're ready to come in and work for democracy with me."

"I haven't changed my mind."

"Filippa liked you."

"We met for five minutes."

"But you're so easy to like. And you should see the equipment they've given us. The budget I got approved. I think you . . ."

"How did it go with Jill Lopez?" Tom interrupted.

Long silence.

Tom smirked. So, it was possible to shut Mattias up.

"We met," Mattias replied vaguely. "What about you? Anything between you and Ambra?"

Tom thought about everything that had happened in Kiruna, the ice-skating on Saturday, the incredible sex, the intense messaging. "We've spoken a few times," he replied equally vaguely.

More silence.

He knew he should hang up, not be drawn into Mattias's conversation. But he still had some way to drive. And Mattias knew things, was much more experienced when it came to certain subjects. Tom sighed, really not comfortable with this conversation. But he didn't have many other options. Unless he Googled the subject, which felt even more pathetic somehow. He cleared his throat, his eyes fixed on the road ahead, and said as formally as he could, "I was wondering whether I should get in touch with her or not."

Mattias was silent for so long that Tom had to ask whether he was still there.

"Yeah, yeah, I'm just trying to recover from the shock of you asking for dating advice. What exactly do you want to know?"

Tom looked straight ahead. Clenched his jaw. "Whether I should call Ambra after we . . . You know."

"I'll take that as meaning you did more than just talk."

"Yeah."

"I see. And you like her?"

He didn't even need to think about it. "Yeah."

"Then it's simple. If you want to get in touch, get in touch."

Tom indicated and turned off. That sounded logical, in and of itself. "I just don't know what to say." Jesus, he sounded like a teenager.

"Tom, dating a woman is a process. You get to know one another. Think balance. If the last time you saw her was very intense, maybe you can do something more easygoing next time. Or vice versa."

Hmm. He hadn't thought of it as dating, and he still had no idea whether that was what they were doing. But Mattias was right, he should call her. Maybe suggest a walk, or a coffee? Or should he send her something? Flowers? Though that might scare her. He managed to stop himself from asking Mattias. There were limits to how much he wanted to embarrass himself in front of his former friend. Or current friend. Ah, he didn't know any longer.

"I've gotta hang up now," he said.

"Talk later."

Tom hung up without another word. He was almost there. He turned off into the driveway and parked outside the garage of his childhood home.

He stayed sitting in the car.

This was the yellow house where he grew up. His sisters had left, one by one, built families of their own. Dad was long since dead.

But Mom still lived there.

Tom couldn't remember when he was last here. He hadn't expected to be so powerfully affected. He climbed out of the car and headed toward the door. The driveway was freshly cleared and sanded, a huge lantern hung from the roof, and there was a green wreath on the door. The house was newly painted, and everything looked neat and well tended. There were strings of electrical lights in the trees, as always this time of year. His mother wasn't old, she wasn't even sixty, and her well-kept home was partly a result of her being very handy, partly having a husband who could fix things. He should have gotten in touch, Tom thought as he walked the short distance to the door. Should have asked if she needed help with anything. He was good with his hands, and strong, and his own mother should feel that she could call him. But his mother didn't like to ask for help, always wanted to handle things on her own.

They were similar in that respect, he realized. He rang the bell and the door opened, as though she had been waiting in the hallway.

"Tom! Come in."

She moved to one side. He stepped in and gave her a pat on the arm, kissed her on the cheek. They weren't particularly physical with one another, but he noticed that her eyes were glistening. She pulled her cardigan around her against the cold. He closed the door behind him.

"It's so good to see you. I'm so happy you could come."

He stamped the snow from his feet and started to unbutton his coat. "You aren't working today?"

"I'm marking papers for a colleague. I can do it from home."

"Do you have time then?"

"I always have time for you. Come on in."

Tom hung up his coat and followed her into the kitchen. He sat down at the table, a table into which he had once carved his initials, much to his parents' anger. His mother took out some seeded crisp bread, low-fat cheese, and various vegetables. That was his mother to a T: healthy, no midweek excesses. When he took the coffee cup she held out to him, he noticed her hands had aged, developed tiny liver spots.

"The girls are dying to see you. They wanted me to say hello from all of them."

"Thanks."

He was grateful she didn't pry. He had never told her exactly what he did, always wanted to protect her, but not knowing could also be difficult. She looked older than he remembered. The shock when she'd found out that her son had died in Chad must have been awful. Of everything he had subjected her to, that was the worst. No parent should have to go through that. "How are you, Mom?"

"I'm fine. A little tired. I've cut back on my hours at work, actually."

She always used to have so much energy. "Is that so?" She wasn't sick, was she?

She made a dismissive gesture and added some cheese and pepper to a piece of crisp bread. "I'm just so happy to see you. I know you've been angry with me."

He didn't say anything. He probably had been.

"You were so angry and disappointed that I divorced your father, that I met Charles, and I haven't always handled that like I should. But I want you to know how important you are to me. That you're here, that you came back. It's a miracle."

He felt a lump in his throat and got up from the table, embarrassed. He went over to the dresser where she kept her photos, pausing in front of a picture of him and his sisters. It was taken that first summer after the divorce, and he had never seen it before. "How old were you here?" he asked, studying his gangly body and set face. Yes, he had been angry at her.

She came over to him. "You were fourteen, so I must've been about to turn thirty-four."

Only thirty-three, four years older than Ambra was now. Alone with four kids. He had never reflected on how tough that must have been for her.

"Wasn't Charles there?" he asked.

"Then? No, I hadn't met Charles yet."

"I always thought that was why you and Dad divorced. Because you met Charles." For a while, he'd hated her because of it.

"No, that wasn't why we got divorced, your dad and I. Did you think that?"

She never let on, but it must have been a struggle, to keep the house running, to keep them clean and fed, all while working full-time. Dad had just disappeared into his own work, didn't have time for them.

"Mom, did Dad drink?" he asked, though he suspected he knew the answer.

She bit her lip, leaned forward, played with the wax of the candle she'd just lit. She nodded. "Sometimes I cried with worry at night. I wanted you to be secure, and I fought so hard to keep us together, to keep the house. All the debts I had to pay off, worries about you. I loved you all so much, trying to do the best for you."

"I had no idea."

"I'm glad. I didn't want you to know, any of you."

"It would've been better if you'd let us in. We could have helped out."

"Maybe. But being a parent isn't easy. There's no manual."

He hadn't exactly made things easier for her.

"I know you blamed me for Dad's death," she said.

"No," he replied, but that wasn't quite true. Mom and Charles got married, and not long after that, his father died. For a long time, he did blame her, assumed that his father died of a broken heart.

"I'm sorry, Mom."

"I know you loved your father, that he was your idol. And he loved you all. He wasn't unkind, he was a good father."

"But not a good husband?"

She slowly shook her head. "He did the best he could. And I tried until the very end. Getting divorced was the hardest thing I ever did. When I saw the effect it had on you, the way you missed your dad, I had so many doubts I thought I would break down. You and your father were so close. Sometimes it feels like I put my own happiness before yours."

She trailed off and raised a hand to her mouth.

Tom had seen his mother cry only once before, he realized.

When he was about to leave for his first foreign operation. Silent and pale, she gave him a ride to the airport. He was exhilarated, tense, hadn't been allowed to say where he was going, but she understood that it wasn't to some safe part of the world.

She had hugged him tight and cried, for the first and only time. And he was just eager to get away.

"I'm sorry, Mom. For causing so much trouble."

"You're one of those people who actually tries to make a difference. You have to know how proud I am of that. You have such a strong sense of right and wrong. Your father did, too, in many ways."

She took a handkerchief from her pocket and wiped her nose. "And you haven't caused any trouble. My dear Tom, sometimes I don't think you realize how important you are to us, how much you mean to your family."

"You mean a lot to me too," he managed to say.

She patted him on the cheek and sat back down at the table. "I know that. How is Ellinor? Is she still . . . ?"

"With Nilas? Yeah."

"She told me over the summer. I'm so sorry. I know how much you always loved Ellinor." She fell silent, wiped a few crumbs from the tablecloth into her palm, and then dropped them onto her napkin.

"Mom? I thought you liked her," he said in surprise.

His whole family knew Ellinor well, had met her, spent time with her. Tom had always assumed they liked her and that she fitted in perfectly.

"I do, absolutely," she said, though her tone wasn't entirely convincing.

He wondered whether she somehow knew that Ellinor had cheated on him. Not only with Nilas, but also once before. He hadn't told anyone, it wasn't anyone else's business, but maybe his mom suspected something nonetheless.

"I've been on a few dates with another girl," he said hesitantly.

She placed her hands in her lap and gave him an encouraging look.

"I don't know whether you would like her."

"Why not?"

"She's completely different from Ellinor," he said. Though maybe that didn't have to be a negative. "Her name is Ambra."

"Pretty name."

"She's a journalist. A little younger."

A shadow crossed her face. "Not too young?"

He laughed. "No, Mom, she's not too young. It's probably nothing serious, so please don't tell the others. I just thought you might want to know that there's hope."

"That makes me happy," she said, and her eyes glistened again.

They spent the rest of his visit talking about the garden and his sisters, and toward the end Tom found himself promising to stop by again soon.

They hugged when he left. "Take care, Mom. Call me if you need any help. And get some rest."

He drove back into town. Halfway there, he had a sudden thought, turned off toward the center, and parked in the garage beneath the posh NK—Nordiska Kompaniet—department store. He went up to the home décor department and picked out some pillows, a few ceramic pots, curtains, and an everyday dinnerware set. When he spotted a brightly colored blanket, he grabbed that too. It reminded him of Ambra's apartment. He arranged home delivery for everything but the blanket, which he took with him there and then. Afterward he went down to the menswear department and bought a suit, shirts, and underwear. His hands full of bags, he caught sight of a sign for the toy section. He went up again and found a shop assistant.

"I want a gift for a boy. He's about eight, but I have no idea what he likes. Just nothing with guns."

"Lego is always popular."

"Sounds good. It should be something big, too. Can I get it gift-wrapped?"

Tom left the department store with the enormous parcel beneath one arm and bags in both hands. He would go home and drop everything off, and then he would make an appointment for a haircut.

Last fall, he had returned from the dead.

But it was only now that he finally felt alive again.

Chapter 45

Ambra stared at the screen with aching eyes and tried to focus on the newsfeed. She hadn't planned to work today, but when Grace, sounding pressed for time, asked whether she could do another shift, she'd said yes. Though now she was starting to feel the effects of not having gotten much sleep lately. The newsroom was always stressful, but with so many people out sick, she barely had time to use the bathroom or eat; she just sat at her desk drinking gallons of coffee. She wanted to binge on something, but she didn't even have time for that. She had three pieces waiting to be written and roughly twenty-five phone calls and messages to answer. None of them from Tom.

She'd sent him a brief reply when he'd texted her yesterday, but after that she went out like a light and then he'd stopped writing to her. She tried to pretend it didn't bother her at all, but she couldn't. What if he had given up? Did he regret inviting her to the party on Friday? She should write something, maybe call him, she should just . . .

The screen on her cell phone lit up and she looked down at it, hoping it would be him. But it wasn't Tom, it was Elsa.

I saw Esaias today. He was talking to a man. I took a picture. Can I attach that to this message?

Ambra replied with the clearest instructions she could, and a picture soon arrived.

Do you know who that is? I feel like a TV detective.

Ambra studied the blurred photo of the tall man dressed in dark colors that Elsa had attached. She had never seen him before.

Nope. Be careful, Elsa. Don't overexert yourself.

Imagine if something happened to Elsa. The woman was almost one hundred.

She sent Ambra a happy face in reply.

Ambra studied the picture of the man again. It was a fuzzy, bad picture, and he was only half facing the camera. It could be anyone. But there was something in his posture that set an alarm bell ringing at the very back of her mind. Could she do an image search, maybe? She just had time to add it to her mental list of Things-I-Need-To-Do before she looked up and saw Oliver Holm approaching her desk.

He had a smirk on his face, and those broad shoulders, that shiny hair, the bounce in his step, made him look like a Disney prince. He was good looking, and several of the women watched as he saun-tered past with his bulging biceps and carefully orchestrated scruffi-ness. Several of the men, too, actually.

Oliver stopped several desks away. From the corner of her eye, Ambra saw him exchange a few words with one of the editors. They laughed, then Oliver ran a hand through his hair and was given a thump on the back in reply to something he said.

After he said *"sup,"* he took a few more steps and stuck his head around the door into Investigative. Ambra couldn't help eavesdropping a little now, but all she could hear was a low murmur. She tried to focus on her work, but it was impossible. What could he be talking about with them for so long?

"Cool, we'll talk later!" he said loudly, and Ambra hurried to look down at her computer, pretending she hadn't seen him. Oliver moved on, like a victor striding through the office, like someone who had won the lottery and was just waiting for the money to clear his account.

If she had a nemesis, it was probably Oliver Holm.

He approached her desk and she lowered her head even farther toward her computer, as though the letters on her screen contained the meaning of life.

Don't stop, don't stop, don't stop.

Oliver stopped.

Of course he stopped.

"How's it going here? Writing a bit?"

Ambra didn't reply, just looked up at him, wished she could say he was nothing but a blond bimbo. Sadly, he was a little too sharp for that.

"I just thought you might want to know that I've got something really good on the go. I was just in with Investigative, sounding it out with them, and they were pretty damn interested. What about you? You doing another of your socio-realistic sob stories? More emotional clickbait?"

Oliver's eyes lingered on Ambra's notes, where she had written *Social Services* in huge letters.

She turned the pad over. "All fine here. What about you, offered the boss any cigs lately?"

Oliver smirked. "No need to be bitter. Who knows, there might be a quota to bring you in somewhere else?" He laughed, as though they were just standing there telling jokes.

"Yeah, since I don't have any relatives to give me a leg up here, I guess I'll cross my fingers for that."

"Poor little Ambra. Must be tough that I cut you out all the time."

And for the first time, Ambra thought that maybe Oliver was right. Maybe he was the better journalist. She was just about to say something to snub him, or at least try to come up with something intelligent, when Oliver raised his hand in greeting to someone behind her. She turned around. Karsten Lundqvist, the security expert, was coming toward them.

"Hey, man," Oliver said.

Karsten studied him over the top of his glasses and didn't reciprocate the greeting. "Ambra, do you have a moment?" was all he said.

"Oliver was just leaving," she said, and she couldn't stop herself from feeling a sense of schadenfreude when she saw her nemesis's face. Karsten was one of the heavyweights at the paper. He'd won awards, been stolen from the competition, and was immune to fawning.

Karsten straightened his glasses and gave Oliver a dismissing look. Ambra could have hugged him. Irritated, Oliver left her desk.

Karsten pulled up a chair and straightened his glasses again. "I've been thinking about what you said."

"About Chad?" Ambra had almost forgotten that they'd talked about it almost two weeks earlier, had been satisfied with Tom's explanations. Thinking more about sex than private wars, if she was honest. But now she felt slightly ashamed. How professional was that, really?

"Something there doesn't add up," Karsten said.

"What?"

"Something did happen in the area we were talking about. There are a ton of rumors. My contact is going to get back to me, if you're still interested."

"But why hasn't anyone written about it?"

"The Central News Agency did actually write a paragraph. But a tiny battle in Chad isn't really a priority, if that makes sense. Russia, Syria, Isis, yes—the Western world has its hands full."

Ambra scratched her forehead. "What do you think? Could there be a link to Sweden?"

"No idea. I don't have time to get into it. You want the information I have?"

Ambra nodded. She would look into it later. One more thing to add to her list of things she didn't have time for. It was getting long.

Close to tears from exhaustion, Ambra walked home late that night after working several hours' overtime. It was snowing, and she was so focused on not slipping on the treacherous ground that she forgot she hadn't bought any food. It was only as she started to climb the stairs that she realized she didn't have anything to eat at home. But she was too tired to turn around.

As she climbed the last flight of stairs, she saw that there was something outside her door.

A brown paper bag. She paused. Her first thought was that it could be a threat of some kind. She had never received anything like that before, not at her home, but she knew several female colleagues who had.

She cautiously approached the bag, bent down, and looked inside. She saw a bouquet of flowers and a basket wrapped in cellophane. Hardly a threat. With a renewed sense of energy, she picked up the bag, unlocked the door, and hurried into the kitchen without taking off her coat. She put it down on the table and unpacked the gifts.

It was a deli basket full of cheese, biscuits, grapes, baby plum tomatoes, and a bag of expensive candy. The bouquet was made up of tulips in every color: purple, yellow, pink, multicolored, double and single, an orgy of colors. She read the card attached:

> *These flowers reminded me of your apartment, of color and joy.*
> *Looking forward to Friday.*
> *Don't work yourself to death.*
> *Tom*

It was the perfect present. The perfect note. Personal, luxurious, considerate, but without being over the top or pushy. She filled a vase with water and placed the flowers in it. Then Ambra opened one of the cheeses, cut a thick slice, and added it to a crisp salt biscuit. She licked her fingers, took the flowers and the basket into the living room, placed everything on the coffee table, and then went back into the hall to take off her coat.

While she ate and looked at the flowers, she couldn't help but think that if Tom didn't want anything serious, he'd chosen the wrong way to go about it. To her, this felt like more than something temporary, more than just a fling. Did he realize that? And did he feel the same?

Chapter 46

Mattias rubbed his chin. It was almost fifteen hours since he'd started work now, and his stubble bristled beneath the fingers. But it had been a good day. He and his new team had managed to fight an aggressive attack from a Russian troll factory spreading rumors about Swedish politicians. He'd also given the security police a reprimand, discussed questions of national security with the government, and had met with the head of the military.

He'd had time to think about Jill, too, and to check her Instagram account roughly twenty times. It was . . . He didn't know what he would call this behavior. What was he going to do about her? He had sent her two messages since their dinner but hadn't received a reply.

On one hand, Jill seemed like a busy woman. She recorded songs, posed for photographs, and appeared on TV, so maybe she just didn't have time to reply. But on the other, Mattias suspected she was annoyed that he'd left her outside the Grand Hôtel in the middle of the night.

Not that he blamed her. And not that it was the first time. Work had always come before relationships with him. It wasn't something he planned, it was just how it always turned out. But he found himself thinking about Jill, and often. And now he was in the habit of checking her Instagram account, following her life, laughing at her occasionally hysterical posts, and worrying about some of the comments.

He told himself it was just about keeping an eye on her trolls. Every time a hateful or threatening comment appeared, he would check it against the list of names Filippa gave him; several cropped

up time and time again. The more he looked into it, the more he realized he would have to dig deep if he wanted to find the net trolls'
real identities. He would talk to Filippa about it, see what she could
find on the deep web, the invisible part of the Internet almost five
times the size of the ordinary web. He opened Jill's latest picture. A
selfie uploaded just a few hours earlier. Glistening red lips, full Holly-
wood hair, a low-cut top. His eyes fixed on that mouth of hers.

Mattias had rules when it came to his love life. He didn't date anyone for longer than two months or so, counted from the day of their
first date. Only the best restaurants would do. He initiated things
when it came to sex, thought it was more respectful that way, but he
also didn't have anything against being seduced. In conversation, he
was personable but private, would talk about anything but his family
or his job. He was careful to be clear about what he was looking for:
closeness, company, sex. And also what he wasn't: a long-term relationship, a shared future.

Stockholm was full of women with similar hopes and values. Busy,
sophisticated women who enjoyed an easygoing existence, interesting conversations, and mutually beneficial sex. Maybe the odd weekend in Paris or an expensive ski trip. Then he would end things
before anyone had time to get hurt and before he was asked any
questions he had no desire to answer. It was neat, practical, enough.
Words he somehow couldn't get to make sense when it came to Jill
Lopez.

He really should drop all thoughts of her. Just last week, he met a
nice academic, a researcher in molecular medicine, at dinner at a colleague's place. He should ask her out rather than spend his time pin-
ing for an ultraglamorous superstar diva.

Mattias tried to drum up some sort of enthusiasm for calling the
researcher but found himself getting caught up in Jill's Instagram account again.

He went into the kitchen and opened a bottle of 2001 Château
Moulin de Lagnet, which he'd bought in France. He let it breathe
while he took out a wineglass. Then he took the lid from a container
of meat stew he had cooked and frozen, tipped it into a pot, and put
it on a low heat. He poured a little wine and tasted it. When the food
was ready, he took his plate and glass into the living room and turned
on the late news. Ordinarily, he didn't have trouble concentrating,

but now he just sat there playing with his phone while the stew cooled on the table.

Eventually, he decided to throw dignity to the wind and write her a message, kept it neutral but friendly: *Hope everything's good with you.*

If she still didn't reply, he would stop bothering her, he decided, would accept that it was over before it even began. Maybe he'd call the researcher after all. He sighed.

Her reply arrived just before the weather report: *Been better.*

Mattias frowned. What did that mean?

Did something happen?

He waited while the little bubble containing three dots worked away. It took a while. Like she was writing a long answer. Or like she was trying to decide what to say. Eventually, she replied: *The police are coming.*

Mattias turned off the TV and dialed her number. Jill answered immediately. Something contracted in his chest when he heard her deep, husky voice.

"Hey, what's going on?" he asked.

He heard her take a deep breath. "Nothing serious. I'm okay." She sounded calm and slightly dismissive, but he noticed something else in her voice, something shaken.

"Tell me."

"Uh."

Mattias said nothing. Silence and patience were an interrogation leader's best weapons.

"When I got home today there was someone outside my door. I got scared."

"Are you hurt?" He didn't mean to sound so sharp, but he couldn't hide his worry. Jill didn't sound at all like herself. She sounded small and scared.

"No. He disappeared."

"Do you know who he was?"

"No, but he had a knife, so I called the police. They're on the way now. Unless they deprioritize me. God, I just want to go to bed."

"Jill, do you have anyone with you?" He was processing her words. A knife-wielding man. Shit.

"What do you mean?"

"Did you lock all the doors? Are you alone? You shouldn't be alone. Could you call your sister?" He glanced around, as though there might be something in his apartment that could help.

"I'm alone. I don't want to call Ambra."

She hadn't called anyone, it struck him, only the police, and she regretted that already. Jill wasn't the type of person to ask for help.

"You want me to come over?" he asked, his wallet and keys already in his hand.

"You don't have to," she replied, but her voice trembled and he went out into the hall. Jill was in shock, even if she didn't realize it herself. She needed someone there. Not just the police.

"I'm coming over," he said, had already convinced himself there was no other option. Jill needed someone, and he was more than happy to be that person.

Ten minutes later, he was on the way to Djursholm. The cab pulled up outside a huge white villa. There was a wall surrounding the property, and a gate opened silently as the car approached. Mattias paid, climbed out, and waited until the cab left and the gate swung shut behind him. Christ. He knew Jill was wealthy and that she lived at one of the most expensive addresses in Djursholm, the most expensive suburb in all of Sweden, but he still hadn't been expecting this.

"Impressive," he mumbled to himself as he walked the last few meters to the house. The building seemed to be on its own peninsula, surrounded by water. A substantial wall looped around the garden, and he had already noticed several cameras. Jill should be safe here, but it was never possible to protect yourself completely. Not from crazy people. He swore, hurried over to the house, wanted to make sure Jill was fine with his own eyes.

There was a patrol car parked outside, and when he rang the bell it was a police officer who opened the door.

Jill was in the living room. She looked small and fragile next to the two broad-shouldered, oversized officers. Her arms were wrapped around herself.

He gave her a quick hug, and though she didn't quite hug him back, she didn't fight it either. "Are you okay?" he asked, stepping back and giving her a once-over. Physically, she seemed unharmed.

Jill nodded, but her face was pale and tense.

"And who are you?" one of the officers asked. Mattias didn't like the way his eyes wandered over to Jill, an irritated look, as if he was questioning the necessity of being there.

"Mattias. A friend. What do you know? Have you made an arrest?"

The police officer shook his head. "There's no one here. We didn't see anyone." They glanced at one another. They didn't quite roll their eyes, but it wasn't far off.

"This Instagram thing you do—you've never thought about not uploading so many pictures?" one of the officers said. He had bright red hair and was standing with his thumbs hooked into his belt, looking Jill up and down.

"What do you mean by that?" Mattias asked coolly.

"Just some advice."

"It's not against the law to upload pictures to social media. What is against the law is threatening someone. Ms. Lopez says there was someone here, so maybe we should try to focus on the right things?"

The redheaded officer puffed himself up. He looked as if he lived at the gym, a typical young guy who liked to show off whenever he could. Mattias estimated he could take him in three seconds. He was tempted, was so angry that his field of vision became blurred. The police didn't seem to be taking anything Jill said seriously, just staring at her breasts and hinting that she had herself to blame.

"We have no evidence. You'll have to come down to the station if anything else happens," the other officer said.

Jill sighed once they left. "I've been through that before. They never do anything. I don't even know why I called. I was just so scared."

"I can understand that." He wanted to go out and hunt for evidence, identify the perpetrator, make sure no one scared her again.

"They'll drop the investigation," she said. "Waste of taxpayers' money. You want a drink? I need one."

Jill went out into the kitchen. She was happy Mattias was there, even though she still didn't quite know why. When she opened the cupboard door, she noticed her hands were shaking.

But Mattias came up behind her, placed a hand on her shoulder, gave off an air of security. "If you tell me what you want, I can make it," he said quietly.

The cupboard was full of bottles. She didn't even know what she wanted.

"There are glasses here," she said, lacking the energy to make up her mind. She was shaken, would never have expected that of herself. Mattias took out a bottle of red wine and two huge glasses. He poured some and handed her the glass.

"Tell me what happened," he said.

Jill sipped the wine. She had no idea where the bottle was from, but it was perfect, easy to drink, unpretentious. "I got home after working all day and I saw something move. At first I thought it was just a bush or a branch, but then he stepped forward. He had a knife. I think anyway." She suddenly felt unsure, like maybe she had made the whole thing up. She shouldn't have called the police; it didn't achieve anything.

"I'll probably end up in the news now. The police will sell me to some tabloid for a thousand kronor," she said, taking a sip of her wine. She was skeptical of everything. Of herself. Of men. Of Mattias. Plus, it was late. She was completely exhausted and didn't have the energy to be sexy and seductive, to play Jill Lopez. She wanted to try to unwind. Watch trash TV. Eat something forbidden, full of fast carbs, like toast or Maryland cookies, the kind of thing she kept secret from her personal trainer. "I'm tired. I think I'm going to take out my lenses and wash my face," she said, hoping Mattias would get the hint.

"Go for it. Is it okay if I sit down in the living room for now?"

She didn't have the energy to care. She was too tired, too fragile, and headed to her dressing room. Once there, she hesitated for a moment but then pulled on her favorite sweatpants: faded gray shorts that made her ass look big but were also the most comfortable thing she owned. She pulled her hair up into a ponytail and took out her lenses. Without them, she was almost blind, and so she put on her glasses, though they were hideous. Then she pulled on a soft T-shirt, not bothering with a bra, let her breasts hang however they wanted. Mattias would have to cope with the sight of her drooping boobs. If he didn't like them, it was just as well she got it over and done with now, before she did something stupid like fall for him. He confused her. No one had ever done this before—stood up for her, unconditionally. No man anyway. Not without being a paid employee.

Mattias was waiting for her by the bookcase. He was looking at her CDs, pulled out a thin case.

"That's from an acoustic show I did in Malmö. It's not on Spotify."

"Can we listen?"

She put it into the CD player—Bang & Olufsen's most expensive stereo unit—and the sound of her voice filled the room.

Mattias handed her the glass and they sat down on the couch, listening.

"Did you write this too?" he asked.

She nodded.

"You're really gifted."

She didn't reply this time. Was she? Gifted? She took a sip of her wine.

"Sorry that I left you at the hotel the other night," he said.

"Don't worry. It was just unexpected," she said quietly. Though she was a little annoyed. Felt like she had been dismissed by a man she was starting to like. She wasn't so good at feeling like that, she realized, took it very personally. So when he wrote to her afterward, she wanted to punish him, make him feel as bad as she had. But it was good to have him here now. And she forgave him immediately.

"I'm not really in control of that, but I'm still sorry," he said.

"Are you ever going to tell me what you do?" she asked, even though she suspected it was top secret.

"I work for the Intelligence and Security Service," he said. He was silent for a moment, but then he added: "That's almost the entire truth."

Jill left it at that, suspecting it was more than he usually said. She was sitting cross-legged and her shorts rode up slightly, so she pulled them back self-consciously.

His index finger stroked the edge of the fabric, and it almost felt like he was drawing a short, hot line across her skin.

"I'm glad you came over," she said, her eyes following the movement of his finger. The touch sent small shockwaves up her legs, into her thighs, stomach. She swallowed. Drank more wine. Then she pulled at her shorts again, feeling a little uncomfortable.

"Sorry," he said.

"Don't worry. I'm just sensitive."

"I understand. I think. What are we talking about?"

She pulled her leg in close. "My cellulite."

His fingers followed the movement. "What's that? These? These tiny dimples? I think they're completely charming."

"You're insane. No one likes cellulite. And no one says charming."

Mattias moved his large palm onto her thigh and stroked it lovingly. He had insanely sensual hands—big, strong, and rough. She was perfectly still, felt his touch right between her thighs. He really was sexy. And the way he handled those cocky police officers. He was on her side, she could feel it. It was a good feeling. Having Mattias Ceder in her corner.

"I do. Especially yours. It's beautiful."

It was a stupid compliment, but Jill felt a small lump in her throat. "It's hereditary, did you know that?"

His hand moved gently over her skin. Maybe he wasn't even aware of the way he affected her. "I like to think I got it from my biological mother." It was dumb, but the cellulite made her feel closer to the woman who gave her life and whose name she didn't even know.

"Do you think about her often?"

"No," she lied. The minute she'd turned eighteen, she'd changed her name to Lopez to honor her origins. And because she didn't want anything from her adoptive Swedish parents.

They looked at each other. She knew he wouldn't do any more unless she took the initiative. And though she was attracted to him, she didn't have the energy right now. She hadn't waxed in a while, and she was tired and needed a shower. She just wanted to sit there, looking into his warm eyes and feeling safe, secure.

"Can you stay awhile?" she asked.

"I'll stay as long as you want," he said simply, and she knew he meant it. He might be a secret agent or master spy or whatever it was he did, but he wasn't lying about that. No one had ever cared about her like this. The record label fawned on her, her assistants fawned on her, and Ambra cared, in her own way. But this everyday care, concern without any ulterior motive, it was foreign to her. Maybe it was just that she had never allowed it before. Because it could be dangerous to give in to, dangerous to get used to.

"Do you have any idea who he was?" Mattias asked.

"No. There are so many crazy people out there."

"Do you think it was one of the people who harass you online?"

"Don't know." She really had no idea, doubted she would ever find out. Men had been threatening her since she was sixteen. Not a single one had ever been charged. It was as if it wasn't even considered a crime.

She sipped her wine and moved closer to him. He put an arm around her. It was a considerate gesture, not erotic. Jill leaned her head against his shoulder, heard her own voice fill the room. It was restful, sitting there like this. She closed her eyes. Didn't care about her cellulite, glasses, or sex appeal. She was just Jill.

Chapter 47

"What are you doing?" Mattias asked.

Tom studied his face in the mirror, turned, and tried not to drop his cell phone into the sink. "Shaving."

"You getting rid of the beard?"

"Yeah, I'm going to a party." Tom dragged the razor across his cheek, cutting a path through the foam. He shook it off over the sink and repeated the process.

"So you're still in Stockholm?"

Tom didn't reply. He was fairly sure Mattias knew exactly where he was. Mattias wasn't the type of man to sit around waiting for information. He got hold of it himself.

"Did you go into work yet?" Mattias asked.

Tom lifted his chin to start on his throat. "Yeah."

He had been in to the office that week. It went unexpectedly well. The majority of his team was ex-military, plus a few former police officers, and they acted like it was no big deal when he showed up, which felt good. Maybe he would be able to go back after all.

"I hired Filippa," said Mattias.

"The hacker?"

"Yeah. Plus a cryptologist I interviewed this week. Competent and smart, a real asset. It's going to be a great team, maybe the best I've ever formed. But I want you too. We need your skills. *I* need them."

But Tom's mind was made up. He didn't want anything to do with Mattias or the Armed Forces. They would have to find his skills somewhere else. He pulled the razor across his skin again, didn't say anything.

Mattias, who always did have an unnatural ability to know precisely what Tom was thinking, said, "Tom, how many times do I have to apologize? Can't you get over what happened? We're soldiers; sometimes we just have to accept what happened."

Tom swore. "I'm getting shaving foam all over the phone."

"Is Ambra going to the party?" Mattias asked.

"Bye." Tom put down the phone, finished shaving, and rinsed his face. He checked that he hadn't missed anything, patted aftershave onto his skin, and thoughtfully studied his reflection.

He had said he would go. But if he didn't have plans to meet Ambra at the party tonight, he would have been tempted to cancel. It was a long time since he'd last had a real anxiety attack, but seeing so many people, exposing himself to popping corks and bright camera flashes, was that really so smart? He didn't want to embarrass himself, particularly not in front of David Hammar or Alexander De la Grip. Oddly enough, he wasn't all that worried about embarrassing himself in front of Ambra. She had witnessed his panic attacks before, and he wasn't worried about what she would think of him. But the others . . .

He combed gel through his hair and started to get dressed. It was a long time since he'd last worn a suit, but it was a festive occasion and he wasn't completely without vanity. He cut off the price tags, then put on his watch and a new pair of cufflinks, black obsidian. He wanted to look good tonight. For Ambra's sake.

It was cold today in Stockholm, colder than Kiruna, ironically enough. The thermometer was approaching four below zero, and it was windy, so he pulled on a thick coat over his suit and picked up the handmade shoes he had bought; he could take off his boots when he got there. He took the enormous gift beneath one arm, grabbed his cell phone and wallet, and left the apartment. He glanced at his watch in the elevator. He would be early. Good. He hated being late.

When Tom pulled up outside the Gardens of Rosendal, the parking lot was already full. Expensive cars, some even with private chauffeurs, and a line of cabs. Long red carpets unrolled on the snow. There were huge iron drums full of burning wood, and the fires sent cascades of sparks soaring into the night sky. The pink castle that had given the gardens their name was visible in the light of the fires.

There were people everywhere, he noticed as he locked the car. Men in suits and women in long, colorful dresses and thick coats, shoe bags in their hands as they walked down the red carpet toward the party—an enormous greenhouse. Crystal chandeliers and small strings of lights lit up the glass building in the darkness, making it look like a glittering, hovering vessel studded with billions of stars. Music and the scent of food made their way out into the winter chill.

There was a line to get inside, and Tom joined the end, waited patiently for his turn. There was an elegant couple with a child in front of him, a pair of celebrities behind, talking admiringly about the luxurious setting for the party. Ambra had said she would take a cab, so he was waiting alone among the couples and occasional family with small children.

Alexander De la Grip was welcoming the guests at the entrance. His wife, Isobel, was by his side. They were shaking hands and smiling at everyone. The two were a strikingly beautiful couple, and their love almost seemed to cast a glow around them. It was obvious in every gesture, every glance. As Tom approached, he saw the child between them, a slim, serious boy in glasses. Marius. Tom hoped the boy wouldn't remember him.

Alexander caught sight of Tom, and his face lit up. He gave Tom a long, firm handshake. "I'm so glad you could come. It's been far too long."

"Thanks for the invite," Tom said. He hadn't liked Alexander when he'd first met him, thought he was a superficial, spoiled, jet-setting brat, someone born with a silver spoon in his mouth, interested only in himself and having fun. But for once Tom was wrong, and Alexander proved to be much more than the handsome playboy everyone thought him. When Isobel went missing, it was Alexander who started the search for her. He paid for the entire rescue operation and even flew to Chad to take an active role in her rescue. Something, Tom was forced to admit, few civilian men could have done.

Alexander had demonstrated that he was more than capable, and had ultimately contributed to the success of Isobel's rescue mission. Tom couldn't feel anything but respect for a man willing to give everything he had for the person he loved.

Isobel shook Tom's hand too. "Like Alex said, it's great to see you. I really hope we can get together more often now." Her voice was warm, but it wasn't pushy. They didn't really know one another, but the fact was he had saved her life, and that kind of thing bound people together. He himself was indebted to a number of people for similar reasons.

Isobel's father had been in the military, he knew, just like her grandfather. And there was something genuine about her, something he respected. She was one of those people who made a difference in the world. Plus, she had a powerful handshake. And the reddest hair Tom had ever seen. He was pleased for her and Alexander—they seemed so happy.

"Congratulations on your marriage," he said, meaning every word. The couple didn't want gifts, and so he had donated a large sum to Isobel's pediatric hospital and an equally large amount to Doctors Without Borders.

Tom looked down at the boy standing between them, with Alexander's large, protective hand on one shoulder. Marius looked up at Tom with a curious expression on his face, and his eyes repeatedly darted to the package Tom was still holding under his arm. He held it out to the boy. Marius's eyes widened.

"This is for you," Tom said. It wasn't much compensation for what he'd done to the boy back in Chad, but it was better than nothing. The parcel was so big that Marius teetered under its weight. Alexander hurried to help him.

"Thanks so much," Marius said in perfect Swedish. The boy had been in Sweden for only six months, but he was eight, going to school, and was, according to a not entirely objective Alexander, a genius.

Tom patted Marius on the shoulder, nodded to Alexander and Isobel, and moved inside. The meeting had gone well after all.

He was handed a glass of champagne and glanced around for Ambra. They hadn't seen one another since Sunday morning. It was now Friday evening, and he was longing for her. But Ambra had sent him a message to say she was running a little late, so he would have to wait. Just as long as she hadn't changed her mind.

That second part was on repeat in his mind. *As long as she hadn't changed her mind.*

Since it was only twenty seconds since he last glanced at his watch, he resisted the impulse to do it again.

He looked around the room, making judgments and running analyses in his mind, kept his back to the wall and tried to look normal. Then he spotted David Hammar. His friend was on the other side of the room, exuding his usual aura of power and arrogance. Tom knew plenty of financiers, respected very few of them and liked even fewer. But David Hammar was in a league of his own. A working-class kid who, through sheer hard work and a genius for business, had made it to the very top of the Swedish business world. Rude and ruthless according to some, one of the most moral and reliable men in the world according to Tom. David came over to him, and they looked at each other for a long moment without saying a word. Tom held out his hand, but David ignored it and pulled him into a firm bear hug instead. He thumped Tom on the back and held him even tighter.

"Finally," was all David said.

Tom cleared his throat and pulled himself from the embrace. He wasn't sure they had ever hugged before. "Lots of people," he said.

"We missed you at the wedding. I hope you're doing better now. You look good anyway."

David was married to Alexander De la Grip's older sister, Natalia, meaning that the two men were brothers-in-law. It was hard to imagine two more different people, however, at least on the surface: financial shark David and playboy jet-setter Alexander.

"Hey, Tom," Natalia Hammar said. She came over and held out her hand, and Tom shook it. David gave his wife a warm glance. Natalia Hammar was slim, elegant, and incredibly competent within the world of finance herself; she and David were practically made for each other. She was carrying her daughter on one hip, and Tom looked down at the baby.

"How old is she now?" he asked politely. His sisters were always talking about children's ages. And food, and sleep.

"Ten months."

Tom studied the gurgling child. She was sweet in a chubby, toothless kind of way. It was hard to imagine a woman as sophisticated as Natalia Hammar giving birth to a baby that looked so completely ordinary, but both Natalia and David looked at Molly as though her happy gurgles were the height of intelligence, so who was he to judge. New parents were curious creatures. Natalia excused herself, and David watched the two women in his life leave with so much love in his eyes that Tom felt something approaching jealousy.

"Beautiful family you've got," he said.

"Yeah," was all David replied.

They stood like that, each holding a glass of champagne. Tom wasn't overly fond of the drink, but he couldn't see anywhere to put it down.

"How long will you be in town?" David asked.

"I'm not sure."

There were other children running around, snatching candy and chips, chasing one another. Despite the exclusive guest list, the party was relaxed, not the least bit staid. There were a few camera flashes, but he noticed that they weren't really affecting him. Neither did the buzz of the crowd or the heat. He felt relatively calm. He jumped at one loud noise, but then he began to relax again and his pulse was almost back to normal. Despite that, he could feel his mood worsening with every minute that passed. Would Ambra show up? He checked the time again.

"Ellinor's coming, too, huh?" David asked.

"No."

David seemed confused. "I thought . . ."

Tom interrupted him, didn't want to go into the details. "No, I invited someone else. She should be here any minute."

I hope.

She had sent him a message to say thanks for the deli basket and the flowers, but what if she thought he was too pushy, too demanding? He had no idea.

"Want me to take that?" David asked, nodding to the full champagne glass in Tom's hand. He waved over a waitress, and soon enough they each had a bottle of beer in hand.

"Cheers." They toasted.

"So, who is she?"

"Who?" Tom asked bluntly.

David gave him an amused look. "Your guest. Whoever you're

waiting for. She's the reason you keep checking your watch every other second, no? I'm assuming it's a she."

Tom took a swig of his beer. "I don't know if she's coming," he admitted.

"There are plenty of single girls here if she doesn't," David said with a shrug that irritated Tom enormously. As though Ambra was replaceable. Tom wasn't interested in anyone else. If Ambra didn't come, he would go home. His eyes followed a group of kids rushing forward.

And then, finally, he spotted her.

Though, at first, he wasn't even sure it was really her.

The room was full, there were people everywhere, the volume was loud, and the many candles created shadows and dark corners, which made it difficult to see clearly. But he was good at identifying people, and the woman looked like Ambra, moved like her.

His heart started to beat a little quicker.

It *was* Ambra. But some new version of her. The same Ambra, but not. For one thing, he had never seen her in a dress before, was used to seeing her in baggy sweaters, hats, and coats. He knew she was a woman, of course. They'd slept together; he was well aware that she had both breasts and an ass. He had seen her naked, could probably remember every inch of her body, recount in detail how the various parts of her smelled, how smooth the inside of her thighs were, how soft her buttocks were.

But he had never seen her like *this*.

She was dressed in blue, in a shining sheath dress that hugged her waist and hips. She was talking to a tall man in a suit and hadn't caught sight of Tom yet. She must have done something to her hair, because it was glossy and bouncy and shone every time she moved her head even slightly, as though she was covered in stardust. She seemed taller than normal, and when his eyes moved down her legs he saw her heels, which made her legs look incredibly sexy. This was a glamorous being, experienced and cool. And she was here for him.

The man she was talking with was standing close to her and had just placed a hand on her bare arm. Tom's eyes didn't leave them for a second.

"That her?" Tom had completely forgotten about David. His friend sounded like he was holding back a laugh.

Tom forced his shoulders to relax, tried to smooth out his facial features. He wasn't used to feelings like these, barely had any right to be jealous. He *wasn't* jealous. Not much anyway.

"Yeah," he said, still staring. Ambra was laughing now. She looked like a princess tonight. Gone was the eager reporter, the vulnerable young woman. The person in front of him, wearing sky-high heels and a close-fitting dress, her hair glimmering and her back straight, was another creature entirely.

"She looks nice," David said neutrally, *too* neutrally. Tom gave him a suspicious look. His friend still seemed to be struggling to hold back a laugh.

"What are you laughing at?" he asked.

David thumped him on the back. "Nothing. I'm just happy to see you like this. Like a mere mortal." He took a swig of his beer and seemed to be having fun. "You could go over and talk to her. Instead of standing here staring, I mean."

Tom didn't budge. Ambra moved her slender arm, and her wrist glittered. Everything about her glittered.

David patted him on the shoulder. "Go now, before you explode. But, hey?"

"Yeah?"

"Try a smile. And breathe."

Tom shook off his hand. But he did take a deep breath.

And he smiled. It felt strange. But he did it for Ambra.

Chapter 48

Ambra nodded at what the man was saying. She didn't know him, couldn't even remember his name, but he knew who she was, had introduced himself and was now blabbering away about himself and a "super-hot project."

She wasn't even listening.

There were always people who did this. Threw themselves at her the minute they heard she worked for *Aftonbladet*, hoping for some free PR by talking nonstop about themselves, which wasn't exactly how it worked.

Usually she wasn't even polite enough to listen, but the truth was that the sky-high heels she was wearing made it difficult to walk normally, which meant it was easier just to stay put and pretend to listen. She was in a good mood, so she could stand there nodding for a while.

The shoes really were difficult to walk or stand in, but she had been practicing all week, and while there were plenty of things to be said about the impracticality of ten-centimeter heels, she felt damn hot in them. They did something to her legs and her posture. Every time she caught a glimpse of herself in a reflection somewhere, she noted that she really did look good. And judging by the way the man—he was in advertising, or possibly finance, something to do with opportunities and thinking outside of the box—kept sneaking looks at her breasts, she was a hit tonight. She fluttered her eyelashes, just because she could. The man was self-obsessed, but he was also rather good looking, and she had knocked back her welcome drink and felt positively inclined to the entire world.

The advertising/finance man's face lit up. He placed an eager hand on her arm and then continued his monologue about himself. She would let him go on until she spotted Tom, she decided. She was planning to believe everything Jill said—that she was pretty, that the dress suited her, that she could have whomever she wanted. And she wanted Tom. She ran her hand over the thin silk on her hip, adjusted her grip on the silver clutch, checked her nail polish. She *did* look beautiful and attractive tonight, even if it had taken a good deal of help. She had spent hours in the chair at Jill's hairdresser, a celebrity place where it was apparently impossible to get an appointment. He used products she had never heard of and cut her hair strand by strand before doing something with tongs, heat, and even more products. She had to admit, it made her curls look more glamorous and elegant than ever before.

After the hairdresser, she ended up at a makeup artist, who gave her dusky, defined eyes, matte skin, and glossy lips. It looked so good she never wanted to wash it off. She was just getting ready to dump the chatterbox when she heard a deep voice behind her, one that made her feel giddy.

"Hi," Tom said. His voice was amazing, calm and deep, serious and controlled.

She slowly turned around. Oh my God. She couldn't stop staring. She wasn't the only one who had fixed herself up for the party.

Tom's hair was freshly cut, and he was wearing an extremely well-cut suit, a dark shirt, and no tie. He smelled great, of aftershave and outdoors and new clothes. And he had . . . Ambra reached out and touched his cheek.

"You got rid of your beard," she said, completely fascinated by how different he looked. Younger, happier. Much, much more handsome. So handsome she actually felt weak at the knees.

Tom caught her hand and pressed his lips to her palm. "You like it?" he mumbled into her skin, kissing it again. The kiss hurtled like an express train to every erogenous zone in her body, and she smiled. If she had been the fainting type, she probably would have done it right then.

Had he been longing to see her as much as she had him? It felt that way, judging by the glimmer in his eyes, the way he kissed the inside of her hand without tearing his eyes from her. It felt like she was worth it, like she deserved to be desired. What if they were meant to be together after all? She found herself being sucked into his dark, laughing eyes. She'd never believed all that talk about finding your soul mate, but if she did have one, then it was Tom Lexington. He was the one she wanted.

"Would you like something to drink?" he asked, waving over a waiter.

The man Ambra was talking to, whom she had completely forgotten about, cleared his throat. "Excuse me, but we were actually talking," he said.

Tom gave the man a tranquil look. He didn't say anything, but something happened between them, and the man practically shrank back, turned on his heel, and walked away.

Ambra took the glass of champagne that Tom handed her. His eyes moved over her, openly appreciative. "You look fantastic," he said, and his gaze made her hot inside.

She sipped her champagne. "You forgot to mention this was a wedding party," she said accusingly.

"Is that bad?" Tom asked, without looking the least bit guilty.

"You could've told me," she said.

She had shaken hands with Alexander De la Grip when she arrived, which was a slightly surreal feeling. Alexander was famous, after all, or infamous depending on how you looked at it. As a former entertainment reporter, she had half expected to be thrown out. But he just greeted her politely and wished her a good evening. Isobel was polite too, and said she was glad that their misunderstanding had been straightened out.

Tom reached out and touched a lock of her hair. When he turned on the charm, she just wanted to glide into him, press her body against his, whisper indecent things in his ear, get drunk on his scent. She sipped her champagne again, allowed the bubbles to fizz in her mouth before she swallowed them in small sips.

Since her entire afternoon was spent being fixed up, made up, and getting dressed, she hadn't eaten, and she could already feel the effect of the alcohol. She laid a hand on Tom's arm.

"Who was the man you were talking to?" Tom asked nonchalantly.

Ambra shrugged, had already forgotten him. But wait. Tom wasn't jealous, was he? Of that guy? She studied him more closely, didn't know what to think. This was all so strange, the way a person could be no one special to begin with, someone you didn't know or think of, someone without any importance at all, only to become the only person you wanted to spend time with, do things with, the only one you wanted to see and talk with. The only one who determined whether a party would be fun. She sipped her champagne. She had fallen for Tom, she knew that already, but imagine if he had fallen for her too?

"Hi there, you planning on introducing me to your guest?" she heard a man's voice say.

David Hammar had come over to them. Ambra recognized him immediately. He was carrying a child in his arms, but he still managed to look slightly dictatorial. She could see why he and Tom liked one another. There was something austere and solid about them both.

"David, this is Ambra Vinter. Ambra, this is David Hammar and his daughter, Molly. And here's Natalia," he added when an elegant dark-haired woman appeared next to them. Ambra shook hands with them both. David and Natalia studied her with curiosity in their eyes. Something told her they both knew Ellinor but were far too polite to let on.

"Nice to meet you, Ambra," Natalia said in her modulated upper-class voice. Everything about her screamed money and elite, from the seemingly simple hairstyle to the expensive dress and enormous engagement ring. But her eyes were kind, and she looked at Ambra with what seemed like genuine warmth. "I recognize your name," she said questioningly.

"I'm a journalist, a reporter with *Aftonbladet*. Though I'm here as a private individual," she quickly reassured them as one of Sweden's biggest sports stars sailed by.

Natalia smiled again. "That may be just as well. My little brother's very good at organizing parties. Things tend to get a little wild once the kids go home to bed."

"And all the kids' parents," David added, shifting his daughter in his arms. Another guest came over and tried to gain the Hammars' attention, and they excused themselves and moved on.

"Everyone's so beautiful here," Ambra whispered as she followed David and Natalia with her eyes.

"But you're the most beautiful," Tom said.

She grinned. It was an over-the-top compliment, but she decided to take it. Tom placed a hand at the base of her spine and guided her through the crowd.

"Where are we going?" she asked.

He didn't reply, just gently pushed her through the room, in through a door, through another room and another door, and out into a room full of coats on hangers. He turned to her, firmly pushed her backward, until she bumped into a wall and couldn't get away from his intense eyes. Her heart was beating expectantly, and he placed one hand on her cheek, used his other to caress the nape of her neck, and then he kissed her. Gently, intensely, properly.

"Finally," she mumbled into his mouth.

Finally, she thought, allowing herself to be swallowed up by his kiss.

They stood there, kissing in the coatroom. Heard the murmur of the party, the occasional rustle of someone coming and going, but back there, in their little corner, the two of them were alone. He pulled away, touched her mouth, caressed her with his gaze. "Hi," he said quietly.

"Hi," she said, smiling, and her heart swelled. She felt the desire coursing through her body, happiness that they had found one another, and that maybe, just maybe, there could be something between them after all. It was in the air, this newness. He had introduced her to his friends. He kissed her as if she was the most desirable woman in the world. That had to mean something.

"I need to fix my makeup," she said. Her lips felt swollen, and her hair probably looked more ruffled than elegant.

"You're perfect," he said, a finger tracing her jawline down to her neck.

She shivered. "But still."

He glanced around, stepped forward, and pulled a heavy velvet drape she hadn't noticed before to one side. "Will this do?" he asked.

Ambra peered into the room behind the curtain and saw an enormous golden mirror, candles, and a velvet stool.

Tom followed her in, stood behind her as she checked her eyes and searched for powder and lip gloss in her bag. He kissed her neck and she leaned back, enjoying the sight of the two of them together in the mirror.

"You're so sexy," he said, kissing her shoulder. "You have such pretty shoulders." He kissed her again. "And a sexy neck." His hand moved up her back and around her rib cage.

They stared at one another. The air in the tiny room had practically vanished. It was as though everything around them was charged, had started to vibrate.

She could barely breathe. She placed her hands on the little dresser in front of her and met his eyes in the mirror.

"Tom," she breathed.

With one fluid movement, he pulled the drapes closed. The fabric was so thick and heavy that it dampened the murmur of the party. But it was just fabric, and if anyone came in . . . Tom's hand moved down over her ass, gentle on the thin fabric. Ambra shuddered, clutched the little dresser tight. His hand caressed her, and she fumbled behind her back, grabbed his other hand, and moved it to her breast. A shockwave of desire rushed down her thighs, pooling in her stomach.

His eyes looked back at her in the mirror, completely black. The candles flickered. Slowly, he pulled her dress up over her hips, and groaned quietly when he saw her garter belt—it wasn't all that comfortable, but judging by Tom's eyes when he studied her legs in her new underwear, it was worth the discomfort. His finger moved along the top of her stocking and then he cupped her, between her legs.

"I waxed," she mumbled. It was an incredibly sexy feeling, actually, and when he touched her through her panties the feeling was more intense than before.

"For me?" he asked.

A smile tugged at her lips. "Not for anyone else, anyway," she said. "Just a little. And I started taking birth control," she added.

He touched her again. It was so incredibly arousing to feel the friction of the rough lace.

Ambra moaned, would never have thought she would be turned on by the risk of being found, and at a party like this. But she moved her ass backward until she came into contact with his body, gently ground against him and felt his arousal through the various layers of fabric.

"God, Ambra," he managed to groan.

She replied by pressing herself more firmly against him.

He unbuttoned his trousers, pushed her panties to one side and moved toward her, caressed her opening, soft, questioning. She trembled, clung to the dresser.

He raised his hand to her cheek again, and she turned her head and took his middle finger in her mouth, sucked it. He groaned, placed a hand on her hip, and pushed into her. Slowly, he moved inside, filled her until she panted.

"Is that okay?" he asked.

God, yes. It was beyond okay. She nodded, hoped her dress would survive.

He pulled his finger from her mouth and ran his hand down to her breast, stomach, and between her legs, all while he moved inside her with slow, deep thrusts. He made her part her legs and began to touch her.

"Tom," she panted.

It felt so good. Warmth spread through her, she was nothing but body, desire. She gripped the dresser and saw herself bounce with every thrust, saw her own eyes become veiled, glossy, saw his hands, his fingers moving. She tightened her hold on the dresser and came, against his hand, around his body, shook and shuddered, saw his eyes fixed on her as she came, saw how it turned him on to see her like that, to watch them in the mirror. She felt herself tighten around him, draw him in.

He placed both hands on her hips and held her tight, thrust so hard that she had to support herself on the wall using one hand.

"Yes," she whimpered. God, she was going to come again, it felt so good—he was everywhere—and then he came too. At the very moment she exploded again, he came deep inside her, held on to her, stopped moving inside her, still without tearing his eyes from her face in the mirror.

They stood there like that, panting, staring. She could barely believe it was true, that it was really happening.

Tom stroked her shoulder, kissed her neck. She shivered.

He found a paper napkin and handed it to her. "In case you want it."

A primitive part of her didn't want to, wanted to keep his scent and smell on her, but while he discreetly looked away, she quickly wiped herself off and then straightened her panties and dress.

"Good party," she said, slightly embarrassed, slightly giggly. She had never done anything like this before, never experienced anything like it.

"One of the best I've been to." He smiled, pulling back the drape when she nodded she was ready. Cool air rushed in.

"Wait a second, I forgot to fix my lip gloss," she said with a laugh.

His eyes lingered on her lips. "They look perfect," he mumbled. "Like you've been properly kissed." He bent down and kissed her again. "I'll wait out here."

But Ambra shook her head. "Let's meet back out there. I want more champagne."

"Hurry then," he said.

Ambra paused in the alcove. She stared at herself in the mirror, smiled at the woman looking back at her, a sexy, exciting woman in love. Yes, she was in love with Tom. She fixed her makeup. Plumped up her hair, adjusted her breasts in her bra, and straightened the strap on one shoe. Once she was happy with her appearance and had checked and double-checked everything was how it should be, she made her way back out to the party.

She spotted Tom's broad back, felt another flutter in her chest. He was standing with David, and it seemed they were talking about something important. Their shoulders were tense, their gestures brief. David caught sight of her. He smiled, but his eyes looked concerned, and then he turned away and shook his head. Tom looked up and seemed distressed. Had someone heard them behind the drapes? Was David angry? No, it was something else; she knew it instinctively. Suddenly, the hair on the back of her arms stood on end. The closer she got, the more she felt that something wasn't right. Tom gave her a serious look. All his happiness was gone, all his desire and carefree pleasure. Worry crept up her spine. Whatever was going on, she wasn't going to like it.

David rubbed his chin. Ambra tried to catch Tom's eye. What was happening?

"Ambra, I'm so sorry . . ." he began, and his face seemed pained, as though he had done something he was ashamed of. Or regretted.

Anxiety had her heart in its iron grip now.

"What's going on?" she asked.

Tom opened his mouth, closed it. Opened it again. "Ambra, I . . ." he began.

And then she caught sight of a blond head behind him. A cold shiver ran down her spine.

It couldn't be.

But deep down, Ambra knew she was fooling herself. She had been so confident. Had started to think she was someone, that she had the right to more than she'd already been given. For a brief, fantastic moment, she had been arrogant enough to think she might actually mean something to someone, that she would get to be a completely ordinary person. To be someone's first choice. It was so stupid of her. And now here it was.

Her punishment.

Tom moved to one side.

The blond head turned, and Ambra looked straight into Ellinor's blue eyes.

"Hi, Ambra," Ellinor said. Her lips curled into what might have been meant as a smile, but there was an aggression in her eyes, a sharpness Ambra had never noticed before. She slurred slightly, and her blue eyes were shining. She looked pretty in her pale yellow evening dress, a real beauty actually. Next to Tom's broad-shouldered masculinity, she looked like an angel, bright and sweet. "You're here? Tom didn't say anything about that." She leaned against Tom's arm, as though she had the right. Ambra couldn't help but notice that Tom didn't pull away.

"What are you doing here?" Ambra asked, though part of her already knew the answer.

Ellinor laughed. "I was invited, of course. Tom asked me if I wanted to come with him." She squeezed his arm. "So here I am." She looked straight into Ambra's eyes, a challenge, and delivered the death blow: "I left Nilas."

Chapter 49

Ambra looked at Tom in shock. His face was twisted in anguish. But he let Ellinor cling to him and didn't say a word. Ambra tried to think of something intelligent to say. The whole situation was utterly bizarre.

Ellinor pressed herself against Tom, her breasts against his bicep, the way women have done for hundreds of years. Ambra didn't know where to look. At Tom's grim face or Ellinor's curvy body. Ellinor had a strange glimmer in her eye; she looked almost manic. Was she drunk? And why the hell was she here?

"What are you doing here, Ambra? Are you here for work? Writing about all the lovely guests? What a coincidence," Ellinor said.

"Isn't it. I didn't know you were in Stockholm," Ambra said tensely. She couldn't bring herself to look at Tom.

Ellinor teetered and Tom's arm shot out, moving protectively behind her back. It was a gesture Ambra found physically painful, like a knife to the heart. "Tom invited me, so I couldn't resist coming down, seeing so many old friends. Plus, I needed a change of scenery." Ellinor's mouth was smiling, but the look in her eyes was . . . Ambra tried to read it. Insecure?

"I didn't know Tom invited you," Ambra said. This time, she looked up at him. His jaw was tense.

"I almost didn't recognize him at first," Ellinor continued. Her voice was slightly shrill, a little forced. "Can you believe he finally shaved off that beard? So handsome." She turned her face to him. "Thank you, darling."

Tom didn't deny a thing.

Why was she even surprised? She had duped herself and now here she was, getting humiliated. It wasn't Tom's fault. She only had herself to blame.

Ellinor swayed again; she really did seem drunk. Her dress was close-fitting around her hips, and the heels on her feminine shoes were slim and high. Ambra couldn't help but notice how the same hand that had recently clutched her thigh in passion as he thrust into her in the small powder room now gripped Ellinor's shoulders, familiar and comfortable. And why shouldn't it? Everything Tom had ever wanted was standing right next to him.

Once again, she had been dropped. He had wanted Ellinor back the entire time, never hid that fact from her. It was just that she'd been stupid enough to forget it.

"I hope you're a little happy to see me anyway," Ellinor said to Tom. She turned to Ambra and explained: "We were texting one another these past few days, and I suddenly felt like I wanted to be here. Sometimes you just need to be reminded of how you really feel."

"Absolutely," Ambra said. For what was a little electric passion in the long run? She should have learned by now. That no one would ever choose her. That there would always be someone else who was prettier, sweeter, and easier to spend time with. Ambra Vinter was replaceable. Easy to leave. Easy to get tired of. She looked over to Tom. He met her eye, but his expression was impossible to read. She couldn't figure the man out. Did he feel sorry for her? Was he embarrassed? Did he care? She had no damn idea anymore.

Ellinor leaned in to Tom's chest, and the gesture cut through Ambra like a long, tortured jolt, as though someone were sawing her in half. *She* wanted to lean against Tom's chest, *she* wanted him. It was all so humiliating. Still wanting him despite the fact that he was literally standing in front of her, choosing Ellinor before her eyes. Of course, Ellinor wanted him back. Ambra knew how it felt to be with Tom. Ellinor must have experienced it hundreds, maybe even thousands of times.

The jealousy was like an animal inside her—it tore at her stomach, her chest. Cut her to shreds from the inside. She was nothing but sex. A rebound lay. A quickie in a cupboard. Ellinor was everything else. Blond, beautiful Ellinor, with her feminine body and her helpless behavior. It was obvious that she activated Tom's core values: his concern, protective instincts, loyalty.

Suddenly, Ambra felt dirty. The expensive dress and the sky-high heels, the luxurious underwear, the jewelry—none of it felt sophisticated and elegant any longer; it felt slutty and fake. It wasn't her; it felt like a costume.

"I'm glad I came, anyway," Ellinor said stubbornly.

"Of course," Tom said. His voice was like rocks rubbing against one another. Ellinor flashed Ambra a quick look, and Ambra could have sworn she saw triumph in those drunk blue eyes.

It hurt so much that she thought she was about to break down. She gripped her purse tightly, forced herself to stand up straight, to swallow her humiliation, disappointment, and all those other embarrassing, unwanted feelings.

"Ambra, I . . ." he said.

But she interrupted him with a firm shake of the head. Enough. She took a deep breath and then forced a smile, hoped it looked somewhat genuine and not just like humiliation and teeth. She *wasn't* going to cry, wasn't going to cause a scene. She still had some pride left. "I'm sure you have a lot to talk about, so I'll just . . ." She made a vague gesture to the rest of the room.

But she didn't know anyone else here, she thought, on the verge of panic. She turned and left with as much dignity as she could muster, not too quick and not too slow. But as she squeezed her purse tight and tried to swallow the lump in her throat, she realized that she needed to get away. She heard Tom shout something behind her. Against her better judgment, she was still hoping he would come after her, choose her. But since this was reality, not a movie or TV show, of course he stayed with Ellinor.

Ambra glanced around. What should she do? She spotted the advertising guy she'd been talking with earlier. He was now deep in conversation with a famous actress. She started to feel genuinely desperate, clutched her bag tighter and tighter, fought to control her breathing. She was dangerously close to . . . to . . .

"Hey, it is you! I thought I recognized you!" She couldn't place the voice and spun around. Thankfully, Tom and Ellinor had been swallowed up by the crowd. She saw a man who seemed familiar.

He hit his chest gently and grinned. "It's me. Henrik Stål."

"Who?" She couldn't make the connection at all.

"We met on Twitter," he said, drawing air quotes around the word "met." "We were supposed to go for a coffee IRL, but I was at a poetry festival in Svalbard. Sorry I didn't reply to your messages."

The journalist from *Dagens Nyheter,* she had completely forgotten about him. She studied Henrik more closely. He seemed to be her age, maybe a couple years older, and he was neat and tidy with an easy, cheerful smile. He looked nice. Someone who went to poetry festivals couldn't be a bad person. And his eyes seemed appreciative. Maybe it was a sign. "They really have poetry festivals on Svalbard?" she asked suspiciously.

"I guess it's a matter of definition. Where are you going?" he asked.

She had been planning to make a run for it, but now she reconsidered. She would stay, show she didn't care. "To the bar. Want to join me?"

Henrik grinned. "Is the Pope a Catholic?"

She liked him already. They installed themselves at the bar and ordered shots.

"Shots are just what I need," Ambra said after her second.

"Better than antidepressants," he said with a smile. He was flirty, but not pushy. Smart in that way cultural journalists often are, but without the self-importance they also usually have. He was, in other words, just what she needed. And finally, she started to get properly drunk. Finally, that terrible feeling in her chest started to fade. It was still there, but the alcohol dulled it.

"How did you end up here?" she asked, slurring slightly.

"No idea," he replied cheerily. "But I'm good at partying, and I used to hang with Alexander in the past. Before he got married and became normal anyway."

"I think I hate normal people."

"They're unbearable," Henrik agreed. "Want to drink more?"

She nodded. It was an open bar, and she had lost count of how much she had drunk, only knew it wasn't enough. There was no sign of Tom. Maybe he'd gone home with Ellinoooooor. Like she cared.

"You have a girlfriend?" she asked over a bowl of olives that had suddenly appeared. They should probably go over to the buffet, but she didn't have the energy.

"Nah," he said, and she suddenly couldn't remember what they were talking about.

Henrik took her hand, the one holding an olive, raised it to his mouth, and sucked the olive from her fingers. Only a month earlier, he might have been her dream man. Kind, funny, sexy. But today, only two hours earlier, Ambra had realized she loved Tom.

"Damn it," she said.

He nodded.

"Life is shit," she explained.

"Absolutely."

"If one of your exes turned up and wanted you back, would you dump me?" she asked as she tucked into a bowl of roasted peanuts. She handed him one.

He took the nut and pushed it into his mouth. "Hardly. Besides, all my exes hate me."

"Sorry."

"Doesn't matter. I hate them too," he said with indifference.

"Should we order more?"

"Sure we should." His eyes moved over her. "Have I told you you're shit hot?"

"Only eight times."

"Is that all? I should be ashamed. You're shit hot." He handed her the next drink.

Ambra sipped it. She barely felt anything anymore. "Alcohol is great stuff," she stated.

He laughed. "No protests here."

Tom couldn't help but look over to the bar where Ambra was sitting, perched on a stool, next to a man. The two of them had been there awhile now, seeming completely absorbed by one another.

Ellinor put a hand on his chest. "I really thought you'd be glad I came."

He placed his hand on top of hers. "I am," he said. Because he was, wasn't he? But it had all happened so quickly. He didn't have time to keep up.

"I mean, you moved to Kiruna for my sake. You called me. We had such good conversations. You took Freja. I thought . . . Tom, we were together so long."

"But Nilas . . ."

"You and I have taken a break before. We always came back to one another. I let you down. But now I'm here. And I really want to give us another chance."

Tom looked over to Ambra again. The man had his arm on the back of her stool now. Ambra leaned in to his shoulder, and they laughed. Tom looked away.

"You have no idea what it means that you fought for me all fall," Ellinor continued.

But now Tom had dropped the thread. It was so warm, he was sweating. "Sorry. What did you say?"

"You fought for me, the whole time. Wanted me back, even though I hurt you. I would never admit it if I hadn't drunk so much, but it made me happy."

"Happy?" He tried to concentrate. He should be exhilarated, ecstatic. Ellinor was standing in front of him, saying she wanted to try again.

But he and Ambra had come here together. They'd just had sex, for God's sake. Ellinor shouldn't be here; she should be in Kiruna, far away. He pulled at the neck of his shirt.

"How's Freja?" he asked.

"She's fine. I left her with a neighbor." She laid her head against his chest. Her hair tickled his nose.

He looked over at Ambra again. Jesus, she was sitting so close to that man.

"Sorry for turning up like this. I really thought you would appreciate it. I couldn't even imagine anything else. And I didn't know Ambra would be here. Did I do something wrong?" Ellinor looked up; she seemed distraught.

Tom glanced over to the bar again. It was as if he didn't know anything anymore. "You didn't do anything wrong," he said. It was his fault, no one else's. But he couldn't trust his feelings. He had loved Ellinor for so long. He had known Ambra only a few weeks. Ambra was so hot, and the sex they had was insane. Was she an infatuation? Absolutely, but was she more than that? They didn't know one another, not the way he and Ellinor did. Ambra wasn't the one he wanted. She couldn't be.

Ellinor was in a state, and he needed to take care of her. He had no choice. Besides, it seemed as if Ambra was ignoring him completely. He looked over to her. She and the man were feeding one another now. They were smiling and laughing.

"Ow, Tom," Ellinor said, pulling her hand away with a grimace. "You were squeezing my hand so hard."

"Sorry," he said, trying to tear his eyes away from Ambra. He couldn't. It was like being in hell, this situation. He couldn't breathe. Ever since he'd met Ambra, he had been impulsive and irrational, which was so unlike him. He pulled at the neck of his shirt again. Jesus, it was difficult to breathe.

"I shouldn't have come." Ellinor sounded close to tears. "I drank when I got here because I was so nervous, but now I feel terrible. Forgive me. I should probably go." She looked like a wreck.

This was *Ellinor,* for God's sake. The woman he had spent months trying to win back. Who had now left Nilas for his sake. She needed him. He had to take care of her; it was his responsibility. "I'll go with you," he said.

Her face softened in relief. "Sure? I don't even know where I'm going to stay. I just came down. I feel so ashamed."

"You can stay with me," Tom said reluctantly.

"Oh, thank you!" She hugged him.

He put an arm around her. "I just need to say good-bye."

He spoke to David. To Natalia. To Alex and Isobel. No one said anything, but he knew they were wondering. He'd come with one woman and was leaving with another. He hesitated, but it was just as well to get it over and done with. He approached the bar.

"Tom!" Ambra shouted. Her cheeks were red, her eyes glossy, but she didn't seem especially sad. In fact, she seemed to be having a great time. That should ease his conscience a little.

It didn't.

"Ambra, I have to go with Ellinor. She's not feeling so great," he said quietly, ignoring the man who was unashamedly listening in on their conversation.

Ambra speared the olive in her drink, ate it, and then waved the cocktail stick in the air. "Fine."

"Will you be okay if I go?" He didn't want to leave her. He wanted to explain that it was just because Ellinor needed him, that he and Ellinor had so much to straighten out. That she was practically his family. He swallowed, already knew he was about to make a mistake, wanted Ambra to ask him to stay.

But she just gave him an indifferent look and a gentle shrug of her silk-covered shoulders. "Didn't you just say you *had* to go?"

She glanced at the man beside her, and he nodded supportively. "Yeah, he did," he slurred. Tom fought the urge to plant a fist in the man's face.

Ambra looked up at him again. "If you *have* to go, then go. You don't need my permission. You're a big boy. You do what you want." She raised a long eyebrow and gave him an impersonal smile.

"Please, Ambra. I didn't think she would come. I'm sorry."

She shook her hair back. "Oh, well then. If you're sorry, every-thing's fine."

Her smile had stiffened, and her green eyes flashed. She was angry. It wasn't that he blamed her. But on the other hand, he thought self-righteously, hadn't she been more or less glued to her new date these past few hours while he comforted Ellinor, talked to her, worried? Did what they had mean so little to her? He could still smell her on his fingers, for God's sake. Ellinor had been part of his life for years; he couldn't just ignore her. Ambra had to understand that.

"Ambra . . ." he began.

"*What*, Tom? What do you want me to say?" She climbed down from her bar stool and stood with her face close to his, continuing in such a quiet voice that only he could hear her. "You had sex with me just hours ago. I was your date tonight, *me*. So if you're saying you need to leave with your ex, go for it. But you can't expect me to give you a medal."

"You don't understand. We . . ."

"No, I understand perfectly well. The love of your life turned up and fluttered her eyelashes and now you're doing whatever she wants you to do." She put her hand on her hip. "Have you met my new best friend Henrik, by the way?"

The man got up and held out his hand. Tom ignored him.

"Ellinor and I were together . . ." he started.

"If you tell me you were together half your lives one more time, I'll scream."

"Hello?" Ellinor's voice sounded behind him.

Ambra sneered at Tom.

Henrik placed a heavy arm around her shoulders. Tom took a step forward. It was as if a red mist had clouded his eyes when he saw that arm. He couldn't think at all.

The man held up a hand, and Tom stopped. Not because Henrik represented any kind of threat. Tom could have ripped him to shreds if he wanted to. But he managed to calm himself down.

"You've done enough, leave her be," the man continued, and there was a sudden sharpness in his inebriated voice.

"Please, can we go?" It was Ellinor, pleading behind him, and it was insane, but for a brief moment Tom had completely forgotten she was even there. He gave Ambra one last look. She stared back, her chin held high, and they stood there like that for a moment. It was over now, he knew it. It was entirely his own fault, but that didn't make it feel any better. He opened his mouth to say something, but there was nothing left to say, not really, and he closed it again. He turned around, took Ellinor by the elbow, and steered her through the room without looking back.

"Is everything okay?" Ellinor asked.

He thought about Ambra's chalk-white face. The way she'd told him about all those times she was abandoned. The way they'd made love, what she had meant to him these past few weeks. He thought about all that. But all he said was: "Everything's fine."

Chapter 50

The day after the party, Ambra woke up with a hangover that went straight to the top spot on her list of Worst Hangovers I've Ever Had.

She would never drink again. It was undignified to feel like this.

For a while, she didn't dare move her head, because she couldn't remember how she got home and had a terrible feeling that she might have brought—oh God, she couldn't even remember his name. Fredrik? Patrik? Henrik—right. She blinked and made the effort to turn her head. Thankfully, she was alone in bed. Right, she and Henrik had parted ways not long after they left the party.

Ambra took a cab home, cried the whole way from Djurgården to the Old Town, cried in the hallway, in the bedroom, and into her pillow.

She could barely even blink now. Barely breathe. Everything was swollen.

But everything was also over, so it made no difference how she looked or felt.

"How was the party?" Jill asked when she called just after lunch. By then, Ambra had been taking painkillers since she got up and was lying on the couch watching *Lyxfällan—What Happened Next?*

Ambra muted the sound on the TV and pulled the blanket up to her chin. She was freezing. "It was good. Aside from the fact that Tom's ex turned up and that he dumped me and spent the whole evening with her. But apart from that, it was totally fine."

Jill was silent. "How are you?" she eventually asked, quietly.

"You know."

Jill sighed. "Did you sleep together again?"

Ambra thought back to the sex they had in the powder room yesterday.

The truth was, it had been magical. There was no other word for it. The way Tom looked at her in the mirror, the way he touched her, it felt like they were so close, not just physically but mentally too. Not like they were *just* having sex. But what was magical for her had been nothing but physical desire and release for him. Now there was nothing to do but try to be an adult about it.

"No," she lied. Jill would be angry, and Ambra couldn't handle any criticism today.

"He treated you like shit," Jill said.

"Yup," Ambra replied. Jill was right, she had duped herself.

"You want to know what I think?" Jill asked.

Ambra was fairly sure she didn't.

"You need to meet someone else as fast as you can. That way, you'll forget all about him."

She should never have talked to Jill about Tom. Jill's advice was terrible. "Can't you see how crazy that sounds? People aren't interchangeable like that. You're messed up."

"Maybe. But am I the one feeling sorry for myself at home? No, exactly. You need to toughen up a little. Men are idiots."

"*I'm* an idiot," Ambra said. It was just as well it had happened now, she told herself. Before she developed any stronger feelings. She ignored the fact that her feelings were already strong and that she wasn't sure how many more times she could handle being abandoned.

Ambra rolled onto her back and stared listlessly up at the ceiling of her living room.

"Did you wear the dress? The shoes?"

"What the hell, Jill, it has nothing to do with what I was wearing. The love of his life turned up and looked at him with those fawning eyes and he left me without blinking."

"Some men can't resist a damsel in distress. Maybe he has some kind of hero complex?"

"Definitely."

"Those macho men. They know girls love them, and they exploit it."

Ambra pulled the blanket over her head. "No one's been exploited. I knew what I was doing. But I don't have the energy to talk anymore. I'm working tomorrow," she said, and hung up. She needed to pull herself together somehow, she thought, curling up on the couch and crying beneath the blanket until she could barely breathe. Tom called her for the tenth time that day, but she rejected the call and then he stopped trying. That was good.

Early the next morning, Ambra started her new five-day shift. From today on, for eleven hours a day, *Aftonbladet* owned her. They could send her wherever they wanted, to practically anywhere in the world, and demand her to work overtime.

She dumped her bag on the chair, stretched, and yawned. The office looked like it always did. Sleepy reporters, cleaners, and a super-energetic Grace clip-clopping around in a pencil skirt, fitted Armani jacket, and Louboutin heels.

Ambra poured herself a coffee, hid yet another yawn, and tried to shake some life into herself. It felt like she was still hungover, like she was in a haze. Henrik had been in touch to see how she was feeling. He really was a good guy. She wished she could be interested in him instead of stupid Tom, that he had replied the first time she'd sent him a message, that they had met up, dated, made out. Then it might have been him she was in love with by now.

She held her head in her hand, wishing deeply she had never gone to Kiruna, never met Tom. Maybe one day, in ten or so years, she would be grateful she had met him after all. But not today. Now all she had was regret, shame, and a hollow feeling in her chest that felt far too much like unbearable sadness.

Tom had called again, but she couldn't bring herself to talk to him.

She wrote a short piece about a dating app while she wondered what he was doing. Was he with Ellinor? Were they still in Stockholm? Had they slept together? While she scanned through the Central News Agency's press reports, she thought about how she wanted to go and spy on them, *do* something, anything to stop it being so damn painful. Though of course she did nothing of the sort. She just kept working, obsessing, and internalizing her feelings as much as she could. She wanted to ask Jill to find out if Mattias knew anything. But she didn't do that either. She just tried to cope.

Back in the saddle, Ambra.

By lunch, she had tackled the majority of her unread messages, deleted all the hate mail—Lord_Brutal9000 was in a particularly vile mood today—and replied to a few normal readers' messages.

As she sat there, staring at her screen, a message from Karsten Lundqvist, the security expert, appeared. Jesus, she had completely forgotten about him.

The subject line read: *Got new info, can we talk?* She didn't even have time to reply before she saw him striding toward her. He was wearing corduroy trousers and a wrinkled shirt, and as he came closer she noticed he sported one brown sock and one blue.

"Do you have a minute?" he asked.

Ambra nodded for him to sit down opposite her. He folded his tall body into the chair and slid closer.

"Are you still interested in Chad?" he asked.

"What did you find out?" she replied, without revealing that she hadn't given Chad a single thought lately.

"That area we talked about. Apparently there was some kind of attack there."

"What kind of attack?"

"Rumor is that foreign soldiers turned up, killed civilians, raped women. Awful." Karsten leaned back and studied her with a thoughtful look. There was more, she could see it.

"There are links to a Swedish security firm, which makes the whole thing considerably more interesting from our point of view. You asked me about Swedish security firms before?"

Ambra nodded, couldn't bring herself to say anything. Had Tom's unit murdered civilians in Chad? Raped women? It couldn't be true. Tom had talked about his morals, guaranteed that no innocents were killed, and she had believed him. Had he lied to her? How many Chadian lives was one Swedish doctor worth? Did Isobel know? David Hammar? If this was true, it was dynamite.

Karsten continued in a thoughtful tone. "I did some research. It does actually seem that individuals from a Swedish security company may have been in the area at the time the attack took place. I guess you already suspect which?"

"Say it anyway." Her voice was weak. She grabbed her coffee and drank the last ice-cold drops. And she hadn't thought her day could get any worse. It was like Grace always said: Things could always be worse.

"Lodestar Security Group," he said.

She wanted to throw up.

Jesus Christ.

She stared at Karsten, didn't know what to say.

She needed time to process all this. There were so many uncertain variables, of course.

But still.

It was awful.

Tom Lexington must be dumb if he didn't realize she would find this information.

"What are your sources?" she asked, because that was crucial in this context.

"They're weak," he said. "Plenty of it's unconfirmed. That was why I wanted to check with you. I wouldn't write anything based on this alone, but maybe you have more." He got up and stretched his long arms. "I've gotta get back," he said, disappearing.

Ambra remained where she was, trying to process the facts as objectively as she could. The information was uncertain, to say the least. There were so many people who tried to spread disinformation. She needed a second opinion. She looked over to Grace. "Could we talk? I need to bounce an idea off you."

They sat down in one of the conference rooms, and she told Grace everything.

Aside from the fact that she had slept with Tom, of course. And nothing about them dating. Or going to a party, or a sauna, or watching the Northern Lights together; almost everything, in other words.

Grace leaned back, looked up at the ceiling, and closed her eyes: "A Swedish former elite soldier who first raped and killed civilians abroad, then got held captive? And a Swedish woman being rescued? I'm not going to deny, it's interesting." She opened her eyes and looked at Ambra. "Do you want to write it? An 'Aftonbladet Reveals,' maybe? It could be really damn good. And just between us, this is precisely what you need."

Yes, Ambra had thought the same. A report like this would almost guarantee her a place on the Investigative desk and recognition from

Dan Persson. Maybe even the Swedish Grand Prize for Journalism, her own private Holy Grail. "I'm not sure. I think I want to wait until I know more."

"Okay," Grace said, taking her feet down from the table and getting up. "But it does sound interesting."

"Grace, while I'm here anyway . . ." Ambra started. But Grace must have known where she was heading. She sighed loudly. "If it's that foster home thing again, then no, no, and no."

"What if I get more info?" Ambra couldn't give up; it felt more important than anything.

Grace waved her hand absentmindedly. "Sure, fine, maybe we can talk again then. You need to go now. I'm being interviewed by one of those damn weekly four-color magazines."

Back at her desk, Ambra wrote a quick article about the weather—she wondered how many of those she had written over the years—and then, just before the second editorial meeting of the day, she got a message. It was from Elsa.

Heard anything else about the picture I sent?

She had completely forgotten it. Ugh, falling in love sucked. It took up far too much time. How could she have forgotten the girls? She was ashamed.

Not yet.

Ambra opened the picture Elsa had sent a few days earlier, the unknown man Esaias was talking to. Again, a small bell started ringing at the very back of her mind, as though she really had seen him before. She drummed her fingers impatiently.

She went over to the coffee machine. Stood there awhile, eavesdropping on different conversations. Thinking. Came up with something. Quickly went back to her desk, put in her earphones, and dialed Henrik Ståhl's number.

"Hey," he replied warmly. "How are you?"

"I'm calling about work," she said apologetically.

"Shoot."

Something he'd said while they sat together getting drunk had made its way through the alcohol haze and popped into her head. "You mentioned you had an advanced image search program, right? Is it something I could borrow?"

"Send me the picture and I'll run it for you."

"You sure? Even though we're competitors?"

"Let me be your knight in shining armor—it's not often that we *Dagens Nyheter,* Daily News, guys get the chance."

Ambra sent him the picture. Not long after, as she was on her way to the afternoon's editorial meeting, he replied:

> *His name's Uno Aalto. Barely a trace online.*
> *But we managed to do a deep web search and*
> *then he turned up. He's a so-called "demon exor-*
> *cist" from Finland.*

For a moment, she thought Henrik was messing with her. But she opened the information he sent her, scrolled through everything while the others sat down. It was true. Uno Aalto was a genuine, old-fashioned, crazy Laestadian exorcist. Who associated with Esaias. And she remembered where she had seen him before. On the notice board outside the church. Every warning bell in her body was ringing.

"Ambra?" The voice belonged to Grace; she sounded insistent. Apparently she'd asked a question.

"Sorry, I didn't hear," she was forced to say. Oliver gave her a snide look while Grace repeated the question. How had she ended up on the same shift as Oliver Holm? There were so many reporters she never got to see. Couldn't Oliver take one of their shifts instead?

With a dark look at Ambra, Grace continued the meeting. They talked about headlines, front pages, and angles, things Ambra usually loved to discuss, but she was finding it difficult to concentrate.

Oliver droned on about something he wanted to write. Ambra yawned into her hand; she was exhausted.

"What about you, Ambra? Do you have anything?" Grace's voice shook her. It felt almost as if she'd nodded out.

"I just found out that an exorcist has arrived in Kiruna. I want to investigate that."

Grace raised a slender eyebrow.

Oliver snorted. "Isn't that the same old rope? Didn't we finish off that one last time?"

Ambra gave Oliver her most poisonous look. She knew she wasn't at her most socially competent that afternoon, but she was hungover, being provoked, and in love with someone who might well be a crazy psychopath; she didn't have the energy to be nice to Oliver on top of that.

She *had* to find something, otherwise she could forget about that job on the Investigative desk.

"It's an important story about kids who are at risk," she said coolly.

"Could you tell us about Chad instead?" Grace suggested.

Ambra gave her a startled look and shook her head. She had said she wanted to wait.

"It's too good not to keep digging. Illegal. Secret. That kind of article is precisely what we want. *That's* evening paper material."

"But I don't want to write it, not yet."

It was still unconfirmed, felt speculative, almost dirty. All the same, it was truly ironic that she was sitting here, possibly sacrificing her career, all so as not to tar a man who had been so careless with her feelings.

If Tom and his men were responsible for those attacks, then they would be charged, of course. But so far, the details were too vague. And she couldn't actually believe Tom would have been involved in something like that.

Once the meeting was over, everyone left the room. Everyone but Oliver, who stayed behind with Grace. Ambra watched them talk, intensely, and she left with the sense that she was missing something vital.

She grabbed her phone the minute she was out of the room.

This time, Lotta answered immediately. "Yes?" she said, curt and distant.

"Did you get my message?" Ambra asked. She had texted earlier, sent the picture.

She received a long-drawn-out sigh in response. "I thought it was a bad joke. An exorcist? You need to stop this."

"But you need to keep an eye on those two kids. This changes the situation."

"Except for the fact there are no exorcists."

"I can send you the information I have," Ambra offered.

"Or you can listen to me: If you don't stop calling, I'll report you."

And with those words, Lotta hung up.

Ambra spent the rest of the afternoon writing, anxiety like a knot in her chest. When she left the office, Oliver was still at his desk.

Grace was bent over him, and they were having a hushed conversation.

The next day passed in much the same way, other than the fact that Tom didn't try to call her. She worked, went home. Then she slept, uneasily; got up early; and walked through the cold winter air to work. Yawned, turned on her computer, checked what was going on in the world.

The first hour was quiet.

But at eight o'clock, all hell broke loose.

The morning's lead article rolled out with huge, black, roaring letters:

SWEDISH MERCENARIES MURDER CIVILIANS.
TERROR IN CHAD.

Ambra read the headline and frowned. It couldn't be . . . ?

No.

She brought up the article. Read it with a growing sense of panic. This was her story. But in different words. With a spin she would never have chosen. Harsh word choices, insinuating angles, aggressive claims.

About Tom. About Lodestar Security Group. About secret military units, private elite soldiers. About weapons and illegal operations. And pictures, dear God, *her* pictures. The ones she'd taken in Tom's study in Kiruna.

Ambra's heart was beating so hard as she read that she thought she would explode. Words and phrases jumped out at her like accusing index fingers.

Doctor Isobel De la Grip was kidnapped.

Aftonbladet has tried to reach Tom Lexington for comment.

Je–sus. Christ.

Oliver Holm's name appeared in the byline. He had a new author photo, she noticed, much bigger than before. It was his name on the article. But the information, the pictures, the responsibility, that was all hers.

This was nothing less than a catastrophe.

She looked over at Grace, who was standing by her screen, absorbed by it. "What have you done?"

There was still a part of her that thought it was all a macabre joke, a cruel prank, or maybe a nightmare.

"Oliver Holm wanted to write that piece. He's done something similar before, he had a source within the Ministry for Foreign Affairs, so we decided to go ahead. You said you didn't want it, so I gave it to him."

"I told you I wasn't sure about the information," Ambra said as sharply as she could, but her voice trembled toward the end.

"Oliver talked to Karsten and came to a different conclusion. He wanted to write it. I gave him the green light and all the info. It doesn't belong to you."

"What about the pictures?" Those were hers, at the very least. Then she remembered she had emptied her cell phone. Had the pictures ended up on the paper's server? Shit.

Grace's dark eyes narrowed, a boss's look. "You took those pictures for the paper, Ambra, on your work phone. *Aftonbladet* owns them. Oliver took them from your work computer. But you've been given all picture credit."

That wasn't quite Ambra's point.

So now her name was linked to an article that would hit Tom like a grenade. The headline was already online, but that was just the beginning. She knew that. This had the potential to develop into a full-blown mass media storm, a veritable massacre. And the victim would be Tom. She didn't know what she was most afraid of, that the information was correct or that it was an exaggeration. Both scenarios were catastrophes, just in different ways.

By nine that morning, the phones started to ring. The media industry and news agencies had woken up and smelled blood.

Ambra just wanted to hide. But this wasn't even the worst part.

What would happen when Tom read it?

Chapter 51

Tom had just left the apartment for the gym when his cell phone started to vibrate in his pocket. It was work. He answered and heard a noticeably shaken Johanna on the other end of the line. There were raised voices in the background, which was unusual in itself. Lodestar Security Group distinguished itself by its calm discretion. Tom had never even heard anyone raise their voice—they were professionals, and people listened without their needing to shout.

"Have you seen the papers?" Johanna asked.

"No. What's going on?"

"We're about to be hanged by *Aftonbladet*."

He stopped. "What?"

"It's completely crazy here," said Johanna. Her voice almost broke.

"I'm coming in."

"Yeah, I think it's probably best if you do," she said, hanging up without a good-bye.

When Tom made it to the office twenty minutes later, he was angrier than he ever remembered being. He had scanned through aftonbladet.se before he climbed into the car, been forced to turn his phone to silent, but he listened to the news on the radio as he drove. There was a piece on them. It was surreal. So this was what Ambra had been up to while she wasn't answering his calls.

"The phones are going crazy," Johanna said the minute he stepped into the office. There were phones ringing everywhere, people talking into headsets, and the noise level was high. People who had been to war, worked under the worst conditions imaginable, now looked shaken.

"That's not even the worst thing," Johanna said with a gloomy frown.

"Clients have started jumping ship?" Tom asked.

She nodded. "That too. But even worse: We've had to call off an operation in Haiti. We couldn't guarantee our operatives any longer."

"We'll have to call people home. We need to go through every operation, check who we have out in the field. As soon as we know that, someone needs to start looking at plane tickets."

"I've prepared the big conference room. The others are waiting in there."

"Thanks, Johanna."

"No problem, boss. Good to have you here, despite the circumstances."

Tom greeted his colleagues and coworkers in the conference room. Ordinarily, things would have been relaxed, but today the room was filled with downcast faces and tense jaws. As people spread out around the table, the seat at the end was left free. Tom sat down there. He had been their boss for so long, they trusted him and expected him to take charge. And Tom knew it was his fault this had even happened. It wasn't Ambra's name beneath the article, but much of the material had come from her. And as though he needed any further proof of her involvement, her name appeared beneath several of the images illustrating the report. One of which she must have taken in the house in Kiruna.

He was so damn angry that he was almost afraid of what he would do.

"The net's already run amok. We'll do what we can, but it doesn't look good," one of their IT experts said. "All of our bigger clients have been in touch. They want explanations."

"We need to call each of the clients," Tom said. They would have to draw up a list of priorities to limit the damage. It would take years to undo what Ambra had done.

Their Iraq chief got up and started to write everyone's suggestions on the whiteboard. They would also have to call every single one of their operatives, they decided, those men and women working out in the world, and come up with an action plan for each of them.

"We need someone handling the media," the head of human resources pointed out.

Tom pulled a face. They didn't have a press officer for the simple reason that they wanted nothing to do with the press, but that was hardly an option right now. They decided Johanna would be responsible for that. She nodded grimly, and Tom felt a rush of pride. These people he worked with, they were the best on earth. There was no fucking way he was going to let a sensation-seeking journalist ruin it for them. They did important work, hadn't done anything wrong, and he wouldn't let them be dragged through the dirt. He was so furious that he wanted to head down to *Aftonbladet* and scream at Ambra until she was so shamed that she crept back into the sewer.

When they took a short break, Alexander De la Grip called.

"What's going on?" he asked in a concerned tone.

"I'm sorry about all this," said Tom. "We're working to control the damage now."

"Isobel is a total wreck. She's terrified she's going to lose Marius."

"I know. I'm already working on it."

"I'd appreciate it if you kept me updated."

Goddamn it. This didn't just affect him. It had an impact on a huge number of others. How could he have failed to see this coming?

David Hammar called next. "I just wanted to say that I'm here, if you need anything," he said.

"Thanks, it's a fucking mess."

"Do you know where they got the information from?" He didn't say any more, but Tom knew he must have seen Ambra's name. His anger mixed with feelings of guilt.

"This is my fault."

"Okay. Understood. Let me know if there's anything I can do."

They continued the meeting in the conference room, ordered in salads, drew up guidelines on the whiteboard. Every now and then, someone would disappear to make an important call. Information continued to flow in during the day. They lost another two clients, but they also managed to reach all of their operatives, and Tom breathed a sigh of relief once each of them reported back that they were safe. By six that evening, even the most stubborn journalists stopped calling. Other stories had taken over.

Some of the staff went home, a few went away to work out. Tom was reading through reports and protocols when he realized his cell phone was ringing. The sound was muted, but when he saw it was his mother, he answered with a stifled sigh. He had completely forgotten her.

"Tom? What exactly is going on?"

"Did the press call you?" He felt ice cold, hadn't thought about that. But his mother had changed her name when she married, his sisters, too, so they should be safe. If Ambra had put his family in danger, he didn't know whether he could be responsible for his actions. He ran his hand over his face.

"No, I'm just calling because I'm worried. You're still my boy."

That made him smile. He was almost two meters tall, weighed just shy of 250 pounds, and had enemies on four continents. "A journalist set me up."

"Didn't she have a similar name, the girl you were seeing?"

Johanna came in and gave him a questioning glance. "I'm trying to fix it. I have to get back to work, Mom."

"We'll see what happens tomorrow," Johanna said once he hung up. "Maybe you should make a statement after all?"

"Yeah," he agreed, feeling a new wave of irritation. He had always managed to keep a low profile, but suddenly his name and picture were everywhere. It felt goddamn uncomfortable.

"How is your family taking it?" Johanna asked.

He shrugged. Ellinor had called, but he'd sent her a message telling her not to worry and she hadn't been in touch since.

He glanced at his watch. It was probably time to do the one thing he had been putting off all day. He took out his cell phone, grabbed a bottle of water, moved over to the window, and called Ambra. He heard the rings, one after one, and he wondered whether she would be a coward and avoid him. But the call went through.

"Hi," she said. Her voice was composed.

"Are you happy now? You got your scoop."

"I don't know what to say. I know you're upset."

"Upset? That's one way of putting it."

"I can hear that you're angry, and I understand that. But would you let me explain? They took the story away from me."

"You took pictures in Kiruna. And you talked about things I told you in confidence, didn't you? Or did I misunderstand that too?" How did she have the stomach to try to push this onto others?

"The picture was a mistake. I took it for my own personal use. I'm sorry. And I confided in my boss, that's all. You have no idea what it's like at the paper. Oliver Holm wants the same job I do, and he went behind my back. I'm as shocked as you are."

He very much doubted that. "So now you're risking other people's lives for a story? One that's false?"

"But is it? Can't I at least write that, if that's the case? Put everything right?"

"You've got some fucking nerve. Are you sure this isn't just revenge on your part?"

"For what?"

"Don't play dumb. Ellinor turns up and then I'm hung out to dry in your rag? I didn't expect it from you, that you could be so fake, so two-faced."

"But I . . ."

"You know what?" he interrupted her. "I hope that Oliver guy gets the job. And I hope you go to hell." He was shaking as he hung up.

"Is everything okay?" Johanna had stuck her head around the door.

Tom turned around. "Fine, thanks. Good work today."

She blushed slightly. He didn't think he had seen Johanna blush before. "Are you headed home?" he asked.

"Unless you need anything else?"

"You go," he said. There were still plenty of people in the office, but the atmosphere was slightly calmer now. His employees were at their most focused when they were surrounded by chaos, so after the initial shock they had shifted into another gear. Even those who weren't scheduled to work had come in to help out. Everyone had been incredible, and he was proud of them.

His phone buzzed on the desk. He turned it over. A message from Mattias: *Want to grab a beer?*

He was about to say no, automatically. But then he felt it could be good to talk to someone who knew how it was. Say what you liked about Mattias, but he would understand this kind of thing. Tom replied that it sounded good.

A few hours later, Tom was sitting with his back to the wall in a bar on Hornsgatan. The place was practically empty.

Mattias had chosen the bar deliberately, Tom was sure of it. They used to come here when they were younger. The food was cheap, the portions were big, and the beer was good. He was smart like that, Mattias. He was also manipulative and stubborn. But Tom was tired of being angry, he realized.

"Tough day?" Mattias asked.

"Ambra tricked me," Tom said, rubbing his forehead.

"Oh? How?"

Tom gave him an incredulous look. "Don't tell me you haven't heard?"

Mattias slowly put down his glass. "Depends what you're talking about. I read a long article by an Oliver Holm in *Aftonbladet*."

"Ambra has to be behind it," was all Tom said.

Mattias gave him a long, thoughtful look. "So, let me guess. You've broken it off."

"And you think that's wrong?"

"It's not my place to think anything."

"Lay off. Of course you think. It's the only thing you do."

"You do have a tendency to do this," Mattias said.

"What are you talking about?"

"You did it to me."

"You betrayed me." Did he really have to point that out again?

Mattias stroked his chin and looked as if he was about to explain something to a stubborn child. "Okay, listen to me now. When I gave evidence against you—about a hundred years ago now—I did it to protect the unit. We wouldn't have survived a scandal like that. I was told to do it."

Tom stared at him. "So why didn't you say anything?"

Mattias sighed deeply. "Tom, I did, several times. But you wouldn't listen. Sometimes, when you get hurt, or offended, you don't *listen*. You made up your mind to feel betrayed. And you were, I know that.

But I did it for the sake of the unit. I think you would have done the same."

"No, I would never have sold you out. I would've damn well died for you, for my men."

Mattias lifted a peanut to his mouth and chewed slowly. "You've always had a dramatic side. I know you would've given your life for a comrade. I would've too, at least for you. But if it was a choice between betraying a friend or saving the unit? Think about it. Plus, things have gone well for you, and it was a long time ago. When are you planning to get over it?"

"Now you're making it sound like I bear a grudge." Tom had never thought of himself like that.

"Sometimes you do," Mattias said evenly.

Tom took a swig of his beer. "You lied."

Mattias shrugged. "We're a lying bunch."

"You sold me out."

"For the unit. You do the same, every day. Sacrifice the individual for the good of the group. You're one of the best people I've ever met. You know the difference between right and wrong, you have ideals, you do the right thing without looking for confirmation, you fight for a better world."

"But?"

"Sometimes you can be a tad self-righteous."

Tom leaned back against the wall. Stared at Mattias and felt himself yield. Was he self-righteous? "I don't know if I can forgive," he said.

"Of course you can. You just have to decide to."

"I can't think about it now anyway. I have more important things on my mind."

"The paper? To hell with it. It'll blow over."

Their food arrived, huge burgers with french fries. Mattias ordered two more beers. They waited until they were alone again.

It felt good to sit there like that. He had missed Mattias, much more than he realized. Imagine if he followed Mattias's advice? Maybe he could decide to move on, force himself to?

They ate their food and didn't talk about anything in particular. It was surprisingly easy to fall back into old routines. To relax. To be friends.

"That was good," Tom said, studying his friend. But Mattias had something else on his chest, he could feel it. He waved to the waiter for more beers, and waited.

"I've been thinking about something," Mattias said after a moment, confirming his suspicions.

"What?"

"A domestic operation."

"Military?" Tom asked. It was a long time since Mattias was last active in the field.

Mattias frowned. "Not exactly. I want to go after Swedish net haters."

"You?"

"Yeah."

"In the field?"

"Yeah."

Something didn't quite fit. "You and your new team?"

"No, it's a private initiative."

"From who?"

"From me."

Tom gave Mattias a questioning look. "Is this a sanctioned operation we're talking about?" he eventually asked.

Mattias shook his head. His eyes didn't leave Tom's.

"Is it legal?" Tom asked, though he suspected he knew the answer. Against his will, he was curious.

"Not even slightly."

"How big a team are we talking about?"

"What do you think?"

Tom couldn't help it—his old instinct reared its head. He and Mattias had done that kind of thing before, domestic operations. Though never without the law on their side. "What does it involve?"

"I'm going to make sure justice is done. I've managed to localize several of the worst online trolls in Sweden. These are people who threaten and harass women."

"Sounds like something for the police. The military doesn't get involved in that kind of thing."

Mattias waved his hand dismissively. "The police had their chance. These are cases that get dropped, for lack of evidence or resources. But I have addresses. I know who they are. It would practically be an act of charity to disarm them. Our job is to protect democracy, not practice it."

"But we're not some vigilante group."

"True."

Tom was silent. It was tempting, he had to admit it.

"What's the goal?"

"Just to scare the shit out of them, make them stop."

"Like some kind of social deed, then?"

"Exactly."

"A small team. Someone keeping watch, someone driving? And then us."

"Yup. I think you'll find one of the target names particularly interesting. A man who's been at it for years. He's harassed a number of female journalists, among other things. He doesn't post anything under his own name, but he's one of the leading voices on a right-wing extremist opinion site called Avpixlat, as well as various closed Facebook groups. I'd say he's a real threat to democracy."

"What's his name?"

Mattias smirked. "You're really going to like this."

Chapter 52

A mbra hadn't thought she could feel any worse than she already did, but that presumption was proved wrong the very next day. Oliver Holm continued his revelations about Lodestar and Tom, using the knife of investigative journalism to tear his victim to shreds. And regardless of what Ambra thought of Oliver as a person, he knew how to do his job.

He interviewed military researchers and various other experts who, without exception, spoke negatively about private security firms. Key phrases like "violence without responsibility" and "moral gray zones" were bandied about over and over again. If you read his reports carefully, between the lines, it became clear that Lodestar Security Group had never been involved in any of the worrying examples the experts brought up, but it made no difference. Because of the context and the angle of the text, the firm still took the hit.

This was the downside to the kind of paper she worked for, and the thing Ambra hated most of all about her own profession: the sensationalism and pursuit of the victim whenever the press smelled blood. It was one thing to watch and criticize power—that was their job, and she did it at least as ruthlessly as Oliver Holm—but it was something entirely different to shape sentences and hide facts to support your own theory.

She scrolled through the report with a rock in her stomach. Two images of Tom kept reoccurring. First, the one she'd found when she'd Googled David Hammar. Tom was still bearded there. The picture had been blown up and was slightly grainy, but it was so familiar that she wanted to reach out and stroke the screen. And then the picture she'd taken using her cell phone, for her own personal use. How could they publish that?

Tom would never forgive her. They had published what little information they had in a small text box. Tom's age. His middle name. The fact he used to work abroad. Oliver hadn't found any more than that. But it was enough. Ambra's heart ached. That private, serious man who had endured so much. Exposed and strung up, and all because of her stupidity. She placed a hand on her chest and massaged. It hurt so much.

She checked her phone, was waiting for a message from a press secretary, but noticed she had a message from an unknown number instead. She opened it and gasped for breath.

You fucking whore. Do everyone a favor and kill yourself.

She didn't want to look at the image they had sent, but she saw it anyway. An awful picture of a dead woman hanging from a rope. With shaking fingers, she deleted it from her screen.

"Is everything okay?" It was Grace who asked. She had appeared by Ambra's desk without a sound.

Ambra turned over her phone, suppressed her reaction, had no desire to appear frightened or vulnerable in front of Grace. Instead, she nodded to the computer screen, where the report was open. "How long is this going to go on?"

Grace crossed her arms. "Their lawyer called. Threatened to sue us."

"Can they?"

"No, I checked with our lawyers. We haven't printed any false information."

"But the angle is so ugly."

"This is a tabloid. But we won't do any more."

"That didn't wash?"

"It did, but not for more than we've already printed."

"I regret saying anything to you."

"And I wish you'd written it." Grace thoughtfully glanced at the screen and shook her head. "It's a damn good story. You should've taken the chance. I just found out that we're having a reorganization in spring. Everyone will have to reapply for their jobs."

Ambra had to assume that would be the death blow for her career. Oliver had stolen her story. The one Grace thought she was too much of a coward to write. That she just wasn't hungry enough.

"They didn't kill any civilians in Chad," Ambra said.

"You know that?"

She nodded. "Tom told me."

"And you trust him?"

"Yeah, I do. I also talked to Karsten this morning. The killings happened a thousand kilometers away. I told you I wanted to wait."

"Hmm. There you have it. Still, we haven't formally done anything wrong."

Other than dragging Tom and Lodestar through the dirt in the country's biggest paper.

Grace walked away. Ambra remained where she was, feeling totally downcast.

Jesus, she really had blown it now. Even if she had sat down and written a plan for The Best Way to Destroy My Life, she wouldn't have managed quite so well. Somehow, she had lost both Tom and, in all likelihood, her job.

What had Ellinor and Tom been doing since Friday? Making love, laughing? Talking and straightening things out? Gotten engaged again, maybe? At least they could hate her together now. These thoughts hurt so much, they were the mental equivalent of poking at an open wound.

He had been so angry. She guessed she should be angry in return. And she was, but most of all, she was sad.

AMBRA VINTER DUMPED AGAIN.

That was the headline of her life.

Chapter 53

Mattias was thinking about Jill. He did that nowadays, had spoken with her every day since he'd gone out to her house. At first it was with the excuse that he wanted to see how she was doing after the intruder, the police, and that whole debacle. But by the third evening, Jill was firm in her claim that she was over it now, and ever since he had been calling just because he enjoyed talking with her.

They had even been out for dinner again, when he'd taken her to his favorite place at Östermalm, so he supposed he could say that they were dating now. They hadn't had sex that evening, but it had definitely been in the air.

Jill was the first woman in his life for some time, and he liked her a lot. They seemed to be on roughly the same wavelength—busy, experienced, focused. The question was how well she would fit into his heavily regulated love life. He realized it sounded a little self-important, but no one had ever complained.

He opened the computer, loaded Skype, and called her. She was the one to suggest they use Skype that evening. He'd protested automatically.

"I'm not at all comfortable leaving a digital trail like that," he'd argued.

Jill had burst out laughing and said something about how the government probably had more interesting conversations to eavesdrop on, and that was that.

Her face flickered onto the screen. She was dressed in white, her dark hair flowing over her shoulders, her lips glistening; she looked as gorgeous as a *Vogue* cover. He had to admit, he liked to be able to see her when they talked.

"How are you?" he asked. He could see the hotel room behind her and thought he could make out Gothenburg in the background, knew she was over on the west coast.

"Tired. We got here yesterday and had meetings with different collaborators all day."

"We?" Mattias loosened his tie and leaned back in his chair. Jill was always surrounded by so many people. He didn't know how she did it.

"My PR person, my assistant Ludvig, my manager, a rep from the record label, and someone else I already forgot. There are always tons of people with opinions on everything I do. They're my team."

"You're probably the only person I know with their own team."

She laughed. "What are you doing?"

"Thinking about you," he replied truthfully.

She smiled, and Mattias felt himself smile back—a broad, unsophisticated wolf's grin. He could make out her breasts at the top of her white blouse. His eyes lingered on her golden skin.

"I'll be in Stockholm tomorrow. Are we going to see each other?" she asked.

"I was just going to ask. I'm invited to an opening—want to join me?"

She seemed to pause.

"We can do something else if you prefer."

"No, no, an opening is good."

The next evening, Mattias searched for a shirt he could wear on his date with Jill. Every time he closed his eyes, he could hear her husky laugh, smell her warm scent. Going by his time scheme, they had at least another month and a half to enjoy each other's company.

Plenty of time, in other words.

He put a lot of thought into his choice of clothes, shaved carefully, and was looking forward to an interesting and pleasant evening in the company of a beautiful woman. But more than that, he was looking forward to seeing *Jill*. Hearing about her week, listening to her hilarious stories, being infected by her laugh, enjoying her uncomplicated company. Maybe even kissing her? The thought of seducing her, slowly and carefully, seeing her melt with pleasure, that filled him with expectation. That golden skin of hers, those soft curves, the voluptuous figure. He stopped himself with a hand in the air, saw a vision of himself in bed with Jill. Was she passionate? Or inhibited, perhaps? Some of the women who played so openly on their sexuality could be almost paradoxically prudish in private.

He cast one last glance in the mirror and left the apartment. If Jill wanted to, he would be more than happy to move their relationship on to the next phase.

Jill put in her lenses, blinked them into place, and finally she could see again. She brushed her newly short hair with firm strokes, twisted and turned her head. She'd had her extensions taken out today and agreed to let the hairdresser cut off a good length of her hair. Now she had a soft, wavy bob just above her shoulders. It was a cute, modern cut, but sadly it made her look a little older. She liked it, or she had for the first hour. But the people from the record label went crazy when they saw it. They demanded she go back to her old look.

She had given them a snide remark, refused to let herself be pushed around by her label, those damn parasites; but inside, the panic rose steadily. They were right. She looked older. Or rather: she looked her age.

Against her better judgment, she scrolled through her Instagram feed. She had uploaded a picture of her new hair. Many of her followers gave her compliments and encouragement, but it was the hateful comments that stuck in her mind, like tar on her soul.

You look old.
Show us your tits instead.
Stop being so pathetic.

And so on. She felt incredibly fragile, didn't understand it; she could usually shake off this kind of thing. Was her period about to start, or what? She stared at her reflection in the mirror and forced her mouth into a smile. It was something she'd once read in *Elle*. If you smiled, it made you happy. If you thought positive thoughts, saw solutions rather than problems, visualized success, affirmed your circumstances and all that crap, it came *true*.

She continued to smile until her cheeks ached. But that wasn't the problem, she realized.

She didn't like how much she was thinking about Mattias.

Didn't like that he had that kind of power over her. The way she found herself comparing him to other men, longing for his messages, looking forward to talking on Skype. She had to regain control of the situation, she thought as she started to apply her makeup. Her first impulse was to go for an understated look, because Mattias would prefer it. She stared at herself. *Pull it together, Jill Lopez.* She applied heavier makeup instead, with glitter on her eyelids, a thick layer of mascara, and plenty of blusher. She gave herself another stern look in the mirror. Don't go falling for Mattias, now. But she still pulled on the same dress she had worn to their dinner in Kiruna, with Tom and Ambra; she could remember the way Mattias devoured her with his eyes. She grabbed her keys, turned on the alarm, and went out to the waiting cab.

When Jill stepped out of the cab at the Moderna Museet, the Swedish national museum of modern and contemporary art, her mood had picked up, and the smile she gave Mattias was genuine. He smiled, kissed her on the cheek; he smelled great and looked impeccable. She could control this. Mattias was only a man, and she knew how to handle men.

"It's really elegant," he commented, admiring her hair.

"Thanks. Do you come here often?" It was her first time; she had never understood the point of museums.

"I saw the Klee exhibition last week. Have you seen it? Otherwise I come from time to time. To keep up my general knowledge."

"Of course," she said, with no intention of revealing that she had no idea who Klee was. The lobby was full of people, the majority considerably older than she. Not exactly a gala feel to the evening. She straightened her scarf, the bracelets on her arms jingled, and someone turned around and gave her a puzzled look.

"Who are these people?" Jesus, some of the women weren't even wearing makeup.

Mattias handed her a plastic glass of wine. "People in the arts, academics, critics, I guess. We can leave if you think it's boring."

"No, no, I love the cultural elite," she mumbled, sipping her wine.

Mattias went over to a couple he knew. Sober, gray, older people who spoke in low, cultivated voices. They greeted Jill politely but didn't seem to know who she was. Jill took another glass of wine and tried to follow their conversation. It seemed to be about a book. Or a play. Or two books written by famous people who hated each other.

She wasn't quite sure. She emptied the plastic glass. Not a celebrity as far as she could see, no one under thirty-five either. She stood out like a damn peacock in her heels, jewelry, and red lips.

Mattias shook hands with yet another man and his wife, a woman with short nails and a badly fitting dress who actually pursed her lips when she was introduced to Jill. No one had done that to her in years.

"We were at Berwaldhallen yesterday. The violin concert."

"I've sung at Berwaldhallen," Jill said. She received a blank look in response before they continued to talk about Brahms and Dvořák as though she didn't exist. Jill grabbed another glass.

"That's your third glass," Mattias pointed out quietly.

"And?"

"You aren't going to eat first?"

"Why?"

Mattias excused himself, took her by the elbow, and led her over to a high cocktail table. "Is everything okay?" he asked quietly.

"Yeah."

"We can go somewhere else."

"No, no, it's fine. I love talking about dead composers and incomprehensible art."

"Is that Mattias Ceder? It's been an eternity," she heard a woman's voice chirp.

"If you'll excuse me, I'm just going to powder my nose," said Jill.

"We'll talk more then," Mattias replied.

"Sure." She snuck off, found the ladies' room, closed the door, and sat down on the lid. Dear God. She took a deep breath. Wished she had brought her wine with her. At least that way she could have stayed there, ignoring all these pretentious people. She didn't understand why she cared so much, but she did. She heard the door to the ladies' room open, heard the murmur before it closed again.

"Were you waiting for me?" a woman said. There were at least two of them then.

"I saw you talking to Mattias Ceder. Did you see the woman he had with him?"

"Wonder where on earth he found her."

Jill held her breath while she eavesdropped.

"I would never have thought it of him."

"Didn't you two date?"

"Yes. He was the one who took me to that place in Östermalm, you know."

"Esperanto?"

Jill bit her lip. They had been there recently, she and Mattias. He clearly had his regular haunts.

"You know about his two-month rule, don't you?"

"That he always ends things after two months?"

"Yes, it's some thing he has. The question is whether she will even last that long."

"What did you think about those breasts—they can't be real?"

"Maybe he felt like something exotic. I wonder if she even speaks Swedish."

"Maybe they don't do all that much talking."

Their mean laughter echoed through the ladies' room.

This was just too much. Jill got up, opened the stall door, and stared at the women.

Their eyes widened. Then they glanced at each other and burst into embarrassed laughter before they hurried away. Jill stared at the closed door. It was like being thirteen again. People had talked about her like that at school, whispered behind her back.

She washed her hands. Her chest felt completely hollow. What was she doing; why was she here?

When she came back out, Mattias was talking to a small group of people. There was no sign of the gossiping women. She hesitantly approached, heard them talking about some debate going on in some paper. She hadn't even heard of it. All her life she had struggled with these feelings, with feeling stupid, ignorant, simple. How many times had her adoptive mother told her she was vulgar, that she must have been born in the gutter? How many social workers had looked at her with the exact same look Mattias's friends were now giving her? As if she were worth nothing.

"What happened?" Mattias asked with concerned creases around his eyes. Coming here had been a mistake. In fact, ever flirting with him had been a mistake. They came from two different worlds.

"Is it true you date women for only two months?" she asked. She didn't really know why that bothered her if it was true. She hadn't even thought that far ahead herself.

He gave her a long look. "Do we have to talk about that now?" he eventually said.

"We don't have to talk about it at all. This isn't working anyway."

He grabbed her arm. "Don't be ridiculous."

She pulled away from him. "Let go of me," she said coolly, and he immediately did as she asked.

"I don't understand what's going on."

"Nothing is going on, but this was a mistake and I'm leaving now."

"Should I go with you?"

She wanted him to. Wanted him to leave these snobby, lofty people behind. But she couldn't bring herself to say it, she just couldn't.

"No," she said, turning on her heel and stalking out.

Mattias didn't follow her. Most men didn't.

Chapter 54

"Come in," Ellinor said, opening the door for Tom. She looked pale but composed.

"We need to talk," he said.

"If you like. Let's sit."

They each sat down in a chair.

"Why did you come to Stockholm?" he began.

"Don't really know. I've really been thinking, up there in Kiruna. I panicked. You disappeared. I wanted to be here."

"In Stockholm? Or with me?"

"Both. I missed our life, and I thought you did too."

He'd thought the same. Had been convinced that he knew what love felt like and that Ellinor was the one he wanted.

"I got the impression you were happy with Nilas," he said.

"And I was. But then you were gone and I suddenly felt completely suffocated up there. All I could think about was you and the life we used to have. It felt as if I'd thrown away all our years together."

You did, he came close to saying, but it made no difference now, not to him.

She'd been in such a state in the car on the way back from the party—tired, sad, and drunker than he'd ever seen her. It was only once he was halfway home that he realized it wouldn't work, that he couldn't take Ellinor back to his place.

He had turned around and checked her into a suite at the Clarion Sign instead. Which was where she had been ever since. Alone. They talked and talked. Ellinor spoke as if it was obvious they would get back together and as though he should be ecstatic. But he wasn't.

"We . . ." he began, but he trailed off, unsure of how to continue. It was so difficult; there were so many invisible threads that bound them together.

Though not anymore, he realized. Those threads had been cut, one by one.

"It was good for me to come here. I saw some friends, did a little shopping, sorted out a few things. I really regret cheating on you. You deserve better. I wanted to say that. I'm so sorry."

"It doesn't matter anymore," he said, and he meant it.

"It was all about me, never you. I want you to know that. And I got my punishment," she said, giving him a lopsided smile.

"What do you mean?"

"You forgave me so easily," she said with a hint of something he had never heard from her before: bitterness. "All my friends said I should be grateful, but I just felt unimportant."

"I can understand that." Maybe it was a sign that he hadn't felt all that much after all?

"I guess this is because of Ambra."

Tom shook his head. It was important to him that no matter what happened in the future, he and Ellinor were a closed chapter. They didn't belong together.

"I don't even know if she wants me anymore. I haven't been so good to her."

"But do you want her?"

"Yes," he said simply.

"She's tough. Good, too." Her eyes focused somewhere in the air. She was beautiful. And he didn't feel a thing.

"Things were bad between us even before Nilas, weren't they?"

"Yeah."

It was the first time he had ever admitted it. But things *had* been bad between them. They hadn't been able to talk, the mood was tense. On one level he'd probably known it was over even then. It was just that Ellinor had realized it a lot sooner. "That's why I went to Chad. Not only that, of course, because it was an important job. But it felt good to get away."

"We've been a big part of each other's lives."

"Yeah. And it was thoughts of you that kept me alive when I was being held prisoner. I created a dream image of you and our relationship. When I came home, I didn't want to give that up, even though you had moved on."

"I can understand that," said Ellinor. "I'm sorry. That I acted like this. Maybe I can blame it on an early midlife crisis?"

"I want to apologize too. For acting so strange, for following you up there. That wasn't cool. Thanks for your patience. And thanks for Freja. I hope I can keep her?"

"Of course. Having a dog suits you."

"Are you going to tell Nilas why you were here?" he asked.

"Guess I may as well be honest. I'm flying home tonight, on the last plane."

"Good luck," he said, but he didn't offer to give her a ride. "You deserve to be with someone who can love you with a full heart."

"You too."

Tom left the hotel room. It was over. Completely.

Chapter 55

Ambra was mad at Tom. It took her three days, but the anger had finally appeared. It was incredibly refreshing not to feel like a dumped victim anymore but a justifiably angry and proactive woman, she thought as she furiously typed.

Tom had *chased* her, sent flowers and bought gifts. They'd had an insane amount of sex. In her world, that meant something. And then he went and chose Ellinor over her.

She hammered away at the keys. Tom was an asshole, and she was entitled to her feelings. She had tried to protect him and still got shit from every direction. Idiot. She hit Enter, sent the piece, and immediately began the next one. Her rage tinged her articles, but no one complained, and it felt good to let out a little anger when she wrote about abused women, murdered women, and inadequate rape sentences. She hated all men today, she decided, glancing at the time. Almost lunch, she thought just as she received a message.

From Tom. What did the idiot want now? Her pulse picked up, but it was just anger. Nothing else. That was it.

I'm in reception. Can we talk? Could you come down?

Her jaw dropped. How arrogant could he be? She was at work and didn't have time for him. He couldn't just turn up and assume she would drop everything for his sake. Angrily, she wrote: *Go to hell.*

But then she hesitated, deleted it, and wrote: *Coming.*

Because, she realized, she needed to talk too. She actually had quite a lot to say.

* * *

Tom was still absorbed by everything he'd done yesterday. He had, face-to-face, drawn a clear line under everything he'd once had with Ellinor. He felt strong, and he wanted Ambra. Was finally ready to stop dithering, to choose her. Imagine that it could be so simple. He was looking forward to seeing her face when he told her. He impatiently waited for her to come down, ignoring the security guards manning reception who kept glancing over to him. Suddenly there she was, bouncing down the stairs, those unruly locks of hers dancing.

She stopped in front of him with her arms crossed. "What do you want?"

"It's over between Ellinor and me."

"Aha. And?"

He frowned. "I don't love her anymore. It's over," he explained.

She didn't say anything. Just stood there with her arms crossed, glaring at him like an angry tiger. Slowly it started to dawn on him that he might have miscalculated. "Are you angry?" he asked, though he knew even before she exploded that it was the wrong thing to say.

"Am I angry? You dumped me, yelled at me, and accused me of taking revenge on you through the paper. And then you turn up wanting to *talk?* You've been flip-flopping between me and Ellinor for weeks now, but it's too late. You can go to hell."

"Ambra, I'm sorry."

"Sorry?" she said, her voice rising. "You're so fucking self-righteous. Did you hear that? Self-righteous." She practically screamed that last part. People were staring at them. He stepped toward her.

"Calm down a little," he said.

"I don't want to calm down. I'm leaving."

"If you can take it easy a moment, I'll explain," he said, grabbing her arm.

Smack!

He hadn't seen it coming at all, but he definitely felt it. Ambra had slapped him, square on the face.

"What the hell . . ." he said in surprise. It was incredible how quick she was. And strong.

"Fuck. Off," she said coolly, turning on her heel and storming away. He remained where he was.

The guards in reception were now watching him with slack jaws. Phones were ringing, but no one was picking them up. The other people in the lobby were staring too. It wouldn't be an exaggeration to say that things hadn't quite gone according to plan. He would go home and regroup. He gave the people staring at him a stern look and managed to avoid rubbing his cheek before he made it out onto the street. Christ, she was strong.

"So I guess you could say I've really blown it now," Ambra said to Jill. Her hand was still smarting a bit; she had put everything she had into the slap. She gloomily played with a rose petal that had fallen from the enormous bouquet on the table in Jill's dressing room at Konserthuset, the Stockholm Concert hall. She watched Jill struggle out of the tight dress she wore onstage. Ludvig floated around them like a blond shadow. He took the dress and hung it up.

"Serves him right. People should slap other people more often." Jill took off her earrings and bracelets. "Did you manage to catch any of the show?"

Ambra shook her head. "Sorry. I was at work. I got here after the break, but they wouldn't let me in. Though I could hear from the applause that they loved you. Sorry."

"It's a long time since you last saw my show. It would be fun if you came sometime," Jill said stiffly.

"Sorry. It's all been a bit much. The trip to Kiruna brought back so many tough memories, and I'm worried about those girls with the Sventins. Then this whole thing with Tom . . ."

Jill rolled her eyes in the mirror. "Dwelling on it won't make it any better. I told you he was no good for you, didn't I?"

Ambra puffed up her cheeks. Of course, Jill had to remind her of that.

"I'll go get some vases," Ludvig said with a quick look at Jill. He gathered the paper and cellophane and left the dressing room.

Jill pulled on a loose sweater and a pair of white velour sweatpants. "They're from my new collection. They came today."

Jill had a number of different collections that she swore she helped design, but Ambra knew she just put her name on them and then earned a fortune: perfumes, jewelry, underwear. She glanced at the thin, pale velour.

"Hard to imagine that would suit anyone but you. Bloggers with eating disorders, maybe?"

"What the hell, Ambra, do you have to whine so much? First you get here late, and now you're just sitting here moaning. Such bad vibes. Stop being so depressing. Pull yourself together."

"I don't have the energy for that today. And I hate that expression."

"You hate all expressions."

The door opened, and Ludvig came back in. "You got flowers from the prince and his wife," he said, holding up a vase of luxurious roses. He took a picture and uploaded it to Instagram.

"Should I take one of the two of you?" he asked, holding up the cell phone.

Ambra shook her head. She was completely exhausted. Her shift had finished today, which meant she now had five free, gray, endless days ahead of her.

"My sister doesn't want to be seen with me," Jill said. She sat down in front of the mirror and started brushing her hair with quick movements. Irritation hung heavy in the air between them.

"You look more mature with that hairstyle. It suits you," Ambra said, thinking that would help to smooth things over.

Jill paused and gave Ambra a look she didn't understand.

"What?" she asked. What had she said *now?*

"Nothing." Jill went back to brushing her hair with those same jerky movements.

"How are things with you and Mattias?" Ambra hated that one of the main reasons she wanted to know was because Mattias was a link to Tom. She hated Tom, of course, but still.

Jill shook her head. "There's nothing between us. It's over. We weren't a good match."

"Are you sad?"

Harder brushing now. "No. No reason to be."

Ambra studied her back. She was so pretty, her foster sister. "I wish I was more like you, that I could just move on," she said, more or less honestly.

Jill put down the brush with a thud and turned around. "What's that supposed to mean? That I'm more superficial? Dumber?"

"Relax," Ambra said. "That you're positive, you can handle breakups, move on without dwelling on things, that's what I meant."

"For someone who studied so much, you aren't so smart. Some-

times you don't get a thing." Jill started making a noise with the pots
and brushes on her dressing table.

"Come on, what's up with you?" Ambra couldn't handle Jill's
moodiness today, couldn't bring herself to smooth things over.

"With me? Nothing. You're the one who came here and started
moaning. You and your own problems, which are so important you
can't come to *one* single show."

"I was busy at work," she snapped. Grace had been hounding her
all afternoon. Oliver had been throwing taunts around. *Everyone*
was on her case right now. Jill, too, apparently.

"Men are idiots," Jill continued, still making a noise. "What did
you expect?"

"Nothing. Let's talk about something other than my problems if it
is bothering you so much. You, maybe? Because that's what you
mean, isn't it? That everything should be about you and your interesting life and your fucking shows. I've heard your songs hundreds
of times. I don't have the patience to listen to them again. But you
think only of yourself and your problems, even ignore my birthday.
It's all you, you, you." Ambra hadn't even realized that she felt like
this, that she was still angry, that she was hurt, but the words were
out there now and she had no desire to take them back. Jill *was* selfish.

Jill's eyes narrowed. "I knew you were still pissed about that. Why
can't you admit it right away rather than being annoyed forever? I
apologized. I bought you super-expensive clothes, you might remember. But clearly that's not enough."

Ambra jumped up, felt the anger rush through her body. "Yeah, I
know they were super-expensive. I knew I would get to hear about
that. You bought yourself out of that one. Like always. And then I'm
meant to be so fucking grateful and bow down. I hate it. I never
asked for that."

"I'm a generous person. Is that wrong all of a sudden?"

"But it isn't generosity. Don't you see? You control people with
your money. You give them stuff and then expect gratitude. That's
not being generous."

Jill's eyes flashed. "Fine, I promise not to give you another
penny. Why do you have to be so fucking difficult? Did I do something to you?"

Ambra held up her hands. "Sorry, sorry. I forgot you only talk about fun, positive things. God forbid we might have a serious conversation."

"Lay off with the self-important tone. Is it so wrong that I don't want to dig deep into everything all the time? Are *you* happy because you get bogged down in all kinds of crap? You're depressed the whole damn time. What's the point of always being unhappy? Can you tell me that?"

Ambra ran her hand through her hair in frustration. Why couldn't Jill understand this? "I didn't *choose* to be sad. It's a normal reaction, Jill. People get sad. Is it so strange that I feel like crap after being dumped by a man I like?"

"Ah. But you have a choice. I don't believe in all this talking about difficult things all the time, going to psychologists, dwelling. It just makes people feel like crap. Look at you. What good does being sad do? All for this damn Tom's sake."

"You don't get a thing."

"No, probably because I'm so bloody stupid."

"Do you want me to say it? Because I will. You're dumb, Jill. Only ever write about stupid stuff on Instagram, don't take a position on anything. You're uneducated, egocentric, and manipulative. Just like you've always been."

Jill pointed to the door. "I don't need to listen to this shit. Get out. You aren't my sister, you aren't my family, my blood, you have no right to talk to me like that. You have no idea what pressure I'm always under to deliver new material, to perform. Get out. And stay out!"

Ambra grabbed her jacket and purse. "I'm leaving. You can go to hell."

Ambra walked away from the concert hall as though in a daze. She didn't even remember how she got home. She was suddenly just on her street, on Västerlånggatan. She blinked away a snowflake, wiped her cheek with her glove, and got cold and wet.

It didn't feel like they would be able to repair what they'd just broken, she and Jill. This was the first time they had ever fought like that. They'd always swept and swept, brushing everything under the carpet until finally there was no room for anything else. She looked up, was standing outside her door. It was locked, and for a moment she panicked that she couldn't remember the code. When she finally remembered the numbers, it took an eternity before she managed to type them in. Her hands were shaking so much that she had to start over several times before the locking mechanism clicked open and a green light told her it was unlocked. She dragged herself up the stairs, clinging to the handrail, and searched her purse for her keys.

No mail, she saw when she opened the door, not even any junk. There was nothing waiting for her, and that was the final straw. No one sent her anything. No one called or sent messages. The tears stung behind her eyelids. No one cared. She dropped her coat, gloves, and hat onto the hallway floor; kicked off her shoes; went into the living room; lay facedown on the couch; and gave herself over to loud, ugly sobs. She cried for a while, caught her breath, and then started up again. No one loved her.

Her nose was soon so swollen that she could breathe only through her mouth. When she sat up to gasp for air, she heard a buzzing sound. It was her cell phone. She wiped her nose with her arm, hurried out into the hallway, and fished it from her purse. Hoped it would be Jill after all. She didn't know how she would cope without her sister. She had to wipe her eyes before she could see who'd sent the message. It was Elsa.

I'm not doing too well. Think it's my heart.

Oh God, not that too. She replied: *What happened?*

Her eyes didn't leave the screen.

I collapsed. I'm in the hospital. But don't worry.

But it was too late. Ambra pressed her hand to her mouth, but she couldn't stop the tears. Elsa. She had forgotten Elsa. There was no point crying anymore; she had to come up with a plan. That was always the best way forward. She sniffed, knew what she needed to do. She was going to Elsa's side. Back to Kiruna. Again.

Chapter 56

"It's actually fucking depressing," Tom said as he scanned the list of names.

"In what way?" Mattias asked as he placed a black bag on the table.

Mattias's copy of the list was already burned, the smell of smoke still hanging in the air. Each of them knew it by heart, and Tom would burn his copy before they set off.

"In every way, I guess," Tom replied, tearing the scrap of paper to shreds and dropping it into an empty jar. "But the fact they're ordinary people, guys we'd meet every day. It's disturbing."

He had expected they would be mentally unstable people who hated and threatened any woman who took up space, disturbed men removed from society. But the names on their list were ordinary men with ordinary jobs.

A doctor who wrote such hate-filled threats that Tom initially thought he must be psychotic. A local politician with extreme right-wing views who regularly threatened female journalists, bloggers, and other prominent women with rape, mutilation, and torture. A guy in finance who spent his nights on the Flashback forums, a journalist who was also the leading agitator on online right-wing opinion sites like Avpixlat and Fria Tider. A cultured, middle-aged man who seemed to hate feminists as much as he loved girls who were far too young for him.

Using a lighter, Tom set fire to the pieces of paper in the jar. Sometimes he lost faith in his own sex. "There are people who think men should have their voting rights taken away for a few years," he pondered. It was something he had read somewhere. Or maybe Ambra had said it to him once. A feeling of gloom washed over him.

"Probably wouldn't do any harm," Mattias said, but Tom had forgotten what they were talking about. He watched the last few scraps of paper burn and remembered that they were discussing men who behaved like assholes. He just wished he had been a little less of an asshole to Ambra. The best he could do right now was to take all those feelings and channel them into this new task. "It's messed up that these douchebags can carry on like they do. There's so little we can actually do about it. But aside from that . . ." He trailed off, made sure everything was burned.

Mattias grinned as he dropped a map of Sweden into his bag. "I know. Aside from the fact this is all so much fun."

Tom nodded. It *was* fun. Illegal, possibly foolhardy. Crazy even, but *cool*. Mattias would lose his job if it ever came out, and Tom would probably be dragged through the press again. But he wasn't worried. They could do this. Calculated risks and secret operations were their life's blood, their field of expertise.

They had checked and double-checked the list, added some names and taken others away. Thought about it and come up with tough inclusion criteria that they bounced back and forth. There had to be serious, specific threats, they decided, not just generalized, confused hatred. The threats had to have been systematic and made over a long period. The people making the threats also had to be legal adults, and they had set a lower age limit of twenty-five, just to be on the safe side, and an upper limit of sixty. The men must have been told to stop several times but refused.

After they came up with a list of the hundred worst online trolls and haters in Sweden, they had to sift through them again, and now their list consisted of a handful of the very worst men in the country. Men who genuinely threatened freedom of speech and democracy. Men who systematically silenced female voices and whom the judicial system couldn't, or hadn't, tried to touch.

"Not one of them threatens other men."

"No, it's totally messed up. I've looked carefully. But it's as though they *hate* women. Lots of them hate immigrants and Muslims, too—it seems to go hand in hand—but it's the women they go after. Sev-

eral of them have criminal records, of course. Almost exclusively violence against girlfriends or wives. Assholes, like we said."

After they'd compiled their list, they had planned their raids,
brought in a couple of old friends, come up with a time line and alternative plans. They found themselves easily slipping back into their old
areas of expertise. Tom weighed a knife in his hand. He and Mattias
had been on hundreds of similar missions, both smaller and considerably larger operations. This wasn't even particularly difficult. He
shoved the knife into a holster on his back and studied the equipment on the table in front of him, which they were now going
through one last time. It was always a case of balance, what they took
with them on an operation, trying to work out what they might need,
weighing the pros and cons of each item. He grabbed a set of brass
knuckles. They looked painful.

"Just to frighten them," Mattias explained. Tom turned over the
heavy weapon in his hand, tried to remember whether he had ever
used one. He put it down and picked up a pistol.

"If we get arrested, this could be tricky to explain," he said drily.

"You planning to get arrested?"

Tom felt the weight of the pistol, a Glock 17, in his hand. He was
rarely armed, but it was a good weapon—simple and robust. "I guess
it could be good to have. But no shooting, right?"

"Obviously not. You can stop worrying now," Mattias replied,
bending down over a map of southern Sweden. They had looked
into construction, planned alternate routes and agreed on meeting
places in case they got separated. It was a simple job, but they were
experienced enough to know that even the simplest of operations
could escalate into catastrophe, and so they checked, double-
checked, and triple-checked everything.

Tom opened a package containing a brand-new cell phone. They
would be leaving their own phones in Stockholm, and each had
bought a burner phone with a prepaid SIM from a different store.
They would use one for each operation and then destroy them and
throw them in the trash. Mattias checked his usual smartphone, turned
the sound on and off, as though he was making sure it worked.

"How are things with Jill?" Tom asked. He assumed that was what
it was about, mostly because he realized he had done something similar several times over the past few days. It was lucky he had both this

operation and the crisis at work to deal with. Otherwise he probably wouldn't have done anything else.

Mattias looked up. "Honestly, I don't know."

"But you like her?"

Mattias looked at the hoods, ropes, and tools with a concerned frown. "I don't have the option of a relationship with anyone. And with a woman like Jill, it's impossible. She uploads everything she does to social media. She's completely unpredictable, not my type at all." His voice didn't sound convinced.

"So you've fallen for her?" Tom said.

Mattias shook his head. "It would never work out."

"Nah, guess not," Tom said.

"What about your women, then?"

Tom pulled a face at his choice of words, regretted telling Mattias that Ellinor had turned up.

"I don't want to talk about it," was all he said.

"But things are over between you and Ambra?"

Tom paused. He really hoped not. He couldn't imagine life without her. It was almost a relief to feel this way. That she meant everything to him. That he would, without a moment's thought, do anything for her, wouldn't hesitate to give his life. But he didn't answer Mattias's question; it was no one else's business. He just continued to pack the equipment they needed. Then he closed the bag. "Ready?" he asked. They were already wearing dark clothes. Nondescript black pants, sturdy boots. Coats without any distinguishing features. They had bought an anonymous old car with thick winter tires, an engine preheater, and a powerful motor. Put on stolen plates and planned to scrap it afterward. Just like in the past.

"Weapons, equipment, maps. Anything else?" Mattias asked while he cast one last glance at his wallet and smartphone on the kitchen table. Tom did the same. They were taking only cash. The fewer things to identify them, the better.

"That's everything."

"Then let's go," said Mattias.

They would start in Skåne, in the south of Sweden, and work their way north.

"Yup. Southward, off to war with the online trolls."

*　　*　　*

They arrived in Skåne just after midnight. Pulled into the small villa neighborhood, found the right address, and settled down in the car to wait.

"Where are our guys?" Mattias asked. They had sent two of Tom's employees ahead to watch the targets, learn their routines, and explore the surroundings. They would keep watch while Tom and Mattias committed the actual crime.

"They're in place. Everything seems calm."

At two in the morning, Tom and Mattias climbed out of the car. Slipped over to the house.

"There's no alarm," Tom whispered. "This isn't even a challenge." They were inside in under twenty seconds. Then again, they had been on similar maneuvers before. Broken into houses and rooms; grabbed the enemy; hauled terrorists, clan leaders, and local criminals back out with them. More often in war zones than quiet residential neighborhoods. A well-nourished, middle-class white man used to peace was no match for them. They made their way into the bedroom and dragged the half-sleeping man from his bed. The men on their list were all single; they didn't want to affect any innocent parties. They taped his mouth shut, pulled a hood over his head, dragged him into the kitchen, pushed him down onto a chair, and secured his hands and feet with cable ties. They didn't hear a sound from the rest of the house. The man's children were grown up and studying abroad, and his wife had left him a few years earlier. Smart woman.

Mattias crossed his arms and stared through the holes in his ski mask.

"So, Stig. Know why we're here?"

Stig shook his head firmly.

"We're here to talk about your online presence. You haven't been nice."

Stig shouted something from behind the tape. Mattias stepped forward and pulled off the hood. Stig abruptly fell silent and stared wildly, was probably more used to being the one with the advantage. Tom had seen the police report in which his latest girlfriend accused him of assault. She'd been beaten black and blue. The case was dropped.

"Now I want you to listen carefully, Stig. You need to stop with all your accounts on Flashback, Facebook, and Instagram. Yes, that's right, we know about your lame alias, and you're never going to write another word in another comment box, not on Facebook, not in any closed groups, not in any debate or column. You're not going to talk on a podcast. Not one unkind word or we'll be back. And then we'll be annoyed. Won't be quite as friendly as we are now, you understand?"

Stig was motionless.

"He seem to understand?" Mattias asked over his shoulder.

Tom snorted. Mattias hit Stig hard in the face. He knew just where to hit, and sure enough, the blood started pouring from Stig's nose.

"Understand?" Mattias asked.

Stig sniffed and nodded.

"I'll take this off now. If you scream . . ." Mattias took his pistol from the holster and held it up in front of the man. His face was covered in sweat. Mattias pulled off the silver tape in one firm tug.

"I'll report you to the police" was the first thing he said. Mattias turned to Tom and rolled his eyes. Tom grabbed the baseball bat and hit it against his palm a few times before he placed it on the table. Then he pulled a nail gun from his bag. He had trouble stifling a laugh behind his balaclava; he'd bought it from Bauhaus and would never use it on anyone. He wasn't much of a fan of torturing people, not even online trolls, but it looked frightening and that was the point. Mattias took the nail gun and held it up in front of Stig's face. Stig made a sound like a trapped animal, and a wet patch spread across his pajama pants.

Any hint of resistance vanished from his face.

That was the good thing about bullies—they were easy to break.

"We're zero tolerance, so you don't get any more chances," Mattias said, still holding the nail gun a few centimeters from Stig's face.

"Okay, okay."

"Are you going to write any more?"

Stig shook his head.

"Because we can make life so damn tough for you, you have no idea."

"I only wrote what everyone else is thinking. We do actually live in a democracy."

Tom pulled the pistol from the waistband of his pants and placed it against Stig's kneecap. Stig started to whimper and Tom fixed his eyes on him, allowed him to see the violence he was capable of.

Stig passed out in the chair. His head slumped forward.

"What a fucking idiot. He's going to suffocate himself if he passes out like that."

They untied him and placed him flat, on his side. They packed up their equipment and left the house as silently as they'd arrived.

They took turns sleeping and driving, and they were back in Stockholm just after the morning rush.

"You working today?" Mattias asked with a yawn. Tom nodded. He would get a few hours' sleep and then head in to Lodestar.

"See you tonight," he said after he gave Mattias a ride home.

Next time, they drove to a red brick villa in Linköping, bordered by neat snow-covered hedges and with a brand-new BMW Cabriolet in the garage.

The confrontation was almost identical. Stefan was a senior physician and a psychiatrist. Newly divorced, childless, and fond of harassing young women online. Plus, he regularly posted about patients with Muslim backgrounds on Flashback and used a pseudonym to write posts urging the murder of the "vermin." Using one of his aliases on Avpixlat, he boasted about having assaulted beggars and unaccompanied refugee minors during a weekend trip to Stockholm.

When they pulled the silver tape from his mouth, he squealed like a pig in a slaughterhouse, and not even two quick slaps from Mattias was enough to shut him up. The doctor continued to spew his bile until Tom had had enough and covered his mouth with tape again. "I'm pretty tempted to cover your nose, too," he muttered.

Mattias sat on the kitchen table, one of his legs dangling beneath him, and went through the threatening and hateful activities the doctor had been busy with over the years. While he did, Tom took out the various tools and did his very best to look as sadistic as he could. As the gravity of the situation started to dawn on the doctor, he turned paste white. And when Tom pulled out the electric saw, he finally broke down.

"How do we check that they aren't still doing it?" Tom asked once they finally left the unharmed doctor and were driving back toward Stockholm.

"Filippa created an algorithm. It's the digital equivalent of a pain in their asses. They can't do a thing without us knowing, and they'll get regular reminders of that. She's pretty creative when given free rein."

"Is that legal?"

"We're classing them as a threat to democracy, terrorists. That gives us plenty of room to maneuver. It's a drop in the ocean, but it's a start."

"Not everyone can do everything, but everyone can do something?" Tom said drily.

"Exactly. These particular men are digitally castrated for good. I'm going to make it my personal mission to ensure they never threaten anyone again."

"Speaking of personal. The doctor you were angry with. What did he do?"

"He's been threatening Jill for years. She reported him to the police several times. He threatened to cut off her breasts, for example, and to share her address online. The other night, there was an armed man outside her house."

"Jesus."

"Yeah. We'll pay our next two upper-class candidates a visit tomorrow."

"So far they've all been pretty receptive," Tom said. He was well aware that they were operating in a moral gray zone and that he shouldn't be finding the whole thing quite so much fun. But it felt incredibly good to actually *do* something.

"Yeah, it's amazing how people suddenly see sense when they get a visit from a baseball bat," Mattias agreed.

The two following visits played out in much the same way as the first, and Tom even found himself yawning when one of the Östermalm guys broke down crying. If he hadn't read the man's serious sexual threats and calls to burn down asylum seekers' accommodations, Tom might even have felt sorry for him. He dutifully waved the brass knuckles, the nail gun, and the electric saw in the air, but it was clear the man would never dare say anything negative about either women or foreigners again.

"Why do you think everyone who hates women also hates immigrants and gay people?" Tom asked while they packed the car.

"I'm sure there's some long, intelligent answer to that, but the short one has to be that they're idiots. We'll take the last one tomorrow, but then I need to get back to work, sadly."

"Same."

"How's it going at Lodestar?"

"Things have calmed down a little."

"Feel good to be working again?"

"Yeah, very."

Tom looked out the car window, saw the slush and gray sky. It did him good to be back at work, and it was going unexpectedly well. But this was fun too. And when he thought of the last name on their list, he grinned maliciously. He was looking forward to that particular visit.

Chapter 57

For the third time in just over a month, Ambra landed at the windy, snowy airport in Kiruna; walked the short, ice-cold distance from the plane to the terminal building; and stamped the snow from her feet once inside. This time she wouldn't be leaving Kiruna until she got the answers she wanted. She grabbed her bags and went out. Just like last time, she was met by piles of snow, a wind so cold it made her gasp for air, and howling sled dogs. The airport bus opened its steaming doors, and she climbed onboard and took a window seat. It was snowing so hard she could barely see the road.

The bus shook and Ambra braced herself with a hand on the seat in front. She looked out, thought of the two foster girls. How were they doing?

She remembered falling in the garden once, twisting her foot beneath her. Esaias and Rakel had forced her to stand on that foot, to walk on it. It hurt so much that she passed out. When she woke, they forced her up again, smothered her in creams, and prayed to God. When that didn't help, they shouted at her as she was lying on the floor in tears, and they said she wouldn't allow God to help her. The school nurse sent her to the hospital, and an X-ray showed a fracture.

It was unbearable to think that something similar—or worse— could be happening to those girls right now. She'd felt so alone and abandoned while she lived in Kiruna that she didn't have the words for it. Finding out now, years later, that people had known what was going on and still had done nothing was terrible. Knowing that didn't give her any comfort. In fact, it filled her with rage. And it filled her with a dire conviction. She would fix this.

Somehow she had to put everything right. Because she knew that two children were suffering with Esaias and Rakel Sventin, and she was worried about what they had planned with the exorcist. She couldn't shut her eyes or turn away. And even if she lost her job as a result—or worse—she would still do everything in her power. What had happened to her simply couldn't be allowed to happen again.

She saw the now-familiar road signs and landmarks pass by, and twenty minutes later she checked in to the Scandic Ferrum once again. The receptionist recognized her and gave her a different room this time, higher up and with a better view. She could make out the mountain in the distance, and through all the snow she could see a pink sky kissing the hilltops. Within an hour or so, it would be dark.

Ambra grabbed her new rucksack and her thick, new gloves. She buttoned her new winter coat up to her chin. It was a miracle. She didn't feel cold at all.

This time, she was ready and equipped for Kiruna.

The hospital was within walking distance of the hotel, and Ambra asked for help finding the wing Elsa was in.

Ambra knocked gently on the door, suddenly terrified at what she might see. What if Elsa was hooked up to all kinds of wires? If she was dying? Unconscious? But when she opened the door, her worries vanished. Elsa's face lit up like a lantern when she saw her. "Darling child, you didn't need to come all the way up here for my sake!"

Ambra took a step into the room. It smelled like a hospital, and there was a drip next to Elsa's bed, but otherwise it didn't seem so bad. "You look well," she said.

Elsa reached out, and Ambra squeezed her hand tight. The old lady sat up against the pillows. "How nice to see you. It's good to see a young person. How are you? Are you hungry?"

"I brought supplies," Ambra said, holding up the box she'd bought on the way.

"Wonderful! What is it?"

"A mix. Cream buns, almond cakes, seven types of cookies."

Elsa clapped her hands. "Kaffeeklatsch! I feel better already."

"How are you doing?" Ambra asked while she took out the baked goods, fetched two mugs of coffee, grabbed a vase, and placed the small bunch of tulips she'd bought into it.

"Much better now."

"I was so worried," said Ambra. She pulled out a chair and sat down by the bed. Elsa sipped her coffee and tucked into the sweet things.

A nurse came in. "And how is Elsa today?" she asked in a hearty voice.

"Fine, especially now I have a special visitor."

"Is this your granddaughter?"

"She could be," Elsa said warmly.

The nurse disappeared, and Elsa smiled at Ambra. "No more talking about me. How are you, dear Ambra? Do you really have time to be up here?"

"It's all fine," she said dismissively.

Elsa put down her cup and clasped her hands on top of the hospital blanket. There was a needle taped to the back of her hand. "Tell me."

"I don't want to talk about myself," Ambra protested. "Everything's fine, I want to talk about you, about the girls, about that picture you sent."

Elsa shook her head. "Is it the man you talked about?"

Ambra twisted in her seat. "How did you know?"

Elsa gestured with her hands. The drip line followed her movement. "It's always a man. Or a woman."

Ambra brushed a crumb from her knee. "We fought."

"Ah, I'm sorry."

"I slapped him."

"Good, that might knock a little sense into the man," Elsa said firmly, and Ambra had to smile. It felt good to have someone so unconditionally on her side. She would survive this, too. In the grand scheme of things, a broken heart wasn't such a big deal.

Ambra got up, straightened a tulip, and gave Elsa a reassuring smile. "He's an idiot."

"He really is if he can't appreciate you."

"Thanks."

It felt good to be back in Kiruna, she realized with slight surprise. It *was* restful to be so far away from Tom, Ellinor, and Stockholm. Knowing she wouldn't bump into a grim-faced Tom or an ever-smiling Ellinor the minute she turned the corner.

"Are you sure that's the end, though? It seemed like you two had something special. This is the young man with the Northern Lights and the dog? The one you talked about?"

Ambra smiled, but she shook her head. "I don't think so. I fought with my sister, too," she said, taking another cookie. The fight with Jill was hanging over her like a huge cloud of despair.

"My dear, you've had a tough time lately."

"Elsa, I came here to see you, to see how you were doing. I was so worried. But I also came because of the picture you sent," she said.

"Did you find out who he is?"

"Yeah. And it's not good. Have you ever heard about the Laestadians performing exorcisms?"

Elsa frowned. "Ingrid mentioned it once. Awful."

"His name is Uno Aalto. He's from Finland. An eastern Laestadian who travels around and preaches. And drives out evil spirits."

"My goodness. And he's here? Do you think he will attack the girls?"

"That's what I'm afraid of. But I feel completely powerless. No one believes me when I tell them. It's so frustrating."

She had called social services again, and the police, and had tried to find and contact the school the girls attended, but all without success. It was like coming up against a wall of mistrust. The voices of the various officials had become increasingly irritated, until eventually they were openly hostile, treating her as if she were a madwoman. She had almost started to believe it herself, that she had become one of those clichés: a crazy journalist, a crank.

"I believe you."

"Thank you."

"You're an incredibly smart woman. I just wish you could see it yourself." Elsa took Ambra's hand and squeezed it. Ambra squeezed back. Elsa's hand was so thin. God, the woman was ninety-two; she could be dying. Wasn't everyone, by definition, dying by the time they approached one hundred?

"What are you going to do now?" Elsa asked.

Ambra looked out the hospital window. All she had were a few blurry pictures taken by Elsa and a half confirmation from Lotta the social worker that the girls were foster children. There wasn't really much she could do with so little information.

But she remembered how many times she had been sent to Esaias's basement, how desperate she was. How she cried and hoped someone would save her, though she should have given up any hope long before. All those times she prayed intensely to her mom and dad, whispered that if they existed, if they were thinking of her up there in heaven, they should give her a sign. No sign ever came. Not a single person on earth cared whether she lived or died. But those two girls would be saved. She would save them. Anyone who tried to stop her could go to hell.

She gave Elsa a serious look. "I'm going to go over there. Talk to Esaias. I have to."

"I think you do have to. But be careful, promise me that."

Ambra nodded. "I promise."

She got up from her seat, full of a new, angry energy. She would do this. Everything was falling into place.

She turned to Elsa. "Can you promise me something too?"

Elsa turned her pale, wrinkled face to her. When she smiled, the expression formed a web of lines and furrows. "Anything, my dear."

"Promise not to die before I come back."

Elsa nodded solemnly. "I'll try."

Chapter 58

Tom studied the picture of their last troll. It was an image of a man he had more than one reason to dislike.

Oliver Holm, the reporter from *Aftonbladet*.

"Have you met him before?" Mattias asked as he hauled the bag up onto the table.

"Nope," Tom replied.

Though it felt like he had.

After he and Mattias had parted ways the day before, Tom went home, showered, and got a few hours' sleep. He went into work for a while after that, and then spent the rest of the day going through the information they had on Oliver Holm. It wasn't exactly an uplifting read. Oliver currently worked the same shift pattern as Ambra, had the same free days as her, and shared some of the same bosses (though there were a lot of different-level bosses at the paper, Tom noted). Oliver and Ambra were almost the same age and had been working at *Aftonbladet* for almost the same length of time.

But there, the similarities ended.

Oliver portrayed himself as a hard-nosed journalist, with edgy pieces on motorcycle gangs, expensive cars, and portraits of primarily male sports stars on his merit list. He lived alone in an expensive condo at Liljeholmsstranden—a new and flashy area—and was seen as a star on the rise. On the surface, in other words, Oliver Holm was a successful journalist. According to his Instagram account, he worked out five times a week, and the same source also claimed he drank champagne and expensive cocktails in Stockholm's coolest spots. He was a member of a number of Facebook groups where music, films, and electronic gadgets were discussed in a raw, manly fashion. The jokes he shared were almost exclusively sexist, and he made the occasional comment about "militant feminists," but otherwise there was nothing remarkable about him. He had a son who lived with him every other week. On the surface, he was a perfectly average guy.

But beneath the surface, a completely different person emerged. Tom leafed through the documents. Extracts from police reports, copies of lists of IP addresses, printouts of SMS conversations, messages from closed groups on Facebook, decoded posts on Flashback. Things Oliver had probably thought were impossible to trace but that were now in a neat pile in front of Tom.

"Filippa's good," Tom remarked as he scanned through a fraction of the messages Oliver had sent to Ambra under a pseudonym.

> *I'll shove a chainsaw up your disgusting feminist pussy.*
> *You traitorous bitch. You think you're something. Why don't you just give up and throw yourself under a train?*

There were a huge number of similar messages. To Ambra and other women. What a fucking scumbag.

"My whole team's great," Mattias said. "Best in Sweden, and definitely top class internationally. The elite of the elite. And nice, too. You'd fit in."

Tom didn't reply to that. What he and Mattias were doing, it was a one-off; he had no intention of carrying out illegal threats on a permanent basis. Lodestar was where he belonged. But that didn't mean this wasn't important. Because if you looked behind the neat facade, Oliver Holm was a real pig. Under various usernames, he moved between a number of different sites like a predator. He was good at making young girls feel appreciated, at winning their trust. Time and time again, he managed to make defenseless and often vulnerable girls gradually expose themselves to him, both psychologically and physically. Little by little, until they were caught in his web. He made them show their breasts, send nude pictures, pose for the web camera, and then he made them do worse and worse things by threatening to publish the material. His accounts had been reported several times, but every single investigation had been dropped.

It was a depressing illustration of the way the legal system failed to safeguard the very youngest online. But degrading and breaking teenage girls wasn't the only thing Oliver got up to on the Internet. As Filippa dug deeper, she found more and more evidence of serious crimes. Tom had seen the very worst sides of humanity. He knew what people were capable of doing to one another, had seen cruelties that, thankfully, the majority couldn't even imagine. There were those who argued that hate against women was stronger in other cultures, but Tom didn't agree with that at all. This everyday misogyny of Oliver and his peers was no different; it was just a question of degree. Bad men doing whatever they could get away with. A guy like Oliver would continue his attacks, threats, and disgusting behavior as long as he felt he would get away with it. Just like those who tortured their fellow citizens, raped women, or acted like animals during war.

"Everyone has a choice whether to be a pig or not," said Tom.

"And Oliver has chosen to be," Mattias replied. "It's not just Ambra and those young girls that he harassed. He's one of Jill's haters too. That's how I found him."

"Figures," Tom said, feeling his dislike of Oliver grow.

"We'll have to try hard not to kill him."

"Guess so. Shame."

"Real shame. You got everything?" Mattias asked.

Tom nodded. It was time again.

They drove out to Liljeholmen in concentrated silence. There were two men already waiting for them out there. They had decided to try to get to Oliver during the daytime. He lived in a residential area where very few people were around during the day. They had studied the plans to his apartment. It was a sturdy, new-build condo, and if he started to scream no one would hear them.

"Is he home?" Tom asked after they met the others.

"Since last night. Alone."

The two guys waited outside, guarding the car and the building, while Tom and Mattias made it in through the front door without any trouble. They pulled on their balaclavas, rang the buzzer, and heard a faint murmur from inside before Oliver Holm unlocked and opened the door. A ruffled head appeared. "Yeah?" he said grumpily.

Without a word, they forced their way into the apartment. Tom placed a hand over Oliver's mouth, Mattias closed and locked the door, and they had him taped and on the floor in three seconds.

Mattias went in to secure the apartment while Tom kept an eye on their prisoner. Oliver fought back. He was unexpectedly strong, no doubt a combination of all the working out and a serious adrenaline rush.

His arms and legs kicked out, and he managed to strike Tom just above the eyebrow.

"Motherfucker," Tom swore as the blood started to pour, temporarily clouding his field of vision. In that same moment, the idiot managed to pull the tape from his mouth and took a deep breath to yell.

Tom, who wasn't exactly in a good mood now that he was bleeding heavily, swung at the side of Oliver's head, making him lose his breath. He managed to retape his mouth.

"The place is empty. What do we do now?" Mattias asked when he returned.

"He's going to hurt himself if he keeps on like this. Calm down, for fuck's sake!" Tom barked, shaking Oliver.

Oliver shouted something that was stifled by the tape. It sounded like: "I'm a journalist. You can't do this."

They dragged him into the living room, where Mattias had pulled out a heavy leather seat. They fastened Oliver's wrists with cable ties at the back of the chair. He pulled and tore at them so hard that he almost tipped it over. But eventually, they had him secure and sitting still, breathless, sweating, and furious behind the silver tape.

Tom went out into the kitchen, found paper towels, and shoved them beneath his balaclava, pressed against the cut on his brow. They would have to make sure to clean up any blood. They couldn't leave behind anything that could be tested for DNA.

Mattias studied Oliver. "We just want to talk to you. If you keep your mouth shut, I'll take the tape off. But if you shout, my friend here will make you regret it."

Tom didn't even need to exert himself to look threatening. Just the thought that this man had tormented Ambra made his blood boil.

Mattias pulled away the silver tape.

"What do you want? I don't have any money here," Oliver insisted.

"We're here because of things you wrote."

"Are you kidding?"

"Not in the paper," Mattias explained.

Oliver seemed confused, as if he genuinely had no idea what Mattias was talking about.

"Online," Mattias said patiently.

Oliver snorted. "You're insane. You actually care? Are you from TV or what? There are real criminals out there. Let me go. I haven't done shit."

"Tell that to the girls whose lives you ruined."

Oliver made another snorting sound. "Those sluts. They only have themselves to blame if they're that stupid."

The fact that Oliver placed the blame with his victims didn't make Tom any more favorable toward him. He forced himself to take a step back. If he got too close, there was a risk he would end up wringing the asshole's neck.

Mattias started to go through some of the worst things Filippa had found, and gratifyingly, the mocking look on Oliver's face was replaced by fear when Mattias read out quotes of his posts to Flashback.

When Tom eventually started the electric saw, Oliver bounced back and they had to tape his mouth again, because he started to yell.

After they scared him with the saw and the nail gun, they moved on to threatening him in different ways. It didn't take long for his arrogance to disappear, and he started crying like a baby. Since Tom had seen pictures of the girls he'd harassed, the youngest of them twelve, Oliver's tears didn't wake an ounce of compassion.

Mattias cast a glance at Tom, who nodded in reply. It was time to finish up.

"We'll be back if we suspect you're even thinking of reoffending."

Oliver had sweated and cried so much that the tape had come loose from his mouth. "It's not illegal to think," he whined.

Tom, who had definitely had enough of Oliver Holm and his crappy opinions, hit him in the face. "In your case it is," was all he said.

They packed up their things while Oliver sank into silence.

"Are you from that firm I wrote about? Lodestar?" he asked after a while, studying them through swollen eyes.

They ignored him, but Oliver continued.

"Are you Tom Lexington?" He nodded toward Tom, who was the taller of the two. "Ambra protected you, God knows why. You're just a thug. She'll probably lose the job she wanted because of you." He laughed. "Typical Ambra, she's always been a loser."

It was as if someone had drawn a dark veil before Tom's eyes. All he could see was black. His fist flew through the air like an unstoppable projectile, and it landed on Oliver's jaw with such force that both he and the chair tipped backward. Oliver roared.

"What the hell." Mattias gave Tom an irritated look.

Tom forced himself to calm down. Mattias was right, of course. There was no point losing it like that. Tom shook his head. He could feel the punch in his knuckles. Good. He waited until Oliver stopped whimpering. "You're going to write to every single journalist you've harassed and apologize, understand?"

"You're crazy."

Tom brought his face close to Oliver's, and Oliver jumped. "You're going to apologize and you're going to grovel. Otherwise I'll come back and throw you off the balcony. Consider that a promise."

Oliver's Adam's apple bobbed. He looked away. But he also nodded.

"We're leaving now," Mattias said. "You go first, I'll follow you."

Tom grabbed the bag and stomped out of the apartment.

Damn it. Oliver was an idiot and an asshole, but his drivel only confirmed what Tom already knew. That Ambra hadn't lied. That Oliver and her boss had gone over her head. She hadn't betrayed him. He clutched the handle of the bag. But that wasn't even the worst part. The worst part was that it had cost Ambra what she wanted most of all: the investigative job. She would lose the one thing he knew she held most dear, and it was all *his* fault. She'd told the truth and he'd punished her for it.

"I'll drive," he said, catching the keys Mattias threw to him.

They pulled the door closed behind them and hurried down the stairs.

"How long before he gets loose?" Tom asked.

Mattias threw the bag into the trunk. "Thirty minutes maybe? I loosened the ties, so he should be able to get free. If he sacrifices a little skin. What happened up there?"

Tom didn't reply; he just started the engine and pulled out of the parking lot. They nodded to their colleagues, who left just as discreetly, taking the highway south, while Tom drove toward the center of Stockholm.

He had treated Ambra badly, and he knew what he had to do.

"It went well anyway," Mattias said after they sat in silence all the way into Stockholm.

"I've really blown things."

"What are you talking about?"

"Not work. That was fun, and I think we did good. But with Ambra."

"So she's the one you want?"

"Yeah."

"Can you fix it?"

"I really don't know." He struggled to say the words, but he had to be realistic.

"Women." Mattias sighed.

"Yeah."

They drove on in silence.

"You going to work?"

"Yeah. But now that we're on the subject. I think I like Jill," said Mattias.

"Like? Are you twelve, or what?"

"You're in no position to act superior when it comes to women. Didn't you just ruin two relationships?"

"Guess so. Tell me about Jill."

"I've never felt like this before. Intellectually I know she's wrong for me, but she feels so right."

Tom listened to Mattias's torment with one ear. He was deep in his own anguished thoughts about Ambra. He had been wrong, done wrong, reacted wrong. He had to try to straighten things out.

"Are you even listening?"

Tom stopped the car suddenly. "I'll drop you off here. I need to go home."

"But . . ."

"We can talk more later," he said, pulling the door closed the minute Mattias was out. He had an important call to make.

Chapter 59

When Ambra left Elsa and the hospital, she noticed that the battery on her cell phone was already empty. Her brand-new, technically advanced smartphone didn't stand a chance against the bitter Norrland chill. It went from fully charged to empty in just a few short hours.

"Weakling," she muttered.

She swung by the hotel to quickly charge it in her room. While she waited for the battery to fill up, she lay down on the bed and breathed calmly. Her phone buzzed, as though it wanted to assure her it was working away. She closed her eyes and tried to picture how the next few hours would play out. She had no idea. And she had no one to talk it over with. She missed Tom. And Jill. She sniffed but refused to start crying, not now. She had to be strong and focused. She had a job to do.

People must have been trying to call her while her phone was dead, because now that it was charging it was pinging away angrily. She was so tired. Couldn't bring herself to check it. She would lie here for ten minutes and wait. Be mindful and calm. But only a minute later, she got up; she couldn't be mindful even if lives were at stake. Her phone was charged to nineteen percent, and she had two missed calls.

Both were from Tom.

At first, she thought it was a mistake. Old messages popping up when her phone restarted. But he had called. And recently.

Her mouth was so dry she couldn't swallow. Her first impulse was to call him back, immediately. But then she hesitated. Why was he calling her? She wasn't sure she had the strength to talk to him right now. One harsh word from Tom and she would fall to pieces. She couldn't afford that. She would wait and see. She had some pride left after all.

Once her cell phone was fully charged, she dropped it into her pocket, brushed all thoughts of Tom to one side, closed the door to her room, and walked toward the church in the icy air. She glanced up at the red building, opened the door, and slipped into one of the pews at the very back. She would have to mentally charge herself for what she had come to do. The sermon was about to begin.

It was dark, just like last time. Although the church was almost full, it was quiet, nothing but a low murmur and the occasional child's cry rising up to the ceiling, quickly silenced by a nervous mother. Row after row of serious faces. The women with long hair and skirts, their hair tucked beneath plain headscarves and colorless shawls. The men in shirts or knitted sweaters. They probably never laughed. To some of the strictest Laestadians, laughter was a sin, and Ambra assumed that those sitting here waiting for the day's sermon probably weren't the most liberal.

The room grew quiet. The first preacher of the day took his place. They didn't have priests, the Laestadians; they had preachers, and they were always men. These were open, violent opponents to female priests. Serious men with monotonous voices who talked about sin and the devil, repeated the same doomsday prophecies over and over again.

". . . and Hell is awaiting them. Because man is born evil," he droned on, and anger bubbled up inside Ambra. Hell and the original sin were something the Swedish church kept at a distance. It was a scandal that this sect was allowed to use the church building to spread its antihuman message.

". . . homosexual intercourse is a sin, the evil of demons. You must see that we are being attacked from every direction. The homodevil is everywhere."

Ambra twisted in her seat, but his droning voice cut straight into her. Everyone else in the church was unmoving on their pews, paying great attention to the preacher. Some cried silently. The children sat with their parents and relatives, their faces pale and their eyes frightened. Ambra remembered it well. Families with ten, maybe even fifteen children. Birth control was forbidden, motherhood was the lot of women, and the most praised mothers gave birth to one child a year. Their daughters dreamed of having many babies of their own. Their sons learned that the man of the family's word was law. Laestadian women were meant to make themselves constantly available for pregnancy; they had no control over their own bodies. It was incredible that such a sect could exist in an enlightened and secular country like Sweden.

"Has she not proven herself to be a strumpet?" the preacher's voice thundered, now talking about a sixteen-year-old girl who had apparently worn makeup and would now be frozen out of the congregation. Ambra glanced around the church and wondered whether the poor girl was present. There was no love here, no reconciliation, none of the good that faith could bring. Although maybe she was looking at everything through the gray filter of her own childhood. Maybe there were people here who didn't hit or torment, good people who believed in God and were kind to those around them. Maybe.

But even among the more enlightened Laestadians, there was a constant battle against the sinful temptations of the world around them. Music, TV, and video games were obviously banned. So were colorful clothes, drapes, jewelry, makeup, and the Internet. Getting an education and reading were sins, as was taking part in hobbies or sports, because it took time from God. It all seemed so wrong to her.

"Now we welcome Uno Aalto. He has come all the way from Finland and our brothers there. He is the apostle and he is revival. The prophet come down to us. We are blessed."

Ambra pressed the small of her back against the hard wooden bench, squinted in the dim lighting. It really was the man from Elsa's photo. He was taller than he looked in the picture and walked with heavy, slightly dragging steps. He had unusually long arms, and every time he swallowed, his enormous Adam's apple bobbed beneath his wrinkled skin. When Uno Aalto opened his mouth to speak, Ambra saw his grayish-brown teeth. They looked dirty, but she couldn't actually remember whether toothpaste was another sin. He was carrying a well-thumbed black Bible. Every Laestadian whom Ambra had ever met was a silent, unassuming person, eternally weighed down by all of the sins they had committed. But the silence that fell when

Uno Aalto took to the pulpit was striking all the same. Several people already looked as if they were about to faint.

Uno Aalto looked out at the congregation. The two images she had seen didn't do him justice. He was tall, with short hair, almost restrained in his movements, but he had a radiance, the type of intensity people always said sect leaders possessed.

He breathed in, waited, and then began his sermon. He spoke Swedish but with a Finnish accent. It always began in the same way, with a tribute to God and Christianity, a speech about love and unity, then moved on to increasingly sharp words about damnation. "It is a revival for our fellow man. A revival for those who live in sin," he said, and his sullen, toneless, old-fashioned voice made her skin crawl. It was so joyless, so unforgiving. It felt so nineteenth century, all judgment and Hell.

"And as the exterior, so the interior," he continued, launching into a long, dreary monologue about alcohol, women's clothing, and the different ways the devil worked on earth. When Ambra glanced at her watch, she saw he had been going for thirty minutes already.

The Laestadian women sat with their heads bowed. Several sniffed loudly. It wasn't so strange: Thanks to their sex, they were automatic bearers of sin. Uno Aalto had really gotten going now. The words poured out of him like a dark maelstrom of admonitions, threats, and hatred toward women. Sinful clothes, sinful towns, sinful temptresses. Sin, sin, sin.

"These perversions enable the devil to take hold. With his terrible claws, he tears his way into the sinner's heart. No one is spared, not the old, not women, nor children." He fell silent. It was hard to tell if it was a deliberate pause for effect or whether he just needed to catch his breath. Ambra glanced around the church. How could they bear to listen to this rubbish?

His thundering voice filled the hall once more: "You must be especially vigilant of sins in the young. For their minds are easy to lead astray."

It was like listening to Esaias talk to her. Neither he nor Rakel was here today, as far as she could tell, but listening to Uno Aalto talk about the sins of the young threw her straight back to her time with them.

They used to have a radio in their kitchen, and she had once turned the round dial until she found a station that played both music and ads. She was so caught up in the music that she didn't hear Esaias coming.

"What are you doing? You wretched whore, what are you doing?"

"Nothing." She'd been so afraid that the words almost caught in her throat.

"And lying, too. You bring sin into my house."

The slap had struck her on the cheek and sent her flying into one of the kitchen chairs. She had huddled down to protect herself from more.

Ambra took a deep breath and forced herself back to the here and now, away from Esaias's kitchen and the abuse that went on all evening.

Esaias had accused her of being sinful so many times that a small part of her had thought maybe he was right after all. That the fault was in her. But now that she was here, listening to Uno Aalto talking about demons and evil, she could see the absurdity of it all. Hitting a child to drive out the devil. Telling a ten-year-old whose mother had died that she was possessed by evil spirits. What kind of God permitted such things?

Ambra glanced at her watch again; more than two hours had passed. But it sounded like Uno Aalto was nearing the end of his sermon. His voice trembled, his face was flushed, and he raised his fist to the congregation from time to time, as though to emphasize how lost they were.

"Amen," he eventually said.

"Amen," the congregation mumbled quietly.

Ambra felt anger and determination rise up inside her. The sixteen-year-olds who were labeled whores, the women forced to bear child after child, and the foster children who were mistreated. Someone had to stop these madmen, and right now that someone seemed to be her.

After the service, people lined up to speak to the preachers, to be touched and blessed. Again and again, Uno Aalto shook the men's hands. The women stood to one side, humble and silent.

Ambra got up from her bench, stepped into the shadows, and moved slowly through the church. No one paid any attention to her.

That was what they did in this sect; they ignored and froze out those who didn't belong. But being ignored could also be a protection. If you kept quiet, didn't make a fuss, it was as though you didn't exist.

Every now and again, the strange acoustics of the church carried fragments of hushed conversations over to her. Words and sentences exchanged by people as others began to drop away, the women with the smallest children first.

Ambra moved behind a pillar and saw Uno Aalto take an old, square cell phone from his pocket. The Internet was a sin, so no Laestadians owned smartphones. But in his elderly hands, next to his old-fashioned clothing, it looked almost anachronistic. As though he were an actor in some period film, talking on the phone between takes.

Uno Aalto turned to one side, his face toward Ambra, as he talked over the line.

She snuck even closer and listened with pricked ears.

". . . we need to carry it out as soon as possible."

She leaned forward and listened to his Finnish accent.

"From your description, Esaias, it sounds as though the devil is strong in them." He shook his head in concern. "Yes." And then silence, while he listened to the person on the other end with a frown. Could he be talking to Esaias Sventin? It wasn't impossible. She had seen them in the same picture, after all.

Impatiently, breathlessly, she waited for Uno Aalto to say something more.

"Yes, that may be the case. The girls egg one another on. The devil is cunning like that. And he is strong. Particularly when they are on the threshold. I understand your concerns. I am worried too."

He trailed off and listened with a sententious expression. Ambra was increasingly convinced that he was talking to Esaias Sventin.

"Yes, that sounds wise. It's precisely that impurity that makes them receptive to sin. You have done what you can, but now you need help. Do you have anywhere we can go?"

Yet another fraught silence as Uno nodded.

Whatever they were talking about, it was something complicated and serious. Ambra managed to move closer without being seen, and she almost jumped when she heard Uno Aalto's monotonous voice again, much closer this time: "The basement will be fine. It can take a long time, as you know, and we need to be undisturbed. If Satan is as strong in them as you say, we must be prepared to fight the demons. This is a test, brother. You need to be strong. Yes, tomorrow will be fine."

Uno Aalto ended the call.

Ambra moved back behind the pillar and tried to make sense of what she had just heard. She didn't want to believe it was true, but no matter which way she twisted and turned it, she came to the same conclusion. They were planning to exorcise the girls living with Esaias and Rakel Sventin. In their basement, starting tomorrow. And the worst part was that she knew exactly what they had planned. She had gone through it herself. It existed in all religions. In its most innocuous form, it was a remedy. In its worst, an attack that could involve torture, even death. Uno and Esaias were planning to drive out demons, no matter what it took.

Chapter 60

Jill glanced at the display on her cell phone. Her personal trainer again. He had been calling like crazy since yesterday, but she rejected the call and stuck her hand into the bowl of chips instead. She had just discovered truffle-flavored chips, and nothing was going to come between them and her today, particularly not her overly energetic PT. She couldn't bear to be scolded, pepped up, or judged, not today.

Jill ate whenever she felt blue. She hated those people who lost their appetite and couldn't eat a thing as soon as they felt worried. It was so damn unfair. Those were the same people who uploaded pictures of ice cream and candy to Instagram but who would never eat it. They panicked the minute they tasted fat or sugar. But Jill had clear memories of starving as a child. No, she loved to eat.

Maybe she could work out at home as compensation? There were people who did that kind of thing.

She spread out a blanket on the floor, sat down, put her feet on the couch, and tried to do a halfhearted sit up before she gave in. She balanced the bowl of chips on her stomach instead and continued to eat. She hated being in this kind of mood. Irritable, depressed, negative. She wanted to be positive, but she couldn't. It had nothing to do with Mattias, she told herself as she shoved a fistful of chips into her mouth. It was just as well it was all over between them. They were too different. She thoughtfully chewed the last few crumbs.

It was because of Ambra, she realized.

How could Ambra claim she used her money to control people? It was crazy. She didn't do that.

Right?

Jill wiggled her toes and thought, tried to be as honest with herself as she could. Had she ended things with Mattias because he wouldn't allow her to control him? Had she used what she'd heard during that failed date as an excuse to run from a man who refused to let her decide everything?

Maybe.

If she was going to start thinking about difficult things like that, then chips wouldn't be nearly enough, she decided. With some effort, she got up from the floor and went into the kitchen. From her ultramodern cabinets, she took out tequila, Cointreau, lime, sugar, and ice cubes. She grabbed her chrome cocktail shaker and then made a batch of frozen margaritas. She reached for a glass, moistened the edge with a slice of lime, dipped it in salt, filled the glass to the brim with the slushy mix, and then went back to the couch. She peered around her enormous living room.

This house really was too big for one person, but once you had been poor, you liked expensive things. At least she did. She loved her extravagant house, one of the most expensive in Djursholm. Every now and then she would upload pictures of it to Instagram. She had shared the custom-made white couches, the expensive rugs, the small decorative items, and her insanely luxurious kitchen. Her fans appreciated it, almost demanded it of her. It really was a strange world she worked in. She finished off her drink, went back to the kitchen, refilled her glass, then moved to another part of the house. There were two rooms she never shared publicly, two private rooms that were hers alone. A study with a window looking out onto a lilac tree and a smaller living room full of bright colors that she had decorated herself and never let any designer touch. In that room, she kept a few things from Colombia. There was nothing Colombian anywhere else in the house. She kept that part of her life to herself. This was where she wrote her songs.

She went into her study and sat down at the computer. She needed to work, but she'd found herself hitting a wall. Was she done now? Her eyes fell on a blurry photograph, a snapshot in an expensive frame. It was of her and Ambra when they were teenagers, angry with the world. In a way, they probably still were. Little Ambra, she thought, on the verge of tears. Maybe it was just the margarita talking, but they were so different. Jill was terrified of being dependent on anyone else. The idea that someone else might try to control her was her nightmare scenario. Not having complete power over her own life. But Jill knew Ambra dreamed of belonging, of being part of a team with someone else. It was hard to say which of them was loneliest. She continued to drink, felt her mind start to go numb. Her laptop was open and turned on. Her screensaver was a slideshow of images from Colombia. She moved the mouse, and the pictures were replaced by the desktop. Skype made its familiar bubbling sound. Someone had been trying to get in touch. She clicked the icon.

It was Mattias.

Hmm.

She sipped her drink. Crunched the ice between her teeth. After a long pause, she took the laptop with her into the white living room, needing the security that her impersonal ostentatiousness gave her. She fetched more margarita, sat down, and clicked on his name.

His picture appeared immediately, as if he really had been sitting there waiting for her. "Hi," he said quietly.

She studied the room where he was sitting. Rows and rows of files and books behind him, a tall-backed desk chair.

"Where are you?" she asked.

"At work. How are you doing?"

Jill held up her glass. "The glass is half full, at least."

He laughed. "I'm glad you accepted the call. I wasn't sure whether you wanted to talk to me anymore."

"Mmm-hmm."

"I wanted to apologize for the other night. I'm sorry for . . . well, everything."

"Don't worry," she said, and she really meant it. What did she care about two jealous old hags in a restroom.

"That thing about me ending things after two months . . ." He trailed off.

That didn't matter either. She was, if she was brutally honest with herself, quite similar to him there. Would rather break things off than get tangled up. Even if part of her wouldn't have had too much against getting tangled up with Mattias Ceder. He looked handsome on her screen. Ruffled hair, intelligent eyes, a smart suit. "Listen, we went out only a few times. You don't have to explain anything to me."

He was quiet for a moment and gave her a thoughtful look. "Is that how you see us? Because I feel like I want to get to know you better."

The words made her chest flutter, as if she was at the very top of a roller coaster about to come hurtling down.

She took a sip of her drink and felt her lips sting from the lime juice. Part of her just wanted to hang up.

"I would be open to seeing you again," she said instead, taking the brakes off and allowing the car to go speeding down the tracks.

Her words made Mattias smile, and appealing lines appeared around his eyes. He looked pale and slightly sallow, as if he had spent the past year indoors. She wondered what he would look like with a tan, when he was relaxed. If the sun would bring out the blond in his hair. She smiled.

"When?" he asked. He didn't sound eager exactly, more encouraging. He was already starting to take control. She found that she didn't hate it instantly, though she wasn't entirely convinced.

"You're looking at me now."

"But I want to *see* you. Be with you."

She smiled. Maybe she had half the power here after all. "What would you do if you were here?" she asked, moving a finger along the neckline of her blouse. She slowly undid one of the fabric-covered buttons. Then another. Mattias's eyes didn't leave her for a second. She was drunk but not so intoxicated that she didn't know what she was doing. This was something she wanted to try, something she had never done before. Mattias leaned forward, toward the screen. He seemed to have stopped blinking.

"Want me to continue?" she asked.

He nodded.

"Unbutton your shirt first," she said.

"Why?"

"Because I want to see you," she said, and that was almost the whole truth.

She needed to see whether he trusted her, needed to force him to do something she was sure he had also never done before.

Mattias slowly loosened the tie around his neck. Then he paused.

Jill cocked her head and waited. His hands moved toward the buttons.

"Wait. Take off your tie first. And the jacket."

She watched him pull the tie off over his head, and then drop it and the jacket out of sight. He settled in the chair again. "Happy?"

"Not quite yet," she said, nodding for him to continue.

He undid his shirt, button by button. She caught sight of his chest, covered in dark blond hair, his nipples, that flat stomach. She put down the glass, felt a rush of expectation in her lower belly and the inside of her thighs. How far would he let her boss him around?

"Untuck your shirt from your pants," she ordered, hearing how husky her voice sounded.

Mattias did as she said. His chest was rising and falling.

"Take it off," she said.

He did it without a word. They studied one another from either side of the screen.

"Your turn," he said quietly.

Jill pulled her blouse from her waistband and let it drop down. She stroked her pale brown stomach, her fingers playing on the soft skin. It made no difference how much her PT hounded her, she didn't have a single firm muscle there.

"What's that?" he asked.

She pointed to the glittering piercing in her belly button.

"You like it?" she asked. Maybe he thought it was vulgar.

But he nodded.

Jill would never have done this with anyone else. She had grown up with the Internet and social media, and she knew how quickly things could spread. There were no naked pictures of her anywhere. Plenty of lovers and men who thought they were her boyfriends had wanted to take pictures or shoot films over the years. Plenty of so-called photographers had reassured her they only wanted to take tasteful images (sex-crazed old creeps, all of them). Eager men, promising it was only for their private use. But she had never agreed, never trusted anyone. She wondered whether Mattias realized she was literally putting her career in his hands when she ran her hand over her body in front of the glowing screen. Though maybe he was doing the same? No matter what kind of secrets he worked with, broadcasting live sex from his office probably wouldn't go down too well. The level of trust between them was arousing. And he was handsome, too, of course. Strong and muscular; a warrior dressed up as a bureaucrat. A man, not a boy.

She raised a hand to the lace on her bra, ran her palm back and forth across her entire breast in a soft, circling motion. Then, using three fingers, she concentrated on her nipple. Mattias's eyes didn't leave her for a second, seemed to be saving what he was seeing for later use. She pushed one bra strap down from her shoulder, folded back the cup, and stroked the breast rising out of it, gently and tenderly, taking the time she needed. Mattias leaned toward her, followed her movements. She touched her nipple again, squeezed it gently between her finger and thumb. It was like he was spellbound.

"Could you take off your bra?" he asked.

She paused, but then she reached to unhook the clasp behind her back. It had taken many years of her life for her to become comfortable with her breasts. She accepted that men liked big breasts, even though she couldn't quite understand it. Hers had developed early, and she hated how they'd affected the boys around her, the way they stared, groped, mocked, called her whore and skank. Even now, she occasionally felt slutty, dirty. But not right now. Slowly, she allowed one of her breasts to fall out, then the other. She dropped her bra and sat naked, allowing him to look at her.

"You're so beautiful," he said huskily.

"Is this turning you on?" she asked.

He nodded. "Yeah. A lot."

"Lean back. Touch yourself through your pants."

He did as she said. He was noticeably aroused, sitting with his legs wide apart. His broad chest heaved up and down. She heard a repressed groan, and the sound made her tremble with anticipation. She glanced at his crotch, saw the promising bulge he was stroking.

"Unbutton them," she ordered.

He gave her a hesitant look, and she noticed that caution was fighting his desire. It was one thing to take off his shirt in his office, another to take off his pants. She waited. He obeyed, took off his shoes and socks first, which she appreciated—there were few things less attractive than a man wearing nothing but socks—followed by his pants and his underwear. He sat back down again, hard and aroused. She studied his dick. It was big, slightly bent. His glans glistened against his flat, muscular stomach. Her nipples contracted, and she could feel herself getting wet. She found herself wondering whether his door was locked.

"Touch yourself," she said.

"Jill . . ." He shook his head.

"I will if you will," she said.

His eyes narrowed, and Jill stood up and took off her trousers and her white lace panties. He exhaled. She was waxed clean, other than a small dark strip just above her opening.

"You like it?" she asked once she sat back down on the couch. Men usually did, but she was unsure about Mattias. He wasn't like other men.

"It's beautiful," he said, looking her in the eye. "*You're* beautiful. Can you show me how you like to be touched?"

"You do the same," she said.

A smile tugged at his lips. "I will, I promise. It's just I want to last longer than two seconds."

Jill readjusted her computer, leaned back on the couch, and her hand pressed between her legs. This was madness. But strangely enough, it didn't feel crazy. It felt intimate and exciting. She slowly began to move her fingers, in a circular motion. She liked to masturbate, preferred the control that doing it herself gave her. She liked to have orgasms, and men weren't always reliable on that score.

Mattias watched her intently. She parted her legs slightly and saw him start to satisfy himself, moving his hand up and down.

Her hand was moving more quickly now, completely focused on her own enjoyment. She had masturbated in front of many men, making it a whole performance with groans and nimble fingers. It was a simple way of taking control in a relationship, but this was different; she was focused on her own enjoyment and was genuinely turned on, didn't care what she looked like. Her other hand moved to her breast, and she began to gently massage herself.

Mattias was breathing through his mouth now. His chest was rising and falling more powerfully, and his fist was working increasingly quickly. It was hot to see him approach climax, the way he lost control over himself on the other side of the screen. She kept her eyes fixed on him, and inserted one finger, imagined it was him moving inside her, stretching her, making love to her. She paused for a moment. But she had a brand-new manicure, with short nails, and she wanted to try it. She pulled out her index finger and moved it downward, saw his eyes glued to the movement. She brought it up again, collected some of her own wetness, and rubbed it onto herself. Then she shifted downward slightly and slowly pushed her finger into her ass. Would he be shocked? She moaned gently, touched herself with her other hand, pushing the tip of her index finger carefully in and out as she moved her other hand, quicker and quicker, and then she came in a powerful orgasm. "Oh God," she panted. She could feel it way down in her thighs, through her whole pelvis, in her ass, and deep within her body. Jesus, it felt good. It took her a moment to return to the living room. She opened her eyes and saw Mattias, still hard and unsatisfied, as though he had been waiting for her. His eyes burned. She continued to touch herself, more slowly now, allowed the orgasm to ebb out, trembling from its after effects.

Mattias tugged at himself a few more times, and that was all it took for him to come too. His body tensed, his hand moved frantically, and he came into his hand and onto his stomach. He was handsome when he found release, sexy, like an animal. Her body responded to what she was seeing and she felt a second orgasm approaching, a pleasant encore that spread warmth through her body. Mattias breathed out. Jill slumped back on the couch, pushed her hair from her face, and pulled her legs beneath her. "Good?" she asked.

"Very," he replied hoarsely. "Jesus, Jill, what a damn thing. That was fantastic. How was it for you?"

"It was really good," she replied honestly. Though now she wished he was actually here. It felt a little lonely.

Mattias disappeared from the screen, and when he returned he had wiped himself off and pulled on his pants.

Jill covered herself with a blanket. The tension in Mattias's face was completely gone now, and he seemed much more relaxed. She drank the last of her margarita and felt how relaxed she was too.

"I'd like to come over," he said quietly.

"Here?"

"Yeah."

She paused, but then made up her mind. "Do it then."

*   *   *

Just under an hour later, Mattias stepped out of a cab outside Jill's manor-like luxury villa for the second time. By then he was already aroused again, had spent the entire car trip reliving what they had done together.

She opened the door the minute he knocked. She was wearing a long, loose-fitting dress, but he had no trouble recalling the way she had looked onscreen—naked, curvy, sensual. He would carry that image with him for the rest of his life.

"Hi," she said, and her deep, husky voice was breathless. "Come in." She stepped to one side. Her cheeks were flushed, and she was barefoot. He wrapped an arm around her waist and kissed her, had been longing to touch her and kiss her ever since she'd made him undress and masturbate in front of the computer in his office. His bosses probably wouldn't have appreciated it quite as much as she had. It had been a crazy risk. But she was worth it.

Jill reciprocated his kiss, practically wound herself around him. His hands moved up to her breasts, and she groaned into his mouth. He fumbled behind her, pulled the door closed, kissed her as she backed into the house.

"I need to have you," he said, tugging at her dress. She let him pull it off. She was completely naked beneath it, and he kissed her breasts tenderly. While they continued to kiss, he undressed and dropped his clothes to her luxurious floor. They ended up in the living room, and he spotted the wide, white couch. He pushed her over to it, parted her legs firmly using his knees. She pulled his head toward her, but he resisted, wanted to watch as he entered her. And she let him take over, take control. She raised her knees and he moved between them and slid into her, saw her eyes mist over as he filled her. He made love to her passionately, heatedly, forced her to touch herself the way she had before while he thrust away at her. Her hips moved forward and back, she shouted his name, and then came in a powerful orgasm; a second later he pulled out and came, too, onto her stomach and breasts. She closed her eyes and panted.

He supported himself on shaking arms and realized that he'd made a mess on her. Would she be annoyed?

She opened her eyes. "I love that you let loose," she said. "Kiss me and then go get us margaritas."

He did as he was told, kissed her deeply and then made his way to the kitchen. He grabbed kitchen roll, the cocktail shaker, and glasses. He carefully cleaned her before he poured two cocktails. They toasted.

"Mmm," he said appreciatively after he tried the drink. He reached out for her. She looked so beautiful with shorter hair.

"I'd like to start over," he said as she sat cross-legged, naked, on the white couch. He forced his eyes back up to her face. "I want to act like a normal man who wants to be with a normal woman. No stupid time limits."

"But I'm not normal," she said.

"No?"

"No. I'm a mess. In relationships, with food, completely crazy. I'll probably get fat any day now."

"Okay," he said.

Her eyes narrowed. "You like fat women? I doubt that."

"I wouldn't like you any less if your weight went up."

"And I'm old," she said, looking down. She swirled her glass.

Mattias smiled. "I know exactly how old you are, so you can't use that as a reason."

Jill shook her head. "I'm older than you think. My birth date isn't right. They made a mistake when I came to Sweden, because I was so small that they thought I was younger. I saw the papers when I was eighteen, but I never told anyone. I'm actually thirty. I'll turn thirty-one this year." She whispered the last part. "I never told anyone that before. Not even Ambra knows." She looked away, as if she had just revealed that she made her living selling drugs to kids.

Silence stretched out between them.

"Jill?"

"Yeah?" Her voice sounded stifled, and she still wouldn't look at him.

Mattias took her glass, placed it on the table, and took her in his arms. She pressed her face against his chest, and all he knew was that this felt *right*. "I like you. Your strange life, your secrets, who you are."

She sniffed against his chest. "I'm almost blind, too."

His grip tightened; tenderness almost overwhelmed him. "I know, I saw your glasses."

"Is that how you see me, as a project? You think I have development potential?"

"No. I actually think you're fine as you are."

"We've only known each other a month."

"I know. But I've never felt this way before."

"What do you mean?"

As though he could love her. "Like two months isn't nearly enough. I want to spend more time with you, much more."

"You don't know anything about me."

"I'm looking forward to getting to know you. But I already know some. You're afraid of being abandoned. You hate working out, you love chocolate, and you get sad though you never show it." He took hold of her chin, lifted her face, and kissed her gently.

"I don't think I can love anyone," she mumbled into his mouth.

His nose brushed hers. "You love Ambra."

"Yeah," she agreed. "But we had a terrible argument."

"That's what siblings do," he said. He had two brothers.

She shook her head. "We never fought like that before. She said horrible things to me. But I said terrible things to her, too. What if we never make up?"

"You love one another. You're family." He had seen them together, knew what they meant to one another. Mattias's cell phone suddenly rang.

"I need to see who it is," he apologized. "Technically I'm still on duty." He pulled out his phone and glanced at the screen. "It's Tom. Is it okay if I answer?"

Jill nodded. She liked that he asked for permission, that he cared about her, that he was *here*. While he disappeared, she took out a pack of microwave popcorn and made an entire bowl. Mattias returned with a frown.

"Jill, when did you last hear from Ambra?" he asked. "Tom wants to know," he added.

Tom Lexington, that damn heartbreaker. What did he want with Ambra now? "A few days ago. Why?"

"He doesn't know where she is."

Jill put down the bowl and felt a pang of worry. "Has something happened?"

Mattias pressed the cell phone to his chest, covered the microphone. "He wants to come over."

"Here?" she said in surprise, but then she nodded. Of course he could come if it was about Ambra.

* * *

Thirty minutes later, Jill opened the door for Tom. She had forgotten how big he was. He filled the entire hallway, bringing a chill and snow in with him. He had a frown on his face, but the beard was gone and he looked less scruffy now. Jill was reluctantly forced to admit that she could see why Ambra had fallen for him. Because she had, Jill was suddenly sure of it. Damn it, she should have realized, been kinder to Ambra. What if Ambra had done something stupid? If anything happened to her . . . Jill searched for Mattias's hand and squeezed it tight.

"What do you mean you haven't spoken?" Tom sounded angry.

"Take it easy," Mattias warned him.

Jill smiled. It was cute that he was defending her. Nerdy and unnecessary, but cute.

Tom gave a quick nod. "Sorry, I didn't mean to snap. Do you have any idea where she could be? She isn't at home, she's not at work, isn't answering her cell."

"She said you yelled at her, told her to get lost," Jill couldn't stop herself from saying.

Tom's jaws tensed. "We fought. I overreacted."

Jill already thought he was quite scary when he looked like this, and she couldn't help but wonder what he looked like when he overreacted. But she could also see her brave sister standing up to him.

Suddenly, her protective instincts came to life. Her anger was gone. If this big lump really had broken Ambra's heart, she would never forgive him.

"Doesn't her boss know where she is?" Mattias asked.

"No, Ambra isn't working right now. And she's not at home. Her mail is piled up in the hallway."

"She said something about Kiruna last time we spoke," Jill remembered. "About how that awful foster family had new kids. Do you think she could be up there?"

Tom took a minute to think. "She hates Kiruna. Hates being cold. But maybe. For the sake of those kids. It would be typical of her. I'll call the hotel."

A quick call later, and Tom confirmed it: "She's checked into the Ferrum. She's in Kiruna."

Jill breathed out in relief.

"But she still isn't answering her phone."

"I'll call her," Jill said. Ambra might just be ignoring Tom's calls. But the phone didn't even ring; it went straight to voice mail. Jill sent her a message instead.

Call me. Please!

"That woman she interviewed in Kiruna? Could she know?" Jill suddenly asked. She glanced at her watch; it was almost ten-thirty.

"Elsa Svensson, good idea," Tom said. He found her number using his smartphone.

"Shall I call?" Jill asked, but Tom shook his head and called her from his phone. He did, at least, turn on the loudspeaker.

"Hello?" They heard a bright voice.

"Hi, my name is Tom Lexington. I'm sorry for calling so late."

"Don't worry, I couldn't sleep anyway. Tom, did you say?"

"I wonder if you know where Ambra Vintner is? You know each other?"

"Yes. Ambra is here in Kiruna."

"Have you seen her?"

"Yes." There was a long silence. "But I am actually starting to get worried about the girl. You know, Tom, I've tried calling her, but I can't get through. Yes, I'm very worried now. She went away to talk to her old foster father and now I can't reach her. I don't know what to do."

Jill felt her throat tighten with worry. Tom thanked Elsa and hung up.

"She sounded really worried," said Jill.

"It doesn't have to mean anything," Mattias said, though his voice didn't sound convinced.

Ordinarily, Ambra could look after herself. But she hadn't been her usual self lately. What if everything had come crashing down on her? Jill bit her lip, could feel the sobs burning her throat.

Tom got abruptly to his feet. There was a new darkness in his eyes.

"What are you going to do?" Mattias asked.

"What do you think?" he replied. His voice was rough.

Mattias nodded. "Call me as soon as you know anything."

Tom left them with long strides. Jill stared after him. He was an extremely annoying man. "What's he going to do?"

"He's going to find her."

"In Kiruna? How do you know?"

"Because that's who he is."

"But it's a hell of a long way."

"I guess he already has a plan."

Tom drove to the hangar where the helicopter he occasionally borrowed was kept. He unlocked the building, turned off the alarm, and went inside. Stopped dead. Breathed in the familiar smell of fuel, oil, and metal.

Suddenly, and without warning, it felt as though he were running out of air as his throat tightened and it became difficult to breathe. It was his first attack in weeks. He closed his eyes, forced himself to relax. He didn't have time for anxiety. Not now. He would just have to struggle through it, he thought grimly, pulling off the cover. He studied the sleek, silent machine, took control of his body, forced his muscles to behave. The last time he was in a helicopter, he crashed. The scars from his injuries were still visible. He still woke drenched with sweat after nightmares about a ball of flames stinking of jet fuel.

A bullet had hit the rear rotor blade. By then, his sniper was already dead. The helicopter started to spin, and the crash was violent. In normal circumstances, of course, you didn't just assume someone was dead, you didn't leave your comrades behind. You wanted to take home any bodies. But the scene had been chaotic, and the mission's primary objective was to rescue Isobel, so they made the decision to leave him. He understood their thinking. People usually died in that kind of crash; the fire became explosive. But when the helicopter hit the ground, the seat he was strapped into had been thrown almost fifty meters from the impact site and he'd survived.

There were burns on his hands and face. Both hands were sprained, and he had huge bruises from the four straps of his seat belt. For a long time, he floated between life and death with those criminals, until suddenly they sold him to an even worse group of bandits. But his new captors did, at least, manage to get in touch with Sweden and Lodestar, and demanded a ransom. His insurance had covered the ten million they'd asked for and so he'd been released at last.

He finally managed to bring his breathing under control. Wiped the sweat from his forehead. It wasn't just the PTSD and the panic attacks he'd brought back from Chad. He also found it difficult to fly. Confined spaces were hard; it felt hugely uncomfortable to strap himself in. And the sound of helicopters . . . He shuddered. But he had no other option. It was around 750 miles to Kiruna. The helicopter could manage just over 110 miles per hour, which meant a little over seven hours, including two stops to refuel along the way. Since he was flying at night, he would have to call ahead and ask the refueling stations to open. He would have to pay bribes and keep in contact with air traffic control the whole time. So long as he didn't have another panic attack, he should be there before dawn. The plus side was that he could land by the house and pick up the snowmobile immediately.

He went through his plan once more while he changed into overalls and a thick jacket and pulled on his helmet. He stared at the gleaming machine. Placed his hand on the curved glass. Took a deep breath.

"Well then, now it's just you and me, you beast."

Chapter 61

"I'll report you for threatening a government official!"

The head of social services in Kiruna, Ingemar Borg, was shouting so loudly that Ambra had to hold her cell phone away from her ear.

"I'm not threatening anyone, but you need to check on those kids," she said, trying to stay calm. It was just a simple conversation; she hadn't harassed or threatened him.

But Ingemar Borg didn't even want to talk about the girls. "What's your problem? You're spreading lies about us up here. I'm going to talk to your boss and make sure you lose your job, sue you."

Yeah yeah, tell me something I haven't heard a thousand times before.

"But Uno Aalto is . . ." Ambra began. Then suddenly all she heard was silence on the other end. Ingemar Borg had simply hung up on her.

For a while Ambra thought about calling him back. But Ingemar Borg seemed to be a dead end. She could hardly count on any help from his direction.

She glanced at the time. Jill had called and sent messages last night, but she hadn't had the energy to respond. She loved Jill, but they had so much to straighten out that it would have to wait. Once she was done here, she would talk with her. And Tom, he had called again, though he hadn't left a message. He would have to wait, too, she thought bullishly. She called Elsa instead.

"Everything okay?"

"Yes, my dear," Elsa chirped. "Everything is just fine."

They said good-bye and Ambra shook off the strange feeling that

Elsa was hiding something from her. She impatiently dialed the number for the Kiruna police again, let it ring at least twenty times before she gave up. She doubted they would be particularly helpful either. Their earlier conversations hadn't exactly ended in mutual understanding.

Her fingers drummed the wheel of the car she had rented, and she felt the powerlessness surrounding her. What the hell should she do? She didn't know anyone in Kiruna, other than a bed-bound old lady in the hospital. She drummed a little more, glanced at the snow outside, tried to come up with a plan. Her thoughts turned to calling Tom after all, finding out what he wanted, but she didn't want to risk any more bad news. What if he just wanted to ease his bad conscience? Or even worse, wanted to tell her he was going back to Ellinor after all. No, not now. She needed to solve this thing. But wait . . . Ambra grabbed the wheel when the thought came to her. She sat upright in the seat. Tareq! She did know someone in Kiruna! The freelance photographer, Tareq.

With her eyes on the snowy road, she managed to bring up his number on her phone.

Please, please answer.

"Hello?"

Yes! Ambra bounced with relief in her seat. "Hey, Tareq! It's Ambra Vinter. I'm in Kiruna. Can you help me out with something? It's nothing official, and it might be crazy, but I need pictures. I need your equipment and I need you."

"I agree, it sounds a little crazy. *You* sound a little crazy," he said.

"But you owe me for this because you dumped me at that gay bar. Bring your film camera, too. Send me your address and I'll come get you right now. Pleasepleaseplease."

Tareq laughed. "Woman in need. Not even I can resist that. Give me half an hour."

Ambra managed to find Tareq's house and waited impatiently outside. When he came out, he dumped his equipment in the car, climbed into the front seat, and gave her a quick hug. "So, what're you up to now?"

"There's a Finnish sect leader who's going to carry out an exorcism on two girls being fostered by a religious fanatic. I need pictures."

"Aha, of course," Tareq said, pulling off his gloves and scratching his forehead.

Ambra took off the hand brake and pulled away. She did a U-turn and drove down toward the main road. It was a four-wheel drive Volvo, like the one Tom had—*don't think about Tom now*—powerful as a wild animal and a pure joy to drive. "Thanks for helping me out."

"It sounded too exciting not to, plus I have nothing booked today. Is this through *Aftonbladet?*"

"I wouldn't say that," she replied, thinking that there was a real risk she wouldn't even have a job to go back to if this went wrong.

"Understood," Tareq said, sounding completely unfazed.

"Sorry if I put pressure on you before."

"No, it'll be an adventure. But tell me everything now."

And so Ambra gave him a broad outline of the foster children, crazy sects, and Finnish exorcists. Tareq shook his head and said Jesus Christ over and over again.

After driving for ten minutes, she managed to find the right exit and turned off onto a smaller road.

They pulled up some distance away from the house. Ambra turned off the motor, and everything went dark.

"What do we do now?" Tareq asked as he took pictures through the windshield like a regular private detective.

"Wait, I guess." She stared at the dark house, wished that she knew how to do this kind of thing. But she wasn't going to leave here without saving those girls and getting evidence of what was going on. They wouldn't be abandoned. She would do for them what no one had done for her.

"A car's coming," Tareq whispered. His camera clicked away quietly.

"I can see," Ambra whispered back. The car stopped outside the house, and Uno Aalto stepped out.

"That's him, the exorcist."

"Ugh, God, what a creep," Tareq said quietly.

Ambra nodded. His full support was a huge comfort. "Thanks for believing me," she whispered.

"Of course. There are crazies like that everywhere. If you knew how many times my mom was told to take me to a mullah to drive out the homosexuality in me."

"Shit."

"I know. Fanaticism is depressingly similar across religious lines."

Tareq took a series of images as they watched Uno knock on the front door. The house had been in complete darkness, but a flickering light suddenly appeared in one of the windows, just as Esaias Sventin opened the door. There was also a shadow in the window, just behind the faint glow. It could be Rakel.

"Someone else is coming," Tareq whispered as the noise of a loud engine approached. A snowmobile pulled up, and two more men entered the house.

"What do you think they'll do to the girls?" Tareq asked with a concerned look. "I mean specifically."

Ambra had read everything she could find about exorcisms. And she had been subject to Esaias's rage herself. "In many cases, it's about praying for the 'afflicted' one. There are clips on YouTube. The exorcists scream at the possessed person, wave the Bible in the air, hit the victim, hold them down. It's often young women who need to be 'controlled.' But there are cases where people have died after the spirits have been 'driven out,' as they put it."

"Not recently, though?" Tareq's handsome face was pale.

"Yeah, sadly. Small children abused until they die while exorcists try to drive out the devil."

"My God."

"It's so awful, because it often happens over a long period of time. And no one steps in. There are several cases where young women have been starved and beaten for months because their families thought they were possessed and that it was the only way to cure them. It happens in the name of some kind of twisted love."

Tareq looked like he was going to be sick, but Ambra continued. She had spent the last few weeks reading, taking in everything. "One woman was found to have severe epilepsy during her autopsy. That produced the symptoms that the preachers and family interpreted as evil spirits. The woman starved and froze to death after months of abuse in her own home."

"Jesus."

"Yeah. And this all happened recently. There's a long list of cases, and those are just the ones we know about. Like I said, it's depressing."

"We should call the police," said Tareq.

"We need evidence. Plus, I did call them. Several times." She added that last part guiltily.

Tareq grinned at her. "Are they sick of you?"

"A little."

He raised the camera again and pointed it at the house. It clicked away. "Then you and I need to go see what evidence we can get."

Ambra nodded and looked out the window. There were moments in life that defined who you really were as a person. Moments that forced you to choose what kind of person you wanted to be.

And as she sat there in the warm Volvo on the edge of Kiruna, a memory came back to her.

She was four years old, standing between her mother and father. One hand in her mother's warm grip, and one in her father's secure palm, with a wildly happy feeling in her chest.

They were outdoors, standing by an especially fun-looking playground. The sand looked soft and smooth, and there were yellow buckets and blue spades dotted around. There was a red slide and a set of shining swings, and it was full of laughing children.

"Want to go down, my love?" her father asked, nodding toward the red slide. His voice was happiness and laughter and promises of ice cream in the sunshine.

Ambra nodded, and then she began to slide, quickly, with a giddy feeling in her stomach and bubbling laughter in her throat. He caught her just as she reached the bottom and lifted her up in the air.

"Where's Mommy?" she asked, wrapping her arms around his neck.

Her father carried her to a bench where her mom was sitting with a girl who'd hurt herself.

"Where are her mommy and daddy?" Ambra asked.

"We'll try to find them, but until then we'll wait here. A sad child is everyone's responsibility."

And Ambra nodded, because she really did understand. And she'd felt proud of her parents for helping other children.

Ambra didn't remember what happened after that. But she did remember what her parents had impressed on her, as early as they could. That it was a person's duty to stand up for those who needed help.

"We need better pictures," Tareq said.

"Yeah," she agreed. "They're probably in the basement."

They climbed out of the car and crept over toward the house. "Man, it's cold," Tareq whispered. Ambra agreed. The temperature had dropped quickly. They moved around the snow-covered building. It was deathly quiet, and she felt a sudden hesitation. What if this whole circus she had started was just a hysterical overreaction? It could just as easily be an innocent gathering of old men going on in there.

"If they're in the basement, there should be a window around here that we can look in," she said, trying to remember where. Her eyes swept along the edge of the house. There was so much snow. "Here, I think," she said, dropping to her knees and starting to dig. Tareq helped her.

"Look, a window," she whispered. She gently dug her way down to the windowpane. It seemed to be covered with some kind of dark fabric, but they could make out a faint light through it.

"I can't see a thing," Tareq whispered just as they heard a loud scream from inside. "Do you think that's them?" he asked.

"Don't know. But it did sound like a kid."

Yet another scream.

"Tareq, you have to take pictures, no matter what happens. That's your main job. As many pictures as you can."

"What are you going to do?"

She knew what she had to do, just hoped she had the nerve. "I'm going to try to get in."

"You don't want me to follow you?" he protested.

"No," she said firmly. If anyone was going to break the law and end up in trouble, it would be her, not Tareq. "I'll try to get rid of the fabric so you can see in."

"Be careful," he whispered as she rounded the corner.

Ambra took hold of the handle and pressed it down. The door swung open, and after she took a deep breath, filling her lungs with air and courage, she stepped over the threshold.

The house looked just like before. The walls, the simple pictures, the furniture. She had to stop. She'd forgotten the smells, the everyday scent of food, bodies, textiles, all of which threw her back to that time. She heard a creaking sound and almost jumped out of her skin. Technically, she was breaking and entering.

She crept on, toward the basement. She was so afraid that she took a wrong turn at first, went left instead of right, started to sweat, thought she heard another sound, stopped, could barely hear anything but her heartbeat. Breathlessly, and with a thousand thoughts racing through her head, she waited, but after a moment she realized it was just the house creaking and sighing, and she moved on. Eventually, she found the door to the basement. As carefully as she could, she went down the stairs, remembering how afraid she had been of it, its dark wood, slippery steps. It smelled like sawdust and untreated wood, and oil from the lamp. She heard mumbled men's voices through the door at the very back, approached it, stopped, so damn afraid. They were there, on the other side. She bent down. There was no key in the lock, and she peered through the keyhole.

She could see the men and the two girls. Clenched men's fists and thin children's arms.

"In the name of Christ, I command you to come out." The voice belonged to Uno Aalto.

He pressed a cross to the girl's forehead. She was crying silently. The other girl started to scream. Esaias raised his Bible in the air and brought it down on her head. The other men were making faint sounds, as though they were saying mass.

Ambra didn't want to remember, but she couldn't prevent the memories of her own torment from washing over her. Abuse with the Bible, the hitting, the beatings with the belt. The total power Esaias held over her. She breathed in, breathed out. Focus on the here and now. Not on then. With shaking hands, she fumbled for her phone, had to try to take pictures.

"Hello?"

The voice came from behind her, and it gave Ambra such a shock that she dropped her cell phone, which clattered to the ground. She turned around and stared at the gray-haired woman who had snuck up behind her without a sound. It was Rakel Sventin.

"Who are you? What are you doing here?" Rakel asked.

Ambra tried to bend down to grab her phone, but Rakel moved closer and she quickly stood up again.

"How did you get in? What are you doing here?"

"I'm here for the girls' sake."

"Yes, those poor things. I hope we'll succeed. The devil is strong in them."

Ambra wanted to grab Rakel by the arms, shake her. "They're children. Don't you realize what you're doing to them?"

Rakel pulled her cardigan tight around her. A stubborn glimmer appeared in her eyes. Ambra remembered it well. Once Rakel made up her mind about something, she wouldn't change it again, whether that meant forcing foster children to eat rancid blood pudding or believing that someone was possessed. "It's for their own good. For the sake of their souls."

Before Ambra had time to say anything else, she heard another scream from inside the room.

"Rakel, we have to help them."

For a second, Rakel looked doubtful, but then something went out in her eyes. "No," she said abruptly, moving past her and opening the door into the room. She gave Ambra a push, and Ambra fell into the room. The smell of fear lay heavy in the air.

"Who is this?" Uno Aalto asked.

"She was sneaking around down here."

Part of Ambra just wanted to run away. But she could see the hope in the terrified girls' eyes and knew she couldn't leave them behind. She tried to appear as authoritative as she could.

"I've come for the girls," she said, looking at them both, trying to communicate with her eyes that she was on their side, that she could save them from the four men now spread out around the room. She sensed Rakel was somewhere behind her, but she didn't dare turn around. "I'm not alone," she warned.

The men were getting closer.

"Tareq!" she shouted, looking up at the window, wondering whether he was out there, whether he heard her.

Esaias gestured toward the door with his head. "Rakel, out."

The others started to move toward the door, and she tried to work out what they had planned. The room was full of candles, and when Esaias turned his back to her and closed the door, one candle fell to a rug, which caught fire. He was the last to leave the room and had closed the door behind him.

Ambra quickly stamped on the rug and managed to put out the fire. "Don't worry," she reassured the girls. "It's not on fire anymore."

She heard Esaias lock the door from the outside. That damn man. He was completely crazy. What was he hoping to achieve by that?

"My friend is out there. He'll let us out. It'll be okay. My name is Ambra." She smiled at the girls, who stared at her with terrified eyes.

"Let's see," she said, pulling out a box from one corner. She placed it beneath the window and pulled down the fabric. The window was built into the wall and couldn't be opened. She pounded on the glass. "Tareq! Are you there?"

Had Tareq called the police? And if so, had he managed to get through? She banged on the glass again. Tareq's face suddenly appeared on the other side.

She almost laughed with relief. Everything would be fine. "I have the girls here. We're locked in."

"Ambra, it looks like there's smoke coming from the house. Can you get out? You need to hurry."

Ambra felt a rush of fear.

"No, we're locked in." She turned around and saw the girls' terrified faces. "Don't worry," she said firmly. They would fix this.

"I'm coming in," Tareq shouted. He disappeared, and a minute later she heard him pulling at the handle and banging on the door. "The others have left—we're the only ones here," he yelled.

"Is it still on fire?"

"I tried to put it out, but it spread too quickly. Could the guy have set fire to his own house? Why would he do that?"

To kill the demons. Because he hated her. Because he'd panicked.

"You need to get out. Now!" Tareq yelled.

"Can you see a key anywhere?" Ambra asked

There was a long silence. "No! Shit, what are we going to do?"

"The window," Ambra said. "Smash the window."

Tareq disappeared outside again.

"We'll be okay," Ambra said, praying it was true. Tareq's face reappeared on the other side of the glass. He was out of breath, sweating. She met his eye and felt the panic grow in her stomach.

"Get back," he yelled. A moment later, he kicked in the window. Shards of glass rained down across the floor. Ice-cold air rushed in.

"You need to get out, quick!"

He pulled out the girls, one by one. Lifted their too-thin bodies through the hole, heard them whimper as the glass cut them.

"Come on, Ambra," he shouted. But there was no way; she had known it all along. The window was too narrow for her.

"The fire department is on the way," he said.

"Where's the fire?

"A couch, I think. It's smoky as hell. But they'll be here soon."

"Yeah. I need to do something, see whether there's anything I can use to get out. Tareq, promise me you won't come in. The smoke is dangerous. Promise me."

"What the hell, Ambra!"

"Promise me."

"I promise."

"And will you tell Jill I love her? That I know she loves me." Jill had to know that.

"Ambra, don't give up. The fire department is coming. They'll get you out."

Right then, they heard an explosion. The heat caused the windows to crack. Fresh oxygen would fuel the fire.

She hadn't given up, but panic made her voice tremble. "How are the girls?"

"They're fine. How is it going? Did you find anything?"

She looked around the terrible, familiar room. How was it possible that she was locked up here again, in this basement she hated so much?

Her eyes scanned the rough shelves. It couldn't be true. But she couldn't see a thing, absolutely nothing to open a door with. She ripped open a cardboard box, but there was nothing but old papers inside it. Was she really about to die? Was this it? At least she had saved the girls. But she had wanted to do more, be more. *I don't want to die.*

She should have told Tareq to tell Tom she loved him. If she hadn't dropped her phone out there, she would have sent messages herself. To Tom. To Jill. And to Elsa. Maybe even to Grace. But there was no one else. How fucking tragic. She heard a hysterical snort and realized it had come from her.

She spotted a small box in one corner, covered in dust, damaged on one corner. It seemed so familiar. She took a closer look. Could it really be? The box she had put all of Mom and Dad's things into? Esaias had told her it was gone, but he must have stolen it, kept it for himself, and now it was here.

She opened it and studied the treasures inside. Saw her parents' faces in old pictures. Stroked their wedding rings and the velvet pouch with . . . And then she recognized the little case. Dad's case, containing the antique watchmaking tools. She opened it. Inside, there was a small knife and a set of tiny screwdrivers. She grabbed the longest of them and stuck it into the lock, coughed, tried to pick it open, the sweat running down between her eyes. She screamed in frustration, took a deep breath, and heard the lock click open. But as she opened the door she realized her mistake. Smoke was curling into the room. As she pushed it shut again, she felt her field of vision blur at the edges, and then she collapsed with the box beneath her.

Chapter 62

Tom had got the address of the house Ambra had gone to from Elsa. He'd landed the helicopter in the snow, grabbed the snowmobile, and set off. Could he smell smoke?

He accelerated as hard as he could, stood up, followed the ups and downs of the terrain as he approached the house. He heard the sirens the moment he turned off the motor, far, far in the distance.

He recognized the waving, sooty figure meeting him as Tareq, who seemed to have aged ten years. There were two filthy, blood-covered girls standing behind him. Tom glanced around.

"Where's Ambra?" he asked, hoping against hope that she had never come here. But of course she had.

Tareq shook his head; his face seemed frozen. "She's stuck inside. Locked in the basement. I haven't heard anything from her for a few minutes, and it's pitch black." He shook his head.

Tom looked over to the house. Smoke was pouring out of the cracked windows.

"Where?" was all he asked.

"A room in the basement. I really tried. But the door was locked, and we couldn't get it open. She was going to try again, but then she just disappeared. I shouted, but nothing. The fire department is on the way." He covered his face with his hand.

Tom ran back to the snowmobile and tore a blanket from his bag. He rushed off toward the house.

"You can't go in!" Tareq shouted.

But for Tom there was no choice.

It was something his father used to say. He was full of sayings and quotes, had one for every occasion. Usually, Tom didn't listen. But he remembered the very last time they saw one another, the way they sat drinking beer together. His father had probably had a little too much to drink. "Tom, when you want something you've never had before, you must do something you've never done before to get it. And if you're not willing to risk everything you have for it, maybe you just don't want it enough. You understand?"

Tom looked at the burning house. The question was: What was he willing to risk for Ambra?

And the answer was easy.

Everything.

And so he pulled the blanket over his head and pressed it to his mouth. He hunched down in the compact darkness. "Ambra!"

No reply. The smoke was filling the house, and so he crouched as he ran. He wouldn't leave without her—it was that simple. And as though by a miracle, he found the staircase leading down to the basement. He practically flew down the steps, could feel the smoke following him like a snaking, black monster. He held his breath. Tareq had said it was the very end room, so he ran over and found the locked door.

"Ambra!" he shouted, though he didn't expect an answer. His throat and eyes were stinging. It was a matter of seconds now. He pushed the door. It was no longer locked, but something was blocking it, and he realized it was Ambra. He bent down, placed the blanket over her unconscious body, picked her up, and ran back up the stairs with her in his arms. His lungs were burning. Finally, he was outside. He dropped to his knees, let go of her, and collapsed flat out, onto his back. Just lay there for a few seconds, filling his lungs with air. Jesus, he'd made it. During all his years as an operative, he'd never done anything even half as crazy as that. You didn't go into a fire. Ever. But he had made it. Jesus Christ. He started to laugh and then coughed so hard that he threw up. On the ground next to him, Ambra began to cough, too. She had a couple of scratches on her face, and she was covered in soot, but she was alive. It was a miracle.

He turned his head to her.

"Tom?" she croaked, and it was the best sound he'd ever heard. "What are you doing here?" she said with a cough.

"Do you know where you are?" he asked as he got to his knees and pushed the hair from her sooty brow.

"Kiruna. There was a fire. The girls?"

"They're fine."

"But you're here? Why?"

"You didn't answer the phone. People were worried."

"People? Who?"

He stroked her forehead, couldn't stop smiling. She was alive. The relief he felt was like a drug; he was lightheaded and wanted to laugh. "Your sister. And Elsa. She said you were coming out here. She was worried about you. I was worried."

"Did you just save my life again?"

He nodded. "I flew up from Stockholm. Because Elsa seemed so worried."

"Wow. Lucky for me." She rubbed her nose with her hand. The Northern Lights flickered above.

"Lucky for *me*. Ambra, I lov . . ."

But he was interrupted when Ambra caught sight of Tareq. She started to wave and point. "Take pictures!" she screamed. "Tareq—pictures!"

The moment had passed, but Tom was relieved that Ambra was back to her usual self. He helped her up. The fire had taken on an explosive nature, and Tom found himself thinking that it was as if hell itself had opened up. Maybe that was fitting.

The area around the house was filling up with fire trucks, ambulances, and police cars. "Come on," he said, taking her under the arm, supporting her. "I want them to check you out, make sure you're okay."

"I'm fine," she protested with her smoke-damaged voice.

"Do it for me," he pleaded, and she nodded.

They moved over to the ambulance, where the girls had already been cleaned up. Ambra sat down next to them, and Tom watched while a paramedic shone a light into her eyes, took her blood pressure, and listened to her lungs; they also gave her oxygen. He declined to be examined, felt more alive than he had in a long time, but he took the oxygen.

"Why aren't they putting the fire out?" Ambra asked, nodding toward the firefighters, who were just watching the flames.

"They can't. It's so cold that the water freezes in the hose. They'll let it burn to the ground."

"Just as well," said Ambra.

A black car was approaching. It squealed to a stop, and a woman threw herself out. It looked like she was wearing pajamas beneath her coat.

"Lotta," Ambra said grimly. She wrapped her arms around the girls' shoulders, pulled them toward her protectively.

"I came as soon as I heard," Lotta panted.

Ambra's eyes narrowed. She looked like a tigress whose cubs were being threatened. "I have proof. You'll need to find new homes for them now." The girls pressed against her.

"I have an even better solution. I found their mom. She's healthy now, and desperate to meet them," Lotta said, and her voice broke toward the end. "So much abuse has happened here. How did we miss it? I'll have to write up a full report. But first, the girls need to be with their mom." She looked Ambra straight in the eye. "Thank you. And I'm so sorry for doubting you. I swear, on everything I hold dear, I'll fix this."

She sounded genuine.

"I'm going to write about this," Ambra said, and there was a warning in her voice.

Tom couldn't help it; he smiled. Ambra was magnificent when she was fighting for those who couldn't fight for themselves.

"Do it," said Lotta. "I'll give a statement."

"With your name?"

"With whatever you want."

"They've suffered enough," said Ambra.

"I agree."

Ambra gave the social worker one last skeptical look. Tom studied the woman whose life he had saved twice. There was nothing he wouldn't do for her; he had literally walked through fire for her. Someone up there clearly thought he deserved her. Now he just hoped they would have the rest of their lives together so he could prove it.

Chapter 63

Ambra was inside the *Aftonbladet* newsroom, standing in front of the online editor's desk. Adrenaline was pumping through her veins.

"Ready?" Grace asked from beside her.

Goose bumps started to appear on Ambra's arms. She must have published thousands of articles since she'd first begun working as a reporter, but this was different.

This was big.

Ambra had been working practically nonstop since the fire, started writing while she was still in Kiruna. There were a couple of scrapes on her forehead, and she was aching all over, but she was otherwise unhurt. A stinging throat and painful lungs, but that was all. As soon as she was done answering the police officers' questions, she sat down and wrote all night. Talked more with the girls—whose names were Siri and Simone—and spoke on the phone with their mom. Then she left for Stockholm. She'd had a total of four hours' sleep over the past few days, had produced several shorter pieces while she worked on her larger article. But she wasn't tired; she was high on excitement and endorphins.

"Then let's hit Send," Grace said, giving the online editor a nod. A second later, and her piece was on the home page. At the same time, a flash update was sent to every news agency in the world, to every TV station and news office in Sweden. To readers' cell phones and computers.

Click, click, click.

They stood in silence for a few seconds. Enjoying the moment. It was, without doubt, the best thing Ambra had ever written. When she'd really started digging into the case, she found a huge number of abuses in the social services system. Children and parents who had been systematically kept apart, children who had suffered, lived in misery, and been abused. It was an important scoop, a story with a fantastic amount of drama. The two defenseless girls who'd suffered so terribly at the hands of social services. The bizarre exorcisms. The terrible conditions living with the Sventin family, stretching way back in time. The head of social services resigned. And then there was the interview with the girls' biological mother, the reunion, the happy ending. It was the best kind of investigative journalism, the kind that would change lives and laws.

Ambra and Grace looked at each other, sharing the sense of having done something important. Ambra felt ready to pass out from lack of sleep. She was wound up and needed a shower. But she was also proud. Grace gave her a nod of confirmation. For a second, Ambra felt invincible.

And then everything returned to normal. It was a newsroom, after all: The news continued to pour in, day in and day out. Grace disappeared, and Ambra started on the next piece in the series, which they had titled:

AFTONBLADET REVEALS: SECT'S EXORCISM OF SWEDISH CHILDREN

Her cell phone buzzed, and when she looked down, she saw it was a message from Elsa.

On the way back from the hospital. Everything fine. Will read your article soon. So proud of you.

Ambra sent a heart in reply. She felt morally obliged to be annoyed that Elsa had deliberately lied for Tom, but it was no good. If he hadn't flown up to Kiruna, she wouldn't be standing here today.

She hadn't managed to talk properly with him since he'd saved her from the burning house, just exchanged a few quick messages, and it felt incredibly frustrating.

Back in Kiruna, she'd interrupted him just as he was about to say . . . something. She felt like hitting herself in the head. In that moment when she'd shouted to Tareq, she realized what it was he was about to say. But then it was too late, and she couldn't exactly ask, So, it sounded like you were about to say you loved me, is that right? Maybe it was just something he wanted to say in the heat of the moment. She was a coward and felt ashamed of it. But rather a coward than rejected.

She opened her e-mails, scanned through them. There were a number of messages from critical readers, but in general it was praise that was pouring in. One e-mail was from Lord_Brutal900. She paused, but then decided to open it:

> *Read your article. It was very good. I'm sorry for everything I put you through. I've been disgusting. It'll never happen again. Sorry.*

She read through the message twice, but it still didn't make any sense. She looked up, and Grace caught her eye.

"Did you hear that Dan Persson wants to talk to you?" she shouted.

"Why?" Being called in to see the big boss was never good.

But Grace simply shrugged and turned away.

Ambra closed the strange e-mail and started to make her way toward Dan Persson's corner office, her feet dragging beneath her. But she was proud of what she had done. If he wanted to cut her down, then she would leave with her head held high. She determinedly knocked on the pane of glass.

"Come in!"

Ambra forced herself to keep a nonchalant expression and opened the door to the luxurious office she had been inside exactly once before.

Dan Persson waved for her to sit down while he continued talking with someone on the phone.

"You've been busy," he said when he hung up.

"Yeah," she replied. Was it meant as praise or criticism? But there was nothing to criticize. Her reports were faultless. Strong. Full of pathos. A battle between the little man and the state. The perfect piece. She was about to start bouncing her foot when she stopped herself and sat up straight. *Leave with your head held high.*

"Grace wants to run it over several days," he continued.

"Yeah."

Dan leaned back in his chair and brought his fingers into a triangle. "I don't know if you heard, but we'll have a free position on Investigative."

She twisted in her seat. What was he doing? Was he messing with her?

"I heard," she replied neutrally.

"I spoke with the editor. We're in agreement. The position is yours, if you want it. You should be proud of yourself. It's people like you *Aftonbladet* wants to champion."

"Not Oliver Holm?" she blurted out before she had time to stop herself.

Dan looked confused. "No, he was never in the running, as far as I know."

He took out a flat plastic package and pressed out a piece of square gum. "Nicotine gum," he explained, putting it in his mouth. "I stopped smoking; it's a disgusting habit. Ah yes, I thought we should arrange a meeting for a long-term plan, too. We want to keep you here at *Aftonbladet,* not lose one of our star reporters to a competitor. So we need to talk wages, future, and development. How does that sound?"

"That sounds great."

"Perfect. My secretary will book you. I like this. I want more women on our site. These are new times we live in, and the paper needs to reflect that. Writing more about breast cancer and women being harassed. You know. More feminism." Ambra considered it such a personal victory that she managed not to snort at his words.

When Ambra left Dan's office a while later, she smiled all the way back to her desk. Grace looked up. "Good meeting?"

"Perfectly fine," Ambra replied breezily.

"Good, but now we need to work. The phones are going crazy."

"Because of my article?"

"Oh yes. Because of that. Let's go."

By three that afternoon, Ambra managed to make it to the bathroom for the first time. She took her cell phone with her and checked Jill's Instagram account. Her sister was performing in Norway. Ambra wrote a comment beneath the latest picture and added a heart. She waited.

Her phone started to ring. "I'm sorry," said Jill.

"Me too. Can you forgive me?"

"Of course, but listen, I just snuck off in the middle of something, I need to get back. Thanks for writing."

"Thanks for calling."

Ambra remained where she was on the toilet. Everything was fine between them. This was completely new. The idea they could fight, say unkind things to one another, and then reconcile. Maybe other people learned that kind of thing automatically, knew that it was human to be stupid and that forgiveness was possible, but for her it was completely revolutionary. For Jill, too, in all likelihood. She washed her hands and headed back to her desk.

At six that evening, Ambra noticed that Grace was looking at her with a thoughtful expression. When the clock struck quarter past seven, Grace said, "You finished fifteen minutes ago. Time to go home."

"But . . ." Ambra didn't want to go home, and Grace didn't normally have anything against her working overtime. This time, however, Grace's expression was firm.

"That's an order. Go."

As Ambra took the elevator downstairs, she realized how tired she was. She avoided looking in the mirror, knew she had huge dark circles beneath her eyes, that she was dehydrated and slightly manic from too much coffee and too little—well, too little of everything else. She zipped up her coat and clutched the bag containing her laptop against her side.

A few of the cool guys were standing outside. They were smoking in the cold air and seemed lost now that the leader of their flock had abandoned them. Ambra walked past them and allowed herself a malicious inner laugh. She had beaten them all. With a report about women and children. And she had bagged herself the most exciting position at the entire paper. Hooray for Ambra Vinter. She just wished she had someone to celebrate with.

"Hi there."

Ambra stopped dead at that low, familiar voice. She wondered if she had been working so much and sleeping so little that she was now hallucinating.

But it was him.

Tom.

He was standing there. In front of her. Here, in Stockholm. And doing that thing he always did. Looking fantastic. Huge and dressed in black, overwhelming and present.

They stared at one another.

"Hi," she eventually said, wondering if she sounded quite as breathless as she thought. "I didn't know you were in Stockholm."

"Do you have time to talk?" he asked.

"How did you know when I finished?" she asked, but then she realized: "Grace?"

"Yeah."

"You could have called. Sent a message."

He shrugged in reply. He was probably standing a meter away from her, yet Ambra still felt as if he was against her, inside her. His warm skin, the scent of him. The rough black hair beneath her fingers, his stubble on her cheek. What did he want? To talk? What did that mean?

Tom raised his hand, held up a car key. "I have the car here. Is that okay?"

She nodded, and he opened the door for her. Their coats rustled against one another as she moved past him, and Ambra closed her eyes, breathed in his familiar scent before she sat down in the passenger seat. He walked around the car, started the engine, and pulled away.

"Where are we going?" she asked as he drove toward Kungsholmen. She was far too tired for a serious conversation, too unshowered and too overworked. And he was so quiet, so lost in himself. "Tom, I . . ."

"To my place," was all he said. Ambra looked out the window, couldn't think of anything else to say.

He parked, walked around the car, and opened the door for her again. She followed him in through a doorway and into an elevator. They went high, high up. The air in the small elevator was so heavy, so saturated, that she found it hard to breathe. Tom reached out to her, and the air practically sparked as she leaned forward. And then the elevator stopped and his hand dropped.

He stepped to one side and let her go first, and it felt like he inhaled as she passed. She couldn't wrap her head around the strange atmosphere.

He unlocked the front door, where she saw a nameplate reading Lexington, took her coat and hung it up, walked ahead of her, and said, "This is the living room."

"Ohh," she said when she spotted the windows. She walked over to them while he moved around the room lighting candles in huge holders. The windows were tall, with low ledges. No plants, no drapes, the decor was fairly minimal. But it wasn't cold, just restrained and masculine, exactly like Tom. And the view out onto the canal and Karlberg Castle, the city in the distance, with all its glittering lights, was so pretty.

She turned around. "It's so nice," she said, wondering whether he used to live here with Ellinor. Somehow, it didn't feel like it. There was nothing feminine about the place. The apartment felt like it was Tom's and Tom's alone. Shelves of books, big, modern furniture, pillows, and throws that looked brand new. She sniffed the air. "Something smells fantastic," she said, feeling her stomach rumble.

"I thought you might be hungry. It's almost ready," he said. There was a high counter at one end of the living room, and she could make out a kitchen behind it. Tom disappeared behind the counter, opened an enormous refrigerator, and returned with an ice-cold beer. Their fingers brushed when he handed it to her. She took the beer. Didn't want to start feeling hopeful. But what if . . . This was what it could be like to have someone in your life, a man like Tom. Someone to come home to, who made food for you, who lit candles and handed you beers. These were dangerous fantasies, wanting to be important to someone. He seemed so serious, and she had no idea what he was thinking or feeling. She raised the bottle of beer to her lips and took a swig. No matter what happened tonight, she would remember the good parts. And remind herself that she was a competent working woman, a hell of a journalist. That she could survive anything. She wiped her mouth with the back of her hand.

"I've been thinking these past few days. About us," he began.

She nodded, drank more beer, both did and didn't want to hear what he had to say.

He scratched his chin, and his stubble bristled quietly. "Lately . . . These months after Chad, in Kiruna, everything with Ellinor—it's been . . . I don't know what to say. It's been a lot to deal with." He trailed off.

"Yeah," she agreed as a cool sensation started to spread through her. Tom's serious voice, those impenetrable eyes. This didn't bode well. It was so stupid of her to come here, to allow herself all these hopes and expectations. She took another swig of beer, thought that he should have just sent her a message instead.

"Ambra, I'm sorry if I hurt you. I know I did."

"I guess we hurt each other," she said, happy she sounded so calm, so cool. She was. Cool Ambra Vinter. She took another swig of her drink. It was low-alcohol beer. She couldn't even get drunk.

"But I'm actually pleased Ellinor turned up like she did," he said.

Well, how nice for you.

Tom continued. "I was so afraid of my feelings, repressed them for so long. After Chad, yes, but even before that. And when I met you, Ambra, so many feelings came to the surface. I couldn't control them, and that scared me. I thought it was a sign I wasn't doing so well, that I *felt* so much. That such strong feelings were a sign it couldn't be real."

"You don't need to explain."

"But I *want* to. I need to say this. Nothing happened between Ellinor and me—I want to say that, first of all."

"No?" She wanted to believe him, but . . .

Tom shook his head, firmly. "No. Nothing. It's over, and it has been for a long time. I don't want Ellinor. I want you. Only you. I think I have since the first time I saw you."

"Really?" she asked skeptically, remembering their first meeting.

Tom grinned. "Maybe the second or third time then. But I never felt like this before. It sounds so cliché, so insufficient. But I've fallen for you so damn hard. I didn't even know it was possible to feel this way. It's so different from anything I ever experienced before, so it took me a while to figure things out."

Her stupid, illogical heart began to pound in her chest. "And have you? Figured things out?" she asked.

"Yeah. You're right. I've been self-righteous. Mattias called me that and said I tend to bear a grudge. But I want to be better. I'd like to keep seeing you. To be together."

She drank more of her beer. Breathed, tried to think.

"Ambra? Say something."

She looked straight at him. Stood tall, met his eye. This was the decisive moment. "I have something I need to say to you, too."

A shadow crossed his face. "Okay."

She readied herself. And then she took the leap. "I love you," she said. It might have sounded stiff and polite. But the words were foreign to her. She hadn't said them to anyone before. Ever. She and Jill never used those words, and there had never been anyone else she cared about.

She would get better at it, she decided. Being brave, not just at work but also in her private life. Daring to show love, to expose herself, to wear her heart on her sleeve and keep it there.

"I love you, Tom," she repeated, and the strange thing was that it felt good to say it. It was how she felt and she wanted to shout it out. In a sense, she was no longer free. She loved him, and he had her trapped like that. "Regardless of what you feel and what happens next, that's that."

Tom Lexington, the man who so rarely smiled, broke into an enormous grin. "That's good," he said. "Because I love you."

Her heart leaped with joy. "I thought I'd ruined everything. With that awful article."

"No, I already loved you by then."

"Maybe you aren't so self-righteous after all."

"So long as I'm good enough for you, I'm happy."

"You are."

He took a step toward her, and their lips met softly.

"Ambra," he said, and then he kissed her neck, her forehead, her nose.

"Yeah?"

"I love you." He slowly undid the top button on her blouse, kissed her neck, unbuttoned another, placed his palm on her skin. They undressed one another, one item of clothing at a time. They were in no rush; kissing and caressing each other as they did it, but eventually they were left facing one another, naked. There was a new gravity between them now that the words had been said. Her hands moved across his chest. Unlike her, there was almost no trace of the fire on his body.

He looked at her with concern.

"It's not as bad as it looks," she mumbled, aware that she was covered in both bruises and scrapes.

"I'm so sorry," he said quietly.

"It's not your fault, and I'm fine, I swear. Kiss me instead." She gently took his head in her hands and pulled him toward her. She pressed herself against the hand cupping her breast, slowly rubbed her nipple against his hot, rough palm. She panted when his hand moved down, between her thighs, as a finger found its way in. She moaned quietly, backed up until her shoulder blades were against the wall, and she pressed herself against his hand. Another finger, and he was kissing her seriously now. She clung to him. "Tom," she breathed, following the rhythm he created with his fingers, his hands, his mouth. She lifted one leg, wrapped it around his hip. He grabbed the other and lifted her as though she weighed nothing.

"Oh," she gasped. It was so sexy, and she had no intention of worrying about whether she was heavy or whether the position was uncomfortable for him. Whether he would drop her. She trusted him.

"I've got you," he said, holding her steady. "I've got you, Ambra," he repeated, and then she felt him enter her, slowly, deliberately, that incredible warm hardness that fit her so well. She leaned back against the wall and kept her eyes fixed on him, felt him fill her. From this angle, he reached new places inside her, and she caught her breath. His hips began to move, and then his tongue was in her mouth, in and out, in time with his thrusts.

"Tom," she whispered, catching his dark eyes. He was carrying her entire weight as he made love to her.

"I love you," he said, entering her again. He repeated it over and over as he thrust into her, kissed her, held her, hugged her. "I love you, Ambra Vinter," he whispered hoarsely. She closed her eyes, it was almost too intense. He kissed her gently, on the lips, on her neck, her breastbone, beneath her ear, mumbled more loving words. She was so close now. He followed her every movement, held her steady, reliably. Ambra felt herself coming, opened her eyes, looked Tom deep in the eye, and gave herself over to the orgasm that was overwhelming her like a tidal wave, like a warm release. Her eyes welled up, her body shook, and he whispered her name as he, too, came, deep inside her. His arms hugged her tight as he buried his face in her neck, kissed her there, nibbled, mumbled. She closed her eyes and breathed him in, didn't want to cry, but she felt so raw from all her emotions that a sob left her throat.

"I don't know if my legs will support me," she eventually whispered. Her thighs had started to shake considerably in the unusual position, but at the same time she wanted to be surrounded by his body, filled by him, close, skin to skin, chest to chest. Instead of putting her down, Tom carried her awkwardly over to the couch, where he gently lowered her onto it.

"Don't go anywhere," he said.

Tom studied his satisfied woman before he went to fetch a small towel, which he handed to her. Afterward he took the colorful new blanket he'd bought, the one that reminded him of her apartment in the Old Town, and draped it over her.

"Thanks," she said softly, smiling up at him. He would pull the moon and the stars from the sky for that smile. Jesus, he'd come so close to losing her, the love of his life, his soul mate. But she was here, in his apartment. She was alive and had said she loved him, and there was no reason to think about what might have gone wrong. Twice now, he had saved her life. But in truth, she was the one who had saved him. Before he'd met Ambra, he wasn't living.

"Want to eat?" he asked.

She stretched, supple as a cat. "Thought you'd never ask."

He puttered around in the kitchen, casting glances over his shoulder and watching her as she half lay on his couch. As he got everything ready, she padded over to him with the blanket trailing behind her. Her hands found his waist, and he felt her cheek against his back.

"It smells incredible," she said.

He dished up salad and bread, saw her lick her lips, enjoyed the simple, everyday miracle of having her here.

He would soon tell her that he had decided to join Mattias and his nation-saving team. Ambra defended democracy in her way, and he would do it in his. He would make this corner of the world a safer place, so that people like her could do what needed to be done. Give a voice to those who needed to be heard.

But first, they would eat, then he would tuck her into bed, watch over her, give her what she wanted: dessert, sleep, sex, a hot bath. Whatever she wanted or needed, he would give it to her. That was his main task.

And it would end like it was meant to.

Happily.

Epilogue

Roughly one year later

Ambra was back in Norrbotten. Even further north this time, in Abisko. It was a place polar researchers, hikers, and snow lovers from all over the world flocked to. And now her.

It was dark, with only the odd star lighting up the otherwise ink-black sky. If she squinted through the window, she could make out Lapporten, the mighty U-shaped valley in the distance. And high above her, perched on top of Nuolja Mountain, was the Aurora Sky Station, one of the best places on earth to experience the Northern Lights. At this time of year, with meter-deep snow and arctic temperatures, the only way to get up there was to use the chairlift.

Around the Abisko Mountain Lodge, the hotel where Ambra was staying, the staff had placed hundreds of lanterns made from clear ice. They glittered against the snow like small earthbound stars. The sight of them was so beautiful it almost hurt. Ambra turned from the window back to the room.

"Are you nervous?" Jill asked. She was standing by one of the room's two full-length mirrors, pulling at her low neckline. The dress she was wearing was Swedish haute couture, made especially for her, and she was shimmering as if this were an Oscars gala.

Ambra studied her glamorous sister. "I'm more worried your dress will blind everyone. You couldn't have chosen something a little more discreet?"

Jill waved her hand. "This *is* the discreet version. Don't worry, today is your day, no one's going to outshine you." She adjusted her bust, which was pushed up above the dazzling fabric. "I hope," she mumbled.

Ambra peered at herself in the other mirror. The dress she was wearing was actually made up of two separate parts. The white silk brocade skirt shimmered with a heavy, expensive glow. The bodice was snow-white jersey, a fabric that fit her like a second skin. The two parts met at the waist, with a wide duchesse band tied in a bow behind her back, and there was a pocket hidden at either side. It was at once modern and romantic. And it was definitely the most gorgeous thing she had ever worn.

"You aren't regretting choosing a winter wedding?" Jill asked, taking out her phone, fluffing up her hair, and snapping a series of selfies.

"No, but I regret not banning you from Instagram."

"Stop being so anti-progress. Tell me some gossip instead. Any drama, or has everyone been behaving?"

"Everything's been fine," Ambra said as she rocked her hips, making her skirt swing. The sixty wedding guests had been flown by helicopter from the airport in Kiruna. They'd been kept entertained with outdoor hot tubs, snowmobile rides, and skiing. Some of them had taken a helicopter ride to the top of Mount Kebnekaise; others had gone ice-fishing. Yesterday, they all ate dinner together in the Aurora Sky Station. When Ambra left the party at two a.m., the band was still playing. One of Tom's sisters had been particularly enthusiastic about dealing out advice on raising children, a cousin had talked about nothing but the dangers of plastic containers, and Grace had gotten into a heated debate about the death penalty with one of Tom's military friends. But other than that, the mood had been as relaxed and familiar as she could have hoped for. The fact that Jill hadn't arrived until today had probably helped maintain the general feeling of peace, she thought disloyally as she listened to the faint murmur of the guests taking their seats in the adjacent room.

Everyone she cared about was here today. Elsa and her new girlfriend. And her son, the social worker. Simone and Siri, the girls Ambra had saved from the burning house, along with their mother. A few colleagues from *Aftonbladet*. And then her new family, of course. She still had trouble getting used to the fact that she was a part of it now: Tom's mother, sisters, cousins, and various others who had married into the family.

Jill placed a hand on her hip and nonchalantly said, "I thought I might go out to see the guests. Alexander De la Grip, he really is sexy. I could see whether he needs anything."

"Stay here, you man-eater. You're my bridesmaid. Leave Alexander in peace."

"He only has eyes for his wife and kids anyway. It would be sweet if it wasn't so annoying."

"And if you didn't have a boyfriend. Mattias, remember him?" Ambra reminded her.

"Yeah, yeah."

They heard a baby crying from the other side of the door, and Jill raised an eyebrow at the sound. The room was full of kids. Alexander and Isobel had come with Marius and their new baby. Natalia and David arrived with the soon-to-be two Molly. And several of the other guests had also brought children of various ages. It was how Ambra wanted it, a lively and inclusive wedding. It had felt like a good idea while she was planning it, but now it just woke a whole host of unwelcome emotions.

"What is it? Why are you sighing like that?" asked Jill, who had developed new, empathetic powers of observation this past year. Honestly, it was disturbing.

Ambra didn't reply immediately. Instead, she met her own gaze in the mirror. The hairdresser had pinned up her curls on one side using a clip shaped like a snowflake. It was a gentle, flattering hairstyle, her dress was a dream, and even her makeup looked like it should. Purely objectively, she had never looked more beautiful. She leaned in close and studied her face. It was so strange that it didn't show on the surface, everything she felt inside. Although that was true of everyone, really. Alexander and Isobel, sitting outside with their perfect family, for example, also had internal scars. Isobel had confessed that they were worried about the increasingly harsh tone of society. How Marius—sweet, kind Marius—was often subjected to racial abuse when they were out. And Natalia and David Hammar, a successful couple who seemed to have everything, had gone through a miscarriage only a few weeks earlier. It hit them so hard that they weren't sure whether they would make it to the wedding right up to the last minute. And Jill, that goddess-like star who was praised and admired by everyone, her soul bore such deep scars that she still couldn't quite believe Mattias really loved her. Life wasn't only what was visible. Life was complex and fragile.

Jill came over to her, suddenly serious. She placed her hands on Ambra's upper arms. "Ambra, what is it? You're so pale. Did something happen? I'm on your side, you know that, right? If you want to call the whole thing off and fly home, we'll do it. Right away. You know I still don't think he deserves you."

"Nutcase. I don't want to call it off," Ambra replied, but her voice broke.

Jill's grip tightened, and Ambra glimpsed panic in her sister's eyes. Always this readiness for catastrophe. That was something they had in common, and it was something they would probably never quite get over. Both were too damaged, too aware of how quickly everything could change.

"So what is it? You're scaring me. Are you dying?" Jill's eyes looked as if they were about to well up. Her nails dug into the silk jersey of Ambra's dress.

"I'm not dying," Ambra hurried to reply. "I swear. Sorry for alarming you."

Jill's death grip loosened. She breathed out. "Jesus, you had me scared there. Tell me."

Ambra turned around, face-to-face. "Tom wants to have kids."

Jill was silent. "But you don't?" she eventually asked.

Ambra looked down, could barely meet Jill's eye. She almost whispered, "What if I can't be a mother? If I don't know what to do?"

She had never dared say it aloud before, but the thought had always been there, and it had grown stronger over the past few months. With her childhood, how could she possible give a baby everything it needed?

"Do you think I'm being stupid?" she asked.

"Very. Listen to me now: You'll be a fantastic mother. You hear me? You're passionate about those who are in need. Christ, you saved the life of those girls, and you have a man who worships the ground you walk on."

Ambra nodded at the last part. "Tom would be a great father."

"Yeah, he probably won't mess up your kids too much," Jill agreed before she continued. "So stop feeling sorry for yourself. The plan is for this to be the happiest evening of your life."

Jill held out a tissue. Ambra took it and blew her nose just as someone knocked at the door. Tom came in.

"How's it going?" he asked. Damn, he looked so handsome.

"Ambra changed her mind, she wants to call the whole thing off," said Jill.

Tom didn't miss a beat. "Mattias is flirting with one of the waitresses."

Jill's eyes flashed and she took a step toward the doorway. "I'll kill him," she said doggedly.

"Jill, he's joking, you know that, right?" Ambra said with a stifled laugh.

Jill gave Tom a sharp look. "It's hard to tell, considering he doesn't have a sense of humor."

"But I do have plenty of other qualities," Tom said, unruffled.

"You do," Ambra agreed, looking down at the bracelet on her wrist.

When Tom had carried her out of the burning building, he'd also rescued her box. "You were holding it in an iron grip, so I thought it must be important," he said with a shrug. Inside, she found the beloved charm bracelet her father had given her mother when Ambra was born. She shook her hand and the charms rattled.

A mournful sound caught Ambra's attention. Suddenly Freja appeared at Tom's side and howled pitifully.

"She doesn't like the flowers," Tom explained. The dog was wearing a green-and-white flower garland around her neck, the same colors as Ambra's bouquet and Tom's corsage. She looked deeply unhappy and gave Ambra a pleading dog look. *Take it off me,* her eyes seemed to be saying. Ambra scratched the dog under the chin. "Soon," she whispered.

"Unless you've changed your mind, it's time," Tom said, taking a step toward her. His tone was breezy, but she saw a quick flash of worry pass over his freshly shaven face. His dark eyes bored into hers, and she almost struggled to breathe. This was what it was all about. Not dresses and candles and floral wreaths. *This.* A life-and-death kind of love. Fidelity. Loyalty. For this man who dared run into a burning house for her sake, who had saved her life *twice*. Who would give his life for her, who would never let her down.

"I haven't changed my mind," she said.

Tom took a step toward her, placed a hand on the back of her neck, and kissed her, eagerly, dominantly, as though to reassure himself that she was serious. Ambra reciprocated his kiss, pressed herself to his chest, his new suit, pulled him to her until she was dizzy and warm and breathless.

Jill groaned.

Freja joined in with a howl.

Tom smiled. "So what do you say? Should we go out and get married?"

She nodded and held out her hand to him.

In front of their family, friends, and the civil officiator, Tom carefully pushed the diamond ring onto Ambra's slender finger. The rock glittered, and he felt his throat tighten. Then he held out his own hand and watched as Ambra pushed the smooth ring onto his finger. Their eyes met, and though the room was full of people, all they could see was each other.

"You have now entered into marriage with one another, and confirmed this before the witnesses gathered here today," the officiator said ceremonially.

Tom breathed out. It was official. Ambra was his. And he was hers. Finally. He gave her a kiss, brushed his mouth against those soft lips of hers, felt her smile. The guests laughed, applauded, and wolf whistled. Music started to play, and Jill Lopez began singing her latest song for them. It was a powerful ballad, a song about the love between two sisters, a smash hit Jill had written after they made up and that had been at the top of the charts all fall.

Tom squeezed Ambra's hand.

"Lucky she isn't stealing the spotlight," Ambra whispered.

"She loves you," he said.

"Yeah."

"And *I* love you," he said.

She squeezed his hand and leaned her head gently against his shoulder. His wife.

*   *   *

Long after the dinner, the speeches, the cake, and the wedding dance, Tom and Ambra stood in the middle of the dance floor. All around them, the party was in full swing, but they were standing still, close together, kissing gently, whispering, breathing each other in.

"Want to dance again?" Tom asked quietly.

Ambra shook her head. Her soft hair tickled his nose. He was determined that her wedding day should be exactly how she wanted it. But he was also longing to be alone with her. "Do you want to talk to anyone else? Jill? Elsa?" he asked.

"I really don't. I've talked so much my throat hurts."

That decided it. "Let's sneak out."

"Where are we going?" she asked as they stole away. Her dress rustled slightly.

"Put this on," he said as they reached the lobby. He draped a thick winter coat over her, wrapped a scarf around her neck, and handed her a hat, which she carefully pulled down over her curls. "We're going out? I'm wearing heels," she protested. But her eyes glistened with curiosity. That was his wife. Always curious. She changed into the warm boots he handed her.

"Come on."

The cold air hit them as Tom opened the door. The dogs began to howl the minute they stepped outside. "A dogsled!" she exclaimed. A team of jumping, barking, gray-and-white dogs was awaiting them. He helped her into the sled, beneath the furs. "So pretty," she mumbled. And it really was. The stars in the sky and the ice lanterns lining their way, until the sled driver called for the dogs to stop. Ambra shivered and looked up, toward the mountain. "Are we really going up there?"

He nodded. "It'll be cold," he said apologetically. She climbed into the chairlift, and he covered her with a fur, sat down next to her, and took her hand. The chair lift silently began its climb. They left the bright lights of the hotel and the glittering lanterns behind them, floated higher and higher until they reached the top of the mountain. The cold was piercing, and they ran the short distance to the station hand in hand.

"Are we the only ones here?" she asked as they stepped inside.

"Yeah." He had reserved the entire mountaintop station for her, for them. He hung up their coats while she glanced around. It was a simple room; the view was the main attraction. She looked at the furs on the floor by the window, the lanterns and the rose petals sprinkled all around. She looked at him. "Rose petals?"

"Is it too much?" he asked.

"A little," she said, but she smiled and her eyes twinkled.

She moved over to one of the windows and paused with her nose to the glass.

"It's like looking down at the whole world," she said. Her voice was low, almost reverential. Millions of stars lit up the sky; they were surrounded by mountains, with the heavens above them, in all their endlessness. He moved behind her, kissed the back of her neck, and felt her tremble. He placed a hand on her back, playing with the line of small buttons on her spine, bent down and kissed her shoulder blade. He undid a button and kissed her again, repeated the procedure until every button was undone and she was breathing with quick, shallow pants. He found the fastening on her skirt and unhooked it. It practically rolled off her, and suddenly it was pooled around her feet like a sea of silk. She wasn't wearing an underskirt. Only underwear. Tom studied her for a long moment.

"Darling?" he eventually asked. He didn't know quite what he had been expecting from her underwear; maybe a little lace, maybe he'd even been hoping for an old-fashioned corset with hooks and eyes and buttons he could slowly get to work on. But this?

"Yes?"

"Are you wearing long johns under your wedding dress?"

She nodded with satisfaction. "They're fleece. So cozy. Are you getting undressed?"

She helped him take off his clothes as he pulled down her long johns. They lay on the animal furs, and she giggled until his hand moved between her legs. Then she gasped for breath instead. He knelt over her, kissed her stomach. Pulled off her panties, which did actually have a little lace on them. Kissed her again, mumbled into her warm skin, and kissed her again and again until she was panting beneath him.

* * *

That night, the Northern Lights danced above Abisko in a way they rarely ever do. In fact, there were many who could confirm that it was an extraordinary show. Perhaps the biggest ever. The kind the papers would write about and the wedding guests would talk about for years to come. But Ambra and Tom saw none of it. They were otherwise engaged.

**Don't miss the other High Stakes novels by
international bestselling author Simona Ahrnstedt!**

ALL IN

Trust is the most precious commodity of all . . .

In the cutthroat world of Sweden's financial elite, no one knows
that better than corporate raider David Hammar. Ruthless. Notori-
ous. Unstoppable. He's out to hijack the ultimate prize: Investum.
After years of planning, all the players are in place; he needs just one
member of the aristocratic owning family on his side—Natalia De la
Grip.

Elegant, brilliant, driven to succeed in a man's world, Natalia is curious about David's unexpected invitation to lunch. Everyone knows
that he is rich, dangerous, and unethical. But she soon discovers he
is also deeply scarred.

The attraction between these two is impossible, but the long
Swedish nights unfold an affair that will bring to light shocking secrets, forever alter a family, and force both Natalia and David to con-
front their innermost fears and desires.

Praise for *All In*

"A compelling story that has heat and heart."
—*New York Times* bestselling author Sandra Brown

"*All In* is sexy, smart, and completely unputdownable.
Breathtaking, from start to finish."
—*New York Times* bestselling author Tessa Dare

"Everything a reader could want!"
—*New York Times* bestselling author Eloisa James

"I've been searching for this feeling all year:
this book left me absolutely breathless."
—*New York Times* bestselling author Christina Lauren

"Fast-paced, sexy and smart!"
—*New York Times* bestselling author Lori Foster

FALLING

A gripping, glittering novel of scandal and suspense that ranges from Sweden to New York City to Africa, from the bestselling author of All In . . .

Alexander de la Grip is known in the tabloids and gossip blogs as a rich, decadent, jet-setting playboy who spends most of his days recovering from the night before. With a string of beautiful conquests, he seems to care about nothing and no one.

Isobel Sørensen has treated patients in refugee camps and war zones, and is about to depart Sweden for a pediatric hospital in Chad. Devoted to her humanitarian work, she cares almost too deeply. Especially when she learns that Alexander is withholding desperately needed funds from her aid foundation.

Is it because she's the only woman who ever told him to go to hell?

As the two push each other's boundaries to the breaking point, the truth turns out to be much more complicated. Pain, love, trust, betrayal. Which will triumph when safety is nothing but an empty word?

Praise for FALLING

"Outstanding . . . Complex, fully realized characters, settings that range from Swedish castles to a barely equipped hospital with exhausted personnel and dying children, and a dangerous rescue mission with a breathtaking finale make this a page turner to savor."
—*Publishers Weekly* STARRED REVIEW

"One of Ahrnstedt's greatest strengths is her ability to recognize the romantic potential in the smallest of everyday details, and it is one of those details that makes both the romantic story lines in this second High Stakes novel so compelling."—*RT Book Reviews*

Connect with

Us

Visit us online at
KensingtonBooks.com
to read more from your favorite authors, see books
by series, view reading group guides, and more.

Join us on social media

for sneak peeks, chances to win books and prize packs,
and to share your thoughts with other readers.

**facebook.com/kensingtonpublishing
twitter.com/kensingtonbooks**

Tell us what you think!

To share your thoughts, submit a review,
or sign up for our eNewsletters, please visit:
KensingtonBooks.com/TellUs.